PENGUIN MODERN CLASSICS

LARK RISE TO CANDLEFORD

Flora Jane Thompson was born in 1876 at Juniper Hill, a hamlet on the borders of Oxfordshire and Northamptonshire. After leaving school she was sent as assistant to the postmistress (who also kept the forge) to a town eight miles away, and was for some time employed to carry the letters locked in a leather bag to the big house nearby. So began her long connection with the Post Office. She married young and her husband later became a postmaster. His work then took them to Bournemouth, where she obtained from the public library the Greek and Roman Classics in translation, as well as Ibsen and the English poets, novelists and critics – especially Shaw and Yeats. Her first book was a collection of poems, *Bog Myrtle and Peat*. However, she is best remembered for three autobiographical volumes: *Lark Rise* (1939), *Over to Candleford* (1941) and *Candleford Green* (1943), reissued in one volume as *Lark Rise to Candleford* (1945). A fourth volume, *Still Glides the Stream*, was published posthumously in 1948. Flora Thompson died at Brixham, Devon, on 21 May 1947.

Harold John Massingham was born in 1888, the eldest son of the journalist H. W. Massingham. He published many works reflecting a great appreciation of the English countryside and natural history, including *The English Countryman* (1942). He died in 1952.

Lark Rise to Candleford is available as a Penguin Audiobook, read by Judi Dench.

FLORA THOMPSON

Lark Rise to Candleford

A Trilogy

With an Introduction by
H. J. Massingham

PENGUIN BOOKS

PENGUIN CLASSICS

Published by the Penguin Group
Penguin Books Ltd, 80 Strand, London WC2R 0RL, England
Penguin Group (USA) Inc., 375 Hudson Street, New York, New York 10014, USA
Penguin Group (Canada), 90 Eglinton Avenue East, Suite 700, Toronto,
Ontario, Canada M4P 2Y3 (a division of Pearson Penguin Canada Inc.)
Penguin Ireland, 25 St Stephen's Green, Dublin 2, Ireland (a division of Penguin Books Ltd)
Penguin Group (Australia), 250 Camberwell Road, Camberwell,
Victoria 3124, Australia (a division of Pearson Australia Group Pty Ltd)
Penguin Books India Pvt Ltd, 11 Community Centre,
Panchsheel Park, New Delhi – 110 017, India
Penguin Group (NZ), 67 Apollo Drive, Rosedale, North Shore 0632, New Zealand
(a division of Pearson New Zealand Ltd)
Penguin Books (South Africa) (Pty) Ltd, 24 Sturdee Avenue,
Rosebank, Johannesburg 2196, South Africa

Penguin Books Ltd, Registered Offices: 80 Strand, London WC2R 0RL, England

www.penguin.com

Lark Rise was first published by Oxford University Press 1939;
Over to Candleford in 1941; *Candleford Green* in 1943
Issued together under the present title 1945
Published in Penguin Books 1973
Reprinted in Penguin Classics 2000
This film and TV tie-in edition published 2008
By arrangement with the BBC
BBC © BBC 1996
The BBC logo is a registered trademark of the
British Broadcasting Corporation and is used under license.
10

Copyright 1939, 1941 and 1943 by Flora Thompson
All rights reserved

Printed in England by Clays Ltd, St Ives plc

978-0-141-03719-6

www.greenpenguin.co.uk

Contents

Introduction

By absolute values, a true writer can never be other than what he is. But in our imperfect world his living light will only shine among men if it appears at precisely the right time. If it does so appear, it is not merely good luck, because the truth should also possess a super-sentive probe (like the woodcock's bill) for testing the subsoil of what it works on. This is something very different from what is called 'appealing to the popular imagination'. Flora Thompson possesses the attributes both of sympathetic presentation and literary power to such a degree of quality and beauty that her claims upon posterity can hardly be questioned. Her lovers guessed it when her three memorial volumes, *Lark Rise, Over to Candleford*, and *Candleford Green*, were published separately; now that they form a trilogy, each part illuminating and reflecting the others in a delicate interplay, the time of speculation is over. This wholeness, they will say, is a triune achievement: a triumph of evocation in the resurrecting of an age that, being transitional, was the most difficult to catch as it flew; another in diversity of rural portraiture engagingly blended with autobiography; and the last in the overtones and implications of a set of values which is the author's 'message'.

Nor will these lovers be deceived by the limitations of her range, her personal simplicity and humility of spirit and the excellent lowness of her voice as the narrator of these quiet annals, into withholding from her the full measure of what is her due. Is that range so restricted? The trilogy enables us to appreciate for the first time what she has done both for literature and social history. By the playing of these soft pipes the hamlet, the village, and the small market town are reawakened at the very moment when the rich, glowing life and culture of an immemorial design for living was passing from them, at the precise point of meeting when the beginnings of what was to be touched the last lingering evidences of what was departing. Of late years memorial books, I might almost say by the score, have strained to overhear the few fading syllables of that country civilization of which the younger generation of today knows and can know nothing. A few of these have been of high distinction. I have only to mention the names of George Bourne, Adrian Bell, Walter Rose, W. R. Mottram, and the author of *How Green was My Valley*. But none of these authors singly achieved the triple revelation of the hamlet, the village, and the market town; none, with the possible exception of the last, has, like Flora Thompson, chronicled the individual life as an integral part of the group life and as the more of an individual one for it.

Again, by these three books being subdued into sections of one whole, Laura now emerges into her full selfhood and as the chorus of the complete drama. Now for the first time Flora Thompson's master work in portrait-painting is seen to be herself. But we keep on forgetting that Laura is her own self, so subtly has our author's spiritual humility contributed to the fineness of the self-portrait. She has lost her life to another and so exquisitely regained it that the personal quality of Laura, which is the key to the whole and diffuses over it a tranquil radiance, is never mistaken as other than that of a separate person. As remote from the present day as Uncle Tom, Queenie, or Dorcas Lane, she is yet more living even than they. At the same time, she is something else than the Cranfordian Miss, 'quaint and oldfashioned', as another character calls her, something else than the lover of Nature and of books, the questing contemplative, the solitary in the Wordsworthian, quite un-Cranfordian sense. She is the recorder of hamlet, village, and country town who was of them but detached from them, and whose observation of their inmates by intimacy by no means clouded precision of insight and an objective capacity to grasp in a few sentences the essentials of character. One of the very best things Laura ever did was to become assistant post-mistress at Candleford Green. The post-office magnetized the whole village.

When George Bourne described Bettesworth and the craftsmen of his wheelwright's shop, he made them the vehicle of an immensely valuable inquiry into social conditions now made obsolete by urban invasion. Flora Thompson's method is entirely different. But the result is the same in both writers. It is the revelation of a local self-acting society living by a fixed pattern of behaviour and with its roots warmly bedded in the soil. The pattern was disintegrating and the roots were loosening, but enough remained for sure inferences to be drawn from it. Flora Thompson does not reconstruct the shattered fabric like a historian nor illustrate and analyse it like a sociologist: she reanimates it.

In this tripartite book we distinguish three strata of social and economic period, cross-hatched by differences of social degree. In terms of geological time, the lowest stratum is the old order of rural England surviving rare but intact from a pre-industrial and pre-Enclosure past almost timeless in its continuity. The middle stratum, particularly represented in *Lark Rise*, discloses the old order impoverished, reduced in status, dispropertied but still clinging to the old values, loyalties, and domestic stabilities. The top stratum, symbolized in the row of new villas that began to link up Candleford Green with Candleford Town, is modern suburbia. This wholly novel class in itself had shed the older differentiations and possessed no rural background other than the accident of place. It was the vanguard of the city blackcoats and proletariat, governed by the mass-mind.

Nor is the stratification a simple one. The two lower layers are not only hierarchical in many grades between squire and labourer, but the upper one of the pair is dyed a different colour from that of the natural deposit. This is the sombre tint of Victorian moralism, quite different from the social ethics of the old order to which it was alien. Puritanism in rural England was never a home-brew; it was always imported from the town. The topmost layer of the three had and has no fixed principles; its aim was quantitative imitation and to 'keep up appearances'. Mr Green of *Candleford Green*, who read Nat Gould and Marie Corelli because everybody did, considered the expert craftsman as inferior in status to himself, sitting on a stool and adding up figures.

It is clear, then, that Flora Thompson's simple-seeming

chronicles of life in hamlet, village, and market town are, when regarded as an index to social change, of great complexity and heavy with revolutionary meaning. But this you do not notice until you look below the surface. The surface is the family lives and characters of Laura and her neighbours at Lark Rise, inhabited by ex-peasants, and the two Candlefords, where society is more mixed and occupation more varied. But the surface is transparent, and there are threatening depths of dislocation and frustration below it. Flora Thompson's method of revealing them is a literary one, as was George Eliot's; that is to say, by the selective representation of domestic interiors in which living personages pass their daily lives. The social document is a by-product of people's normal activities and intercourse intensely localized, just as beauty is a by-product of the craftsman's utility-work for his neighbours.

Thus, the commonest occurrences, the lightest of words, the very ordinariness of the home-task are pregnant with a dual meaning. This is the reverse of a photographic method like that of the fashionable 'mass-observation' because it looks inward to human character and outward to changes in environment affecting the whole structure of society and modifying, even distorting, the way people think and act. Her art is in fact universalized by its very particularity, its very confinement to small places and the people Laura knew. It all seems a placid water-colour of the English school, delicately and reticently painted in and charmed by the character of Laura herself. But it is not. What Flora Thompson depicts is the utter ruin of a closely knit organic society with a richly interwoven and traditional culture that had defied every change, every aggression, except the one that established the modern world. It is notable that, though husbandry itself plays little part in the trilogy, it is the story of the irreparable calamity of the English fields. In the shell of her concealed art we hear the thunder of an ocean of change, a change tragic indeed, since nothing has taken and nothing can take the place of what has gone.

On the bottom layer once rested all England. In the perfect economy of a few deft and happy strokes, *Lark Rise* reveals it as surviving principally in two households, those of Queenie, the lace-maker and bee-mistress, and 'Old Sally', whose grand-father built her house 'before the open heathland had been cut up into fenced fields' and the community of cooperative self-help destroyed by the Enclosures. Old Sally is so closely identified with her house and furniture, its two-feet-thick walls making a snuggery for the gate-legged table, the dresser with its pewter and willow-pattern ware and the grandfather's clock, that they can no more be prised apart than the snail from its shell. In remembering the Rise when it was common land, Sally was carrying in her mind the England of small properties based on the land, the England whose native land belonged to its own people, not to a State masquerading as such, not even to the manorial lords who exacted services, but not from a landless proletariat. Still less to big business whose *latifundia* are the modern plan. Sally is self-supporting peasant England, the bed-rock of all, solid as her furniture, enduring as her walls, the last of the longest of all lines.

Moving on to Candleford, we find in Uncle Tom, the cobbler with his apprentices, the representative of the master-craftsman who did quite literally build England, the England that Laura at Candleford Green saw *in articulo mortis*. Uncle Tom is a townsman, but his spiritual brother of the fields was the yeoman. Farm and workshop both were husbanded as a re-sponsible stewardship and according to inalienable first prin-ciples. For both, yeoman and master-craftsman, the holding of property was the guarantee of economic freedom and a dutiful right. Home, as the centre alike of the family and of industry and the nucleus of neighbourliness, was the ruling concept for them both. *Over to Candleford* devotes special pains to the portraiture of Uncle Tom and his household. The interaction between his social value to the life of the little town and his personal integrity, his pride in his work and virile personality are described with the intent of revealing good living and the good life as an historical unity of the older England. In a line, Laura looking back and seeing herself, the other Laura, reading to Uncle Tom in his workshop-cum-home, sums up his end, both as a symbol and a living-figure. If he were alive now, she says, he would be the manager of a chain-store.

In *Candleford Green* the same parable of the past is spoken, with a difference. Dorcas Lane, the post-mistress, and her household-workshop with Matthew the foreman of the farriery, the smithy and the wheelwright's shop and the journeymen sitting below the salt at Miss Lane's table, other symbols of 'an age-old discipline', these have an obvious affinity with Uncle Tom and *his* little commonwealth. She too has her willow-pattern plate and other bygones. But this household seems embalmed, a show-piece, and we feel it would be a blunder to speak of Old Sally's and Uncle Tom's possessions as 'bygones'. Dorcas's 'modernism', her sceptical outlook and partiality for reading Darwin lends point to the sense of preservation, not use.

In *Candleford Green*, again, Mr Coulsdon, the Vicar, and Sir Timothy, the Squire, are held momentarily in the light before they too pass into limbo. But both of them cast a shadow, however soft the illumination of Laura's lamp. They are Victorianized, and it was Victoria's reign that, partly through their agency, but mainly by the growth of the industrial town and the industrial mentality, ended the self-sufficient England of peasant and craftsman. The supreme value of Flora Thompson's presentation is that she makes us see the passing of this England, not as a milestone along the road of inevitable progress, but as the attempted murder of something timeless in and quintessential to the spirit of man. A design for living has become unravelled, and there can be no substitute, because, however imperfect the pattern, it was part of the essential constitution of human nature. The fatal flaw of the modern theory of progress is that it is untrue to historical reality. The frustrations and convulsions of our own time are the effect of aiming this mortal blow at the core of man's integral nature, which can be perverted, but not destroyed.

In *Lark Rise* especially, we receive an unforgettable impression of the transitional state between the old stable, work-pleasure England and the modern world. *World* because non-differentiation is the mark of it, and all modern industrial States have a common likeness such as that of Manchester to Stalingrad, Paris to Buenos Aires. The society of *Lark Rise* is one of

land-labourers' families – only they are now all landless. They
have lost that which made them what they are in Part I of the
trilogy; and the whole point of it is that the reader is given a
picture of a peasant class which is still a peasantry in everything
but the one thing that makes it so – the holding of land and
stock. Here, the labourers are dispropertied, though they still
have gardens; here, they are wage-earners only, keeping their
families on ten shillings a week, though in 1540 their forefathers
in another village not a score of miles from Lark Rise, and
exactly the same class as that from which they were descended,
paid the lord of the manor £46,000 as copyholders to be free of
all dues and services to him. Lark Rise in the 'eighties of last
century, admittedly but a hamlet, could certainly not have collected 46,000 farthings.

Though pauperized, they were still craftsmanly men: the day
of an emptied country-side harvested by machines and chemi-
cals and of mass, mobile, skill-less labour in the towns serving
the combine at the assembly line was yet to come. It is
significant that Lark Rise still called the older geneiation
'master' not 'mister'. Though landless, they still kept the cottage
pig, which served a social no less than a material need. The
women still went leazing in the stubble fields and fed their families the winter through on whole-grain bread baked by themselves, not yet bleached and a broken reed instead of the staff of
life. The hedgerows were still utilized for wines and jellies, the
gardens for fresh vegetables and herbs. They even made mead
and 'yarb (yarrow) beer'. Of Candleford Green our author
writes:

'The community was largely self-supporting. Every household
grew its own vegetables, produced its new-laid eggs and cured its
own bacon. Jams and jellies, wines and pickles, were made at home
as a matter of course. Most gardens had a row of beehives. In the
houses of the well-to-do there was an abundance of such foods, and
even the poor enjoyed a rough plenty.'

The last words are true of the hamlet of Lark Rise. Because they
were still an organic community, subsisting on the food, however scanty and monotonous, they raised themselves, they enjoyed good health and so, in spite of grinding poverty, no

money to spend on amusements and hardly any for necessities, happiness. They still sang out-of-doors and kept May Day and Harvest Home. The songs were travesties of the traditional ones, but their blurred echoes and the remnants of the old salty country speech had not yet died and left the fields to their modern silence. The songs came from their own lips, not out of a box.

Charity (in the old sense) survived, and what Laura's mother called the 'seemliness' of a too industrious life. Yet the tradition of the old order was crumbling fast. What suffered most visibly was the inborn aesthetic faculty, once a common possession of all countrymen. Almanacs for samplers, the 'Present from Brighton' for willow-pattern, novelettes for the Bible, Richardson and travel books, coarse, machined embroidery for point-lace, cheap shoddy for oak and mahogany. The instalment system was beginning. The manor and the rectory ever since the Enclosures were felt to be against the people. The more amenable of these were now regarded as 'the deserving poor' and Cobbett's 'the commons of England' had become 'the lower orders'. When Laura's mother was outraged at Edmund, her son, wanting to go on the land, the end was in sight. The end of what? Of a self-sufficient country England living by the land, cultivating it by husbandry and associating liberty with the small property. It was not poverty that broke it – that was a secondary cause. It was not even imported cheap and foodless foods. It was that the Industrial Revolution and the Enclosures between them demolished the structure and the pattern of country life. Their traces long lingered like those of old ploughed fields on grassland in the rays of the setting sun. But they have been all but effaced today, and now we plough and sow and reap an empty land. One thing only can ever re-people it – the restoration of the peasantry. But that industrialism does not understand. Catastrophe alone can teach it to understand.

It has been Flora Thompson's mission to represent this great tragic epic obliquely, and by the medium of humdrum but highly individualized country people living their ordinary lives in their own homes. As I said at the opening of this Introduction, she has conveyed it at just the right time – namely, when the triumphs of industrial progress are beginning to be seen for what they are. Or, as a recent correspondent to *The Times* expressed it, 'peace and beauty must inevitably give way to progress'. She has conveyed this profound tragedy through so delicate a mastery, with so beguiling an air and by so tender an elegy, that what she has to tell is 'felt along the heart' rather than as a spectacular eclipse. I regard this as an achievement in literature that will outlive her own life. Or, as the gipsy said who told Laura's fortune at Candleford Green – 'You are going to be loved by people you've never seen and never will see.'

H. J. MASSINGHAM

Reddings, Long Crendon, Bucks.
August 1944

LARK RISE

I

Poor People's Houses

THE hamlet stood on a gentle rise in the flat, wheat-growing north-east corner of Oxfordshire. We will call it Lark Rise because of the great number of skylarks which made the surrounding fields their springboard and nested on the bare earth between the rows of green corn.

All around, from every quarter, the stiff, clayey soil of the arable fields crept up; bare, brown and windswept for eight months out of the twelve. Spring brought a flush of green wheat and there were violets under the hedges and pussy-willows out beside the brook at the bottom of the 'Hundred Acres'; but only for a few weeks in later summer had the landscape real beauty. Then the ripened cornfields rippled up to the doorsteps of the cottages and the hamlet became an island in a sea of dark gold.

To a child it seemed that it must always have been so; but the ploughing and sowing and reaping were recent innovations. Old men could remember when the Rise, covered with juniper bushes, stood in the midst of a furzy heath – common land, which had come under the plough after the passing of the Enclosure Acts. Some of the ancients still occupied cottages on land which had been ceded to their fathers as 'squatters' rights', and probably all the small plots upon which the houses stood had originally been so ceded. In the eighteen-eighties the hamlet consisted of about thirty cottages and an inn, not built in rows, but dotted down anywhere within a more or less circular group. A deeply rutted cart track surrounded the whole, and separate houses or groups of houses were connected by a network of pathways. Going from one part of the hamlet to another was called 'going round the Rise', and the plural of 'house' was not 'houses', but 'housen'. The only shop was a small general one kept in the back kitchen of the inn. The church and school were in the mother village, a mile and a half away.

A road flattened the circle at one point. It had been cut when the heath was enclosed, for convenience in fieldwork and to connect the main Oxford road with the mother village and a series of other villages beyond. From the hamlet it led on the one hand to church and school, and on the other to the main road, or the turnpike, as it was still called, and so to the market town where the Saturday shopping was done. It brought little traffic past the hamlet. An occasional farm wagon, piled with sacks or square-cut bundles of hay; a farmer on horseback or in his gig; the baker's little old white-tiled van; a string of blanketed hunters with grooms, exercising in the early morning; and a carriage with gentry out paying calls in the afternoon were about the sum of it. No motors, no buses, and only one of the old penny-farthing high bicycles at rare intervals. People still rushed to their cottage doors to see one of the latter come past.

A few of the houses had thatched roofs, whitewashed outer walls and diamond-paned windows, but the majority were just stone or brick boxes with blue-slated roofs. The older houses were relics of pre-enclosure days and were still occupied by descendants of the original squatters, themselves at that time elderly people. One old couple owned a donkey and cart, which they used to carry their vegetables, eggs, and honey to the market town and sometimes hired out at sixpence a day to their neighbours. One house was occupied by a retired farm bailiff, who was reported to have 'well feathered his own nest' during his years of stewardship. Another aged man owned and worked upon about an acre of land. These, the innkeeper, and one other man, a stonemason who walked the three miles to and from his work in the town every day, were the only ones not employed as agricultural labourers.

Some of the cottages had two bedrooms, others only one, in which case it had to be divided by a screen or curtain to accommodate parents and children. Often the big boys of a family slept downstairs, or were put out to sleep in the second bedroom of an elderly couple whose own children were out in the world. Except at holiday times, there were no big girls to provide for, as they were all out in service. Still, it was often a tight fit, for children swarmed, eight, ten, or even more in some families, and although they were seldom all at home together, the eldest often being married before the youngest was born, beds and shakedowns were often so closely packed that the inmates had to climb over one bed to get into another.

But Lark Rise must not be thought of as a slum set down in the country. The inhabitants lived an open-air life; the cottages were kept clean by much scrubbing with soap and water, and doors and windows stood wide open when the weather permitted. When the wind cut across the flat land to the east, or came roaring down from the north, doors and windows had to be closed; but then, as the hamlet people said, they got more than enough fresh air through the keyhole.

There were two epidemics of measles during the decade, and two men had accidents in the harvest field and were taken to hospital; but, for years together, the doctor was only seen there when one of the ancients was dying of old age, or some difficult first confinement baffled the skill of the old woman who, as she said, saw the beginning and end of everybody. There was no cripple or mental defective in the hamlet, and, except for a few months when a poor woman was dying of cancer, no invalid. Though food was rough and teeth were neglected, indigestion was unknown, while nervous troubles, there as elsewhere, had yet to be invented. The very word 'nerve' was used in a different sense to the modern one. 'My word! An' 'aven't she got a nerve!' they would say of any one who expected more than was reasonable.

In nearly all the cottages there was but one room downstairs, and many of these were poor and bare, with only a table and a few chairs and stools for furniture and a superannuated potato-sack thrown down by way of hearthrug. Other rooms were bright and cosy, with dressers of crockery, cushioned chairs, pictures on the walls and brightly coloured hand-made rag rugs on the floor. In these there would be pots of geraniums, fuchsias, and old-fashioned sweet-smelling musk on the window-sills. In the older cottages there were grandfathers' clocks, gate-legged tables, and rows of pewter, relics of a time when life was easier for country folk.

The interiors varied, according to the number of mouths to be fed and the thrift and skill of the housewife, or the lack of those qualities; but the income in all was precisely the same, for ten shillings a week was the standard wage of the farm labourer at that time in that district.

Looking at the hamlet from a distance, one house would have been seen, a little apart, and turning its back on its neighbours, as though about to run away into the fields. It was a small grey stone cottage with a thatched roof, a green-painted door and a plum tree trained up the wall to the eaves. This was called the 'end house' and was the home of the stonemason and his family. At the beginning of the decade there were two children: Laura, aged three, and Edmund, a year and a half younger. In some respects these children, while small, were more fortunate than their neighbours. Their father earned a little more money than the labourers. Their mother had been a children's nurse and they were well looked after. They were taught good manners and taken for walks, milk was bought for them, and they were bathed regularly on Saturday nights and, after 'Gentle Jesus' was said, were tucked up in bed with a peppermint or clove ball to suck. They had tidier clothes, too, for their mother had taste and skill with her needle and better-off relations sent them parcels of outgrown clothes. The other children used to tease the little girl about the lace on her drawers and led her such a life that she once took them off and hid them in a haystack.

Their mother at that time used to say that she dreaded the day when they would have to go to school; children got so wild and rude and tore their clothes to shreds going the mile and a half backwards and forwards. But when the time came for them to go she was glad, for, after a break of five years, more babies had begun to arrive, and, by the end of the 'eighties, there were six children at the end house.

As they grew, the two elder children would ask questions of anybody and everybody willing or unwilling to answer them.

Who planted the buttercups? Why did God let the wheat get blighted? Who lived in this house before we did, and what were their children's names? What's the sea like? Is it bigger than Cottisloe Pond? *Why* can't we go to Heaven in the donkey-cart? Is it farther than Banbury? And so on, taking their bearings in that small corner of the world they had somehow got into.

This asking of questions teased their mother and made them unpopular with the neighbours. 'Little children should be seen and not heard', they were told at home. Out of doors it would more often be 'Ask no questions and you'll be told no lies.' One old woman once handed the little girl a leaf from a pot-plant on her window-sill. 'What's it called?' was the inevitable question. ' 'Tis called mind your own business,' was the reply; 'an' I think I'd better give a slip of it to your mother to plant in a pot for you.' But no such reproofs could cure them of the habit, although they soon learned who and who not to question.

In this way they learned the little that was known of the past of the hamlet and of places beyond. They had no need to ask the names of the birds, flowers, and trees they saw every day, for they had already learned these unconsciously, and neither could remember a time when they did not know an oak from an ash, wheat from barley, or a Jenny wren from a blue-tit. Of what was going on around them, not much was hidden, for the gossips talked freely before children, evidently considering them not meant to hear as well as not to be heard, and, as every house was open to them and their own home was open to most people, there was not much that escaped their sharp ears.

The first charge on the labourers' ten shillings was house rent. Most of the cottages belonged to small tradesmen in the market town and the weekly rents ranged from one shilling to half a crown. Some labourers in other villages worked on farms or estates where they had their cottages rent free; but the hamlet people did not envy them, for 'Stands to reason,' they said, 'they've allus got to do just what they be told, or out they goes, neck and crop, bag and baggage.' A shilling, or even two shillings a week, they felt, was not too much to pay for the freedom to live and vote as they liked and to go to church or chapel or neither as they preferred.

Every house had a good vegetable garden and there were allotments for all; but only three of the thirty cottages had their own water supply. The less fortunate tenants obtained their water from a well on a vacant plot on the outskirts of the hamlet, from which the cottage had disappeared. There was no public well or pump. They just had to get their water where and how they could; the landlords did not undertake to supply water.

Against the wall of every well-kept cottage stood a tarred or green-painted water butt to catch and store the rain-water from the roof. This saved many journeys to the well with buckets, as it could be used for cleaning and washing clothes and for watering small, precious things in the garden. It was also valued for toilet purposes and women would hoard the last drops for themselves and their children to wash in. Rain-water was supposed to be good for the complexion, and, though they had no money to spend upon beautifying themselves, they were not too far gone in poverty to neglect such means as they had to that end.

For drinking water, and for cleaning water, too, when the water butts failed, the women went to the well in all weathers, drawing up the buckets with a windlass and carting them home suspended from their shoulders by a yoke. Those were weary journeys 'round the Rise' for water, and many were the rests and endless was the gossip, as they stood at corners in their big white aprons and crossover shawls.

A few of the younger, more recently married women who had been in good service and had not yet given up the attempt to hold themselves a little aloof would get their husbands to fill the big red store crock with water at night. But this was said by others to be 'a sin and a shame', for, after his hard day's work, a man wanted his rest, not to do ' 'ooman's work'. Later on in the decade it became the fashion for the men to fetch water at night, and then, of course, it was quite right that they should do so and a woman who 'dragged her guts out' fetching more than an occasional load from the well was looked upon as a traitor to her sex.

In dry summers, when the hamlet wells failed, water had to

be fetched from a pump at some farm buildings half a mile distant. Those who had wells in their gardens would not give away a spot, as they feared if they did theirs, too, would run dry, so they fastened down the lids with padlocks and disregarded all hints.

The only sanitary arrangement known in the hamlet was housed either in a little beehive-shaped building at the bottom of the garden or in a corner of the wood and toolshed known as 'the hovel'. It was not even an earth closet; but merely a deep pit with a seat set over it, the half-yearly emptying of which caused every door and window in the vicinity to be sealed. Unfortunately, there was no means of sealing the chimneys!

The 'privies' were as good an index as any to the characters of their owners. Some were horrible holes; others were fairly decent, while some, and these not a few, were kept well cleared, with the seat scrubbed to snow-whiteness and the brick floor raddled. One old woman even went so far as to nail up a text as a finishing touch, 'Thou God seest me' – most embarrassing to a Victorian child who had been taught that no one must even see her approach the door.

In other such places health and sanitary maxims were scrawled with lead pencil or yellow chalk on the whitewashed walls. Most of them embodied sound sense and some were expressed in sound verse, but few were so worded as to be printable. One short and pithy maxim may pass: 'Eat well, work well, sleep well, and — well once a day.'

On the wall of the 'little house' at Laura's home pictures cut from the newspapers were pasted. These were changed when the walls were whitewashed and in succession they were 'The Bombardment of Alexandria', all clouds of smoke, flying fragments, and flashes of explosives; 'Glasgow's Mournful Disaster: Plunges from Life from the *Daphne*', and 'The Tay Bridge Disaster', with the end of the train dangling from the broken bridge over a boiling sea. It was before the day of Press photography and the artists were able to give their imagination full play. Later, the place of honour in the 'little house' was occupied by 'Our Political Leaders', two rows of portraits on one print; Mr Gladstone, with hawk-like countenance and flashing eyes, in the middle of the top row, and kind, sleepy-looking Lord Salisbury in the other. Laura loved that picture because Lord Randolph Churchill was there. She thought he must be the most handsome man in the world.

At the back or side of each cottage was a lean-to pigsty and the house refuse was thrown on a nearby pile called 'the muck'll'. This was so situated that the oozings from the sty could drain into it; the manure was also thrown there when the sty was cleared, and the whole formed a nasty, smelly eyesore to have within a few feet of the windows. 'The wind's in the so-and-so,' some woman indoors would say, 'I can smell th' muck'll,' and she would often be reminded of the saying, 'Pigs for health', or told that the smell was a healthy one.

It was in a sense a healthy smell for them; for a good pig fattening in the sty promised a good winter. During its lifetime the pig was an important member of the family, and its health and condition were regularly reported in letters to children away from home, together with news of their brothers and sisters. Men callers on Sunday afternoons came, not to see the family, but the pig, and would lounge with its owner against the pigsty door for an hour, scratching piggy's back and praising his points or turning up their own noses in criticism. Ten to fifteen shillings was the price paid for a pigling when weaned, and they all delighted in getting a bargain. Some men swore by the 'dilling', as the smallest of a litter was called, saying it was little and good, and would soon catch up; others preferred to give a few shillings more for a larger young pig.

The family pig was everybody's pride and everybody's business. Mother spent hours boiling up the 'little taturs' to mash and mix with the pot-liquor, in which food had been cooked, to feed to the pig for its evening meal and help out the expensive barley meal. The children, on their way home from school, would fill their arms with sow thistle, dandelion, and choice long grass, or roam along the hedgerows on wet evenings collecting snails in a pail for the pig's supper. These piggy crunched up with great relish. 'Feyther', over and above farming out the sty, bedding down, doctoring, and so on, would even go without his nightly half-pint when, towards the end, the barley-meal mounted until 'it fair frightened anybody'.

Sometimes, when the weekly income would not run to a sufficient quantity of fattening food, an arrangement would be made with the baker or miller that he should give credit now, and when the pig was killed receive a portion of the meat in payment. More often than not one-half the pig-meat would be mortgaged in this way, and it was no uncommon thing to hear a woman say, 'Us be going to kill half a pig, please God, come Friday,' leaving the uninitiated to conclude that the other half would still run about in the sty.

Some of the families killed two separate half pigs a year; others one, or even two, whole ones, and the meat provided them with bacon for the winter or longer. Fresh meat was a luxury only seen in a few of the cottages on Sunday, when six-pennyworth of pieces would be bought to make a meat pudding. If a small joint came their way as a Saturday night bargain, those without oven grates would roast it by suspending it on a string before the fire, with one of the children in attendance as turnspit. Or a 'pot-roast' would be made by placing the meat with a little lard or other fat in an iron saucepan and keeping it well shaken over the fire. But, after all, as they said, there was nothing to beat a 'toad'. For this the meat was enclosed whole in a suet crust and well boiled, a method which preserved all the delicious juices of the meat and provided a good pudding into the bargain. When some superior person tried to give them a hint, the women used to say, 'You tell us how to get the victuals; we can cook it all right when we've got it'; and they could.

When the pig was fattened – and the fatter the better – the date of execution had to be decided upon. It had to take place some time during the first two quarters of the moon; for, if the pig was killed when the moon was waning the bacon would shrink in cooking, and they wanted it to 'plimp up'. The next thing was to engage the travelling pork butcher, or pig-sticker, and, as he was a thatcher by day, he always had to kill after dark, the scene being lighted with lanterns and the fire of burning straw which at a later stage of the proceedings was to singe the bristles off the victim.

The killing was a noisy, bloody business, in the course of which the animal was hoisted to a rough bench that it might bleed thoroughly and so preserve the quality of the meat. The job was often bungled, the pig sometimes getting away and having to be chased; but country people of that day had little sympathy for the sufferings of animals, and men, women, and children would gather round to see the sight.

After the carcass had been singed, the pig-sticker would pull off the detachable, gristly, outer coverings of the toes, known locally as 'the shoes', and fling them among the children, who scrambled for, then sucked and gnawed them, straight from the filth of the sty and blackened by fire as they were.

The whole scene, with its mud and blood, flaring lights and dark shadows, was as savage as anything to be seen in an African jungle. The children at the end house would steal out of bed to the window. 'Look! Look! It's hell, and those are the devils,' Edmund would whisper, pointing to the men tossing the burning straw with their pitchforks; but Laura felt sick and would creep back into bed and cry: she was sorry for the pig.

But, hidden from the children, there was another aspect of the pig-killing. Months of hard work and self-denial were brought on that night to a successful conclusion. It was a time to rejoice, and rejoice they did, with beer flowing freely and the first delicious dish of pig's fry sizzling in the frying-pan.

The next day, when the carcass had been cut up, joints of pork were distributed to those neighbours who had sent similar ones at their own pig-killing. Small plates of fry and other oddments were sent to others as a pure compliment, and no one who happened to be ill or down on his luck at these occasions was ever forgotten.

Then the housewife 'got down to it', as she said. Hams and sides of bacon were salted, to be taken out of the brine later and hung on the wall near the fireplace to dry. Lard was dried out, hog's puddings were made, and the chitterlings were cleaned and turned three days in succession under running water, according to ancient ritual. It was a busy time, but a happy one, with the larder full and something over to give away, and all the pride and importance of owning such riches.

On the following Sunday came the official 'pig feast', when fathers and mothers, sisters and brothers, married children and grandchildren who lived within walking distance arrived to dinner.

If the house had no oven, permission was obtained from an old couple in one of the thatched cottages to heat up the big bread-baking oven in their wash-house. This was like a large cupboard with an iron door, lined with brick and going far back into the wall. Faggots of wood were lighted inside and the door was closed upon them until the oven was well heated. Then the ashes were swept out and baking tins with joints of pork, potatoes, batter puddings, pork pies, and sometimes a cake or two, were popped inside and left to bake without further attention.

Meanwhile, at home, three or four different kinds of vegetables would be cooked, and always a meat pudding, made in a basin. No feast and few Sunday dinners were considered complete without that item, which was eaten alone, without vegetables, when a joint was to follow. On ordinary days the pudding would be a roly-poly containing fruit, currants, or jam; but it still appeared as a first course, the idea being that it took the edge off the appetite. At the pig feast there would be no sweet pudding, for that could be had any day, and who wanted sweet things when there was plenty of meat to be had!

But this glorious plenty only came once or at most twice a year, and there were all the other days to provide for. How was it done on ten shillings a week? Well, for one thing, food was much cheaper than it is today. Then, in addition to the bacon, all vegetables, including potatoes, were home-grown and grown in abundance. The men took great pride in their gardens and allotments and there was always competition amongst them as to who should have the earliest and choicest of each kind. Fat green peas, broad beans as big as a halfpenny, cauliflowers a child could make an armchair of, runner beans and cabbage and kale, all in their seasons went into the pot with the roly-poly and slip of bacon.

Then they ate plenty of green food, all home-grown and freshly pulled; lettuce and radishes and young onions with

pearly heads and leaves like fine grass. A few slices of bread and
home-made lard, flavoured with rosemary, and plenty of green
food 'went down good' as they used to say.

Bread had to be bought, and that was a heavy item, with so
many growing children to be fed; but flour for the daily
pudding and an occasional plain cake could be laid in for the
winter without any cash outlay. After the harvest had been
carried from the fields, the women and children swarmed over
the stubble picking up the ears of wheat the horse-rake had
missed. Gleaning, or 'leazing', as it was called locally.

Up and down and over and over the stubble they hurried,
backs bent, eyes on the ground, one hand outstretched to pick
up the ears, the other resting on the small of the back with the
'handful'. When this had been completed, it was bound round
with a wisp of straw and erected with others in a double rank,
like the harvesters erected their sheaves in shocks, beside the
leazer's water-can and dinner-basket. It was hard work, from as
soon as possible after daybreak until nightfall, with only two
short breaks for refreshment; but the single ears mounted, and
a woman with four or five strong, well-disciplined children
would carry a good load home on the head every night. And
they enjoyed doing it, for it was pleasant in the fields under the
pale blue August sky, with the clover springing green in the
stubble and the hedges bright with hips and haws and feathery
with traveller's joy. When the rest-hour came, the children
would wander off down the hedgerows gathering crab-apples or
sloes, or searching for mushrooms, while the mothers reclined
and suckled their babes and drank their cold tea and gossiped or
dozed until it was time to be at it again.

At the end of the fortnight or three weeks that the leazing
lasted, the corn would be thrashed out at home and sent to the
miller, who paid himself for grinding by taking toll of the flour.
Great was the excitement in a good year when the flour came
home – one bushel, two bushels, or even more in large, industrious families. The mealy-white sack with its contents was
often kept for a time on show on a chair in the living-room and
it was a common thing for a passer-by to be invited to 'step
inside an' see our little bit o' leazings'. They liked to have the

product of their labour before their own eyes and to let others admire it, just as the artist likes to show his picture and the composer to hear his opus played. 'Them's better'n any o' yer oil-paintin's,' a man would say, pointing to the flitches on his wall, and the women felt the same about the leazings.

Here, then, were the three chief ingredients of the one hot meal a day, bacon from the flitch, vegetables from the garden, and flour for the roly-poly. This meal, called 'tea', was taken in the evening, when the men were home from the fields and the children from school, for neither could get home at midday.

About four o'clock, smoke would go up from the chimneys, as the fire was made up and the big iron boiler, or the three-legged pot, was slung on the hook of the chimney-chain. Everything was cooked in the one utensil; the square of bacon, amounting to little more than a taste each; cabbage, or other green vegetables in one net, potatoes in another, and the roly-poly swathed in a cloth. It sounds a haphazard method in these days of gas and electric cookers; but it answered its purpose, for, by carefully timing the putting in of each item and keeping the simmering of the pot well regulated, each item was kept intact and an appetising meal was produced. The water in which the food had been cooked, the potato parings, and other vegetable trimmings were the pig's share.

When the men came home from work they would find the table spread with a clean whitey-brown cloth, upon which would be knives and two-pronged steel forks with buckhorn handles. The vegetables would then be turned out into big round yellow crockery dishes and the bacon cut into dice, with much the largest cube upon Feyther's plate, and the whole family would sit down to the chief meal of the day. True, it was seldom that all could find places at the central table; but some of the smaller children could sit upon stools with the seat of a chair for a table, or on the doorstep with their plates on their laps.

Good manners prevailed. The children were given their share of the food, there was no picking and choosing, and they were expected to eat it in silence. 'Please' and 'Thank you' were permitted, but nothing more. Father and Mother might talk if they wanted to; but usually they were content to concentrate upon their enjoyment of the meal. Father might shovel green peas into his mouth with his knife, Mother might drink her tea from her saucer, and some of the children might lick their plates when the food was devoured; but who could eat peas with a two-pronged fork, or wait for tea to cool after the heat and flurry of cooking, and licking the plates passed as a graceful compliment to Mother's good dinner. 'Thank God for my good dinner. Thank Father and Mother. Amen' was the grace used in one family, and it certainly had the merit of giving credit where credit was due.

For other meals they depended largely on bread and butter, or, more often, bread and lard, eaten with any relish that happened to be at hand. Fresh butter was too costly for general use, but a pound was sometimes purchased in the summer, when it cost tenpence. Margarine, then called 'butterine', was already on the market, but was little used there, as most people preferred lard, especially when it was their own home-made lard flavoured with rosemary leaves. In summer there was always plenty of green food from the garden and home-made jam as long as it lasted, and sometimes an egg or two, where fowls were kept, or when eggs were plentiful and sold at twenty a shilling.

When bread and lard appeared alone, the men would spread mustard on their slices and the children would be given a scraping of black treacle or a sprinkling of brown sugar. Some children, who preferred it, would have 'sop' – bread steeped in boiling water, then strained and sugar added.

Milk was a rare luxury, as it had to be fetched a mile and a half from the farmhouse. The cost was not great: a penny a jug or can, irrespective of size. It was, of course, skimmed milk, but hand-skimmed, not separated, and so still had some small proportion of cream left. A few families fetched it daily; but many did not bother about it. The women said they preferred their tea neat, and it did not seem to occur to them that the children needed milk. Many of them never tasted it from the time they were weaned until they went out in the world. Yet they were stout-limbed and rosy-cheeked and full of life and mischief.

The skimmed milk was supposed by the farmer to be sold at a penny a pint, that remaining unsold going to feed his own calves and pigs. But the dairymaid did not trouble to measure it; she just filled the proffered vessel and let it go as 'a pen'orth'. Of course, the jugs and cans got larger and larger. One old woman increased the size of her vessels by degrees until she had the impudence to take a small, new, tin cooking boiler which was filled without question. The children at the end house wondered what she could do with so much milk, as she had only her husband and herself at home. 'That'll make you a nice big rice pudding. Queenie,' one of them said tentatively.

'Pudden! Lor' bless 'ee!' was Queenie's reply. 'I don't ever make no rice puddens. That milk's for my pig's supper, an', my! ain't 'ee just about thrivin' on it. Can't hardly see out of his eyes, bless him!'

'Poverty's no disgrace, but 'tis a great inconvenience' was a common saying among the Lark Rise people; but that put the case too mildly, for their poverty was no less than a hampering drag upon them. Everybody had enough to eat and a shelter which, though it fell far short of modern requirements, satisfied them. Coal at a shilling a hundredweight and a pint of paraffin for lighting *had* to be squeezed out of the weekly wage; but for boots, clothes, illness, holidays, amusements, and household renewals there was no provision whatever. How did they manage?

Boots were often bought with the extra money the men earned in the harvest field. When that was paid, those lucky families which were not in arrears with their rent would have a new pair all round, from the father's hobnailed dreadnoughts to little pink kid slippers for the baby. Then some careful housewives paid a few pence every week into the boot club run by a shopkeeper in the market town. This helped; but it was not sufficient, and how to get a pair of new boots for 'our young Ern or Alf' was a problem which kept many a mother awake at night.

Girls needed boots, too, and good, stout, nailed ones for those rough and muddy roads; but they were not particular, any boots would do. At a confirmation class which Laura attended, the clergyman's daughter, after weeks of careful preparation, asked her catechumens: 'Now, are you sure you are all of you thoroughly prepared for tomorrow. Is there anything you would like to ask me?'

'Yes, miss,' piped up a voice in a corner, 'me mother says have you got a pair of your old boots you could give me, for I haven't got any fit to go in.'

Alice got her boots on that occasion; but there was not a confirmation every day. Still, boots were obtained somehow; nobody went barefoot, even though some of the toes might sometimes stick out beyond the toe of the boot.

To obtain clothes was an even more difficult matter. Mothers of families sometimes said in despair that they supposed they would have to black their own backsides and go naked. They never quite came to that; but it was difficult to keep decently covered, and that was a pity because they did dearly love what they called 'anything a bit dressy'. This taste was not encouraged by the garments made by the girls in school from material given by the Rectory people – roomy chemises and wide-legged drawers made of unbleached calico, beautifully sewn, but without an inch of trimming; harsh, but strong flannel petticoats and worsted stockings that would almost stand up with no legs in them – although these were gratefully received and had their merits, for they wore for years and the calico improved with washing.

For outer garments they had to depend upon daughters, sisters, and aunts away in service, who all sent parcels, not only of their own clothes, but also of those they could beg from their mistresses. These were worn and altered and dyed and turned and ultimately patched and darned as long as the threads hung together.

But, in spite of their poverty and the worry and anxiety attending it, they were not unhappy, and, though poor, there was nothing sordid about their lives. 'The nearer the bone the sweeter the meat', they used to say, and they were getting very near the bone from which their country ancestors had fed. Their children and children's children would have to depend wholly upon whatever was carved for them from the communal

joint, and for their pleasure upon the mass enjoyments of a new
era. But for that generation there was still a small picking left to
supplement the weekly wage. They had their home-cured
bacon, their 'bit o' leazings', their small wheat or barley patch
on the allotment; their knowledge of herbs for their homely
simples, and the wild fruits and berries of the countryside for
jam, jellies, and wine, and round about them as part of their
lives were the last relics of country customs and the last echoes
of country songs, ballads, and game rhymes. This last picking,
though meagre, was sweet.

II

A Hamlet Childhood

OXFORD was only nineteen miles distant. The children at the
end house knew that, for, while they were small, they were
often taken by their mother for a walk along the turnpike and
would never pass the milestone until the inscription had been
read to them: OXFORD XIX MILES.

They often wondered what Oxford was like and asked questions about it. One answer was that it was 'a gert big town'
where a man might earn as much as five and twenty shillings a
week; but as he would have to pay 'pretty near' half of it in
house rent and have nowhere to keep a pig or to grow many
vegetables, he'd be a fool to go there.

One girl who had actually been there on a visit said you could
buy a long stick of pink-and-white rock for a penny and that
one of her aunt's young gentlemen lodgers had given her a
whole shilling for cleaning his shoes. Their mother said it was
called a city because a bishop lived there, and that a big fair was
held there once a year, and that was all she seemed to know
about it. They did not ask their father, although he had lived
there as a child, when his parents had kept an hotel in the city
(his relations spoke of it as an hotel, but his wife once called it a
pot-house, so probably it was an ordinary public-house). They
already had to be careful not to ask their father too many

questions, and when their mother said, 'Your father's cross again', they found it was better not to talk at all.

So, for some time, Oxford remained to them a dim blur of bishops (they had seen a picture of one with big white sleeves, sitting in a high-backed chair) and swings and shows and coconut shies (for they knew what a fair was like) and little girls sucking pink-and-white rock and polishing shoes. To imagine a place without pigsties and vegetable gardens was more difficult. With no bacon or cabbage, what could people have to eat?

But the Oxford road with the milestone they had known as long as they could remember. Round the Rise and up the narrow hamlet road they would go until they came to the turning, their mother pushing the baby carriage ('pram' was a word of the future) with Edmund strapped in the high, slippery seat, or, later, little May, who was born when Edmund was five, and Laura holding on at the side or darting hither and thither to pick flowers.

The baby carriage was made of black wickerwork, something like an old-fashioned bath-chair in shape, running on three wheels and pushed from behind. It wobbled and creaked and rattled over the stones, for rubber tyres were not yet invented and its springs, if springs it had, were of the most primitive kind. Yet it was one of the most cherished of the family possessions, for there was only one other baby carriage in the hamlet, the up-to-date new bassinet which the young wife at the inn had recently purchased. The other mothers carried their babies on one arm, tightly rolled in shawls, with only the face showing.

As soon as the turning was passed, the flat, brown fields were left behind and they were in a different world with a different atmosphere and even different flowers. Up and down went the white main road between wide grass margins, thick, berried hedgerows and overhanging trees. After the dark mire of the hamlet ways, even the milky-white road surface pleased them, and they would splash up the thin, pale mud, like uncooked batter, or drag their feet through the smooth white dust until their mother got cross and slapped them.

Although it was a main road, there was scarcely any traffic,

for the market town lay in the opposite direction along it, the
next village was five miles on, and with Oxford there was no
road communication from that distant point in those days of
horse-drawn vehicles. Today, past that same spot, a first-class,
tar-sprayed road, thronged with motor traffic, runs between
low, closely trimmed hedges. Last year a girl of eighteen was
knocked down and killed by a passing car at that very turning.
At that time it was deserted for hours together. Three miles
away trains roared over a viaduct, carrying those who would,
had they lived a few years before or later, have used the turnpike. People were saying that far too much money was being
spent on keeping such roads in repair, for their day was over;
they were only needed now for people going from village to
village. Sometimes the children and their mother would meet a
tradesman's van, delivering goods from the market town at
some country mansion, or the doctor's tall gig, or the smart
turn-out of a brewer's traveller; but often they walked their
mile along the turnpike and back without seeing anything on
wheels.

The white tails of rabbits bobbed in and out of the hedgerows; stoats crossed the road in front of the children's feet —
swift, silent, stealthy creatures which made them shudder; there
were squirrels in the oak-trees, and once they even saw a fox
curled up asleep in the ditch beneath thick overhanging ivy.
Bands of little blue butterflies flitted here and there or poised
themselves with quivering wings on the long grass bents; bees
hummed in the white clover blooms, and over all a deep silence
brooded. It seemed as though the road had been made ages
before, then forgotten.

The children were allowed to run freely on the grass verges,
as wide as a small meadow in places. 'Keep to the grinsard,'
their mother would call. 'Don't go on the road. Keep to the
grinsard!' and it was many years before Laura realized that that
name for the grass verges, in general use there, was a worn
survival of the old English 'greensward'.

It was no hardship to her to be obliged to keep to the greensward, for flowers strange to the hamlet soil flourished there,
eyebright and harebell, sunset-coloured patches of lady's-glove,

and succory with vivid blue flowers and stems like black wire.

In one little roadside dell mushrooms might ·sometimes be found, small button mushrooms with beaded moisture on their cold milk-white skins. The dell was the farthest point of their walk; after searching the long grass for mushrooms, in season and out of season – for they would not give up hope – they turned back and never reached the second milestone.

Once or twice when they reached the dell they got a greater thrill than even the discovery of a mushroom could give; for the gipsies were there, their painted caravan drawn up, their poor old skeleton horse turned loose to graze, and their fire with a cooking pot over it, as though the whole road belonged to them. With men making pegs, women combing their hair or making cabbage nets, and boys and girls and dogs sprawling around, the dell was full of dark, wild life, foreign to the hamlet children and fascinating, yet terrifying.

When they saw the gipsies they drew back behind their mother and the baby carriage, for there was a tradition that once, years before, a child from a neighbouring village had been stolen by them. Even the cold ashes where a gipsy's fire had been sent little squiggles of fear down Laura's spine, for how could she knew that they were not still lurking near with designs upon her own person? Her mother laughed at her fears and said, 'Surely to goodness they've got children enough of their own,' but Laura would not be reassured. She never really enjoyed the game the hamlet children played going home from school, when one of them went on before to hide and the others followed slowly, hand in hand, singing:

> 'I hope we shan't meet any gipsies tonight!
> I hope we shan't meet any gipsies tonight!'

And when the hiding-place was reached and the supposed gipsy sprung out and grabbed the nearest, she always shrieked, although she knew it was only a game.

But in those early days of the walks fear only gave spice to excitement, for Mother was there, Mother in her pretty maize-coloured gown with the rows and rows of narrow brown velvet sewn round the long skirt, which stuck out like a bell, and her second-best hat with the honeysuckle. She was still in her twenties and still very pretty, with her neat little figure, rose-leaf complexion and hair which was brown in some lights and golden in others. When her family grew larger and troubles crowded upon her and the rose-leaf complexion had faded and the last of the pre-marriage wardrobe had worn out, the walks were given up; but by that time Edmund and Laura were old enough to go where they liked, and, though they usually preferred to go farther afield on Saturdays and other school holidays, they would sometimes go to the turnpike to jump over and over the milestone and scramble about in the hedges for blackberries and crab-apples.

It was while they were still small they were walking there one day with a visiting aunt; Edmund and Laura, both in clean, white, starched clothes, holding on to a hand on either side. The children were a little shy, for they did not remember seeing this aunt before. She was married to a master builder in Yorkshire and only visited her brother and his family at long intervals. But they liked her, although Laura had already sensed that their mother did not. Jane was too dressy and 'set up' for her taste, she said. That morning, her luggage being still at the railway station, she was wearing the clothes she had travelled in, a long, pleated dove-coloured gown with an apron arrangement drawn round and up and puffed over a bustle at the back, and, on her head, a tiny toque made entirely of purple velvet pansies.

Swish, swish, swish, went her long skirt over the grass verges; but every time they crossed the road she would relinquish Laura's hand to gather it up from the dust, thus revealing to the child's delighted gaze a frilly purple petticoat. When she was grown up she would have a frock and petticoat just like those, she decided.

But Edmund was not interested in clothes. Being a polite little boy, he was trying to make conversation. He had already shown his aunt the spot where they had found the dead hedgehog and the bush where the thrush had built last spring and told her the distant rumble they heard was a train going over the viaduct, when they came to the milestone.

'Aunt Jenny,' he said, 'what's Oxford like?'

'Well, it's all old buildings, churches and colleges where rich people's sons go to school when they're grown up.'

'What do they learn there?' demanded Laura.

'Oh, Latin and Greek and suchlike, I suppose.'

'Do they all go there?' asked Edmund seriously.

'Well, no. Some go to Cambridge; there are colleges there as well. Some go to one and some to the other,' said the aunt with a smile that meant 'Whatever will these children want to know next?'

Four-year-old Edmund pondered a few moments, then said, 'Which college shall I go to when I am grown up, Oxford or Cambridge?' and his expression of innocent good faith checked his aunt's inclination to laugh.

'There won't be any college for you, my poor little man,' she explained. 'You'll have to go to work as soon as you leave school; but if I could have *my* way, you should go to the very best college in Oxford,' and, for the rest of the walk she entertained them with stories of her mother's family, the Wallingtons.

She said one of her uncles had written a book and she thought Edmund might turn out to be clever, like him. But when they told their mother what she had said she tossed her head and said she had never heard about any book, and what if he had, wasting his time. It was not as if he was like Shakespeare or Miss Braddon or anybody like that. And she hoped Edmund would not turn out to be clever. Brains were no good to a working man; they only made him discontented and saucy and lose his jobs. She'd seen it happen again and again.

Yet she had brains of her own and her education had been above the average in her station in life. She had been born and brought up in a cottage standing in the churchyard of a neighbouring village, 'just like the little girl in *We are Seven*', she used to tell her own children. At the time when she was a small girl in the churchyard cottage the incumbent of the parish had been an old man and with him had lived his still more aged sister. This lady, whose name was Miss Lowe, had become very fond of the pretty, fair-haired little girl at the churchyard cottage and had had her at the Rectory every day out of school hours. Little Emma had a sweet voice and she was supposed to go there for singing lessons; but she had learned other things, too, including old-world manners and to write a beautiful antique hand with delicate, open-looped pointed letters and long 's's', such as her instructress and other young ladies had been taught in the last quarter of the eighteenth century.

Miss Lowe was then nearly eighty, and had long been dead when Laura, at two and a half years old, had been taken by her mother to see the by then very aged Rector. The visit was one of her earliest memories, which survived as an indistinct impression of twilight in a room with dark green walls and the branch of a tree against the outside of the window; and, more distinctly, a pair of trembling, veiny hands putting something smooth and cold and round into her own. The smooth cold roundness was accounted for afterwards. The old gentleman, it appeared, had given her a china mug which had been his sister's in her nursery days. It had stood on the mantelpiece at the end house for years, a beautiful old piece with a design of heavy green foliage on a ground of translucent whiteness. Afterwards it got broken, which was strange in that careful home; but Laura carried the design in her mind's eye for the rest of her life and would sometimes wonder if it accounted for her lifelong love of green and white in conjunction.

Their mother would often tell the children about the Rectory and her own home in the churchyard, and how the choir, in which her father played the violin, would bring their instruments and practise there in the evening. But she liked better to tell of that other rectory where she had been nurse to the children. The living was small and the Rector was poor, but three maids had been possible in those days, a cook-general, a young housemaid, and Nurse Emma. They must have been needed in that large, rambling old house, in which lived the Rector and his wife, their nine children, three maids, and often three or four young men pupils. They had all had such jolly, happy times she said; all of them, family and maids and pupils, singing glees and part songs in the drawing-room in the evening. But what thrilled Laura most was that she herself had had a narrow escape from ever having been born at all. Some relatives of the family who had settled in New South Wales had come to England on a visit and nearly persuaded Nurse Emma to go back with them. Indeed, it was all settled when, one night, they began talking about snakes, which, according to their account, infested their Australian bungalow and garden. 'Then,' said Emma, 'I shan't go, for I can't abear the horrid creatures,' and she did not go, but got married instead and became the mother of Edmund and Laura. But it seems that the call was genuine, that Australia had something for, or required something of, her descendants; for of the next generation her own second son became a fruit-farmer in Queensland, and of the next a son of Laura's is now an engineer in Brisbane.

The little Johnstones were always held up as an example to the end-house children. They were always kind to each other and obedient to their elders, never grubby or rowdy or incon-siderate. Perhaps they deteriorated after Nurse Emma left, for Laura remembered being taken to see them before they left the neighbourhood for good, when one of the big boys pulled her hair and made faces at her and buried her doll beneath a tree in the orchard, with one of the cook's aprons tied round his neck by way of a surplice.

The eldest girl, Miss Lily, then about nineteen, walked miles of the way back home with them and returned alone in the twilight (so Victorian young ladies were not always as carefully guarded as they are now supposed to have been!). Laura re-membered the low murmur of conversation behind her as she rode for a lift on the front of the baby carriage with her heels dangling over the front wheel. Both a Sir George and a Mr Looker, it appeared, were paying Miss Lily 'particular atten-tion' at the time, and their rival advantages were under dis-cussion. Every now and then Miss Lily would protest, 'But, Emma, Sir George paid me *particular attention*. Many re-marked upon it to Mamma,' and Emma would say, 'But, Miss Lily, my dear, do you think he is serious?' Perhaps he was, for Miss Lily was a lovely girl; but it was as Mrs Looker she became a kind of fairy godmother to the end-house family. A Christmas parcel of books and toys came from her regularly, and although she never saw her old nurse again, they were still writing to each other in the nineteen-twenties.

Around the hamlet cottages played many little children, too young to go to school. Every morning they were bundled into a piece of old shawl crossed on the chest and tied in a hard knot at the back, a slice of food was thrust into their hands and they were told to 'go play' while their mothers got on with the housework. In winter, their little limbs purple-mottled with cold, they would stamp around playing horses or engines. In summer they would make mud pies in the dust, moistening them from their own most intimate water supply. If they fell down or hurt themselves in any other way, they did not run indoors for comfort, for they knew that all they would get would be 'Sarves ye right. You should've looked where you wer' a-goin'!'

They were like little foals turned out to grass, and received about as much attention. They might, and often did, have running noses and chilblains on hands, feet and ear-tips; but they hardly ever were ill enough to have to stay indoors, and grew sturdy and strong, so the system must have suited them. 'Makes 'em hardy,' their mothers said, and hardy, indeed, they became, just as the men and women and older boys and girls of the hamlet were hardy, in body and spirit.

Sometimes Laura and Edmund would go out to play with the other children. Their father did not like this; he said they were little savages already. But their mother maintained that, as they would have to go to school soon, it was better for them to fall in at once with the hamlet ways. 'Besides,' she would say, 'why shouldn't they? There's nothing the matter with Lark Rise folks but poverty, and that's no crime. If it was, we should likely be hung ourselves.'

So the children went out to play and often had happy times, outlining houses with scraps of broken crockery and furnishing them with moss and stones; or lying on their stomachs in the dust to peer down into the deep cracks dry weather always produced in that stiff, clayey soil; or making snow men or sliding on puddles in winter.

Other times were not so pleasant, for a quarrel would arise and kicks and blows would fly freely, and how hard those little two-year-old fists could hit out! To say that a child was as broad as it was long was considered a compliment by the hamlet mothers, and some of those toddlers in their knotted woollen wrappings were as near square as anything human can be. One little girl named Rosie Phillips fascinated Laura. She was plump and hard and as rosy-cheeked as an apple, with the deepest of dimples and hair like bronze wire. No matter how hard the other children bumped into her in the games, she stood four-square, as firm as a little rock. She was a very hard hitter and had little, pointed, white teeth that bit. The two tamer children always came out worst in these conflicts. Then they would make a dash on their long stalky legs for their own garden gate, followed by stones and cries of 'Long-shanks! Cowardy, cowardy custards!'

During those early years at the end house plans were always being made and discussed. Edmund must be apprenticed to a good trade – a carpenter's, perhaps – for if a man had a good trade in his hands he was always sure of a living. Laura might become a school-teacher, or, if that proved impossible, a children's nurse in a good family. But, first and foremost, the family must move from Lark Rise to a house in the market town. It had always been the parents' intention to leave. When he met and married his wife the father was a stranger in the neighbourhood, working for a few months on the restoration of the church in a neighbouring parish and the end house had been taken as a temporary home. Then the children had come and other things had happened to delay the removal. They could not give notice until Michaelmas Day, or another baby was coming, or they must wait until the pig was killed or the allotment crops were brought in; there was always some obstacle, and at the end of seven years they were still at the end house and still talking almost daily about leaving it. Fifty years later the father had died there and the mother was living there alone.

When Laura approached school-going age the discussions became more urgent. Her father did not want the children to go to school with the hamlet children and for once her mother agreed with him. Not because, as he said, they ought to have a better education than they could get at Lark Rise; but because she feared they would tear their clothes and catch cold and get dirty heads going the mile and a half to and from the school in the mother village. So vacant cottages in the market town were inspected and often it seemed that the next week or the next month they would be leaving Lark Rise for ever; but, again, each time something would happen to prevent the removal, and, gradually, a new idea arose. To gain time, their father would teach the two eldest children to read and write, so that, if approached by the School Attendance Office, their mother could say they were leaving the hamlet shortly and, in the meantime, were being taught at home.

So their father brought home two copies of Mavor's First Reader and taught them the alphabet; but just as Laura was beginning on words of one syllable, he was sent away to work on a distant job, only coming home at week-ends. Laura, left at the 'C-a-t s-i-t-s on the m-a-t' stage, had then to carry her book round after her mother as she went about her housework, asking: 'Please, Mother, what does h-o-u-s-e spell?' or 'W-a-l-k, Mother, what is that?' Often when her mother was too busy or too irritated to attend to her, she would sit and gaze on a page that might as well have been printed in Hebrew for all she could make of it, frowning and poring over the print as though she would wring out the meaning by force of concentration.

After weeks of this, there came a day when, quite suddenly, as it seemed to her, the printed characters took on a meaning. There were still many words, even in the first pages of that simple primer, she could not decipher; but she could skip those and yet make sense of the whole. 'I'm reading! I'm reading!' she cried aloud. 'Oh, Mother! Oh, Edmund! I'm reading!'

There were not many books in the house, although in this respect the family was better off than its neighbours; for, in addition to 'Father's books', mostly unreadable as yet, and Mother's Bible and *Pilgrim's Progress*, there were a few children's books which the Johnstones had turned out from their nursery when they left the neighbourhood. So, in time, she was able to read Grimms' *Fairy Tales*, *Gulliver's Travels*, *The Daisy Chain*, and Mrs Molesworth's *Cuckoo Clock* and *Carrots*.

As she was seldom seen without an open book in her hand, it was not long before the neighbours knew she could read. They did not approve of this at all. None of their children had learned to read before they went to school, and then only under compulsion, and they thought that Laura, by doing so, had stolen a march on them. So they attacked her mother about it, her father conveniently being away. 'He'd no business to teach the child himself,' they said. 'Schools be the places for teaching, and you'll likely get wrong for him doing it when governess finds out.' Others, more kindly disposed, said Laura was trying her eyes and begged her mother to put an end to her studies; but, as fast as one book was hidden away from her, she found another, for anything in print drew her eyes as a magnet drew steel.

Edmund did not learn to read quite so early; but when he did, he learned more thoroughly. No skipping unknown words for him and guessing what they meant by the context; he mastered every page before he turned over, and his mother was more patient with his inquiries, for Edmund was her darling.

If the two children could have gone on as they were doing, and have had access to suitable books as they advanced, they would probably have learnt more than they did during their brief schooldays. But that happy time of discovery did not last. A woman, the frequent absences from school of whose child had brought the dreaded Attendance Officer to her door, informed him of the end-house scandal, and he went there and threatened Laura's mother with all manner of penalties if Laura was not in school at nine o'clock the next Monday morning.

So there was to be no Oxford or Cambridge for Edmund. No school other than the National School for either. They would have to pick up what learning they could like chickens pecking for grain – a little at school, more from books, and some by dipping into the store of others.

Sometimes, later, when they read about children whose lives were very different from their own, children who had nurseries with rocking-horses and went to parties and for sea-side holidays and were encouraged to do and praised for doing just those things they themselves were thought odd for, they wondered why they had alighted at birth upon such an unpromising spot as Lark Rise.

That was indoors. Outside there was plenty to see and hear and learn, for the hamlet people were interesting, and almost every one of them interesting in some different way to the others, and to Laura the old people were the most interesting of all, for they told her about the old times and could sing old songs and remember old customs, although they could never remember enough to satisfy her. She sometimes wished she could make the earth and stones speak and tell her about all the dead people who had trodden upon them. She was fond of collecting stones of all shapes and colours, and for years played with the idea that, one day, she would touch a secret spring and a stone would fly open and reveal a parchment which would tell her exactly what the world was like when it was written and placed there.

There were no bought pleasures, and, if there had been, there was no money to pay for them; but there were the sights, sounds and scents of the different seasons: spring with its fields of young wheat-blades bending in the wind as the cloud-shadows swept over them; summer with its ripening grain and its flowers and fruit and its thunder-storms, and how the thunder growled and rattled over that flat land and what boiling, sizzling downpours it brought! With August came the harvest and the fields settled down to the long winter rest, when the snow was often piled high and frozen, so that the buried hedges could be walked over, and strange birds came for crumbs to the cottage doors and hares in search of food left their spoor round the pigsties.

The children at the end house had their own private amusements, such as guarding the clump of white violets they found blooming in a cleft of the brook bank and called their 'holy secret', or pretending the scabious, which bloomed in abundance there, had fallen in a shower from the mid-summer sky, which was exactly the same dim, dreamy blue. Another favourite game was to creep silently up behind birds which had perched on a rail or twig and try to touch their tails. Laura once succeeded in this, but she was alone at the time and nobody believed she had done it.

A little later, remembering man's earthy origin, 'dust thou art and to dust thou shalt return', they liked to fancy themselves bubbles of earth. When alone in the fields, with no one to see them, they would hop, skip and jump, touching the ground as lightly as possible and crying 'We are bubbles of earth! Bubbles of earth! Bubbles of earth!'

But although they had these private fancies, unknown to their elders, they did not grow into the ultra-sensitive, misunderstood, and thwarted adolescents who, according to present-day writers, were a feature of that era. Perhaps, being of mixed birth with a large proportion of peasant blood in them, they were tougher in fibre than some. When their bottoms were soundly smacked, as they often were, their reaction was to make a mental note not to repeat the offence which had caused the smacking, rather than to lay up for themselves complexes to spoil their later lives; and when Laura, at about twelve years old, stumbled into a rickyard where a bull was in the act of justifying its existence, the sight did not warp her nature. She neither peeped from behind a rick, nor fled, horrified, across country; but merely thought in her old-fashioned way, 'Dear me! I had better slip quietly away before the men see me.' The bull to her was but a bull performing a necessary function if there was to be butter on the bread and bread and milk for breakfast, and she thought it quite natural that the men in attendance at such functions should prefer not to have women or little girls as spectators. They would have felt, as they would have said, 'a bit okkard'. She just withdrew and went another way round without so much as a kink in her subconscious.

From the time the two children began school they were merged in the hamlet life, sharing the work and play and mischief of their younger companions and taking harsh or kind words from their elders according to circumstances. Yet, although they shared in the pleasures, limitations, and hardships of the hamlet, some peculiarity of mental outlook prevented them from accepting everything that existed or happened there as a matter of course, as the other children did. Small things which passed unnoticed by others interested, delighted, or saddened them. Nothing that took place around them went unnoted; words spoken and forgotten the next moment by the speaker were recorded in their memories, and the actions and reactions of others were impressed on their minds, until a clear, indelible impression of their little world remained with them for life.

Their own lives were to carry them far from the hamlet. Edmund's to South Africa, India, Canada, and, lastly, to his soldier's grave in Belgium. Their credentials presented, they will only appear in this book as observers of and commentators upon the country scene of their birth and early years.

III

Men Afield

A MILE and a half up the straight, narrow road in the opposite direction to that of the turnpike, round a corner, just out of sight of the hamlet, lay the mother village of Fordlow. Here, again, as soon as the turning of the road was passed, the scene changed, and the large open fields gave place to meadows and elm trees and tiny trickling streams.

The village was a little, lost, lonely place, much smaller than the hamlet, without a shop, an inn, or a post office, and six miles from a railway station. The little squat church, without spire or tower, crouched back in a tiny churchyard that centuries of use had raised many feet above the road, and the whole was surrounded by tall, windy elms in which a colony of rooks kept up a perpetual cawing. Next came the Rectory, so buried in orchards and shrubberies that only the chimney stacks were visible from the road; then the old Tudor farmhouse with its stone, mullioned windows and reputed dungeon. These, with the school and about a dozen cottages occupied by the shepherd, carter, blacksmith, and a few other superior farm-workers, made up the village. Even these few buildings were strung out along the roadside, so far between and so sunken in greenery that there seemed no village at all. It was a standing joke in the hamlet that a stranger had once asked the way to Fordlow after he had walked right through it. The hamlet laughed at the village as 'stuck up'; while the village looked down on 'that gipsy lot' at the hamlet.

Excepting the two or three men who frequented the inn in the evening, the villagers seldom visited the hamlet, which to them represented the outer wilds, beyond the bounds of civilization. The hamlet people, on the other hand, knew the road between the two places by heart, for the church and the school and the farmhouse which was the men's working headquarters were all in the village. The hamlet had only the inn.

Very early in the morning, before daybreak for the greater part of the year, the hamlet men would throw on their clothes, breakfast on bread and lard, snatch the dinner-baskets which had been packed for them overnight, and hurry off across fields and over stiles to the farm. Getting the boys off was a more difficult matter. Mothers would have to call and shake and sometimes pull boys of eleven or twelve out of their warm beds on a winter morning. Then boots which had been drying inside the fender all night and had become shrunk and hard as boards in the process would have to be coaxed on over chilblains. Sometimes a very small boy would cry over this and his mother to cheer him would remind him that they were only boots, not breeches. 'Good thing you didn't live when breeches wer' made o' leather,' she would say, and tell him about the boy of a previous generation whose leather breeches were so baked up in drying that it took him an hour to get into them. 'Patience! Have patience, my son', his mother had exhorted. 'Remember Job.' 'Job!' scoffed the boy. 'What did he know about patience? He didn't have to wear no leather breeches.'

Leather breeches had disappeared in the 'eighties and were only remembered in telling that story. The carter, shepherd, and a few of the older labourers still wore the traditional smock-frock topped by a round black felt hat, like those formerly worn by clergymen. But this old country style of dress was already out of date; most of the men wore suits of stiff, dark brown corduroy, or, in summer, corduroy trousers and an unbleached drill jacket known as a 'sloppy'.

Most of the young and those in the prime of life were thick-

set, red-faced men of good medium height and enormous
strength who prided themselves on the weights they could carry
and boasted of never having had 'an e-ache nor a pa-in' in their
lives. The elders stooped, had gnarled and swollen hands and
walked badly, for they felt the effects of a life spent out of
doors in all weathers and of the rheumatism which tried most of
them. These elders wore a fringe of grey whisker beneath the
jaw, extending from ear to ear. The younger men sported
drooping walrus moustaches. One or two, in advance of the
fashion of their day, were clean-shaven; but as Sunday was the
only shaving day, the effect of either style became blurred by
the end of the week.

They still spoke the dialect, in which the vowels were not only
broadened, but in many words doubled. 'Boy' was 'boo-oy',
'coal', 'coo-al', 'pail', 'pay-ull', and so on. In other words, syllables were slurred, and words were run together, as 'brenbu'er'
for bread and butter. They had hundreds of proverbs and
sayings and their talk was stiff with simile. Nothing was simply
hot, cold, or coloured; it was 'as hot as hell', 'as cold as ice', 'as
green as grass', or 'as yellow as a guinea'. A botched-up job
done with insufficient materials was 'like Dick's hat-band that
went half-way round and tucked'; to try to persuade or encourage one who did not respond was 'putting a poultice on
wooden leg'. To be nervy was to be 'like a cat on hot bricks'; to
be angry, 'mad as a bull'; or any one might be 'poor as a rat',
'sick as a dog', 'hoarse as a crow', 'as ugly as sin', 'full of the
milk of human kindness', or 'stinking with pride'. A tempera-
mental person was said to be 'one o' them as is either up on the
roof or down the well'. The dialect was heard at its best on the
lips of the few middle-aged men, who had good natural voices,
plenty of sense, and a grave, dignified delivery. Mr Frederick
Grisewood of the BBC gave a perfect rendering of the old
Oxfordshire dialect in some broadcast sketches a few years ago.
Usually, such imitations are maddening to the native born; but
he made the past live again for one listener.

The men's incomes were the same to a penny; their circumstances, pleasures, and their daily field work were shared in
common; but in themselves they differed, as other men of their

day differed, in country and town. Some were intelligent, others slow at the uptake; some were kind and helpful, others selfish, some vivacious, others taciturn. If a stranger had gone there looking for the conventional Hodge, he would not have found him.

Nor would he have found the dry humour of the Scottish peasant, or the racy wit and wisdom of Thomas Hardy's Wessex. These men's minds were cast in a heavier mould and moved more slowly. Yet there were occasional gleams of quiet fun. One man who had found Edmund crying because his magpie, let out for her daily exercise, had not returned to her wicker cage, said: 'Doo'nt 'ee take on like that, my man. You goo an' tell Mrs Andrews about it [naming the village gossip] an' you'll hear where your Maggie's been seen, if 'tis as far away as Stratton.'

Their favourite virtue was endurance. Not to flinch from pain or hardship was their ideal. A man would say, 'He says, says he, that field o' oo-ats's got to come in afore night, for there's a rain a-comin'. But we didn't flinch, not we! Got the last loo-ad under cover by midnight. A'moost too fagged-out to walk home; but we didn't flinch. We done it!' Or, 'Ole bull he comes for me, wi's head down. But I didn't flinch. I ripped off a bit o' loose rail an' went for he. 'Twas him as did th' flinchin'. He! he!' Or a woman would say, 'I set up wi' my poor old mother six nights runnin'; never had me clothes off. But I didn't flinch, an' I pulled her through, for she didn't flinch neither.' Or a young wife would say to the midwife after her first confinement, 'I didn't flinch, did I? Oh, I do hope I didn't flinch.'

The farm was large, extending far beyond the parish boundaries; being, in fact, several farms, formerly in separate occupancy, but now thrown into one and ruled over by the rich old man at the Tudor farmhouse. The meadows around the farmstead sufficed for the carthorses' grazing and to support the store cattle and a couple of milking cows which supplied the farmer's family and those of a few of his immediate neighbours with butter and milk. A few fields were sown with grass seed for hay, and sainfoin and rye were grown and cut green for cattle food. The rest was arable land producing corn and root crops, chiefly wheat.

Around the farmhouse were grouped the farm buildings; stables for the great stamping shaggy-fetlocked carthorses; barns with doors so wide and high that a load of hay could be driven through; sheds for the yellow-and-blue painted farm wagons, granaries with outdoor staircases; and sheds for storing oilcake, artificial manures, and agricultural implements. In the rickyard, tall, pointed, elaborately thatched ricks stood on stone straddles; the dairy indoors, though small, was a model one; there was a profusion of all that was necessary or desirable for good farming.

Labour, too, was lavishly used. Boys leaving school were taken on at the farm as a matter of course, and no time-expired soldier or settler on marriage was ever refused a job. As the farmer said, he could always do with an extra hand, for labour was cheap and the land was well tilled up to the last inch.

When the men and boys from the hamlet reached the farm-yard in the morning, the carter and his assistant had been at work for an hour, feeding and getting ready the horses. After giving any help required, the men and boys would harness and lead out their teams and file off to the field where their day's work was to be done.

If it rained, they donned sacks, split up one side to form a hood and cloak combined. If it was frosty, they blew upon their nails and thumped their arms across their chest to warm them. If they felt hungry after their bread-and-lard breakfast, they would pare a turnip and munch it, or try a bite or two of the rich, dark brown oilcake provided for the cattle. Some of the boys would sample the tallow candles belonging to the stable lanterns; but that was done more out of devilry than from hunger, for, whoever went short, the mothers took care that their Tom or Dicky should have 'a bit o' summat to peck at between meals' – half a cold pancake or the end of yesterday's roly-poly.

With 'Gee!' and 'Wert up!' and 'Who-a-a, now!' the teams would draw out. The boys were hoisted to the backs of the tall carthorses, and the men, walking alongside, filled their clay pipes with shag and drew the first precious puffs of the day, as with cracking of whips, clopping of hooves and jingling of harness, the teams went tramping along the muddy byways.

The field names gave the clue to the fields' history. Near the farmhouse, 'Moat Piece', 'Fishponds', 'Duffus [i.e. dovehouse] Piece', 'Kennels', and 'Warren Piece' spoke of a time before the Tudor house took the place of another and older establishment. Farther on, 'Lark Hill', 'Cuckoos' Clump', 'The Osiers', and 'Pond Piece' were named after natural features, while 'Gibbard's Piece' and 'Blackwell's' probably commemorated otherwise long-forgotten former occupants. The large new fields round the hamlet had been cut too late to be named and were known as 'The Hundred Acres', 'The Sixty Acres', and so on according to their acreage. One or two of the ancients persisted in calling one of these 'The Heath' and another 'The Racecourse'.

One name was as good as another to most of the men; to them it was just a name and meant nothing. What mattered to them about the fields in which they happened to be working was whether the road was good or bad which led from the farm to it; or if it was comparatively sheltered or one of those bleak open places which the wind hurtled through, driving the rain through the clothes to the very pores; and was the soil easily workable or of back-breaking heaviness or so bound together with that 'hemmed' twitch that a ploughshare could scarcely get through it.

There were usually three or four ploughs to a field, each of them drawn by a team of three horses, with a boy at the head of the leader and the ploughman behind at the shafts. All day, up and down they would go, ribbing the pale stubble with stripes of dark furrows, which, as the day advanced, would get wider and nearer together, until, at length, the whole field lay a rich velvety plum-colour.

Each plough had its following of rooks, searching the clods with sidelong glances for worms and grubs. Little hedgerow birds flitted hither and thither, intent upon getting their tiny share of whatever was going. Sheep, penned in a neighbouring field, bleated complainingly; and above the ma-a-ing and cawing and twittering rose the immemorial cries of the landworker: 'Wert up!' 'Who-o-o-a!' 'Go it, Poppet!' 'Go it, Lightfoot!' 'Boo-oy, be you deaf, or be you hard of hearin', dang ye!'

After the plough had done its part, the horse-drawn roller was used to break down the clods; then the harrow to comb out and leave in neat piles the weeds and the twitch grass which infested those fields, to be fired later and fill the air with the light blue haze and the scent that can haunt for a lifetime. Then seed was sown, crops were thinned out and hoed and, in time, mown, and the whole process began again.

Machinery was just coming into use on the land. Every autumn appeared a pair of large traction engines, which, posted one on each side of a field, drew a plough across and across by means of a cable. These toured the district under their own steam for hire on the different farms, and the outfit included a small caravan, known as 'the box', for the two drivers to live and sleep in. In the 'nineties, when they had decided to emigrate and wanted to learn all that was possible about farming, both Laura's brothers, in turn, did a spell with the steam plough, horrifying the other hamlet people, who looked upon such nomads as social outcasts. Their ideas had not then been extended to include mechanics as a class apart and they were lumped as inferiors with sweeps and tinkers and others whose work made their faces and clothes black. On the other hand, clerks and salesmen of every grade, whose clean smartness might have been expected to ensure respect, were looked down upon as 'counter-jumpers'. Their recognized world was made up of landowners, farmers, publicans, and farm labourers, with the butcher, the baker, the miller, and the grocer as subsidiaries.

Such machinery as the farmer owned was horse-drawn and was only in partial use. In some fields a horse-drawn drill would sow the seed in rows, in others a human sower would walk up and down with a basket suspended from his neck and fling the seed with both hands broadcast. In harvest time the mechanical reaper was already a familiar sight, but it only did a small part of the work; men were still mowing with scythes and a few women were still reaping with sickles. A thrashing machine on hire went from farm to farm and its use was more general; but men at home still thrashed out their allotment crops and their wives' leazings with a flail and winnowed the corn by pouring from sieve to sieve in the wind.

The labourers worked hard and well when they considered the occasion demanded it and kept up a good steady pace at all times. Some were better workmen than others, of course; but the majority took a pride in their craft and were fond of explaining to an outsider that field work was not the fool's job that some townsmen considered it. Things must be done just so and at the exact moment, they said; there were ins and outs in good land work which took a man's lifetime to learn. A few of less admirable build would boast: 'We gets ten bob a week, a' we yarns every penny of it; but we doesn't yarn no more; we takes hemmed good care o' that!' But at team work, at least, such 'slack-twisted 'uns' had to keep in step, and the pace, if slow, was steady.

While the ploughmen were in charge of the teams, other men went singly, or in twos or threes, to hoe, harrow, or spread manure in other fields; others cleared ditches and saw to drains, or sawed wood or cut chaff or did other odd jobs about the farmstead. Two or three highly skilled middle-aged men were sometimes put upon piecework, hedging and ditching, sheep-shearing, thatching, or mowing, according to the season. The carter, shepherd, stockman, and blacksmith had each his own specialized job. Important men, these, with two shillings a week extra on their wages and a cottage rent free near the farmstead.

When the ploughmen shouted to each other across the furrows, they did not call 'Miller' or 'Gaskins' or 'Tuffrey' or even 'Bill', 'Tom' or 'Dick', for they all had nicknames and answered more readily to 'Bishie' or 'Pumpkin' or 'Boamer'. The origin of many of these names was forgotten, even by the bearers; but a few were traceable to personal peculiarities. 'Cockie' or 'Cock-eye' had a slight cast; 'Old Stut' stuttered, while 'Bayour' was so called because when he fancied a snack between meals he would say 'I must just have my mouthful of bavour', using the old name for a snack, which was rapidly becoming modernized into 'lunch' or 'luncheon'.

When, a few years later, Edmund worked in the fields for a time, the carter, having asked him some question and being struck with the aptness of his reply, exclaimed: 'Why, boo-oy, you be as wise as Solomon, an' Solomon I shall call 'ee!' and Solomon he was until he left the hamlet. A younger brother was called 'Fisher'; but the origin of this name was a mystery. His mother, who was fonder of boys than girls, used to call him her 'kingfisher'.

Sometimes afield, instead of the friendly shout, a low hissing whistle would pass between the ploughs. It was a warning note that meant that 'Old Monday', the farm bailiff, had been sighted. He would come riding across the furrows on his little long-tailed grey pony, himself so tall and his steed so dumpy that his feet almost touched the ground, a rosy, shrivelled, nut-cracker-faced old fellow, swishing his ash stick and shouting, 'Hi, men! Ho, men! What do you reckon you're doing!'

He questioned them sharply and found fault here and there, but was in the main fairly just in his dealings with them. He had one great fault in their eyes, however; he was always in a hurry himself and he tried to hurry them, and that was a thing they detested.

The nickname of 'Old Monday', or 'Old Monday Morning', had been bestowed upon him years before when some hitch had occurred and he was said to have cried: 'Ten o'clock Monday morning! Today's Monday, tomorrow's Tuesday, next day's Wednesday – half the week gone and nothing done!' This name, of course, was reserved for his absence; while he was with them it was 'Yes, Muster Morris' and 'No, Muster Morris', and 'I'll see what I can do, Muster Morris'. A few of the tamer-spirited even called him 'sir'. Then, as soon as his back was turned, some wag would point to it with one hand and slap his own buttocks with the other, saying, but not too loudly, 'My elbow to you, you ole devil!'

At twelve by the sun, or by signal from the possessor of one of the old turnip-faced watches which descended from father to son, the teams would knock off for the dinner-hour. Horses were unyoked, led to the shelter of a hedge or a rick and given their nosebags, and men and boys threw themselves down on

sacks spread out beside them and tin bottles of cold tea were
uncorked and red handkerchiefs of food unwrapped. The lucky
ones had bread and cold bacon, perhaps the top or the bottom
of a cottage loaf, on which the small cube of bacon was placed,
with a finger of bread on top, called the thumbpiece, to keep the
meat untouched by hand and in position for manipulation with
a clasp-knife. The consumption of this food was managed
neatly and decently, a small sliver of bacon and chunk of
bread being cut and conveyed to the mouth in one movement.
The less fortunate ones munched their bread and lard or morsel
of cheese; and the boys with their ends of cold pudding were
jokingly bidden not to get 'that 'ere treacle' in their ears.

The food soon vanished, the crumbs from the red handkerchiefs were shaken out for the birds, the men lighted their pipes
and the boys wandered off with their catapults down the hedgerows. Often the elders would sit out their hour of leisure dis
cussing politics, the latest murder story, or local affairs; but at
other times, especially when one man noted for that kind of
thing was present, they would while away the time in repeating
what the women spoke of with shamed voices as 'men's tales'.

These stories, which were kept strictly to the fields and never
repeated elsewhere, formed a kind of rustic *Decameron*, which
seemed to have been in existence for centuries and increased
like a snowball as it rolled down the generations. The tales were
supposed to be extremely indecent, and elderly men would say
after such a sitting, 'I got up an' went over to th' osses, for I
couldn't stand no more on't. The brimstone fair come out o'
their mouths as they put their rascally heads together.' What
they were really like only the men knew; but probably they
were coarse rather than filthy. Judging by a few stray specimens
which leaked through the channel of eavesdropping juniors,
they consisted chiefly of 'he said' and 'she said', together with a
lavish enumeration of those parts of the human body then
known as 'the unmentionables'.

Songs and snatches on the same lines were bawled at the
plough-tail and under hedges and never heard elsewhere. Some
of these ribald rhymes were so neatly turned that those who
have studied the subject have attributed their authorship to some

graceless son of the Rectory or Hall. It may be that some of these young scamps had a hand in them, but it is just as likely that they sprung direct from the soil, for, in those days of general churchgoing, the men's minds were well stored with hymns and psalms and some of them were very good at parodying them.

There was 'The Parish Clerk's Daughter', for instance. This damsel was sent one Christmas morning to the church to inform her father that the Christmas present of beef had arrived after he left home. When she reached the church the service had begun and the congregation, led by her father, was half-way through the psalms. Nothing daunted, she sidled up to her father and intoned:

'Feyther, the me-a-at's come, an' what's me mother to d-o-o-o w'it?'

And the answer came pat: 'Tell her to roast the thick an' boil th' thin, an' me-ak a pudden o' th' su-u-u-u-et.'

But such simple entertainment did not suit the man already mentioned. He would drag out the filthiest of the stock rhymes, then go on to improvise, dragging in the names of honest lovers and making a mock of fathers of first children. Though nine out of ten of his listeners disapproved and felt thoroughly uncomfortable, they did nothing to check him beyond a mild 'Look out, or them boo-oys'll hear 'ee!' or 'Careful! some 'ooman may be comin' along th' roo-ad.'

But the lewd scandalizer did not always have everything his own way. There came a day when a young ex-soldier, home from his five years' service in India, sat next to him. He sat through one or two such extemporized songs, then, eyeing the singer, said shortly, 'You'd better go and wash out your dirty mouth.'

The answer was a bawled stanza in which the objector's name figured. At that the ex-soldier sprung to his feet, seized the singer by the scruff of his neck, dragged him to the ground and, after a scuffle, forced earth and small stones between his teeth. 'There, that's a lot cleaner!' he said, administering a final kick on the buttocks as the fellow slunk, coughing and spitting, behind the hedge.

A few women still did field work, not with the men, or even in the same field as a rule, but at their own special tasks, weeding and hoeing, picking up stones, and topping and tailing turnips and mangel; or, in wet weather, mending sacks in a barn. Formerly, it was said, there had been a large gang of field women, lawless, slatternly creatures, some of whom had thought nothing of having four or five children out of wedlock. Their day was over; but the reputation they had left behind them had given most country-women a distaste for 'goin' afield'. In the 'eighties about half a dozen of the hamlet women did field work, most of them being respectable middle-aged women who, having got their families off hand, had spare time, a liking for an open-air life, and a longing for a few shillings a week they could call their own.

Their hours, arranged that they might do their housework before they left home in the morning and cook their husband's meal after they returned, were from ten to four, with an hour off for dinner. Their wage was four shillings a week. They worked in sunbonnets, hobnailed boots and men's coats, with coarse aprons of sacking enveloping the lower part of their bodies. One, a Mrs Spicer, was a pioneer in the wearing of trousers; she sported a pair of her husband's corduroys. The others compromised with ends of old trouser legs worn as gaiters. Strong, healthy, weather-beaten, hard as nails, they worked through all but the very worst weathers and declared they would go 'stark, staring mad' if they had to be shut up in a house all day.

To a passer-by, seeing them bent over their work in a row, they might have appeared as alike as peas in a pod. They were not. There was Lily, the only unmarried one, big and strong and clumsy as a carthorse and dark as a gipsy, her skin ingrained with field mould and the smell of the earth about her, even indoors. Years before she had been betrayed by a man and had sworn she would never marry until she had brought up the boy she had had by him – a quite superfluous oath, her neighbours thought, for she was one of the very few really ugly people in the world.

The 'eighties found her a woman of fifty, a creature of earth, earthy, whose life was a round of working, eating, and sleeping. She lived alone in a tiny cottage, in which, as she boasted, she could get her meals, eat them, and put the things away·without leaving her seat by the hearth. She could read a little, but had forgotten how to write, and Laura's mother wrote her letters to her soldier son in India.

Then there was Mrs Spicer, the wearer of the trousers, a rough-tongued old body, but independent and upright, who kept her home spotless and boasted that she owed no man a penny and wanted nothing from anybody. Her gentle, hen-pecked, little husband adored her.

Very different from either was the comfortable, pink-cheeked Mrs Braby, who always carried an apple or a paper of pep-permints in her pocket, in case she should meet a child she favoured. In her spare time she was a great reader of novelettes and out of her four shillings subscribed to *Bow Bells* and the *Family Herald*. Once when Laura, coming home from school, happened to overtake her, she enlivened the rest of the journey with the synopsis of a serial she was reading, called *His Ice Queen*, telling her how the heroine, rich, lovely, and icily virtu-ous in her white velvet and swansdown, almost broke the heart of the hero by her cool aloofness; then, suddenly melting, threw herself into his arms. But, after all, the plot could not have been quite as simple as that, for there was a villainous colonel in it. 'Oh! I do just about hate that colonel!' Mrs Braby ejaculated at intervals. She pronounced it 'col-on-el', as spelt, which so worked upon Laura that at last she ventured, 'But don't they call that word "colonel", Mrs Braby?' Which led to a spelling lesson: 'Col-on-el; that's as plain as the nose on your face. What-ever be you a-thinkin' of, child? They don't seem to teach you much at school these days!' She was distinctly offended and did not offer Laura a peppermint for weeks, which served her right, for she should not have tried to correct her elders.

One man worked with the field women or in the same field. He was a poor, weedy creature, getting old and not very strong and they had put him upon half-pay. He was known as 'Algy' and was not a native, but had appeared there suddenly, years before, out of a past he never mentioned. He was tall and thin and stooping, with watery blue eyes and long ginger side-whiskers of the kind then known as 'weepers'. Sometimes, when he straightened his back, the last vestiges of a military bearing might be detected, and there were other grounds for supposing he had at some time been in the Army. When tipsy, or nearly so, he would begin, 'When I was in the Grenadier Guards ...' a sentence that always tailed off into silence. Although his voice broke on the high notes and often deteriorated into a squeak, it still bore the same vague resemblance to that of a man of culture as his bearing did to that of a soldier. Then, instead of swearing with 'd—s' and 'b—s' as the other men did, he would, when surprised, burst into a 'Bai Jove!' which amused everybody, but threw little light on his mystery.

Twenty years before, when his present wife had been a widow of a few weeks' standing, he had knocked at her door during a thunderstorm and asked for a night's lodging, and had been there ever since, never receiving a letter or speaking of his past, even to his wife. It was said that during his first days at field work his hands had blistered and bled from softness. There must have been great curiosity in the hamlet about him at first; but it had long died down and by the 'eighties he was accepted as 'a poor, slack-twisted crittur', useful for cracking jokes on. He kept his own counsel and worked contentedly to the best of his power. The only thing that disturbed him was the rare visit of the German band. As soon as he heard the brass instruments strike up and the 'pom, pom' of the drum, he would stick his fingers in his ears and run, across fields, anywhere, and not be seen again that day.

On Friday evening, when work was done, the men trooped up to the farmhouse for their wages. These were handed out of a window to them by the farmer himself and acknowledged by a rustic scraping of feet and pulling of forelocks. The farmer had grown too old and too stout to ride horseback, and, although he still made the circuit of his land in his high dogcart every day, he had to keep to the roads, and pay-day was the only time he saw many of his men. Then, if there was cause for complaint, was the time they heard of it. 'You, there! What were you up to in Causey Spinney last Monday, when you were supposed to be clearing the runnels?' was a type of complaint that could always be countered by pleading. 'Call o' Nature, please, sir.' Less frequent and harder to answer was: 'I hear you've not been too smart about your work lately, Stimson. 'Twon't do, you know, 'twon't do! You've got to earn your money if you're going to stay here.' But, just as often, it would be: 'There, Boamer, there you are, my lad, a bright and shining golden half-sovereign for you. Take care you don't go spending it all at once!' or an inquiry about some wife in childbed or one of the ancients' rheumatism. He could afford to be jolly and affable: he paid poor old Monday Morning to do his dirty work for him.

Apart from that, he was not a bad-hearted man and had no idea he was sweating his labourers. Did they not get the full standard wage, with no deduction for standing by in bad weather? How they managed to live and keep their families on such a sum was their own affair. After all, they did not need much, they were not used to luxuries. He liked a cut off a juicy sirloin and a glass of good port himself; but bacon and beans were better to work on. 'Hard liver, hard worker' was a sound old country maxim, and the labouring men did well to follow it. Besides, was there not at least one good blow-out for everybody once a year at his harvest-home dinner, and the joint of beef at Christmas, when he killed a beast and distributed the meat, and soup and milk-puddings for anybody who was ill; they had only to ask for and fetch them.

He never interfered with his men as long as they did their work well. Not he! He was a staunch Conservative himself, a true blue, and they knew his colour when they went to vote; but he never tried to influence them at election times and never inquired afterwards which way they had voted. Some masters did it, he knew, but it was a dirty, low-down trick, in his opinion. As to getting them to go to church – that was the parson's job.

Although they hoodwinked him whenever possible and referred to him behind his back as 'God a'mighty', the farmer was liked by his men. 'Not a bad ole sort,' they said; 'an' does his bit by the land.' All their rancour was reserved for the bailiff.

There is something exhilarating about pay-day, even when the pay is poor and already mortgaged for necessities. With that

morsel of gold in their pockets, the men stepped out more
briskly and their voices were cheerier than ordinary. When
they reached home they handed the half-sovereign straight over
to their wives, who gave them back a shilling for the next
week's pocket-money. That was the custom of the countryside.
The men worked for the money and the women had the spending of it. The men had the best of the bargain. They earned
their half-sovereign by hard toil, it is true, but in the open air, at
work they liked and took an interest in, and in congenial
company. The women, kept close at home, with cooking, cleaning, washing, and mending to do, plus their constant preg-
nancies and a tribe of children to look after, had also the worry
of ways and means on an insufficient income.

Many husbands boasted that they never asked their wives
what they did with the money. As long as there was food
enough, clothes to cover everybody, and a roof over their
heads, they were satisfied, they said, and they seemed to make a
virtue of this and think what generous, trusting, fine-hearted
fellows they were. If a wife got in debt or complained, she was
told: 'You must larn to cut your coat accordin' to your cloth,
my gal.' The coats not only needed expert cutting, but should
have been made of elastic.

On light evenings, after their tea-supper, the men worked for
an hour or two in their gardens or on the allotments. They were
first-class gardeners and it was their pride to have the earliest
and best of the different kinds of vegetables. They were helped
in this by good soil and plenty of manure from their pigsties;
but good tilling also played its part. They considered keeping
the soil constantly stirred about the roots of growing things the
secret of success and used the Dutch hoe a good deal for this
purpose. The process was called 'tickling'. 'Tickle up old
Mother Earth and make her bear!' they would shout to each
other across the plots, or salute a busy neighbour in passing
with: 'Just tickling her up a bit, Jack?'

The energy they brought to their gardening after a hard day's
work in the fields was marvellous. They grudged no effort and
seemed never to tire. Often, on moonlight nights in spring, the
solitary fork of some one who had not been able to tear himself

away would be heard and the scent of his twitch fire smoke would float in at the windows. It was pleasant, too, in summer twilight, perhaps in hot weather when water was scarce, to hear the *swish* of water on parched earth in a garden – water which had been fetched from the brook a quarter of a mile distant. 'It's no good stintin' th' land,' they would say. 'If you wants anything out you've got to put summat in, if 'tis only elbow-grease.'

The allotment plots were divided into two, and one half planted with potatoes and the other half with wheat or barley. The garden was reserved for green vegetables, currant and gooseberry bushes, and a few old-fashioned flowers. Proud as they were of their celery, peas and beans, cauliflowers and marrows, and fine as were the specimens they could show of these, their potatoes were their special care, for they had to grow enough to last the year round. They grew all the old-fashioned varieties – ashleaf kidney, early rose, American rose, magnum bonum, and the huge misshaped white elephant. Everybody knew the elephant was an unsatisfactory potato, that it was awkward to handle when paring, and that it boiled down to a white pulp in cooking; but it produced tubers of such astonishing size that none of the men could resist the temptation to plant it. Every year specimens were taken to the inn to be weighed on the only pair of scales in the hamlet, then handed round for guesses to be made of the weight. As the men said, when a patch of elephants was dug up and spread out, 'You'd got summat to put in your eye and look at.'

Very little money was spent on seed; there was little to spend, and they depended mainly upon the seed saved from the previous year. Sometimes, to secure the advantage of fresh soil, they would exchange a bag of seed potatoes with friends living at a distance, and sometimes a gardener at one of the big houses around would give one of them a few tubers of a new variety. These would be carefully planted and tended, and, when the crop was dug up, specimens would be presented to neighbours.

Most of the men sang or whistled as they dug or hoed. There was a good deal of outdoor singing in those days. Workmen

sang at their jobs; men with horses and carts sang on the road;
the baker, the miller's man, and the fish-hawker sang as they
went from door to door; even the doctor and parson on their
rounds hummed a tune between their teeth. People were poorer
and had not the comforts, amusements, or knowledge we have
today; but they were happier. Which seems to suggest that happiness depends more upon the state of mind – and body,
perhaps – than upon circumstances and events.

IV

At the 'Wagon and Horses'

FORDLOW might boast of its church, its school, its annual
concert, and its quarterly penny reading, but the hamlet did not
envy it these amenities, for it had its own social centre, warmer,
more human, and altogether preferable, in the taproom of the
'Wagon and Horses'.

There the adult male population gathered every evening, to
sip its half-pints, drop by drop, to make them last, and to
discuss local events, wrangle over politics or farming methods,
or to sing a few songs 'to oblige'.

It was an innocent gathering. None of them got drunk; they
had not money enough, even with beer, and good beer, at twopence a pint. Yet the parson preached from the pulpit against
it, going so far on one occasion as to call it a den of iniquity.
' 'Tis a great pity he can't come an' see what it's like for his own
self,' said one of the older men on the way home from church.
'Pity he can't mind his own business,' retorted a younger one.
While one of the ancients put in pacifically, 'Well, 'tis his
business, come to think on't. The man's paid to preach, an' he's
got to find summat to preach against, stands to reason.'

Only about half a dozen men held aloof from the circle and
those were either known to 'have religion', or suspected of being
'close wi' their ha'pence'.

The others went as a matter of course, appropriating their
own special seats on settle or bench. It was as much their home

as their own cottages, and far more homelike than many of them, with its roaring fire, red window curtains, and well-scoured pewter.

To spend their evenings there was, indeed, as the men argued, a saving, for, with no man in the house, the fire at home could be let die down and the rest of the family could go to bed when the room got cold. So the men's spending money was fixed at a shilling a week, sevenpence for the nightly half-pint and the balance for other expenses. An ounce of tobacco, Nigger Head brand, was bought for them by their wives with the groceries.

It was exclusively a men's gathering. Their wives never accompanied them; though sometimes a woman who had got her family off hand, and so had a few halfpence to spend on herself, would knock at the back door with a bottle or jug and perhaps linger a little, herself, unseen, to listen to what was going on within. Children also knocked at the back door to buy candles or treacle or cheese, for the innkeeper ran a small shop at the back of his premises, and the children, too, liked to hear what was going on. Indoors, the innkeeper's children would steal out of bed and sit on the stairs in their nightgowns. The stairs went up from the taproom, with only the back of the settle between, and it gave the men a bit of a shock one night when what looked at first sight like a big white bird came flopping down among them. It was little Florrie, who had gone to sleep on the stairs and fallen. They nursed her on their knees, held her feet to the fire, and soon dried her tears, for she was not hurt, only frightened.

The children heard no bad language beyond an occasional 'B—' or 'd—', for their mother was greatly respected and the merest hint of anything stronger was hushed by nudges and whispers of 'Don't forget Landlady', or 'Mind! 'Ooman present'. Nor were the smutty songs and stories of the fields ever repeated there; they were kept for their own time and place.

Politics was a favourite topic, for, under the recently extended franchise, every householder was a voter, and they took their new responsibility seriously. A mild Liberalism prevailed, a Liberalism that would be regarded as hide-bound Toryism now, but was daring enough in those days. One man who had been to work in Northampton proclaimed himself a Radical; but he was cancelled out by the landlord, who called himself a 'true blue'. With the collaboration of this Left and Right, questions of the moment were thrashed out and settled to the satisfaction of the majority.

'Three Acres and a Cow', 'The Secret Ballot', 'The Parnell Commission and Crime', 'Disestablishment of the Church', were catchwords that flew about freely. Sometimes a speech by Gladstone or some other leader would be read aloud from a newspaper and punctuated by the fervent 'Hear! Hear!' of the company. Or Sam, the man with advanced opinions, would relate with reverent pride the story of his meeting and shaking hands with Joseph Arch, the farm-worker's champion. 'Joseph Arch!' he would cry. 'Joseph Arch is the man for the farm labourer!' and knock on the table and wave aloft his pewter mug, very carefully, for every drop was precious.

Then the landlord, standing back to the fireplace with legs astride, would say with the authority of one in his own house, 'It's no good you chaps think'n you're goin' against the gentry. They've got the land and they've got the money, *an'* they'll keep it. Where'd *you* be without them to give you work an' pay your wages, I'd like to know?' and this, as yet, unanswerable question would cast a chill over the company until some one conjured it away with the name of Gladstone. Gladstone! The Grand Old Man! The People's William! Their faith in his power was touching, and all voices would join in singing:

> God bless the people's William,
>   Long may he lead the van
> Of Liberty and Freedom,
>   God bless the Grand Old Man.

But the children, listening, without and within, liked better the evenings of tale-telling; when, with curdling blood and creeping spine, they would hear about the turnpike ghost, which, only a mile away from the spot where they stood, had been seen in the form of a lighted lantern, bobbing up and down in the path of a solitary wayfarer, the bearer, if any, invisible. And the man in a neighbouring village who, on his six-mile walk in the dark to fetch medicine for his sick wife, met a huge black dog with eyes of fire – the devil, evidently. Or perhaps the talk would turn to the old sheep-stealing days and the ghost which was said still to haunt the spot where the gibbet had stood; or the lady dressed in white and riding a white horse, but minus her head, who, every night as the clock struck twelve, rode over a bridge on the way to the market town.

One cold winter night, as this tale was being told, the doctor, an old man of eighty, who still attended the sick in the villages for miles around, stopped his dogcart at the inn gate and came in for hot brandy and water.

'You, sir, now,' said one of the men. 'You've been over Lady Bridge at midnight many's the time, I'll warrant. Can you say as you've ever seen anything?'

The doctor shook his head. 'No,' he replied, 'I can't say that I have. But,' and he paused to weigh his words, 'well, it's rather a curious thing. During the fifty years I've been amongst you I've had many horses, as you know, and not one of them have I got over that bridge at night without urging. Whether they can see more than we can see, of course, I don't know; but there it is for what it is worth. Good night, men.'

In addition to these public and well-known ghost stories, there were family tales of death warnings, or of a father, mother, or wife who had appeared after death to warn, counsel, or accuse. But it was all entertainment; nobody really believed in ghosts, though few would have chosen to go at night to haunted spots, and it all ended in: 'Well, well, if the livin' don't hurt us, the dead can't. The good wouldn't want to come back, an' the bad wouldn't be let to.'

The newspapers furnished other tales of dread. Jack the Ripper was stalking the streets of East London by night, and one poor wretched woman after another was found murdered and butchered. These crimes were discussed for hours together in the hamlet and everybody had some theory as to the identity and motive of the elusive murderer. To the children the name was indeed one of dread and the cause of much anguished sleeplessness. Father might be hammering away in the shed and Mother quietly busy with her sewing downstairs; but the

Ripper! the Ripper! he might be nearer still, for he might have crept in during the day and be hiding in the cupboard on the landing!

One curious tale had to do with natural phenomena. Some years before, the people in the hamlet had seen a regiment of soldiers marching in the sky, all complete with drum and fife band. Upon inquiry it had been found that such a regiment had been passing at the time along a road near Bicester, six miles away, and it was concluded that the apparition in the sky must have been a freak reflection.

Some of the tales related practical jokes, often cruel ones, for even in the 'eighties the sense of humour there was not over-refined, and it had, in past times, been cruder still. It was still the practice there to annoy certain people by shouting after them a nickname or a catchword, and one old and very harm-less woman was known as 'Thick and thin'. One winter night, years before, when the snowdrifts were knee-high and it was still snowing, a party of thoughtless youths had knocked at her cottage door and got her and her husband out of bed by telling them that their daughter, married and living three miles away, was brought to bed and had sent for her mother.

The old couple huddled on all the clothes they possessed, lighted their lantern, and set out, the practical jokers shadowing them. They struggled through the snowdrifts for some distance, but the road was all but impassable, and the old man was for turning back. Not so the mother. Determined to reach her child in her hour of need, she struggled onward, encouraging her husband the while by coaxing, 'Come on John. Through thick and thin!' and 'Thick and thin' she was ever after.

But tastes were changing, if slowly, by the 'eighties, and such a story, though it might be still current, no longer produced the loud guffaws it had formerly done. A few sniggers, perhaps, then silence; or 'I calls it a shame, sarvin' poor old people like that. Now let's have a song to te-ake the taste of it out of our mouths.'

All times are times of transition; but the eighteen-eighties were so in a special sense, for the world was at the beginning of a new era, the era of machinery and scientific discovery. Values and conditions of life were changing everywhere. Even to simple country people the change was apparent. The railways had brought distant parts of the country nearer; newspapers were coming into every home; machinery was superseding hand labour, even on the farms to some extent; food bought at shops, much of it from distant countries, was replacing the home-made and home-grown. Horizons were widening; a stranger from a village five miles away was no longer looked upon as 'a furriner'.

But, side by side with these changes, the old country civilization lingered. Traditions and customs which had lasted for centuries did not die out in a moment. State-educated children still played the old country rhyme games; women still went leazing, although the field had been cut by the mechanical reaper; and men and boys still sang the old country ballads and songs, as well as the latest music-hall successes. So, when a few songs were called for at the 'Wagon and Horses', the programme was apt to be a curious mixture of old and new.

While the talking was going on, the few younger men, 'boy-chaps', as they were called until they were married, would not have taken a great part in it. Had they shown any inclination to do so, they would have been checked, for the age of youthful dominance was still to come; and, as the women used to say, 'The old cocks don't like it when the young cocks begin to crow.' But, when singing began they came into their own, for they represented the novel.

They usually had first innings with such songs of the day as had percolated so far. 'Over the Garden Wall', with its many parodies, 'Tommy, Make Room for Your Uncle', 'Two Lovely Black Eyes', and other 'comic' or 'sentimental' songs of the moment. The most popular of these would have arrived complete with tune from the outer world; others, culled from the penny song-book they most of them carried, would have to have a tune fitted to them by the singer. They had good lusty voices and bawled them out with spirit. There were no crooners in those days.

The men of middle age inclined more to long and usually mournful stories in verse, of thwarted lovers, children buried in snowdrifts, dead maidens, and motherless homes. Sometimes they would vary these with songs of a high moral tone, such as:

> Waste not, want not,
>   Some maxim I would teach;
> Let your watchword be never despair
>   And practise what you preach.
> Do not let your chances like the sunbeams pass you by,
> For you'll never miss the water till the well runs dry.

But this dolorous singing was not allowed to continue long. 'Now, then, all together, boys,' some one would shout, and the company would revert to old favourites. Of these, one was 'The Barleymow'. Trolled out in chorus, the first verse went:

> Oh, when we drink out of our noggins, my boys,
>   We'll drink to the barleymow.
> We'll drink to the barleymow, my boys,
>   We'll drink to the barleymow.
> So knock your pint on the settle's back;
>   Fill again, in again, Hannah Brown,
> We'll drink to the barleymow, my boys,
>   We'll drink now the barley's mown.

So they went on, increasing the measure in each stanza, from noggins to half-pints, pints, quarters, gallons, barrels, hogsheads, brooks, ponds, rivers, seas, and oceans. That song could be made to last a whole evening, or it could be dropped as soon as they got tired of it.

Another favourite for singing in chorus was 'King Arthur', which was also a favourite for outdoor singing and was often heard to the accompaniment of the jingling of harness and cracking of whips as the teams went afield. It was also sung by solitary wayfarers to keep up their spirits on dark nights. It ran:

> When King Arthur first did reign
>   He ru-led like a king;
> He bought three sacks of barley meal
>   To make a plum pud-ding.

> The pudding it was made
> 　And duly stuffed with plums,
> And lumps of suet put in it
> 　As big as my two thumbs.

> The king and queen sat down to it
> 　And all the lords beside;
> And what they couldn't eat that night
> 　The queen next morning fried.

Every time Laura heard this sung she saw the queen, a gold crown on her head, her train over her arm, and her sleeves rolled up, holding the frying-pan over the fire. Of course, a queen *would* have fried pudding for breakfast: ordinary common people seldom had any left over to fry.

Then Lukey, the only bachelor of mature age in the hamlet, would oblige with:

> Me feyther's a hedger and ditcher,
> 　An' me mother does nothing but spin,
> But I'm a pretty young girl and
> 　The money comes slowly in.
> 　　Oh, dear! what can the matter be?
> 　　Oh, dear! what shall I do?
> 　For there's nobody coming to marry,
> 　　And there's nobody coming to woo.

> They say I shall die an old maid,
> 　Oh, dear! how shocking the thought!
> For then all my beauty will fade,
> 　And I'm sure it won't be my own fault.
> 　　Oh, dear! what can the matter be?
> 　　Oh, dear! what shall I do?
> 　There's nobody coming to marry,
> 　　And there's nobody coming to woo!

This was given point by Luke's own unmarried state. He sang it as a comic song and his rendering certainly made it one. Perhaps, then, for a change, poor old Algy, the mystery man, would be asked for a song and he would sing in a cracked

falsetto, which seemed to call for the tinkling notes of a piano
as accompaniment:

> Have you ever been on the Penin-su-lah?
> If not, I advise you to stay where you haw,
>   For should you adore a
>   Sweet Spanish senor-ah,
> She may prove what some might call sin-gu-lah.

Then there were snatches that any one might break out with
at any time when no one else happened to be singing:

> I wish, I wish, 'twer all in vain,
> I wish I were a maid again!
> A maid again I ne'er shall be
> Till oranges grow on an apple tree

or:

> Now all you young chaps, take a warning by me,
> And do not build your nest at the top of any tree,
> For the green leaves they will wither and the flowers they will
>   will decay,
> And the beauty of that fair maid will soon pass away.

One comparatively recent settler, who had only lived at the
hamlet about a quarter of a century, had composed a snatch for
himself, to sing when he felt homesick. It ran:

> Where be Dedington boo-oys, where be they now?
> They be at Dedington at the 'Plough';
> If they be-ent, they be at home,
> And this is the 'Wagon and Horses'.

But, always, sooner or later, came the cry, 'Let's give the old
'uns a turn. Here you, Master Price, what about "It was my
father's custom and always shall be mine", or "Lord Lovell
stood", or summat of that sort as has stood the testing o' time?'
and Master Price would rise from his corner of the settle, using
the stick he called his 'third leg' to support his bent figure as he
sang:

> Lord Lovell stood at his castle gate,
>   Calming his milk-white steed,
> When up came Lady Nancy Bell
>   To wish her lover God-speed.

'And where are you going, Lord Lovell?' she said.
'And where are you going?' said she.
'Oh, I'm going away from my Nancy Bell,
Away to a far country-tre-tre;
Away to a far coun-tre.'

'And when will you come back, Lord Lovell?' she said,
'When will you come back?' said she.
'Oh, I will come back in a year and a day,
Back to my Lady Nancy-ce-ce-ce.
Back to my Lady Nan-cee.'

But Lord Lovell was gone more than his year and a day, much longer, and when he did at last return, the church bells were tolling:

'And who is it dead?' Lord Lovell, he said.
'And who is it dead,' said he.
And some said, 'Lady Nancy Bell,'
And some said, 'Lady Nancy-ce-ce-ce,
And some said, 'Lady Nan-cee.'

Lady Nancy died as it were to-day;
And Lord Lovell, he died to-morrow,
And she, she died for pure, pure grief,
And he, he died for sorrow.

And they buried her in the chancel high,
And they buried him in the choir;
And out of her grave sprung a red, red rose,
And out of his sprung a briar.

And they grew till they grew to the church roof,
And then they couldn't grow any higher;
So they twined themselves in a true lovers' knot,
For all lovers true to admire.

After that they would all look thoughtfully into their mugs. Partly because the old song had saddened them, and partly because by that time the beer was getting low and the one half-pint had to be made to last until closing time. Then some would

say, 'What's old Master Tuffrey up to, over in his corner there?
Ain't heard him strike up tonight', and there would be calls for
old David's 'Outlandish Knight'; not because they wanted particularly to hear it – indeed, they had heard it so often they all
knew it by heart – but because, as they said, 'Poor old feller be
eighty-three. Let 'un sing while he can.'

So David would have his turn. He only knew the one ballad,
and that, he said, his grandfather had sung, and had said that he
had heard his own grandfather sing it. Probably a long chain of
grandfathers had sung it; but David was fated to be the last of
them. It was out of date, even then, and only tolerated on account of his age. It ran:

> An outlandish knight, all from the north lands,
>   A-wooing came to me,
> He said he would take me to the north lands
>   And there he would marry me.
>
> 'Go, fetch me some of your father's gold
>   And some of your mother's fee,
> And two of the best nags out of the stable
>   Where there stand thirty and three.'
>
> She fetched him some of her father's gold
>   And some of her mother's fee,
> And two of the best nags out of the stable
>   Where there stood thirty and three.
>
> And then she mounted her milk-white steed
>   And he the dapple grey,
> And they rode until they came to the sea-shore,
>   Three hours before it was day.
>
> 'Get off, get off thy milk-white steed
>   And deliver it unto me,
> For six pretty maids I have drowned here
>   And thou the seventh shall be.
>
> 'Take off, take off, thy silken gown,
>   And deliver it unto me,
> For I think it is too rich and too good
>   To rot in the salt sea.'

'If I must take off my silken gown,
    Pray turn thy back to me,
For I think it's not fitting a ruffian like you
    A naked woman should see.'

He turned his back towards her
    To view the leaves so green,
And she took hold of his middle so small
    And tumbled him into the stream.

And he sank high and he sank low
    Until he came to the side.
'Take hold of my hand, my pretty ladye,
    And I will make you my bride.'

'Lie there, lie there, you false-hearted man,
    Lie there instead of me,
For six pretty maids hast thou drowned here
    And the seventh hath drowned thee.'

So then she mounted the milk-white steed
    And led the dapple grey,
And she rode till she came to her own father's door,
    An hour before it was day.

As this last song was piped out in the aged voice, women at their cottage doors on summer evenings would say: 'They'll soon be out now. Poor old Dave's just singing his "Outlandish Knight".'

Songs and singers all have gone, and in their places the wireless blares out variety and swing music, or informs the company in cultured tones of what is happening in China or Spain. Children no longer listen outside. There are very few who could listen, for the thirty or forty which throve there in those days have dwindled to about half a dozen, and these, happily, have books, wireless, and a good fire in their own homes. But, to one of an older generation, it seems that a faint echo of those songs must still linger round the inn doorway. The singers were rude and untaught and poor beyond modern imagining; but they deserve to be remembered, for they knew the now lost secret of being happy on little.

Survivals

THERE were three distinct types of home in the hamlet. Those of the old couples in comfortable circumstances, those of the married people with growing families, and the few new homes which had recently been established. The old people who were not in comfortable circumstances had no homes at all worth mentioning, for, as soon as they got past work, they had either to go to the workhouse or find accommodation in the already overcrowded cottages of their children. A father or a mother could usually be squeezed in, but there was never room for both, so one child would take one parent and another the other, and even then, as they used to say, there was always the in-law to be dealt with. It was a common thing to hear ageing people say that they hoped God would be pleased to take them before they got past work and became a trouble to anybody.

But the homes of the more fortunate aged were the most comfortable in the hamlet, and one of the most attractive of these was known as 'Old Sally's'. Never as 'Old Dick's', although Sally's husband, Dick, might have been seen at any hour of the day, digging and hoeing and watering and planting his garden, as much a part of the landscape as his own row of beehives.

He was a little, dry, withered old man, who always wore his smock-frock rolled up round his waist and the trousers on his thin legs gartered with buckled straps. Sally was tall and broad, not fat, but massive, and her large, beamingly good-natured face, with its well-defined moustache and tight, coal-black curls bobbing over each ear, was framed in a white cap frill; for Sally, though still strong and active, was over eighty, and had remained faithful to the fashions of her youth.

She was the dominating partner. If Dick was called upon to decide any question whatever, he would edge nervously aside and say, 'I'll just step indoors and see what Sally thinks about it,' or 'All depends upon what Sally says.' The house was hers and she carried the purse; but Dick was a willing subject and enjoyed her dominion over him. It saved him a lot of thinking, and left him free to give all his time and attention to the growing things in his garden.

Old Sally's was a long, low, thatched cottage with diamond-paned windows winking under the eaves and a rustic porch smothered in honeysuckle. Excepting the inn, it was the largest house in the hamlet, and of the two downstair rooms one was used as a kind of kitchen-storeroom, with pots and pans and a big red crockery water vessel at one end, and potatoes in sacks and peas and beans spread out to dry at the other. The apple crop was stored on racks suspended beneath the ceiling and bunches of herbs dangled below. In one corner stood the big brewing copper in which Sally still brewed with good malt and hops once a quarter. The scent of the last brewing hung over the place till the next and mingled with apple and onion and dried thyme and sage smells, with a dash of soap-suds thrown in, to compound the aroma which remained in the children's memories for life and caused a whiff of any two of the component parts in any part of the world to be recognized with an appreciative sniff and a mental ejaculation of 'Old Sally's!'

The inner room – 'the house', as it was called – was a perfect snuggery, with walls two feet thick and outside shutters to close at night and a padding of rag rugs, red curtains and feather cushions within. There was a good oak, gate-legged table, a dresser with pewter and willow-pattern plates, and a grandfather's clock that not only told the time, but the day of the week as well. It had even once told the changes of the moon; but the works belonging to that part had stopped and only the fat, full face, painted with eyes, nose and mouth, looked out from the square where the four quarters should have rotated. The clock portion kept such good time that half the hamlet set its own clocks by it. The other half preferred to follow the hooter at the brewery in the market town, which could be heard when the wind was in the right quarter. So there were two times in the hamlet and people would say when asking the hour, 'Is that hooter time, or Old Sally's?'

The garden was a large one, tailing off at the bottom into a little field where Dick grew his corn crop. Nearer the cottage were fruit trees, then the yew hedge, close and solid as a wall, which sheltered the beehives and enclosed the flower garden. Sally had such flowers, and so many of them, and nearly all of them sweet-scented! Wallflowers and tulips, lavender and sweet william, and pinks and old-world roses with enchanting names — Seven Sisters, Maiden's Blush, moss rose, monthly rose, cabbage rose, blood rose, and, most thrilling of all to the children, a big bush of the York and Lancaster rose, in the blooms of which the rival roses mingled in a pied white and red. It seemed as though all the roses in Lark Rise had gathered together in that one garden. Most of the gardens had only one poor starveling bush or none; but, then, nobody else had so much of anything as Sally.

A continual subject for speculation was as to how Dick and Sally managed to live so comfortably with no visible means of support beyond their garden and beehives and the few shillings their two soldier sons might be supposed to send them, and Sally in her black silk on Sundays and Dick never without a few ha'pence for garden seeds or to fill his tobacco pouch. 'Wish they'd tell me how 'tis done,' somebody would grumble. 'I could do wi' a leaf out o' their book.'

But Dick and Sally did not talk about their affairs. All that was known of them was that the house belonged to Sally, and that it had been built by her grandfather before the open heath had been cut up into fenced fields and the newer houses had been built to accommodate the labourers who came to work in them. It was only when Laura was old enough to write their letters for them that she learned more. They could both read and Dick could write well enough to exchange letters with their own children; but one day they received a business letter that puzzled them, and Laura was called in, sworn to secrecy, and consulted. It was one of the nicest things that happened to her as a child, to be chosen out of the whole hamlet for their confidence and to know that Dick and Sally liked her, though so few other people did. After that, at twelve years old, she became their little woman of business, writing letters to seedsmen and fetch-

ing postal orders from the market town to put in them and
helping Dick to calculate the interest due on their savings bank
account. From them she learned a great deal about the past life
of the hamlet.

Sally could just remember the Rise when it still stood in a
wide expanse of open heath, with juniper bushes and furze
thickets and close, springly, rabbit-bitten turf. There were only
six houses then and they stood in a ring round an open green, all
with large gardens and fruit trees and faggot piles. Laura could
pick out most of the houses, still in a ring, but lost to sight of
each other among the newer, meaner dwellings that had sprung
up around and between them. Some of the houses had been
built on and made into two, others had lost their lean-tos and
outbuildings. Only Sally's remained the same, and Sally was
eighty. Laura in her lifetime was to see a ploughed field where
Sally's stood; but had she been told that she would not have
believed it.

Country people had not been so poor when Sally was a girl,
or their prospects so hopeless. Sally's father had kept a cow,
geese, poultry, pigs, and a donkey-cart to carry his produce to
the market town. He could do this because he had commoners'
rights and could turn his animals out to graze, and cut furze for
firing and even turf to make a lawn for one of his customers.
Her mother made butter, for themselves and to sell, baked their
own bread, and made candles for lighting. Not much of a light,
Sally said, but it cost next to nothing, and, of course, they went
to bed early.

Sometimes her father would do a day's work for wages,
thatching a rick, cutting and laying a hedge, or helping with the
shearing or the harvest. This provided them with ready money
for boots and clothes; for food they relied almost entirely on
home produce. Tea was a luxury seldom indulged in for it cost
five shillings a pound. But country people then had not acquired
the taste for tea; they preferred home-brewed.

Everybody worked; the father and mother from daybreak to
dark. Sally's job was to mind the cow and drive the geese to the
best grass patches. It was strange to picture Sally, a little girl,
running with her switch after the great hissing birds on the

common, especially as both common and geese had vanished
as completely as though they never had been.

Sally had never been to school, for, when she was a child,
there was no dame school near enough for her to attend; but
her brother had gone to a night school run by the vicar of an
adjoining parish, walking the three miles each way after his
day's work was done, and he had taught Sally to spell out a few
words in her mother's Bible. After that, she had been left
to tread the path of learning alone and had only managed to
reach the point where she could write her own name and
read the Bible or newspaper by skipping words of more
than two syllables. Dick was a little more advanced, for
he had had the benefit of the night-school education at first
hand.

It was surprising to find how many of the old people in the
hamlet who had had no regular schooling could yet read a little.
A parent had taught some; others had attended a dame school or
the night school, and a few had made their own children teach
them in later life. Statistics of illiteracy of that period are often
misleading, for many who could read and write sufficiently well
for their own humble needs would modestly disclaim any pretensions to being what they called 'scholards'. Some who could
write their own name quite well would make a cross as signature
to a document out of nervousness or modesty.

After Sally's mother died, she became her father's right hand,
indoors and out. When the old man became feeble, Dick used
to come sometimes to do a bit of hard digging or to farm out
the pigsties, and Sally had many tales to tell of the fun they had
had carting their bit of hay or hunting for eggs in the loft.
When, at a great age, the father died, he left the house and
furniture and his seventy-five pounds in the savings bank to
Sally, for, by that time, both her brothers were thriving and
needed no share. So Dick and Sally were married and had lived
there together for nearly sixty years. It had been a hard, frugal,
but happy life. For most of the time Dick had worked as a farm
labourer while Sally saw to things about home, for the cow,
geese and other stock had long gone the way of the common.
But when Dick retired from wage-earning the seventy-five

pounds was not only intact, but had been added to. It had been
their rule, Sally said, to save something every week, if only a
penny or twopence, and the result of their hard work and self-
denial was their present comfortable circumstances. 'But us
couldn't've done it if us'd gone havin' a great tribe o' children,'
Sally would say. 'I didn't never hold wi' havin' a lot o' poor
brats and nothin' to put into their bellies. Took us all our time
to bring up our two.' She was very bitter about the huge families around her and no doubt would have said more had she
been talking to one of maturer age.

They had their little capital reckoned up and allotted: they
could manage on so much a year in addition to the earnings of
their garden, fowls, and beehives, and that much, and no more,
was drawn every year from the bank. 'Reckon it'll about last
our time,' they used to say, and it did, although both lived well
on into the eighties.

After they had gone, their house stood empty for years. The
population of the hamlet was falling and none of the young
newly married couples cared for the thatched roof and stone
floors. People who lived near used the well; it saved them many
a journey. And many were not above taking the railings or the
beehive bench or anything made of wood for firing, or gathering the apples or using the poor tattered remnant of the flower
garden as a nursery. But nobody wanted to live there.

When Laura visited the hamlet just before the War, the roof
had fallen in, the yew hedge had run wild and the flowers were
gone, excepting one pink rose which was shedding its petals
over the ruin. Today, all has gone, and only the limy whiteness
of the soil in a corner of a ploughed field is left to show that a
cottage once stood there.

Sally and Dick were survivals from the earliest hamlet days.
Queenie represented another phase of its life which had also
ended and been forgotten by most people. She lived in a tiny,
thatched cottage at the back of the end house, which, although
it was not in line, was always spoken of as 'next door'. She
seemed very old to the children, for she was a little, wrinkled,
yellow-faced old woman in a sunbonnet; but she cannot have
been nearly as old as Sally. Queenie and her husband were not

in such comfortable circumstances as Sally and Dick; but old Master Macey, commonly called 'Twister', was still able to work part of the time, and they managed to keep their home going.

It was a pleasant home, though bare, for Queenie kept it spotless, scrubbing her deal table and whitening her floor with hearthstone every morning and keeping the two brass candle-sticks on her mantelpiece polished till they looked like gold. The cottage faced south and, in summer, the window and door stood open all day to the sunshine. When the children from the end house passed close by her doorway, as they had to do every time they went beyond their own garden, they would pause a moment to listen to Queenie's old sheep's-head clock ticking. There was no other sound; for, after she had finished her house-work, Queenie was never indoors while the sun shone. If the children had a message for her, they were told to go round to the beehives, and there they would find her, sitting on a low stool with her lace-pillow on her lap, sometimes working and sometimes dozing with her lilac sunbonnet drawn down over her face to shield it from the sun.

Every fine day, throughout the summer, she sat there 'watch-ing the bees'. She was combining duty and pleasure, for, if they swarmed, she was making sure of not losing the swarm; and, if they did not, it was still, as she said, 'a trate' to sit there, feeling the warmth of the sun, smelling the flowers, and watching 'the craturs' go in and out of the hives.

When, at last, the long-looked-for swarm rose into the air, Queenie would seize her coal shovel and iron spoon and follow it over cabbage beds and down pea-stick alleys, her own or, if necessary, other peoples', tanging the spoon on the shovel: *Tang tang-tangety-tang!*

She said it was the law that, if they were not tanged, and they settled beyond her own garden bounds, she would have no further claim to them. Where they settled, they belonged. That would have been a serious loss, especially in early summer, for, as she reminded the children:

> A swarm in May's worth a rick of hay;
> And a swarm in June's worth a silver spoon;

while

A swarm in July isn't worth a fly.

So she would follow and leave her shovel to mark her claim, then go back home for the straw skep and her long green veil and sheepskin gloves to protect her face and hands while she hived her swarm.

In winter she fed her bees with a mixture of sugar and water and might often have been seen at that time of the year with her ear pressed to one of the red pan roofs of the hives, listening. 'The craturs! The poor little craturs,' she would say, 'they must be a'most frozed. If I could have *my* way I'd take 'em all indoors and set 'em in rows in front of a good fire.'

Queenie at her lace-making was a constant attraction to the children. They loved to see the bobbins tossed hither and thither, at random it seemed to them, every bobbin weighted with its bunch of bright beads and every bunch with its own story, which they had heard so many times that they knew it by heart, how this bunch had been part of a blue bead necklace worn by her little sister who had died at five years old, and this other one had belonged to her mother, and that black one had been found, after she was dead, in a work-box belonging to a woman who was reputed to have been a witch.

There had been a time, it appeared, when lace-making was a regular industry in the hamlet. Queenie, in her childhood, had been 'brought up to the pillow', sitting among the women at eight years old and learning to fling her bobbins with the best of them. They would gather in one cottage in winter for warmth, she said, each one bringing her faggot or shovel of coals for the fire, and there they would sit all day, working, gossiping, singing old songs, and telling old tales till it was time to run home and put on the pots for their husbands' suppers. These were the older women and the young unmarried girls; the women with little children did what lace-making they could at home. In very cold winter weather the lace-makers would have a small earthen pot with a lid, called a 'pipkin', containing hot embers, at which they warmed their hands and feet and sometimes sat upon.

In the summer they would sit in the shade behind one of the

'housen', and, as they gossiped, the bobbins flew and the lovely, delicate pattern lengthened until the piece was completed and wrapped in blue paper and stored away to await the great day when the year's work was taken to Banbury Fair and sold to the dealer.

'Them wer' the days!' she would sigh. 'Money to spend.' And she would tell of the bargains she had bought with her earnings. Good brown calico and linsey-woolsey, and a certain chocolate print sprigged with white, her favourite gown, of which she could still show a pattern in her big patchwork quilt. Then there was a fairing to be bought for those at home – pipes and packets of shag tobacco for the men, rag dolls and ginger-bread for the 'little 'uns', and snuff for the old grannies. And the home-coming, loaded with treasure, and money in the pocket besides. Tripe. They always bought tripe; it was the only time in the year they could get it, and it was soon heated up, with onions and a nice bit of thickening; and after supper there was hot, spiced elderberry wine, and so to bed, everybody happy.

Now, of course, things were different. She didn't know what the world was coming to. This nasty machine-made stuff had killed the lace-making; the dealer had not been to the Fair for the last ten years; nobody knew a bit of good stuff when they saw it. Said they liked the Nottingham lace better; it was wider and had more pattern to it! She still did a bit to keep her hand in. One or two old ladies still used it to trim their shifts, and it was handy to give as presents to such as the children's mother; but, as for living by it, no, those days were over.

So it emerged from her talk that there had been a second period in the hamlet more prosperous than the present. Perhaps the women's earnings at lace-making had helped to tide them over the Hungry 'Forties, for no one seemed to remember that time of general hardship in country villages; but memories were short there, and it may have been that life had always been such a struggle they had noticed no difference in those lean years.

Queenie's ideal of happiness was to have a pound a week coming in. 'If I had a pound a week,' she would say, 'I 'udn't care if it rained hatchets and hammers.' Laura's mother longed

for thirty shillings a week, and would say, 'If I could depend on
thirty shillings, regular, I could keep you all so nice and tidy,
and keep *such* a table!'

Queenie's income fell far short of even half of the pound a
week she dreamed of, for her husband, Twister, was what was
known in the hamlet as 'a slack-twisted sort o' chap', one who
'whatever he died on, 'uldn't kill hisself wi' hard work'. He was
fond of a bit of sport and always managed to get taken on as a
beater at shoots, and took care never to have a job on hand
when hounds were meeting in the neighbourhood. Best of all, he
liked to go round with one of the brewers' travellers, perched
precariously on the back seat of the high dogcart, to open and
shut the gates they had to pass through and to hold the horse
outside public houses. But, although he had retired from regular farm labour on account of age and chronic rheumatism, he
still went to the farm and lent a hand when he had nothing more
exciting to do. The farmer must have liked him, for he had
given orders that whenever Twister was working about the
farmstead he was to have a daily half-pint on demand. That
half-pint was the salvation of Queenie's house-keeping, for, in
spite of his varied interests, there were many days when Twister
must either work or thirst.

He was a small, thin-legged, jackdaw-eyed old fellow, and
dressed in an old velveteen coat that had once belong to a gamekeeper, with a peacock's feather stuck in the band of his battered old bowler and a red-and-yellow neckerchief knotted
under one ear. The neckerchief was a relic of the days when he
had taken baskets of nuts to fairs, and, taking up his stand
among the booths and roundabouts, had shouted: 'Bassalonies
big as ponies!' until his throat felt dry. Then he had adjourned
to the nearest public house and spent his takings and distributed
the rest of his stock, gratis. That venture soon came to an end
for want of capital.

To serve his own purposes, Twister would sometimes pose as
a half-wit; but, as the children's father said, he was no fool
where his own interests were concerned. He was ready at any
time to clown in public for the sake of a pint of beer; but at
home he was morose – one of those people who 'hang their

fiddle up at the door when they go home', as the saying went there.

But in old age Queenie had him well in hand. He knew that he had to produce at least a few shillings on Saturday night, or, when Sunday dinner-time came, Queenie would spread the bare cloth on the table and they would just have to sit down and look at each other; there would be no food.

Forty-five years before she had served him with a dish even less to his taste. He had got drunk and beaten her cruelly with the strap with which he used to keep up his trousers. Poor Queenie had gone to bed sobbing; but she was not too overcome to think, and she decided to try an old country cure for such offences.

The next morning when he came to dress, his strap was missing. Probably already ashamed of himself, he said nothing, but hitched up his trousers with string and slunk off to work, leaving Queenie apparently still asleep.

At night, when he came home to tea, a handsome pie was placed before him, baked a beautiful golden-brown and with a pastry tulip on the top; such a pie as must have seemed to him to illustrate the old saying: '*A woman, a dog and a walnut tree, the more you beat 'em the better they be.*'

'You cut it, Tom,' said a smiling Queenie. 'I made it a-purpose for you. Come, don't 'ee be afraid on it. 'Tis all for you.' And she turned her back and pretended to be hunting for something in the cupboard.

Tom cut it; then recoiled, for, curled up inside, was the leather strap with which he had beaten his wife. 'A just went as white as a ghoo-ost, an' got up an' went out,' said Queenie all those years later. 'But it cured 'en, for's not so much as laid a finger on me from that day to this!'

Perhaps Twister's clowning was not all affected; for, in later years, he became a little mad and took to walking about talking to himself, with a large, open clasp-knife in his hand. Nobody thought of getting a doctor to examine him; but everybody in the hamlet suddenly became very polite to him.

It was at this time he gave the children's mother the fright of her life. She had gone out to hang out some clothes in the garden, leaving one of her younger children alone, asleep in his cradle. When she came back, Twister was stooping over the child with his head inside the hood of the cradle, completely hiding the babe from her sight. As she rushed forward, fearing the worst, the poor, silly old man looked up at her with his eyes full of tears. 'Ain't 'ee like little Jesus? Ain't 'ee just like little Jesus?' he said, and the little baby of two months woke up at that moment and smiled. It was the first time he had been known to smile.

But Twister's exploits did not always end as happily. He had begun to torture animals and was showing an inclination to turn nudist, and people were telling Queenie he ought to be 'put away' when the great snowstorm came. For days the hamlet was cut off from the outer world by great drifts which filled the narrow hamlet road to the tops of the hedges in places. In digging a way out they found a cart with the horse still between the shafts and still alive; but there was no trace of the boy who was known to have been in charge. Men, women, and children turned out to dig, expecting to find a dead body, and Twister was one of the foremost amongst them. They said he worked then as he had never worked before in his life; his strength and energy were marvellous. They did not find the boy, alive or dead, for the very good reason that he had, at the height of the storm, deserted the cart, forgotten the horse, and scrambled across country to his home in another village; but poor old Twister got pneumonia and was dead within a fortnight.

On the evening of the day he died, Edmund was round at the back of the end house banking up his rabbit-hutches with straw for the night, when he saw Queenie come out of her door and go towards her beehives. For some reason or other, Edmund followed her. She tapped on the roof of each hive in turn, like knocking at a door, and said, *'Bees, bees, your master's dead, an' now you must work for your missis.'* Then, seeing the little boy, she explained: 'I 'ad to tell 'em, you know or they'd all've died, poor craturs.' So Edmund really heard bees seriously told of a death.

Afterwards, with parish relief and a little help here and there from her children and friends, Queenie managed to live. Her chief difficulty was to get her ounce of snuff a week, and that was the one thing she could not do without; it was as necessary to her as tobacco is to a smoker.

All the women over fifty took snuff. It was the one luxury in their hard lives. 'I couldn't do wi'out my pinch o' snuff,' they used to say. ' 'Tis meat an' drink to me,' and, tapping the sides of their snuffboxes, ' 'Ave a pinch, me dear.'

Most of the younger women pulled a face of disgust as they refused the invitation, for snuff-taking had gone out of fashion and was looked upon as a dirty habit; but Laura's mother would dip her thumb and forefinger into the box and sniff at them delicately, 'for manners' sake', as she said. Queenie's snuffbox had a picture of Queen Victoria and the Prince Consort on the lid. Sometimes, when every grain of the powder was gone, she would sniff at the empty box and say, 'Ah! That's better. The ghost o' good snuff's better nor nothin'.'

She still had one great day every year, when, every autumn, the dealer came to purchase the produce of her beehives. Then, in her pantry doorway, a large muslin bag was suspended to drain the honey from the broken pieces of comb into a large, red pan which stood beneath, while, on her doorstep, the end house children waited to see 'the honeyman' carry out and weigh the whole combs. One year – one never-to-be-forgotten year – he had handed to each of them a rich, dripping fragment of comb. He never did it again; but they always waited, for the hope was almost as sweet as the honey.

There had been, when Laura was small, one bachelor's establishment near her home. This had belonged to 'the Major', who, as his nickname denoted, had been in the Army. He had served in many lands and then returned to his native place to set up house and do for himself in a neat, orderly, soldier-like manner. All went well until he became old and feeble. Even then, for some years, he struggled on alone in his little home, for he had a small pension. Then he was ill and spent some weeks in Oxford Infirmary. Before he went there, as he had no relatives or special friends, Laura's mother nursed him and helped him to get together the few necessities he had to take with him. She would have visited him at the hospital had it been possible; but money was scarce and her children were too young to be left, so she wrote him a few letters and sent him the newspaper every week. It was, as she said, 'the least anybody could do for the poor old fellow'. But the Major had seen the world and knew its ways and he did not take such small kindnesses as a matter of course.

He came home from the hospital late one Saturday night, after the children were in bed, and, next morning, Laura, waking at early dawn, thought she saw some strange object on her pillow. She dozed and woke again. It was still there. A small wooden box. She sat up in bed and opened it. Inside was a set of doll's dishes with painted wax food upon them – chops and green peas and new potatoes, and a jam tart with criss-cross pastry. Where could it have come from? It was not Christmas or her birthday. Then Edmund awoke and called out he had found an engine. It was a tiny tin engine, perhaps a penny one, but his delight was unbounded. Then Mother came into their room and said that the Major had brought the presents from Oxford. She had a little red silk handkerchief, such as were worn inside the coat-collar at that time for extra warmth. It was before fur collars were thought of. Father had a pipe and the baby a rattle. It was amazing. To be thought of! To be brought presents, and such presents, by one who was not even a relative! The good, kind Major was in no danger of being forgotten by the family at the end house. Mother made his bed and tidied his room, and Laura was sent with covered plates whenever there was anything special for dinner. She would knock at his door and go in and say in her demure little way, 'Please, Mr Sharman, Mother say could you fancy a little of so-and-so?'

But the Major was too old and ill to be able to live alone much longer, even with such help as the children's mother and other kind neighbours could give. The day came when the doctor called in the relieving officer. The old man was seriously ill; he had no relatives. There was only one place where he could be properly looked after, and that was the workhouse infirmary. They were right in their decision. He was not able to look after himself; he had no relatives or friends able to undertake the responsibility; the workhouse *was* the best place for him. But they made one terrible mistake. They were dealing with a man of intelligence and spirit, and they treated him as they might have done one in the extreme of senile decay. They did not consult him or tell him what they had decided; but ordered the carrier's cart to call at his house the next morning and wait at a short distance while they, in the doctor's gig, drove up to his door. When they entered, the Major had just dressed and dragged himself to his chair by the fire. 'It's a nice morning, and we've come to take you for a drive,' announced the doctor cheerfully, and, in spite of his protests, they hustled on his coat and had him out and in the carrier's cart in a very few minutes.

Laura saw the carrier touch up his horse with the whip and the cart turn, and she always wished afterwards she had not, for, as soon as he realized where he was being taken, the old soldier, the independent old bachelor, the kind family friend, collapsed and cried like a child. He was beaten. But not for long. Before six weeks were over he was back in the parish and all his troubles were over, for he came in his coffin.

As he had no relatives to be informed, the time appointed for his funeral was not known in the hamlet, or no doubt a few of his old neighbours would have gathered in the churchyard. As it was, Laura, standing back among the graves, a milk-can in her hand, was the only spectator, and that quite by chance. No mourner followed the coffin into the church, and she was far too shy to come forward; but when it was brought out and carried towards the open grave it was no longer unac-companied, for the clergyman's middle-aged daughter walked behind it, an open prayer-book in her hand and an expression of gentle pity in her eyes. She could barely have known him in life, for he was not a churchgoer; but she had seen the solitary coffin arrive and had hurried across from her home to the church that he might at least have one fellow human being to say 'Farewell' to him. In after years, when Laura heard her spoken of slightingly, and, indeed, often felt irritated herself by her inter-fering ways, she thought of that graceful action.

The children's grandparents lived in a funny little house out in the fields. It was a round house, tapering off at the top, so there were two rooms downstairs and only one – and that a kind of a loft, with a sloping ceiling – above them. The garden did not adjoin the house, but was shut away between high hedges on the other side of the cart track which led to it. It was full of currant and gooseberry bushes, raspberry canes, and old hardy flowers run wild, almost solid with greenery, for, since the gardener had grown old and stiff in the joints, he had not been able to do much pruning or trimming. There Laura spent many happy hours, supposed to be picking fruit for jam, but for the better part of the time reading or dreaming. One corner, overhung by a damson tree and walled in with bushes and flowers, she called her 'green study'.

Laura's grandfather was a tall old man with snow-white hair and beard and the bluest eyes imaginable. He must at that time have been well on in the seventies, for her mother had been his youngest child and a late-comer. One of her outstanding distinctions in the eyes of her own children was that she had been born an aunt, and, as soon as she could talk, had insisted upon her two nieces, both older than herself, addressing her as 'Aunt Emma'.

Before he retired from active life, the grandfather had followed the old country calling of an eggler, travelling the countryside with a little horse and trap, buying up eggs from farms and cottages and selling them at markets and to shopkeepers. At the back of the round house stood the little lean-to stable in which his pony Dobbin had lived. The children loved to lie in the manger and climb about among the rafters. The death of Dobbin of old age had put an end to his master's eggling, for he had no capital with which to buy another horse. Far from it. Moreover, by that time he was himself suffering from Dobbin's complaint; so he settled down to doing what he could in his garden and making a private daily round on his own feet, from his home to the end house, from the end house to church, and back home again.

At the church he not only attended every service, Sunday and weekday, but, when there was no service, he would go there alone to pray and meditate, for he was a deeply religious man. At one time he had been a local preacher, and had walked miles on Sunday evenings to conduct, in turn with others, the services at the cottage meeting houses in the different villages. In old age he had returned to the Church of England, not because of any change of opinion, for creeds did not trouble him – his feet were too firmly planted on the Rock upon which they are all founded – but because the parish church was near enough for him to attend its services, was always open for his private devotions, and the music there, poor as it was, was all the music left to him.

Some members of his old meeting-house congregations still remembered what they considered his inspired preaching 'of the Word'. 'You did ought to be a better gal, wi' such a gran'fer,' said a Methodist woman to Laura one day when she saw her crawl through a gap in a hedge and tear her new pinafore. But Laura was not old enough to appreciate her grandfather, for he died when she was ten, and his loving care for her mother, his youngest and dearest child, led to many lectures and reproofs. Had he seen the torn pinafore, it would certainly have provoked both. However, she had just sufficient discrimination to know he was better than most people.

As has already been mentioned, he had at one time played the violin in one of the last instrumental church choirs in the district. He had also played it at gatherings at home and in neighbours' houses and, in his earlier, unregenerate days, at weddings and feasts and fairs. Laura, happening to think of this one day, said to her mother, 'Why doesn't Grandfather ever play his fiddle now! What's he done with it?'

'Oh,' said her mother in a matter-of-fact tone. 'He hasn't got it any longer. He sold it once when Granny was ill and they were a bit short of money. It was a good fiddle and he got five pounds for it.'

She spoke as though there was no more in selling your fiddle than in selling half a pig or a spare sack of potatoes in an emergency; but Laura, though so much younger, felt differently about it. Though devoid of the most rudimentary musical instinct herself, she had imagination enough to know that to a musician his musical instrument must be a most precious possession. So, when she was alone with her grandfather one day, she said, 'Didn't you miss your fiddle, Granda?'

The old man gave her a quick, searching look, then smiled sadly. 'I did, my maid, more than anything I've ever had to part with, and that's not a little, and I miss it still and always shall. But it went for a good cause, and we can't have everything we want in this world. It wouldn't be good for us.' But Laura did not agree. She thought it would have been good for him to have his dear old fiddle. That wretched money, or rather the lack of it, seemed the cause of everybody's troubles.

The fiddle was not the only thing he had had to give up. He had given up smoking when he retired and they had to live on their tiny savings and the small allowance from a brother who had prospered as a coal-merchant. Perhaps what he felt most keenly of all was that he had had to give up giving, for he loved to give.

One of Laura's earliest memories was of her grandfather coming through the gate and up the end house garden in his old-fashioned close-fitting black overcoat and bowler hat, his beard nicely trimmed and shining, with a huge vegetable marrow under his arm. He came every morning and seldom came empty-handed. He would bring a little basket of early raspberries or green peas, already shelled, or a tight little bunch of sweet williams and moss rosebuds, or a baby rabbit, which someone else had given him – always something. He would come indoors, and if anything in the house was broken, he would mend it, or he would take a stocking out of his pocket and sit down and knit, and all the time he was working he would talk in a kind, gentle voice to his daughter, calling her 'Emmie'. Sometimes she would cry as she told him of her troubles, and he would get up and smooth her hair and wipe her eyes and say, 'That's better! That's better! Now you're going to be my own brave little wench! And remember, my dear, there's One above who knows what's best for us, though we may not see it ourselves at the time.'

By the middle of the 'eighties the daily visits had ceased, for the chronic rheumatism against which he had fought was getting the better of him. First, the church was too far for him; then the end house; then his own garden across the road; and at last his world narrowed down to the bed upon which he was lying. That bed was not the four-poster with the silk-and-satin patchwork quilt in rich shades of red and brown and orange which stood in the best downstairs bedroom, but the plain white bed beneath the sloping ceiling in the little whitewashed room under the roof. He had slept there for years, leaving his wife the downstairs room, that she might not be disturbed by his fevered tossing during his rheumatic attacks, and also because, like many old people, he woke early, and liked to get up and light the fire and read his Bible before his wife was ready for her cup of tea to be taken to her.

Gradually, his limbs became so locked he could not turn over in bed without help. Giving to and doing for others was over for him. He would lie upon his back for hours, his tired old blue eyes fixed upon the picture nailed on the wall at the foot of his bed. It was the only coloured thing in the room; the rest was bare whiteness. It was of the Crucifixion, and, printed above the crown of thorns were the words:

This have I done for thee.

And underneath the pierced and bleeding feet:

What hast thou done for me?

His two years' uncomplaining endurance of excruciating pain answered for him.

When her husband was asleep, or lying, washed and tended, gazing at his picture, Laura's grandmother would sit among her feather cushions downstairs reading *Bow Bells* or the *Princess Novelettes* or the *Family Herald*. Except when engaged in housework, she was never seen without a book in her hand. It was always a novelette, and she had a large assortment of these which she kept tied up in flat parcels, ready to exchange with other novelette readers.

She had been very pretty when she was young. 'The Belle of Hornton', they had called her in her native village, and she often told Laura of the time when her hair had reached down to her knees, like a great yellow cape, she said, which covered her. Another of her favourite stories was of the day when she had danced with a real lord. It was at his coming-of-age celebrations, and a great honour, for he had passed over his own friends and the daughters of his tenants in favour of one who was but a gamekeeper's daughter. Before the evening was over he had whispered in her ear that she was the prettiest girl in the country, and she had cherished the compliment all her life. There were no further developments. My Lord was My Lord, and Hannah Pollard was Hannah Pollard, a poor girl, but the daughter of decent parents. No further developments were possible in real life, though such affairs ended differently in her novelettes. Perhaps that was why she enjoyed them.

It was difficult for Laura to connect the long, yellow hair and the white frock with blue ribbons worn at the coming-of-age fête with her grandmother, for she saw her only as a thin, frail old woman who wore her grey hair parted like curtains and looped at the ears with little combs. Still, there was something which made her worth looking at. Laura's mother said it was because her features were good. 'My mother,' she would say, 'will look handsome in her coffin. Colour goes and the hair turns grey, but the framework lasts.'

Laura's mother was greatly disappointed in her little daughter's looks. Her own mother had been an acknowledged belle, she herself had been charmingly pretty, and she naturally expected her children to carry on the tradition. But Laura was a plain, thin child: 'Like a moll heron, all legs and wings,' she was told in the hamlet, and her dark eyes and wide mouth looked too large for her small face. The only compliment ever paid her in childhood was that of a curate who said she was 'intelligent looking'. Those around her would have preferred curly hair and a rosebud mouth to all the intelligence in the world.

Laura's grandmother had never tramped ten miles on a Sunday night to hear her husband preach in a village chapel. She had gone to church once every Sunday, unless it rained or was too hot, or she had a cold, or some article of her attire was too shabby. She was particular about her clothes and liked to have everything handsome about her. In her bedroom there were pictures and ornaments, as well as the feather cushions and silk patchwork quilt.

When she came to the end house, the best chair was placed by the fire for her and the best possible tea put on the table, and Laura's mother did not whisper her troubles to her as she did to her father. If some little thing did leak out, she would only say, 'All men need a bit of humouring.'

Some women, too, thought Laura, for she could see that her grandmother had always been the one to be indulged and spared all trouble and unpleasantness. If the fiddle had belonged to her, it would never have been sold; the whole family would have combined to buy a handsome new case for it.

After her husband died, she went away to live with her eldest son, and the round house shared the fate of Sally's. Where it stood is now a ploughed field. The husband's sacrifices, the wife's romance, are as though they had never been – 'melted into air, into thin air'.

Those were a few of the old men and women to whom the Rector referred as 'our old folks' and visiting townsmen lumped together as 'a lot of old yokels'. There were a few other homes of old people in the hamlet; that of Master Ashley, for instance, who, like Sally, had descended from one of the original squatters and still owned the ancestral cottage and strip of land. He must have been one of the last people to use a breast-plough, a primitive implement consisting of a ploughshare at one end of a stout stick and a cross-piece of shaped wood at the other which the user pressed to his breast to drive the share through the soil. On his land stood the only surviving specimen of the old furze and daub building which had once been common in the neighbourhood. The walls were of furze branches closely pressed together and daubed with a mixture of mud and mortar. It was said that the first settlers built their cottages of these materials with their own hands.

Then there were one or two poorer couples, just holding on to their homes, but in daily fear of the workhouse. The Poor Law authorities allowed old people past work a small weekly sum as outdoor relief; but it was not sufficient to live upon, and, unless they had more than usually prosperous children to help support them, there came a time when the home had to be broken up. When, twenty years later, the Old Age Pensions began, life was transformed for such aged cottagers. They were relieved of anxiety. They were suddenly rich. Independent for life! At first when they went to the Post Office to draw it, tears of gratitude would run down the cheeks of some, and they would say as they picked up their money, 'God bless that Lord George! [for they could not believe one so powerful and munificent could be a plain 'Mr'] and God bless *you*, miss!' and there were flowers from their gardens and apples from their trees for the girl who merely handed them the money.

VI

The Besieged Generation

To Laura, as a child, the hamlet once appeared as a fortress. She was coming home alone from school one wild, grey, March afternoon, and, looking up from her battling against the wind, got a swift new impression of the cluster of stark walls and slated roofs on the Rise, with rooks tumbling and clouds hurrying overhead, smoke beating down from the chimneys, and clothes on clothes-lines straining away in the wind.

'It's a fort! It's a fort!' she cried, and she went on up the road, singing in her flat, tuneless little voice the Salvation Army hymn of the day, 'Hold the fort, for I am coming'.

There was a deeper likeness than that of her childish vision. The hamlet was indeed in a state of siege, and its chief assailant was Want. Yet, like other citizens during a long, but not too desperate siege, its inhabitants had become accustomed to their hard conditions and were able to snatch at any small passing pleasure and even at times to turn their very straits to laughter.

To go from the homes of the older people to those of the besieged generation was to step into another chapter of the hamlet's history. All the graces and simple luxuries of the older style of living had disappeared. They were poor people's houses rich only in children, strong, healthy children, who, in a few years, would be ready to take their part in the work of the world and to provide good, healthy blood for the regeneration

of city populations; but, in the meantime, their parents had to
give their all in order to feed and clothe them.

In their houses the good, solid, hand-made furniture of their
forefathers had given place to the cheap and ugly products of
the early machine age. A deal table, the top ribbed and softened
by much scrubbing; four or five windsor chairs with the varnish
blistered and flaking; a side table for the family photographs
and ornaments, and a few stools for fireside seats, together with
the beds upstairs, made up the collection spoken of by its
owners as 'our few sticks of furniture'.

If the father had a special chair in which to rest after his day's
work was done, it would be but a rather larger replica of the
hard windsors with wooden arms added. The clock, if any, was
a cheap, foreign timepiece, standing on the mantelshelf – one
which could seldom be relied upon to keep correct time for
twelve hours together. Those who had no clock depended upon
the husband's watch for getting up in the morning. The watch
then went to work with him, an arrangement which must have
been a great inconvenience to most wives; but was a boon to the
gossips, who could then knock at a neighbour's door and ask the
time when they felt inclined for a chat.

The few poor crocks were not good enough to keep on show
and were hidden away in the pantry between mealtimes. Pewter
plates and dishes as ornaments had gone. There were still plenty
of them to be found, kicked about around gardens and pigsties.
Sometimes a travelling tinker would spy one of these and beg or
buy it for a few coppers, to melt down and use in his trade.
Other casual callers at the cottages would buy a set of hand-
wrought, brass drop-handles from an inherited chest of drawers
for sixpence; or a corner cupboard, or a gate-legged table which
had become slightly infirm, for half a crown. Other such articles
of furniture were put out of doors and spoilt by the weather, for
the newer generation did not value such things; it preferred the
products of its own day, and, gradually, the hamlet was being
stripped of such relics.

As ornaments for their mantelpieces and side tables the
women liked gaudy glass vases, pottery images of animals,
shell-covered boxes and plush photograph frames. The most

valued ornaments of all were the white china mugs inscribed in gilt lettering 'A Present for a Good Child', or 'A Present from Brighton', or some other sea-side place. Those who had daughters in service to bring them would accumulate quite a collection of these, which were hung by the handles in rows from the edge of a shelf, and were a source of great pride in the owner and of envy in the neighbours.

Those who could find the necessary cash covered their walls with wall-paper in big, sprawling, brightly coloured flower designs. Those who could not, used whitewash or pasted up newspaper sheets. On the wall space near the hearth hung the flitch or flitches of bacon, and every house had a few pictures, mostly coloured ones given by grocers as almanacks and framed at home. These had to be in pairs, and lovers' meetings lovers' partings, brides in their wedding gowns, widows standing by newly made graves, children begging in the snow or playing with puppies or kittens in nurseries were the favourite subjects.

Yet, even out of these unpromising materials, in a room which was kitchen, living-room, nursery, and wash-house combined, some women would contrive to make a pleasant, attractive-looking home. A well-whitened hearth, a home-made rag rug in bright colours, and a few geraniums on the window-sill would cost nothing, but make a great difference to the general effect. Others despised these finishing touches. What was the good of breaking your back pegging rugs for the children to mess up when an old sack thrown down would serve the same purpose, they said. As to flowers in pots, they didn't hold with the nasty, messy things. But they did, at least, believe in cleaning up their houses once a day, for public opinion demanded that of them. There were plenty of bare, comfortless homes in the hamlet, but there was not one really dirty one.

Every morning, as soon as the men had been packed off to work, the older children to school, the smaller ones to play, and the baby had been bathed and put to sleep in its cradle, rugs and mats were carried out of doors and banged against walls, fire-places were 'ridded up', and tables and floors were scrubbed. In wet weather, before scrubbing, the stone floor had often to be

scraped with an old knife-blade to loosen the trodden-in mud;
for, although there was a scraper for shoes beside every doorstep, some of the stiff, clayey mud would stick to the insteps and
uppers of boots and be brought indoors.

To avoid bringing in more during the day, the women wore
pattens over their shoes to go to the well or the pigsty. The
patten consisted of a wooden sole with a leather toepiece, raised
about two inches from the ground on an iron ring. *Clack!*
Clack! Clack! over the stones, and *Slush! Slush! Slush!* through
the mud went the patten rings. You could not keep your movements secret if you wore pattens to keep yourself dry shod.

A pair of pattens only cost tenpence and lasted for years. But
the patten was doomed. Vicarage ladies and farmers' wives no
longer wore them to go to and fro between their dairies and
poultry yards, and newly married cottagers no longer provided
themselves with a pair. 'Too proud to wear pattens' was already
becoming a proverb at the beginning of the decade, and by the
end of it they had practically disappeared.

The morning cleaning proceeded to the accompaniment of
neighbourly greetings and shouting across garden and fences,
for the first sound of the banging of mats was a signal for others
to bring out theirs, and it would be 'Have 'ee heard this?' and
'What d'ye think of that?' until industrious housewives declared
that they would take to banging their mats overnight, for they
never knew if it was going to take them two minutes or two
hours.

Nicknames were not used among the women, and only the
aged were spoken of by their Christian names, Old Sally or Old
Queenie or sometimes Dame – Dame Mercer or Dame Morris.
The other married women were Mrs This or Mrs That, even
with those who had known them from their cradles. Old men
were called Master, not Mister. Younger men were known by
their nicknames or their Christian names, excepting a few who
were more than usually respected. Children were carefully
taught to address all as Mr or Mrs.

Cleaning began at about the same time in every house, but
the time of finishing varied. Some housewives would have
everything spick-and-span and themselves 'tidied up' by noon;

others would still be at it at tea-time. 'A slut's work's never done' was a saying among the good housewives.

It puzzled Laura that, although everybody cleaned up every day, some houses looked what they called there 'a pictur' and others a muddle. She remarked on this to her mother.

'Come here,' was the answer. 'See this grate I'm cleaning? Looks done, doesn't it? But you wait.'

Up and down and round and round and between the bars went the brush; then: 'Now look. Looks different, doesn't it?' It did. It had been passably polished before; now it was resplendent. 'There!' said her mother. 'That's the secret; just that bit of extra elbow-grease after some folks would consider a thing done.'

But that final polish, the giving of which came naturally to Laura's mother, could not have been possible to all. Pregnancy and nursing and continual money worries must have worn down the strength and energy of many. Taking these drawbacks into account, together with the inconvenience and over-crowding of the cottages, the general standard of cleanliness was marvellous.

There was one postal delivery a day, and towards ten o'clock, the heads of the women beating their mats would be turned towards the allotment path to watch for 'Old Postie'. Some days there were two, or even three, letters for Lark Rise; quite as often there were none; but there were few women who did not gaze longingly. This longing for letters was called 'yearning' (pronounced 'yarnin' '); 'No, I be-ant expectin' nothin', but I be so yarnin'' one woman would say to another as they watched the old postman dawdle over the stile and between the allotment plots. On wet days he carried an old green gig umbrella with whalebone ribs, and, beneath its immense circumference he seemed to make no more progress than an overgrown mushroom. But at last he would reach and usually pass the spot where the watchers were standing.

'No, I ain't got nothin' for you, Mrs Parish,' he would call. 'Your young Annie wrote to you only last week. She's got summat else to do besides sittin' down on her arse writing home all the time.' Or, waving his arm for some woman to meet him,

for he did not intend to go a step further than he was obliged:
'One for you, Mrs Knowles, and, my! ain't it a thin-roed 'un!
Not much time to write to her mother these days. I took a good
fat 'un from her to young Chad Gubbins.'

So he went on, always leaving a sting behind, a gloomy,
grumpy old man who seemed to resent having to serve such
humble people. He had been a postman forty years and had
walked an incredible number of miles in all weathers, so
perhaps the resulting flat feet and rheumaticky limbs were to
blame; but the whole hamlet rejoiced when at last he was pensioned off and a smart, obliging young postman took his place
on the Lark Rise round.

Delighted as the women were with the letters from their
daughters, it was the occasional parcels of clothing they sent
that caused the greatest excitement. As soon as a parcel was
taken indoors, neighbours who had seen Old Postie arrive with
it would drop in, as though by accident, and stay to admire, or
sometimes to criticize, the contents.

All except the aged women, who wore what they had been
accustomed to wearing and were satisfied, were very particular
about their clothes. Anything did for everyday wear, as long as
it was clean and whole and could be covered with a decent
white apron; it was the 'Sunday best' that had to be just so.
'Better be out of the world than out of the fashion' was one of
their sayings. To be appreciated, the hat or coat contained in the
parcel had to be in the fashion, and the hamlet had a fashion of
its own, a year or two behind outside standards, and strictly
limited as to style and colour.

The daughter's or other kinswoman's clothes were sure to be
appreciated, for they had usually already been seen and
admired when the girl was at home for her holiday, and had
indeed helped to set the standard of what was worn. The garments bestowed by the mistresses were unfamiliar and often
somewhat in advance of the hamlet vogue, and so were often
rejected for personal wear as 'a bit queer' and cut down for the
children; though the mothers often wished a year or two later
when that particular fashion arrived that they had kept them
for themselves. Then they had colour prejudices. A red frock!

Only a fast hussy would wear red. Or green – sure to bring any wearer bad luck! There was a positive taboo on green in the hamlet; nobody would wear it until it had been home-dyed navy or brown. Yellow ranked with red as immodest; but there was not much yellow worn anywhere in the 'eighties. On the whole, they preferred dark or neutral colours; but there was one exception; blue had nothing against it. Marine and sky blue were the favourite shades, both very bright and crude.

Much prettier were the colours of the servant girls' print morning dresses – lilac, or pink, or buff, sprigged with white – which were cut down for the little girls to wear on May Day and for churchgoing throughout the summer.

To the mothers the cut was even more important than the colour. If sleeves were worn wide they liked them to be very wide; if narrow, skin tight. Skirts in those days did not vary in length; they were made to touch the ground. But they were sometimes trimmed with frills or flounces or bunched up at the back, and the women would spend days altering this trimming to make it just right, or turning gathers into pleats or pleats into gathers.

The hamlet's fashion lag was the salvation of its wardrobes, for a style became 'all the go' there just as the outer world was discarding it, and good, little-worn specimens came that way by means of the parcels. *The* Sunday garment at the beginning of the decade was the tippet, a little shoulder cape of black silk or satin with a long, dangling fringe. All the women and some of the girls had these, and they were worn proudly to church or Sunday school with a posy of roses or geraniums pinned in front.

Hats were of the chimney-pot variety, a tall cylinder of straw, with a very narrow brim and a spray of artificial flowers trained up the front. Later in the decade, the shape changed to wide brims and squashed crowns. The chimney-pot hat had had its day, and the women declared they would not be seen going to the privy in one.

Then there were the bustles, at first looked upon with horror, and no wonder! but after a year or two the most popular fashion ever known in the hamlet and the one which lasted longest. They cost nothing, as they could be made at home from any piece of old cloth rolled up into a cushion and worn under any frock. Soon all the women, excepting the aged, and all the girls, excepting the tiniest, were peacocking in their bustles, and they wore them so long that Edmund was old enough in the day of their decline to say that he had seen the last bustle on earth going round the Rise on a woman with a bucket of pig-wash.

This devotion to fashion gave a spice to life and helped to make bearable the underlying poverty. But the poverty was there; one might have a velvet tippet and no shoes worth mentioning; or a smart frock, but no coat; and the same applied to the children's clothes and the sheets and towels and cups and saucepans. There was never enough of anything, except food.

Monday was washing-day, and then the place fairly hummed with activity. 'What d'ye think of the weather?' 'Shall we get 'em dry?' were the questions shouted across gardens, or asked as the women met going to and from the well for water. There was no gossiping at corners that morning. It was before the days of patent soaps and washing powders, and much hard rubbing was involved. There were no washing coppers, and the clothes had to be boiled in the big cooking pots over the fire. Often these inadequate vessels would boil over and fill the house with ashes and steam. The small children would hang round their mothers' skirts and hinder them, and tempers grew short and nerves frayed long before the clothes, well blued, were hung on the lines or spread on the hedges. In wet weather they had to be dried indoors, and no one who has not experienced it can imagine the misery of living for several days with a firmament of drying clothes on lines overhead.

After their meagre midday meal, the women allowed themselves a little leisure. In summer, some of them would take out their sewing and do it in company with others in the shade of one of the houses. Others would sew or read indoors, or carry their babies out in the garden for an airing. A few who had no very young children liked to have what they called 'a bit of a lay down' on the bed. With their doors locked and window-blinds drawn, they, at least, escaped the gossips, who began to get busy at this hour.

One of the most dreaded of these was Mrs Mullins, a thin, pale, elderly woman who wore her iron-grey hair thrust into a black chenille net at the back of her head and wore a little black shawl over her shoulders, summer and winter alike. She was one of the most common sights of the hamlet, going round the Rise in her pattens, with her door-key dangling from her fingers.

That door-key was looked upon as a bad sign, for she only locked her door when she intended to be away some time. 'Where's she a prowlin' off to?' one woman would ask another as they rested with their water-buckets at a corner. 'God knows, an' He won't tell us,' was likely to be the reply. 'But, thanks be, she won't be a goin' to our place now she's seen me here.'

She visited every cottage in turn, knocking at the door and asking the correct time, or for the loan of a few matches, or the gift of a pin – anything to make an opening. Some housewives only opened the door a crack, hoping to get rid of her, but she usually managed to cross the threshold, and, once within, would stand just inside the door, twisting her door-key and talking.

She talked no scandal. Had she done so, her visits might have been less unwelcome. She just babbled on, about the weather, or her sons' last letters, or her pig, or something she had read in the Sunday newspaper. There was a saying in the hamlet: 'Standing gossipers stay longest', and Mrs Mullins was a standing example of this. 'Won't you sit down, Mrs Mullins?' Laura's mother would say if she happened herself to be seated. But it was always, 'No, oh no, thankee. I mustn't stop a minute'; but her minutes always mounted up to an hour or more, and at last her unwilling hostess would say 'Excuse me, I must just run round to the well,' or 'I'd nearly forgotten that I'd got to fetch a cabbage from the allotment,' and, even then, the chances were that Mrs Mullins would insist upon accompanying her, talking them both to a standstill every few yards.

Poor Mrs Mullins! With her children all out in the world, her home must have seemed to her unbearably silent, and, having no resources of her own and a great longing to hear her own voice, she was forced out in search of company. Nobody wanted her, for she had nothing interesting to say, and yet talked too much to allow her listener a fair share of the conversation. She was the worst of all bores, a melancholy bore, and at the sight of her door-key and little black shawl the pleasantest of little gossiping groups would scatter.

Mrs Andrews was an even greater talker; but, although most people objected to her visits on principle, they did not glance at the clock every two minutes while she was there or invent errands for themselves in order to get rid of her. Like Mrs Mullins, she had got her family off hand and so had unlimited leisure; but, unlike her, she had always something of interest to relate. If nothing had happened in the hamlet since her last call, she was quite capable of inventing something. More often, she would take up some stray, unimportant fact, blow it up like a balloon, tie it neatly with circumstantial detail and present it to her listener, ready to be launched on the air of the hamlet. She would watch the clothes-line of some expectant mother, and if no small garments appeared on it in what she considered due time, it would be: 'There's that Mrs Wren, only a month from her time, and not a stitch put into a rag yet.' If she saw a well-dressed stranger call at one of the cottages, she would know 'for a fac' ' that he was the bailiff with a County Court summons, or that he had been to tell the parents that 'their young Jim', who was working up-country, had got into trouble with the police over some money. She 'sized up' every girl at home on holiday and thought that most of them looked pregnant. She took care to say 'thought' and 'looked' in those cases, because she knew that in ninety-nine cases out of a hundred time would prove her suspicions to have been groundless.

Sometimes she would widen her field and tell of the doings in high society. She 'knew for a fac' ' that the then Prince of Wales had given one of his ladies a necklace with pearls the size of pigeon's eggs, and that the poor old Queen, with her crown on her head and tears streaming down her cheeks, had gone down on her knees to beg him to turn the whole lot of saucy hussies out of Windsor Castle. It was said in the hamlet that, when Mrs Andrews spoke, you could see the lies coming out of her mouth like steam, and nobody believed a word she said, even when, occasionally, she spoke the truth. Yet most of the women enjoyed a chat with her. As they said, it 'made a bit of a change'. Laura's mother was too hard on her when she called her a pest, or interrupted one of her stories at a crucial point to ask, 'Are you sure that is right, Mrs Andrews?' In a community without cinemas or wireless and with very little reading matter, she had her uses.

Borrowers were another nuisance. Most of the women borrowed at some time, and a few families lived entirely on borrowing the day before pay-day. There would come a shy, low-down, little knock at the door, and when it was opened, a child's voice would say, 'Oh, please Mrs So-and-So, could you oblige me mother with a spoonful of tea [or a cup of sugar, or half a loaf] till me Dad gets his money?' If the required article could not be spared at the first house, she would go from door to door repeating her request until she got what she wanted, for such were her instructions.

The borrowings were usually repaid, or there would soon have been nowhere to borrow from; but often an insufficient quantity or an inferior quality were returned, and the result was a smouldering resentment against the habitual borrowers. But no word of direct complaint was uttered. Had it been, the borrower might have taken offence, and the women wished above all things to be on good terms with their neighbours.

Laura's mother detested the borrowing habit. She said that when she had first set up housekeeping she had made it her rule when a borrower came to the door to say, 'Tell your mother I never borrow myself and I never lend. But here's the tea. I don't want it back again. Tell your mother she's welcome to it.' The plan did not work. The same borrower came again and again, until she had to say, 'Tell your mother I must have it back this time.' Again the plan did not work. Laura once heard her mother say to Queenie, 'Here's half a loaf, Queenie, if it's any good to you. But I won't deceive you about it; it's one that Mrs Knowles sent back that she'd borrowed from me, and I can't fancy it myself, out of her house. If you don't have it, it'll have to go in the pig-tub.'

'That's all right, me dear,' was Queenie's smiling response.

'It'll do fine for our Tom's tea. He won't know where it's been, an' 'ould'nt care if he did. All he cares about's a full belly.'

However, there were other friends and neighbours to whom it was a pleasure to lend, or to give on the rare occasions when that was possible. They seldom asked directly for a loan, but would say, 'My poor old tea-caddy's empty,' or 'I ain't got a mossel o' bread till the baker comes.' They spoke of this kind of approach as 'a nint' and said that if anybody liked to take it they could; if not, no harm was done, for they hadn't demeaned themselves by asking.

As well as the noted gossips, there were in Lark Rise, as elsewhere, women who, by means of a dropped hint or a subtle suggestion, could poison another's mind, and others who wished no harm to anybody, yet loved to discuss their neighbours' affairs and were apt to babble confidences. But, though few of the women were averse to a little scandal at times, most of them grew restive when it passed a certain point. 'Let's give it a rest,' they would say, or 'Well, I think we've plucked enough feathers out of her wings for one day,' and they would change the subject and talk about their children, or the rising prices, or the servant problem – from the maid's standpoint.

Those of the younger set who were what they called 'folks together', meaning friendly, would sometimes meet in the afternoon in one of their cottages to sip strong, sweet, milkless tea and talk things over. These tea-drinkings were never premeditated. One neighbour would drop in, then another, and another would be beckoned to from the doorway or fetched in to settle some disputed point. Then some one would say, 'How about a cup o' tay?' and they would all run home to fetch a spoonful, with a few leaves over to help make up the spoonful for the pot.

Those who assembled thus were those under forty. The older women did not care for the little tea-parties, nor for light, pleasant chit-chat; there was more of the salt of the earth in their conversation and they were apt to express things in terms which the others, who had all been in good service, considered coarse and countrified.

As they settled around the room to enjoy their cup of tea,

some would have babies at the breast or toddlers playing 'bo-peep' with their aprons, and others would have sewing or knitting in their hands. They were pleasant to look at, with their large clean white aprons and smoothly plaited hair, parted in the middle. The best clothes were kept folded away in their boxes from Sunday to Sunday, and a clean apron was full dress on week-days.

It was not a countryside noted for feminine good looks and there were plenty of wide mouths, high cheekbones, and snub noses among them; but they nearly all had the country-bred woman's clear eyes, strong, white teeth and fresh colour. Their height was above that of the average working-class towns-woman, and, when not obscured by pregnancy, their figures were straight and supple, though inclining to thickness.

This tea-drinking time was the women's hour. Soon the children would be rushing in from school; then would come the men, with their loud voices and coarse jokes and corduroys reeking of earth and sweat. In the meantime, the wives and mothers were free to crook their little fingers genteelly as they sipped from their tea-cups and talked about the, to them, latest fashion, or discussed the serial then running in the novelette they were reading.

Most of the younger women and some of the older ones were fond of what they called 'a bit of a read', and their mental fare consisted almost exclusively of the novelette. Several of the hamlet women took in one of these weekly, as published, for the price was but one penny, and these were handed round until the pages were thin and frayed with use. Copies of others found their way there from neighbouring villages, or from daughters in service, and there was always quite a library of them in circulation.

The novelette of the 'eighties was a romantic love story, in which the poor governess always married the duke, or the lady of title the gamekeeper, who always turned out to be a duke or an earl in disguise. Midway through the story there had to be a description of a ball, at which the heroine in her simple white gown attracted all the men in the room; or the gamekeeper, commandeered to help serve, made love to the daughter of the

house in the conservatory. The stories were often prettily written and as innocent as sugared milk and water; but, although
they devoured them, the women looked upon novelette reading
as a vice, to be hidden from their menfolk and only discussed
with fellow devotees.

The novelettes were as carefully kept out of the children's
way as the advanced modern novel is, or should be, today; but
children who wanted to read them knew where to find them, on
the top shelf of the cupboard or under the bed, and managed to
read them in secret. An ordinarily intelligent child of eight or
nine found them cloying; but they did the women good, for, as
they said, they took them out of themselves.

There had been a time when the hamlet readers had fed on
stronger food, and Biblical words and imagery still coloured the
speech of some of the older people. Though unread, every well-
kept cottage had still its little row of books, neatly arranged on
the side table with the lamp, the clothes brush and the family
photographs. Some of these collections consisted solely of the
family Bible and a prayer-book or two; others had a few extra
volumes which had either belonged to parents or been bought
with other oddments for a few pence at a sale – *The Pilgrim's
Progress, Drelincourt on Death*, Richardson's *Pamela, Anna
Lee: The Maiden Wife and Mother*, and old books of travel
and sermons. Laura's greatest find was a battered old copy of
Belzoni's *Travels* propping open somebody's pantry window.
When she asked for the loan of it, it was generously given to
her, and she had the, to her, intense pleasure of exploring the
burial chambers of the pyramids with her author.

Some of the imported books had their original owner's book-
plate, or an inscription in faded copper-plate handwriting inside
the covers, while the family ones, in a ruder hand, would pro-
claim:

> George Welby, his book:
> Give me grace therein to look,
> And not only to look, but to understand,
> For learning is better than houses and land
> When land is lost and money spent
> Then learning is most excellent.

Or:

> George Welby is my name,
>   England is my nation,
> Lark Rise is my dwelling place
>   And Christ is my salvation.
>
> When I am dead and in my grave
>   And all my bones are rotten,
> Take this book and think of me
>   And mind I'm not forgotten.

Another favourite inscription was the warning:

> Steal not this book for fear of shame,
> For in it doth stand the owner's name,
> And at the last day God will say
> 'Where is that book you stole away?'
> And if you, 'I cannot tell,'
> He'll say, 'Thou cursed, go to hell.'

All or any of these books were freely lent, for none of the owners wanted to read them. The women had their novelettes, and it took the men all their time to get through their Sunday newspapers, one of which came into almost every house, either by purchase or borrowing. The *Weekly Despatch*, *Reynolds's News*, and *Lloyd's News* were their favourites, though a few remained faithful to that fine old local newspaper, the *Bicester Herald*.

Laura's father, as well as his *Weekly Despatch*, took the *Carpenter and Builder*, through which the children got their first instruction to Shakespeare, for there was a controversy in it as to Hamlet's words, 'I know a hawk from a handsaw'. It appeared that some scholar had suggested that it should read, 'I know a hawk from a heron, pshaw!' and the carpenters and builders were up in arms. *Of course*, the hawk was the mason's and plasterer's tool of that time, and the handsaw was *just* a handsaw. Although that line and a few extracts that she afterwards found in the school readers were all that Laura was to know of Shakespeare's works for some time, she sided warmly with the carpenters and builders, and her mother, when appealed to, agreed, for she said 'that heron, pshaw!' certainly sounded a bit left-handed.

While the novelette readers, who represented the genteel section of the community, were enjoying their tea, there would be livelier gatherings at another of the cottages. The hostess, Caroline Arless, was at that time about forty-five, and a tall, fine, upstanding woman with flashing dark eyes, hair like crinkled black wire, and cheeks the colour of a ripe apricot. She was not a native of the hamlet, but had come there as a bride, and it was said that she had gipsy blood in her.

Although she was herself a grandmother, she still produced a child of her own every eighteen months or so, a proceeding regarded as bad form in the hamlet, for the saying ran, 'When the young 'uns begin, 'tis time for the old 'uns to finish.' But Mrs Arless recognized no rules, excepting those of Nature. She welcomed each new arrival, cared for it tenderly while it was helpless, swept it out of doors to play as soon as it could toddle, to school at three, and to work at ten or eleven. Some of the girls married at seventeen and the boys at nineteen or twenty.

Ways and means did not trouble her. Husband and sons at work 'brassed up' on Friday nights, and daughters in service sent home at least half of their wages. One night she would fry steak and onions for supper and make the hamlet's mouth water; another night there would be nothing but bread and lard on her table. When she had money she spent it, and when she had none she got things on credit or went without. 'I shall feather the foam,' she used to say. 'I have before an' I shall again, and what's the good of worrying.' She always did manage to feather it, and usually to have a few coppers in her pocket as well, although she was known to be deeply in debt. When she received a postal order from one of her daughters she would say to any one who happened to be standing by when she opened the letter, 'I be-ant goin' to squander this bit o' money in paying me debts.'

Her idea of wise spending was to call in a few neighbours of like mind, seat them round a roaring fire, and dispatch one of her toddlers to the inn with the beer can. They none of them got drunk, or even fuddled, for there was not very much each, even when the can went round to the inn a second or a third time. But there was just enough to hearten them up and make them forget their troubles, and the talk and laughter and scraps of song which floated on the air from 'that there Mrs Arless's house' were shocking to the more sedate matrons. Nobody crooked their finger round the handle of a teacup or 'talked genteel' at Mrs Arless's gatherings, herself least of all. She was so charged with sex vitality that with her all subjects of conversation led to it – not in its filthy or furtive aspects, but as the one great central fact of life.

Yet no one could dislike Mrs Arless, however much she might offend their taste and sense of fitness. She was so full of life and vigour and so overflowing with good nature that she would force anything she had upon any one she thought needed it, regardless of the fact that it was not and never would be paid for. She knew the inside of a County Court well, and made no secret of her knowledge, for a County Court summons was to her but an invitation to a day's outing from which she would return victorious, having persuaded the judge that she was a model wife and mother who only got into debt because her family was so large and she herself was so generous. It was her creditor who retired discomfited.

Another woman who lived in the hamlet and yet stood somewhat aside from its ordinary life was Hannah Ashley. She was the daughter-in-law of the old Methodist who drove the breast plough, and she and her husband were also Methodists. She was a little brown mouse of a woman who took no part in the hamlet gossip or the hamlet disputes. Indeed, she was seldom seen on week-days, for her cottage stood somewhat apart from the others and had its own well in the garden. But on Sunday evenings her house was used as a Methodist meeting place, and then all her week-day reserve was put aside and all who cared to come were made welcome. As she listened to the preacher, or joined in the hymns and prayers, she would look round on the tiny congregation, and those whose eyes met hers would see such a glow of love in them that they could never again think, much less say, ill of her, beyond 'Well, she's a

Methody', as though that explained and excused anything strange about her.

These younger Ashleys had one child, a son, about Edmund's age, and the children at the end house sometimes played with him. When Laura called at his home for him one Saturday morning she saw a picture which stamped itself upon her mind for life. It was the hour when every other house in the hamlet was being turned inside out for the Saturday cleaning. The older children, home from school, were running in and out of their homes, or quarrelling over their games outside. Mothers were scolding and babies were crying during the process of being rolled in their shawls for an outing on the arm of an older sister. It was the kind of day Laura detested, for there was no corner indoors for her and her book, and outside she was in danger of being dragged into games that either pulled her to pieces or bored her.

Inside Freddy Ashley's home all was peace and quiet and spotless purity. The walls were freshly whitewashed, the table and board floor were scrubbed to a pale straw colour, the beautifully polished grate glowed crimson, for the oven was being heated, and placed half-way over the table was a snowy cloth with paste-board and rolling-pin upon it. Freddy was helping his mother make biscuits, cutting the pastry she had rolled into shapes with a little tin cutter. Their two faces, both so plain and yet so pleasant, were close together above the paste-board, and their two voices as they bade Laura come in and sit by the fire sounded like angels' voices after the tumult outside.

It was a brief glimpse into a different world from the one she was accustomed to, but the picture remained with her as something quiet and pure and lovely. She thought that the home at Nazareth must have been something like Freddy's.

The women never worked in the vegetable gardens or on the allotments, even when they had their children off hand and had plenty of spare time, for there was a strict division of labour and that was 'men's work'. Victorian ideas, too, had penetrated to some extent, and any work outside the home was considered unwomanly. But even that code permitted a woman to cultivate

a flower garden, and most of the houses had at least a narrow
border beside the pathway. As no money could be spared for
seeds or plants, they had to depend upon roots and cuttings
given by their neighbours, and there was little variety; but they
grew all the sweet old-fashioned cottage garden flowers, pinks
and sweet williams and love-in-a-mist, wallflowers and forget-
me-nots in spring and hollyhocks and Michaelmas daisies in
autumn. Then there were lavender and sweetbriar bushes, and
southern-wood, sometimes called 'lad's love', but known there
as 'old man'.

Almost every garden had its rose bush; but there were no
coloured roses amongst them. Only Old Sally had those; the
other people had to be content with that meek, old-fashioned
white rose with a pink flush at the heart known as the 'maiden's
blush'. Laura used to wonder who had imported the first bush,
for evidently slips of it had been handed round from house to
house.

As well as their flower garden, the women cultivated a herb
corner, stocked with thyme and parsley and sage for cooking,
rosemary to flavour the home-made lard, lavender to scent the
best clothes, and peppermint, pennyroyal, horehound, camomile, tansy, balm, and rue for physic. They made a good deal
of camomile tea, which they drank freely to ward off colds, to
soothe the nerves, and as a general tonic. A large jug of this was
always prepared and stood ready for heating up after
confinements. The horehound was used with honey in a preparation to be taken for sore throats and colds on the chest.
Peppermint tea was made rather as a luxury than a medicine; it
was brought out on special occasions and drunk from wine-
glasses; and the women had a private use for the pennyroyal,
though, judging from appearances, it was not very effective.

As well as the garden herbs, still in general use, some of the
older women used wild ones, which they gathered in their
seasons and dried. But the knowledge and use of these was
dying out; most people depended upon their garden stock.
Yarrow, or milleflower, was an exception; everybody still gathered that in large quantities to make 'yarb beer'. Gallons of this
were brewed and taken to work in their tea cans by the men and

stood aside in the pantry for the mother and children to drink whenever thirsty. The finest yarrow grew beside the turnpike, and in dry weather the whole plant became so saturated with white dust that the beer, when brewed, had a milky tinge. If the children remarked on this they were told, 'Us've all got to eat a peck o' dust before we dies, an' it'll slip down easy in this good yarb beer.'

The children at the end house used to wonder how they would ever obtain their peck of dust, for their mother was fastidiously particular. Such things as lettuce and watercress she washed in three waters, instead of giving them the dip and shake considered sufficient by most other people. Watercress had almost to be washed away, because of the story of the man who had swallowed a tadpole which had grown to a full-sized frog in his stomach. There was an abundance of watercress to be had for the picking, and a good deal of it was eaten in the spring, before it got tough and people got tired of it. Perhaps they owed much of their good health to such food.

All kinds of home-made wines were brewed by all but the poorest. Sloes and blackberries and elderberries could be picked from the hedgerows, dandelions and coltsfoot and cowslips from the fields, and the garden provided rhubarb, currants and gooseberries and parsnips. Jam was made from garden and hedgerow fruit. This had to be made over an open fire and needed great care in the making; but the result was generally good – too good, the women said, for the jam disappeared too soon. Some notable housewives made jelly. Crab-apple jelly was a speciality at the end house. Crab-apple trees abounded in the hedgerows and the children knew just where to go for red crabs, red-and-yellow streaked crabs, or crabs which hung like ropes of green onions on the branches.

It seemed to Laura a miracle when a basket of these, with nothing but sugar and water added, turned into jelly as clear and bright as a ruby. She did not take into account the long stewing, tedious straining, and careful measuring, boiling up and clarifying that went to the filling of the row of glass jars which cast a glow of red light on the whitewash at the back of the pantry shelf.

A quickly made delicacy was cowslip tea. This was made by picking the golden pips from a handful of cowslips, pouring boiling water over them, and letting the tea stand a few minutes to infuse. It could then be drunk either with or without sugar as preferred.

Cowslip balls were made for the children. These were fashioned by taking a great fragrant handful of the flowers, tying the stalks tightly with string, and pulling down the blooms to cover the stems. The bunch was then almost round, and made the loveliest ball imaginable.

Some of the older people who kept bees made mead, known there as 'metheglin'. It was a drink almost superstitiously esteemed, and the offer of a glass was regarded as a great compliment. Those who made it liked to make a little mystery of the process; but it was really very simple. Three pounds of honey were allowed to every gallon of spring water. This had to be running spring water, and was obtained from a place in the brook where the water bubbled up; never from the well. The honey and water were boiled together, and skimmed and strained and worked with a little yeast; then kept in a barrel for six months, when the metheglin was ready for bottling.

Old Sally said that some folks messed up their metheglin with lemons, bay leaves, and suchlike; but all she could say was that folks who'd add anything to honey didn't deserve to have bees to work for them.

Old metheglin was supposed to be the most intoxicating drink on earth, and it was certainly potent, as a small girl once found when, staying up to welcome home a soldier uncle from Egypt, she was invited to take a sip from his glass and took a pull.

All the evening it had been 'Yes, please, Uncle Reuben', and 'Very well, thank you, Uncle Reuben' with her; but as she went upstairs to bed she astonished every one by calling pertly: 'Uncle Reuby is a booby!' It was the mead speaking, not her. There was a dash in her direction; but, fortunately for her, it was stayed by Sergeant Reuben draining his glass, smacking his lips, and declaring: 'Well, I've tasted some liquors in my time; but this beats all!' and under cover of the fresh uncorking and pouring out, she tumbled sleepily into bed with her white, starched finery still on her.

The hamlet people never invited each other to a meal; but when it was necessary to offer tea to an important caller, or to friends from a distance, the women had their resources. If, as often happened, there was no butter in the house, a child would be sent to the shop at the inn for a quarter of the best fresh, even if it had to 'go down on the book' until pay-day. Thin bread and butter, cut and arranged as in their old days in service, with a pot of homemade jam, which had been hidden away for such an occasion, and a dish of lettuce, fresh from the garden and garnished with little rosy radishes, made an attractive little meal, fit, as they said, to put before anybody.

In winter, salt butter would be sent for and toast would be made and eaten with celery. Toast was a favourite dish for family consumption. 'I've made 'em a stack o' toast as high as up to their knees', a mother would say on a winter Sunday afternoon before her hungry brood came in from church. Another dish upon which they prided themselves was thin slices of cold, boiled streaky bacon on toast, a dish so delicious that it deserves to be more widely popular.

The few visitors from the outer world who came that way enjoyed such simple food, with a cup of tea; and a glass of homemade wine at their departure; and the women enjoyed entertaining them, and especially enjoyed the feeling that they, themselves, were equal to the occasion. 'You don't want to be poor and look poor, too,' they would say; and 'We've got our pride. Yes, we've got our pride.'

VII

Callers

CALLERS made a pleasant diversion in the hamlet women's day, and there were more of these than might have been expected. The first to arrive on Monday morning was old Jerry Parish with his cartload of fish and fruit. As he served some of the big houses on his round, Jerry carried quite a large stock; but the only goods he took round to the doors at Lark Rise were a box of bloaters and a basket of small, sour oranges. The bloaters were sold at a penny each and the oranges at three a penny. Even at these prices they were luxuries; but, as it was still only Monday and a few coppers might remain in a few purses, the women felt at liberty to crowd round his cart to examine and criticize his wares, even if they bought nothing.

Two or three of them would be tempted to buy a bloater for their midday meal, but it had to be a soft-roed one, for, in nearly every house there were children under school age at home; so the bloater had to be shared, and the soft roes spread upon bread for the smallest ones.

'Lor' blime me!' Jerry used to say. 'Never knowed such a lot in me life for soft roes. Good job I ain't a soft-roed 'un or I should've got aten up meself before now.' And he pinched the bloaters between his great red fingers, pretended to consider the matter with his head on one side, then declared each separate fish had the softest of soft roes, whether it had or not. 'Oozin', simply oozin' with goodness, I tell ye!' and oozing it certainly was when released from his grip. 'But what's the good of one bloater amongst the lot of ye? Tell ye what I'll do,' he would urge. 'I'll put ye in these three whoppers for tuppence-ha'penny.'

It was no good. The twopence-halfpenny was never forth-coming; even the penny could so ill be spared that the purchaser often felt selfish and greedy after she had parted with it; but, after a morning at the washtub, she needed a treat so badly, and a bloater made a tasty change from her usually monotonous diet.

The oranges were tempting, too, for the children loved them. It was one of their greatest treats to find oranges on the mantelshelf when they came home from school in winter. Sour they might be and hard and skinny within; but without how rich and glowing! and what a strange foreign scent pervaded the room when their mother divided each one into quarters and distributed them. Even when the pulp had been eaten, the peel remained, to be dried on the hob and taken to school to chew in class or 'swopped' for conkers or string or some other desirable object.

Jerry's cart had a great attraction for Laura. At the sound of his wheels she would run out to feast her eyes on the lovely rich colours of grapes and pears and peaches. She loved to see the fish, too, with their cool colours and queer shapes, and would imagine them swimming about in the sea or resting among the seaweed. 'What is that one called?' she asked one day, pointing to a particularly queer-looking one.

'That's a John Dory, me dear. See them black marks? Look like finger-marks, don't 'em? An' they do say that they be finger-marks. *He* made 'em, that night, ye know, when they was fishin' ye know, an' *He* took some an' cooked 'em all ready for 'em, an' ever since, they say, that ivery John Dory as comes out o' th' sea have got *His* finger-marks on 'un.'

Laura was puzzled, for Jerry had mentioned no name and he was, moreover, a drinking, swearing old man, little likely, as she thought, to repeat a sacred legend.

'Do you mean the Sea of Galilee?' she asked timidly.

'That's it, me dear. That's what they say, whether true or not, of course, I *don't* know; but there be the finger-marks, right enough, an' that's what they say in our trade.'

It was on Jerry's cart tomatoes first appeared in the hamlet. They had not long been introduced into this country and were slowly making their way into favour. The fruit was flatter in shape then than now and deeply grooved and indented from the stem, giving it an almost starlike appearance. There were bright yellow ones, too, as well as the scarlet; but, after a few years, the yellow ones disappeared from the market and the red ones became rounder and smoother, as we see them now.

At first sight, the basket of red and yellow fruit attracted Laura's colour-loving eye. 'What are those?' she asked old Jerry.

'Love-apples, me dear. Love-apples, they be; though some hignorant folks be a callin' 'em tommytoes. But you don't want any o' they – nasty sour things, they be, as only gentry can eat. You have a nice sweet orange wi' your penny.' But Laura felt she must taste the love-apples and insisted upon having one.

Such daring created quite a sensation among the onlookers.
'Don't 'ee go tryin' to eat it, now,' one woman urged. 'It'll only
make 'ee sick. I know because I had one of the nasty horrid
things at our Minnie's.' And nasty, horrid things tomatoes remained in the popular estimation for years; though most people
today would prefer them as they were then, with the real
tomato flavour pronounced, to the watery insipidity of our
larger, smoother tomato.

Mr Wilkins, the baker, came three times a week. His long,
lank figure, girded by a white apron which always seemed about
to slip down over his hips, was a familiar one at the end house.
He always stayed there for a cup of tea, for which he propped
himself up against the end of the dresser. He would never sit
down; he said he had not time, and that was why he did not stop
to change his flour-dusty bakehouse clothes before he started on
his round.

He was no ordinary baker, but a ship's carpenter by trade
who had come to the neighbouring village on a visit to relatives,
met his present wife, married her, and cast anchor inland. Her
father was old, she was the only child, and the family business
had to be attended to; so, partly for love and partly for future
gain he had given up the sea, but he still remained a sailor at
heart.

He would stand in the doorway of Laura's home and look
out at the wheatfields billowing in the breeze and the white
clouds hurrying over them, and say: 'All very fine; but it seems
a bit dead to me, right away from the sea, like this.' And he
would tell the children how the waves pile up in a storm, 'like
the wall of a house coming down on your ship', and about other
seas, calm and bright as a looking-glass, with little islands and
palm trees – but treacherous, too – and treacherous little men
living in palm leaf huts, 'their faces as brown as your frock,
Laura.' Once he had been shipwrecked and spent nine days in
an open boat, the last two without water. His tongue had stuck
to the roof of his mouth and he had spent weeks after rescue in
hospital.

'And yet,' he would say, 'I'd dearly love just one more trip;
but my dear wife would cry her eyes out if I mentioned it, and

the business, of course, couldn't be left. No. I've swallowed the anchor, all right. I've swallowed the anchor.'

Mr Wilkins brought the image of the real living sea to the end house; otherwise the children would have only known it in pictures. True, their mother in her nursing days had been to the seaside with her charges and had many pleasant stories to tell of walks on piers, digging on sands, gathering seaweed, and shrimping with nets. But the seaside was different – delightful in its way, no doubt, but nothing like the wide tumbling ocean with ships on it.

The only portion of the sea which came their way was contained in a medicine bottle which a hamlet girl in service at Brighton brought home as a curiosity. In time the bottle of sea-water became the property of a younger sister, a school-fellow of Laura's, who was persuaded to barter it for a hunch of cake and a blue-bead necklace. Laura treasured it for years.

Many casual callers passed through the hamlet. Travelling tinkers with their barrows, braziers, and twirling grindstones turned aside from the main road and came singing:

> Any razors or scissors to grind?
> Or anything else in the tinker's line?
> Any old pots or kettles to mend?

After squinting into any leaking vessel against the light, or trying the edges of razors or scissors upon the hard skin of their palms, they would squat by the side of the road to work, or start their emery wheel whizzing, to the delight of the hamlet children, who always formed a ring around any such operations.

Gipsy women with cabbage-nets and clothes-pegs to sell were more frequent callers for they had a camping-place only a mile away and no place was too poor to yield them a harvest. When a door was opened to them, if the housewife appeared to be under forty, they would ask in a wheedling voice: 'Is your mother at home, my dear?' Then, when the position was explained, they would exclaim in astonished tones: 'You don't mean to tell me you *be* the mother? Look at that, now. I shouldn't have taken you to be a day over twenty.'

No matter how often repeated, this compliment was swallowed whole, and made a favourable opening for a long conversation, in the course of which the wily 'Egyptian' not only learned the full history of the woman's own family, but also a good deal about those of her neighbours, which was duly noted for future use. Then would come a request for 'handful of little 'taters, or an onion or two for the pot', and, if these were given, as they usually were, 'My pretty lady' would be asked for an old shift of her own or an old shirt of her husband's, or anything that the children might have left off, and, poverty-stricken though the hamlet was, a few worn-out garments would be secured to swell the size of the bundle which, afterwards, would be sold to the rag merchant.

Sometimes the gipsies would offer to tell fortunes; but this offer was always refused, not out of scepticism or lack of curiosity about the future, but because the necessary silver coin was not available. 'No, thank 'ee,' the women would say. 'I don't want nothink of that sort. My fortune's already told.'

'Ah, my lady! you med think so; but them as has got childern never knows. You be born, but you ain't dead yet, an' you may dress in silks and ride in your own carriage yet. You wait till that fine strappin' boy o' yourn gets rich. He won't forget his mother, I'll bet!' and after this free prognostication, they would trail off to the next house, leaving behind a scent as strong as a vixen's.

The gipsies paid in entertainment for what they received. Their calls made a welcome break in the day. Those of the tramps only harrowed the feelings and left the depressed in spirit even more depressed.

There must have been hundreds of tramps on the roads at that time. It was a common sight, when out for a walk, to see a dirty, unshaven man, his rags topped with a battered bowler, lighting a fire of sticks by the roadside to boil his tea-can. Sometimes he would have a poor bedraggled woman with him and she would be lighting the fire while he lolled at ease on the turf or picked out the best pieces from the bag of food they had collected at their last place of call.

Some of them carried small, worthless things to sell — matches, shoe-laces, or dried-lavender bags. The children's mother often bought from these out of pity; but never from the man who sold oranges, for they had seen him on one of their walks, spitting on his oranges and polishing them with a filthy rag. Then there was the woman who, very early one morning, knocked at the door with small slabs of tree-bark in her apron. She was cleaner and better dressed than the ordinary tramp and brought with her a strong scent of lavender. The bark appeared to be such as could have been hacked with a clasp-knife from the nearest pine tree; but she claimed for it a very different origin. It was the famous lavender bark, she said, brought from foreign parts by her sailor son. One fragment kept among clothes was not only an everlasting perfume, but it was also death to moths. 'You just smell it, my dears,' she said, handing pieces to the mother and the children, who had crowded to the door.

It certainly smelt strongly of lavender. The children handled it lovingly, fascinated by a substance which had travelled so far and smelt so sweetly.

She asked sixpence a slab; but obligingly came down to two-pence, and three pieces were purchased and placed in a fancy bowl on the side table to perfume the room and to be exhibited as a rarity.

Alas! the vendor had barely time to clear out of the hamlet before all the perfume had evaporated and the bark became what it had been before she sprinkled it with oil of lavender – just ordinary bark from a pine trunk!

Such brilliance was exceptional. Most of the tramps were plain beggars. 'Please could you give me a morsel of bread, for I be so hungry. I'm telling God I haven't put a bite between my lips since yesterday morning' was a regular formula with them when they knocked at the door of a cottage; and, although many of them looked well-nourished, they were never turned away. Thick slices, which could ill be spared, were plastered with lard; the cold potatoes which the housewife had intended to fry for her own dinner were wrapped in newspaper, and by the time they left the hamlet they were insured against starvation for at least a week. The only reward for such generosity, beyond the whining professional 'God bless ye', was the cheering reflection that however badly off one might be oneself, there were others poorer.

Where all these wayfarers came from or how they had fallen so low in the social scale was uncertain. According to their own account, they had been ordinary decent working people with homes 'just such another as yourn, mum'; but their houses had been burned down or flooded, or they had fallen out of work, or spent a long time in hospital and had never been able to start again. Many of the women pleaded that their husbands were dead, and several men came begging with the plea that, having lost their wives, they had the children to look after and could not leave them to work for their living.

Sometimes whole families took to the road with their bags and bundles and tea-cans, begging their food as they went and sleeping in casual wards or under ricks or in ditches. Laura's father, coming home from work at dusk one night, thought he heard a rustling in the ditch by the roadside. When he looked down into it, a row of white faces looked up at him, belonging to a mother, a father, and three or four children. He said that in the half light only their faces were visible and that they looked like a set of silver coins, ranging from a florin to a threepenny bit. Though late in the summer, the night was not cold. 'Thank God for that!' said the children's mother when she heard about them, for, had it been cold, he might have brought them all home with him. He had brought home tramps before and had them sit at table with the family, to his wife's disgust, for he had what she considered peculiar ideas on hospitality and the brotherhood of man.

There was no tallyman, or Johnny Fortnight, in those parts; but once, for a few months, a man who kept a small furniture shop in a neighbouring town came round selling his wares on the instalment plan. On his first visit to Lark Rise he got no order at all; but on his second one of the women, more daring than the rest, ordered a small wooden washstand and a zinc bath for washing day. Immediately washstands and zinc baths became the rage. None of the women could think how they had managed to exist so long without a washstand in their bedroom. They were quite satisfied with the buckets and basins of water in the pantry or by the fireside or out of doors for their own use; but supposing someone fell ill and the doctor had to wash his hands in a basin placed on a clean towel on the kitchen table! or supposing some of their town relatives came on a visit, those with a real sink and water laid on! They felt they would die with mortification if they had to apologize for having no washstand. As to the zinc bath, that seemed even more necessary. That wooden tub their mother had used was 'a girt okkard old thing'. Although they had not noticed its weight much before, it seemed almost to break their backs when they could see a bright, shining new bath hanging under the eaves of the next-door barn.

It was not long before practically every house had a new bath and washstand. A few mothers of young children went farther and ordered a fireguard as well. Then the fortnightly payments began. One-and-six was the specified instalment, and, for the first few fortnights, this was forthcoming. But it was so difficult to get that eighteenpence together. A few pence had always to be used out of the first week's ninepence, then in the second week some urgent need for cash would occur. The instalments fell to a shilling. Then to sixpence. A few gave up the struggle and defaulted.

Month after month the salesman came round and collected what he could; but he did not try to tempt them to buy anything more, for he could see that he would never be paid for it. He was a good-hearted man who listened to their tales of woe and never bullied or threatened to County Court them. Perhaps the debts were not as important to him as they appeared to his customers; or he may have felt he was to blame for tempting them to order things they could not afford. He continued calling until he had collected as much as he thought possible, then disappeared from the scene.

A more amusing episode was that of the barrels of beer. At that time in that part of the country, brewers' travellers, known locally as 'outriders', called for orders at farm-houses and superior cottages, as well as at inns. No experienced outrider visited farm labourers' cottages; but the time came when a beginner, full of youthful enthusiasm and burning to fill up his order book, had the brilliant idea of canvassing the hamlet for orders.

Wouldn't it be splendid, he asked the women, to have their own nine-gallon cask of good ale in for Christmas, and only have to go into the pantry and turn the tap to get a glass for their husband and friends. The ale cost far less by the barrel than when bought at the inn. It would be an economy in the long run, and how well it would look to bring out a jug of foaming ale from their own barrel for their friends. As to payment, they sent in their bills quarterly, so there would be plenty of time to save up.

The women agreed that it would, indeed, be splendid to have their own barrel, and even the men, when told of the project at night, were impressed by the difference in price when buying by the nine-gallon cask. Some of them worked it out on paper and were satisfied that, considering that they would be spending a few shillings extra at Christmas in any case, and that the missus had been looking rather peaked lately and a glass of good beer cost less than doctor's physic, and that maybe a daughter in service would be sending a postal order, they might venture to order the cask.

Others did not trouble to work it out; but, enchanted with the idea, gave the order lightheartedly. After all, as the outrider said, Christmas came but once a year, and this year they would have a jolly one. Of course there were kill-joys, like Laura's father, who said sardonically: 'They'll laugh the other side of their faces when it comes to paying for it.'

The barrels came and were tapped and the beer was handed around. The barrels were empty and the brewer's carter in his leather apron heaved them into the van behind his steaming, stamping horses; but none of the mustard or cocoa tins hidden away in secret places contained more than a few coppers towards paying the bill. When the day of reckoning came only three of the purchasers had the money ready. But time was allowed. Next month would do; but, mind! it must be forthcoming then. Most of the women tried hard to get that money together; but, of course, they could not. The traveller called again and again, each time growing more threatening, and, after some months, the brewer took the matter to the County Court, where the judge, after hearing the circumstances of sale and the income of the purchasers, ordered them all to pay twopence weekly off the debt. So ended the great excitement of having one's own barrel of beer on tap.

The packman, or pedlar, once a familiar figure in that part of the country, was seldom seen in the 'eighties. People had taken to buying their clothes at the shops in the market town, where fashions were newer and prices lower. But one last survivor of the once numerous clan still visited the hamlet at long and irregular intervals.

He would turn aside from the turnpike and come plodding down the narrow hamlet road, an old white-headed, white-bearded man, still hale and rosy, although almost bent double under the heavy, black canvas-covered pack he carried strapped on his shoulders. 'Anything out of the pack today?' he would ask at each house, and, at the least encouragement, fling down his load and open it on the doorstep. He carried a tempting variety of goods: dress-lengths and shirt-lengths and remnants to make up for the children; aprons and pinafores, plain and fancy; corduroys for the men, and coloured scarves and ribbons for Sunday wear.

'That's a bit of right good stuff, ma'am, that is,' he would say, holding up some dress-length to exhibit it. 'A gown made of this piece'd last anybody for ever and then make 'em a good petticoat afterwards.' Few of the hamlet women could afford to test the quality of his piece goods; cottons or tapes, or a paper of pins, were their usual purchases; but his dress-lengths and other fabrics were of excellent quality and wore much longer than anyone would wish anything to wear in these days of rapidly changing fashions. It was from his pack the soft, warm woollen, grey with a white fleck in it, came to make the frock Laura wore with a little black satin apron and a bunch of snowdrops pinned to the breast when she went to sell stamps in the post office.

Once every summer a German band passed through the hamlet and halted outside the inn to play. It was composed of an entire family, a father and his six sons, the latter graded in size like a set of jugs, from the tall young man who played the cornet to the chubby pink-faced little boy who beat the drum.

Drawn up in the semicircle in their neat, green uniforms, they would blow away at their instruments until their chubby German cheeks seemed near to bursting point. Most of the music they played was above the heads of the hamlet folks, who said they liked something with a bit more 'chune' in it; but when, at the end of the performance, they gave *God Save the Queen* the standers-by joined with gusto in singing it.

That was the sign for the landlord to come out in his shirt-sleeves with three frothing beer mugs. One for the father, who poured the beer down his throat like water down a sink, and the other two to be passed politely from son to son. Unless a farmer's gig or a tradesman's trap happened to pull up at the inn gate during the performance, the beer was their only reward for the entertainment. They did not take their collecting bag round to the women and children who had gathered to listen, for they knew from experience there were no stray half-pence for German bands in a farm labourer's wife's pocket. So after shaking the saliva from their brass instruments, they bowed, clicked their heels, and marched off up the dusty road to the mother village. It was good beer and they were hot and thirsty, so perhaps the reward was sufficient.

The only other travelling entertainment which came there was known as the dancing dolls. These, alas! did not dance in the open, but in a cottage to which a penny admission was charged, and, as the cottage was not of the cleanest, Laura was never allowed to witness this performance. Those who had seen them said the dolls were on wires and that the man who exhibited them said the words for them, so it must have been some kind of marionette show.

Once, very early in their school life, the end house children met a man with a dancing bear. The man, apparently a foreigner, saw that the children were afraid to pass, and, to reassure them, set his bear dancing. With a long pole balanced across its front paws, it waltzed heavily to the tune hummed by its master, then shouldered the pole and did exercises at his word of command. The elders of the hamlet said the bear had appeared there at long intervals for many years; but that was its last appearance. Poor Bruin, with his mangy fur and hot, tainted breath, was never seen in those parts again. Perhaps he died of old age.

The greatest thrill of all and the one longest remembered in the hamlet, was provided by the visit of a cheap-jack about half-way through the decade. One autumn evening, just before dusk, he arrived with his cartload of crockery and tinware and set out his stock on the grass by the roadside before a back-cloth painted with icebergs and penguins and polar bears. Soon he had his naphtha lamps flaring and was clashing his basins together like bells and calling: 'Come buy! Come buy!'

It was the first visit of a cheap-jack to the hamlet and there was great excitement. Men, women, and children rushed from the houses and crowded around in the circle of light to listen to his patter and admire his wares. And what bargains he had! The tea-service decorated with fat, full-blown pink roses: twenty-one pieces and not a flaw in any one of them. The Queen had purchased its fellow set for Buckingham Palace it appeared. The teapots, the trays, the nests of dishes and basins, and the set of bedroom china which made everyone blush when he selected the most intimate utensil to rap with his knuckles to show it rang true.

'Two bob!' he shouted. 'Only two bob for this handsome set of jugs. Here's one for your beer and one for your milk and another in case you break one of the other two. Nobody willing to speculate? Then what about this here set of trays, straight from Japan and the peonies hand-painted; or this lot of basins, exact replicas of the one the Princess of Wales supped her gruel from when Prince George was born. Why damme, they cost me more n'r that. I could get twice the price I'm asking in Banbury tomorrow; but I'll give 'em to you, for you can't call it selling, because I like your faces and me load's heavy for me 'oss. Alarming bargains! Tremendous sacrifices! Come buy! Come buy!'

But there were scarcely any offers. A woman here and there would give threepence for a large pudding-basin or sixpence for a tin saucepan. The children's mother bought a penny nutmeg-grater and a set of wooden spoons for cooking; the innkeeper's wife ran to a dozen tumblers and a ball of string; then there was a long pause during which the vendor kept up a continual stream of jokes and anecdotes which sent his audience into fits of laughter. Once he broke into song:

> There was a man in his garden walked
> And cut his throat with a lump of chalk;
> His wife, she knew not what she did,
> She strangled herself with the saucepan lid.
> There was a man and a fine young fellow
> Who poisoned himself with an umbrella.
> Even Joey in his cradle shot himself dead with a silver ladle.
> When you hear this horrible tale
> It makes your faces all turn pale,
> Your eyes go green, you're overcome,
> So tweedle, tweedle, tweedle twum.

All very fine entertainment; but it brought him no money and he began to suspect that he would draw a blank at Lark Rise.

'Never let it be said,' he implored, 'that this is the poverty-strickenist place on God's earth. Buy something, if only for your own credit's sake. Here!' snatching up a pile of odd plates. 'Good dinner-plates for you. Everyone a left-over from a first-class service. Buy one of these and you'll have the satisfaction of knowing you're eating off the same ware as lords and dukes. Only three-halfpence each. Who'll buy? Who'll buy?'

There was a scramble for the plates, for nearly every one could muster three-halfpence; but every time anything more costly was produced there was dead silence. Some of the women began to feel uncomfortable. 'Don't be poor and look poor, too' was their motto, and here they were looking poor indeed, for who, with money in their pockets, could have resisted such wonderful bargains.

Then the glorious unexpected happened. The man had brought the pink rose tea-service forward again and was handing one of the cups round. 'You just look at the light through it – and you, ma'am – and you. Ain't it lovely china, thin as an eggshell, practically transparent, and with every one

of them roses hand-painted with a brush? You can't let a set like
that go out of the place, now can you? I can see all your mouths
a-watering. You run home, my dears, and bring out them stockings from under the mattress and the first one to get back shall
have it for twelve bob.'

Each woman in turn handled the cup lovingly, then shook her
head and passed it on. None of them had stockings of savings
hidden away. But, just as the man was receiving back the cup, a
little roughly, for he was getting discouraged, a voice spoke up
in the background.

'How much did you say, mister? Twelve bob? I'll give you
ten.' It was John Price, who, only the night before, had returned
from his soldiering in India. A very ordinary sort of chap at
most times, for he was a teetotaller and stood no drinks at the
inn, as a returned soldier should have done; but now, suddenly,
he became important. All eyes were upon him. The credit of the
hamlet was at stake.

'I'll give you ten bob.'

'Can't be done, matey. Cost me more nor that. But, look see,
tell you what I will do. You give me eleven and six and I'll
throw in this handsome silver-gilt vase for your mantelpiece.'

'Done!' The bargain was concluded; the money changed
hands, and the reputation of the hamlet was rehabilitated. Willing hands helped John carry the tea-service to his home.
Indeed, it was considered an honour to be trusted with a cup.
His bride-to-be was still away in service and little knew how
many were envying her that night. To have such a lovely service
awaiting her return, no cracked or odd pieces, every piece alike
and all so lovely; lucky, lucky, Lucy! But though they could not
help envying her a little, they shared in her triumph, for surely
such a purchase must shed a glow of reflected prosperity on the
whole hamlet. Though it might not be convenient to all of them
to buy very much on that particular night, the man must see
there *was* a bit of money in the place and folks who knew how
to spend it.

What came after was anti-climax, and yet very pleasant from
the end house children's point of view. A set of pretty little
dishes, suitable for holding jam, butter or fruit, according to

size, was being exhibited. The price had gone down from half a crown to a shilling without response, when once more a voice spoke up in the background. 'Pass them over, please. I expect my wife can find a use for them,' and, behold, it was the children's father who had halted on his way home from work to see what the lights and the crowd meant.

Perhaps in all the man took a pound that night, which was fifteen shillings more than any one could have foretold; but it was not sufficient to tempt him to come again, and thenceforth the year was dated as 'that time the cheap-jack came'.

VIII

'The Box'

A FAMILIAR sight at Lark Rise was that of a young girl – any young girl between ten and thirteen – pushing one of the two perambulators in the hamlet round the Rise with a smallish-sized, oak clothes box with black handles lashed to the seat. Those not already informed who met her would read the signs and inquire: 'How is your mother' – or your sister or your aunt – 'getting on?' and she, well-primed, would answer demurely, 'As well as can be expected under the circumstances, thank you, Mrs So-and-So.'

She had been to the Rectory for THE BOX, which appeared almost simultaneously with every new baby, and a gruelling time she would have had pushing her load the mile and a half and, at the same time, keeping it from slipping from its narrow perch. But, very soon, such small drawbacks would be forgotten in the pleasure of seeing it unpacked. It contained half a dozen of everything – tiny shirts, swathes, long flannel barrows, nighties, and napkins, made, kept in repair, and lent for every confinement by the clergyman's daughter. In addition to the loaned clothes, it would contain, as a gift, packets of tea and sugar and a tin of patent groats for making gruel.

The box was a popular institution. Any farm labourer's wife, whether she attended church or not, was made welcome to the

loan of it. It appeared in most of the cottages at regular intervals and seemed to the children as much a feature of family life
as the new babies. It was so constantly in demand that it had to
have an understudy, known as 'the second-best box', altogether
inferior, which fell to the lot of those careless matrons who had
neglected to bespeak the loan the moment they 'knew their luck
again'.

The boxes were supposed to be returned at the end of a
month with the clothes freshly laundered; but, if no one else
required them, an extension could be had, and many mothers
were allowed to keep their box until, at six or seven weeks old,
the baby was big enough to be put into short clothes; so saving
them the cost of preparing a layette other than the one set of
clothes got ready for the infant's arrival. Even that might be
borrowed. The stock at the end house was several times called
for in what, by a polite fiction, passed as an emergency. Other
women had their own baby clothes, beautifully sewn and laundered; but there was scarcely one who did not require the
clothes in the box to supplement them. For some reason or
other, the box was never allowed to go out until the baby had
arrived.

The little garments on loan were all good quality and nicely
trimmed with embroidery and hand tucking. The clergyman's
daughter also kept two christening robes to lend to the mothers,
and made a new frock, as a gift, for every baby's 'shortening'.
Summer or winter, these little frocks were made of flowered
print, blue for the boys and pink for the girls, and every one of
the tiny, strong stitches in them were done by her own hands.
She got little credit for this. The mothers, like the children,
looked upon the small garments, both loaned and given, as a
provision of Nature. Indeed, they were rather inclined to criticize. One woman ripped off the deep flounce of old Buck-
inghamshire lace from the second-best christening robe and
substituted a frill of coarse, machine-made embroidery, saying
she was not going to take her child to church 'trigged out' in
that old-fashioned trash. As she had not troubled to unpick the
stitches, the lace was torn beyond repair, and the gown ever
after was decidedly second-best, for the best one was the old

Rectory family christening robe and made of the finest lawn, tucked and inserted all over with real Valenciennes.

When the hamlet babies arrived, they found good clothes awaiting them, and the best of all nourishment – Nature's own. The mothers did not fare so well. It was the fashion at that time to keep maternity patients on low diet for the first three days, and the hamlet women found no difficulty in following this régime; water gruel, dry toast, and weak tea was their menu. When the time came for more nourishing diet, the parson's daughter made for every patient one large sago pudding, followed up by a jug of veal broth. After these were consumed they returned to their ordinary food, with a half-pint of stout a day for those who could afford it. No milk was taken, and yet their own milk supply was abundant. Once, when a bottle-fed baby was brought on a visit to the hamlet, its bottle was held up as a curiosity. It had a long, thin rubber tube for the baby to suck through which must have been impossible to clean.

The only cash outlay in an ordinary confinement was half a crown, the fee of the old woman who, as she said, saw the beginning and end of everybody. She was, of course, not a certified midwife; but she was a decent, intelligent old body, clean in her person and methods and very kind. For the half-crown she officiated at the birth and came every morning for ten days to bath the baby and make the mother comfortable. She also tried hard to keep the patient in bed for the ten days; but with little success. Some mothers refused to stay there because they knew they were needed downstairs; others because they felt so strong and fit they saw no reason to lie there. Some women actually got up on the third day, and, as far as could be seen at the time, suffered no ill effects.

Complications at birth were rare; but in the two or three cases where they did occur during her practice, old Mrs Quinton had sufficient skill to recognize the symptoms and send post haste for the doctor. No mother lost her life in childbed during the decade.

In these more enlightened days the mere mention of the old, untrained village midwife raises a vision of some dirty, drink-sodden old hag without skill or conscience. But not all of them were Sairey Gamps. The great majority were clean, knowledge-able old women who took a pride in their office. Nor had many of them been entirely without instruction. The country doctor of that day valued a good midwife in an outlying village and did not begrudge time and trouble in training her. Such a one would save him many a six or eight mile drive over bad roads at night, and, if a summons did come, he would know that his presence was necessary.

The trained district nurses, when they came a few years later, were a great blessing in country districts; but the old midwife also had her good points, for which she now receives no credit. She was no superior person coming into the house to strain its resources to the utmost and shame the patient by forced con-fessions that she did not possess this or that; but a neighbour, poor like herself, who could make do with what there was, or, if not, knew where to send to borrow it. This Mrs Quinton pos-sessed quite a stock of the things she knew she would not find in every house, and might often be met with a baby's little round bath in her hand, or a clothes-horse, for airing, slung over her arm.

Other days, other ways; and, although they have now been greatly improved upon, the old country midwives did at least succeed in bringing into the world many generations of our forefathers, or where should we be now?

The general health of the hamlet was excellent. The healthy, open-air life and the abundance of coarse but wholesome food must have been largely responsible for that; but lack of im-agination may also have played a part. Such people at that time did not look for or expect illness, and there were not as many patent medicine advertisements then as now to teach them to search for symptoms of minor ailments in themselves. Bee-cham's and Holloway's Pills were already familiar to all news-paper readers, and a booklet advertising Mother Siegel's Syrup arrived by post at every house once a year. But only Beecham's Pills were patronized, and those only by a few; the majority relied upon an occasional dose of Epsom salts to cure all ills. One old man, then nearly eighty, had for years drunk a tea-cupful of frothing soap-suds every Sunday morning. 'Them cleans the outers,' he would say, 'an' stands to reason they must clean th' innards, too.' His dose did not appear to do him any harm; but he made no converts.

Although only babies and very small children had baths, the hamlet folks were cleanly in their persons. The women would lock their cottage doors for a whole afternoon once a week to have what they called 'a good clean up'. This consisted of stripping to the waist and washing downward; then stepping into a footbath and washing upward. 'Well, I feels all the better for that,' some woman would say complacently. 'I've washed up as far as possible and down as far as possible,' and the ribald would inquire what poor 'possible' had done that that should not be included.

Toothbrushes were not in general use; few could afford to buy such luxuries; but the women took a pride in their strong white teeth and cleaned them with a scrap of clean, wet rag dipped in salt. Some of the men used soot as a tooth-powder.

After a confinement, if the eldest girl was too young and there was no other relative available, the housework, cooking, and washing would be shared among the neighbours, who would be repaid in kind when they themselves were in like case.

Babies, especially young babies, were adored by their parents and loved and petted and often spoilt by the whole family until another arrived; then, as they used to say, its 'nose was put out of joint'; all the adoration was centred on the newcomer and the ex-baby was fortunate if it had a still devoted elder sister to stand by it.

In the production of their large families the parents appeared reckless. One obvious method of birth control, culled from the Old Testament, was known in the hamlet and practised by one couple, which had managed to keep their family down to four. The wife told their secret to another woman, thinking to help her; but it only brought scorn down on her own head. 'Did you ever! Fancy begrudging a little child a bit o' food, the nasty greedy selfish hussy, her!' was the general verdict. But, although they protested so volubly, and bore their own frequent confinements with courage and cheerfulness, they must have sometimes rebelled in secret, for there was great bitterness in the tone in which in another mood they would say: 'The wife ought to have the first child and the husband the second, then there wouldn't ever be any more.'

That showed how the land lay, as Laura's mother said to her in later life. She herself lived to see the decline in the birth-rate, and, when she discussed it with her daughter in the early 1930s, laughed heartily at some of the explanations advanced by the learned, and said: 'If they knew what it meant to carry and bear and bring up a child themselves, they wouldn't expect the women to be in a hurry to have a second or third now they've got a say in the matter. Now, if they made it a bit easier for people, dividing it out a bit, so to speak, by taking over some of the money worry. It's never seemed fair to my mind that the one who's got to go through all a confinement means should have to scrape and pinch beforehand to save a bit as well. Then there's the other child or children. What mother wants to rob those she's already got by bringing in another to share what there's too little of already?'

None of the unmarried hamlet girls had babies in the 'eighties, although there must have been quite a crop of illegitimate births a few years earlier, for when the attendance register was called out at school the eldest children of several families answered to another surname than that borne by their brothers and sisters and by which they themselves were commonly known. These would be the children of couples who had married after the birth of their first child, a common happening at that time and little thought of.

In the 'eighties a young woman of thirty came from Birmingham to have her illegitimate baby at her sister's home in the hamlet, and a widow who had already three legitimate children and afterwards married again managed to produce two children between her two marriages. These births passed without much comment; but when a young girl of sixteen whose home was out in the fields near the hamlet was known to be 'in trouble' public feeling was stirred.

One evening, a few weeks before the birth, Emily passed through the hamlet with her father on their way to interview the young man she had named as responsible for her condition. It

was a sad little sight. Emily, who had so recently been romping
with the other children, going slowly, unwillingly, and red-eyed
from crying, her tell-tale figure enveloped in her mother's plaid
shawl, and her respectable, grey-headed father in his Sunday
suit urging her to 'Come on!' as though longing to be through
with a disagreeable business. Women came to their cottage
gates and children left their play to watch them pass by, for
every one knew or guessed their errand, and much sympathy
was felt towards them on account of Emily's youth and her
parents' respectability.

The interview turned out even more mortifying than the
father could have expected, for Emily had named the young son
of the house where she had been in service, and he not only
repudiated the charge, but was able to prove that he had been
away from home for some time before and after the crucial
date. Yet, in spite of the evidence, the neighbours still believed
Emily's version of the story and treated her as a wronged heroine, to be petted and made much of. Perhaps they made too
much of her, for what should have been an episode turned into
a habit, and, although she never married, Emily had quite a
good-sized family.

The hamlet women's attitude towards the unmarried mother
was contradictory. If one of them brought her baby on a visit to
the hamlet they all went out of their way to pet and fuss over
them. 'The pretty dear!' they would cry. 'How ever can anybody say such a one as him ought not to be born. Ain't he a
beauty! Ain't he a size! They always say, you know, that that
sort of child is the finest. An' don't you go mindin' what folks
says about you, me dear. It's only the good girls, like you, that
has 'em; the others is too artful!'

But they did not want their own daughters to have babies
before they were married. 'I allus tells my gals,' one woman
would say confidentially to another, 'that if they goes getting
theirselves into trouble they'll have to go to th' work'us, for I
won't have 'em at home.' And the other would agree, saying,
'So I tells mine, an' I allus think that's why I've had no trouble
with 'em.'

To those who knew the girls, the pity was that their own

mothers should so misjudge their motives for keeping chaste;
but there was little room for their finer feelings in the hamlet
mother's life. All her strength, invention and understanding
were absorbed in caring for her children's bodies; their mental
and spiritual qualities were outside her range. At the same time,
if one of the girls had got into trouble, as they called it, the
mother would almost certainly have had her home and cared
for her. There was more than one home in the hamlet where the
mother was bringing up a grandchild with her own younger
children, the grandchild calling the grandmother 'Mother'.

If, as sometimes happened, a girl had to be married in haste,
she was thought none the worse of on that account. She had
secured her man. All was well. ' 'Tis but Nature' was the general verdict.

But though they were lenient with such slips, especially when
not in their own families, anything in the way of what they
called 'loose living' was detested by them. Only once in the
history of the hamlet had a case of adultery been known to the
general public, and, although that had occurred ten or twelve
years before, it was still talked of in the 'eighties. The guilty
couple had been treated to 'rough music'. Effigies of the pair
had been made and carried aloft on poles by torchlight to the
house of the woman, to the accompaniment of the banging of
pots, pans, and coal-shovels, the screeching of tin whistles and
mouth-organs, and cat-calls, hoots, and jeers. The man, who
was a lodger at the woman's house, disappeared before daybreak the next morning, and soon afterwards the woman and
her husband followed him.

About the middle of the decade, the memory of that historic
night was revived when an unmarried woman with four illegitimate children moved into a vacant house in the hamlet. Her
coming raised a fury of indignation. Words hitherto only heard
by the children when the Lessons were read in church were
flung about freely: 'harlot' was one of the mildest. The more
ardent moralists were for stoning her or driving her out of the
place with rough music. The more moderate proposed getting
her landlord to turn her out as a bad character. However, upon
closer acquaintance, she turned out to be so clean, quiet, and

well-spoken, that her sins, which she had apparently abandoned, were forgiven her, and one after another of the neighbours began 'passing the time of day' with her when they met. Then, as though willing to do anything in reason to conform to their standard, she got married to a man who had been navvying on a stretch of new railway line and then settled down to farm labour. So there were wedding bells instead of rough music and the family gradually merged into ordinary hamlet life.

It was the hamlet's gain. One of the boys was musical, an aunt had bought him a good melodeon, and, every light evening, he played it for hours on the youths' gathering round in front of the 'Wagon and Horses'.

Before his arrival there had been no musical instrumer of any kind at Lark Rise, and, in those days before gramophones or wireless, any one who liked 'a bit of a tune' had to go to church to hear it, and then it would only be a hymn tune wheezed out by an ancient harmonium. Now they could have all the old favourites – 'Home Sweet Home', 'Annie Laurie', 'Barbara Allen', and 'Silver Threads Among the Gold' – they had only to ask for what they fancied. Alf played well and had a marvellous ear. If the baker or any other caller hummed the tune of a new popular song in his hearing, Alf would be playing it that night on his melodeon.

Women stood at their cottage gates, men leaned out of the inn window, and children left their play and gathered around him to listen. Often he played dance tunes, and the youths would foot it with each other as partners, for there was seldom a grown-up girl at home and the little ones they despised. So the little girls, too, had to dance with each other. One stout old woman, who was said to have been gay in her time, would come out and give them hints, or she would take a turn herself, gliding around alone, her feet hidden by her long skirts, massively graceful.

Sometimes they would sing to the dance music, and the standers-by would join in:

> I have a bonnet, trimmed with blue,
> Why don't you wear it? So I do.
> When do you wear it? When I can,
> When I go out with my young man.

> My young man is gone to sea
> With silver buckles on his knee,
> With his blue coat and yellow hose,
> And that's the way the polka goes.

Or perhaps it would be:

> Step and fetch her, step and fetch her,
>   Step and fetch her, pretty little dear.
> Do not tease her, try and please her,
>   Step and fetch her, pretty little dear.

And so they would dance and sing through the long summer evenings, until dusk fell and the stars came out and they all went laughing and panting home, a community simple enough to be made happy by one little boy with a melodeon.

IX

Country Playtime

'SHALL we dance tonight or shall we have a game?' was a frequent question among the girls after Alf's arrival. Until the novelty of the dancing wore off, the old country games were eclipsed; but their day was not over. Some of the quieter girls always preferred the games, and, later, on those evenings when Alf was away, playing for dancers in other villages, they all went back to the games.

Then, beneath the long summer sunsets, the girls would gather on one of the green open spaces between the houses and bow and curtsey and sweep to and fro in their ankle-length frocks as they went through the game movements and sang the game rhymes as their mothers and grandmothers had done before them.

How long the games had been played and how they originated no one knew, for they had been handed down for a time long before living memory and accepted by each succeeding generation as a natural part of its childhood. No one inquired the meaning of the words of the game rhymes; many of the girls, indeed, barely mastered them, but went through the movements to the accompaniment of an indistinct babbling. But the rhymes had been preserved; breaking down into doggerel in places; but still sufficiently intact to have spoken to the discerning, had any such been present, of an older, sweeter country civilization than had survived, excepting in a few such fragments.

Of all the generations that had played the games, that of the 'eighties was to be the last. Already those children had one foot in the national school and one on the village green. Their children and grandchildren would have left the village green behind them; new and as yet undreamed-of pleasures and excitements would be theirs. In ten years' time the games would be neglected, and in twenty forgotten. But all through the 'eighties the games went on and seemed to the children themselves and to onlookers part of a life that always had been and always would be.

The Lark Rise children had a large repertoire, including the well-known games still met with at children's parties, such as 'Oranges and Lemons', 'London Bridge', and 'Here We Go Round the Mulberry Bush'; but also including others which appear to have been peculiar to that part of the country. Some of these were played by forming a ring, others by taking sides, and all had distinctive rhymes, which were chanted rather than sung.

The boys of the hamlet did not join in them, for the amusement was too formal and restrained for their taste, and even some of the rougher girls when playing would spoil a game, for the movements were stately and all was done by rule. Only at the end of some of the games, where the verse had deteriorated into doggerel, did the play break down into a romp. Most of the girls when playing revealed graces unsuspected in them at other times; their movements became dignified and their voices softer and sweeter than ordinarily, and when hauteur was demanded by the part, they became, as they would have said, 'regular duchesses'. It is probable that carriage and voice inflexion had been handed down with the words.

One old favourite was 'Here Come Three Tinkers'. For this

all but two of the players, a big girl and a little one, joined
hands in a row, and the bigger girl out took up her stand about
a dozen paces in front of the row with the smaller one lying on
the turf behind her feigning sleep. Then three of the line of
players detached themselves and, hand in hand, tripped forward, singing:

> Here come three tinkers, three by three,
> To court your daughter, fair ladye,
> Oh, can we have a lodging here, here, here?
> Oh, can we have a lodging here?

Upon which the fair lady (pronounced 'far-la-dee') admonished
her sleeping daughter:

> Sleep, sleep, my daughter. Do not wake.
> Here come three tinkers you can't take.

Then, severely, to the tinkers:

> You cannot have a lodging here, here, here.
> You cannot have a lodging here.

And the tinkers returned to the line, and three others came
forward, calling themselves tailors, soldiers, sailors, gardeners,
bricklayers, or policemen, according to fancy, the rhymes being
sung for each three, until it was time for the climax, and, putting fresh spirit into their tones, the conquering candidates came
forward, singing:

> Here come three princes, three by three,
> To court your daughter fair ladye,
> Oh, can we have a lodging here, here, here?
> Oh, can we have a lodging here?

At the mere mention of the rank of the princes the scene
changed. The fair lady became all becks and nods and smiles,
and, lifting up her supposedly sleeping daughter, sang:

> Oh, wake, my daughter, wake, wake, wake.
> Here come three princes you can take.

And, turning to the princes:

> Oh, you can have a lodging here, here, here.
> Oh, you can have a lodging here.

Then, finally, leading forward and presenting her daughter, she said:

> Here is my daughter, safe and sound,
> And in her pocket five thousand pound,
> And on her finger a gay gold ring,
> And I'm sure she's fit to walk with a king.

For 'Isabella' a ring was formed with one of the players standing alone in the centre. Then circling slowly, the girls sang:

> Isabella, Isabella, Isabella, farewell.
>> Last night when we parted
>> I left you broken-hearted,
> And on the green gravel there stands a young man.

> Isabella, Isabella, Isabella, farewell.
> Take your choice, love, take your choice, love,
> Take your choice, love. Farewell.

The girl in the middle of the ring then chose another who took up her position inside with her, while the singers continued:

> Put the banns up, put the banns up,
> Put the banns up. Farewell.
> Come to church, love, come to church, love. Farewell.

> Put the ring on, put the ring on,
> Put the ring on, Farewell.

> Come to supper, love, come to supper, love,
> Come to supper, love. Farewell.

> Now to bed, love, now to bed, love,
> Now to bed, love. Farewell.

With other instructions, all of which were carried out in dumb show by the couple in the middle of the ring. Having got the pair wedded and bedded, the spirit of the piece changed. The stately game became a romp. Jumping up and down, still with joined hands, round the two in the middle, the girls shouted:

> Now they're married we wish them joy,
> First a girl and then a boy,
> Sixpence married sevenpence's daughter,
> Kiss the couple over and over.

In that game the Isabella of the sad farewell to whom the sweet plaintive tune of the rhyme originally belonged had somehow got mixed up in a country courtship and wedding.

A pretty, graceful game to watch was 'Thread the Tailor's Needle'. For this two girls joined both hands and elevated them to form an arch or bridge, and the other players, in single file and holding on to each other's skirts, passed under, singing:

> Thread the tailor's needle,
> Thread the tailor's needle.
> The tailor's blind and he can't see,
> So thread the tailor's needle.

As the end of the file passed under the arch the last two girls detached themselves, took up their stand by the original two and joined their hands and elevated them, thus widening the arch, and this was repeated until the arch became a tunnel. As the file passing under grew shorter, the tune was quickened, until, towards the end, the game became a merry whirl.

A grim little game often played by the younger children was called 'Daddy'. For this a ring was formed, one of the players remaining outside it, and the outside player stalked stealthily round the silent and motionless ring and chose another girl by striking her on the shoulder. The chosen one burst from the ring and rushed round it, closely pursued by the first player, the others chanting meanwhile:

> Round a ring to catch a king,
> Round a ring to catch a king,
> Round a ring to catch a king –

and, as the pursuer caught up with the pursued and struck her neck with the edge of her hand:

> Down falls Daddy!

At the stroke on the neck the second player fell flat on the turf, beheaded, and the game continued until all were stretched on the turf.

Round *what* ring, to catch *what* king? And who was Daddy? Was the game founded on some tale dished up for the commonality of the end of one who 'nothing common did or mean'? The players did not know or care, and we can only guess.

'Honeypots' was another small children's game. For this the children squatted down with their hands clasped tightly under their buttocks and two taller girls approached them, singing:

> Honeypots, honeypots, all in a row!
> Who will buy my honeypots, O?

One on each side of a squatting child, they 'tried' it by swinging by the arms, the child's hands still being clasped under its buttocks. If the hands gave way, the honeypot was cast away as broken; if they held, it was adjudged a good pot.

A homely game was 'The Old Woman from Cumberland'. For this a row of girls stood hand in hand with a bigger one in the middle to represent the old woman from Cumberland. Another bigger girl stood alone a few paces in front. She was known as the 'mistress'. Then the row of girls tripped forward, singing:

> Here comes an old woman from Cumberland
> With all her children in her hand.
> And please do you want a servant to-day?

'What can they do?' demanded the mistress as they drew up before her. Then the old woman of Cumberland detached herself and walked down the row, placing a hand on the heads of one after another of her children as she said:

> This can brew, and this can bake,
> This can make a wedding cake,
> This can wear a gay gold ring,
> This can sit in the barn and sing,
> This can go to bed with a king,
> And this one can do everything.

'Oh! I will have that one,' said the mistress, pointing to the one who could do everything, who then went over to her. The pro-

ceedings were repeated until half the girls had gone over, when
the two sides had a tug-of-war.

'The Old Woman from Cumberland' was a brisk, businesslike game; but most of the rhymes of the others were long-
drawn-out and sad, and saddest of all was 'Poor Mary is A-
weeping', which went:

Poor Mary is a-weeping, a-weeping, a-weeping,
Poor Mary is a-weeping on a bright summer's day.

And what's poor Mary a-weeping for, a-weeping for, a-weeping for?
Oh, what's poor Mary a-weeping for on a bright summer's day?

She's weeping for her own true love on a bright summer's own true
    love.
She's weeping for her own true love on a bright summer's day.

Then let her choose another love, another love, another love.
Then let her choose another love on a bright summer's day.

'Waly, Waly, Wallflower' ran 'Poor Mary' close in gentle
melancholy; but the original verse in this seems to have broken
down after the fourth line. The Lark Rise version ran:

>   Waly, waly, wallflower, growing up so high.
>   We're all maidens, we must all die,
>   Excepting So-and-So [*naming one of the players*]
>   And she's the youngest maid.

Then, the tune changing to a livelier air:

>   She can hop and she can skip,
>   She can play the candlestick,
>   Fie! Fie! Fie!
>   Turn your face to the wall again.

All clasping hands and jumping up and down:

All the boys in this town
    Lead a happy life,
Excepting So-and-So [*naming some hamlet boy, not necessarily
    present*]
    And he wants a wife.
A wife he shall have and a-courting he shall go,
Along with So-and-So; because he loves her so.

He kissed her, he cuddled her, he sat her on his knee,
And he said 'My dearest So-and-So, how happy we shall be.'
First he bought the frying-pan and then he bought the cradle
And then he bought the knives and forks and set them on the table.

> So-and-So made a pudding, she made it very sweet,
> She daren't stick the knife in till So-and-So came home at night.
> Taste, So-and-So, taste, and do not be afraid,
> Next Monday morning the wedding day shall be,
> And the cat shall sing and the bells shall ring
> And we'll all clap hands together.

Evidently in the course of the centuries 'Waly, Waly, Wallflower' had become mixed with something else. The youngest maid of the first verse would never have played the candlestick or been courted by such a lover. Her destiny was very different. But what?

'Green Gravel' was another ring game. The words were:

> Green gravel, green gravel, the grass is so green,
> The fairest young damsel that ever was seen,
> Sweet So-and-So, sweet So-and-So, your true love is dead,
> I send you a letter, so turn round your head.

And as each name was mentioned the bearer turned outwards from the middle of the ring and, still holding hands with the others, went on revolving. When all had turned, the girls jigged up and down, shouting:

> Bunch o' rags! Bunch o' rags! Bunch o' rags!

until all fell down.

Then there was 'Sally, Sally Waters', who 'sprinkled in the pan'; and 'Queen Anne, Queen Anne', who 'sat in the sun'. The local version of the first verse of the latter ran:

> Queen Anne, Queen Anne, she sat in the sun,
> She had a pair of ringlets on.
> She shook them off, she shook them on,
> She shook them into Scotland.

Which seems to suggest that the Queen Anne intended was Anne of Denmark, consort of our James the First, and not the last of our Stuart monarchs, as sometimes supposed. When the founders of the new royal house first arrived in England, there would certainly be gossip about them, and Queen Anne would most probably be supposed to favour Scotland, Scots, and things Scottish.

The brisk and rather disagreeable little game known as 'Queen Caroline' must have been of comparatively recent date. For this two lines of girls stood facing each other, while one other one ran the gauntlet. As she dashed between the lines the girls on both sides 'buffeted' her with hands, pinafores and handkerchiefs, singing:

> Queen, Queen Caroline,
> Dipped her head in turpentine.
> Why did she look so fine?
> Because she wore a crinoline.

An echo of the coronation scene of George IV?

Contemporary with that was 'The Sheepfold', which began:

> Who's that going round my sheepfold?
> Oh, it's only your poor neighbour Dick.
> Do not steal my sheep while I am fast asleep.

But that was not a favourite and no one seemed to know the whole of it. Then there were 'How Many Miles to Banbury Town?', 'Blind Man's Buff', and many other games. The children could play for hours without repeating a game.

As well as the country games, a few others, probably as old, but better known, were played by the hamlet children. Marbles, peg-tops, and skipping-ropes appeared in their season, and when there happened to be a ball available a game called 'Tip-it' was played. There was not always a ball to be had; for the smallest rubber one cost a penny, and pennies were scarce. Even marbles, at twenty a penny, were seldom bought, although there were a good many in circulation, for the hamlet boys were champion marble players and thought nothing of walking five or six miles on a Saturday to play with the boys of other villages and replenish their own store with their winnings. Some of them owned as trophies the scarce and valued glass marbles, called 'alleys'. These were of clear glass enclosing bright, wavy, multi-coloured threads, and they looked very handsome among the dingy-coloured clay ones. The girls skipped with any odd length of rope, usually a piece of their mothers' old clothes-lines.

A simple form of hopscotch was played, for which three lines, or steps, enclosed in an oblong were scratched in the dust. The elaborate hopscotch diagrams, resembling an astrological horoscope, still to be seen chalked on the roads in the West Country were unknown there.

'Dibs' was a girls' game, played with five small, smooth pebbles, which had to be kept in the air at the same time and caught on the back of the hand. Laura, who was clumsy with her hands, never mastered this game; nor could she play marbles or spin tops or catch balls, or play hopscotch. She was by common consent 'a duffer'. Skipping and running were her only accomplishments.

Sometimes in the summer the 'pin-a-sight' was all the rage, and no girl would feel herself properly equipped unless she had one secreted about her. To make a 'pin-a-sight' two small sheets of glass, a piece of brown paper, and plenty of flowers were required. Then the petals were stripped from the flowers and arranged on one of the sheets of glass with the other sheet placed over it to form a kind of floral sandwich, and the whole was enveloped in brown paper, in which a little square window was cut, with a flap left hanging to act as a drop-scene. Within the opening then appeared a multi-coloured medley of flower petals, and that was the 'pin-a-sight'. No design was aimed at; the object being to show as many and as brightly coloured petals as possible; but Laura, when alone, loved to arrange her petals as little pictures, building up a geranium or a rose, or even a little house, against a background of green leaves.

Usually the girls only showed their 'pin-a-sights' to each other; but sometimes they would approach one of the women. or knock at a door, singing:

> A pin to see a pin-a-sight,
> All the ladies dressed in white.
> A pin behind and a pin before,
> And a pin to knock at the lady's door.

They would then lift the flap and show the 'pin-a-sight', for which they expected to be rewarded with a pin. When this was forthcoming, it was stuck with any others that might be received on the front of the pinafore. There was always a competition as to who should get the longest row of pins.

After they reached school-going age, the boys no longer played with the girls, but found themselves a separate pitch on which to play marbles or spin tops or kick an old tin about by way of a football. Or they would hunt in couples along the hedgerows, shooting at birds with their catapults, climbing trees, or looking for birds' nests, mushrooms, or chestnuts, according to the season.

The birds'-nesting was a cruel sport, for not only was every egg taken from every nest they found, but the nests themselves were demolished and all the soft moss and lining feathers were left torn and scattered around on the grass and bushes.

'Oh, dear! What must the poor bird have felt when she saw that!' was Laura's cry when she came upon that, to her, saddest of all sad sights, and once she even dared to remonstrate with some boys she had found in the act. They only laughed and pushed her aside. To them, the idea that anything so small as a mother chaffinch could feel was ridiculous. They were thinking of the lovely long string of threaded eggshells, blue and speckled and pearly white, they hoped to collect and hang up at home as an ornament. The tiny whites and yolks which would come from the eggs when blown they would make their mothers whip up and stir into their own cup of tea as a delicacy, and their mothers would be pleased and say what kind, thoughtful boys they had, for they, like the boys, did not consider the birds' point of view.

No one in authority told them that such wholesale robbery of birds' nests was cruel. Even the Rector, when he called at the cottages, would admire the collections and sometimes even condescend to accept a rare specimen. Ordinary country people at that time, though not actively cruel to animals, were indifferent to their sufferings. 'Where there's no sense there's no feeling,' they would say when they had hurt some creature by accident or through carelessness. By sense they meant wits or understanding, and these they imagined purely human attributes.

A few birds were sacred. No boy would rob a robin's or a wren's nest; nor would they have wrecked a swallow's nest if they could have reached one, for they believed that:

> The robin and the wrens
> Be God Almighty's friends.
> And the martin and the swallow
> Be God Almighty's birds to follow.

And those four were safe from molestation. Their cruelty to the other birds and to some other animals was due to an utter lack of imagination, not to bad-heartedness. When, a little later, country boys were taught in school to show mercy to animals and especially to birds, one egg only from a clutch became the general rule. Then came the splendid Boy Scout movement, which has done more than all the Preservation of Wild Birds Acts to prevent the wholesale raiding of nests, by teaching the boys mercy and kindness.

In winter in the 'eighties the youths and big boys of the hamlet would go out on dark nights 'spadgering'. For this a large net upon four poles was carried; two bearers going on one side of a hedge and two on the other. When they came to a spot where a flock of sparrows or other small birds was roosting, the net was dropped over the hedge and drawn tight and the birds enclosed were slaughtered by lantern light. One boy would often bring home as many as twenty sparrows, which his mother would pluck and make into a pudding. A small number of birds, or a single bird, would be toasted in front of the fire. Many of the children and some of the women set traps for birds in their gardens. This was done by strewing crumbs or corn around and beneath a sieve or a shallow box set up endways. To the top of the trap as it stood, one end of a length of fine twine was attached and the other end was held by someone lurking in a barn doorway or behind a hedge or wall. When a bird was in a favourable position, the trap was jerked down upon it. One old woman in particular excelled as a bird-trapper, and, even in snowy weather, she might often have been seen sitting in her barn doorway with the string of a trap in her hand. Had a kindly disposed stranger seen her, his heart would have bled with pity for the poor old soul, so starving that she spent hours in the snow snaring a sparrow for her supper. His pity would have been wasted. She was quite comfortably off according to hamlet standards, and often did not trouble to pluck and cook her bag. She was out for the sport.

In one way and another a bird, or a few birds, were a regular feature of the hamlet menu. But there were birds and birds. 'Do you think you could fancy a bird, me dear?' a man would say to his ailing wife or child, and if they thought they would the bird would appear; but it would not be a sparrow, or even a thrush or a lark. It would be a much bigger bird with a plump breast; but it would never be named and no feathers would be left lying about by which to identify it. The hamlet men were not habitual poachers. They called poaching 'a mug's game' and laughed at those who practised it. 'One month in quod and one out,' as they said. But, when the necessity arose, they knew where the game birds were and how to get them.

Edmund and Laura once witnessed a neat bit of poaching. They had climbed a ladder they had found set against the side of a haystack which had been unthatched, ready for removal, and, after an exciting hour of sticking out their heads and making faces to represent gargoyles on a tower, they were lying, hidden from below, while the men on their way home from work passed along the footpath beneath the rick.

It was near sunset and the low, level light searched the path and the stubble and aftermath on either side of it. The men sauntered along in twos and threes, smoking and talking, then disappeared, group by group, over the stile at the farther side of the field. Just as the last group was nearing the stile and the children were breathing a sigh of relief at not having been seen and scolded, a hare broke from one of the hedges and went bounding and capering across the field in the headlong way hares have. It looked for a moment as if it would land under the feet of the last group of men, who were nearing the stile; but, suddenly, it scented danger and drew up and squatted motionless behind a tuft of green clover a few feet from the pathway. Just then one of the men fell behind to tie his bootlace: the others passed over the stile. The moment they were out of sight, in one movement, the man left behind rose and flung himself sideways over the clover clump where the hare was hiding. There was a short scuffle, a slight raising of dust; then the limp form was pressed into a dinner-basket, and, after a good look round to make sure his action had not been observed, the man followed his workmates.

X

Daughters of the Hamlet

A STRANGER coming to Lark Rise would have looked in vain for the sweet country girl of tradition, with her sunbonnet, hay-rake, and air of rustic coquetry. If he had, by chance, seen a girl well on in her teens, she would be dressed in town clothes, complete with gloves and veil, for she would be home from service for her fortnight's holiday, and her mother would insist upon her wearing her best every time she went out of doors, in order to impress the neighbours.

There was no girl over twelve or thirteen living permanently at home. Some were sent out to their first place at eleven. The way they were pushed out into the world at that tender age might have seemed heartless to a casual observer. As soon as a little girl approached school-leaving age, her mother would say, 'About time you was earnin' your own livin', me gal,' or, to a neighbour, 'I shan't be sorry when our young So-and-So gets her knees under somebody else's table. Five slices for breakfast this mornin', if you please!' From that time onward the child was made to feel herself one too many in the overcrowded home; while her brothers, when they left school and began to bring home a few shillings weekly, were treated with a new consideration and made much of. The parents did not want the boys to leave home. Later on, if they wished to strike out for themselves, they might even meet with opposition, for their money, though barely sufficient to keep them in food, made a little more in the family purse, and every shilling was precious. The girls, while at home, could earn nothing.

Then there was the sleeping problem. None of the cottages had more than two bedrooms, and when children of both sexes were entering their teens it was difficult to arrange matters, and the departure of even one small girl of twelve made a little more room for those remaining.

When the older boys of a family began to grow up, the second bedroom became the boys' room. Boys, big and little were packed into it, and the girls still at home had to sleep in the parents' room. They had their own standard of decency; a screen was placed or a curtain was drawn to form a partition between the parents' and children's beds; but it was, at best, a poor makeshift arrangement, irritating, cramped, and inconvenient. If there happened to be one big boy, with several girls following him in age, he would sleep downstairs on a bed made up every night and the second bedroom would be the girls' room. When the girls came home from service for their summer holiday, it was the custom for the father to sleep downstairs that the girl might share her mother's bed. It is common now to hear people say, when looking at some little old cottage, 'And they brought up ten children there. Where on earth did they sleep?' And the answer is, or should be, that they did not all sleep there at the same time. Obviously they could not. By the time the youngest of such a family was born, the eldest would probably be twenty and have been out in the world for years, as would those who came immediately after in age. The overcrowding was bad enough; but not quite as bad as people imagine.

Then, again, as the children grew up, they required more and more food, and the mother was often at her wits' end to provide it. It was no wonder her thoughts and hopes sprang ahead to the time when one, at least, of her brood would be self-supporting. She should not have spoken her thoughts aloud, for many a poor, sensitive, little girl must have suffered. But the same mother would often at mealtimes slip the morsel of meat from her own to her child's plate, with a 'I don't seem to feel peckish tonight. You have it. You're growing.'

After the girls left school at ten or eleven, they were usually kept at home for a year to help with the younger children, then

places were found for them locally in the households of tradesmen, schoolmasters, stud grooms, or farm bailiffs. Employment
in a public house was looked upon with horror by the hamlet
mothers, and farm-house servants were a class apart. 'Once a
farm-house servant, always a farm-house servant' they used to
say, and they were more ambitious for their daughters.

The first places were called 'petty places' and looked upon as
stepping-stones to better things. It was considered unwise to
allow a girl to remain in her petty place more than a year; but a
year she must stay whether she liked it or not, for that was the
custom. The food in such places was good and abundant, and in
a year a girl of thirteen would grow tall and strong enough for
the desired 'gentlemen's service', her wages would buy her a few
clothes, and she would be learning.

The employers were usually very kind to these small maids.
In some houses they were treated as one of the family; in others
they were put into caps and aprons and ate in the kitchen, often
with one or two of the younger children of the house to keep
them company. The wages were small, often only a shilling a
week; but the remuneration did not end with the money payment. Material, already cut out and placed, was given them to
make their underwear, and the Christmas gift of a best frock or
a winter coat was common. Caps and aprons and morning print
dresses, if worn, were provided by the employer. 'She shan't
want for anything while she is with me' was a promise frequently made by a shopkeeper's wife when engaging a girl, and
many were even better than their word in that respect. They
worked with the girls themselves and trained them; then as they
said, just as they were becoming useful they left to 'better themselves'.

The mothers' attitude towards these mistresses of small
households was peculiar. If one of them had formerly been in
service herself, her situation was avoided, for 'a good servant
makes a bad missis' they said. In any case they considered it a
favour to allow their small untrained daughters to 'oblige' (it
was always spoke of as 'obliging') in a small household. They
were jealous of their children's rights, and ready to rush in and
cause an upset if anything happened of which they did not

approve; and they did not like it if the small maid became fond of her employer or her family, or wished to remain in her petty place after her year was up. One girl who had been sent out at eleven as maid to an elderly couple and had insisted upon remaining there through her teens, was always spoken of by her mother as 'our poor Em'. 'When I sees t'other girls and how they keeps on improvin' an' think of our poor Em wastin' her life in a petty place, I could sit down an' howl like a dog, that I could', she would say, long after Em had been adopted as a daughter by the people to whom she had become attached.

Of course there were queer places and a few definitely bad places; but these were the exception and soon became known and avoided. Laura once accompanied a schoolfellow to interview a mistress who was said to require a maid. At ordinary times a mother took her daughter to such interviews; but Mrs Beamish was near her time, and it was not thought safe for her to venture so far from home. So Martha and Laura set out, accompanied by a younger brother of Martha's, aged about ten. Martha in her mother's best coat with the sleeves turned back to the elbows and with her hair, done up for the first time that morning, plaited into an inverted saucer at the back of her head and bristling with black hairpins. Laura in a chimney-pot hat, a short brown cape, and buttoned boots reaching nearly to her knees. The little brother wore a pale grey astrakan coat, many sizes too small, a huge red knitted scarf, and carried no pocket-handkerchief.

It was a mild, grey November day with wisps of mist floating over the ploughed fields and water drops hanging on every twig and thorn of the hedgerows. The lonely country house they were bound for was said to be four miles from the hamlet; but, long before they reached it, the distance seemed to them more like forty. It was all cross-country going; over field-paths and stiles, through spinneys and past villages. They asked the way of everybody they met or saw working in the fields and were always directed to some short cut or other, which seemed to bring them out at the same place as before. Then there were delays. Martha's newly done-up hair kept tumbling down and Laura had to take out all the hairpins and adjust it. The little brother got stones in his shoes, and all their feet felt tired from the rough travelling and the stiff mud which caked their insteps. The mud was a special source of worry to Laura, because she had put on her best boots without asking permission, and knew she would get into trouble about it when she returned.

Still, such small vexations and hindrances could not quite spoil her pleasure in the veiled grey day and the new fields and woods and villages, of which she did not even know the names.

It was late afternoon when, coming out of a deep, narrow lane with a stream trickling down the middle, they saw before them a grey-stone mansion with twisted chimney-stacks and a sundial standing in long grass before the front door. Martha and Laura were appalled at the size of the house. Gentry must live there. Which door should they go to and what should they say?

In a paved yard a man was brushing down a horse, hissing so loudly as he did so that he did not hear their first timid inquiry. When it was repeated he raised his head and smiled. 'Ho! Ho!' he said. 'Yes, yes, it's Missis at the house there you'll be wanting, I'll warrant.'

'Please does she want a maid?'

'I dare say she do. She generally do. But where's the maid? Goin' to roll yourselves up into one, all three of ye? You go on round by that harness-room and across the lawn by the big pear trees and you'll find the back door. Go on; don't be afraid. She's not agoin' to eat ye.'

In response to their timid knock, the door was opened by a youngish woman. She was like no one Laura had ever seen. Very slight – she would have been called 'scraggy' in the hamlet – with a dead white face, dark, arched brows, and black hair brushed straight back from her forehead, and with all this black and whiteness set off by a little scarlet jacket that, when Laura described it to her mother later, was identified as a garibaldi. She seemed glad to see the children, though she looked doubtful when she heard their errand and saw Martha's size.

'So you want a place?' she asked as she conducted them into a kitchen as large as a church and not unlike one with its stone-paved floor and central pillar. Yes, she wanted a maid, and she thought Martha might do. How old was she? Twelve? And what could she do? Anything she was told? Well, that was right. It was not a hard place, for, although there were sixteen rooms, only three or four of them were in use. Could she get up at six without being called? There would be the kitchen range to light and the flues to be swept once a week, and the dining-room to be swept and dusted and the fire lighted before breakfast. She herself would be down in time to cook breakfast. No cooking was required, beyond preparing vegetables. After breakfast Martha would help her with the beds, turning out the rooms, paring the potatoes and so on; and after dinner there was plenty to do – washing up, cleaning knives and boots and polishing silver. And so she went on, mapping out Martha's day, until at nine o'clock she would be free to go to bed, after placing hot water in her mistress's bedroom.

Laura could see that Martha was bewildered. She stood, twisting her scarf, curtseying, and saying 'Yes, mum' to everything.

'Then, as wages, I can offer you two pounds ten a year. It is not a great wage, but you are very small, and you'll have an easy place and a comfortable home. How do you like your kitchen?'

Martha's gaze wandered round the huge place, and once more she said, 'Yes, mum.'

'You'll find it nice and cosy here, eating your meals by the fire. You won't feel lonely, will you?'

This time Martha said, 'No, mum.'

'Tell your mother I shall expect her to fit you out well. You will want caps and aprons. I like my maids to look neat. And tell her to let you bring plenty of changes, for we only wash once in six weeks. I have a woman in to do it all up,' and although Martha knew her mother had not a penny to spend on her outfit, and that she had been told the last thing before she left home that morning to ask her prospective employer to send her mother her first month's wages in advance to buy necessaries, once again she said, 'Yes, mum.'

'Well, I shall expect you next Monday, then. And, now, are

you hungry?' and for the first time there was feeling in Martha's tone as she answered, 'Yes, mum.'

Soon a huge sirloin of cold beef was placed on the table and liberal helpings were being carved for the three children. It was such a joint of beef as one only sees in old pictures with an abbot carving; immense, and so rich in flavour and so tender that it seemed to melt in the mouth. The three plates were clean in a twinkling.

'Would any of you like another helping?'

Laura, conscious that she was no principal in the affair, and only invited to partake out of courtesy, declined wistfully but firmly; Martha said she would like a little more if 'mum' pleased, and the little brother merely pushed his plate forward. Martha, mindful of her manners, refused a third helping. But the little brother had no such scruples; he was famishing, and accepted a third and a fourth plateful, the mistress of the house standing by with an amused smile on her face. She must have remembered him for the rest of her life as the little boy with the large appetite.

It was dark before they reached home, and Laura got into trouble, not only for spoiling her best boots, but still more for telling a lie, for she had led her mother to believe they were going into the market town shopping. But even when she lay in bed supperless she felt the experience was worth the punishment, for she had been where she had never been before and seen the old house and the lady in the scarlet jacket and tasted the beef and seen Tommy Beamish eat four large helpings.

After all, Martha did not go to live there. Her mother was not satisfied with her account of the place and her father heard the next day that the house was haunted. 'She shan't goo there while we've got a crust for her,' said her Dad. 'Not as I believes in Ghostesses – lot o' rubbish I calls 'em – but the child might think she seed summat and be scared out of her wits an' maybe catch her death o' cold in that girt, draughty, old kitchen.'

So Martha waited until two sisters, milliners in the market town, wanted a maid; and, once there, grew strong and rosy and, according to their report, learned to say a great deal more than 'Yes, mum'; for their only complaint against her was that she was inclined to be saucy and sang so loudly about her work that the customers in the shop could hear her.

When the girls had been in their petty places a year, their mothers began to say it was time they 'bettered themselves' and the clergyman's daughter was consulted. Did she know if a scullery-maid or a tweeny was required at any of the big country houses around? If not, she would wait until she had two or three such candidates for promotion on her list, then advertise in the *Morning Post* or the *Church Times* for situations for them. Other girls secured places through sisters or friends already serving in large establishments.

When the place was found, the girl set out alone on what was usually her first train journey, with her yellow tin trunk tied up with thick cord, her bunch of flowers and brown paper parcel bursting with left-overs.

The tin trunk would be sent on to the railway station by the carrier and the mother would walk the three miles to the station with her daughter. They would leave Lark Rise, perhaps before it was quite light on a winter morning, the girl in her best, would-be fashionable clothes and the mother carrying the baby of the family, rolled in its shawl. Neighbours would come to their garden gates to see them off and call after them 'Pleasant journey! Hope you'll have a good place!' or 'Mind you be a good gal, now, an' does just as you be told!' or, more comfortingly, 'You'll be back for y'r holidays before you knows where you are and then there won't be no holdin' you, you'll have got that London proud!' and the two would go off in good spirits, turning and waving repeatedly.

Laura once saw the departure of such a couple, the mother enveloped in a large plaid shawl, with her baby's face looking out from its folds, and the girl in a bright blue, poplin frock which had been bought at the second-hand clothes shop in the town – a frock made in the extreme fashion of three years before, but by that time ridiculously obsolete. Laura's mother, foreseeing the impression it would make at the journey's end, shook her head and clicked her tongue and said, 'Why ever couldn't they spend the money on a bit of good navy serge!' But they, poor innocents, were delighted with it.

They went off cheerfully, even proudly; but, some hours later, Laura met the mother returning alone. She was limping, for the sole of one of her old boots had parted company with the upper, and the eighteen-months-old child must have hung heavily on her arm. When asked if Aggie had gone off all right, she nodded, but could not answer; her heart was too full. After all, she was just a mother who had sent her young daughter into the unknown and was tormented with doubts and fears for her.

What the girl, bound for a strange and distant part of the country to live a new, strange life among strangers, felt when the train moved off with her can only be imagined. Probably those who saw her round, stolid little face and found her slow in learning her new duties for the next few days would have been surprised and even a little touched if they could have read her thoughts.

The girls who 'went into the kitchen' began as scullerymaids, washing up stacks of dishes, cleaning saucepans and dish covers, preparing vegetables, and doing the kitchen scrubbing and other rough work. After a year or two of this, they became under kitchen-maids and worked up gradually until they were second in command to the cook. When they reached that point, they did much of the actual cooking under supervision; sometimes they did it without any, for there were stories of cooks who never put hand to a dish, but, having taught the kitchenmaid, left all the cooking to her, expecting some spectacular dish for a dinner party. This pleased the ambitious kitchenmaid, for she was gaining experience and would soon be a professional cook herself; then, if she attained the summit of her ambition, cook-housekeeper.

Some girls preferred house to kitchen work, and they would be found a place in some mansion as third or fourth house-maid and work upward. Troops of men and maid-servants were kept in large town and country houses in those days.

The maids on the lower rungs of the ladder seldom saw their employers. If they happened to meet one or other of them about the house, her ladyship would ask kindly how they were getting on and how their parents were; or his lordship would

smile and make some mild joke if he happened to be in a good
humour. The upper servants were their real mistresses, and they
treated beginners as a sergeant treated recruits, drilling them
well in their duties by dint of much scolding; but the girl who
was anxious to learn and did not mind hard work or hard words
and could keep a respectful tongue in her head had nothing to
fear from them.

The food of the maids in those large establishments was
wholesome and abundant, though far from dainty. In some
houses they would be given cold beef or mutton, or even hot
Irish stew for breakfast, and the midday meal was always a
heavy one, with suet pudding following a cut from a hot joint.
Their bedrooms were poor according to modern standards; but,
sleeping in a large attic, shared with two or three others, was not
then looked upon as a hardship, provided they had a bed each
and their own chest of drawers and washstands. The maids had
no bathroom. Often their employers had none either. Some
families had installed one for their own use; others preferred
the individual tub in the bedroom. A hip-bath was part of the
furniture of the maids' room. Like the children of the family,
they had no evenings out, unless they had somewhere definite to
go and obtained special leave. They had to go to church on
Sunday, whether they wanted to or not, and had to leave their
best hats with the red roses and ostrich tips in the boxes under
their beds and 'make frights of themselves' in funny little flat
bonnets. When the Princess of Wales, afterwards Queen Alexandra, set the fashion of wearing the hair in a curled fringe
over the forehead, and the fashion spread until it became uni-
versal, a fringe was forbidden to maids. They must wear their
hair brushed straight back from their brows. A great hardship.

The wages paid would amuse the young housekeepers of
today. At her petty place, a girl was paid from one to two
shillings a week. A grown-up servant in a tradesman's family
received seven pounds a year, and that was about the wage of a
farm-house servant. The Rectory cook had sixteen pounds a
year; the Rectory house-maid twelve; both excellent servants.
The under-servants in big houses began at seven pounds a year,

which was increased at each advancement, until, as head house-maid, they might receive as much as thirty. A good cook could ask fifty, and even obtain another five by threatening to leave. 'Everybody who was anything,' as they used to say, kept a maid in those days – stud grooms' wives, village schoolmasters' wives, and, of course, inn-keepers' and shopkeepers' wives. Even the wives of carpenters and masons paid a girl sixpence to clean the knives and boots and take out the children on Saturday.

As soon as a mother had even one daughter in service, the strain upon herself slackened a little. Not only was there one mouth less to feed, one pair of feet less to be shod, and a tiny space left free in the cramped sleeping quarters; but, every month, when the girl received her wages, a shilling or more would be sent to 'our Mum', and, as the wages increased, the mother's portion grew larger. In addition to presents, some of the older girls undertook to pay their parents' rent; others to give them a ton of coal for the winter; and all sent Christmas and birthday presents and parcels of left-off clothing.

The unselfish generosity of these poor girls was astonishing. It was said in the hamlet that some of them stripped themselves to help those at home. One girl did so literally. She had come for her holidays in her new best frock – a pale grey cashmere with white lace collar and cuffs. It had been much admired and she had obviously enjoyed wearing it during her fortnight at home; but when Laura said, 'I do like your new frock, Clem,' she replied in what was meant for an off-hand tone, 'Oh, that! I'm leaving that for our young Sally. She hasn't got hardly any-thing, and it don't matter what I wear when I'm away. There's nobody I care about to see it,' and Clem went back in her second-best navy serge and Sally wore the pale grey to church the next Sunday.

Many of them must have kept themselves very short of money, for they would send half or even more of their wages home. Laura's mother used to say that she would rather have starved than allow a child of hers to be placed at such a dis-advantage among other girls at their places in service, not to mention the temptations to which they might be exposed through poverty. But the mothers were so poor, so barely able to feed their families and keep out of debt, that it was only human of them to take what their children sent and sometimes even pressed upon them.

Strange to say, although they were grateful to and fond of their daughters, their boys, who were always at home and whose money barely paid for their keep, seemed always to come first with them. If there was any inconvenience, it must not fall on the boys; if there was a limited quantity of anything, the boys must still have their full share; the boys' best clothes must be brushed and put away for them; their shirts must be specially well ironed, and tit-bits must always be saved for their luncheon afield. No wonder the fathers were jealous at times and exclaimed, 'Our Mum, she do make a reg'lar fool o' that boo-oy!'

A few of the girls were engaged to youths at home, and, after several years of courtship, mostly conducted by letter, for they seldom met except during the girl's summer holiday, they would marry and settle in or near the hamlet. Others married and settled away. Butchers and milkmen were favoured as husbands, perhaps because these were frequent callers at the houses where the girls were employed. A hamlet girl would marry a milkman or a butcher's roundsman in London, or some other distant part of the country, and, after a few years, the couple would acquire a business of their own and become quite prosperous. One married a butler and with him set up an apartment house on the East Coast; another married a shopkeeper and, with astonishing want of tact, brought a nursemaid to help look after her children when she visited her parents. The nursemaid was invited into most of the cottages and well pumped for information about the home life; but Susie herself was eyed coldly; she had departed from the normal. The girls who had married away remained faithful to the old custom of spending a summer fortnight with their parents, and the outward and visible signs of their prosperity must have been trying to those who had married farm labourers and returned to the old style of living.

With the girls away, the young men of the hamlet would have had a dull time had there not been other girls from other homes in service within walking distance. On Sunday afternoons, those who were free would be off, dressed in their best, with their boots well polished and a flower stuck in the band of their Sunday hats, to court the dairy-maids at neighbouring farms or the under-servants at the big country houses. Those who were pledged would go upstairs to write their weekly love-letter, and a face might often be seen at an upper window, chewing a pen-holder and gazing sadly out at what must have appeared an empty world.

There were then no dances at village halls and no cinemas or cheap excursions to lead to the picking up of casual acquaint-ances; but, from time to time, one or other of the engaged youths would shock public opinion by walking out with another girl while his sweetheart was away. When taxed with not being 'true to Nell', he would declare it was only friendship or only a bit of fun; but Nell's mother and his mother would think other-wise and upbraid him until the meetings were dropped or grew furtive.

But such sideslips were never mentioned when, at last, Nellie herself came home for her holiday. Then, every evening, neigh-bours peeping from behind window-curtains would see the couple come out of their respective homes and stroll in the same direction, but not together as yet, for that would have been thought too brazen. As soon as they were out of sight of the windows, they would link up, arm in arm, and saunter along field-paths between the ripening corn, or stand at stiles, whis-pering and kissing and making love until the dusk deepened and it was time for the girl to go home, for no respectable girl was supposed to be out after ten. Only fourteen nights of such bliss, and all the other nights of the year blank, and this not for one year, but for six or seven or eight. Poor lovers!

Mistresses used to say – and probably those who are for-tunate enough to keep their maids from year to year still say – that the girls are sullen and absent-minded for the first few days after they return to their duties. No doubt they are, for their thoughts must still be with the dear ones left behind and the coming months must stretch out, an endless seeming blank, before they will see them again. That is the time for a little

extra patience and a little human sympathy to help them to adjust themselves, and if this is forthcoming, as it still is in many
homes, in spite of newspaper correspondence, the young mind
will soon turn from memories of the past to hopes for the future.

The hamlet children saw little of such love-making. Had they
attempted to follow or watch such couples, the young man
would have threatened them with what he would have called 'a
good sock on the ear'ole'; but there was always a country courtship on view if they felt curious to witness it. This was that of
an elderly pair called Chokey and Bess, who had at that time
been walking out together for ten or twelve years and still had
another five or six to go before they were married. Bessie, then
about forty, was supposed not to be strong enough for service
and lived at home, doing the housework for her mother, who
was the last of the lacemakers. Chokey was a farm labourer, a
great lumbering fellow who could lift a sack of wheat with ease,
but was supposed to be 'a bit soft in the upper storey'. He lived
in a neighbouring village and came over every Sunday.

Bessie's mother sat at the window with her lace-pillow all day
long; but her earnings must have been small, for, although her
husband received the same wages as the men who had families
and they had only Bess, they were terribly poor. It was said that
when the two women fried a rasher for their midday meal, the
father being away at work, they took it in turn to have the
rasher, the other one dipping her bread in the fat, day and day
about. When they went out, they wore clothes of a bygone
fashion, shawls and bonnets, instead of coats and hats, and
short skirts and white stockings, when the rest of the hamlet
world wore black stockings and skirts touching the ground. To
see them set off to the market town for their Saturday shopping
always raised a smile among the beholders; the mother carrying
an old green gig umbrella and Bessie a double-lidded marketing
basket over her arm. They were both long-faced and pale, and
the mother lifted her feet high and touched earth with her umbrella at every step, while Bess trailed along a little in the rear
with the point of her shawl dangling below her skirt at the back.
'For all the world like an old white mare an' her foal,' as the
hamlet funny man said.

Every Sunday evening, Chokey and Bess would appear, he in his best pale grey suit and pink tie, with a geranium, rose, or dahlia stuck in his hat. She in her Paisley shawl and little black bonnet with velvet strings tied in a bow under her chin. They were not shy. It was arm in arm with them from the door, and often a pale grey arm round the Paisley shawl before they were out of sight of the windows; although, to be sure, nobody took the trouble to watch, the sight was too familiar.

They always made for the turnpike and strolled a certain distance along it, then turned back and went to Bessie's home. They seldom walked unattended; a little band of hamlet children usually accompanied them, walking about a dozen paces behind, stopping when they stopped and walking on when they walked on. 'Going with Chokey and Bess' was a favourite Sunday evening diversion. As one batch of children grew up, another took its place; though what amusement they found in following them was a mystery, for the lovers would walk a mile without exchanging a remark, and when they did it would only be: 'Seems to me there's rain in the air', or 'My! ain't it hot!' They did not seem to resent being followed. They would sometimes address a friendly remark to one of the children, or Chokey would say as he shut the garden gate on setting out, 'Comin' our way tonight?'

At last came their funny little wedding, with Bess still in the Paisley shawl, and only her father and mother to follow them on foot through the allotments and over the stile to church. After a wedding breakfast of sausages, they went to live in a funny little house with a thatched roof and a magpie in a wicker cage hanging beside the door.

The up-to-date lovers asked more of life than did Chokey and his Bess. More than their own parents had done.

There was a local saying, 'Nobody ever dies at Lark Rise and nobody goes away.' Had this been exact, there would have been no new homes in the hamlet; but, although no building had been done there for many years and there was no migration of families, a few aged people died, and from time to time a cottage was left vacant. It did not stand empty long, for there was always at least one young man waiting to get married and the joyful news of a house to let brought his bride-to-be home from service as soon as the requisite month's notice to her employer had expired.

The homes of these newly married couples illustrated a new phase in the hamlet's history. The furniture to be found in them might lack the solidity and comeliness of that belonging to their grandparents; but it showed a marked improvement on their parents' possessions.

It had become the custom for the bride to buy the bulk of the furniture with her savings in service, while the bridegroom re-decorated the interior of the house, planted the vegetable garden and put a pig, or a couple of pigs, in the sty. When the bride bought the furniture, she would try to obtain things as nearly as possible like those in the houses in which she had been em-ployed. Instead of the hard windsor chairs of her childhood's home, she would have small 'parlour' chairs with round backs and seats covered with horsehair or American cloth. The deal centre table would be covered with a brightly coloured woollen cloth between meals and cookery operations. On the chest of drawers which served as a sideboard, her wedding presents from her employers and fellow servants would be displayed – a best tea-service, a shaded lamp, a case of silver tea-spoons with the lid propped open, or a pair of owl pepper-boxes with green-glass eyes and holes at the top of the head for the pepper to come through. Somewhere in the room would be seen a few books and a vase or two of flowers. The two wicker arm-chairs by the hearth would have cushions and antimacassars of the bride's own working.

Except in a few cases, and those growing fewer, where the first child of a marriage followed immediately on the ceremony, the babies did not pour so quickly into these new homes as into the older ones. Often more than a year would elapse before the first child appeared, to be followed at reasonable intervals by four or five more. Families were beginning to be reckoned in half-dozens rather than dozens.

Those belonging to this new generation of housewives were well-trained in household work. Many of them were highly skilled in one or other of its branches. The young woman laying her own simple dinner table with knives and forks only could have told just how many knives, forks, spoons, and glasses were proper to each place at a dinner party and the order in which they should be placed. Another, blowing on her finger-tips to cool them as she unswathed the inevitable roly-poly, must have thought of the seven-course dinners she had cooked and dished up in other days. But, except for a few small innovations, such as a regular Sunday joint, roasted before the fire if no oven were available, and an Irish stew once in the week, they mostly reverted to the old hamlet dishes and style of cooking them. The square of bacon was cut, the roly-poly made, and the black cooking-pot was slung over the fire at four o'clock; for wages still stood at ten shillings a week and they knew that their mothers' way was the only way to nourish their husbands and children on so small a sum.

In decorating their homes and managing their housework, they were able to let themselves go a little more. There were fancy touches, hitherto unknown in the hamlet. Cosy corners were built of old boxes and covered with cretonne; gridirons were covered with pink wool and tinsel and hung up to serve as letter racks; Japanese fans appeared above picture frames and window curtains were tied back with ribbon bows. Blue or pink ribbon bows figured largely in these new decorative schemes. There were bows on the curtains, on the corners of cushion covers, on the cloth that covered the chest of drawers, and sometimes even on photograph frames. Some of the older men used to say that one bride, an outstanding example of the new refinement, had actually put the blue ribbon bows on the handle of her bedroom utensil. Another joke concerned the vase of flowers the same girl placed on her table at mealtimes. Her father-in-law, it was said, being entertained to tea at the new home, exclaimed, 'Hemmed if I've ever heard of eatin' flowers before!' and the mother-in-law passed the vase to her son, saying, 'Here, Georgie. Have a mouthful of sweet peas.' But the brides only laughed and tossed their heads at such ignorance. The old hamlet ways were all very well, some of them; but they had seen the world and knew how things were done. It was their day now.

Changing ideas in the outer world were also reflected in the relationship between husband and wife. Marriage was becoming more of a partnership. The man of the house was no longer absolved of all further responsibility when he had brought his week's wages home; he was made to feel that he had an interest in the management of the home and the bringing up of the children. A good, steady husband who could be depended upon was encouraged to keep part of his wages, out of which he paid the rent, bought the pig's food, and often the family footwear. He would chop the wood, sweep the path and fetch water from the well.

'So you be takin' a turn at 'ooman's work?' the older men would say teasingly, and the older women had plenty to say about the lazy, good-for-nothing wenches of these days; but the good example was not lost; the better-natured among the older men began to do odd jobs about their homes, and though, at first, their wives would tell them to 'keep out o' th' road', and say that they could do it themselves in half the time, they soon learned to appreciate, then to expect it.

Then the young wives, unused to never having a penny of their own and sorely tried by their straitened housekeeping, began to look round for some way of adding to the family income. One, with the remains of her savings, bought a few fowls and fowl-houses and sold the eggs to the grocer in the market town. Another who was clever with her needle made frocks for the servants at the neighbouring farm-houses; another left her only child with her mother and did the Rectory charring twice a week. The old country tradition of self-help was reviving; but, although there was a little extra money and there were fewer mouths to feed, the income was still woefully inadequate. Whichever way the young housewife turned, she was, as she said, 'up against it'. 'If only we had more money!' was still the cry.

Early in the 'nineties some measure of relief came, for then the weekly wage was raised to fifteen shillings; but rising prices and new requirements soon absorbed this rise and it took a world war to obtain for them anything like a living wage.

XI

School

SCHOOL began at nine o'clock, but the hamlet children set out on their mile-and-a-half walk there as soon as possible after their seven o'clock breakfast, partly because they liked plenty of time to play on the road and partly because their mothers wanted them out of the way before house-cleaning began.

Up the long, straight road they straggled, in twos and threes and in gangs, their flat, rush dinner-baskets over their shoulders and their shabby little coats on their arms against rain. In cold weather some of them carried two hot potatoes which had been in the oven, or in the ashes, all night, to warm their hands on the way and to serve as a light lunch on arrival.

They were strong, lusty children, let loose from control, and there was plenty of shouting, quarrelling, and often fighting among them. In more peaceful moments they would squat in the dust of the road and play marbles, or sit on a stone heap and play dibs with pebbles, or climb into the hedges after birds' nests or blackberries, or to pull long trails of bryony to wreathe round their hats. In winter they would slide on the ice on the puddles, or make snowballs – soft ones for their friends, and hard ones with a stone inside for their enemies.

After the first mile or so the dinner-baskets would be raided; or they would creep through the bars of the padlocked field gates for turnips to pare with the teeth and munch, or for handfuls of green pea shucks, or ears of wheat, to rub out the sweet, milky grain between the hands and devour. In spring they ate the young green from the hawthorn hedges, which they called 'bread and cheese', and sorrel leaves from the wayside, which they called 'sour grass', and in autumn there was an abundance of haws and blackberries and sloes and crab-apples for them to feast upon. There was always something to eat, and they ate, not so much because they were hungry as from habit and relish of the wild food.

At that early hour there was little traffic upon the road. Sometimes, in winter, the children would hear the pounding of galloping hoofs and a string of hunters, blanketed up to the ears and ridden and led by grooms, would loom up out of the mist and thunder past on the grass verges. At other times the steady tramp and jingle of the teams going afield would approach, and, as they passed, fathers would pretend to flick their offspring with whips, saying. 'There! that's for that time you deserved it an' didn't get it'; while elder brothers, themselves at school only a few months before, would look patronizingly down from the horses' backs and call: 'Get out o' th' way, you kids!'

Going home in the afternoon there was more to be seen. A farmer's gig, on the way home from market, would stir up the dust; or the miller's van or the brewer's dray, drawn by four immense, hairy-legged, satin-backed carthorses. More exciting was the rare sight of Squire Harrison's four-in-hand, with ladies in bright, summer dresses, like a garden of flowers, on the top of the coach, and Squire himself, pink-cheeked and white-hatted, handling the four greys. When the four-in-hand passed, the children drew back and saluted, the Squire would gravely touch the brim of his hat with his whip, and the ladies would lean from their high seats to smile on the curtseying children.

A more familiar sight was the lady on a white horse who rode slowly on the same grass verge in the same direction every Monday and Thursday. It was whispered among the children that she was engaged to a farmer living at a distance, and that they met half-way between their two homes. If so, it must have been a long engagement, for she rode past at exactly the same hour twice a week throughout Laura's schooldays, her face getting whiter and her figure getting fuller and her old white horse also putting on weight.

It has been said that every child is born a little savage and has to be civilized. The process of civilization had not gone very far with some of the hamlet children; although one civilization had them in hand at home and another at school, they were able to throw off both on the road between the two places and revert to a state of Nature. A favourite amusement with these was to fall in a body upon some unoffending companion, usually a small girl in a clean frock, and to 'run her', as they called it. This meant chasing her until they caught her, then dragging her down and sitting upon her, tearing her clothes, smudging her face, and tousling her hair in the process. She might scream and cry and say she would 'tell on' them; they took no notice until, tiring of the sport, they would run whooping off, leaving her sobbing and exhausted.

The persecuted one never 'told on' them, even when reproved by the schoolmistress for her dishevelled condition, for she knew that, if she had, there would have been a worse 'running' to endure on the way home, and one that went to the tune of:

> Tell-tale tit!
> Cut her tongue a-slit,
> And every little puppy-dog shall have a little bit!

It was no good telling the mothers either, for it was the rule of the hamlet never to interfere in the children's quarrels. 'Let 'em fight it out among theirselves,' the woman would say; and if a child complained the only response would be: 'You must've been doin' summat to them. If you'd've left them alone, they'd've left you alone; so don't come bringing your tales home to me!' It was harsh schooling; but the majority seemed to thrive upon it, and the few quieter and more sensitive children soon learned either to start early and get to school first, or to linger behind, dipping under bushes and lurking inside field gates until the main body had passed.

When Edmund was about to start school, Laura was afraid for him. He was such a quiet, gentle little boy, inclined to sit gazing into space, thinking his own thoughts and dreaming his own dreams. What would he do among the rough, noisy crowd? In imagination she saw him struggling in the dust with the runners sitting on his small, slender body, while she stood by, powerless to help.

At first she took him to school by a field path, a mile or more round; but bad weather and growing crops soon put an end to that and the day came when they had to take the road with the other children. But, beyond snatching his cap and flinging it into the hedge as they passed, the bigger boys paid no attention to

him, while the younger ones were definitely friendly, especially
when he invited them to have a blow each on the whistle which
hung on a white cord from the, neck of his sailor suit. They
accepted him, in fact, as one of themselves, allowing him to join
in their games and saluting him with a grunted 'Hello, Ted,'
when they passed.

When the clash came at last and a quarrel arose, and Laura,
looking back, saw Edmund in the thick of a struggling group
and heard his voice shouting loudly and rudely, not gentle at all,
'I shan't! I won't! Stop it, I tell you!' and rushed back, if not to
rescue, to be near him, she found Edmund, her gentle little
Edmund, with face as red as a turkey-cock, hitting out with
clenched fists at such a rate that some of the bigger boys, standing near, started applauding.

So Edmund was not a coward, like she was! Edmund could
fight! Though where and how he had learned to do so was a
mystery. Perhaps, being a boy, it came to him naturally. At any
rate, fight he did, so often and so well that soon no one near his
own age risked. offending him. His elders gave him an occasional cuff, just to keep him in his place; but in scuffles with
others they took his part, perhaps because they knew he was
likely to win. So all was well with Edmund. He was accepted
inside the circle, and the only drawback, from Laura's point of
view, was that she was still outside.

Although they started to school so early, the hamlet children
took so much time on the way that the last quarter of a mile was
always a race, and they would rush, panting and dishevelled,
into school just as the bell stopped, and the other children, spick
and span, fresh from their mothers' hands, would eye them
sourly. 'That gipsy lot from Lark Rise!' they would
murmur.

Fordlow National School was a small grey one-storied building, standing at the cross-roads at the entrance to the village.
The one large classroom which served all purposes was well
lighted with several windows, including the large one which
filled the end of the building which faced the road. Beside, and
joined on to the school, was a tiny two-roomed cottage for the
schoolmistress, and beyond that a playground with birch trees

and turf, bald in places, the whole being enclosed within pointed, white-painted palings.

The only other building in sight was a row of model cottages occupied by the shepherd, the blacksmith, and other superior farm-workers. The school had probably been built at the same time as the houses and by the same model landlord; for, though it would seem a hovel compared to a modern council school, it must at that time have been fairly up-to-date. It had a lobby with pegs for clothes, boys' and girls' earth-closets, and a back-yard with fixed wash-basins, although there was no water laid on. The water supply was contained in a small bucket, filled every morning by the old woman who cleaned the schoolroom, and every morning she grumbled because the children had been so extravagant that she had to 'fill 'un again'.

The average attendance was about forty-five. Ten or twelve of the children lived near the school, a few others came from cottages in the fields, and the rest were the Lark Rise children. Even then, to an outsider, it would have appeared a quaint, old-fashioned little gathering; the girls in their ankle-length frocks and long, straight pinafores, with their hair strained back from their brows and secured on their crowns by a ribbon or black tape or a bootlace; the bigger boys in corduroys and hobnailed boots, and the smaller ones in home-made sailor suits or, until they were six or seven, in petticoats.

Baptismal names were such as the children's parents and grandparents had borne. The fashion in Christian names was changing; babies were being christened Mabel and Gladys and Doreen and Percy and Stanley; but the change was too recent to have affected the names of the older children. Mary Ann, Sarah Ann, Eliza, Martha, Annie, Jane, Amy, and Rose were favourite girls' names. There was a Mary Ann in almost every family, and Eliza was nearly as popular. But none of them were called by their proper names. Mary Ann and Sarah Ann were contracted to Mar'ann and Sar'ann. Mary, apart from Ann, had, by stages, descended through Molly and Polly to Poll. Eliza had become Liza, then Tiza, then Tize; Martha was Mat or Pat; Jane was Jin; and every Amy had at least one 'Aim' in life, of which she had constant reminder. The few more uncommon names were also distorted. Two sisters named at the font Beatrice and Agnes, went through life as Beat and Agg, Laura was Lor, or Low, and Edmund was Ned or Ted.

Laura's mother disliked this cheapening of names and named her third child May, thinking it would not lend itself to a diminutive. However, while still in her cradle, the child became Mayie among the neighbours.

There was no Victoria in the school, nor was there a Miss Victoria or a Lady Victoria in any of the farm-houses, rectories, or mansions in the district, nor did Laura ever meet a Victoria in later life. That great name was sacred to the Queen and was not copied by her subjects to the extent imagined by period novelists of today.

The schoolmistress in charge of the Fordlow school at the beginning of the 'eighties had held that position for fifteen years and seemed to her pupils as much a fixture as the school building; but for most of that time she had been engaged to the squire's head gardener and her long reign was drawing to a close.

She was, at that time, about forty, and was a small, neat little body with a pale, slightly pock-marked face, snaky black curls hanging down to her shoulders, and eyebrows arched into a perpetual inquiry. She wore in school stiffly starched, holland aprons with bibs, one embroidered with red one week, and one with blue the next, and was seldom seen without a posy of flowers pinned on her breast and another tucked into her hair.

Every morning, when school had assembled, and Governess, with her starched apron and bobbing curls appeared in the doorway, there was a great rustling and scraping of curtseying and pulling of forelocks. 'Good morning, children,' 'Good morning, ma'am,' were the formal, old-fashioned greetings. Then, under her determined fingers the harmonium wheezed out 'Once in Royal', or 'We are but little children weak', prayers followed, and the day's work began.

Reading, writing, and arithmetic were the principal subjects, with a Scripture lesson every morning, and needlework every afternoon for the girls. There was no assistant mistress; Governess taught all the classes simultaneously, assisted only by two monitors – ex-scholars, aged about twelve, who were paid a shilling a week each for their services.

Every morning at ten o'clock the Rector arrived to take the older children for Scripture. He was a parson of the old school; a commanding figure, tall and stout, with white hair, ruddy cheeks and an aristocratically beaked nose, and he was as far as possible removed by birth, education, and worldly circumstances from the lambs of his flock. He spoke to them from a great height, physical, mental, and spiritual. 'To order myself lowly and reverently before my betters' was the clause he underlined in the Church Catechism, for had he not been divinely appointed pastor and master to those little rustics and was it not one of his chief duties to teach them to realize this? As a man, he was kindly disposed – a giver of blankets and coals at Christmas, and of soup and milk puddings to the sick.

His lesson consisted of Bible reading, turn and turn about round the class, of reciting from memory the names of the kings of Israel and repeating the Church Catechism. After that, he would deliver a little lecture on morals and behaviour. The children must not lie or steal or be discontented or envious. God had placed them just where they were in the social order and given them their own special work to do; to envy others or to try to change their own lot in life was a sin of which he hoped they would never be guilty. From his lips the children heard nothing of that God who is Truth and Beauty and Love; but they learned for him and repeated to him long passages from the Authorized Version, thus laying up treasure for themselves; so the lessons, in spite of much aridity, were valuable.

Scripture over and the Rector bowed and curtsied out of the door, ordinary lessons began. Arithmetic was considered the most important of the subjects taught, and those who were good at figures ranked high in their classes. It was very simple arithmetic, extending only to the first four rules, with the money sums, known as 'bills of parcels', for the most advanced pupils.

The writing lesson consisted of the copying of copperplate maxims: 'A fool and his money are soon parted'; 'Waste not, want not'; 'Count ten before you speak', and so on. Once a week composition would be set, usually in the form of writing a letter describing some recent event. This was regarded chiefly as a spelling test.

History was not taught formally; but history readers were in use containing such picturesque stories as those of King Alfred and the cakes, King Canute commanding the waves, the loss of the White Ship, and Raleigh spreading his cloak for Queen Elizabeth.

There were no geography readers and, excepting what could be gleaned from the descriptions of different parts of the world in the ordinary readers, no geography was taught. But, for some reason or other, on the walls of the schoolroom were hung splendid maps: The World, Europe, North America, South America, England, Ireland, and Scotland. During long waits in class for her turn to read, or to have her copy or sewing examined, Laura would gaze on these maps until the shapes of the countries with their islands and inlets became photographed on her brain. Baffin Bay and the land around the poles were especially fascinating to her.

Once a day, at whatever hour the poor, overworked mistress could find time, a class would be called out to toe the chalked semicircle on the floor for a reading lesson. This lesson, which should have been pleasant, for the reading matter was good, was tedious in the extreme. Many of the children read so slowly and haltingly that Laura, who was impatient by nature, longed to take hold of their words and drag them out of their mouths, and it often seemed to her that her own turn to read would never come. As often as she could do so without being detected, she would turn over and peep between the pages of her own *Royal Reader*, and, studiously holding the book to her nose, pretend to be following the lesson while she was pages ahead.

There was plenty there to enthral any child: 'The Skater Chased by Wolves'; The Siege of Torquilstone', from *Ivanhoe*; Fenimore Cooper's *Prairie on Fire*; and Washington Irving's *Capture of Wild Horses*.

Then there were fascinating descriptions of such far-apart places as Greenland and the Amazon; of the Pacific Ocean with its fairy islands and coral reefs; the snows of Hudson Bay Ter-

ritory and the sterile heights of the Andes. Best of all she loved
the description of the Himalayas, which began: 'Northward of
the great plain of India, and along its whole extent, towers the
sublime mountain region of the Himalayas, ascending gradually until it terminates in a long range of summits wrapped in
perpetual snow.'

Interspersed between the prose readings were poems: 'The
Slave's Dream'; 'Young Lochinvar'; 'The Parting of Douglas
and Marmion'; Tennyson's 'Brook' and 'Ring out, Wild Bells';
Byron's 'Shipwreck'; Hogg's 'Skylark', and many more. 'Lochiel's Warning' was a favourite with Edmund, who often, in bed
at night, might be heard declaiming: 'Lochiel! Lochiel! beware
of the day!' while Laura, at any time, with or without encouragement, was ready to 'look back into other years' with
Henry Glassford Bell, and recite his scenes from the life
of Mary Queen of Scots, reserving her most impressive tone for
the concluding couplet:

> Lapped by a dog. Go think of it in silence and alone,
> Then weigh against a grain of sand the glories of a throne.

But long before their schooldays were over they knew every
piece in the books by heart and it was one of their greatest
pleasures in life to recite them to each other. By that time
Edmund had appropriated Scott and could repeat hundreds of
lines, always showing a preference for scenes of single combat
between warrior chiefs. The selection in the *Royal Readers*,
then, was an education in itself for those who took to it kindly;
but the majority of the children would have none of it; saying
that the prose was 'dry old stuff' and that they hated 'portry'.

Those children who read fluently, and there were several of
them in every class, read in a monotonous sing-song, without
expression, and apparently without interest. Yet there were very
few really stupid children in the school, as is proved by the
success of many of them in after life, and though few were
interested in their lessons, they nearly all showed an intelligent
interest in other things – the boys in field work and crops and
cattle and agricultural machinery; the girls in dress, other
people's love affairs and domestic details.

It is easy to imagine the education authorities of that day, when drawing up the scheme for that simple but sound education, saying, 'Once teach them to read and they will hold the key to all knowledge.' But the scheme did not work out. If the children, by the time they left school, could read well enough to read the newspaper and perhaps an occasional book for amusement, and write well enough to write their own letters, they had no wish to go farther. Their interest was not in books, but in life, and especially the life that lay immediately about them. At school they worked unwillingly, upon compulsion, and the life of the schoolmistress was a hard one.

As Miss Holmes went from class to class, she carried the cane and laid it upon the desk before her; not necessarily for use, but as a reminder, for some of the bigger boys were very unruly. She punished by a smart stroke on each hand. 'Put out your hand,' she would say, and some boys would openly spit on each hand before proffering it. Others murmured and muttered before and after a caning and threatened to 'tell me feyther'; but she remained calm and cool, and after the punishment had been inflicted there was a marked improvement – for a time.

It must be remembered that in those days a boy of eleven was nearing the end of his school life. Soon he would be at work; already he felt himself nearly a man and too old for petticoat government. Moreover, those were country boys, wild and rough, and many of them as tall as she was. Those who had failed to pass Standard IV and so could not leave school until they were eleven, looked upon that last year as a punishment inflicted upon them by the school authorities and behaved accordingly. In this they were encouraged by their parents, for a certain section of these resented their boys being kept at school when they might be earning. 'What do our young Alf want wi' a lot o' book-larnin'?' they would say. 'He can read and write and add up as much money as he's ever likely to get. What more do he want?' Then a neighbour of more advanced views would tell them: 'A good education's everything in these days. You can't get on in the world if you ain't had one,' for they read their newspapers and new ideas were percolating, though slowly. It was only the second generation to be forcibly fed with the fruit of the tree of knowledge: what wonder if it did not always agree with it.

Meanwhile, Miss Holmes carried her cane about with her. A poor method of enforcing discipline, according to modern educational ideas: but it served. It may be that she and her like all over the country at that time were breaking up the ground that other, later comers to the field, with a knowledge of child psychology and with tradition and experiment behind them, might sow the good seed.

She seldom used the cane on the girls and still more seldom on the infants. Standing in a corner with their hands on their heads was their punishment. She gave little treats and encouragements, too, and, although the children called her 'Susie' behind her back, they really liked and respected her. Many times there came a knock at the door and a smartly dressed girl on holidays, or a tall young soldier on leave, in his scarlet tunic and pill-box cap, looked in 'to see Governess'.

That Laura could already read when she went to school was never discovered. 'Do you know your ABC?' the mistress asked her on the first morning. 'Come, let me hear you say it: A – B – C – '

'A – B – C – ' Laura began; but when she got to F she stumbled, for she had never memorized the letters in order. So she was placed in the class known as 'the babies' and joined in chanting the alphabet from A to Z. Alternatively they recited it backward, and Laura soon had that version by heart, for it rhymed:

> Z–Y–X and W–V
> U–T–S and R–Q–P
> O–N–M and L–K–J
> I–H–G and F–E–D
> And C—B—A!

Once started, they were like a watch wound up, and went on alone for hours. The mistress, with all the other classes on her hands, had no time to teach the babies, although she always had a smile for them when she passed and any disturbance or cessation of the chanting would bring her down to them at once.

Even the monitors were usually engaged in giving out dictation to the older children, or in hearing tables or spelling repeated; but, in the afternoon, one of the bigger girls, usually the one who was the poorest needlewoman (it was always Laura in later years) would come down from her own form to point to and name each letter on a wall-sheet, the little ones repeating them after her. Then she would teach them to form pot-hooks and hangers, and, afterwards, letters, on their slates, and this went on for years, as it seemed to Laura, but perhaps it was only one year.

At the end of that time the class was examined and those who knew and could form their letters were moved up into the official 'Infants'. Laura, who by this time was reading *Old St Paul's* at home, simply romped through this Little-Go; but without credit, for it was said she 'gabbled' her letters, and her writing was certainly poor.

It was not until she reached Standard I that her troubles really began. Arithmetic was the subject by which the pupils were placed, and as Laura could not grasp the simplest rule with such small help as the mistress had time to give, she did not even know how to begin working out the sums and was permanently at the bottom of the class. At needlework in the afternoon she was no better. The girls around her in class were making pinafores for themselves, putting in tiny stitches and biting off their cotton like grown women, while she was still struggling with her first hemming strip. And a dingy, crumpled strip it was before she had done with it, punctuated throughout its length with blood spots where she had pricked her fingers.

'Oh, Laura! What a dunce you are!' Miss Holmes used to say every time she examined it, and Laura really was the dunce of the school in those two subjects. However, as time went on, she improved a little, and managed to pass her standard every year with moderate success until she came to Standard V and could go no farther, for that was the highest in the school. By that time the other children she had worked with had left, excepting one girl named Emily Rose, who was an only child and lived in a lonely cottage far out in the fields. For two years Standard V consisted of Laura and Emily Rose. They did few lessons and those few mostly those they could learn from books by themselves, and much of their time was spent in teaching the babies and assisting the schoolmistress generally.

That mistress was not Miss Holmes. She had married her head gardener while Laura was still in the Infants and gone to live in a pretty old cottage which she had renamed 'Malvern Villa'. Immediately after her had come a young teacher, fresh from her training college, with all the latest educational ideas. She was a bright, breezy girl, keen on reform and anxious to be a friend as well as a teacher to her charges.

She came too early. The human material she had to work on was not ready for such methods. On the first morning she began a little speech, meaning to take the children into her confidence:

'Good morning, children. My name is Matilda Annie Higgs, and I want us all to be friends – ' A giggling murmur ran round the school. 'Matilda Annie! Matilda Annie! Did she say Higgs or pigs?' The name made direct appeal to their crude sense of humour, and, as to the offer of friendship, they scented weakness in that, coming from one whose office it was to rule. Thenceforth, Miss Higgs might drive her pigs in the rhyme they shouted in her hearing; but she could neither drive nor lead her pupils. They hid her cane, filled her inkpot with water, put young frogs in her desk, and asked her silly, unnecessary questions about their work. When she answered them, they all coughed in chorus.

The girls were as bad as the boys. Twenty times in one afternoon a hand would shoot upward and it would be: 'Please, miss, can I have this or that from the needlework box?' and poor Miss Higgs, trying to teach a class at the other end of the room, would come and unlock and search the box for something they had already and had hidden.

Several times she appealed to them to show more consideration. Once she burst into tears before the whole school. She told the woman who cleaned that she had never dreamed there were such children anywhere. They were little savages.

One afternoon, when a pitched battle was raging among the big boys in class and the mistress was calling imploringly for order, the Rector appeared in the doorway.

'Silence!' he roared.

The silence was immediate and profound, for they knew he was not one to be trifled with. Like Gulliver among the Lilliputians, he strode into the midst of them, his face flushed with anger, his eyes flashing blue fire. 'Now, what is the meaning of this disgraceful uproar?'

Some of the younger children began to cry; but one look in their direction froze them into silence and they sat, wide-eyed and horrified, while he had the whole class out and caned each boy soundly, including those who had taken no part in the fray. Then, after a heated discourse in which he reminded the children of their lowly position in life and the twin duties of gratitude to and respect towards their superiors, school was dismissed. Trembling hands seized coats and dinner-baskets and frightened little figures made a dash for the gate. But the big boys who had caused the trouble showed a different spirit. 'Who cares for him?' they muttered, 'Who cares? Who cares? He's only an old parson!' Then, when safely out of the playground, one voice shouted:

> Old Charley-wag! Old Charley-wag!
> Ate the pudden and gnawed the bag!

The other children expected the heavens to fall; for Mr Ellison's Christian name was Charles. The shout was meant for him and was one of defiance. He did not recognize it as such. There were several Charleses in the school, and it must have been inconceivable to him that his own Christian name should be intended. Nothing happened, and, after a few moments of tense silence, the rebels trooped off to get their own account of the affair in first at home.

After that, it was not long before the station fly stood at the school gate and Miss Higgs's trunk and bundles and easy-chair were hauled on top. Back came the married Miss Holmes, now Mrs Tenby. Girls curtsied again and boys pulled their forelocks. It was 'Yes, ma'am', and 'No, ma'am', and 'What did you please to say, ma'am?' once more. But either she did not wish to teach again permanently or the education authorities already had a rule against employing married-women teachers, for she only remained a few weeks until a new mistress was engaged.

This turned out to be a sweet, frail-looking, grey-haired, elderly lady named Miss Shepherd, and a gentle shepherd she proved to her flock. Unfortunately, she was but a poor disciplinarian, and the struggle to maintain some degree of order wore her almost to shreds. Again there was always a buzz of whispering in class; stupid and unnecessary questions were asked, and too long intervals elapsed between the word of command and the response. But, unlike Miss Higgs, she did not give up. Perhaps she could not afford to do so at her age and with an invalid sister living with and dependent upon her. She ruled, if she can be said to have ruled at all, by love and patience and ready forgiveness. In time, even the blackest of her sheep realized this and kept within certain limits; just sufficient order was maintained to avoid scandal, and the school settled down under her mild rule for five or six years.

Perhaps these upheavals were a necessary part of the transition which was going on. Under Miss Holmes, the children had been weaned from the old free life; they had become accustomed to regular attendance, to sitting at a desk and concentrating, however imperfectly. Although they had not learned much, they had been learning to learn. But Miss Holmes's ideas belonged to an age that was rapidly passing. She believed in the established order of society, with clear divisions, and had done her best to train the children to accept their lowly lot with gratitude to and humility before their betters. She belonged to the past; the children's lives lay in the future, and they needed a guide with at least some inkling of the changing spirit of the times. The new mistresses, who came from the outside world, brought something of this spirit with them. Even the transient and unappreciated Miss Higgs, having given as a subject for composition one day 'Write a letter to Miss Ellison, telling her what you did at Christmas', when she read over one girl's shoulder the hitherto conventional beginning 'Dear and Honoured Miss', exclaimed 'Oh, no! That's a *very* old-fashioned beginning. Why not say, "Dear Miss Ellison"?' An amendment which was almost revolutionary.

Miss Shepherd went further. She taught the children that it

was not what a man or woman had, but what they were which mattered. That poor people's souls are as valuable and that their hearts may be as good and their minds as capable of cultivation as those of the rich. She even hinted that on the material plane people need not necessarily remain always upon one level. Some boys, born of poor parents, had struck out for themselves and become great men, and everybody had respected them for rising upon their own merits. She would read them the lives of some of these so-called self-made men (there were no women, Laura noticed!) and though their circumstances were too far removed from those of her hearers for them to inspire the ambition she hoped to awaken, they must have done something to widen their outlook on life.

Meanwhile the ordinary lessons went on. Reading, writing, arithmetic, all a little less rather than more well taught and mastered than formerly. In needlework there was a definite falling off. Miss Shepherd was not a great needle-woman herself and was inclined to cut down the sewing time to make way for other work. Infinitesimal stitches no longer provoked delighted exclamations, but more often a 'Child! You will ruin your eyes!' As the bigger girls left who in their time had won county prizes, the standard of the output declined, until, from being known as one of the first needlework schools in the district, Fordlow became one of the last.

XII

Her Majesty's Inspector

HER MAJESTY'S Inspector of Schools came once a year on a date of which previous notice had been given. There was no singing or quarrelling on the way to school that morning. The children, in clean pinafores and well blackened boots, walked deep in thought; or, with open spelling or table books in hand, tried to make up in an hour for all their wasted yesterdays.

Although the date of 'Inspector's' visit had been notified, the time had not. Some years he would come to Fordlow in the morning; other years in the afternoon, having examined another school earlier. So, after prayers, copybooks were given out and the children settled down for a long wait. A few of the more stolid, leaning forward with tongues slightly protruding, would copy laboriously, 'Lightly on the up-strokes, heavy on the down', but most of the children were too apprehensive even to attempt to work and the mistress did not urge them, for she felt even more apprehensive herself and did not want nervously executed copies to witness against her.

Ten – eleven – the hands of the clock dragged on, and forty-odd hearts might almost be heard thumping when at last came the sound of wheels crunching on gravel and two top hats and the top of a whip appeared outside the upper panes of the large end window.

Her Majesty's Inspector was an elderly clergyman, a little man with an immense paunch and tiny grey eyes like gimlets. He had the reputation of being 'strict', but that was a mild way of describing his autocratic demeanour and scathing judgement. His voice was an exasperated roar and his criticism was a blend of outraged learning and sarcasm. Fortunately, nine out of ten of his examinees were proof against the latter. He looked at the rows of children as if he hated them and at the mistress as if he despised her. The Assistant Inspector was also a clergyman, but younger, and, in comparison, almost human. Black eyes and very red lips shone through the bushiness of the whiskers which almost covered his face. The children in the lower classes, which he examined, were considered fortunate.

The mistress did not have to teach a class in front of the great man, as later; her part was to put out the books required and to see that the pupils had the pens and paper they needed. Most of the time she hovered about the Inspector, replying in low tones to his scathing remarks, or, with twitching lips, smiling encouragement at any child who happened to catch her eye.

What kind of a man the Inspector really was it is impossible to say. He may have been a great scholar, a good parish priest, and a good friend and neighbour to people of his own class. One thing, however, is certain, he did not care for or understand children, at least not national school children. In homely language, he was the wrong man for the job. The very sound of his voice scattered the few wits of the less gifted, and even those who could have done better were too terrified in his presence to be able to collect their thoughts or keep their hands from trembling.

But, slowly as the hands of the clock seemed to move, the afternoon wore on. Classes came out and toed the chalk line to read; other classes bent over their sums, or wrote letters to grandmothers describing imaginary summer holidays. Some wrote to the great man's dictation pieces full of hard spelling words. One year he made the confusion of their minds doubly confused by adopting the, to them, new method of giving out the stops by name: 'Water-fowl and other aquatic birds dwell on their banks semicolon while on the surface of the placid water float the wide-spreading leaves of the *Victoria regia* comma and other lilies and water dash plants full stop.'

Of course, they all wrote the names of the stops, which, together with their spelling, would have made their papers rich reading had there been any one there capable of enjoying it.

The composition class made a sad hash of their letters. The children had been told beforehand that they must fill at least one page, so they wrote in a very large hand and spaced their lines well; but what to say was the difficulty! One year the Inspector, observing a small boy sitting bolt upright gazing before him, called savagely: 'Why are you not writing – you at the end of the row? You have your pen and your paper, have you not?'

'Yes, thank you, sir.'

'Then why are you idling?'

'Please, sir, I was only thinking what to say.'

A grunt was the only answer. What other was possible from one who must have known well that pen, ink, and paper were no good without at least a little thinking.

Once he gave out to Laura's class two verses of *The Ancient Mariner*, reading them through first, then dictating them very slowly, with an air of aloof disdain, and yet rolling the lines on his tongue as if he relished them:

'All in a hot and copper sky,' he bawled. Then his voice softened. So perhaps there was another side to his nature.

At last the ordeal was over. No one would know who had passed and who had not for a fortnight; but that did not trouble the children at all. They crept like mice from the presence, and then, what shouting and skipping and tumbling each other in the dust as soon as they were out of sight and hearing!

When the papers arrived and the examination results were read out it was surprising to find what a number had passed. The standard must have been very low, for the children had never been taught some of the work set, and in what they had learned nervous dread had prevented them from reaching their usual poor level.

Another Inspector, also a clergyman, came to examine the school in Scripture. But that was a different matter. On those days the Rector was present, and the mistress, in her best frock, had nothing to do beyond presiding at the harmonium for hymn singing. The examination consisted of Scripture questions, put to a class as a whole and answered by any one who was able to shoot up a hand to show they had the requisite knowledge; or portions of the Church Catechism, repeated from memory in order round the class; and of a written paper on some set Biblical subject. There was little nervous tension on that day, for 'Scripture Inspector' beamed upon and encouraged the children, even to the extent of prompting those who were not word-perfect. While the writing was going on, he and the Rector talked in undertones, laughing aloud at the doings of 'old So-and-So', and, at one point, the mistress slipped away into her cottage and brought them cups of tea on a tray.

The children did reasonably well, for Scripture was the one subject they were thoroughly taught; even the dullest knew most of the Church Catechism by heart. The written paper was the stumbling-block to many; but this was Laura and Edmund's best subject and both succeeded in different years in carrying off the large, calf-bound, gilt-edged 'Book of Common Prayer' which was given as a prize – the only prize given at that school.

Laura won hers by means of a minor miracle. That day, for the first and last time in her life, the gift of words descended upon her. The subject set was 'The Life of Moses', and although up to that moment she had felt no special affection for the great law-giver, a sudden wave of hero-worship surged over her. While her classmates were still wrinkling their brows and biting their pens, she was well away with the baby in the bulrushes scene. Her pen flew over her paper as she filled sheet after sheet, and she had got the Children of Israel through the Red Sea, across the desert, and was well in sight of Pisgah when the little bell on the mistress's table tinkled that time was up.

The Inspector, who had been watching her, was much amused by her verbosity and began reading her paper at once, although, as a rule, he carried the essay away to read. After three or four pages he laughingly declared that he must have more tea as 'that desert' made him feel thirsty.

Such inspiration never visited her again. She returned to her usual pedestrian style of essay writing, in which there were so many alterations and erasures that, although she wrote a fair amount, she got no more marks than those who got stuck at 'My dear Grandmother'.

There was a good deal of jealousy and unkindness among the parents over the passes and still more over the one annual prize for Scripture. Those whose children had not done well in examinations would never believe that the success of others was due to merit. The successful ones were spoken of as 'favourites' and disliked. 'You ain't a-goin' to tell me that that young So-and-So did any better n'r our Jim,' some disappointed mother would say. 'Stands to reason that what he could do our Jimmy could do, *and* better, too. Examinations are all a lot of humbug, if you asks me.' The parents of those who had passed were almost apologetic. ' 'Tis all luck,' they would say. 'Our Tize happened to hit it this time; next year it'll be your Alice's turn.' They showed no pleasure in any small success their own children might have. Indeed, it is doubtful if they felt any, except in the case of a boy who, having passed the fourth standard, could leave school and start work. Their ideal for themselves and their children was to keep to the level of the normal. To them outstanding ability was no better than outstanding stupidity.

Boys who had been morose or rebellious during their later

schooldays were often transformed when they got upon a
horse's back or were promoted to driving a dung-cart afield.
For the first time in their lives, they felt themselves persons of
importance. They bandied lively words with the men and gave
themselves manly airs at home with their younger brothers and
sisters. Sometimes, when two or three boys were working
together, they were too lively, and very little work was done.
'One boy's a boy; two boys be half a boy, and three boys be no
boy at all', ran the old country saying. 'Little gallasses', the men
called them when vexed; and, in more indulgent moods, 'young
dogs'. 'Ain't he a regular young dog?' a fond parent would ask,
when a boy, just starting work, would set his cap at an angle,
cut himself an ash stick, and try to walk like a man.

They were lovable little fellows, in their stiff new corduroys
and hobnailed boots, with their broad, childish faces, powdered
with freckles and ready to break into dimples at a word. For a
few years they were happy enough, for they loved their work
and did not, as yet, feel the pinch of their poverty. The pity of it
was that the calling they were entering should have been so
unappreciated and underpaid. There was nothing the matter
with the work, as work, the men agreed. It was a man's life, and
they laughed scornfully at the occupations of some who looked
down upon them; but the wages were ridiculously low and the
farm labourer was so looked down upon and slighted that the
day was soon to come when a country boy leaving school would
look for any other way of earning a living than on the land.

At that time boys of a roving disposition who wanted to see a
bit of the world before settling down went into the Army.
Nearly every family in the hamlet had its soldier son or uncle or
cousin, and it was a common sight to see a scarlet coat going
round the Rise. After their Army service, most of the hamlet-
bred young men returned and took up the old life on the land;
but a few settled in other parts of the country. One was a policeman in Birmingham, another kept a public house, and a third
was said to be a foreman in a brewery in Staffordshire. A few
other boys left the hamlet to become farm servants in the North
of England. To obtain such situations, they went to Banbury
Fair and stood in the Market to be hired by an agent. They

were engaged for a year and during that time were lodged and
fed with the farmer's family, but received little or no money
until the year was up, when they were paid in a lump sum. They
were usually well treated, especially in the matter of food; but
were glad to return at the end of the year from what was, to
them, a foreign country where, at first, they could barely understand the speech.

At 'the hiring' the different grades of farm workers stood in
groups, according to their occupations – the shepherds with
their crooks, the carters with whips and tufts of horsehair in
their hats, and the maid-servants relying upon their sex to distinguish them. The young boys, not as yet specialists, were
easily picked out by their youth and their innocent, wondering
faces. The maids who secured situations by hiring themselves
out at the Fair were farm-house servants of the rougher kind.
None of the hamlet girls attended the Fair for that purpose.

Squire at the Manor House, known as 'our Squire', not out
of any particular affection or respect, but in contradistinction to
the richer and more important squire in a neighbouring parish,
was at that time unmarried, though verging on middle age, and
his mother still reigned as Lady of the Manor. Two or three
times a year she called at the school to examine the needlework,
a tall, haughty, and still handsome old dame in a long, flowing,
pale-grey silk dustcloak and small, close-fitting, black bonnet,
with two tiny King Charles's spaniels on a leash.

It would be almost impossible for any one born in this century to imagine the pride and importance of such small country
gentlepeople in the 'eighties. As far as was known, the Brace-
wells were connected with no noble family; they had but little
land, kept up but a small establishment, and were said in the
village and hamlet to be 'poor as crows'. Yet, by virtue of
having been born into a particular caste and of living in the 'big
house' of the parish, they expected to reign over their poorer
neighbours and to be treated by them with the deference due to
royalty. Like royalty, too, they could be charming to those who
pleased them. Those who did not had to beware.

A good many of the cottagers still played up to them, the
women curtseying to the ground when their carriage passed and

speaking in awed tones in their presence. Others, conscious of their own independence – for none of the hamlet people worked on their land or occupied their cottages – and having breathed the new free air of democracy, which was then beginning to percolate even into such remote places, were inclined to laugh at their pretensions. 'We don't want nothin' from they,' they would say, 'and us shouldn't get it if us did. Let the old gal stay at home and see that her own tea-caddy's kept locked up, not come nosing round here axin' how many spoonsful we puts in ours.'

Mrs Bracewell knew nothing of such speeches. If she had, she would probably have thought the world – her world – was coming to an end. Which it was. In her girlhood under the Regency, she had been taught her duty towards the cottagers, and that included reproving them for their wasteful habits. It also included certain charities. She was generous out of all proportion to her small means; keeping two aged women pensioners, doling out soup in the winter to those she called 'the deserving poor', and entertaining the school-children to a tea and a magic-lantern entertainment every Christmas.

Meanwhile, as the old servants in and about her house died or were pensioned off, they were not replaced. By the middle of the 'eighties only a cook and a house-parlourmaid sat down to meals in the vast servants' hall where a large staff had formerly feasted. Grass grew between the flagstones in the stable yard where generations of grooms and coachmen had hissed over the grooming of hunters and carriage horses, and the one old mare which drew her wagonette when she paid calls took a turn at drawing the lawn-mower, or even the plough, betweenwhiles.

As she got poorer, she got prouder, more overbearing in manner and more acid in tone, and the girls trembled when she came into school, especially Laura, who knew that her sewing would never pass that eagle eye without stern criticism. She would work slowly along the form, examining each garment, and exclaiming that the sewing was so badly done that she did not know what the world was coming to. Stitches were much too large; the wrong side of the work was not as well finished as the right side; buttonholes were bungled and tapes sewn on

askew; and the feather-stitching looked as though a spider had
crawled over the piece of work. But when she came to examine
the work of one of the prize sewers her face would light up.
'Very neat! Exquisitely sewn!' she would say, and have the
stitching passed round the class as an example.

The schoolmistress attended at her elbow, overawed, like the
children, but trying to appear at her ease. Miss Holmes, in her
day, had called Mrs Bracewell 'ma'am' and sketched a slight
curtsey as she held open the door for her. The later mistresses
called her 'Mrs Bracewell', but not very frequently or with con-
viction.

At that time the position of a village schoolmistress was a
trying one socially. Perhaps it is still trying in some places, for it
is not many years ago that the President of a Women's Institute
wrote: 'We are very democratic here. Our Committee consists
of three ladies, three women, and the village schoolmistress.'
That mistress, though neither lady nor woman, was still placed.
In the 'eighties the schoolmistress was so nearly a new institution that a vicar's wife, in a real dilemma said: 'I should
like to ask Miss So-and-So to tea; but do I ask her to kitchen or
dining-room tea?'

Miss Holmes had settled that question herself when she
became engaged to the squire's gardener. Miss Shepherd was
more ambitious socially. Indeed, democratic as she was in
theory, the dear soul was in practice a little snobbish. She
courted the notice of the betters, though, she was wont to declare, they were only betters when they were better men and
women. An invitation to tea at the Rectory was, to her, something to be fished for before and talked about afterwards, and
when the daughter of a poor, but aristocratic local family set up
as a music teacher, Miss Shepherd at once decided to learn the
violin.

Laura was once the delighted witness of a funny little display
of this weakness. It was the day of the school treat at the Manor
House, and the children had met at the school and were being
marched, two and two, through garden and shrubbery paths to
the back door. Other guests, such as the curate, the doctor's

widow, and the daughters of the rich farmer, who were to have
tea in the drawing-room while the children feasted in the servants' hall, were going to the front door.

Now, Miss Holmes had always marched right in with her
pupils and sipped her own tea and nibbled her cake between
attending to their wants; but Miss Shepherd was more ambitious. When the procession reached a point where the shrubbery path crossed the main drive which led to the front door,
she paused and considered; then said, 'I think I will go to the
front door, dears. I want to see how well you can behave without me,' and off she branched up the drive in her best brown
frock, tight little velvet hip-length jacket, and long fur boa
bound like a snake round her neck, followed by at least one
pair of cynically smiling little eyes.

She had the satisfaction of ringing the front-door bell and
drinking tea in the drawing-room; but it was a short-lived triumph. In a very few minutes she was out in the servants' hall,
passing bread and butter to her charges and whispering to one
of her monitors that 'Dear Mrs Bracewell gave me my tea first,
because, as she said, she knew I was anxious to get back to my
children.'

Squire himself called at the school once a year; but nobody
felt nervous when his red, jovial face appeared in the doorway,
and smiles broke out all around when he told his errand. He was
arranging a concert, to take place in the schoolroom, and would
like some of the children to sing. He took his responsibilities less
seriously than his mother did hers; spending most of his days
roaming the fields and spinneys with a gun under his arm and a
brace of spaniels at his heels, leaving her to manage house and
gardens and what was left of the family estate, as well as to
support the family dignity. His one indoor accomplishment was
playing the banjo and singing Negro songs. He had trained a
few of the village youths to support him in his Negro Minstrel
Troupe, which always formed the backbone of the annual concert programme. A few other items were contributed by his and
his mother's friends and the gaps were filled up by the school-
children.

So, after his visit, the school became animated. What should be sung and who should sing it were the questions of the moment. Finally, it was arranged that everybody should sing something. Even Laura, who had neither voice nor ear for music, was to join in the communal songs.

They sang, very badly, mildly pretty spring and Nature songs from the *School Song Book*, such as they had sung the year before and the year before that, some of them actually the same songs. One year Miss Shepherd thought it 'would be nice' to sing a Primrose League song to 'please Squire'. One verse ran:

> O come, ye Tories, all unite
> To bear the Primrose badge with might,
> And work and hope and strive and fight
> And pray may God defend the right.

When Laura's father heard this, he wrote a stiffly polite little note to the mistress, saying that, as a Liberal of pronounced views, he could not allow a child of his to sing such a song. Laura did not tell him she had already been asked to sing very softly, not to put the other singers out of tune. 'Just move your lips, dear,' the mistress had said. Laura, in fact, was to have gone on to help dress the stage, where all the girls who were taking part in the programme sat in a row throughout the performance, forming a background for the soloists. That year she had the pleasure of sitting among the audience and hearing the criticism, as well as seeing the stage and listening to the programme. A good three-pennyworth ('children, half-price').

When the great night came, the whole population of the neighbourhood assembled, for it was the only public entertainment of the year. Squire and his Negro Minstrel Troupe was the great attraction. They went on, dressed in red and blue, their hands and faces blackened with burnt cork, and rattled their bones and cracked their jokes and sang such songs as:

> A friend of Darwin's came to me,
> A million years ago said he
> You had a tail and no great toe.
> I answered him, 'That may be so,
> But I've one now, I'll let you know—
> G-r-r-r-r out!'

Very few in the audience had heard of Darwin or his theory; but they all knew what 'G-R-R-R-R out!' meant, especially when emphasized by a kick on Tom Binns's backside by Squire's boot. The schoolroom rocked. 'I pretty well busted me sides wi' laughin',' they said afterwards.

After the applause had died down, a little bell would ring and a robust curate from a neighbouring village would announce the next item. Most of these were piano pieces, played singly, or as duets, by young ladies in white evening frocks, cut in a modest V at the neck, and white kid gloves reaching to the elbow. As their contributions to the programme were announced, they would rise from the front seat in the audience; a gentleman – two gentlemen – would spring forward, and between them hand the fair performer up the three shallow steps which led to the platform and hand her over to yet another gentleman, who led her to the piano and held her gloves and fan and turned her music pages.

'Tinkle, tinkle, tinkle' went the piano, and 'Warble, warble, warble' went the voices, as the performers worked their conscientious way through the show piano pieces and popular drawing-room ballads of the moment. Each performer was greeted and dismissed with a round of applause, which served the double purpose of encouraging the singer and relieving the boredom of the audience. Youths and young men in the back seats would sometimes carry this too far, drowning the programme with their stamping and shouting until they had to be reprimanded, when they would subside sulkily, complaining, 'Us've paid our sixpences, ain't we?'

Once, when the athletic curate sang 'You should see Me dance the Polka' he accompanied the song with such violent action that he polked part of the platform down and left the double row of schoolgirls hanging in the air on the backmost planks while he finished his song on the floor:

> You should see me dance the polka,
>   You should see me cover the ground,
> You should see my coat tails flying
>   As I dance my way around.

Edmund and Laura had the words and actions by heart, if not the tune, and polked that night in their mother's bedroom until they woke up the baby and were slapped. A sad ending to an evening of pure bliss.

When the school-children on the platform rose and came forward to sing they, also, were applauded; but their performance and those of the young ladies were but the lettuce in the salad; all the flavour was in the comic items.

Now, Miss Shepherd was a poet, and had several times turned out a neat verse to supplement those of a song she considered too short. One year she took the National Anthem in hand and added a verse. It ran:

> May every village school
> Uphold Victoria's rule,
> To Church and State be true,
> God save the Queen.

Which pleased Squire so much that he talked of sending it to the newspapers.

Going home with lanterns swinging down the long dark road, the groups would discuss the evening's entertainment. Squire's Minstrels and the curate's songs were always unreservedly praised and the young ladies' performances were tolerated, although, often, a man would complain, 'I don't know if I be goin' deaf, or what; but I couldn't hear a dommed word any of 'em said.' As to the school-children's efforts, criticism was applied more to how they looked than to their musical performance. Those who had scuffled or giggled, or even blushed, heard of it from their parents, while such remarks were frequent as: 'Got up to kill, that young Mary Ann Parish was!' or 'I declare I could see the hem o' young Rose Mitchell's breeches showin',' or 'That Em Tuffrey made a poor show. Whatever wer' her mother a thinkin' on?' Taken all in all, they enjoyed the concert almost as much as their grandchildren enjoy the cinema.

XIII

May Day

AFTER the excitement of the concert came the long winter months, when snowstorms left patches on the ploughed fields, like scrapings of sauce on left-over pieces of Christmas pudding, until the rains came and washed them away and the children, carrying old umbrellas to school, had them turned inside out by the wind, and cottage chimneys smoked and washing had to be dried indoors. But at last came spring and spring brought May Day, the greatest day in the year from the children's point of view.

The May garland was all that survived there of the old May Day festivities. The maypole and the May games and May dances in which whole parishes had joined had long been forgotten. Beyond giving flowers for the garland and pointing out how things should be done and telling how they had been done in their own young days, the older people took no part in the revels.

For the children as the day approached all hardships were forgotten and troubles melted away. The only thing that mattered was the weather. 'Will it be fine?' was the constant question, and many an aged eye was turned skyward in response to read the signs of wind and cloud. Fortunately, it was always reasonably fine. Showers there were, of course, at that season, but never a May Day of hopelessly drenching rain, and the May garland was carried in procession every year throughout the eighties.

The garland was made, or 'dressed', in the school-room. Formerly it had been dressed out of doors, or in one of the cottages, or in someone's barn; but dressed it had been and probably in much the same fashion for countless generations.

The foundation of the garland was a light wooden framework of uprights supporting graduated hoops, forming a bell-shaped structure about four feet high. This frame was covered

with flowers, bunched and set closely, after the manner of
wreath-making.

On the last morning of April the children would come to
school with bunches, baskets, arms and pinafores full of flowers
– every blossom they could find in the fields and hedges or beg
from parents and neighbours. On the previous Sunday some of
the bigger boys would have walked six or eight miles to a distant wood where primroses grew. These, with violets from the
hedgerows, cowslips from the meadows, and wallflowers,
oxlips, and sprays of pale red flowering currant from the cottage gardens formed the main supply. A sweetbriar hedge in the
schoolmistress's garden furnished unlimited greenery.

Piled on desks, table, and floor, this supply appeared in-
exhaustible; but the garland was large, and as the work of dressing it proceeded, it soon became plain that the present stock
wouldn't 'hardly go nowheres', as the children said. So foraging
parties were sent out, one to the Rectory, another to Squire's,
and others to outlying farm-houses and cottages. All returned
loaded, for even the most miserly and garden-proud gave liberally to the garland. In time the wooden frame was covered, even
if there had to be solid greenery to fill up at the back, out of
sight. Then the 'Top-knot', consisting of a bunch of crown im-
perial, yellow and brown, was added to crown the whole, and
the fragrant, bowering structure was sprinkled with water and
set aside for the night.

While the garland was being dressed, an older girl, perhaps the May Queen herself, would be busy in a corner making the crown. This always had to be a daisy crown; but,
meadow daisies being considered too common, and also pos-
sessing insufficient staying power, garden daisies, white and
red, were used, with a background of dark, glossy, evergreen
leaves.

The May Queen had been chosen weeks beforehand. She was
supposed to be either the prettiest or the most popular girl in the
parish; but it was more often a case of self-election by the
strongest willed or of taking turns: 'You choose me this year
and I'll choose you next.' However elected, the queens had a
strong resemblance to each other, being stout-limbed, rosy-

cheeked maidens of ten or eleven, with great manes of dark hair frizzed out to support the crown becomingly.

The final touches were given the garland when the children assembled at six o'clock on May Day morning. Then a large china doll in a blue frock was brought forth from the depths of the school needlework chest and arranged in a sitting position on a little ledge in the centre front of the garland. This doll was known as 'the lady', and a doll of some kind was considered essential. Even in those parishes where the garland had degenerated into a shabby nosegay carried aloft at the top of a stick, some dollish image was mixed in with the flowers. The attitude of the children to the lady is interesting. It was understood that the garland was her garland, carried in her honour. The lady must never be roughly handled. If the garland turned turtle, as it was apt to do later in the day, when the road was rough and the bearers were growing weary, the first question was always, 'Is the lady all right?' (Is it possible that the lady was once 'Our Lady', she having in her turn, perhaps, replaced an earlier effigy of some pagan spirit of the newly decked earth?)

The lady comfortably settled in front of the garland, a large white muslin veil or skirt, obviously borrowed from a Victorian dressing-table, was draped over the whole to act as drop-scene and sunshade combined. Then a broomstick was inserted between the hoops for carrying purposes.

All the children in the parish between the ages of seven and eleven were by this time assembled, those girls who possessed them wearing white or light coloured frocks, irrespective of the temperature, and girls and boys alike decked out with bright ribbon knots and bows and sashes, those of the boys worn crosswise over one shoulder. The queen wore her daisy crown with a white veil thrown over it, and the other girls who could procure them also wore white veils. White gloves were traditional, but could seldom be obtained. A pair would sometimes be found for the queen, always many sizes too large; but the empty finger-ends came in handy to suck in a bashful mood when later on, the kissing began.

The procession then formed. It was as follows:

Boy with flag.   Girl with money box.
THE GARLAND with two bearers.
King and queen.
Two maids of honour.
Lord and Lady.
Two maids of honour.
Footman and footman's lady.
Rank and file, walking in twos.
Girl known as 'Mother'.   Boy called 'Ragman'.

The 'Mother' was one of the most dependable of the older girls, who was made responsible for the behaviour of the garlanders. She carried a large, old-fashioned, double-lidded marketing basket over her arm, containing the lunches of the principal actors. The boy called 'Ragman' carried the coats, brought in case of rain, but seldom worn, even during a shower, lest by their poverty and shabbiness they should disgrace the festive attire.

The procession stepped out briskly. Mothers waved and implored their offspring to behave well; some of the little ones left behind lifted up their voices and wept; old people came to cottage gates and said that, though well enough, this year's procession was poor compared to some they had seen. But the garlanders paid no heed; they had their feet on the road at last and vowed they would not turn back now, 'not if it rained cats and dogs'.

The first stop was at the Rectory, where the garland was planted before the front door and the shrill little voices struck up, shyly at first, but gathering confidence as they went on:

> A bunch of may I have brought you
>   And at your door it stands.
> It is but a sprout, but it's well put about
>   By the Lord Almighty's hands.

> God bless the master of this house
>   God bless the mistress too,
> And all the little children
>   That round the table go.

> And now I've sung my short little song
>> I must no longer stay.
> God bless you all, both great and small,
>> And send you a happy May Day.

During the singing of this the Rector's face, wearing its mildest expression, and bedaubed with shaving lather, for it was only as yet seven o'clock, would appear at an upper window and nod approval and admiration of the garland. His daughter would be down and at the door, and for her the veil was lifted and the glory of the garland revealed. She would look, touch and smell, then slip a silver coin into the money-box, and the procession would move on towards Squire's.

There, the lady of the house would bow haughty approval and if there were visiting grandchildren the lady would be detached from the garland and held up to their nursery window to be admired. Then Squire himself would appear in the stable doorway with a brace of sniffing, suspicious spaniels at his heels. 'How many are there of you?' he would call. 'Twenty-seven? Well, here's a five-bob bit for you. Don't quarrel over it. Now let's have a song.'

'Not "A Bunch of May",' the girl called Mother would whisper, impressed by the five-shilling piece; 'not that old-fashioned thing. Something newer,' and something newer, though still not very new, would be selected. Perhaps it would be:

> All hail gentle spring
>> With thy sunshine and showers,
> And welcome the sweet buds
>> That burst in the bowers;
> Again we rejoice as thy light step and free
> Bring leaves to the woodland and flowers to the bee,
> Bounding, bounding, bounding, bounding,
>> Joyful and gay,
> Light and airy, like a fairy
>> Come, come away.

Or it might be:

> Come see our new garland, so green and so gay;
> 'Tis the firstfruits of spring and the glory of May.

Here are cowslips and daisies and hyacinths blue,
Here are buttercups bright and anemones too.

During the singing of the latter song, as each flower was mentioned, a specimen bloom would be pointed to in the garland. It was always a point of honour to have at least one of each named in the several verses; though the hawthorn was always a difficulty, for in the south midlands May's own flower seldom opens before the middle of that month. However, there was always at least one knot of tight green flower buds.

After becoming duty had been paid to the Rectory and Big House, the farm-house and cottages were visited; then the little procession set out along narrow, winding country roads, with tall hedges of blackthorn and bursting leaf-buds on either side, to make its seven-mile circuit. In those days there were no motors to dodge and there was very little other traffic; just a farm cart here and there, or the baker's white-tilted van, or a governess car with nurses and children out for their airing. Sometimes the garlanders would forsake the road for stiles and footpaths across buttercup meadows, or go through parks and gardens to call at some big house or secluded farmstead.

In the ordinary course, country children of that day seldom went beyond their own parish bounds, and this long trek opened up new country to most of them. There was a delightful element of exploration about it. New short cuts would be tried, one year through a wood, another past the fishponds, or across such and such a paddock, where there might, or might not, be a bull. On one pond they passed sailed a solitary swan; on the terrace before one mansion peacocks spread their tails in the sun; the ram which pumped the water to one house mystified them with its subterranean thudding. There were often showers, and to Laura, looking back after fifty years, the whole scene would melt into a blur of wet greenery, with rainbows and cuckoo-calls and, overpowering all other impressions, the wet wallflower and primrose scent of the May garland.

Sometimes on the road a similar procession from another village came into view; but never one with so magnificent a garland. Some of them, indeed, had nothing worth calling a garland at all; only nosegays tied mopwise on sticks. No lord and lady, no king and queen; only a rabble begging with money-boxes. Were the Fordlow and Lark Rise folks sorry for them? No. They stuck out their tongues, and, forgetting their pretty May songs, yelled:

> Old Hardwick skags!
> Come to Fordlow to pick up rags
> To mend their mothers' pudding-bags,
> Yah! Yah!

and the rival troop retaliated in the same strain.

At the front-door calls, the queen and her retinue stood demurely behind the garland and helped with the singing, unless Her Majesty was called forward to have her crown inspected and admired. It was at the back doors of large houses that the fun began. In country houses at that date troops of servants were kept, and the May Day procession would find the courtyard crowded with house-maids and kitchen-maids, dairy-maids and laundry-maids, footmen, grooms, coachmen, and gardeners. The songs were sung, the garland was admired; then, to a chorus of laughter, teasing and urging, one Maid of Honour snatched the cap from the King's head, the other raised the Queen's veil, and a shy, sheepish boy pecked at his companion's rosy cheek, to the huge delight of the beholders.

'Again! Again!' a dozen voices would cry and the kissing was repeated until the royal couple turned sulky and refused to kiss any more, even when offered a penny a kiss. Then the lord saluted his lady and the footman the footman's lady (this couple had probably been introduced in compliment to such patrons), and the money-box was handed round and began to grow heavy with pence.

The menservants, with their respectable side-whiskers, the maids in their little flat caps like crocheted mats on their smoothly parted hair, and their long, billowing lilac or pink print gowns, and the children in their ribbon-decked poverty, alike belong to a bygone order of things. The boys pulled forelocks and the girls dropped curtseys to the upper servants, for they came next in importance to 'the gentry'. Some of them really belonged to a class which would not be found in service today; for at that time there was little hospital nursing, teaching, typing, or shop work to engage the daughters of small farmers, small shopkeepers, innkeepers and farm bailiffs. Most of them had either to go out to service or remain at home.

After the mansion, there were the steward's, the head gardener's and the stud-groom's houses to visit with the garland; then on through gardens and park and woods and fields to the next stopping-place. Things did not always go smoothly. Feet got tired, especially when boots did not fit properly or were worn thin. Squabbles broke out among the boys and sometimes had to be settled by a fight. Often a heavy shower would send the whole party packing under trees for shelter, with the unveiled garland freshening outside in the rain; or some irate gamekeeper would turn the procession back from a short cut, adding miles to the way. But these were slight drawbacks to happiness on a day as near to perfection as anything can be in human life.

There came a point in the circuit when faces were turned towards home, instead of away from it; and at last, at long last, the lights in the Lark Rise windows shone clear through the spring twilight. The great day was over, for ever, as it seemed, for at ten years old a year seems as long as a century. Still, there was the May money to be shared out in school the next morning, and the lady to be stroked before being put back in her box, and the flowers which had survived to be put in water: even tomorrow would not be quite a common day. So the last waking thoughts blended with dreams of swans and peacocks and footmen and sore feet and fat cooks with pink faces wearing daisy crowns which turned into pure gold, then melted away.

XIV

To Church on Sunday

If the Lark Rise people had been asked their religion, the answer of nine out of ten would have been 'Church of England', for practically all of them were christened, married, and buried as such, although, in adult life, few went to church between the baptisms of their offspring. The children were shepherded there after Sunday school and about a dozen of their elders attended regularly; the rest stayed at home, the women cooking and nursing, and the men, after an elaborate Sunday toilet, which included shaving and cutting each other's hair and much puffing and splashing with buckets of water, but stopped short before lacing up boots or putting on a collar and tie, spent the rest of the day eating, sleeping, reading the newspaper, and strolling round to see how their neighbours' pigs and gardens were looking.

There were a few keener spirits. The family at the inn was Catholic and was up and off to early Mass in the next village before others had turned over in bed for an extra Sunday morning snooze. There were also three Methodist families which met in one of their cottages on Sunday evenings for prayer and praise; but most of these attended church as well, thus earning for themselves the name of 'Devil dodgers'.

Every Sunday, morning and afternoon, the two cracked, flat-toned bells at the church in the mother village called the faithful to worship. *Ding-dong, Ding-dong, Ding-dong*, they went, and, when they heard them, the hamlet churchgoers hurried across fields and over stiles, for the Parish Clerk was always threatening to lock the church door when the bells stopped and those outside might stop outside for all he cared.

With the Fordlow cottagers, the Squire's and farmer's families and maids, the Rectory people and the hamlet contingent, the congregation averaged about thirty. Even with this small number, the church was fairly well filled, for it was a tiny place,

about the size of a barn, with nave and chancel only, no side
aisles. The interior was almost as bare as a barn, with its grey,
roughcast walls, plain-glass windows, and flagstone floor. The
cold, damp, earthy odour common to old and unheated
churches pervaded the atmosphere, with occasional whiffs of a
more unpleasant nature said to proceed from the stacks of
mouldering bones in the vault beneath. Who had been buried
there, or when, was unknown, for, excepting one ancient and
mutilated brass in the wall by the font, there were but two
memorial tablets, both of comparatively recent date. The
church, like the village, was old and forgotten, and those buried
in the vault, who must have once been people of importance,
had not left even a name. Only the stained glass window over
the altar, glowing jewel-like amidst the cold greyness, the
broken piscina within the altar rails, and a tall broken shaft of
what had been a cross in the churchyard, remained to witness
mutely to what once had been.

The Squire's and clergyman's families had pews in the chancel, with backs to the wall on either side, and between them
stood two long benches for the schoolchildren, well under the
eyes of authority. Below the steps down into the nave stood the
harmonium, played by the clergyman's daughter, and round it
was ranged the choir of small schoolgirls. Then came the rank
and file of the congregation, nicely graded, with the farmer's
family in the front row, then the Squire's gardener and coachman, the schoolmistress, the maidservants, and the cottagers,
with the Parish Clerk at the back to keep order.

'Clerk Tom', as he was called, was an important man in the
parish. Not only did he dig the graves, record the banns of
marriage, take the chill off the water for winter baptisms, and
stoke the coke stove which stood in the nave at the end of his
seat; but he also took an active and official part in the services.
It was his duty to lead the congregation in the responses and to
intone the 'Amens'. The psalms were not sung or chanted, but
read, verse and verse about, by the Rector and people, and in
these especially Tom's voice so drowned the subdued murmur
of his fellow worshippers that it sounded like a duet between
him and the clergyman – a duet in which Tom won easily, for

his much louder voice would often trip up the Rector before he had quite finished his portion, while he prolonged his own final syllables at will.

The afternoon service, with not a prayer left out or a creed spared, seemed to the children everlasting. The schoolchildren, under the stern eye of the Manor House, dared not so much as wriggle; they sat in their stiff, stuffy, best clothes, their stomachs lined with heavy Sunday dinner, in a kind of waking doze, through which Tom's 'Amens' rang like a bell and the Rector's voice buzzed beelike. Only on the rare occasions when a bat fluttered down from the roof, or a butterfly drifted in at a window, or the Rector's little fox terrier looked in at the door and sidled up the nave, was the tedium lightened.

Edmund and Laura, alone in their grandfather's seat, modestly situated exactly half-way down the nave, were more fortunate, for they sat opposite the church door and, in summer, when it was left open, they could at least watch the birds and the bees and the butterflies crossing the opening and the breezes shaking the boughs of the trees and ruffling the long grass on the graves. It was interesting, too, to observe some woman in the congregation fussing with her back hair, or a man easing his tight collar, or old Dave Pridham, who had a bad bunion, shuffling off a shoe before the sermon began, with one eye all the time upon the clergyman; or to note how closely together some newly married couple were sitting, or to see Clerk Tom's young wife suckling her baby. She wore a fur tippet in winter and her breast hung like a white heather bell between the soft blackness until it was covered up with a white handkerchief, 'for modesty'.

Mr Ellison in the pulpit was the Mr Ellison of the Scripture lessons, plus a white surplice. To him, his congregation were but children of a larger growth, and he preached as he taught. A favourite theme was the duty of regular churchgoing. He would hammer away at that for forty-five minutes, never seeming to realize that he was preaching to the absent, that all those present were regular attendants, and that the stray sheep of his flock were snoring upon their beds a mile and a half away.

Another favourite subject was the supreme rightness of the

social order as it then existed. God, in His infinite wisdom, had appointed a place for every man, woman, and child on this earth and it was their bounden duty to remain contentedly in their niches. A gentleman might seem to some of his listeners to have a pleasant, easy life, compared to theirs at field labour; but he had his duties and responsibilities, which would be far beyond their capabilities. He had to pay taxes, sit on the Bench of Magistrates, oversee his estate, and keep up his position by entertaining. Could they do these things? No. Of course they could not; and he did not suppose that a gentleman could cut as straight a furrow or mow or thatch a rick as expertly as they could. So let them be thankful and rejoice in their physical strength and the bounty of the farmer, who found them work on his land and paid them wages with his money.

Less frequently, he would preach eternal punishment for sin, and touch, more lightly, upon the bliss reserved for those who worked hard, were contented with their lot and showed proper respect to their superiors. The Holy Name was seldom mentioned, nor were human griefs or joys, or the kindly human feelings which bind a man to man. It was not religion he preached, but a narrow code of ethics, imposed from above upon the lower orders, which, even in those days, was out of date.

Once and once only did inspiration move him. It was the Sunday after the polling for the General Election of 1886, and he had begun preaching one of his usual sermons on the duty to social superiors, when, suddenly something, perhaps the memory of the events of the past week, seemed to boil up within him. Flushed with anger – 'righteous anger', he would have called it – and his frosty blue eyes flashing like swords, he cast himself forward across the ledge of his pulpit and roared: 'There are some among you who have lately forgotten that duty, and we know the cause, the *bloody* cause!'

Laura shivered. Bad language in church! and from the Rector! But, later in life, she liked to think that she had lived early enough to have heard a mild and orthodox Liberalism denounced from the pulpit as 'a bloody cause'. It lent her the dignity of an historical survival.

The sermon over, the people sprang to their feet like Jacks-in-a-box. With what gusto they sang the evening hymn, and how their lungs expanded and their tongues wagged as they poured out of the churchyard! Not that they resented anything that was said in the Rector's sermons. They did not listen to them. After the Bloody Cause sermon Laura tried to find out how her elders had reacted to it; but all she could learn was: 'I seems to have lost the thread just then,' or, more frankly, 'I must've been nodding'; the most she could get was one woman's, 'My! didn't th' old parson get worked up today!'

Some of them went to church to show off their best clothes and to see and criticize those of their neighbours; some because they loved to hear their own voices raised in the hymns, or because churchgoing qualified them for the Christmas blankets and coals; and a few to worship. There was at least one saint and mystic in that parish and there were several good Christian men and women, but the majority regarded religion as something proper to extreme old age, for which they themselves had as yet no use.

'About time he wer' thinkin' about his latter end,' they would say of one who showed levity when his head and beard were white, or of anybody who was ill or afflicted. Once a hunchback from another village came to a pig feast and distinguished himself by getting drunk and using bad language; and, because he was a cripple, his conduct was looked upon with horror. Laura's mother was distressed when she heard about it. 'To think of a poor afflicted creature like that cursing and swearing,' she sighed. 'Terrible! Terrible!' and when Edmund, then about ten, looked up from his book and said calmly, 'I should think if anybody's got a right to swear it's a man with a back like that,' she told him he was nearly as bad to say such a thing.

The Catholic minority at the inn was treated with respect, for a landlord could do no wrong, especially the landlord of a free house where such excellent beer was on tap. On Catholicism at large, the Lark Rise people looked with contemptuous intolerance, for they regarded it as a kind of heathenism, and what excuse could there be for that in a Christian country? When, early in life, the end house children asked what Roman Catholics were, they were told they were 'folks as prays to images', and further inquiries elicited the information that they also worshipped the Pope, a bad old man, some said in league with the Devil. Their genuflexions in church and their 'playin' wi' beads' were described as 'monkey tricks'. People who openly said they had no use for religion themselves became quite heated when the Catholics were mentioned. Yet the children's grandfather, when the sound of the Angelus bell was borne on the wind from the chapel in the next village, would take off his hat and, after a moment's silence, murmur, 'In my Father's house are many mansions.' It was all very puzzling.

Later on, when they came to associate more with the other children, on the way to Sunday school they would see horses and traps loaded with families from many miles around on their way to the Catholic church in the next village. 'There go the old Catholics!' the children would cry, and run after the vehicles shouting: 'Old Catholics! Old lick the cats!' until they had to fall behind for want of breath. Sometimes a lady in one of the high dogcarts would smile at them forbearingly, otherwise no notice was taken.

The horses and traps were followed at a distance by the young men and big boys of the families on foot. Always late in starting, yet always in time for the service, how they legged it! The children took good care not to call out after them, for they knew, whatever their haste, the boy Catholics would have time to turn back and cuff them. It had happened before. So they let them get on for quite a distance before they started to mock their gait and recite in a snuffling sing-song:

> 'O dear Father, I've come to confess.'
> 'Well, my child, and what have you done?'
> 'O dear Father, I've killed the cat.'
> 'Well, my child, and what about that?'
> 'O dear Father, what shall I do?'
> 'You kiss me and I'll kiss you.'

a gem which had probably a political origin, for the seeds of their ignorant bigotry must have been sown at some time. Yet, strange to say, some of those very children still said by way of a prayer when they went to bed:

> Matthew, Mark, Luke and John,
> Bless the bed where I lie on.
> Four corners have I to my bed;
> At them four angels nightly spread.
> One to watch and one to pray
> And one to take my soul away.

At that time many words, phrases, and shreds of customs persisted which faded out before the end of the century. When Laura was a child, some of the older mothers and the grandmothers still threatened naughty children with the name of Cromwell. 'If you ain't a good gal, old Oliver Crummell'll have 'ee!' they would say, or 'Here comes old Crummell!' just as the mothers of southern England threatened their children with Napoleon. Napoleon was forgotten there; being far from the sea-coast, such places had never known the fear of invasion. But the armies of the Civil War had fought ten miles to the eastward, and the name still lingered.

The Methodists were a class apart. Provided they did not attempt to convert others, religion in them was tolerated. Every Sunday evening they held a service in one of their cottages, and, whenever she could obtain permission at home, it was Laura's delight to attend. This was not because the service appealed to her; she really preferred the church service; but because Sunday evening at home was a trying time, with the whole family huddled round the fire and Father reading and no one allowed to speak and barely to move.

Permission was hard to get, for her father did not approve of 'the ranters'; nor did he like Laura to be out after dark. But one time out of four or five when she asked, he would grunt and nod, and she would dash off before her mother could raise any objection. Sometimes Edmund would follow her, and they would seat themselves on one of the hard, white-scrubbed benches in the meeting house, prepared to hear all that was to be heard and see all that was to be seen.

The first thing that would have struck any one less accustomed to the place was its marvellous cleanliness. The cottage walls were whitewashed and always fresh and clean. The everyday furniture had been carried out to the barn to make way for the long white wooden benches, and before the window with its drawn white blind stood a table covered with a linen cloth, on which were the lamp, a large Bible, and a glass of water for the visiting preacher, whose seat was behind it. Only the clock and a pair of red china dogs on the mantelpiece remained to show that on other days people lived and cooked and ate in the room. A bright fire always glowed in the grate and there was a smell compounded of lavender, lamp-oil, and packed humanity.

The man of the house stood in the doorway to welcome each arrival with a handshake and a whispered 'God bless you!' His wife, a small woman with a slight spinal curvature which thrust her head forward and gave her a resemblance to an amiable-looking frog, smiled her welcome from her seat near the fireplace. In twos and threes, the brethren filed in and took their accustomed places on the hard, backless benches. With them came a few neighbours, not of their community, but glad to have somewhere to go, especially on wet or cold Sundays.

In the dim lamplight dark Sunday suits and sad-coloured Sunday gowns massed together in a dark huddle against the speckless background, and out of it here and there eyes and cheeks caught the light as the brethren smiled their greetings to each other.

If the visiting preacher happened to be late, which he often was with a long distance to cover on foot, the host would give out a hymn from Sankey and Moody's Hymn-Book, which would be sung without musical accompaniment to one of the droning, long-drawn-out tunes peculiar to the community. At other times one of the brethren would break into extempore prayer, in the course of which he would retail the week's news so far as it affected the gathering, prefacing each statement with 'Thou knowest', or 'As thou knowest, Lord'. It amused Laura and Edmund to hear old Mr Barker telling God that it had not rained for a fortnight and that his carrot bed was getting 'mortal dry'; or that swine fever had broken out at a farm four miles away and that his own pig didn't seem 'no great shakes'; or that somebody had mangled his wrist in a turnip cutter and had come out of hospital, but found it still stiff; for, as they said to each other afterwards, God must know already, as He knew everything. But these one-sided conversations with the Deity were conducted in a spirit of simple faith. 'Cast your care upon Him' was a text they loved and took literally. To them God was a loving Father who loved to listen to His children's confidences. No trouble was too small to bring to 'the Mercy Seat'.

Sometimes a brother or a sister would stand up to 'testify', and then the children opened their eyes and ears, for a misspent youth was the conventional prelude to conversion and who knew what exciting transgressions might not be revealed. Most of them did not amount to much. One would say that before he 'found the Lord' he had been 'a regular beastly drunkard'; but it turned out that he had only taken a pint too much once or twice at a village feast; another claimed to have been a desperate poacher, 'a wild, lawless sort o' chap'; he had snared an occasional rabbit. A sister confessed that in her youth she had not only taken a delight in decking out her vile body, forgetting that it was only the worm that perishes; but, worse still, she had imperilled her immortal soul by dancing on the green at feasts and club outings, keeping it up on one occasion until midnight.

Such mild sins were not in themselves exciting, for plenty of people were still doing such things and they could be observed at first hand; but they were described with such a wealth of detail and with such self-condemnation that the listener was for the moment persuaded that he or she was gazing on the chief of sinners. One man, especially, claimed that pre-eminence. 'I wer' the chief of sinners,' he would cry; 'a real bad lot, a Devil's disciple. Cursing and swearing, drinking and drabbing there were nothing bad as I didn't do. Why, would you believe it, in my sinful pride, I sinned against the Holy Ghost. Aye, that I did,' and the awed silence would be broken by the groans and 'God have mercy's of his hearers while he looked round to observe the effect of his confession before relating how he 'came to the Lord'.

No doubt the second part of his discourse was more edifying

than the first but the children never listened to it; they were too
engrossed in speculations as to the exact nature of his sin
against the Holy Ghost, and wondering if he were really as
thoroughly saved as he thought himself; for, after all, was not
that sin unpardonable? He might yet burn in hell. Terrible yet
fascinating thought!

But the chief interest centred in the travelling preacher, especially if he were a stranger who had not been there before.
Would he preach the Word, or would he be one of those who
rambled on for an hour or more, yet said nothing? Most of
these men, who gave up their Sunday rest and walked miles to
preach at the village meeting houses, were farm labourers or
small shopkeepers. With a very few exceptions they were poor,
uneducated men. 'The blind leading the blind,' Laura's father
said of them. They may have been unenlightened in some respects, but some of them had gifts no education could have
given. There was something fine about their discourses, as they
raised their voices in rustic eloquence and testified to the cleans-
ing power of 'the Blood', forgetting themselves and their own
imperfections of speech in their ardour.

Others were less sincere, and some merely self-seeking
poseurs who took to preaching as the only means of getting a
little limelight shed on their undistinguished lives. One such was
a young shop assistant from the market town, who came,
stylishly dressed, with a bunch of violets in his buttonhole,
smoothing his well-oiled hair with his hand and shaking clouds
of scent from his large white handkerchief. He emphatically did
not preach the Word. His perfume and buttonhole and pseudo-
cultured accent so worked upon the brethren that, after he had
gone, they for once forgot their rule of no criticism and exclaimed: 'Did you ever see such a la-de-da in all your draggings-
up?'

Then there was the elderly man who chose for his text: 'I will
sweep them off the face of the earth with the besom of de-
struction', and proceeded to take each word of his text as a
heading. '*I* will sweep them off the face of the earth. I *will*
sweep them off the face of the earth. I will *sweep* them off the
face of the earth', and so on. By the time he had finished he had

expounded the nature of God and justified His ways to man to his own satisfaction; but he made such a sad mess of it that the children's ears burned with shame for him.

Some managed to be sincere Christians and yet quicker of wit and lighter of hand. The host keeping the door one night was greeted by the arriving minister with 'I would rather be a door-keeper in the house of my God,' and capped it with 'than dwell in the tents of the ungodly.'

Methodism, as known and practised there, was a poor people's religion, simple and crude; but its adherents brought to it more fervour than was shown by the church congregation, and appeared to obtain more comfort and support from it than the church could give. Their lives were exemplary.

Many in the hamlet who attended neither church nor chapel and said they had no use for religion, guided their lives by the light of a few homely precepts, such as 'Pay your way and fear nobody'; 'Right's right and wrong's no man's right'; 'Tell the truth and shame the devil', and 'Honesty is the best policy'.

Strict honesty was the policy of most of them; although there were a few who were said to 'find anything before 'tis lost' and to whom findings were keepings. Children were taught to 'Know it's a sin to steal a pin', and when they brought home some doubtful finding, saying they did not think it belonged to anybody, their mothers would say severely, 'You knowed it didn't belong to you, and what don't belong to you belongs to somebody else. So go and put it back where you found it, before I gets the stick to you.'

Liars were more detested than thieves. 'A liar did ought to have a good memory,' they would say, or, more witheringly, 'You can lock up from a thief, but you can't from a liar.' Any statement which departed in the least degree from plain fact was a lie; any one who ate a plum from an overhanging bough belonging to a neighbour's tree was a thief. It was a stark code in which black was black and white was white; there were no intermediate shades.

For the afflicted or bereaved there was ready sympathy. Had the custom of sending wreaths to funerals been general then, as it is today, they would certainly have subscribed their last halfpenny for the purpose. But, at that time, the coffins of the country poor went flowerless to the grave, and all they could do to mark their respect was to gather outside the house of mourning and watch the clean-scrubbed farm wagon which served as a hearse set out on its slow journey up the long, straight road, with the mourners following on foot behind. At such times the tears of the women spectators flowed freely; little children howled aloud in sympathy, and any man who happened to be near broke into extravagant praise of the departed. 'Never speak ill of the dead' was one of their maxims and they carried it to excess.

In illness or trouble they were ready to help and to give, to the small extent possible. Men who had been working all day would give up their night's rest to sit up with the ill or dying, and women would carry big bundles of bed-linen home to wash with their own.

They carried out St Paul's injunction to weep with those who weep; but when it came to rejoicing with those who rejoiced they were less ready. There was nothing they disliked more than seeing one of their number doing better or having more of anything than themselves. A mother whose child was awarded a prize at school, or whose daughter was doing better than ordinary in service, had to bear many pin-pricks of sarcasm, and if a specially devoted young married couple was mentioned, someone was bound to quote, 'My dear today'll be my devil tomorrow.' They were, in fact, poor fallible human beings.

The Rector visited each cottage in turn, working his way conscientiously round the hamlet from door to door, so that by the end of the year he had called upon everybody. When he tapped with his gold-headed cane at a cottage door there would come a sound of scuffling within, as unseemly objects were hustled out of sight, for the whisper would have gone round that he had been seen getting over the stile and his knock would have been recognized.

The women received him with respectful tolerance. A chair was dusted with an apron and the doing of housework or cooking was suspended while his hostess, seated uncomfortably on the edge of one of her own chairs, waited for him to open the conversation. When the weather had been discussed, the health of the inmates and absent children inquired about, and the progress of the pig and the prospect of the allotment crops, there came an awkward pause, during which both racked their brains to find something to talk about. There was nothing. The Rector never mentioned religion. That was looked upon in the parish as one of his chief virtues, but it limited the possible topics of conversation. Apart from his autocratic ideas, he was a kindly man, and he had come to pay a friendly call, hoping, no doubt, to get to know and to understand his parishioners better. But the gulf between them was too wide; neither he nor his hostess could bridge it. The kindly inquiries made and answered, they had nothing more to say to each other, and, after much 'ah-ing' and 'er-ing', he would rise from his seat, and be shown out with alacrity.

His daughter visited the hamlet more frequently. Any fine afternoon she might have been seen, gathering up her long, full skirts to mount the stile and tripping daintily between the allotment plots. As a widowed clergyman's only daughter, parochial visiting was, to her, a sacred duty; but she did not come in any district-visiting spirit, to criticize household management, or give unasked advice on the bringing up of children; hers, like her father's, were intended to be friendly calls. Considering her many kindnesses to the women, she might have been expected to be more popular than she was. None of them welcomed her visits. Some would lock their doors and pretend to be out; others would rattle their teacups when they saw her coming, hoping she would say, as she sometimes did, 'I hear you are at tea, so I won't come in.'

The only spoken complaint about her was that she talked too much. 'That Miss Ellison; she'd fair talk a donkey's hind leg off,' they would say; but that was a failing they tolerated in others, and one to which they were not averse in her, once she was installed in their best chair and some item of local gossip was being discussed.

Perhaps at the root of their unease in her presence was the subconscious feeling of contrast between her lot and theirs. Her neat little figure, well corseted in; her clear, high-pitched voice, good clothes, and faint scent of lily-of-the-valley perfume put them, in their workaday garb and all blowsed from their cooking or water-fetching, at a disadvantage.

She never suspected she was unwanted. On the contrary, she was most careful to visit each cottage in rotation, lest jealousy should arise. She would inquire about every member of the family in turn, listen to extracts from letters of daughters in service, sympathize with those who had tales of woe to tell, discuss everything that had happened since her last visit, and insist upon nursing the baby the while, and only smile good-naturedly when it wetted the front of her frock.

Her last visit of the day was always to the end house, where, over a cup of tea, she would become quite confidential. She and Laura's mother were 'Miss Margaret' and 'Emma' to each other, for they had known each other from birth, including the time when Emma was nurse to Miss Margaret's young friends at the neighbouring rectory.

Laura, supposed to be deep in her book, but really all ears, learnt that, surprisingly, Miss Ellison, the great Miss Ellison, had her troubles. She had a brother, reputed 'wild', in the parish, whom her father had forbidden the house, and much of their talk was about 'my brother Robert', or 'Master Bobbie', and the length of time since his last letter, and whether he had gone to Brazil, as he had said he should, or whether he was still in London. 'What I feel, Emma, is that he is such a boy, and you know what the world is – what perils – ' Then Emma's cheerful rejoinder: 'Don't you worry yourself, Miss Margaret. He can look after himself all right, Master Bob can.'

Sometimes Emma would venture to admire something Miss Margaret was wearing. 'Excuse me, Miss Margaret, but that mauve muslin really does become you'; and Miss Ellison would look pleased. She had probably few compliments, for one of her type was not likely to be admired in those days of pink and white dollishness, although her clear, healthy pallor, with only the faintest flush of pink, her broad white brow, grey eyes, and dark hair waving back to the knot at her nape were at least distinguished looking. And she could not at that time have been more than thirty, although to Laura she seemed quite old, and the hamlet women called her an old maid.

Such a life as hers must have been is almost unimaginable now. Between playing the harmonium in church, teaching in Sunday school, ordering her father's meals and overseeing the maids, she must have spent hours doing needlework. Coarse, unattractive needlework, too, cross-over shawls and flannel petticoats for the old women, flannel shirts and long, thick knitted stockings for the old men, these, as well as the babies' print frocks, were all made by her own hands. Excepting a fortnight's visit a year to relatives, the only outing she was known to have was a weekly drive to the market town, shopping, in her father's high, yellow-wheeled dogcart, with the fat fox-terrier, Beppo, panting behind.

Half-way through the decade, the Rector began to feel the weight of his seventy odd years, and a succession of curates came to share his work and to provide new subjects of conversation for his parishioners. Several appeared and vanished without leaving any definite impression, beyond those of a new voice in church and an extraordinary bashfulness before the hamlet housewives; but two or three stayed longer and became, for a time, part of the life of the parish. There was Mr Dallas, who was said to be 'in a decline'. A pale, thin wraith of a man, who, in foggy weather wore a respirator, which looked like a heavy black moustache. Laura remembered him chiefly because when she was awarded the prize for Scripture he congratulated her – the first time she was ever congratulated upon anything in her life. On his next visit to her home he asked to see the prize prayer-book, and when she brought it, said: 'The binding is calf – my favourite binding – but it is very susceptible to damp. You must keep it in a room with a fire.' He was talking a language foreign to the children, who knew nothing of bindings or editions, a book to them being simply a book; but his expression and the gentle caressing way in which he turned the pages, told Laura that he, too, was a book-lover.

After he had left came Mr Alport; a big, fat-faced young man, who had been a medical student. He kept a small dispensary at his lodgings and it was his delight to doctor anyone who was ailing, both advice and medicine being gratis. As usual, supply created demand. Before he came, illness had been rare in the hamlet; now, suddenly, nearly everyone had something the matter with them. 'My pink pills', 'my little tablets', 'my mixture', and 'my lotion' became as common in conversation as potatoes or pig's food. People asked each other how their So-and-So was when they met, and, barely waiting for an answer, plunged into a description of their own symptoms.

Mr Alport complained to the children's father that the hamlet people were ignorant, and some of them certainly were, on the subjects in which he was enlightened. One woman particularly. On a visit to her house he noticed that one of her children, a tall, thin girl of eleven or twelve was looking rather pale. 'She is growing too fast, I expect,' he remarked. 'I must give her a tonic'; which he did. But she was not allowed to take it. 'No, she ain't a goin' to take that stuff,' her mother told the neighbours. 'He said she was growin' too tall, an' it's summat to stunt her. I shan't let a child o' mine be stunted. Oh, no!'

When he left the place and the supply of physic failed, all the invalids forgot their ailments. But he left one lasting memorial. Before his coming, the road round the Rise in winter had been a quagmire. 'Mud up to the hocks, and splashes up to the neck,' as they said. Mr Alport, after a few weeks' experience of mud-caked boots and mud-stained trouser-ends, decided to do something. So, perhaps in imitation of Ruskin's road-making at Oxford, he begged cartloads of stones from the farmer and, assisted by the hamlet youths and boys, began, on light evenings, to work with his own hands building a raised foot-path. Laura always remembered him best breaking stones and shovelling mud in his beautifully white shirt-sleeves and red braces, his clerical coat and collar hung on a bush, his big, smooth face damp with perspiration and his spectacles gleaming, as he urged on his fellow workers.

Neither of the curates mentioned ever spoke of religion out of church. Mr Dallas was far too shy, and Mr Alport was too busy ministering to peoples' bodies to have time to spare for their souls. Mr Marley, who came next, considered their souls his special care.

He was surely as strange a curate as ever came to a remote agricultural parish. An old man with a long, grey beard which he buttoned inside his long, close-fitting, black overcoat. Fervour and many fast days had worn away his flesh, and he had hollow cheeks and deep-set, dark eyes which glowed with the flame of fanaticism. He was a fanatic where his Church and his creed were concerned; otherwise he was the kindest and most gentle of men. Too good for this world, some of the women said when they came to know him.

He was what is now known as an Anglo-Catholic. Sunday after Sunday he preached 'One Catholic Apostolic Church' and 'our Holy Religion' to his congregation of rustics. But he did not stop at that: he dealt often with the underlying truths of religion, preaching the gospel of love and forgiveness of sins and the brotherhood of man. He was a wonderful preacher. No listener nodded or 'lost the thread' when he was in the pulpit, and though most of his congregation might not be able to grasp or agree with his doctrine, all responded to the love, sympathy, and sincerity of the preacher and every eye was upon him from his first word to his last. How such a preacher came to be in old age but a curate in a remote country parish is a mystery. His eloquence and fervour would have filled a city church.

The Rector by that time was bedridden, and a scholarly, easy-going, middle-aged son was deputizing for him; otherwise Mr Marley would have had less freedom in the church and parish. When officiating, he openly genuflected to the altar, made the sign of the cross before and after his own silent devotions, made known his willingness to hear confessions, and instituted daily services and weekly instead of monthly Communion.

This in many parishes would have caused scandal; but the Fordlow people rather enjoyed the change, excepting the Methodists, who, quite rightly according to their tenets, left off going to church, and a few other extremists who said he was 'a Pope's man'. He even made a few converts. Miss Ellison was one, and two others, oddly enough, were a navvy and his wife who had recently settled near the hamlet. The latter had formerly been a rowdy couple and it was strange to see them, all cleaned up and dressed in their best on a week-day evening, quietly crossing the allotments on their way to confession.

Of course, Laura's father said they were 'after what they could get out of the poor old fool'. That couple almost certainly were not; but others may have been, for he was a most generous man, who gave with both hands, '*and* running over', as the hamlet people said. Not only to the sick and needy, although those were his first care, but to anybody he thought wanted or wished for a thing or who would be pleased with it. He gave the schoolboys two handsome footballs and the girls a skipping-rope each – fine affairs with painted handles and little bells, such as they had never seen in their lives before. When winter came he bought three of the poorest girls warm, grey ulsters, such as were then fashionable, to go to church in. When he found Edmund loved Scott's poems, but only knew extracts from them, he bought him the *Complete Poetical Works*, and, that Laura might not feel neglected, presented her at the same time with *The Imitation of Christ,* daintily bound in blue and silver. These were only a few of his known kindnesses; there were signs and rumours of dozens of others, and no doubt many more were quite unknown except to himself and the recipient.

He once gave the very shoes off his feet to a woman who had pleaded that she could not go to church for want of a pair, and had added, meaningly, that she took a large size and that a man's pair of light shoes would do very well. He gave her the better of the two pairs he possessed, which he happened to be wearing, stipulating that he should be allowed to walk home in them. The wearing of them home was a concession to convention, for he would have enjoyed walking barefoot over the flints as a follower of his beloved St Francis of Assisi, towards whom he had a special devotion twenty years before the cult of the Little Poor Man became popular. He gave away so much that he could only have kept just enough to keep himself in bare necessaries. His black overcoat, which he wore in all weathers, was threadbare, and the old cassock he wore indoors was green and falling to pieces.

Laura's mother, whose religion was as plain and wholesome as the food she cooked, had little sympathy with his 'bowings and crossings'; but she was genuinely fond of the old man and persuaded him to look in for a cup of tea whenever he visited the hamlet. Over this simple meal he would tell the children about his own childhood. He had been the bad boy of the nursery, he said, selfish and self-willed and given to fits of passionate anger. Once he had hurled a plate at his sister (here the children's mother frowned and shook her head at him and that story trailed off lamely); but on another day he told them of his famous ride, which ever after ranked with them beside Dick Turpin's.

The children of his family had a pony which they were supposed to ride in turn; but, in time, he so monopolized it that it was known as his Moppet, and once, when his elders had insisted that another brother should ride that day, he had waited until the party had gone, then taken his mother's riding horse out of the stable, mounted it with the help of a stable boy who had believed him when he said he had permission to do so, and gone careering across country, giving the horse its head, for he had no control over it. They went like the wind, over rough grass and under trees, where any low-hanging bough might have killed him, and, at that point in the story, the teller leaned forward with such a flush on his cheek and such a light in his eye that, for one moment, Laura could almost see in the ageing man the boy he had once been. The ride ended in broken knees for the horse and a broken crown for the rider. 'And a mercy 'twas nothing worse,' the children's mother commented.

The moral of this story was the danger of selfish recklessness: but he told it with such relish and so much fascinating detail that had the end house children had access to anybody's stable they would have tried to imitate him. Edmund suggested they should try to mount Polly, the innkeeper's old pony, and they even went to the place where she was pegged out to reconnoitre; but Polly had only to rattle her tethering chain to convince them they were not cut out for Dick Turpins.

All was going well and Mr Marley was talking of teaching Edmund Latin, when, in an unfortunate moment, finding the children's father at home, he taxed him with neglect of his religious duties. The father, who never went to church at all and spoke of himself as an agnostic, resented this and a quarrel arose, which ended in Mr Marley being told never to darken that door again. So there were no more of those pleasant teas and talks, although he still remained a kind friend and would sometimes come to the cottage door to speak to the mother, scrupulously remaining outside on the doorstep. Then, in a few months, the Rector died, there were changes, and Mr Marley left the parish.

Five or six years afterwards, when Edmund and Laura were both out in the world, their mother, sitting by her fire one gloomy winter afternoon, heard a knock at her door and opened it to find Mr Marley on her doorstep. Ignoring the old quarrel, she brought him in and insisted upon making tea for him. He was by that time very old and she thought he looked very frail; but in spite of that he had walked many miles across country from the parish where he was doing temporary duty. He sat by the fire while she made toast and they talked of the absent two and of her other children and of neighbours and friends. He stayed a long time, partly because they had so much to say to each other and partly because he was very tired and, as she thought, ill.

Presently the children's father came in from his work and there was a strained moment which ended, to her great relief, in a polite handclasp. The old feud was either forgotten or re-pented of.

The father could see at once that the old man was not in a fit state to walk seven or eight miles at night in that weather and begged him not to think of doing so. But what was to be done? They were far from a railway station, even had there been a convenient train, and there was no vehicle for hire within three miles. Then some one suggested that Master Ashley's donkey-cart would be better than nothing, and the father departed to borrow it. He brought it to the garden gate, for he had to drive it himself, and this, surprisingly, he was ready to do although he had just come in tired and damp from his work and had had no proper meal.

With his knees wrapped round in an old fur coat that had once belonged to the children's grandmother and a hot brick at

his feet, the visitor was about to say 'Farewell', when the
mother, Martha like, exclaimed: 'I'm sorry it's such a poor
turn-out for a gentleman like you to ride in.'

'Poor!' he exclaimed. 'I'm proud of it and shall always remember this day. My Master rode through Jerusalem on one of
these dear patient beasts, you know!'

A fortnight afterwards she read in the local paper that the
Rev Alfred Augustus Peregrine Marley, who was relieving the
Vicar of Such-and-such a parish, had collapsed and died at
the altar while administering Holy Communion.

XV

Harvest Home

IF one of the women was accused of hoarding her best clothes
instead of wearing them, she would laugh and say: 'Ah! I be
savin' they for high days an' holidays an' bonfire nights.' If she
had, they would have lasted a long time, for there were very few
holidays and scarcely any which called for a special toilet.

Christmas Day passed very quietly. The men had a holiday
from work and the children from school and the churchgoers
attended special Christmas services. Mothers who had young
children would buy them an orange each and a handful of nuts;
but, except at the end house and the inn, there was no hanging
up of stockings, and those who had no kind elder sister or aunt
in service to send them parcels got no Christmas presents.

Still, they did manage to make a little festival of it. Every
year the farmer killed an ox for the purpose and gave each of
his men a joint of beef, which duly appeared on the Christmas
dinner-table together with plum pudding – not Christmas
pudding, but suet duff with a good sprinkling of raisins. Ivy and
other evergreens (it was not a holly country) were hung from
the ceiling and over the pictures; a bottle of home-made wine
was uncorked, a good fire was made up, and, with doors and
windows closed against the keen, wintry weather, they all
settled down by their own firesides for a kind of super-Sunday.

There was little visiting of neighbours and there were no family
reunions, for the girls in service could not be spared at that
season, and the few boys who had gone out in the world were
mostly serving abroad in the Army.

There were still bands of mummers in some of the larger
villages, and village choirs went carol-singing about the
countryside; but none of these came to the hamlet, for they
knew the collection to be expected there would not make it
worth their while. A few families, sitting by their own firesides,
would sing carols and songs; that, and more and better food and
a better fire than usual, made up their Christmas cheer.

The Sunday of the Feast was more exciting. Then strangers,
as well as friends, came from far and near to throng the houses
and inn and to promenade on the stretch of road which ran
through the hamlet. On that day the big ovens were heated and
nearly every family managed to have a joint of beef and a
Yorkshire pudding for dinner. The men wore their best suits,
complete with collar and tie, and the women brought out their
treasured finery and wore it, for, even if no relatives from a
distance were expected, some one might be 'popping in', if not
to dinner, to tea or supper. Half a crown, at least, had been
saved from the harvest money for spending at the inn, and the
jugs and beer-cans went merrily round the Rise. 'Arter all, 'tis
the Feast,' they said; 'an't only comes once a year,' and they
enjoyed the extra food and drink and the excitement of seeing
so many people about, never dreaming that they were cele-
brating the dedication five hundred years before of the little
old church in the mother village which so few of them attended.

Those of the Fordlow people who liked to see life had on that
day to go to Lark Rise, for, beyond the extra food, there was no
celebration in the mother village. Some time early in that century the scene of the Feast had shifted from the site of the
church to that of the only inn in the parish.

At least a hundred people, friends and strangers, came from
the market town and surrounding villages; not that there was
anything to do at Lark Rise, or much to see; but because it was
Fordlow Feast and a pleasant walk with a drink at the end was

a good way of spending a fine September Sunday evening.

The Monday of the Feast – for it lasted two days – was kept by women and children only, the men being at work. It was a great day for tea parties; mothers and sisters and aunts and cousins coming in droves from about the neighbourhood. The chief delicacy at these teas was 'baker's cake', a rich, fruity, spicy dough cake, obtained in the following manner. The house-wife provided all the ingredients excepting the dough, putting raisins and currants, lard, sugar, and spice in a basin which she gave to the baker, who added the dough, made and baked the cake, and returned it, beautifully browned in his big oven. The charge was the same as that for a loaf of bread the same size, and the result was delicious. 'There's only one fault wi' these 'ere baker's cakes,' the women used to say; 'they won't keep!' And they would not; they were too good and there were too many children about.

The women made their houses very clean and neat for Feast Monday, and, with hollyhocks nodding in at the open windows and a sight of the clean, yellow stubble of the cleared fields beyond, and the hum of friendly talk and laughter within, the tea parties were very pleasant.

At the beginning of the 'eighties the outside world remembered Fordlow Feast to the extent of sending one old woman with a gingerbread stall. On it were gingerbread babies with currants for eyes, brown-and-white striped peppermint humbugs, sticks of pink-and-white rock, and a few boxes and bottles of other sweets. Even there, on that little old stall with its canvas awning, the first sign of changing taste might have been seen, for, one year, side by side with the gingerbread babies, stood a box filled with thin, dark brown slabs packed in pink paper. 'What is that brown sweet?' asked Laura, spelling out the word 'Chocolate'. A visiting cousin, being fairly well educated and a great reader, already knew it by name. 'Oh, that's choco-late,' he said off-handedly. 'But don't buy any; it's for drinking. They have it for breakfast in France.' A year or two later, chocolate was a favourite sweet even in a place as remote as the hamlet; but it could no longer be bought from the gingerbread stall, for the old woman no longer brought it to the Feast.

Perhaps she had died. Except for the tea-drinkings, Feast
Monday had died, too, as a holiday.

The younger hamlet people still went occasionally to feasts
and club walkings in other villages. In larger places these were
like small fairs, with roundabouts, swings, and coconut shies. At
the club walkings there were brass bands and processions of the
club members, all wearing their club colours in the shape of
rosettes and wide sashes worn across the breast. There was
dancing on the green to the strains of the band, and country
people came from miles around to the village where the feast or
club walking was being held.

Palm Sunday, known locally as Fig Sunday, was a minor
hamlet festival. Sprays of soft gold and silver willow catkins,
called 'palm' in that part of the country, were brought indoors
to decorate the houses and be worn as buttonholes for churchgoing. The children at the end house loved fetching in the palm
and putting it in pots and vases and hanging it over the picture
frames. Better still, they loved the old custom of eating figs on
Palm Sunday. The week before, the innkeeper's wife would get
in a stock to be sold in pennyworths in her small grocery store.
Some of the more expert cooks among the women would use
these to make fig puddings for dinner and the children bought
pennyworths and ate them out of screws of blue sugar paper on
their way to Sunday school.

The gathering of the palm branches must have been a survival from old Catholic days, when, in many English churches,
the willow served for palm to be blessed on Palm Sunday. The
original significance of eating figs on that day had long been
forgotten; but it was regarded as an important duty, and children ordinarily selfish would give one of their figs, or at least a
bite out of one, to the few unfortunates who had been given no
penny.

No such mystery surrounded the making of a bonfire on 5
November. Parents would tell inquiring children all about the
Gunpowder Plot and 'that unked ole Guy Fawkes in his black
mask', as though it had all happened recently; and, the night
before, the boys and youths of the hamlet would go round
knocking at all but the poorest doors and chanting:

Remember, remember, the fifth of November,
    The gunpowder treason and plot.
A stick or a stake, for King James's sake
    Will you please to give us a faggot?
It you won't give us one, we'll take two!
The better for us and the worse for you.

The few housewives who possessed faggot stacks (cut from the undergrowth of woods in the autumn and sold at one and sixpence a score) would give them a bundle or two; others would give them hedge-trimmings, or a piece of old line-post, or anything else that was handy, and, altogether, they managed to collect enough wood to make a modest bonfire which they lit on one of the open spaces and capered and shouted around and roasted potatoes and chestnuts in the ashes, after the manner of boys everywhere.

Harvest time was a natural holiday. 'A hemmed hard-worked 'un,' the men would have said; but they all enjoyed the stir and excitement of getting in the crops and their own importance as skilled and trusted workers, with extra beer at the farmer's expense and extra harvest money to follow.

The 'eighties brought a succession of hot summers and, day after day, as harvest time approached, the children at the end house would wake to the dewy, pearly pink of a fine summer dawn and the *swizzh, swizzh* of the early morning breeze rustling through the ripe corn beyond their doorstep.

Then, very early one morning, the men would come out of their houses, pulling on coats and lighting pipes as they hurried and calling to each other with skyward glances: 'Think weather's a-gooin' to hold?' For three weeks or more during harvest the hamlet was astir before dawn and the homely odours of bacon frying, wood fires and tobacco smoke overpowered the pure, damp, earthy scent of the fields. It would be school holidays then and the children at the end house always wanted to get up hours before their time. There were mushrooms in the meadows around Fordlow and they were sometimes allowed to go picking them to fry for their breakfast. More often they were not; for the dew-soaked grass was bad for their boots. 'Six shillingsworth of good shoe-leather gone for sixpen'orth of mushrooms!' their mother would cry despairingly. But some years old boots had been kept for the purpose and they would dress and creep silently downstairs not to disturb the younger children, and with hunks of bread and butter in their hands steal out into the dewy, morning world.

Against the billowing gold of the fields the hedges stood dark, solid and dew-sleeked; dewdrops beaded the gossamer webs, and the children's feet left long, dark trails on the dewy turf. There were night scents of wheat-straw and flowers and moist earth on the air and the sky was fleeced with pink clouds.

For a few days or a week or a fortnight, the fields stood 'ripe unto harvest'. It was the one perfect period in the hamlet year. The human eye loves to rest upon wide expanses of pure colour: the moors in the purple heyday of the heather, miles of green downland, and the sea when it lies calm and blue and boundless, all delight it; but to some none of these, lovely though they all are, can give the same satisfaction of spirit as acres upon acres of golden corn. *There* is both beauty and bread and the seeds of bread for future generations.

Awed, yet uplifted by the silence and clean-washed loveliness of the dawn, the children would pass along the narrow field paths with rustling wheat on each side. Or Laura would make little dashes into the corn for poppies, or pull trails of the lesser bindweed with its pink-striped trumpets, like clean cotton frocks, to trim her hat and girdle her waist, while Edmund would stump on, red-faced with indignation at her carelessness in making trails in the standing corn.

In the fields where the harvest had begun all was bustle and activity. At that time the mechanical reaper with long, red, revolving arms like windmill sails had already appeared in the locality; but it was looked upon by the men as an auxiliary, a farmers' toy; the scythe still did most of the work and they did not dream it would ever be superseded. So while the red sails revolved in one field and the youth on the driver's seat of the machine called cheerily to his horses and women followed behind to bind the corn into sheaves, in the next field a band of men would be whetting their scythes and mowing by hand as their fathers had done before them.

With no idea that they were at the end of a long tradition, they still kept up the old country custom of choosing as their leader the tallest and most highly skilled man amongst them, who was then called 'King of the Mowers'. For several harvests in the 'eighties they were led by the man known as Boamer. He had served in the Army and was still a fine, well-set-up young fellow with flashing white teeth and a skin darkened by fiercer than English suns.

With a wreath of poppies and green bindweed trails around his wide, rush-plaited hat, he led the band down the swathes as they mowed and decreed when and for how long they should halt for 'a breather' and what drinks should be had from the yellow stone jar they kept under the hedge in a shady corner of the field. They did not rest often or long; for every morning they set themselves to accomplish an amount of work in the day that they knew would tax all their powers till long after sunset. 'Set yourself more than you can do and you'll do it' was one of their maxims, and some of their feats in the harvest field astonished themselves as well as the onlooker.

Old Monday, the bailiff, went riding from field to field on his long-tailed, grey pony. Not at that season to criticize, but rather to encourage, and to carry strung to his saddle the hooped and handled miniature barrel of beer provided by the farmer.

One of the smaller fields was always reserved for any of the women who cared to go reaping. Formerly all the able-bodied women not otherwise occupied had gone as a matter of course; but, by the 'eighties, there were only three or four, beside the regular field women, who could hand the sickle. Often the Irish harvesters had to be called in to finish the field.

Patrick, Dominick, James (never called Jim), Big Mike and Little Mike, and Mr O'Hara seemed to the children as much a part of the harvest scene as the corn itself. They came over from Ireland every year to help with the harvest and slept in the farmer's barn, doing their own cooking and washing at a little fire in the open. They were a wild-looking lot, dressed in odd clothes and speaking a brogue so thick that the natives could only catch a word here and there. When not at work, they went about in a band, talking loudly and usually all together, with the purchases they had made at the inn bundled in blue-and-white check handkerchiefs which they carried over their shoulders at the end of a stick. 'Here comes they jabberin' old Irish,' the country people would say, and some of the women pretended to be afraid of them. They could not have been serious, for the Irishmen showed no disposition to harm any one. All they desired was to earn as much money as possible to send home to their wives, to have enough left for themselves to get drunk on a Saturday night, and to be in time for Mass on a Sunday morning. All these aims were fulfilled; for, as the other men confessed, they were 'gluttons for work' and more work meant more money at that season; there was an excellent inn handy, and a Catholic church within three miles.

After the mowing and reaping and binding came the carrying, the busiest time of all. Every man and boy put his best foot forward then, for, when the corn was cut and dried it was imperative to get it stacked and thatched before the weather broke. All day and far into the twilight the yellow-and-blue painted farm wagons passed and repassed along the roads between the field and the stack-yard. Big cart-horses returning with an empty wagon were made to gallop like two-year-olds. Straws hung on the roadside hedges and many a gate-post was knocked down through hasty driving. In the fields men pitch-forked the sheaves to the one who was building the load on the wagon, and the air resounded with *Hold tights* and *Wert ups* and *Who-o-oas*. The *Hold tight!* was no empty cry; sometimes, in the past, the man on top of the load had not held tight or not tight enough. There were tales of fathers and grandfathers whose necks or backs had been broken by a fall from a load, and of other fatal accidents afield, bad cuts from scythes, pitch-forks passing through feet, to be followed by lockjaw, and of sunstroke; but, happily, nothing of this kind happened on that particular farm in the 'eighties.

At last, in the cool dusk of an August evening, the last load was brought in, with a nest of merry boys' faces among the sheaves on the top, and the men walking alongside with pitch-

forks on shoulders. As they passed along the roads they
shouted:

> Harvest home! Harvest home!
> Merry, merry, merry harvest home!

and women came to their cottage gates and waved, and the few
passers-by looked up and smiled their congratulations. The joy
and pleasure of the labourers in their task well done was pathetic, considering their very small share in the gain. But it was
genuine enough; for they still loved the soil and rejoiced in their
own work and skill in bringing forth the fruits of the soil, and
harvest home put the crown on their year's work.

As they approached the farm-house their song changed to:

> Harvest home! Harvest home!
> Merry, merry, merry harvest home!
> Our bottles are empty, our barrels won't run,
> And we think it's a very dry harvest home.

and the farmer came out, followed by his daughters and maids
with jugs and bottles and mugs, and drinks were handed round
amidst general congratulations. Then the farmer invited the
men to his harvest home dinner, to be held in a few days' time,
and the adult workers dispersed to add up their harvest money
and to rest their weary bones. The boys and youths, who could
never have too much of a good thing, spent the rest of the
evening circling the hamlet and shouting 'Merry, merry, merry
harvest home!' until the stars came out and at last silence fell
upon the fat rickyard and the stripped fields.

On the morning of the harvest home dinner everybody prepared themselves for a tremendous feast, some to the extent of
going without breakfast, that the appetite might not be im-
paired. And what a feast it was! Such a bustling in the farm-
house kitchen for days beforehand; such boiling of hams and
roasting of sirloins; such a stacking of plum puddings, made by
the Christmas recipe; such a tapping of eighteen-gallon casks
and baking of plum loaves would astonish those accustomed to
the appetites of today. By noon the whole parish had assembled,
the workers and their wives and children to feast and the

sprinkling of the better-to-do to help with the serving. The only ones absent were the aged bedridden and their attendants, and to them, the next day, portions, carefully graded in daintiness according to their social standing, were carried by the children from the remnants of the feast. A plum pudding was considered a delicate compliment to an equal of the farmer; slices of beef or ham went to the 'bettermost poor'; and a ham-bone with plenty of meat left upon it or part of a pudding or a can of soup to the commonalty.

Long tables were laid out of doors in the shade of a barn, and soon after twelve o'clock the cottagers sat down to the good cheer, with the farmer carving at the principal table, his wife with her tea urn at another, the daughters of the house and their friends circling the tables with vegetable dishes and beer jugs, and the grandchildren, in their stiff, white, embroidered frocks, dashing hither and thither to see that everybody had what they required. As a background there was the rick-yard with its new yellow stacks and, over all, the mellow sunshine of late summer.

Passers-by on the road stopped their gigs and high dog-carts to wave greetings and shout congratulations on the weather. If a tramp looked wistfully in, he was beckoned to a seat on the straw beneath a rick and a full plate was placed on his knees. It was a picture of plenty and goodwill.

It did not do to look beneath the surface. Laura's father, who did not come into the picture, being a 'tradesman' and so not invited, used to say that the farmer paid his men starvation wages all the year and thought he made it up to them by giving that one good meal. The farmer did not think so, because he did not think at all, and the men did not think either on that day; they were too busy enjoying the food and the fun.

After the dinner there were sports and games, then dancing in the home paddock until twilight, and when, at the end of the day, the farmer, carving indoors for the family supper, paused with knife poised to listen to the last distant 'Hooray!' and exclaimed, 'A lot of good chaps! A lot of good chaps, God bless 'em!' both he and the cheering men were sincere, however mistaken.

But these modest festivals which had figured every year in

everybody's life for generations were eclipsed in 1887 by Queen Victoria's Golden Jubilee.

Up to the middle of the 'eighties the hamlet had taken little intererest in the Royal House. The Queen and the Prince and Princess of Wales were sometimes mentioned, but with little respect and no affection. 'The old Queen', as she was called, was supposed to have shut herself up in Balmoral Castle with a favourite servant named John Brown and to have refused to open Parliament when Mr Gladstone begged her to. The Prince was said to be leading a gay life, and the dear, beautiful Princess, afterwards Queen Alexandra, was celebrated only for her supposed make-up.

By the middle of the decade a new spirit was abroad and had percolated to the hamlet. The Queen, it appeared, had reigned fifty years. She had been a good queen, a wonderful queen, she was soon to celebrate her Jubilee, and, still more exciting, they were going to celebrate it, too, for there was going to be a big 'do' in which three villages would join for tea and sports and dancing and fireworks in the park of a local magnate. Nothing like it had ever been known before.

As the time drew nearer, the Queen and her Jubilee became the chief topic of conversation. The tradesmen gave lovely coloured portraits of her in her crown and garter ribbon on their almanacks, most of which were framed at home and hung up in the cottages. Jam could be bought in glass jugs adorned with her profile in hobnails and inscribed '1837 to 1887. Victoria the Good', and, underneath, the national catchword of the moment: 'Peace and Plenty'. The newspapers were full of the great achievements of her reign: railway travel, the telegraph, Free Trade, exports, progress, prosperity, Peace: all these blessings, it appeared, were due to her inspiration.

Of most of these advantages the hamlet enjoyed but Esau's share; but, as no one reflected upon this, it did not damp the general enthusiasm. 'Fancy her reigning fifty years, the old dear, her!' they said, and bought paper banners inscribed 'Fifty Years, Mother, Wife, and Queen' to put inside their window panes. 'God Bless Her. Victoria the Good. The Mother of Her People.'

Laura was lucky enough to be given a bound volume of
Good Words – or was it *Home Words*? – in which the Queen's
own journal, *Leaves From Her Majesty's Life in the Highlands,*
ran as a serial. She galloped through all the instalments immediately to pick out the places mentioned by her dear Sir Walter
Scott. Afterwards the journal was re-read many times, as everything was re-read in that home of few books. Laura liked the
journal, for although the Queen kept to the level of meals and
drives and seasickness and the 'civility' of her hosts and host-
esses, and only mentioned the scenery (Scott's scenery!) to
repeat what 'Albert said' about it – and he always compared it
to some foreign scene – there was a forthright sincerity about
the writing which revealed a human being behind all the glitter
and fuss.

By the end of May everybody was talking about the weather.
Would it be fine for the great drive through London; and, still
more important, would it be fine for the doings in Skeldon
Park? Of course it would be fine, said the more optimistic.
Providence knew what He was about. It was going to be a glorious June. Queen's weather, they called it. Hadn't the listener
heard that the sun always shone when the Queen drove out?

Then there were rumours of a subscription fund. The women
of England were going to give the Queen a Jubilee present, and,
wonder of wonders, the amount given was not to exceed one
penny. 'Of course we shall give,' they said proudly. 'It'll be our
duty an' our pleasure.' And when the time came for the collection to be made they had all of them their pennies ready.
Bright new ones in most cases, for, although they knew the
coins were to be converted into a piece of plate before reaching
Her Majesty, they felt that only new money was worthy of the
occasion.

The ever-faithful, ever-useful clergyman's daughter collected
the pence. Thinking, perhaps, that the day after pay-day would
be most convenient, she visited Lark Rise on a Saturday, and
Laura, at home from school, was clipping the garden hedge
when she heard one neighbour say to another: 'I want a bucket
of water, but I can't run round to the well till Miss Ellison's
been for the penny.'

'Lordy, dear!' ejaculated the other. 'Why, she's been an' gone this quarter of an hour. She's a-been to my place. Didn't she come to yourn?'

The first speaker flushed to the roots of her hair. She was a woman whose husband had recently had an accident afield and was still in hospital. There were no Insurance benefits then, and it was known she was having a hard struggle to keep her home going; but she had her penny ready and was hurt, terribly hurt, by the suspicion that she had been purposely passed over.

'I s'pose, because I be down on me luck, she thinks I ain't worth a penny,' she cried, and went in and banged the door.

'There's temper for you!' the other woman exclaimed to the world at large and went about her own business. But Laura was distressed. She had seen Mrs Parker's expression and could imagine how her pride was hurt. She, herself, hated to be pitied. But what could she do about it?

She went to the gate. Miss Ellison had finished collecting and was crossing the allotments on her way home. Laura would just have time to run the other way round and meet her at the stile. After a struggle with her own inward shrinking which lasted about two minutes, but was ridiculously intense, she ran off on her long, thin legs, and popped up, like a little jack-in-the-box, on the other side of the stile which the lady was gathering up her long frilly skirts to mount.

'Oh, please, Miss Ellison, you haven't been to Mrs Parker's, and she's got her penny all ready and she wants the Queen to have it so much.'

'But, Laura,' said the lady loftily, surprised at such inter-ference, 'I did not intend to call upon Mrs Parker today. With her husband in hospital, I know she has no penny to spare, poor soul.'

But, although somewhat quelled, Laura persisted: 'But she's got it all polished up and wrapped in tissue paper, Miss Ellison, and 'twill hurt her feelings most awful if you don't go for it, Miss Ellison.'

At that, Miss Ellison grasped the situation and retraced her steps, keeping Laura by her side and talking to her as to another grown-up person.

'Our dear Queen,' she was saying as they passed Twister's turnip patch, 'our dear, good Queen, Laura, is noted for her perfect tact. Once, and I have this on good authority, some church workers were invited to visit her at Osborne. Tea was served in a magnificent drawing-room, the Queen actually partaking of a cup with them, and this, I am told, is very unusual – a great honour, in fact; but no doubt she did it to put them at their ease. But in her confusion, one poor lady, unaccustomed to taking tea with royalty, had the misfortune to drop her slice of cake on the floor. Imagine that, Laura, a slice of cake on the Queen's beautiful carpet; you can understand how the poor lady must have felt, can't you dear? One of the ladies-in-waiting smiled at her discomfiture, which made her still more nervous and trembling; but our dear Queen – she has sharp eyes, God bless her! – saw at once how matters stood. She asked for a slice of cake, then purposely dropped it, and commanded the lady who had smiled to pick up both pieces at once. Which she did quickly, you may be sure, Laura, and there were no more smiles. What a lesson! What a lesson, Laura!'

Cynical little Laura wondered for whom the lesson was intended; but she only said meekly: 'Yes, indeed, Miss Ellison,' and this brought them to Mrs Parker's door, where she had the satisfaction of hearing Miss Ellison say: 'Oh, dear, Mrs Parker, I nearly overlooked your house. I have come for your contribution to the Queen's Jubilee present.'

The great day dawned at last and most of the hamlet people were up in time to see the sun burst in dazzling splendour from the pearly pink east and mount into a sky unflecked by the smallest cloud. Queen's weather indeed! And as the day began it continued. It was very hot; but nobody minded that, for the best hats could be worn without fear of showers, and those who had sunshades put by for just such an occasion could bring them forth in all their glory of deep lace or long, knotted, silk fringe.

By noon all the hamlet children had been scrubbed with soap and water and arrayed in their best clothes. 'Every bit clean, right through to the skin,' as their mothers proudly declared. Then, after a snack, calculated to sustain the family during the walk to the park, but not to spoil the appetite for tea, the mothers went upstairs to take out their own curl papers and don their best clothes. A strong scent of camphor and lavender and closely shut boxes pervaded the atmosphere around them for the rest of the day. The colours and styles did not harmonize too well with the midsummer country scene, and many might have preferred to see them in print frocks and sunbonnets; but they dressed to please themselves, not to please the artistic taste of others, and they were all the happier for it.

Before they started there was much running from house to house and asking: 'Now, *should* you put on another bow just here!' or 'Do you think that ostrich tip our young Em sent me'd improve my hat, or do you think the red roses and black lace is enough?' or 'Now, tell me true, do you like my hair done this way?'

The men and boys with shining faces and in Sunday suits had gone on before to have dinner at the farm before meeting their families at the cross-roads. They would be having cuts off great sirloins and Christmas pudding washed down with beer, just as they did at the harvest home dinner.

The little party from the end house walked alone in the straggling procession; the mother, still rather pale from her recent confinement, pushing the baby carriage with little May and baby Elizabeth; Laura and Edmund, on tiptoe with excitement, helping to shove the carriage over the rough turf of the park. Their father had not come. He did not care for 'do's', and had gone to work at his bench at the shop alone while his work-mates held high holiday. There were as yet no trade union laws to forbid such singularity.

There were more people in the park than the children had ever seen together, and the roundabouts, swings, and coconut shies were doing a roaring trade. Tea was partaken of in a huge marquee in relays, one parish at a time, and the sound of the brass band, roundabout hurdy-gurdy, coconut thwacks, and showmen's shouting surged round the frail, canvas walls like a roaring sea.

Within, the mingled scents of hot tea, dough cake, tobacco smoke, and trampled grass lent a holiday savour to a simple menu. But if the provisions were simple in quality, the quantity was prodigious. Clothes baskets of bread and butter and jam cut in thick slices and watering cans of tea, already milked and sugared, were handed round and disappeared in a twinkling. 'God bless my soul,' one old clergyman exclaimed. 'Where on earth do they put it all!' They put three-fourths of it in the same handy receptacle he himself used for his four-course dinners; but the fourth part went into their pockets. That was their little weakness – not to be satisfied with a bellyful, but to manage somehow to secure a portion to take home for next day.

After tea there were sports, with races, high jumps, dipping heads into tubs of water to retrieve sixpences with the teeth, grinning through horse-collars, the prize going to the one making the most grotesque face, and, to crown all, climbing the greased pole for the prize leg of mutton. This was a tough job, as the pole was as tall and slender as a telephone post and extremely slippery. Prudent wives would not allow their husbands to attempt it on account of spoiling their clothes, so the competition was left to the ragamuffins and a few experts who had had the foresight to bring with them a pair of old trousers. This competition must have run concurrently with the other events, for all the afternoon there was a crowd around it, and first one, then another, would 'have a go'. It was painful to watch the climbers, shinning up a few inches, then slipping back again, and, as one retired, another taking his place, until, late in the afternoon, the champion arrived, climbed slowly but steadily to the top and threw down the joint, which, by the way, must have been already roasted after four or five hours in the burning sun. It was whispered around that he had carried a bag of ashes and sprinkled them on the greasy surface as he ascended.

The local gentlepeople promenaded the ground in parties: stout, red-faced squires, raising their straw hats to mop their foreheads; hunting ladies, incongruously garbed in silks and ostrich-feather boas; young girls in embroidered white muslin and boys in Eton suits. They had kind words for everybody, especially for the poor and lonely, and, from time to time, they would pause before some sight and try to enter into the spirit of the other beholders; but everywhere their arrival hushed the mirth, and there was a sigh of relief when they moved on. After dancing the first dance they disappeared, and 'now we can have some fun', the people said.

All this time Edmund and Laura, with about two hundred other children, had been let loose in the crowd to spend their pennies and watch the fun. They rode on the wooden horses, swung in the swing-boats, pried around coconut shies and shooting booths munching coconut or rock or long strips of black liquorice, until their hands were sticky and their faces grimed.

Laura, who hated crowds and noise, was soon tired of it and looked longingly at the shady trees and woods and spinneys around the big open space where the fair was held. But before she escaped a new and wonderful experience awaited her. Before one of the booths a man was beating a drum and before him two girls were posturing and pirouetting. 'Walk up! Walk up!' he was shouting. 'Walk up and see the tightrope dancing! Only one penny admission. Walk up! Walk up!' Laura paid her penny and walked up, as did about a dozen others, the man and girls came inside, the flap of the tent was drawn, and the show began.

Laura had never heard of tightrope dancing before and she was not sure she was not dreaming it then. The outer tumult beat against the frail walls of the tent, but within was a magic circle of quiet. As she crossed to take her place with the other spectators, her feet sank deep into sawdust; and, in the subdued light which filtered through the canvas, the broad, white, pock-marked face of the man in his faded red satin and the tinsel crowns and tights of the girls seemed as unreal as a dream.

The girl who did the tightrope dancing was a fair, delicate-looking child with grey eyes and fat, pale-brown ringlets, a great contrast to her dark, bouncing gipsy-looking sister, and when she mounted to the rope stretched between two poles and did a few dance steps as she swayed gracefully along it, Laura gazed and gazed, speechless with admiration. To the simple country-bred child the performance was marvellous. It came to an end all too soon for her; for not much could be done to entertain a house which only brought a shilling or so to the box office; but the impression remained with her as a glimpse into a new and fascinating world. There were few five-barred gates in the vicinity of Laura's home on which she did not attempt a little pirouetting along the top bar during the next year or two.

The tightrope dancing was her outstanding memory of the great Queen's Jubilee; but the merrymaking went on for hours after that. All the way home in the twilight, the end house party could hear the popping of fireworks behind them and, turning, see rockets and showers of golden rain above the dark tree-tops. At last, standing at their own garden gate, they heard the roaring of cheers from hundreds of throats and the band playing 'God save the Queen'.

They were first home and the hamlet was in darkness, but the twilight was luminous over the fields and the sky right round to the north was still faintly pink. A cat rubbed itself against their legs and mewed; the pig in the sty woke and grunted a protest against the long day's neglect. A light breeze rustled through the green corn and shivered the garden bushes, releasing the scent of stocks and roses and sunbaked grass and the grosser smells of cabbage beds and pigsties. It had been a great day – the greatest day they were ever likely to see, however long they lived, they were told; but it was over and they were home and home was best.

After the Jubilee nothing ever seemed quite the same. The old Rector died and the farmer, who had seemed immovable excepting by death, had to retire to make way for the heir of the landowning nobleman who intended to farm the family estates himself. He brought with him the new self-binding reaping machine and women were no longer required in the harvest field. At the hamlet several new brides took possession of houses previously occupied by elderly people and brought new ideas into the place. The last of the bustles disappeared and leg-o'-mutton sleeves were 'all the go'. The new Rector's wife took her Mothers' Meeting women for a trip to London. Babies were christened new names; Wanda was one, Gwendolin another. The innkeeper's wife got in cases of tinned salmon and Australian rabbit. The Sanitary Inspector appeared for the first time at the hamlet and shook his head over the pigsties and privies. Wages rose, prices soared, and new needs multiplied. People began to speak of 'before the Jubilee' much as we in the nineteen-twenties spoke of 'before the war', either as a golden time or as one of exploded ideas, according to the age of the speaker.

And all the time boys were being born or growing up in the parish, expecting to follow the plough all their lives, or, at most, to do a little mild soldiering or go to work in a town. Gallipoli? Kut? Vimy Ridge? Ypres? What did they know of such places? But they were to know them, and when the time came they did not flinch. Eleven out of that tiny community never came back again. A brass plate on the wall of the church immediately over the old end house seat is engraved with their names. A double column, five names long, then, last and alone, the name of Edmund.

OVER TO CANDLEFORD

═══

XVI

As They Were

'COME the summer, we'll borrow old Polly and the spring cart from the "Wagon and Horses" and all go over to Candleford,' their father said, for the ten-millionth time, thought Laura. Although he had said it so often they had never been. They had not been anywhere farther than the market town for the Saturday shopping.

Once, when some one asked them how long they had lived in their cottage, Laura had replied, 'Oh, for years and years,' and Edmund had said 'Always'; but his always was only five years and her years and years were barely seven. That was why, when their mother told them that the greatest mistake in life is to be born poor, they did not realize that they themselves had made that initial blunder. They were too young and had no means of comparison.

Their home was one of a group of small cottages surrounded by fields, three miles from the nearest small town and nineteen from a city. All around was rich, flat farming country, which, at the end of a lifetime, remained obstinately in the memory as stretch after stretch of brown-ribbed ploughland patterned with quick-set hedges and hedgerow elms. That picture was permanent; others could be called up at will, of acres of young green wheat swept by chasing cloud-shadows; of the gold of harvest fields, or the billowing whiteness of snow upon which the spoor of hares and foxes could be traced from hedgerow to hedgerow.

On a slight rise in the midst of this brown or green or whiteness stood the hamlet, a huddle of grey stone walls and pale slated roofs with only the bushiness of a fruit-tree or the dark line of a yew hedge to relieve its colourlessness. To a passer-by on the main road a mile away it must often have appeared a lone and desolate place; but it had a warmth of its own, and a closer observer would have found it as seething with interest and activity as a molehill.

All the cottages in the group were occupied by poor families. Some, through old age, or the possession of a larger family than ordinary, had a little less, and two or three in more favourable circumstances had a little more comfort than their neighbours, but in every house money was scarce.

If any one wanted to borrow, they knew better than to ask for more than sixpence, and if the expression with which their request was received was discouraging they would add hurriedly: 'If you can't manage it, I think tuppence'd see me through.' The children were given halfpennies or even farthings to spend on sweets when the travelling grocer's van called. For even the smaller sum they got enough hardbake or peppermint rock to distend their cheeks for hours. It took the parents months to save up to buy a young pig for the sty or a few score of faggots for the winter. Apart from the prudent, who had these small hoards, people were penniless for days towards the end of the week.

But, as they were fond of saying, money isn't everything. Poor as they were, every one of the small cottages, so much alike when seen from the outside, had for its inmates the unique distinction of being 'our place' or 'ho-um'. After working in the pure cold air of the fields all day, the men found it comforting to be met by, and wrapped round in, an atmosphere of chimney-smoke and bacon and cabbage-cooking; to sink into 'feyther's chair' by the hearth, draw off heavy, mud-caked boots, take the latest baby on their knee and sip strong, sweet tea while 'our Mum' dished up the tea-supper.

The elder children were either at school all day or lived out of doors in fine weather; but, as their mothers said, they knew which house to go to when they felt hungry, and towards dusk they made for their supper and bed like homing pigeons, or rabbits scurrying to their burrows.

To the women, home was home in a special sense, for nine-tenths of their lives were spent indoors. There they washed and cooked and cleaned and mended for their teeming families; there they enjoyed their precious half-hour's peace with a cup of tea before the fire in the afternoon, and there they bore their troubles as best they could and cherished their few joys. At times when things did not press too heavily upon them they found pleasure in re-arranging their few poor articles of furniture, in re-papering the walls and making quilts and cushions of scraps of old cloth to adorn their dwelling and add to its comfort, and few were so poor that they had not some treasure to exhibit, some article that had been in the family since 'I dunno when', or had been bought at a sale of furniture at such-and-such a great house, or had been given them when in service.

Such treasures in time gained a reputation of fabulous value. Bill's grandfather had refused an offer of twenty pounds for that corner cupboard, or grandfather's clock, said one; another that a mysterious gentleman had once told her that the immense rubies and emeralds which studded a shabby old metal photograph frame were real stones. She was always saying that she would take it to a jeweller at Sherston and get it valued, 'come Fair time', but she never did. Like the rest of us, she knew better than to put her favourite illusion to the test.

None of the listeners cast doubt upon the value of such treasures. It would not have been 'manners', and, besides, nearly everybody had got some article with a similar legend. At home, the children's father laughed and said that as none of the Braby family had ever had more than twenty shillings at one time in their lives an offer of twenty pounds would soon have been snapped at; and as to Mrs Gaskin's rubies and emeralds, anybody with half an eye could see that they came from the same mine as the stuff used to make penny tumblers.

'What's the odds, if thinking so makes them happy?' asked his wife.

They were a hardworking, self-reliant, passably honest people. 'Providence helps them as has got the sense to look out for theirselves' was a motto often quoted. They had not much original wit, but had inherited a stock of cheerful sayings which passed as such. A neighbour called in to help move a heavy piece of furniture would arrive spitting on his palms and saying, 'Here I be, ready an' willin' to do as much for half a crown as I 'ud for a shillin'.' Which mild joke, besides the jumbled arithmetic, had the added point of the fantastic sum suggested as a reward. A glass of beer, or the price of one, was the current payment for that and some more considerable services.

One who had helped a neighbour to solve some knotty problem would quote the old proverb: 'Two heads be better n'r one,' and the other would retort, 'That's why fools get married,' or, if materially minded, 'Aye, specially if 'um be sheep's heads.' A proverb always had to be capped. No one could say, 'There's more ways of killing a dog than hanging it' without being reminded, 'nor of choking it with a pound of fresh butter', and any reference to money as the root of all evil would be followed, by, 'Same time, I 'udn't say no to anybody as offered me a slip off that root.'

The discussion of their own and their neighbours' affairs took the place occupied by books and films in the modern outlook. Nothing of outside importance ever happened there and their lives were as unlike as possible the modern conception of country life, for Lark Rise was neither a little hotbed of vice nor a garden of all the Arcadian virtues. But the lives of all human beings, however narrow, have room for complications for themselves and entertainment for the onlooker, and many a satisfying little drama was played out on that ten-foot stage.

In their daily life they had none of the conveniences now looked upon as necessities: no water nearer than the communal well, no sanitation beyond the garden closet, and no light but candles and paraffin lamps. It was a hard life, but the hamlet folks did not pity themselves. They kept their pity for those they thought really poor.

The children brought home from the Sunday School Lending Library books about the London slums which their mothers also read. This was then a favourite subject with writers of that class of fiction; their object apparently being not so much to arouse indignation at the terrible conditions as to provide a striking background for some ministering lady or child. Many tears were shed in the hamlet over *Christie's Old Organ* and

Froggy's Little Brother, and everybody wished they could have brought those poor neglected slum children there and shared with them the best they had of everything. 'Poor little mite. If we could have got him here, he could have slept with our young Sammy and this air'd have set him up in no time,' one woman said of Froggy's poor dying little brother, forgetting that he was, as she would have said at another time, 'just somebody in a book'.

But, saddening as it was to read about the poor things, it was also enjoyable, for it gave one a cheering sense of superiority. Thank God, the reader had a whole house to herself with an upstairs and downstairs and did not have to 'pig it' in one room; and real beds, and clean ones, not bundles of rags in corners, to sleep on.

To them, as to the two children learning to live among them, the hamlet life was the normal life. On one side of that norm were the real poor, living in slums, and, on the other, 'the gentry'. They recognized no other division of classes; although, of course, they knew there were a few 'bettermost people' between. The visiting clergyman and that kind friend of them all, the doctor in the market town, had more money and better houses than theirs, and though they were both 'gentlemen born' they did not belong to the aristocracy inhabiting the great country houses or visiting the hunting boxes around. But these were, indulgently, 'th' ole parson', and, affectionately, 'our doctor'; they were not thought of as belonging to any particular class of society.

The gentry flitted across the scene like kingfishers crossing a flock of hedgerow sparrows. They saw them sweeping through the hamlet in their carriages, the ladies billowing in silks and satins, with tiny chenille-fringed parasols held at an angle to protect their complexions. Or riding to hounds in winter, the men in immaculate pink, the women sitting their side-saddles with hour-glass figures encased in skin-tight black habits. *'Looks for all the world as if she'd been melted and poured into it, now don't she?'* On raw, misty mornings they would trot their horses through on their way to the Meet, calling to each other in high-pitched voices it was fun to imitate.

Later in the day they would often be seen galloping full-stretch over the fields and then the men at work there would drop their tools and climb on the five-barred gates for a better view, or stop their teams and straighten their backs at the plough-tail to cup their hands to their mouths and shout: 'Tally-ho: A-gallop, a-gallop, a-lye, a-lye, Tally-ho.'

When the carriages passed through, many of the women would set down the buckets they were carrying and curtsey, and the boys would pull their forelocks and the girls bob their knees, as they had been taught to do at school. This was an awkward moment for Laura, because her father had said, while he had no objection to Edmund saluting any lady – though he hoped, for heaven's sake, he would not do it by pulling his own hair, like pulling a bell-rope – he was determined that no daughter of his should bow the knee, excepting at 'The Name' in church or to Queen Victoria, if ever she happened to pass that way. Their mother laughed. 'When at Rome do as the Romans do,' she said.

'This is not Rome,' their father retorted. 'It's Lark Rise – the spot God made with the left-overs when He'd finished creating the rest of the earth.'

At that their mother tossed her head and clicked her tongue against the roof of her mouth. She had, as she said, no patience with some of his ideas.

Apart from the occasional carriages and the carrier's cart twice a week, there was little traffic on that road beyond the baker's van and the farm carts and wagons. Sometimes a woman from a neighbouring village or hamlet would pass through on foot, shopping basket on arm, on her way to the market town. It was thought nothing of then to walk six or seven miles to purchase a reel of cotton or a packet of tea, or sixpen'orth of pieces from the butcher to make a meat pudding for Sunday. Excepting the carrier's cart, which only came on certain days, there was no other way of travelling. It was thought quite dashing to ride with Old Jimmy, but frightfully extravagant, for the fare was sixpence. Most people preferred to go on foot and keep the sixpence to spend when they got there.

But, although it was not yet realized, the revolution in transport had begun. The first high 'penny-farthing' bicycles were already on the roads, darting and swerving like swallows heralding the summer of the buses and cars and motor cycles which were soon to transform country life. But how fast those new bicycles travelled and how dangerous they looked! Pedestrians backed almost into the hedges when they met one of them, for was there not almost every week in the Sunday newspaper the story of some one being knocked down and killed by a bicycle, and letters from readers saying cyclists ought not to be allowed to use the roads, which, as everybody knew, were provided for people to walk on or to drive on behind horses. 'Bicyclists ought to have roads to themselves, like railway trains' was the general opinion.

Yet it was thrilling to see a man hurtling through space on one high wheel, with another tiny wheel wobbling helplessly behind. You wondered how they managed to keep their balance. No wonder they wore an anxious air. 'Bicyclist's face', the expression was called, and the newspapers foretold a hunch-backed and tortured-faced future generation as a result of the pastime.

Cycling was looked upon as a passing craze and the cyclists in their tight navy knickerbocker suits and pillbox caps with the badge of their club in front were regarded as figures of fun. None of those in the hamlet who rushed out to their gates to see one pass, half hoping for and half fearing a spill, would have believed, if they had been told, that in a few years there would be at least one bicycle in every one of their houses, that the men would ride to work on them and the younger women, when their housework was done, would lightly mount 'the old bike' and pedal away to the market town to see the shops. They would have been still more incredulous had they been told that many of them would live to see every child of school age in the hamlet provided by a kind County Council with a bicycle on which they would ride to school, 'all free, gratis, and for nothing', as they would have said.

In the outer world men were running up tall factory chimneys and covering the green fields for miles with rows of mean little houses to house the workers. Towns which were already towns were throwing out roads and roads of suburban villas. New churches and chapels and railway stations and schools and public houses were being built to meet the needs of a fast-growing population. But the hamlet people saw none of these changes. They were far from the industrial districts and their surroundings remained as they had been from the time of their birth. No cottage had been added to the little group in the fields for many years, and, as it turned out, none were to be added for at least a half century; perhaps never, for the hamlet stands today unchanged in its outward appearance.

Queen Victoria was on the throne. She had been well established there before either of Laura's parents were born, and it seemed to her and her brother that she had always been Queen and always would be. But plenty of elderly people could remember her Coronation and could tell them what church bells had pealed all day in the different villages and what oxen had been roasted whole and what bonfires had been lighted at night.

'Our little English rose', the Rector said had then been her subjects' name for her, and Laura often thought of that when she studied the portrait which hung, framed and glazed, in the place of honour in many of the cottages. It was that of a stout, middle-aged, rather cross-looking lady with a bright blue Garter ribbon across her breast and a crown on her head so tiny that it made her face look large.

'How does she keep it on?' asked Laura, for it looked as if the slightest movement would send it toppling.

'Don't you worry about that,' said her mother comfortably, 'she'll manage to keep that on for a good many more years, you'll see'; and she did, for another twenty.

To the country at large, the Queen was no longer 'Our little English rose'. She had become 'The Queen-Empress' or 'Victoria the Good, the mother of her people'. To the hamlet she was 'th' old Queen', or, sometimes 'th' poor old Queen', for was she not a widow? And it was said she was having none too easy a time with that son of hers, either. But they all agreed she was a good Queen, and when asked why, would reply, 'Because she's brought the price of the quartern loaf down' or 'Well, we have got peace under her, haven't we?'

Peace? Of course there was peace. War was something you read about in books, something rather exciting, if only the poor soldiers had not had to be killed, but all long ago and far away, something that could not possibly happen in our time.

But there had been a war not so very long ago, their father told them. He himself had been born on the day of the Battle of Alma. We had been fighting the Russians then, a hard and cruel lot who had thought might was right, but had found themselves mistaken. They couldn't make slaves of a free people.

Then there was the old man who came round every few months playing a penny whistle and begging. He was known as 'One-eyed Peg-leg' because he had lost an eye and part of a leg fighting before Sebastopol. His trouser leg was cut short at the knee, which was supported by what was then called a 'wooden leg', although it did not resemble a human leg very closely, being but a plain wooden stump, tapering slightly at the bottom, where it was finished off by a ferrule. 'Dot and carry one', they called the sound he made when walking.

Laura once heard old Peg-leg telling a neighbour about the loss of his living member. After a hit with a cannon-ball he had lain for twenty-four hours unattended on the battlefield. Then a surgeon had come and, without more ado, had sawn off the shattered portion. 'And didn't I just holler,' he said; ' 'specially when he dipped the stump into a bucket of boiling tar. That was afore th' nusses come.'

Before the nurses came. Laura knew what that meant, for there was a picture of Florence Nightingale in a book she had and her mother had read to her about 'the Lady with the Lamp', whose shadow was kissed by the wounded.

But these rumours of the war in the Crimea did not seem to the children to bring it any nearer to their own lifetime, and when, later, they read in their old-fashioned story books of families of good children helping their mothers to knit and roll bandages for the soldiers in Russia, it still seemed as unreal as any fairy tale.

The soldiers who had their homes in the hamlet were not

looked upon as fighting men, but as young adventurers who had enlisted as the only way of seeing the world before they settled down to marriage and the plough-tail. Judging from their letters, often read aloud to groups at cottage doors, the only enemies they had to face were sand-storms, mosquitoes, heat stroke, or ague.

The children's Uncle Edmund's trials were of a different nature, because he was in Nova Scotia, where noses got frozen. But he, of course, was in the Royal Engineers, as all the soldiers on their father's side of the family were, for had they not got a trade in their hands? The family was a bit snobbish about this. In those simple days a man whose parents had apprenticed him to a trade was looked upon as established for life. 'Put a trade in his hands and he'll always be sure of a good living,' people would say of a promising boy. They had yet to learn the full meaning of such words as 'depression' and 'unemployment'. So it was always the *Royal* Engineers, even with the mother at the end house. Her own family favoured the Field Artillery, which, to be sure, was Royal, too, although this was not insisted upon.

Both Engineers and Artillery looked down a little on the county regiment, and that, in its turn, looked down on the Militia. No doubt the Militia men had their standards, too; probably they looked down upon the unenterprising youths left at home, 'chaps as hadn't the sprawl to go a-soldiering'. Those who timidly ventured to join the Militia seldom remained in it long. Almost always, before their first season's training was over, they wrote to their parents to say that they found soldiering such a fine life they had decided to transfer to 'the Regulars'. Then they came home on furlough in their scarlet tunics and pill-box caps and strolled around the hamlet twirling their canes and caressing their new moustaches before disappearing overseas to India or Egypt. For those left at home there was little excitement. Christmas, the Harvest Home and the Village Feast were the only holidays. No cinemas, no wireless, no excursions or motor coaches or dances in village halls in those days! A few of the youths and younger men played cricket in the summer. One young man was considered a good bowler locally and he would sometimes get up a team to play one of the neighbouring villages. This once led to a curious little conversation on his doorstep. A lady had alighted from her carriage to ask or, rather, command him to get up a team to play 'the young gentlemen', meaning her sons, on holidays from school, and a few of their friends. Naturally, Frank wanted to know the strength of the team he was to be up against. 'You'd want me to bring a good team, I suppose, ma'am?' he asked respectfully.

'Well, yes,' said the lady. 'The young gentlemen would enjoy a good game. But don't bring *too* good a team. They wouldn't want to be beaten.'

'That's what she calls cricket,' said Frank, grinning broadly at her retreating figure.

This country scene is only a little over fifty years distant from us in time; but in manners, customs and conditions of life, it is centuries away. Except that slates were superseding thatch for roofing and the old open hearth was giving place to the built-in grate, the cottages were as the dwellings of the poor had been for generations. The people still ate the old country fare, preferring it, so far, to such of the new factory-made products as had come their way. The smock frock was still worn by the older men, who declared that one well-made smock would outlast twenty of the new machine-made suits the younger men were buying. The smock, with its elaborately stitched yoke and snow-white home laundering, was certainly more artistic than the coarse, badly-fitting 'reach-me-downs', as they were sometimes called.

The women were more fashion-minded than the men, but their efforts to keep up-to-date were confined to the 'Sunday best' which they seldom took from their boxes upstairs. For everyday wear, they contented themselves with a large, well-ironed white apron to cover their patches and darns. To go to the well, or from house to house in the hamlet, they threw a plaid woollen shawl over their shoulders, or, in bad weather, drew it up to cover their heads. Then, with a strong pair of pattens under their feet, they were ready for anything.

They were still much as their forefathers had been; but change was creeping in, if slowly. A weekly newspaper came into every house, either by purchase or borrowing, and although these were still written by educated men for the educated, and our hamlet intellects had sometimes to reach up a little for their ideas, ideas were slowly percolating.

Having to reach up for ideas came naturally to a generation brought up on the Bible. Their fathers had looked upon 'the Word' as their one unfailing guide in life's difficulties. It was their story book, their treasury of words and sayings, and, for those who could appreciate it, their one book of poetry. Many of the older people still believed every word in the Bible to be literally true. Others were not so sure; that tale of Jonah and the whale, for instance, took a good deal of swallowing. But the newspaper everybody believed in. 'I seed it in the paper, so it must be true' was a saying calculated to clinch any argument.

XVII

A Hamlet Home

LAURA arrived on this scene on a cold December morning when snow lay in deep drifts over the fields and blocked the roads. There were no fireplaces in cottage bedrooms such as her mother's was, and the relays of hot bricks, baked in the oven and swathed in flannel, lost their warmth coming upstairs. 'Oh, we were so cold, so cold,' her mother would say when telling the story, and Laura liked that 'we'. It showed that even a tiny baby who had never been outside the room in which she was born was already a person.

Her parents' life was not quite so hard as that of most of their neighbours, for her father was a stonemason and earned more money than the farm-workers, although in the eighteen-eighties a skilled craftsman, such as he was, received little more in wages than today's unemployment pay.

He was not a native of those parts, but had been brought there a few years earlier by a firm of builders engaged in the restoration of some of the churches of the countryside. He was an expert workman and loved his craft. It was said that he would copy some crumbling detail of carving and fit it in in such a way that the original carver could not have detected the substitution. He did carving at home, too, in the little workshop he had built at the side of their cottage. A few of his attempts stood about as ornaments in the house, a lion, lilies of the valley growing at the base of a tree trunk, and a baby's head, perhaps Edmund's or Laura's. Whether these were well done or not Laura never knew, for before she was old enough to discriminate they had become grimy and been swept off to the rubbish heap; but it pleased her to know that he had at least the impulse to create and the skill to execute, however imperfectly.

By the time the restoration work was finished he had married and had two children and, though he never cared for the hamlet or became one with the little community there, as his wife and children did, he stayed behind when his workmates left and settled down to work as an ordinary stonemason.

There was still a good deal of building in stone going on in that part of the country. One country house had been burnt down and had to be rebuilt; another had a new wing added, and, afterwards, he would make a tombstone, build a cottage or wall, set a grate, or lay a few bricks as required. Workmen were expected to turn their hands to anything within the limits of their trade, and he who could do most was considered the better workman. The day of the specialist was in the future. Each workman must keep to his trade, however. Laura remembered that once, when frost prevented him from working, he happened to say to her mother that the carpenters had plenty to do, and when her mother, knowing that he had been through all the shops, as was the custom with builders' sons at that time, asked why he could not ask to be allowed to do some carpentering, he laughed and said: 'The carpenters would have something to say about that! They would say I was poaching, and tell me to keep to my own trade.'

For thirty-five years he was employed by a firm of builders in the market town, walking the three miles, night and morning, at first; cycling later. His hours were from six in the morning to

five in the afternoon, and to reach his work in time he had for
the greater part of the year to leave home before daylight.

As Laura first remembered him he was a slim, upright young
man in the late twenties, with dark, fiery eyes and raven-black
hair, but fair, fresh-coloured complexion. On account of the
dusty-white nature of his work, he usually wore clothes of some
strong light-grey worsted material. Years after he had died, an
old and embittered man, she could see him, a white apron rolled
up around his middle, a basket of tools slung over his shoulder
and a black billycock hat set at an angle on his head, swinging
along on the crown of the road on his way home from work,
looking, as the hamlet people said, 'as if he had bought all the
land on one side of the road and was thinking of buying that on
the other side'.

Even in darkness his step could be distinguished, for it was
lighter and sharper than that of the other men. His mind moved
more quickly, too, and his tongue was readier, for he belonged
to another breed and had been brought up in another environment.

Some of the neighbours thought him proud and 'set up with
himself', but he was tolerated for his wife's sake and his relations with the neighbours were at least outwardly friendly –
especially at Election time, when he mounted a plank supported
by two beer-barrels and expounded the Gladstonian programme, while Laura, her eyes on a level with his best buttoned
boots, quaked inwardly lest he should be laughed at.

His audience of twenty or so laughed quite a lot, but with
him, not at him, for he was an amusing speaker. None of them
knew and probably he himself had not begun to suspect that
they were listening to a lost and thwarted man, one who
had strayed into a life to which he did not belong and one
whose own weakness would keep him there for the rest of his
days.

Already he was beginning to keep irregular hours. Their
mother, telling them a bedtime story, would glance up at the
clock and say: 'Wherever has Daddy got to?' or, later in the
evening, more severely, 'Your father's staying late again', and
when he came in his face would be flushed and he would be

more than usually talkative. But that was only the beginning of his downfall. Things went well, or fairly well, for several years after that.

Their cottage belonged to a Mrs Herring. She and her husband had lived there for some time before Laura's parents had rented it, but, as he was an ex-stud groom with a pension and she prided herself on her superiority, they had never been happy or popular there. Her superiority might have been borne, or even played up to, for 'you've got to hold a candle to the fire', as some of the neighbours said, but it was accompanied by the to them intolerable vice of meanness. Not only had she kept herself to herself, as she boasted, but she had also kept her belongings to herself, down to the last shred of 'scratchings' when she boiled down her lard and the last cabbage-stalk from the garden. 'She wer' that near she 'udn't give away enough to make a pair of leggings for a skylark' was the reputation she left behind her.

She, on her side, had complained that the hamlet people were a rough, unmannerly lot. There was nobody fit to ask in for a game of cards and she did so like a bit of society, and she had long wanted to go to live near her married daughter, when, one Saturday afternoon, the children's father came, looking for a cottage not too far from his work. She made a great favour of getting out quickly, but her new tenants were not impressed, for she was asking a high rent, half a crown a week, more than anyone else in the hamlet paid. The neighbours had thought she would never let her house, for who could afford to pay that sum?

Laura's parents, with more knowledge of town prices, thought the house was well worth the rent, for it was two small thatched cottages made into one, with two bedrooms and a good garden. Of course, as they said, it had not the conveniences of a town house. Until they themselves had bought an oven grate and put it in the second cottage downstairs room, known as 'the wash-house', there was nowhere to bake the Sunday joint, and it was tiresome to have to draw water up from a well and irritating in wet weather to have to walk under an umbrella half-way down the garden to the earth closet. But the cottage living-room was a pleasant place, with its well-polished furniture, shelves of bright crockery, and red-and-black rugs laid down to 'take the tread' on the raddled tile floor.

In summer the window stood permanently open and hollyhocks and other tall flowers would push their way in and mingle with the geraniums and fuchsias on the window-sill.

This room was the children's nursery. Their mother called it that sometimes when they had been cutting out pictures and left scraps of paper on the floor. 'This room's nothing but a nursery,' she would say, forgetting for the moment that the nurseries she had presided over in her pre-marriage days were usually held up by her as patterns of neatness.

The room had one advantage over most nurseries. The door opened straight out on to the garden path and in fine weather the children were allowed to run in and out as they would. Even when it rained and a board was slipped, country fashion, into grooves in the doorposts to keep them in, they could still lean out over it and feel the rain splash on their hands and see the birds flicking their wings in the puddles and smell the flowers and wet earth while they sang: 'Rain, rain, go away, Come again another day.'

They had more garden than they needed at that time and one corner was given up to a tangle of currant and gooseberry bushes and raspberry canes surrounding an old apple tree. This jungle, as their father called it, was only a few feet square, but a child of five or seven could hide there and pretend it was lost, or hollow out a cave in the greenery and call it its house. Their father kept saying that he must get busy and lop the old unproductive apple tree and cut down the bushes to let in the light and air, but he was so seldom at home in daylight that for a long time nothing was done about it and they still had their hidy-houses and could still swing themselves up and ride astride on the low-hanging limb of the apple tree.

From there they could see the house and their mother going in and out, banging mats and rattling pails and whitening the flagstones around the doorway. Sometimes, when she went to the well, they would run after her and she would hold them tight and let them look down to where, framed in the green-slimy stones, the water reflected their faces, very small and far down.

'You must never come here alone,' she would say. 'I once knew a little boy who was drowned in a well like this.' Then, of course, they wanted to know where and when and why he was drowned, although they had heard the story as long as they could remember. 'Where was his mother?' 'Why was the well lid left open?' 'How did they get him out?' and 'Was he quite, quite dead? As dead as the mole we saw under the hedge one day?'

Beyond their garden in summer were fields of wheat and barley and oats which sighed and rustled and filled the air with sleepy pollen and earth scents. These fields were large and flat and stretched away to a distant line of trees set in the hedgerows. To the children at that time these trees marked the boundary of their world. Tall trees and smaller trees and one big bushy squat tree like a crouching animal – they knew the outline of each one by heart and looked upon them as children in more hilly districts look upon the peaks of distant, unvisited, but familiar mountains.

Beyond their world, enclosed by the trees, there was, they were told, a wider world, with other hamlets and villages and towns and the sea, and, beyond that, other countries where the people spoke languages different from their own. Their father had told them so. But, until they learned to read, they had no mental picture of these, they were but ideas, unrealized; whereas, in their own little world within the tree boundary, everything appeared to them more than life-size and more richly coloured.

They knew every slight rise in the fields and the moist lower places where the young wheat grew taller and greener, and the bank where the white violets grew, and the speciality of every hedgerow – honeysuckle, crab-apples, misty purple sloes, or long trails of white bryony berries through which the sun shone crimson as it did through the window at church: '*But you must not even touch one or your hand will poison your food.*'

And they knew the sounds of the different seasons, the skylarks singing high up out of sight over the green corn; the loud, metallic chirring of the mechanical reaper, the cheerful 'Who-o-as' and 'Werts up' of the ploughmen to their teams, and the rush of wings as the starlings wheeled in flocks over the stripped stubble.

There were other shadows than those of chasing clouds and wheeling bird flocks over those fields. Ghost stories and stories of witchcraft lingered and were half believed. No one cared to go after dark to the cross roads where Dickie Bracknell, the suicide, was buried with a stake through his entrails, or to approach the barn out in the fields where he had hung himself some time at the beginning of the century. Bobbing lights were said to have been seen and gurgling sounds heard there.

Far out in the fields by the side of a wood was a pool which was said to be bottomless and haunted by a monster. No one could say exactly what the monster was like, for no one living had seen it, but the general idea was that it resembled a large newt, perhaps as big as a bullock. Among the children this pool was known as 'the beast's pond' and none of them ever went near it. Few people went that way, for the pond was cut off from the fields by a piece of uncultivated waste, and there was no path anywhere near it. Some fathers and mothers did not believe there was a pond there. It was just a silly old tale, they said, that folks used at one time to frighten themselves with. But there was a pond, for, towards the end of their schooldays, Edmund and Laura plodded over several ploughed fields and scrambled through as many hedges and pushed their way through a waste of dried thistles and ragwort and stood at last by a dark, still, tree-shadowed pool. No monster was there, only dark water, dark trees and a darkening sky and a silence so deep they could hear their own hearts pounding.

Nearer home, beside the brook, was an old elder tree which was said to bleed human blood when cut, and that was because it was no ordinary tree, but a witch. Men and boys of a former generation had caught her listening outside the window of a neighbour's cottage and chased her with pitchforks until she reached the brook. Then, being a witch, she could not cross running water, so had turned herself into an elder tree on the bank. She must have turned herself back again, for, the next morning, she was seen fetching water from the well as usual, a poor, ugly, disagreeable old woman who denied having been outside her own door the night before. But the tree, which hitherto no one had noticed, still stood beside the brook and was still standing there fifty years later. Edmund and Laura once took a table knife, intending to cut it, but their courage failed them. 'What if it should really bleed? And what if the witch came out of it and ran after us?'

'Mother,' asked Laura one day, 'are there any witches now?' and her mother answered seriously, 'No. They seem to have all died out. There haven't been any in my time; but when I was your age there were plenty of old people alive who had known or even been ill-wished by one. And, of course,' she added as an afterthought, 'we know there were witches. We read about them in the Bible.' That settled it. Anything the Bible said must be true.

Edmund was at that time a quiet, thoughtful little boy, apt to ask questions which it puzzled his mother to answer. The neighbours said he thought too much and ought to be made to play more; but they liked him because of his good looks and quaint, old-fashioned good manners. Except when he fired questions at them.

'I shan't tell you,' some one would say when cornered by him. 'If I told you that you'd know as much as I do myself. Besides, what do it matter to you what makes the thunder and lightning. You sees it and hears it and are lucky if you're not struck dead by it, and that ought to be enough for you.' Others, more kindly disposed, or more talkative, would tell him that the thunder was the voice of God. Somebody had been wicked, perhaps Edmund himself, and God was angry; or that thunder was caused by the clouds knocking together; or warn him to keep away from trees during a thunderstorm because they had known a man who was struck dead while sheltering and the watch in his pocket had melted and run like quicksilver down his legs. Others would quote:

> Under oak there comes a stroke,
> Under elm there comes a calm,
> And under ash there comes a crash,

and Edmund would retire into himself to sort out this information.

He was a tall, slender child with blue eyes and regular features. When she had dressed him for their afternoon walk, his mother would kiss him and exclaim: 'I do declare he might be anybody's child. I can't see any difference between him and a young lord, and as for intelligence, he's too intelligent!'

Setting out on these walks, Laura must have looked a prim, old-fashioned little thing in her stiffly starched frock, with a white silk scarf tied in a bow under her chin and a couple of inches of knicker frill showing. 'Odd', the neighbours called her when discussing her in her presence, for she had dark eyes and pale yellow hair, and they did not approve of the mixture. 'Pity she ain't got your eyes,' they would say to her mother whose own eyes were blue; 'or even if she had dark hair like her father, 'twouldn't be so bad, but, as 'tis, she ain't neither one thing nor t'other. Cross-grained, they say them folks is whose eyes and hair don't match. But' – turning to Laura – 'never you mind, my poppet. Good looks ain't everything, and you can't help it if you did happen to be behind the door when they were being given out. And, after all' – comfortingly to her mother – 'she don't hurt, really. She's got a nice bit of colour in her cheeks.'

'You're all right. Always keep yourself clean and neat and try to have a pleasant, good-tempered expression, and you'll pass in a crowd,' her mother told her.

But that did not satisfy Laura. She was bent on improvement. She could not alter her eyes, but she tried to darken her hair with ink, put on in streaks with her father's new toothbrush. That only resulted in a sore bottom and lying in bed by daylight with her newly washed hair in tiny tight plaits which hurt her head. However, to her great joy, her hair soon began to darken naturally, and, after many false alarms, one of which was the fear it was turning red, it became a respectable brown, quite unnoticeable.

Other memories of those early years remained with her as little pictures, without background, and unrelated to anything which went before or came after. One was of walking over frosty fields with her father, her small knitted-gloved hand reaching up to his big knitted-gloved hand and the stubble beneath their feet clinking with little icicles until they came to a pinewood and crept under a rail and walked on deep, soft earth beneath tall, dark trees.

The wood was so dark and silent at first that it was almost frightening; but, soon, they heard the sounds of axes and saws at work and came out into a clearing where men were felling trees. They had built themselves a little house of pine branches and before it a fire was burning. The air was full of the sharp, piny scent of the smoke which drifted across the clearing in blue whorls and lay in sheets about the boughs of the unfelled trees beyond. Laura and her father sat on a tree-trunk before the fire and drank hot tea, which was poured for them from a tin can. Then her father filled the sack he had brought with logs and Laura's little basket was piled with shiny brown pine-cones and they went home. They must have gone home, although no trace of memory remained of the backward journey: only the joy of drinking hot tea so far from a house and the loveliness of shooting flames and blue smoke against blue-green pine boughs survived.

Another memory was of a big girl, with red hair, in a bright blue frock billowing over a green field, looking for mushrooms, and a man at the gate taking his clay pipe from his mouth to whisper behind his hand to a companion: 'That gal'll tumble to bits before they get her to church if they don't look sharp.'

'Patty tumble to bits? Tumble to bits? How could she?' Laura's mother looked rather taken aback when asked, and told her little daughter she must never, never listen to men talking. It was naughty to do that. Then she explained, rather lamely for her, that Patty must have done something wrong. Perhaps she'd told a lie, and Mr Arliss was afraid she might be struck dead, like the man and woman in the Bible. 'You remember them? I told you about them when you said you saw a ghost coming out of the clothes closet upstairs.'

That reference to her own misdeed sent Laura out to creep under the gooseberry bushes in the garden, where she thought it would puzzle even God to find her; but she was not satisfied. Why should Mr Arliss mind if Patty had told a lie? Plenty of

people told them and no one, so far, had been struck dead at
Lark Rise.

Forty years after, her mother laughed when reminded of this.
'Poor old Pat!' she said. 'She was a regular harum-scarum and
no mistake. But they did just manage to get her to church,
although it was said at the time they had to give her a sup of
brandy in the porch. Howsoever, she recovered enough to
dance at the wedding, I heard, and a fine sight she must have
looked in a white frock with blue bows all down the front. I
think that was the last time I ever heard of taking round the hat
to collect for the cradle at a wedding. It used to be quite the
usual thing with that class of people at one time.'

Then there was the picture of a man lying on straw at the
bottom of a farm cart with a white cloth over his face. The cart
had halted outside one of the houses and apparently the news of
its arrival had not got round, for, at first, only Laura was standing by. The tailboard of the cart had been removed and she
could see the man plainly, lying so still, so terribly still, that she
thought he was dead. It seemed a long time to her before his
wife rushed out, climbed into the car, and calling, 'My dear
one! My poor old man!' took the cloth from his face, revealing
a face almost as white, excepting for one long dark gash from
lips to one ear. Then he groaned and Laura's heart began beating again.

The neighbours gathered round and the story spread. He was
a stockman and had been feeding his fattening beasts when one
of them had accidentally caught a horn in his mouth and torn
his cheek open. He was taken at once to the Cottage Hospital in
the market town and his wound soon healed.

An especially vivid memory was of an April evening when
Laura was about three. Her mother had told her that the next
day was May Day and that Alice Shaw was going to be May
Queen and wear a daisy crown. 'I should like to be May Queen
and wear a daisy crown. Can't I have one, too, Mother?' asked
Laura.

'So you shall,' her mother replied. 'You run down to the play
place and pick some daisies and I'll make you a crown. You
shall be our May Queen.'

Off she ran with her little basket, but by the time she reached the plot of rough grass where the hamlet children played their country games it was too late; the sun had set, and the daisies were all asleep. There were thousands and thousands of them, but all screwed up, like tightly shut eyes. Laura was so disappointed that she sat down in the midst of them and cried. Only a few tears and very soon dried, then she began to look about her. The long grass in which she sat was a little wet, perhaps with dew, or perhaps from an April shower, and the pink-tipped daisy buds were a little wet, too, like eyes that had gone to sleep crying. The sky, where the sun had set, was all pink and purple and primrose. There was no one in sight and no sound but the birds singing and, suddenly, Laura realized that it was nice to be there, out of doors by herself, deep in the long grass, with the birds and the sleeping daisies.

A little later in her life came the evening after a pig-killing when she stood alone in the pantry where the dead animal hung suspended from a hook in the ceiling. Her mother was only a few feet away. She could hear her talking cheerfully to Mary Ann, the girl who fetched their milk from the farm and took the children for walks when their mother was busy. Through the thin wooden partition she could hear her distinctive giggle as she poured water from a jug into the long, slippery lengths of chitterlings her mother was manipulating. Out there in the wash-house they were busy and cheerful, but in the pantry where Laura stood was a dead, cold silence.

She had known that pig all its life. Her father had often held her over the door of its sty to scratch its back and she had pushed lettuce and cabbage stalks through the bars for it to enjoy. Only that morning it had routed and grunted and squealed because it had had no breakfast. Her mother had said its noise got on her nerves and her father had looked uncomfortable, although he had passed it off by saying: 'No. No breakfast today, piggy. You're going to have a big operation by and by and there's no breakfast before operations.'

Now it had had its operation and there it hung, cold and stiff and so very, very dead. Not funny at all any more, but in some queer way dignified. The butcher had draped a long, lacy piece of fat from its own interior over one of its forelegs, in the manner in which ladies of that day sometimes carried a white lacy shawl, and that last touch seemed to Laura utterly heartless. She stayed there a long time, patting its hard, cold side and wondering that a thing so recently full of life and noise could be so still. Then, hearing her mother call her, she ran out of the door farthest from where she was working lest she should be scolded for crying over a dead pig.

There was fried liver and fat for supper and when Laura said, 'No, thank you,' her mother looked at her rather suspiciously, then said: 'Well, perhaps better not, just going to bed and all; but here's a nice bit of sweetbread. I was saving it for Daddy, but you have it. You'll like that.' And Laura ate the sweetbread and dipped her bread in the thick, rich gravy and refused to think about the poor pig in the pantry, for, although only five years old, she was learning to live in this world of compromises.

XVIII

'Once Upon a Time'

No one who saw Laura's mother at that time would have wondered at the hasty, youthful marriage which turned her husband's contemplated sojourn of a few months into a permanent abode. She was a slight, graceful girl with a wild-rose complexion and hair the colour of a new penny which she parted in the middle and drew down to a knot at the back of her head because a gentleman of the family, where she had been nurse to the children before her marriage, had told her she ought always to do it like that.

'A pocket Venus,' she said he had called her. 'But quite nicely,' she hastened to assure her listener, 'for he was a married gentleman with no nonsense about him.' Another thing she told her children about her nursing days was that when visitors were staying in the house it was the custom for some member of the family to bring them up to the nursery after dinner to listen to the bed-time stories she was telling the children. 'A regular amusement,' she said it was with them, and her own children did not think that at all strange, for the bed-time stories were now being told to them and they knew how exciting they were.

Some of them were short stories, begun and finished in an evening, fairy stories and animal stories and stories of good and bad children, the good ones rewarded and the bad ones punished, according to the convention of that day. A few of these were part of the stock-in-trade of all tellers of stories to children, but far more of them were of her own invention, for she said it was easier to make up a tale than to try to remember one. The children liked her own stories best. 'Something out of your own head, Mother,' they would beg, and she would wrinkle up her brow and pretend to think hard, then begin: 'Once upon a time.'

One story remained with Laura long after hundreds of others had become a blur of pleasurable memory. Not because it was one of her mother's best, for it was not, but because it had a colour scheme which appealed to a childish taste. It was about a little girl who crept under a bush on a heath, 'just like Hardwick Heath, where we went blackberrying, you know', and found a concealed opening which led to an underground palace in which all the furniture and hangings were pale blue and silver. 'Silver tables and silver chairs and silver plates to eat off and all the cushions and curtains made of pale blue satin.' The heroine had marvellous adventures, but they left no impression on Laura's mind, while the blue and silver, deep down under the earth, shone with a kind of moonlight radiance in her imagination. But when her mother, at her urgent request, tried to tell the story again the magic was gone, although she introduced silver floors and silver ceilings, hoping to please her. Perhaps she overdid it.

Then there were serial stories which went on in nightly instalments for weeks, or perhaps months, for nobody wanted them to end and the teller's invention never flagged. There was one, however, which came to a sudden and tragic conclusion.

One night when it was bedtime, or past bedtime, and the children had begged for more and been given it and were still begging for more, their mother lost patience and startled them both by saying, 'and then he came to the sea and fell in and was eaten by a shark, and that was the end of poor Jimmy', and the end of their story, too, for what further developments were possible?

Then there were the family stories, each one of which they knew by heart and could just as well have told to each other. Their favourite was the one they called 'Granny's Golden Footstool'. It was short and simple enough. Their father's parents had at one time kept a public-house and livery stables in Oxford and the story ran that, either going to, or coming from, the 'Horse and Rider', their grandfather had handed their grandmother into the carriage and placed a box containing a thousand pounds in gold at her feet, saying: 'It's not every lady who can ride in her own carriage with a golden footstool.'

They must have been on their way there with the purchase money, for they can have brought no golden footstool away with them. Before that adventure, made possible by a legacy left to the grandmother by one of her relatives, the grandfather had been a builder in a small way, and, after it, he went back to building again, in a still smaller way, presumably, for by the time Laura was born the family business had disappeared and her father was working for wages.

The thousand pounds had vanished as completely as Jimmy after the shark had eaten him, and all they could do about it was to try to imagine what so much gold together must have looked like and to plan what they would do with such a sum if they had it now. Even their mother liked talking about it, although, as she said, she had no patience with wasteful, extravagant ways, such as some people she knew had got, and them proud and set up when they ought to be ashamed of themselves for coming down in the world.

And, just as they prided themselves on the golden footstool and the accompanying tradition that their grandmother was 'a lady by birth' who had made a runaway marriage with their grandfather, almost every family in the hamlet prided itself upon some family tradition which, in its own estimation, at least, raised it above the common mass of the wholly uninteresting. An uncle or a great-uncle had owned a cottage which, in the course of time, had been magnified into a whole row of houses; or some one in the family had once kept a shop or a public-house, or farmed his own land. Or they boasted of good blood, even if it came illegitimately. One man claimed to be the great-grandson of an earl, 'on the wrong side of the blanket, of course,' he admitted; but he liked to talk about it, and his listener, noticing, perhaps for the first time, his fine figure and big, hooked nose, and considering the reputation of a certain wild young nobleman of a former generation, would feel inclined to believe there was some foundation for his story.

Another of Edmund and Laura's family stories, more fantastic, though not so well substantiated as that of the golden footstool, was that one of their mother's uncles, when a very young man, shut his father in a box and himself ran away to the Australian goldfields. In answer to their questions as to why he had shut his father up in a box, how he had got him into it, and how the father had got out again, their mother could only say that she did not know. It had all happened before her own father was born. It was a large family and he was the youngest. But she had seen the box: it was a long oak coffer that could well have held a man, and that was the story she had been told as long as she could remember.

That must have been eighty years before, and the uncle was never heard of again, but they never tired of talking about him and wondering if he found any gold. Perhaps he had made a fortune at the diggings and died without children and without making a will. Then the money would be theirs, wouldn't it? Perhaps it was even now in Chancery, waiting for them to claim it. Several families in the hamlet had money in Chancery. They knew it was there because one of the Sunday newspapers printed each week a list of names of people who had fortunes waiting, and their names had been there, in print, 'as large as life and twice as natural'. True, as the children's father said, most of their names were common ones, but if this was pointed out to them they were quite offended and hinted that when they could raise a few pounds to 'hire a lawyer chap' to set about claiming it, no disbeliever would participate.

The children had not seen their names in print, but they enjoyed planning what they would do with their Chancery money. Edmund said he would buy a ship and visit every country in the world. Laura thought she would like a house full of books in the middle of a wood, and their mother declared she would be quite satisfied if she had an income of thirty shillings a week, 'paid regular and to be depended upon'.

Their Chancery money was a chimera, and none of them throughout their lives had more than a few pounds at a time, but their wishes were more or less granted. Edmund crossed the sea many times and saw four out of the five continents; Laura had her house full of books, if not actually in a wood, with a wood somewhere handy; and their poor mother, towards the end of her life, got her modest thirty shillings a week, for that was the exact sum to which the Canadian Government made up her small income when granting her her Mother's Pension. The memory of that wish gave an added bitterness to the tears she shed for the first few years when the monthly cheque arrived.

But all that was far in the future on those winter evenings when they sat in the firelight, the two children on little stools at their mother's feet, while she knitted their socks and told them stories or sang. They had had their evening meal and their father's plate stood over a saucepan of water on the hob, keeping warm. Laura loved to watch the warm light flickering on the walls, lighting up one thing after another and casting dark shadows, including their own, more than life-size and excitingly grotesque.

Edmund joined in the chorus of such things as 'There is a Tavern' and 'Little Brown Jug' but Laura refrained, by special request, for she had no ear for music and they said her singing put them out of tune. But she loved to watch the firelight shadows and to hear her mother's voice singing to sweet melancholy airs of a pale host of fair maidens who pined and faded for love. There was 'Lily Lyle, Sweet Lily Lyle', which began:

'Twas a still, calm night and the moon's pale light
     Shone over hill and dale
When friends mute with grief stood around the deathbed
     Of their loved, lost Lily Lyle.
Heart as pure as forest lily,
     Never knowing guile,
Had its home within the bosom
     Of sweet Lily Lyle.

Several other dying maidens were celebrated in similar words to similar airs. Then there was 'The Old Armchair' and 'The Gipsy's Warning' and a group of cottage songs apparently dating from the beginning of the century, such as:

'Twas a fine clear night and the moon shone bright
   When the village clock struck eight
And Mary hastened with delight
   Unto the garden gate.

But what was there that made her sad?
The gate was there, but not the lad,
   Which caused poor Mary to sigh and say,
'He never shall make a goose of me.'

She traced the garden here and there and the village clock struck
     nine,
   Which caused poor Mary to sigh and say
'He never shall be mine.'

She traced the garden here and there and the village clock struck
     ten,
   Young William caught her in his arms,
Never to part again.

Now he'd been to buy the ring that day and he had been such a
     long, long way,
   So how could Mary so cruel prove
As to banish the lad whom she dearly loved?

So down in a cot by the riverside
William and Mary now reside.
And she's blessed the hour that she did wait
For her absent lover at the garden gate.

Sometimes the children would talk about what they would do when they were grown up. Their fortune had already been mapped out for them. Edmund was to be apprenticed to a trade – a carpenter's, their mother thought; it was cleaner work than that of a mason and carpenters did not drink in public-houses as masons did, and people respected them more.

Laura was to go as nursemaid under one of her mother's old nurse friends with whom she had kept up a correspondence. Then, in time, she would be head nurse herself in what was then known as 'a good family'; where, if she did not marry, she would be sure of a home for life, for the imaginary good family her mother had in mind was of the kind where loved old nurses dressed in black silk and had a room of their own in which to receive confidences. But these ideas did not interest the children so much as that of having houses of their own in which they could do as they liked. 'And you'll come to stay with me and I shall spring-clean the house and bake some pies the day before,' promised Laura, who knew from her mother's example what was due to an honoured guest. Edmund's idea was that he would have treacle mixed with milk for dinner without any bread at all, but then he was much younger than she was.

Neither story-telling, singing, nor talking could go on for ever. The time always came, and always came too soon for them, when their mother would whisk them off to bed, 'For your father cannot be much longer now,' and stay to hear them say their prayers, 'Our Father' and 'Gentle Jesus', then 'Gaw-bless dear Mammy an' Daddy an' dear little brother [or sister] an' all kind friends an' alations . . .'

Laura was not sure who the friends were, but she knew that the relations included the Candleford aunts, her father's sisters, who sent them nice parcels at Christmas, and the cousins whose wardrobes she inherited. The aunts were kind – she knew that, for when she opened the parcels her mother would say, 'It's very kind of Edith, I'm sure,' or, more warmly, although the parcel might not be as exciting, 'If ever there was a good kind soul in this world, it's your Aunt Ann.'

Candleford was a wonderful place. Her mother said there were rows of shops there, simply stuffed with toys and sweets

and furs and muffs and watches and chains and other delightful
things. 'You should see them at Christmas,' she said, 'all lit up
like a fair. All you want then is a purseful of money!' The
Candleford people had pursefuls of money, for wages were
higher there, and they had gas to light them to bed and drew
their water out of taps, instead of up from a well. She had heard
her parents say so. 'What he wants is a job at some place such as
Candleford,' her father would say of some promising boy.
'He'd do himself some good there. Here, there's nothing.' This
surprised Laura, for she had thought there were many exciting
things about the hamlet. 'Is there a brook there?' she asked,
rather hoping there was not, and she was told there was a river,
which was wider than any brook and had a stone bridge, instead
of a rickety old plank to cross by. A magnificent place, indeed,
and she hoped soon to see it. 'Come the summer' her father had
said, but the summer had come and gone again and nothing
more had been said about borrowing Polly and the spring cart.
Then, always, something or other happened to push the idea of
Candleford to the back of her mind. One dreary November the
pigs were ill. They refused to eat and became so weak they had
to lean against the rails of their sties for support. Some of them
died and were buried in quicklime, which was said to burn up
their bodies in no time. Horrible thought to be dead and buried
in quicklime and soon nothing left of what had been so much
alive! Her mother said it was a far worse thought that the poor
people had lost their pigs, after paying for their food all those
months, too, and when their own pigs were killed – both had
escaped – she was more than usually generous with the plates of
liver and fat and other oddments always sent to neighbours as a
compliment. Many of the people who had lost their pigs still
owed for the food. They had depended upon being able to pay
for that in kind when the animal was fattened. One man took to
poaching and was caught and sent to prison, then every one had
to take half loaves and small screws of tea and sugar to help his
wife to keep the home going, until the whisper went round that
she had three different lots of butter in the house, given by
different people to whom she had pleaded poverty, and that the
J.P. himself had sent a sovereign. People looked sourly upon

her after that was known, and said, 'Crime seems to pay nowadays.'

XIX

'A Bit of a Tell'

SOMETIMES, instead of saying, 'Here there's nothing,' her
father would say, 'Here there's nobody,' meaning nobody he
thought worth considering. But Laura never tired of considering the hamlet neighbours and, as she grew older, would
listen to, and piece together, the things they said until she had
learned quite a lot from them. She liked the older women best
such as Old Queenie, Old Sally, and Old Mrs Prout, old
countrywomen who still wore sun-bonnets and stayed in their
own homes and gardens and cared not at all about what was in
fashion and very little for gossip. They said they did not hold
with gadding about from house to house. Queenie had her lace-
making and her beehives to watch; Old Sally her brewing and
her bacon to cure; if anybody wanted to see them, they knew
where to find them. 'Crusty old dames,' some of the younger
women called them, especially when one of them had refused to
lend them something. To Laura they seemed like rocks, keeping
firm in their places, while those about them drifted around,
always on the look-out for some new sensation. But only a few
were left who kept to the old country ways, and the other
women were interesting, too. Although they wore much the
same kind of clothes and lived in similar houses, no two of them
were really alike.

In theory all the hamlet women were on friendly terms with
each other, at least as far as 'passing the time of day' when they
met, for they had an almost morbid dread of giving offence and
would go out of their way to be pleasant to other women they
would rather not have seen. As Laura's mother said: 'You can't
afford to be on bad terms with anybody in a small place like
this.' But in that, as in more sophisticated societies, there was a
tendency to form sets. The members of the slightly more pros-

perous of these, consisting mostly of the newly married and those of the older women whose children were grown up and off their hands, would change into a clean apron in the afternoon and stay quietly at home, sewing or ironing, or put on their hats and go out to call upon their friends, carefully knocking at the door before they lifted the latch. The commoner kind burst hatless into their neighbour's houses to borrow something or to relate some breathless item of news, or they would spend the afternoon shouting it across gardens or from doorsteps, or hold long, bantering conversations with the baker, or the oilman, or any one else who happened to call and found themselves unable to get away without downright rudeness.

Laura's mother belonged to the first category and those who came to her house were mostly her own special friends. They had a few other callers, however, and those Laura thought far more interesting than young Mrs Massey, who was always making baby's clothes, although at that time she had no baby (Laura thought afterwards, when a baby arrived for her, it was a lucky coincidence), or Mrs Hadley, who was always talking about her daughter in service, or Mrs Finch, who was 'not too strong' and had to be given the best seat, nearest the fire. The only interesting thing about her was the little blue bottle of smelling-salts she carried, and that ceased to interest after she had handed it to Laura, telling her to give a good sniff, then laughed when the tears ran down her cheeks. Not at all Laura's idea of a joke!

She liked Rachel much better. Although never invited, she would drift in sometimes, 'just to have a tell', as she expressed it. Her 'tells' were worth hearing, for she knew everything that happened, 'and a good lot more, too', her enemies said. 'Ask Rachel,' some one would say with a shrug if the whole of the facts of a happening were not known, and Rachel, when appealed to, if she, too, were not quite sure, would say in her loud, hearty voice, 'Well to tell the truth, I haven't ever quite got to the bottom of that business. But I 'ull know, that I 'ull, for I'll go to th' fountain-head and ax.' And off she would march with all the good-natured effrontery imaginable to ask Mrs Beaby if it was 'a fac'' that her young Em was leaving her place before

her year was up, or Charley's mother if it was true that he and
Nell had quarrelled coming home from church last Sunday, and
had they made it up, or were they still 'off at hooks', as they
called an estrangement.

When Rachel dropped in for a tell, others were sure to
follow. Laura, lying on her stomach on the hearth-rug with a
picture book propped up before her, or cutting out patterns
from paper in a corner, would hear their voices rising and falling or dropping to a whisper when some item they were discussing was not considered suitable for children's ears. She
would sometimes long to ask questions, but dare not, for it was
a strict rule there that children should be seen, but not heard. It
was better not even to laugh when something funny was said,
for that might call attention to oneself and some one might say:
'That child's gettin' too knowin'. I hope she ain't goin' to turn
out one of them forrard sort, for I can't abide 'em.' At that her
mother would bridle and say that, far from being forward, she
was rather young for her age, and as to being knowing, she
didn't suppose she had heard what was said, but had laughed
because they were laughing. At the same time, she took care to
send Laura upstairs, or out into the garden for something, when
she thought the conversation was taking an unsuitable turn.

Sometimes one of them would let fall a remark about the
vague far-distant days before the children were born. 'My ole
gran-fer used to say that all the land between here and the
church wer' left by will to th' poor o' th' parish in the old times;
all common land of turf and fuzz 'twas then; but 'twer' all stole
away an' cut up into fields,' and another would agree, 'Yes, so
I've allus heard.'

Sometimes one of them would bring out some surprising
saying, as Patty Wardup did when the rest of the company were
discussing Mrs Eames's fur cape: she couldn't have bought it
and it certainly did not grow upon her back, yet she had appeared in it last Sunday at church, and not so much as a word to
anybody as to how she had got it. True, as Mrs Baker suggested,
it did look something like a coachman's shoulder tippet – dark,
thick fur, bearskin, they called it – and she had once said she
had a brother who was a coachman somewhere up country.

Then Patty, who had been pensively twisting her doorkey between her fingers and taking no part in the conversation, said quietly: 'The golden ball rolls to everybody's feet once in a lifetime. That's what my Uncle Jarvis used to say and I've seen it myself, over and over.'

What golden ball? And who was her Uncle Jarvis? And what had a golden ball to do with Mrs Eames's fur tippet? No wonder they all laughed and said, 'She's dreaming as usual!'

Patty was not a native of those parts, but had come there only a few years before as housekeeper to an elderly man whose wife had died. As was the custom when no relative was available, he had applied to the Board of Guardians for a housekeeper and Patty had been selected as the most suitable inmate of the workhouse at the time. She was a plump little woman with pale brown, satin-sleek hair and mild blue eyes, well set off on her arrival by the bunch of forget-me-nots in her bonnet. How she had come to be in the workhouse was a mystery, for she was still in the forties, able-bodied, and evidently belonging to a slightly higher stratum of society than her new employer. She told her story to no one and no one asked her for it. 'Ax no questions and you'll be told no lies, although you may hear a few without axing' was the hamlet motto. But she was generally acknowledged to be 'superior', for did she not plait her hair in fives every day, instead of in threes all the week and in fives on Sunday, and exchange her white apron after dinner for a small black satin one with beaded trimming? She was a good cook, too. Amos was lucky. On the very first Sunday after she arrived she made a meat pudding with a crust so light a puff of wind would have blown it away and with thick, rich gravy that gushed out in a stream when the knife was stuck into it. Old Amos said the very smell made his mouth water and began inquiring how soon after his wife's death it would be decent to put up the banns. It was tacitly understood that such engagements would lead to marriage.

But she did not marry Old Amos. He had a son – Old Amos and Young Amos to the hamlet – and Young Amos got in his proposal first and was accepted. The hamlet women did not hold, as they said, with the wife being older than the husband

and Patty was a good ten years older than her intended; but they thought Young Amos had done well for himself, especially when, immediately before the wedding, a cartload of furniture arrived, together with a trunk of clothes which Patty had somehow managed to save from the wreck of her fortunes and hide up somewhere.

They had already thought Patty was superior and they were sure of it when it became known that the furniture included a feather-bed, a leather-covered couch with chairs to match and a stuffed owl in a glass case. Somehow they learned, or perhaps Young Amos told them, for he was inclined to be boastful, that Patty had been married before – to a publican, if you please! And then to come down to the workhouse, poor thing! But what a mercy she'd had the wit to hide up her good things. If she hadn't, the Guardians would have had them.

Patty and Amos were a model couple when they went to the market town to shop on a Saturday night, Patty in her black silk with flounces, her good Paisley shawl and her ivory-handled umbrella, rolled up in its shiny black macintosh case to preserve the silk cover. But, gradually another side of the picture emerged. Patty was fond of her glass of stout. Nobody blamed her for that, for it was well known she could afford it and she must have been used to it in her public-house days. Presently it was noticed that on their marketing nights Amos and Patty came later and later from town, and then, one sad night, somebody passed them on the road and reported that Patty had had so many glasses of stout, or of something stronger, that it was as much as Amos could do to coax her along. Some said he was carrying her. That accounted for the workhouse, they said, and they waited for Amos to begin beating her. But he never did, nor did he ever mention her weakness or complain about her to anybody.

Her lapses occurred only at week-ends and she was not noisy or quarrelsome, only helpless. The hamlet would be in darkness and most of the people in bed when they stole home silently and Amos carried Patty upstairs. He may even have thought that none of the neighbours knew of his wife's failing. If so, it was a vain hope, it sometimes seemed as if the very hedges had eyes and the roadway ears, for, next morning, the whisper ran round as to which public-house Patty had favoured, the nature and number of her drinks, and how far she had got on her home- ward way before her potations overcome her. But if Amos did not mind, why should other folks? 'Twas not as if she'd made a beast of herself in public. So Patty and Amos, with that one reservation, were still looked upon as a model couple.

It was one of the children's treats to be invited into her house to see her stuffed owl and other treasures, which included some pressed flowers from the Holy Land in a frame made of olive wood from the Mount of Olives. Another treasure was a fan made of long white ostrich feathers which she would take out of its case and show them, then fan herself gently as she re- clined on her couch with her feet up. 'I've seen better times,' she would say in her more talkative moods. 'Yes, I've seen better times, but I've never seen a better husband than Amos, and I like this little house where I can shut the door and do as I like. After all, a public's never your own. Anybody who's got two pennies to rub together can come in and out as they like, with- out so much as a knock at the door or a "by your leave", and what's grand furniture as isn't your own, for you can't call it that when other people have the use of it.' And she would curl up on her couch and shut her eyes, for, although she was never known to get tipsy at home, her breath sometimes had a queer, sweetish smell which an older person might have recognized as that of gin. 'Now, run along,' she would say, opening one eye; 'and lock the door behind you and put the key on the window- sill. I don't want any more visitors and I'm not going out. This isn't one of my visiting days.'

Then there was a young married woman named Gertie who passed as a beauty, entirely on the strength of a tiny waist and simpering smile. She was a great reader of novelettes and had romantic ideas. Before her marriage she had been a housemaid at one of the country mansions where men-servants were kept, and their company and compliments had spoiled her for her kind, honest great cart-horse of a husband. She loved to talk about her conquests, telling of the time Mr Pratt, the butler, had danced with her four times at the servants' ball, and how jealous her John had been. He had been invited for her sake but could not dance, and had sat there all the evening, like a great gowk, in his light-grey Sunday suit, with his great red hands hanging down between his knees, and a chrysanthemum in his buttonhole as big as a pancake.

She had worn her white silk, the one she was afterwards married in, and her hair had been curled by a real hairdresser – the maids had clubbed together to pay for his attendance, and he had afterwards stayed for the dancing and paid special attention to Gertrude. 'And you should've seen our John, his eyes simply rolling with jealousy ...' But, if she managed to get so far, she was then interrupted. No one wanted to hear about her conquests, but they were willing to hear about the dresses. What did the cook wear? Black lace over a red silk underslip. That sounded handsome. And the head housemaid and the stillroom maid, and so on, down to the tweeny, who, it had to be confessed, could afford nothing more exciting than her best frock of grey cloth.

Gertie was the only one of them all who discussed her relations with her husband. 'I don't think our Johnny loves me any more,' she would sigh, 'He went off to work this morning without kissing me.' Or, 'Our John's getting a regular chawbacon. He went to sleep and snored in his chair after tea last night. I felt that lonely I could have cried me eyes out.' And the more robust characters would laugh and ask her what more she expected of a man who had been at work in the fields all day, or say, 'Times is changed, my gal. You ain't courtin' no longer.'

Gertie was a fool and the hamlet laughing-stock for a year or so; then young John arrived and the white silk was cut up to make him a christening robe and Gertie forgot her past triumphs in the more recent one of producing such a paragon. 'Isn't he lovely?' she would say, exhibiting her red, shapeless lump of a son, and those who had been most unsympathetic with her former outpourings would be the first to declare him a marvellous boy. 'He's the very spit of his dad; but he's got your eyes, Gertie. My word! He's going to break some hearts when the time comes, you'll see.' As time went on, Gertie grew red and lumpy herself. Gone were the wasp waist and the waxen pallor she had thought so genteel. But she still managed to keep her romantic ideas, and the last time Laura saw her, by that time a middle-aged woman, she assured her that her daughter's recent marriage to a stable-boy was 'a regular romance in real life', although, as far as her listener could gather, it was what the hamlet people of the preceding generation would have called 'a pushed on, hugger-mugger sort of affair'.

Laura did not like Gertie's face. Her features were not bad, but she had protruding pale blue eyes of which the whites were always faintly bloodshot, and her complexion was of a sickly yellowish shade. Even her small mouth, so much admired by some of the hamlet judges of beauty, was repulsive to a child. It was drawn up so close that the lips made tiny wrinkles, like stitches round a buttonhole. 'A mouth like a hen's backside', one rude man said of it.

But there was one visiting neighbour Laura loved to look at, for her face reminded her of that on the cameo brooch her mother used to pin her lace collar on Sundays, and her black hair rippled down from its centre parting as though that also was carved. Her fine head had a slight droop that showed up the line of her neck and shoulders and, although her clothes were no better than those of other people, they looked better on her. She was always in black, for no sooner was the year and a half mourning up for one great-uncle or first or second cousin than another died. Or, failing an actual death, she decided it would not be worth while to 'bring out her colours' with some distant relative over eighty or 'just at the last'. If she knew that black suited her, she was too wise to mention that fact. People would have thought her vain, or peculiar, to wear black for choice, whereas mourning there was no gainsaying.

'Mother,' said Laura one day after this neighbour had gone, 'doesn't Mrs Merton look lovely?'

Her mother laughed. 'Lovely? No. Though some might think her good-looking. She's too pale and melancholy for my taste and her nose is too long.'

Mrs Merton, as Laura remembered her in after years, might have sat for a picture as the Tragic Muse. She was of a melancholy nature. 'I've supped sorrow with a spoon,' she was never tired of saying. 'I've supped sorrow with a spoon and sorrow will always be my lot.' Yet, as the children's mother reminded her, she had little to complain of. She had a good husband and not too large a family. As well as the distant relations, some of whom she had never seen, she had lost one child in infancy and her father had recently died of old age, and the loss of her pig from swine fever two years before was admittedly a serious affliction; but these were losses such as any one might experience. Many had, and yet managed to get over them without talking about supping sorrow.

Does melancholy attract misfortune? Or is it true that past, present and future are one, only divided by our time sense? Mrs Merton was fated to become in her old age the tragic figure she had looked when young. Her husband was already dead when her only son and two grandsons were killed in the 1914–18 War and she was left practically alone in the world.

By that time she had gone to live in another village, and Laura's mother, herself bereaved by the War, walked over to see her and sympathize. She found her a sad but resigned old woman. There was no longer any talk about supping sorrow, no mourning her own woes, but a quiet acceptance of the world as it then was and a resolute attempt at cheerfulness.

It was spring and her room had flowers in pots and vases. The air was rather faint with the scent of them, her visitor noticed; then, looking more closely, she found they were not garden flowers. Every pot and jug and vase was filled with hawthorn blossom.

She was rather shocked at this, for, although less superstitious than many countrywomen, she herself would not have brought may blossom indoors. It might be unlucky, or it might not, but there was no sense in running unnecessary risks.

'Aren't you afraid all this may'll bring you bad luck?' she asked Mrs Merton as they sipped their tea.

Mrs Merton smiled, and a smile from her was almost as unusual as to see may indoors. 'How can it?' she said. 'I've got nobody else to lose. I've always been fond of those flowers. So I thought I'd bring some of them in and enjoy them. My thread's spun as far as luck's concerned.'

Politics were seldom mentioned by the women. If they did come up it was usually by way of comment on some husband's excessive zeal. 'Why can't he leave such things alone? 'Tis no business of his'n,' some wife would say. 'What does it matter to him who governs? Whoever 'tis, they won't give us nothing, and they can't take nothing away from us, for you can't get blood from a stone.'

Some would discriminate and say it was a pity the men had taken up with these Liberal notions. 'If they've got to vote, why not vote Tory and keep in with the gentry? You never hear of Liberals giving the poor a bit of coal or a blanket at Christmas.' As, indeed, you did not, for there was no Liberal in the parish but bought his own coals by the hundredweight and might think himself lucky if his wife had a blanket for each bed.

A few of the older men were equally poor-spirited. One election day the children, coming home from school, met an old, semi-bedridden neighbour, riding, propped up with cushions, in a luxurious carriage to the polling station. A few days afterwards, when Laura had taken him some small delicacy from her mother, he whispered to her at parting: 'Tell y're dad I voted Liberal. He! He! They took th' poor old hoss to th' water, but he didn't drink out o' their trough. Not he!'

When Laura gave her father the message he did not seem as pleased as their neighbour had expected. He said he thought it was 'a bit low down to roll up in anybody's carriage to vote against them'; but her mother laughed and said: 'Serves 'em right for dragging the poor old hunks out of bed in that weather.'

Apart from politics, the hamlet people's attitude towards those they called 'the gentry' was peculiar. They took a pride in their rich and powerful country-house neighbours, especially when titled. The old Earl in the next parish was spoken of as 'our Earl' and when the flag, flown from the tower of his mansion to show he was in residence, could be seen floating above tree-tops they would say: 'I see our family's at home again.'

They sometimes saw him pass through the hamlet in his carriage, an old, old man, sunk deep in cushions and half-buried in rugs, often too comatose to be aware of, or acknowledge, their curtsies. He had never spoken to them or given them anything, for they did not live in his cottages, and in the way of Christmas coals and blankets he had his own parish to attend to; but the men worked on his land, though not directly employed by him, and by some inherited instinct they felt he belonged to them.

For wealth without rank or birth they had small respect. When a rich retired hatter bought a neighbouring estate and set up as a country gentleman, the hamlet was scandalized. 'Who's he?' they said. 'Only a shopkeeper pretending to be gentry. I 'udn't work for him, no, not if he paid me in gold!' One man who had been sent to clean out a well in his stable-yard and had seen him, said: 'I'd a good mind to ask him to sell me a hat'; and that was repeated for weeks as a great joke. Laura was told in after years that their better-educated neighbours were almost as prejudiced; they did not call on the newly rich family. That was before the days when a golden key could open any door.

Landowners of established rank and stern or kindly JPs and their ladies were respected. Some of the sons or grandsons of local families were said to be 'wild young devils' and were looked upon with a kind of horrified admiration. The tradition of the Hell-fire Club had not entirely faded, and one young nobleman was reputed to have 'gambled away' one of his family estates at one sitting. There were hints of more lurid orgies in which a bunch of good-looking country girls were supposed to figure, and a saintly curate, an old white-haired man, went to admonish the young spark, at that time living alone in a wing of the otherwise deserted family mansion. There was no record of the conversation, but the result was known. The older man was pushed or kicked down the front door flight of steps and the door was banged and bolted against him. Then, the story went, he raised himself to his knees and prayed aloud for 'the poor sinful child' within. The gardener, greatly daring, supported him to his cottage and made him rest before attempting to walk home.

But the great majority of the country gentlepeople lived decent, if, according to hamlet standards, not particularly useful lives. In summer the carriage was at the door at three o'clock in the afternoon to take the lady of the house and her grown-up daughters, if any, to pay calls. If they found no one in, they left cards, turned down at the corner, or not turned down, according to etiquette. Or they stayed at home to receive their own callers and played croquet and drank tea under spreading cedars on exquisitely kept lawns. In winter they hunted with the local pack; and, summer and winter, they never failed to attend Sunday morning service at their parish church. They had always a smile and a nod for their poorer neighbours who saluted them, with more substantial favours for those who lived in the cottages on their estates. As to their inner lives, the commonalty knew no more than the Britons knew of the Romans who inhabited the villas dotted about the countryside; and it is doubtful if the county families knew more of their poorer neighbours than the Romans did of theirs, in spite of speaking the same language.

Here and there the barrier of caste was overstepped. Perhaps by some young man or girl who, in advance of their time, realized that the population beyond their park gates were less 'the poor' in a lump than individual men and women who happened to have been born to poverty. Of such it was sometimes said: 'He's different, Master Raymond is; you can say anything to him, he's more like one of ourselves than one of the gentry. Makes you split your sides, he does, with some of his tales, and he's got a feeling heart, too, and don't button his pockets too tight. Good thing if there were more like him.' Or: 'Miss Dorothy, now, she's different. No asking questions and questions when she comes to see anybody; but she sets her down and if you've a mind to tell her anything, you can and know it won't go no further. I udn't mind seeing her come in when I was in the godspeed of washday, and that's saying something.'

On the other hand, there were old nurses and trusted maids who had come to be regarded as individuals and loved as true friends, irrespective of class, by those they served. And the name of 'friend', when applied to them in words, gave them a deeper satisfaction than any material benefit. A retired lady's maid, whom Laura knew later, spoke to her many times with much feeling of what she evidently regarded as the crown of her

experiences. She had been for many years maid to a titled lady
moving in high society, had dressed her for royal courts, un-
dressed and put her to bed in illness, travelled with her, indulged
her innocent vanities, and knew, for she could not help knowing, being so near her person, her most intimate griefs. At last
'Her Ladyship', grown old, lay upon her deathbed and her
maid, who was helping to nurse her, happened to be alone in the
room with her, her relatives, none of whom were very near
ones, being downstairs at dinner. ' "Raise me up," she said, and
I raised her up, and when she put her arms round my neck to
help lift her, she kissed me and said, *"My friend,"* ' and Miss
Wilson, twenty years after, considered that kiss and those two
words a more ample reward for her years of devotion than the
nice cottage and annuity she received under the will of the poor
lady.

XX

Mrs Herring

WHEN Laura said she had seen a ghost coming out of the
clothes closet in the bedroom she had not meant to tell a lie. She
really believed she had seen one. One evening, before it was
quite dark and yet the corners of the room were shadowy her
mother had sent her upstairs to fetch something out of the
chest, and, as she leant over it, with one eye turned apprehen-
sively towards the clothes closet corner, she thought she saw
something move. At the time she felt sure she saw something
move, though she had no clear idea of what it was that was
moving. It may have been a lock of her own hair, or the end of
a window-curtain stirring, or merely a shadow seen sideways;
but, whatever it was, it was sufficient to send her screaming and
stumbling downstairs.

At first, her mother was sorry for her, for she thought she had
fallen down a step or two and hurt herself; but when Laura said
that she had seen a ghost she put her off her lap and began to
ask questions.

At that point the fibbing began. When asked what the ghost was like, she first said it was dark and shaggy, like a bear; then that it was tall and white, adding as an after-thought that it had eyes like lanterns and she thought it was carrying one, but was not sure. 'I don't suppose you are sure,' said her mother dryly. 'If you ask me, it's all a parcel of fibs, and if you don't look out you'll be struck dead, like Ananias and Sapphira in the Bible,' and she proceeded to tell their story as a warning.

After that, Laura never spoke of the closet to any one else but Edmund; but she was still desperately afraid of it, as she had been as long as she could remember. There was something terrifying about a door which was never unlocked, and a door in such a dark corner. Even her mother had never seen inside it, for the contents belonged to their landlady, Mrs Herring, who when she moved out of the house had left some of her belongings there, saying she would fetch them as soon as possible. 'What was inside it?' the children used to ask each other. Edmund thought there was a skeleton, for he had heard his mother say, 'There's a skeleton in every cupboard,' but Laura felt it was nothing as harmless.

After they were in bed and their mother had gone downstairs at night, she would turn her back on the door, but, if she peeped round, as she often did – for how otherwise could she be sure that it was not slowly opening? – all the darkness in the room seemed to be piled up in that corner. There was the window, a grey square, with sometimes a star or two showing, and there were the faint outlines of the chair and the chest, but where the closet door should have been was only darkness.

'Afraid of a locked door!' her mother exclaimed one night when she found her sitting up in bed and shivering. 'What's inside it? Only a lot of old lumber, you may be sure. If there was anything much good, she'd have fetched it before now. Lie down and go to sleep, do, and don't be silly!' *Lumber! Lumber!* What a queer word, especially when said over and over beneath the bedclothes. It meant odds and ends of old rubbish, her mother had explained, but, to her, it sounded more like black shadows come alive and ready to bear down on one.

Her parents disliked the closet, too. They paid the rent of the house and did not see why even a small part of it should be reserved for the landlady's use; and, until the closet was cleared, they could not carry out their plan of removing the front, throwing the extra space into the room, and then running up a wooden partition to make a small separate bedroom for Edmund. So her father wrote to Mrs Herring, and one day she arrived and turned out to be a little, lean old lady with a dark brown mole on one leathery cheek and wearing a black bonnet decorated with jet dangles, like tiny fishing rods. The children's mother had asked her when she arrived if she would not like to take off her bonnet, but she had said she could not, for she had not brought her cap; and, to make it look less formal for indoor wear, she had untied the ribbon bow beneath her chin and flung a bonnet string over each shoulder. Thus unmoored, the bonnet had grown more and more askew, which went oddly with her genteel manner.

Edmund and Laura sat on the bed and watched her shake out old garments and examine them for moth holes and blow the dust off crockery with her bellows which she had borrowed, until the air of the clean, bright room was as thick with dust as that of a lime kiln. 'Plenty of dust!' their mother said, wrinkling her pretty nose distastefully. But Mrs Herring did nothing to abate it. Why should she? She was in her own house; her tenants were privileged to be allowed to live there. At least that was what Laura read in the upward movement of her little pointed nose.

Now that the closet door was thrown back it revealed a deep, whitewashed den going back to the eaves of the cottage. It was crammed with the hoarding of years, with old clothes and shoes, legless chairs, empty picture frames, handleless cups and spout-less teapots. The best things had gone downstairs already; the lace-pillow on a stand, the huge green gig umbrella with whale-bone ribs, and the nest of copper preserving pans that Laura's mother said afterwards were worth a mint of money. From the window, Mr Herring could be seen arranging them in the spring cart, his thin legs straddling in drab gaiters. There would not be room in the cart for everything, and the hire of it for the day was too costly to make another journey possible. The time had come for Mrs Herring to decide what was best worth taking.

'I wonder what I'd better do,' she kept saying to the children's mother, but she got no helpful suggestions from one who detested what she called 'a lot of old clutter laid up in dark corners'.

'She's an old hoarder. A regular old hoarder!' she whispered to Laura when Mrs Herring had gone downstairs to consult her husband. 'And don't let me see you mess with that old rubbish she's given you. Put it down, and when she's gone it can be cleaned or burnt.' They put down their presents reluctantly. Edmund had been pleased with his broken corkscrew and coil of short lengths of string, and Laura had admired her flannel-leaved needlebook with 'Be Diligent' worked in cross-stitch on its canvas cover. The needles inside were all rusty, but that did not matter; it was as a work of art she valued it. But before they had time to protest, Mrs Herring's head appeared round the banisters, her bonnet more than ever askew by that time and her face smutted by cobwebs. 'Would these be any good to you, my dear?' she asked, handing down a coil of light steel hoops from a nail in the wall of the closet.

'It's very kind of you, I'm sure,' was the guarded response; 'but, somehow, I don't see myself wearing a crinoline again.'

'No. Right out of fashion,' Mrs Herring admitted. 'Pity, too, for it was a handy fashion for young married women. I've known some, wearing a good-sized crinoline, go right up to the day of their confinement without so much as their next-door neighbour suspecting. Now look at the brazen trollops! And here's a lovely picture of the Prince Consort, and that's somebody you've never heard of, I'll lay,' turning to the children.

Oh, yes, they had. Their mother had told them that when the Prince Consort died every lady in the land had gone into mourning, and, no matter how often they were told this, they always asked, 'And did you go into mourning, too, Mother?' and were told that she had been only a girl at the time, but she had had a black sash and ribbons. And they knew he had been the Queen's husband, though, oddly enough, not the King, and that he had been so good that nobody had liked him in his lifetime, excepting the Queen, who 'fairly doted'. They had heard all this by degrees because a neighbour called 'Old Queenie' had portraits of him and the Queen on the lid of her snuffbox.

But Mrs Herring was back in the closet and, since she could not take all her things away with her, was determined to be generous. 'Now, here's a nice little beaded footstool. Come out of Tusmore House that time the fire was, so you may be sure it's good. You have it, my dear. I'd like you to have it.' Their mother eyed the little round stool with the claw legs and beaded cover. She would really have liked that, but had made up her mind to accept nothing. Perhaps she reflected, too, that it would be hers in any case, as what Mrs Herring could not take she would have to leave, for she said again: 'It's very kind of you, I'm sure, but I don't know that I've any use for it.'

'Use! Use!' echoed Mrs Herring. 'Keep a thing seven years and you'll always find a use for it! Besides,' she added, rather sharply, 'it's just the thing to have under your feet when you're suckling, and you can't pretend you'll not be doing that again, *and* a good many times, too, at your age.'

Fortunately, at that moment, Mr Herring was heard calling upstairs that the cart was so chock-a-block that he couldn't get so much as another needle in edgeways, and, with a deep sigh his wife said she supposed she'd have to leave the rest. 'Perhaps you could sell some of the best things and send the money on with the rent,' she suggested hopefully, but the children's mother thought a bonfire in the garden would be the best way of disposing of them. However, after she had gone, a number of things were picked out and cleaned and kept, including the beaded footstool, a brass ladle, and a little travelling clock, which, when repaired, delighted the children by playing a little tune after striking the hours. 'Tinkle, tinkle, tinkle, tink, tink, tink' it went, night and day, for another forty years! then, its works worn out at last, retired to a shelf in Laura's attic.

Downstairs, the table was laid with a 'visitor's tea'. There were the best tea things with a fat pink rose on the side of each cup; hearts of lettuce, thin bread and butter, and the crisp little cakes that had been baked in readiness that morning. Edmund and Laura sat very upright in their hard windsor chairs. Bread and butter first. Always bread and butter first: they had been told that so many times that it had the finality of a text of Scripture. But Mr Herring, who was the eldest present and ought to have set a good example, began with the little cakes, picking up and examining each one closely before disposing of it in two bites. However, while there were still a few left, Mrs Herring placed bread and butter on his plate and handed him the lettuce meaningly; and when he twisted the tender young hearts of lettuce into tight rolls and dipped them into the salt-cellar she took the spoon and put salt on the side of his plate.

Mrs Herring ate very genteelly, crumbling her cake on her plate and picking out and putting aside the currants, because, she explained, they did not agree with her. She crooked the little finger of the hand which held her teacup and sipped its contents like a bird, with her eyes turned up to the ceiling.

While they sat there, the door wide open, with the scent of flowers and the humming of bees and the waving of fruit-tree tops seeming to the children to say that the stiff, formal tea-drinking would soon be over and that they were all waiting for them in the garden, a woman paused at the gate, looked the spring cart well over, set down her water-buckets and opened the gate. 'Why, it's Rachel. Whatever can she want?' said the children's mother, rather vexed at the intrusion. What Rachel wanted was to know who the visitors were and why they had come.

'Why, if it ain't Mrs Herring – and Mr Herring, too!' she cried in a tone of joyful recognition as she reached the door. 'An' you've come to clear out that old closet of yours, I'll be bound. I thought to meself when I saw the spring cart at th' gate, "That's Mrs Herring come to fetch away her old lumber at last." But I weren't quite sure, because you've got that water-proof cover over it all. How be ye both, and how do ye like it up yonder?'

During this speech Mrs Herring had frozen visibly. 'We are well, thank you,' she said, 'and we like our present residence very much, though what business it is of yours to inquire, I *don't* know.'

'Oh, no offence intended, no offence,' said Rachel, somewhat abashed. 'I only come to inquire, just friendly like,' and off she stumped down the path, throwing another inquisitive glance at the cart as she passed it.

'There! Did you ever!' Mrs Herring exclaimed. 'I never saw such a lot of heathen Turks in my life! A woman I took good care barely to pass the time of day with when I lived here to come hail-fellow-well-metting me like that!'

'She didn't mean any harm,' apologized Laura's mother. 'There's so little going on here that when anybody does come the folks take more interest than they would in a town.'

'I'd interest her! I'd hail-fellow-well-met her!' exclaimed Mr Herring, who had so far sat mute. 'I'd teach her how to behave to her betters, if I had my way.'

'God knows I did my best to put them in their places when we were living here,' sighed Mrs Herring, her anger subsiding, 'but 'twas no good. Why we ever thought to live in such a place I couldn't tell you if you asked me, unless it was that the house was going cheap at the time Mr Herring retired and a nice bit of ground went with it. It's very different at Candleford. Of course, there are poor people there, but we don't have to associate with them; they keep to their part of the town and we keep to ours. You should see our house: nice iron railings in front and an entry where the stairs go up, not like this, with the door opening straight out on the path and anybody right on top of you before you know where you are. Not but what this is a nice little house,' she added hastily, remembering that she owned it, 'but you know what I mean. Candleford's different. Civilized, that's what my son-in-law calls it, and he works at the biggest grocer's in the town, so he ought to know. It's civilized, he says, and he's right. You can't call a place like this civilized, now can you?'

Laura thought it must be a fine thing to be civilized until, later, she asked her mother what the word meant and her mother replied: 'A civilized place is where the people wear clothes and don't run naked like savages.' So it meant nothing, for everybody in this country wore clothes. One old Lark Rise woman wore three flannel petticoats in winter. She thought that if all the Candleford people were like Mr and Mrs Herring she

would not like them much. How rude they had been to poor
Rachel!

But they were funny. When her father came home from work
that night her mother told him about the visit, imitating first
Mrs Herring's voice, then that of Mr Herring, and making the
one even more carefully genteel than it had been and the other
more sudden and squeaky.

They all laughed a good deal, then her father said: 'I forgot
to tell you I saw Harris last night and he says we can have the
pony and cart any Sunday we like now.'

The children were so pleased they made a little song about
it:

> We're going over to Candleford,
>> To Candleford, to Candleford,
> We're going over to Candleford
>> To see our relations,

and they sang it about the house so often that their mother said
it just about drove her melancholy mad. The loan of the pony
and cart was not everything, it appeared; the half-year's rent
had to be got together and taken because, big as Candleford
was, the Herrings would know they had been. They knew everything, nosy parkers as they were, and if the rent, then about due,
was not taken, they would think their tenants had not the
money. That would never do. 'Don't be poor and look poor,
too,' was a family maxim. Then the Sunday outfits had to be
overhauled and a few small presents purchased to take with
them. Planning a summer Sunday outing in those days meant
more than turning over the leaves of a bus time-table.

XXI

Over to Candleford

VERY early one Sunday morning, while the rest of the hamlet
was still asleep and the sky was still pink and the garden flowers
and currant bushes were still greyish-rough with dew, they

heard the sounds of wheels drawing up at their gate and knew that the innkeeper's old pony had come with the spring cart to take them.

Father and Mother rode on the front seat, Father in his best black coat and grey-striped trousers and Mother resplendent in her pale grey wedding gown with rows and rows of narrow blue velvet ribbon edging its many flounces. The wedding bonnet had long been cast aside, for, as she often said, 'headgear does date so', and on this occasion she wore a tiny blue velvet bonnet, like a little flat mat on her hair, with wide velvet strings tied in a bow under her chin, – a new bonnet, the procuring of which had helped to delay the expedition. Upon her lap she nursed a basket containing the presents; a bottle of her elder-berry wine, a fowl she had specially fattened, and a length of pillow-lace, made to order by a neighbour, which she thought would make nice neckfrills for the cousins' best frocks. Their father, not to be outdone in generosity, at the last moment filled the back of the cart, where Edmund and Laura were to sit, with a selection of his choicest vegetables, so that, throughout the drive, Laura's legs rested higher than her seat on a sack of spring cabbage, the first of the season.

At last the children were strapped into the high, narrow seat with their backs to those of their parents and off they went, their father coaxing the old grey mare past her stable door, which she made determined efforts to enter, with: 'Come on, Polly, old girl. Not tired already. Why, we haven't started yet.' Later on, he lost patience and called her 'a measley old screw', and once, when she stopped dead in the middle of the road, he said, 'Damn the mare!' and their mother looked back over the shoulder as though she feared the animal's owner might hear. Be-tween the stops, she trotted in little bursts, and the children bumped up and down in their seat like rubber balls bouncing. All of which was as exciting to them as a flight in an aeroplane would be to a modern child.

From their high seat they could see over hedges into butter-cup meadows where cows lay munching the wet grass and big cropping cart-horses loomed up out of the morning mist. In one place the first wild roses were out in the hedge and their father

lassoed a spray with his whip and passed it over his shoulder to
Laura. The delicate pale pink cups had dew in them. Farther
on, he stopped Polly, handed the reins to their mother and leapt
down. 'Ah! I thought so!' he said as he plunged his arm into the
hedge at a spot from which he had seen a bird flutter out, and he
came back with two bright blue eggs in his palm and let them
all feel and stroke them before putting them back in the nest.
They were warm and as soft as satin.

'Pat, pat, pat', went Polly's hooves in the dust, 'creak, creak,
creak', went the harness, and 'rattle, rattle, rattle', went the iron-
tyred wheels over the stony places. The road might have been
made entirely for their convenience. There was no other vehicle
upon it. The farm carts and bakers' vans which passed that way
on week-days were standing in yards with their shafts pointing
skyward; the gentry's carriages reposed in lofty, stone-paved
coach-houses, and coachmen and carters and drivers were all
still in bed, for it was Sunday.

The blinds of roadside cottages were drawn and their gardens
were deserted of all but a prowling cat or a thrush cracking a
snail on a stone, and the children bumped and jolted on through
this early morning world with their hearts full of blissful expec-
tation.

They were going over to Candleford. It was always called
'going over', for the country people never spoke of just plain
going anywhere; it had to be going up or down or round or over
to a place, and there were so many ups and downs, so many
small streams to cross and so many gates across roads to open
between their home and Candleford that 'going over' seemed
best to describe the journey.

Towards midday they passed through a village where the
people, in their Sunday best, were streaming towards the lych-
gate of the church. The squire and the farmers wore top hats,
and the squire's head gardener and the schoolmaster and the
village carpenter. The farm labourers wore bowlers, or, the
older men, soft, round black felts. With the top-hatted men
were woman in rich, dark, heavy dresses who clung to their
husband's arms while their children walked meekly in front or,
not so meekly, behind them. Other villagers in work-day

clothes, with very clean shirts and their boots unlaced for
greater Sunday ease, carried their dinners to the baker's, or
stood in a group at the bakehouse door; while slowly up and
down the road in front of them paced a handsome pair of greys
with a carriage behind them and a coachman and a footman on
the box with cockades in their glossy hats. Shepherded by their
teachers, the school-children marched two and two to church
from the Sunday School.

This village was so populous and looked so fine, with its
pretty cottages standing back on each side of an avenue of
young chestnut trees, that Laura thought at first it was Candleford. But, no, she was told; it was Lord So-and-So's place. No
doubt the carriage and greys belonged to him. It was what was
called a model village, with three bedrooms to every house and
a pump to supply water to each group of cottages.

Only good people were allowed to live there, her father said.
That was why so many were going to church. He seemed to
speak seriously, but her mother clicked her tongue, and, to pla-
cate her, he said that he thought the bakehouse was a good idea.
'How would you like to send your Sunday joint out to be baked
and find it just done to a turn when you came out of church?' he
asked their mother. But that did not seem to please her either;
she said more went to the cooking of a good dinner than just
baking the meat, and, besides, how could you be sure of getting
all your dripping? It was a funny thing bakers so often had
dripping to sell. They said they bought it from the cooks at big
houses. But did they?

Soon after the model village was left behind Polly got tired
and stood stockstill in the road, and their mother suggested a
rest and a nosebag for her and some food for them. So they all
got out and sat on a stone-heap like gipsies and ate little cakes
and drank milk out of a bottle while they listened to the skylarks overhead and smelt the wild thyme at their feet. They
were in a new country by then, a country of large grass fields
dotted with trees where herds of bullocks grazed, or peered at
them through the iron railings by the roadside. Their father
pointed out some earthworks, which he said were thrown up by
the Romans and described those old warriors in their brass

helmets so well that the children seemed to see them; but neither he, nor they, dreamed that another field within sight would one day be surrounded by buildings called 'hangars', or that one day, within their own lifetimes, other warriors would soar from it into the sky, armed with more deadly weapons than the Romans ever knew. No, that field lay dreaming in the sunshine, flat and green, waiting for a future of which they knew nothing.

Soon after that Candleford came out to meet them. First, wayside cottages embowered in flower gardens, then cottages in pairs with iron railings enclosing neat little front plots and tiled paths leading up to the doors. Then the gasometer (for they actually had gas at Candleford!) and the railway station, which made the town accessible to all but such cross-country districts as theirs. Then came pavements and lamp-posts and people, more people than they had ever seen together in their lives before. But, while they were still on the outskirts, they felt their mother nudge their father's arm and heard her ejaculate: 'There's pomp for you! Feathers, if you please!' Then, throwing her voice ahead: 'Why, it's Ethel and Alma, coming to meet us. Here are your cousins. Turn round and wave to them, dears!' Still held by the strap, Laura wriggled round and saw, coming towards them, two tall girls in white.

The feathers that had shocked her mother, partly, perhaps, because of the contrast between their richness and Laura's plain little hat of white chip with its pink ribbon tied round in a bow to match her pink frock, were long white ostrich plumes wreathed round floppy leghorn hats. The hats were exactly alike and the feathers of the same fullness down to the last strand. The white embroidered muslin dresses they wore were also replicas of each other, for it was the fashion then to dress sisters alike, regardless of type. But the girls had seen them and came running towards the spring cart with a twinkle of long, black-stockinged legs and shiny patent-leather best shoes. After the health of themselves, their parents, and the rest of the family had been inquired into, they came round to the back of the cart.

'So this is Laura? And this is dear little Edmund? How do

you do? How do you do, dear?' Alma was twelve and Ethel thirteen, but their cool, grown-up manner might have belonged to twenty-five and thirty. Laura began to wish herself back at home as, one blush of embarrassment all over, she answered for herself and Edmund. She could scarcely believe that these two tall, well-dressed, nearly grown-up girls were her cousins. She had expected something quite different.

However, things were easier when their equipage moved on, with Ethel and Alma holding on, one on each side of the tail board, and smiling a little as they answered their uncle's shouted questions. 'Yes, Uncle,' Alma was still at the Candleford school; but Ethel was at Miss Bussell's, a weekly boarder; she came home on Friday night and went back on Monday morning. She was going to stay there until she was old enough to go to the Training College for Schoolteachers. 'That's right!' called Laura's father. 'Stuff your own brains now and you'll be able to stuff other people's hereafter. And Alma, is she going to be a teacher, too?' Oh, no, when she left school she was going to be apprenticed to a Court dressmaker in Oxford. 'That's first rate,' said their uncle. 'Then when Laura is presented at Court she'll be able to make her dress for her.' The girls laughed uncertainly, as if they were not sure if that was meant for a joke or not, and his wife told him not to be 'a great donkey', but Laura felt uncomfortable. The only Court she had heard of was the County Court, to which a neighbour had recently been summoned, and the idea of being presented there was far from pleasant.

It had been arranged that the Lark Rise family should have dinner at Ethel and Alma's home, not because her parents happened to be the most prosperous of their Candleford kin, but because their house came first as they entered the town. Afterwards they were to go on to see another family of cousins. Laura thought her mother would have preferred to go there at once, for, when their arrangements had been discussed at home, she had said something about hating a lot of fuss and show-off, and that money wasn't everything, though some folks who had plenty might think so. 'But,' she had concluded, 'they are your relations, not mine, and I expect you understand them better

than I do. But, for goodness' sake, don't get on to politics with
James, like you did at our wedding. If you two talked till you
were black in the face you'd never agree, so what's the good of
arguing'; and her husband had promised, quite meekly for him,
that he would not be the first to bring up the subject.

Candleford seemed a very large and grand place to Laura,
with its several streets meeting in a square where there were
many large shop windows, with the blinds drawn because it was
Sunday, and a doctor's house with a red lamp over the gate, and
a church with a tall spire, and women and girls in light summer
frocks and men in smart suits and white straw, boater-shaped
hats.

But they were pulling up at a tall white house set back on a
little green with a chestnut tree supporting scaffold poles and
ladders and a sign which informed the public that James Dowland, Builder and Contractor, was ready and competent to
undertake 'Constructions, Renovations, and Sanitary Work. Es-
timates Free'.

Readers have no doubt noticed how seldom builders live in
houses of their own construction. You will find a town or village expanding in all directions with their masterpieces of mod-
ernity in the way of houses and bungalows; but the builder
himself you will usually find living nearer the heart of things,
snugly and comfortably housed in some more substantial, if less
convenient, building of less recent date. Uncle James Dowland's house was probably Georgian. The eight windows with
their clinging wreaths of wistaria were beautifully spaced and
the flight of steps which led up to the hooded front door was
guarded by the low white posts and chains which enclosed the
little green. But, before Laura could get more than a general
impression and think 'what a nice house', she was in the
comfortable arms of her Aunt Edith, who was sure they were
all tired out after that long drive in the hot sun and would be
glad to rest, and Uncle would be here soon. He was a Churchwarden now and had to attend the morning service; and if
Robert would take the horse and cart round to the yard gate –
'You haven't forgotten the way, Robert?' – Alma would call the
boy to see to the pony. 'He comes in for an hour or two on

Sunday mornings to clean the boots and the knives, you know, Emmie, and I've kept him on today on purpose. Now, you come upstairs with me and I'll find some lotion for Laura's freckles; then you must all have a glass of wine to refresh you. It's all of my own making, so you need not be afraid of it for the children. James would never allow intoxicating liquor in this house.'

The inside of the house seemed like a palace to Laura, after their own homely cottage. There were two parlours, one on each side of the front door, and in one of them a table was spread with decanters and wineglasses and dishes of cakes and fruit and biscuits. 'What a lovely dinner,' Laura whispered to her mother when they happened to be alone in the room for a moment.

'That's not dinner. It's refreshments,' she whispered back, and Laura thought 'refreshments' meant an extra nice dinner provided on such occasions. Then her father and Edmund came back from their hand-washing, Edmund bubbling over with some tale of a chain you could pull which brought water pouring down, 'More water than there is in the brook at home,' and their mother said, 'S-s-hush!' and added that she would explain later. Laura had not seen this marvel. She and her mother had taken off their hats and washed their hands in the best bedroom, a magnificent room with a four-poster bed with green curtains and a double washstand with a jug and basin each for them. 'You'll find the commode in that corner,' her auntie had said, and the commode turned out to be a kind of throne with carpeted steps and a lid which opened. But Laura was older than Edmund and knew it was rude to mention such things.

Uncle James Dowland now came in. He was a big man and an important-looking one, and seemed to fill even that large, well-proportioned room with his presence. At his approach Aunt Edith's stream of good-natured chatter ran dry, and Alma, who had been tiptoeing round the table, helping herself to a little from most of the dishes, sank down on the couch and pulled her short skirt over her knees. After she had been greeted by a heavy pat on the head, Laura shrank back behind her mother. Uncle James was so tall and stout and dark, with eyebrows so bushy and so thick a moustache, with so glossy a Sunday suit and so heavy a gold watchchain that, before him, the others present seemed to fade into the background. Except Laura's father, who nearly as tall as he was, though slighter, stood with him on the hearthrug, talking about their trade. It turned out afterwards to be the only safe subject.

Uncle James Dowland was one of those leading spirits found at that time in every country town or large village. In addition to attending to his own not inconsiderable business of building new houses, renovating old ones, and keeping everybody's roofs and drains in order, he was People's Churchwarden, choirman, and occasional organist, a member of every committee, and auditor of all charity accounts. But his chief interest was in the temperance movement, at that time a regular feature of parochial life. His hatred of intoxicating drink amounted to a phobia, and he used to say that if he saw a workman of his entering a public-house, he would not be his workman much longer. But he was not content with ruling his own home and business in this respect; the whole town was his mission field, and if he could coax or bribe some unhappy workman into signing away his nightly half-pint he became as exhilarated as if his tender for building a mansion had been accepted.

To him the smallest child was worth winning as a temperance convert. He would guide their tiny hands as they signed the temperance pledge, and to keep them in the fold he had established a Band of Hope which met once a week to eat buns and drink lemonade at his expense and to sing to his accompaniment on the school harmonium such rousing ditties as 'Pray sell no more drink to my father' or:

> Father, dear Father, come home with me now,
> The clock in the steeple strikes one.
> You promised, dear Father, that you would come home
> As soon as your day's work was done

while, all the time, their own excellent fathers, after a modest half-pint at their favourite inn, were already at home and the singers themselves were likely to get into trouble for being out late.

Edmund and Laura, that first Sunday, wrote their names on a handsome blue-and-gold illuminated pledge card, thereby promising they would henceforth touch no intoxicating liquor, 'so help me God'. They were not quite sure what intoxicating liquor was, but they liked the cards and were pleased when their uncle offered to have them framed to hang over their beds at home.

Their Aunt Edith was more attractive to children. She was pink and plump and had wavy grey hair and kind grey eyes. She was dressed in grey silk and when she stirred there was a faint scent of lavender. She looked kind and was kind; but, that discovered and acknowledged, there was little more to be said about her. Away from her husband and daughters she was talkative, running on from subject to subject, like a brook babbling. She greatly admired her husband, and every moment when alone with Laura's mother was devoted to his praise. It was James says this, and James did that, and stories to show how important and respected he was. In his presence she seemed a little afraid of him and she was certainly afraid of her daughters. It was 'What do you think, dear?' or 'What would you do if you were me?' to the girls before she would express an opinion or make an arrangement. Then, to her sister-in-law, 'Of course, you see, Emmie, they've got different ideas to us, with all this education and getting to know people.' She had already informed her that they sometimes played tennis at the Rectory.

Laura thought the girls were conceited, and, although she could not have put it into words, felt they patronized her mother and her as poor relations; but perhaps she was wrong. It may only have been that they were so far removed in circumstances and interests that they had nothing in common. That was the only time Laura was to meet them upon anything like equal terms. They were away from home at the time of her next visit and grown-up before she saw them again. She was only just in time to catch the last flick of their skirts as they began to climb the social ladder which would take them right out of her own life.

The dinner which speedily followed the refreshments was superlative. At one end of the table was a leg of lamb, roasted before an open fire to conserve the juices; at the other a couple of boiled fowls garnished with slices of ham. There were jellies and cheese-cakes, and gooseberry tart with cream.

'The girl' brought in and cleared away the dishes. The maid in a tradesman's family was then always known as 'the girl', irrespective of age. In this case she was a girl of about fifty, who had been with Aunt Edith from the day she was married and was to remain with her as long as she lived. According to Laura's mother, she was overworked, but, if so, it appeared to agree with her, for she was rosy and round as a tub, and the only complaint she was ever known to make was that 'the Missis' would always make the pastry herself, although she knew that she (Bertha) had a lighter hand with a rolling-pin. She kept the whole of the fair-sized house cleaned and polished and whitestoned, helped the washer-woman on Mondays, cooked the meals, and mended the stockings, and all for twelve pounds a year. She was kind, too. Seeing on that first visit Laura had no appetite for dinner after the refreshments, she whisked her scarcely touched plate away while the others were talking.

It was all very rich and fine, but frightfully dull to a child who had come with such high expectations. They were back in the first parlour. The refreshments had disappeared and there was a green plush cloth on the table. Ethel and Alma had gone to Sunday School, where both took classes, and Laura had been given a book with views of Ramsgate to look at. The window blinds were drawn, for the sun was hot on the panes, and the room smelt of best clothes, furniture polish, and potpourri. Edmund was already asleep on his mother's knee and Laura was getting drowsy when the soft buzz of grown-up conversation which had been going on over her head was broken by sharp cries of 'Ireland', 'Home Rule', 'Gladstone says ...' 'Lord Harrington says ...' 'Joey Chamberlain says ...' The two men had got on to the subject which her mother had dreaded.

'They're subjects of Queen Victoria, ain't they, same as we are,' her uncle insisted. 'Well, then, let 'em behave as such and be thankful to have a decent Government over 'em. Nice thing they'd make of governing themselves, and they no better than a lot of drunken savages.'

'How'd you like it if a foreign country invaded England ...' her father began.

'I'd like to see 'em try it,' interposed her uncle.

'... invaded England and shed blood like water and burnt down your house and workshops and interfered with your religion. You'd want to get rid of 'em, I'll bet, and get back your independence.'

'Well, we did conquer 'em, didn't we? So let 'em learn who's their masters, I say, and if they won't toe the line, let our soldiers go over and make them.'

'How many Irishmen have you ever known personally?'

'If I'd only known one it'd be one too many; but, as a matter of fact, I've had several working for me at different times. Then there was Colonel Dimmock at Bradley, went bankrupt and let me in for more money than you're ever likely to earn.'

'Now, Bob!' pleaded Laura's mother.

'Now, James!' urged her aunt. 'You're not at a meeting now, but at home, and it's Sunday. What's Ireland to either of you. You've never been there and are never likely to, so have done with your arguing.'

Both men laughed a little and seemed ashamed of their vehemence, but her uncle could not forbear a parting shot. 'Tell you what,' he said, probably meaning it for a joke. 'In my opinion, the best way to settle the question would be to send over a shipload of whisky one day and a shipload of guns the next and they'd all get raving drunk and kill one another and save us the trouble.'

Robert stood up and his face was white with anger, but he only said a cold 'Good day' as he made for the door. His wife and sister ran to him and seized an arm each and his brother-in-law told him not to be a fool. 'It's only politics,' he said. 'You take things too seriously. Come, sit down, and Edith'll tell the girl to bring in a cup of tea before you go on to Ann's.' But Robert walked out of the house and away down the street after saying over his shoulder to his wife, 'See you later.'

He had no sense of humour. None of them had at that moment. Laura's mother was all apologies. Her uncle, still angry, but a little ashamed, said he was sorry *for her*. Her aunt wiped her eyes on a pretty lace-edged handkerchief and Laura's needed wiping, for was not their long-looked-for day ruined if their lovely drive behind Polly had only led to this.

It was her mother, who did not pretend to be well-bred, yet always managed to do or say the right thing, who eased the situation by saying: 'Well, he'll have to come back presently to harness the horse and he'll be sorry enough by that time, I dare say, and I think I *will* have that cup of tea, if Bertha's got the kettle boiling. Just a cup to drink. Nothing more to eat, really. Then we must be getting on.'

XXII

Kind Friends and Relations

AFTER a decent interval, during which everybody tried to talk as though nothing had happened, the two children with their mother set out to follow their father to Aunt Ann's, Laura dragging behind a little, for the sun was hot and she was tired and not sure that she liked Candleford.

She soon cheered up; there was so much to see. Houses, houses all the way, not rows of houses, all alike, like peas in a pod, but big and little, tall and low, with old grey walls between with broken bottle-glass on the coping and fruit trees waving in gardens behind, and queer door-knockers and little shed-like porches, and people walking in their thin best shoes on the cobblestones with bunches of flowers, or prayerbooks, or beer jugs in their hands.

Once, at a turning, they caught a glimpse of a narrow lane of poor houses with ragged washing slung on lines between windows and children sitting on doorsteps. 'Is that a slum, Mother?' asked Laura, for she recognized some of the features described in the Sunday-school stories.

'Of course not,' said her mother crossly; then, after they had passed the turning: 'Don't speak so loud. Somebody might hear you and not like it. Folks who live in slums don't call them that. They're used to it and it seems all right to them. And why should you worry about things like that. You'd do better to mind your own business.'

Her own business! Wasn't it her business to be sorry for people who lived in slums and had no food or bed and a drunken father, or a landlord ready to turn them out in the snow. Hadn't her mother herself nearly cried when she read *Froggy's Little Brother* aloud to them? Laura could have cried then, in the middle of Candleford, at the thought of the time when Froggy took home the bloater as a treat and his poor little brother was too ill to eat any.

But they had come to a place where they could see green fields and a winding river with willows beside it. Facing them with its back to the fields was a row of shops, the last in the town on that side, and in the window of the shop they were approaching was nothing but one lady's top boot, beautifully polished and standing on an amber velvet cushion with an amber velvet curtain behind it. Above the window was a notice, unreadable to Laura then, but read by her many times afterwards, which said: 'Ladies' boots and shoes made to order. Best Materials. Perfect Workmanship. Fit Guaranteed. Ladies' Hunting Boots a Speciality.'

Their Uncle Tom had what was at that time called 'a snug little business'. It was a common thing then for people of all classes, excepting the very poorest, to have their footwear made to measure. In a large workshop across the yard at the back of the house and shop, workmen and apprentices scraped and hammered and sewed all day, making and mending. Uncle Tom's own workshop was a back room of the house, with a door opening out on to the yard, across which he came and went dozens of times a day to and from the main workshop. He made the hunting boots there and sewed the uppers of the more delicate makes, and there he fitted the customers, excepting the hunting ladies, who tried their boots on in the best parlour, Uncle Tom kneeling on the carpet before them like a courtier before a queen.

But all this Laura found out afterwards. On that first visit the front door flew open before they had reached it and they were surrounded by cousins and kissed and hugged and led to where Aunt Ann stood in the doorway.

Laura had never known any one like her Aunt Ann. The neighbours at home were kind in their rough way, but they were so bent on doing their best for themselves and those belonging to them that, excepting in times of illness or trouble, they had little feeling to spare for others. Her mother was kind and sensible and loved her children dearly, but she did not believe in showing too much tenderness towards them or in 'giving herself away' to the world at large. Aunt Ann gave herself away with every breath she drew. No one who heard her gentle voice or looked into her fine dark eyes could doubt her loving nature. Her husband laughed at what he called her 'softness' and said that customers calling in a great rage to complain that their shoes had not been delivered to time had stayed to tell the full story of their lives. For her own children she had sweet, pet names, and Edmund was soon her 'little lover' and Laura her 'Pussikins'. Except for her eyes and the dark, satiny hair which rippled in waves flat to her head, she was a plain-looking woman, pale and thin of face and of figure so flat that, with her hair parted in the middle and in the long, straight frocks she wore, she reminded Laura of Mrs Noah in the toy ark she had given Edmund at Christmas. That impression, a bony embrace, and a soft, warm kiss were all Laura had time for before she was borne on a stream of cousins straight through the house to an arbour in the garden where her father and uncle sat with a jug and glasses on a table between them and their pipes in their mouths. They were talking amiably together, although, only that morning, her father had spoken of her uncle as 'a snob' and her mother had protested, 'But he's not a common cobbler, Bob. He's a master man, and he makes more than he mends.'

If Laura's Uncle Tom was a snob by trade, there was nothing else snobbish about him, for he was one of the most liberal-minded men she was ever to know and one of the wisest. He was a Liberal in politics, too, and no doubt that accounted for her father's air of friendliness and ease. They were settling the Irish question, for the old familiar catchwords caught her ear, and it was rather an absent-minded uncle who stroked her hair and told the girls to take her to play in the orchard, but not to let the little boy go tumbling in the river, or their mother would have all those cakes she had been making left on her hands.

The orchard consisted of about a score of old apple and plum trees on a square of rough grass at the bottom of the garden, beyond which ran the small, sluggish stream, half choked with rushes and bordered with willows. Laura, who had felt so tired before, suddenly felt tired no more, but ran and shouted and played 'tig' with the others around the tree trunks. The apple blossom was nearly over and the petals were falling and they all tried to catch a petal or two because one of the cousins said that for every petal they caught they would have a happy month. Then there were small green gooseberries to crunch and forget-me-nots to pick. Laura filled her hands with these and carried them about until they drooped and had to be thrown into the river.

Gradually, she became able to distinguish between the new faces and to discover the name for each. There was Molly, the eldest, a motherly little person with a plump, soft figure, red-gold hair, and freckles on the bridge of her nose. Annie had reddish hair, too, but was smaller than Molly and had no freckles. Nelly was dark, quick in her movements, and said things that made people laugh. 'Sharp as a needle,' said Laura's father afterwards. Amy, the youngest girl, was Laura's own age. She had a red bow on her dark curls, but Laura did not need to look at the bow, except to admire it, because Amy was smaller than the others.

Johnny was the youngest of all, but by far the most important, for he was a boy, and a boy who came at the end of a long string of girls. Johnny must have anything he wanted, no matter to whom it belonged. If Johnny fell down, he must be picked up and comforted, and around Johnny, when he approached the river, red heads and dark heads drew to form a bodyguard. Rather a baby, thought Laura, although the same age as Edmund, who needed no attention at all, but went and stood on the bank and threw down twigs to float and called them ships; then ran, throwing up his heels like a young colt and lay on his back in the grass with his legs sticking up.

A shabby old flat-bottomed boat was moored beneath the bank, and when they were tired of their play, some one sug-

gested that they should go and sit in it. 'But may we?' asked
Laura, rather nervously, for it was the first boat she had seen
outside a picture-book, and the water looked deep and wide to
her, after the brook at home. But Edmund was more enterprising; he slid down the bank into the boat at once, crying:
'Come on! Hurry up! Our ship's just starting to Australia!' So,
with the little boys holding an oar each and pretending to row,
and the girls packed into the stern, well out of the way of
chance knocks with the oars, and the willow leaves silvery
against the blue sky, and the air flavoured with mint and the
raw dankness of water weeds, they set out on their imaginary
voyage. And, all the time, there was that stout, strong rope
holding the boat safely to shore. All the joys of adventure without its perils.

When discussing the family afterwards, Laura's mother said
Molly was a little woman, 'a regular second mother to the
younger ones', and her own mother must have trusted her, for
the children were left to themselves the whole of that afternoon.
Or it may have been that the father and uncle had so much to
settle about Ireland and the mother and aunt were so busy
indoors inspecting wardrobes and discussing family affairs.

The children, too, had plenty to discuss. 'Can you read?'
'When are you going to school?' 'What's Lark Rise like?' 'Only
a few houses – all fields?' 'Where do you buy things if there are
no shops?' 'Do you like Molly's hair? Most people hate red and
they call her "ginger" at school; but Mr Collier, that's our
Vicar, says it's lovely, and a customer told Mother that if she
liked to have it cut off she could sell it for pounds and pounds.
Some ladies would pay anything to have it to put on their own
heads. Yes, didn't you know that some people wear false hair?
Aunt Edith has a switch? I've seen it, hanging on her dressing-
table in the morning; that's what makes her hair bunch out so at
the back.' 'And your hair's nice, too, Laura,' said Molly generously, picking out Laura's best feature. 'I like the way it runs
like water all down your back.'

'My mother can sit on her hair when it's down,' boasted
Laura, and the cousins were impressed, for a great deal was
thought of quantity in those days, of hair as of other things.

All the girls were going to school in the town as yet, but soon Molly and Nellie were to go to Miss Bussell's for a year each to be 'finished'. When, later, Laura asked her father if Johnny would go to Miss Bussell's, too, he laughed and said, 'Of course not. It's a girls' school. For the daughters of gentlemen, says the brass plate on the door, and that means for the daughters of a chimney sweep, if he can afford to pay.'

'Then where will Johnny go?' she persisted, and her father said, 'Eton, I s'pose,' which rather alarmed Laura because she thought he had said 'eaten'. She was relieved when he added, 'But I doubt if that'll be good enough. They'll have to build a special school on purpose for Johnny.'

What surprised Laura most as she listened to her cousins that afternoon was that they spoke of school as if they liked it. The hamlet children hated school. It was prison to them, and from the very beginning they counted the years until they would be able to leave. But Molly and Nellie and Amy said school was great fun. Annie did not like it so much.

'A-h-h! Who's bottom of her class!' laughed Nell.

But Molly said, 'Never mind her, Annie. She may be good at lessons, but she can't sew for nuts, and you're going to get the needlework prize with that baby's frock you're making. Ask her what Miss Pridham said when she examined her herring-boning.'

Then a voice from the upper garden called them in to tea. Just the kind of tea Laura liked, bread and butter and jam and a cake and some little cakes, a little more of everything than they had at home, but not the rich, bewildering abundance of the 'refreshments'.

She liked her cousins' house, too. It was old, with little flights of steps going up or down in unexpected places. Aunt Ann's parlour had a piano across one corner and a soft green carpet the colour of faded moss. The windows were wide open and there was a delicious scent of wallflowers and tea and cake and cobbler's wax. They had tea out of the silver teapot at the large round table in the parlour that day. Afterwards, they always had tea in the kitchen, much the nicest room in the house, with its two windows with window seats and brass warming pans and candlesticks and strips of red-and-blue striped matting on the stone floor.

That day, because they were having tea in the parlour, there was not room at the table for all, and Edmund and Johnny were seated at a side table with their backs to the wall, so that their respective mothers could keep an eye on them. But there was still so much talking going on among the elders that the little boys were forgotten until Johnny asked for more cake. When his mother handed him a slice he said it was too large, and, when halved, too small, and, finally, left the portion he had accepted in crumbs upon his plate, which shocked Edmund and Laura, who, at home, had to eat whatever was put upon their plates, and 'no leavings allowed'.

'Spoilt to death, regularly spoilt' was their mother's verdict when Johnny was spoken of afterwards, and perhaps at that time he was spoilt. He could scarcely escape spoiling, being the only and long-desired boy, coming after so many girls and then turning out to be the only delicate one of the family. He was young for his age and slow in developing; but there was fine stuff in Johnny. As a young man he was deeply religious, a non-smoker, a non-drinker and a non-card-player, and served the altar set up on many a battlefield during the 1914–18 War, and all this needed character in the atmosphere of Army life.

That Sunday afternoon Laura saw only a little boy with a pale, freckled face and thin fair hair. A spoilt child, of whom even his parents looked a little ashamed. But, in after years, she also saw Johnny as a sick soldier shut up in Kut, emaciated by illness and hunger and tormented by heat and flies; and that same soldier, once the adored little boy with his bodyguard of sisters, thrown out bodily after an exchange of sick prisoners with a last kick from his native jailor and a 'You can have this one for a makeweight. He's no good.' Or the same Johnny, lying for a whole summer on a long chair in the orchard, fed, every few minutes, as it seemed, with broth, or eggs beaten up in milk, out of teacups, until home and rest and his mother's nursing had strengthened him sufficient to pass his Board and be sent to the trenches in France. For, as we grow older, we see in memory not only our friends as they appeared to us as children, but also as they were to become in later years. The first sharp impression remains with us as a picture. Subsequent ones as a chain of episodes in a story, less positive, but more enlightening.

XXIII

Sink or Swim

THAT journey to Candleford marked the end of Laura's childhood. Soon afterwards her schooldays began and she passed in one day from a protected home life to one where those who could had to fight for a place and maintain it by fighting.

The National School for the parish had been built in the mother village, a mile and a half from the hamlet. Only about a dozen children lived there and more than three times that number lived at Lark Rise; but, as the Church was there and the Rectory and the Manor House, it far outweighed the hamlet in importance. Up and down the long, straight road between the two places, the hamlet children travelled in bands. No straggling was allowed. An inclination to walk alone, or in twos or threes, was looked upon as an unpleasant eccentricity.

Most of the children were clean and at least moderately tidy when they left home, although garments might be too large or too small or much patched. 'Patch upon patch is better'n holes' was one of the hamlet mothers' maxims. The girls wore large white or coloured print pinafores over their ankle-length frocks, and their hair was worn scraped back from the brow and tied on the crown or plaited into a tight pigtail. Laura appeared on the first morning with her hair pushed back with an Alice in Wonderland comb under a pork-pie hat which had belonged to one of her cousins, but this style of headgear caused so much mirth that she begged that evening to be allowed to wear 'a real hat' and to have her hair plaited.

Her companions were strong, well-grown children between the ages of four and eleven. They ran and shouted and wrestled the whole way, or pushed each other over stoneheaps or into

ditches, or stopped to climb into the hedges, or to make sorties
into fields for turnips or blackberries, or to chase the sheep, if
the shepherd was not handy.

Every one of the stoneheaps which dotted the grass margins
at intervals for road-mending was somebody's castle. 'I'm the
king of the castle. Get down, you dirty rascal!' was the cry of
the first to reach and mount it, and he, or she, would hold it
against all comers with kicks and blows. Loud cries of 'You're a
liar!' 'You're another!' 'You daren't!' 'Yes, I dare, then!' 'Let's
see you do it!' punctuated even their most peaceful games.
There was no 'Sez you', or 'O.K., Chief', for the 'pictures' had
not been invented, and the more civilizing wireless, with its
Children's Hour, was still farther in the future. Even com-
pulsory education was comparatively new. They were an un-
diluted native product.

There were times when they walked quietly, the elder ones
talking like little old men and women, while the younger ones
enlarged their knowledge of life by listening. Perhaps they
would discuss the story of the snake, as thick as a man's thigh
and yards long, which the shepherd had seen crossing that same
road a few feet in front of him as he came home in the early
morning from his lambing fold. Rather a puzzle to older
people, that snake, for snakes are not usually abroad at lambing
time, so it could not have been an English grass snake,
magnified. Yet David was a sober, middle-aged man, unlikely
to have invented the story. He must have seen something. Or
perhaps the children would discuss their own and each other's
chances of passing the next school examination. The shadow of
a coming exam might account for their sedate behaviour. Or
some one would relate how such-and-such a man had treated
the foreman when he had 'tried to come it over him'; or the
news would go round that So-and-So's mother was 'like to have
another', much to the embarrassment of poor So-and-So. They
talked about procreation and birth as soberly as little judges.
'What's the good of having a lot of brats you can't afford to
feed,' one would say. 'When I'm married I shall only have one,
or maybe two, in case one of 'em dies.'

The morning after a death in the hamlet would see them with

serious faces discussing the signs which were supposed to have foretold it: the ticking of a death-watch spider, the unexplained stopping of a clock, the falling of a picture from the wall, or the beating of a bird's wings against the window. The formalities of the death chamber fascinated them. They knew why and in what manner the chin was tied up, of the plate of salt placed on the breast of a corpse, and the new pennies used to weight down the eyelids. This led naturally to ghost stories, and the smaller children on the edge of the group would cease whispering among themselves and press tightly in to the main throng for protection.

They did not mean to be cruel; but they were strong, hardy children, without much imagination, and overflowing with energy and high spirits which had to find an outlet. There was some bullying and a great deal of boisterous teasing.

Once, on their way home from school, they overtook an old man. So old that, as he dragged slowly along, his head was bent to the level of the top of the stick which supported his footsteps. He was a stranger, or the children would never have dared to mock, mob, and insult him as they did. They knew that their parents and the schoolmistress were unlikely to hear of it.

They did not actually strike him, but they hustled and pushed him from behind, shouting: 'Old Benbow! Old Benbow!' Why 'Benbow', nobody knew, unless it was because his back was so bent. At first he pretended to laugh at their attentions as a joke; but, soon, growing tired of the pace they were forcing on him, he stood still with them all about him, looked upward, shook his stick at them and muttered a curse. At that they fell off, laughing, and ran.

It was a grey winter afternoon and, to Laura's eyes, the ancient, solitary figure of the old man stood for a type of extreme desolation. He had been young once, she thought, and strong; they would not have dared to molest him then. Indeed, they were afraid of able-bodied tramps and would run and hide from them. Now he was old and poor and weak, and homeless, perhaps. Nobody cared for him any more. What was the use of living at all if it was to end like this, thought little eight-year-old, and spent the rest of the time going home in making up a story in which he figured as a rich, handsome young man, until ruined by a bank failure (bank failures were frequent in juvenile fiction just then) and his lovely young wife died of smallpox and his only son was drowned at sea.

During her first year or two at school Laura came in for a good deal of teasing which she shared with two or three others whose looks, voices, parents or clothes did not please the majority. Not that there was anything objectionable about them, according to outside standards; it was only that they were a little different in some way from the accepted school pattern.

For instance, long frocks down to the ankles were still the hamlet wear for girls of all ages, while, in the outer world, the fashion had changed and little girls' frocks were worn extremely short. As Laura was fortunate, or unfortunate, enough to have the reversion of her cousins' wardrobes, she was put into short frocks prematurely. She was a little pleased and proud when she started off for school one morning in a cream cotton frock patterned with red dots that just touched her knees, especially as her mother, at the last moment, had found and ironed out a red hair-ribbon to go with it. But her pride had a fall when she was greeted with laughter and cries of 'Hamfrill!' and 'Longshanks!' and was told seriously by a girl who was usually friendly that she wondered that a nice woman like Laura's mother could allow her to go out like that.

She arrived home that evening a deplorable sight, for she had been tripped up and rolled in the dust and had cried so much that her face was streaked, and her mother – sympathetic for once, although she did not fail to remind her that 'sticks and stones break your bones, but calling names hurts nobody' – set to work upon the short frock and lengthened it sufficiently to reach to the calves of her legs. After which, if she stooped a little when any one looked directly at her, it passed muster.

There was one girl named Ethel Parker who at this time made Laura's life a misery to her. She professed friendship and would call for her every morning. 'So nice of Ethel,' Laura's mother said. Then, as soon as they were out of sight of the windows, she would either betray her to the gang – once by telling them Laura was wearing a red flannel petticoat – or force her to follow her through thorn hedges and over ploughed fields for some supposed short cut, or pull her hair, or wrench her arms, 'to try her strength', as she told her.

At the age of ten she was as tall and much stronger than most girls of fourteen. 'Our young Et's as strong as a young bullifant,' her father would say proudly. She was a fair-haired girl with a round, plump face and greenish eyes, the shape and almost the colour of a gooseberry. She had for cold weather a scarlet cloak, a survival of a fashion of some years before, and in this she must have looked a magnificent specimen of country childhood.

One of her pleasures was to make Laura gaze steadily at her. 'Now, see if you can stare me out,' she would say, and Laura would gaze slavishly into those hard, green eyes until her own fell before them. The penalty for flinching was a pinch.

As they grew older she used less physical violence, though she would still handle Laura pretty roughly under the pretence of play. She was what they called there 'an early-ripe' and, as she grew up, Laura's mother did not like her so much and told Laura to have as little to do with her as possible, adding, 'But don't offend her, mind. You can't afford to offend anybody in a place like this.' Then Ethel went away to a place in service and, a year or two later, Laura also left home and did not expect to see Ethel again.

But, fifteen years after, when living in Bournemouth, Laura, walking on the West Cliff one afternoon, a little out of her usual beat on some errand or other, saw coming towards her a large, fair young woman in a smartly-tailored suit with a toy dog under one arm and a pack of tradesmen's books in her hand. It was Ethel, by that time a cook-housekeeper, and out paying the household accounts and giving the family dog an airing.

She was delighted to see Laura, 'such an old friend and playmate'. What splendid times they had had and what scrapes they had got into together! Ah! There were no days like childhood's days and no friends like the old friends. Didn't Laura think so?

She was so enthusiastic and had so obviously forgotten everything unpleasant in their former association that Laura was almost persuaded that they really had been happy together, and was just going to ask Ethel to come to tea with her when the little dog under her arm began to fidget and she gave him a nip in the neck which quieted him. Laura knew that nip which made his eyes bulge, for she herself had felt it many times, and she knew that, beneath the smart clothes and improved manners, there was still the old Ethel. That was the last Laura ever saw of her; but she heard afterwards that she had married an ex-butler and opened a boarding-house. It is to be hoped that her guests were all people of strong character, for it is easy to imagine weaker ones quailing before those gooseberry eyes if they dared to make a request.

But the girls were not all like Ethel. Except when in contact with her and others of her kind, many were friendly, and Laura soon found out that her special mission in life was to listen to confidences. 'You are such a quiet little thing,' they would say, 'I know you won't tell anybody'; and, afterwards: 'We've had such a nice talk,' although they had done every bit of the talking themselves, Laura's part in the conversation being limited to 'Yes' and 'No' and other sympathetic monosyllables.

Those girls who had sweethearts would talk about them by the hour. Did Laura not think Alfie good-looking? And he was strong, so strong that his father said he could carry a sack of potatoes that he himself could scarce lift, and his mother said he ate twice as much as his brothers; and, although you might not think it, he could be very agreeable when he chose. Only 'Saturday was a week' he had allowed the speaker to pick up and hold his catapult while he climbed down from a tree; 'that one in the corner of the meadow where the blacksmith's shop is, you know, Laura; there's nobody else in the school could climb it. That'll show you!' The remarkable thing about these love affairs was that the boys involved were usually unaware of them. A girl picked out a boy to be her sweetheart and sang his praises (to Laura, at least) and dreamed about him at night (or so she said) and treasured some worthless article which had belonged to him, and the utmost the boy did in return was to say 'Hullo!' when they met.

Sometimes it was difficult to decide upon a sweetheart. Then an ash leaf with nine leaflets had to be searched for, and, when found, placed in the seeker's bosom with the incantation:

> Here's an ash leaf with nine leaves on.
>   Take it and press it to your heart
> And the first chap you meet'll be your sweetheart.
> If he's married let him pass by.
> If he's single, let him draw nigh,

and that usually did the trick, as there was but one side to that bargain.

Confidences about quarrels with other girls were even more frequent. What 'she said' and what 'I said', and how long it was since they had spoken to each other. But nearly every one had something to tell, if only what they had had for dinner on Sunday, or about the new frock they hoped to wear to church on Easter Day. This usually began as a red or blue velvet and ended by being 'that one of our young Nell's, turned and made shorter'. Laura would try to get in a word edgeways here, for she was fond of planning clothes. Her ideal frock at that time was a pale blue silk trimmed with white lace, and she always imagined herself riding in the station fly in it, as one of her aunts had ridden from the station when she came to them on a visit.

These confidences were all very well, if sometimes boring; but there were others which filled Laura's thoughts and weighed heavily upon her. Only one girl in the hamlet had a stepmother, and she was a model stepmother, according to hamlet standards, for she had no children of her own, and did not beat or starve her stepchildren. One of Laura's earliest memories was of the day on which Polly's own mother died. Polly, although a little older than Laura, could not remember so far back, and Laura must have been a very small child at the time. She was standing on the doorstep of her home on a misty morning when she heard a cock crow, very loudly and shrilly, and her mother, standing close behind her, said: 'At the house where that cock is crowing a little girl's mammy has died this morning.'

At the time of the school confidences, Polly was an unattractive-looking little girl, fat and pale, with scanty mouse-coloured hair, and heavy and clumsy in her movements. She breathed very heavily and had a way of getting very close to the person to whom she was talking. Laura almost hated herself for not liking her more; but she was really sorry for her. The stepmother, so fair-spoken to outsiders, was a tyrant indoors, and the stepchildren's lives were made miserable by her nagging. Every day – or every day when Polly could buttonhole Laura – there was some fresh story of persecution to be told and listened to. 'I know. I know,' Laura would say sympathetically, meaning that she understood, and Polly would retort, 'No, you don't know. Nobody could but them as has to put up with her,' and Laura would feel that her heart must break with the hopeless misery of it all. Her mother found her crying one day after one of Polly's confidences and demanded to be told the reason. 'Polly's not happy,' was all Laura could say, for she had sworn never to repeat what Polly had told her.

'Polly not happy? I dare say not,' said her mother dryly. 'None of us can be happy all the time; but your being unhappy as well doesn't seem to me to improve matters. It's no good, my girl, you've got to learn you can't take other people's troubles upon you. Do anything you can to help them, by all means, but their troubles are their own and they've got to bear them. You'll have troubles of your own before you have done, and perhaps by that time Polly'll be at the top of the tree of happiness. We all have our turn, and it only weakens us when our turn comes to have always been grieving about things we couldn't help. So, now, dry your eyes and come in and lay the table for tea and don't let me catch you crying again.' But Laura only thought her mother heartless and continued to grieve, until one day it suddenly struck her that it was only when she was alone with herself that Polly was miserable. When in company with the other girls she forgot her troubles and was as cheerful as her nature permitted, and, from that time, she took care to be less often alone with Polly.

No country child could be unhappy for long together. There were happy hours spent blackberrying, or picking bluebells or cowslips with a friend, or sitting in the long meadow grass making daisy or buttercup chains to be worn on the hair as a crown or as necklaces or girdles. When Laura was too old (according to others) to wear these herself, they could still be made for one of the younger children, who would stand, like a little statue, to be hung from head to foot with flowers, including anklets and earrings.

Sliding on the ice in winter was another joy. Not on the big slide, which was as smooth as glass and reached the whole length of the pond. That was for the strong, fighting spirits who could keep up the pace, and when tripped up themselves would be up in a moment and tripping up the tripper. Edmund was soon one of the leaders there, but Laura preferred some small private slide made by herself and a few friends and as near the bank as possible. How the cheeks glowed and the whole body tingled with warmth and excitement in the frosty air! And what fun it was to pretend that the arms stretched out for balance were wings and that the slider was a swallow!

Not such fun for Laura was the time when the ice gave way under her, and she found herself suddenly plunged into icy water. This was not the big pond, but a small, deep pool to which she and two other small girls had gone without asking permission at home. When they saw Laura drowning, as they thought, her companions ran off screaming for help, and Laura, left alone, was in danger of being sucked down under the ice; but she was near the bank and managed to grasp the branch of a bush and pull herself out before she realized her danger.

As she walked home across the fields her wet clothes froze upon her, and when she arrived dripping on the doorstep her mother was so cross that smacks, as well as hot bricks in bed, were administered to warm her. The wetting did her no harm. She did not even have a cold afterwards, although her mother had prophesied pneumonia. Another instance, she was told, of the wicked flourishing like a green bay-tree.

XXIV

Laura Looks On

OCCASIONALLY, during the school hours, something exciting would happen. Once a year the German band came and the children were marched out into the playground to listen. The bandsmen gave of their best at the school, for the mistress not only put a whole shilling in the collecting cap, but gave it with smiles and thanks and told the children to clap, and they clapped heartily, as they would have clapped anything which brought them out into the sunshine for a few minutes. When their shilling programme was finished, before playing 'God Save the Queen', the leader asked in his broken English if there was anything special 'the gracious lady' would like them to play. 'Home, Sweet Home' was the usual choice, but, one year, the mistress asked for 'When the Dewy Light was Fading', a Sankey and Moody hymn which had just then taken the neighbourhood by storm. When the musician shook his head and said, 'Sorry, not know,' his reputation went down considerably.

Once a grand funeral procession passed and the mistress told the children they might go out and watch it. It might be their last opportunity of seeing such a procession, she said, for times were changing and such deep, very deep mourning was becoming out of date.

It was the time of year when the buttercups were out on the road-margins and the hedges were white with may, and between them, at a snail's pace, came swaying a huge black hearse, draped with black velvet and surmounted at the four corners with bunches of black ostrich plumes. It was drawn by four coal-black horses with long, flowing tails, and driven and attended by undertaker's men with melancholy faces and with long black crape streamers floating from their top hats. Behind it came carriage after carriage of mourners, spaced out to make the procession as long as possible, and every carriage was drawn by its own black horse.

It passed slowly between the rows of open-mouthed, wondering children. There was plenty of time to look at it; but to Laura it did not seem real. Against the earth's spring loveliness the heavy black procession looked dream-like, like a great black shadow, Laura thought. And, in spite of the lavish display of mourning, it did not touch her as the country funerals did with their farm-wagon hearse and few poor, walking mourners crying into their handkerchiefs.

But she was so much impressed that she unintentionally started a rumour by saying that she thought such a grand funeral must be that of an earl. There was an aged nobleman living in the neighbourhood whose time must soon come in the course of Nature, and her 'an earl' became 'the earl' before it had been many times repeated. Fortunately for Laura, the schoolmistress heard this and corrected it by telling the children that it was the funeral of a farmer whose family had formerly lived in the parish and had a family burying place in the churchyard. Such a man would now be carried to his last resting-place in one of his own farm wagons and be followed by his near relatives in a couple of cars.

Then there was the day of the General Election, when little school work was done because the children could hear bands of voters passing beneath the school windows and shouts of 'Maclean! Maclean for Freedom! Maclean! Maclean! He be the boy for the farm labourer!' and they wished their schoolroom had been chosen for the polling station instead of the schoolroom in the next village. There was an uneasy feeling, too, because they knew their fathers were voting Liberal, and the mistress was wearing a bright blue rosette, the Conservative colour, which proclaimed her one with the Rectory and the Manor House, and against the villagers. The children were forbidden to wear the deep crimson which stood for the Liberal cause, but most of them carried a scrap of red in their pockets to wear going home and two or three of the more daring girls sported a red hair ribbon. The mistress was at liberty, too, to look out of the window, which they were not, and she made the most of this advantage, tiptoeing to open or shut it or arrange the blind whenever voices were heard. On one of these occasions she

looked round at her scholars and said: 'Here, now, are two respectable men going quietly to vote, and as you may guess they
are voting for law and order. It's a pity more in this parish are
not like Mr Price and Mr Hickman' (the parson's factotum and
the squire's gardener). At that, faces flared up and mouths grew
sulky-looking, for the more intelligent took it as a reflection on
their own fathers; but all such resentment was wiped out when
she said at three o'clock: 'I think we had better dismiss now.
You had better get home early, as it is Election Day.' Although
it was a pity she added 'there may be drunken men about'.

But the most memorable day for Laura was that on which the
Bishop came to consecrate an extension of the churchyard and
walked round it in his big lawn sleeves, with a cross carried
before him and a book in his hands, and the clergy of the
district following. The schoolchildren, wearing their best
clothes, were drawn up to watch. 'It makes a nice change from
school,' somebody said, but to Laura the ceremony was but a
prelude.

For some reason she had lingered after the other children had
gone home, and the schoolmistress, who, after all, had not been
invited to the Rectory to tea as she had hoped, took her round
the church and told her all she knew of its history and archi-
tecture, then took her home to tea.

A small, two-roomed cottage adjoining the school was provided for the schoolmistress, and this the school managers had
furnished in the manner they thought suitable for one of her
degree. 'Very comfortable', they had stated in their advertisement; but to a new tenant it must have looked bare. The
downstairs room had a deal table for meals, four cane-
bottomed chairs of the type until recently seen in bedrooms, a
white marble-topped sideboard stood for luxury and a wicker
armchair by the hearth for comfort. The tiled floor was partly
covered with brown matting.

But Miss Shepherd was 'artistic' and by the time Laura saw
the room a transformation had taken place. A green art serge
cloth with bobble fringe hid the nakedness of the deal centre
table; the backs of the cane chairs were draped with white crocheted lace, tied with blue bows, and the wicker chair was

cushioned and antimacassared. The walls were so crowded with pictures, photographs, Japanese fans, wool-work letter-racks, hanging pincushions, and other trophies of the present tenant's skill that, as the children used to say: 'You couldn't so much as stick a pin in.'

'Don't you think I've made it nice and cosy, dear?' said Miss Shepherd, after Laura had been shown and duly admired each specimen of her handiwork, and Laura agreed heartily, for it seemed to her the very height of elegance.

It was her first invitation to grown-up tea, with biscuits and jam – not spread on her bread for her, as at home, but spooned on to her plate by herself and spread exactly as she had seen her father spread his. After tea, Miss Shepherd played the harmonium and showed Laura her photographs and books, finally presenting her with one called *Ministering Children* and walking part of the way home with her. How thrilled Laura was when, at their parting, she said: 'Well, I think we have had quite a nice little time, after all, Laura.'

But, at the time of that tea-drinking, Laura must have been eleven or twelve, one of Miss Shepherd's 'big girls' and no longer an object of persecution. By that time the play was becoming less rough and bullying rarer, for the older children of her early schooldays had left school and none who came after were quite so belligerent. Civilization was beginning to tame them.

But, even in her earlier days, her life was easier after Edmund began school, for he was better-liked than she was; moreover, he could fight, and, unlike most of the other boys, he was not ashamed to be seen with his sister.

Often, on their way to school, Laura and he would take a field path which led part of the way by a brook backed by a pinewood where wood-pigeons cooed. By leaping the little stream, they could visit 'the graves'. These were two, side by side, in the deepest shade of the pines, and the headstones said: 'In Memory of Rufus' and 'In Memory of Bess'. They both knew very well that Rufus and Bess had been favourite hunters of a former owner of the estate; but they preferred to think of them as human beings – lovers, perhaps, who in life had been used to meet in that deep, mysterious gloom.

On other days they would scramble down the bank of the
brook to pick watercress or forget-me-nots, or to build a dam,
or to fish for minnows with their fingers. But, very often, they
would pass along the bank without seeing anything, they would
be so busy discussing some book they had read. They were
voracious readers, although their books were few and not selected, but came to them by chance. There were the books from
the school library, which, though better than nothing to read,
made little impression upon them, for they were all of the
goody-goody, Sunday-school prize type. But their father had a
few books and others were lent to them, and amongst these
were a few of the Waverley Novels. *The Bride of Lammermoor*
was one of the first books Laura read with absorbed interest.
She adored the Master of Ravenswood, his dark, haughty
beauty, his flowing cloak and his sword, his ruined castle, set
high on its crag by the sea, and his faithful servant Caleb and
the amusing shifts he made to conceal his master's poverty. She
read and re-read *The Bride* and dipped into it between whiles,
until the heathery hills and moors of Scotland became as real to
her as her flat native fields, and the lords and ladies and soldiers
and witches and old retainers as familiar as the sober labouring
people who were her actual neighbours.

At seven years old *The Bride* made such an impression upon
her that she communicated her excitement to Edmund, himself
as yet unable to read, and one night in their mother's bedroom
they enacted the scene in the bridal chamber; Edmund insisting
that he should be Lucy and Laura the bridegroom, although she
had told him that a bridegroom was usually one of his own
sex.

'Take up your bonny bridegroom!' he cried, so realistically
that their mother came running upstairs thinking he was in pain.
She found Laura crouching on the floor in her nightdress while
Edmund stood over her with a dagger which looked very much
like his father's two-foot rule. No wonder she said, 'Whatever
will you two be up to next!' and took *The Bride of Lammermoor* away and hid it.

Then a neighbour who had bought a bundle of old books for
a few pence at a sale lent them *Old Saint Paul's,* and the out-

house door was soon chalked with a cross and the wheelbarrow trundled round the garden to the cry of 'Bring out your dead!'

Between the ages of seven and ten, Laura became such a confirmed reader that, when other books failed, she would read her father's dictionary, until this disappeared because her mother thought the small print was bad for her eyes. There was still the Bible, which could not be forbidden, and she spent many an hour over that, delighting in the Old Testament stories of the Pillar of Fire, and of Ruth and Esther and Samuel and David, and of Jonah and the whale, or learning by heart the parables in the New Testament to repeat at Sunday School. At one time she had a passion for the Psalms, not so much from religious fervour as from sheer delight in the language. She felt these ought to be read aloud, and, as she dare not read them aloud herself, lest she should be overheard, she would persuade Edmund or some other child to read them with her, verse and verse about.

Once, when Edmund was upstairs in bed with measles and her mother was out, she and another girl were having a fine time imitating the parson and clerk reading the Psalms in church, when Edmund, who could hear all that was going on downstairs, called out to ask whose Bible Alice was using. She was using his and when Edmund had his suspicions confirmed he was so enraged that he dashed downstairs in his nightshirt and chased Alice all down the garden to the gate. If his mother could have seen him out of doors with his spots, in his night-shirt, brandishing his Bible and threatening the retreating Alice, she would have been horrified, for measles patients were then told that they must not put so much as a hand out of bed or the spots would 'go inward' and the simple measles would turn to black measles, when they would probably die. But no one saw him and he returned to his bed, apparently not a ha-penny the worse for his airing.

A little later, Scott's poems came into their lives and Edmund would swing along the field path to school reciting 'The way was long, the night was cold', or stop to strike an attitude and declaim,

Come one, come all! this rock shall fly
From its stern base as soon as I,

or wave Laura on with 'Charge, Chester, charge! On, Stanley, on!' At that time their conversation when alone together was tinged with the language of their favourite romances. Sometimes Edmund would amuse his sister and himself by translating, when a battered old zinc bucket became 'ye antique pail', or a tree slightly damaged by the wind 'yon lightning-blasted pine', while some good neighbour of theirs whom they could see working in the fields would have given Edmund what he would have called 'a darned good bommicking' if he had heard himself referred to as 'yon caitiff hind'.

Sometimes they tried their hand at writing a little verse themselves. Laura was guilty of a terrible moral story in rhyme about a good child who gave his birthday sixpence to a beggar, and Edmund wrote a poem about sliding on the ice with the refrain 'Slide, glide, glide, slide, over the slippery pond'. Laura liked that one and used to sing it. She also sang one of her own, beginning, 'The snowdrop comes in winter cold', which ran, with a stanza for every flower, through the seasons, and to which she added yet another stanza every time she saw or remembered a flower hitherto neglected. One day her mother asked her what that 'unked thing' she was trying to sing was about, and, in an unguarded moment, she brought out the scraps of paper on which it was written. She did not scold or even laugh at her folly; but Laura could feel that she was not pleased, and, later that evening, she lectured her soundly on her needlework. 'You can't *afford* to waste your time,' she said. 'Here you are, eleven years old, and just look at this seam!'

Laura looked; then turned away her face to hide her confusion. She did try to sew well; but, however hard she tried, her cotton would knot and her material pucker. She was supposed to be making stays for herself from narrow strips of calico left over from cutting out larger things, which, when finished with buttons and shoulder straps would make a lasting and comfortable garment. Laura always wore such stays; but not of her own making. If she had ever finished those she was working on, they would, by that time, have been too small to go round her. She saw them thirty years later in an old trunk of oddments with the strips puckered and the needle rusted into the material half-way up a seam, and remembered then the happy evening when her mother told her to put it aside and get on with her knitting.

By the eighteen-eighties the fine sewing of the beginning of the century was a lost art. Little children of six were no longer kept indoors to work samplers, whip cambric frills or stitch seams with stitches so tiny that a microscope was needed to examine them. Better uses had been found for young eyesight. But plain sewing was still looked upon as an important part of a girl's education, both at school and at home, for it was expected that for the rest of her life any ordinary girl would have at least to make her own underclothes. Ready-made clothes were beginning to appear in the shops, but those such as working people were able to buy were coarse, ugly, and of inferior quality. Calico stiffened with dressing which would all come out in the wash and leave the material like butter muslin, edging which looked like notched tape, and all put together with the proverbial hot needle and burning thread, tempted few people with self-respect to give up making their own underclothes.

If those who gave up outdoor pleasure and worked so busily in order that they might, as they said, know that all was good 'right to the skin' could have seen in a vision the lovely garments made of rayon and other materials of today, sold at less than their lengths of material cost, and all ready to step into, they would have thought the millennium was approaching.

But perhaps not. They might have thought the material too insubstantial to 'stand the wash' and so filmy it might show the figure through. Their taste ran to plenty of trimming; lace and insertion and feather-stitching on under-garments, flounces on frocks and an erection of ribbon and artificial flowers on hats. Laura's mother showed an almost revolutionary taste when she said: 'I don't care so much for an important-looking hat. I like something small and natty. But,' she would add apologetically to her listener, 'that may be because my face is small. I couldn't carry anything off like you can.'

The masterpiece of fashion during Laura's schooldays was what was known as the kilted frock. The skirt of this, over a

pleated bottom part, had a kind of apron of the same material
drawn up in folds round the hips and bunched out behind. It
was a long time before any one in the hamlet possessed a kilted
frock, but they were seen in church, and the girls in service
came home for their holidays in them; then, as the fashion
waned in the outer world, they began to arrive, either as gifts,
or as copies of gifts made by some village dressmaker. And,
with them, came the story that some great Parisian dress de-
signer had invented the style after seeing a fisherwoman on the
beach with her frock drawn up over her kilted petticoat, just in
that manner. 'It's a corker to me how the de'il these 'oomen get
to know such things,' said the men.

XXV

Summer Holiday

AFTER that first visit to Candleford, it became the custom for
Laura's parents to hire the innkeeper's horse and cart and drive
there one Sunday in every summer; and, every summer, on the
Sunday of the village feast, their Candleford aunt and uncle and
cousins drove over to Lark Rise.

Then, one day when Laura was eleven and Edmund nine
years old, their mother astonished them by asking if they
thought they could walk over, just the two of them, by themselves. They had often walked to the market town and back, she
reminded them. That was six miles and Candleford only eight.
But did they think they could be trusted not to stray from the
road ('No going into fields to pick flowers, Laura!') and would
they be sure not to get into conversation with any strangers they
might meet on the road, or be persuaded to follow them anywhere? It was their summer holiday from school and their Aunt
Ann had written to ask them to spend a week or two with her
and their cousins.

Could they manage the walk? What a question! Of course
they could, and Edmund began to draw a map of the road to
convince her. When could they go? Not before Saturday? What

a long time to wait. But she said she must write to their aunt to tell her they were coming, then, perhaps, some of their cousins would walk out to meet them.

Saturday came at last and their mother waved to them from the gate and called out a last injunction not to forget the turnings, and, above all, not to have anything to do with strange men. She was evidently thinking of a recent kidnapping case which had been front-page news in the Sunday newspaper; but she need not have been afraid, no criminal was likely to be prowling about those unfrequented byways, and, had there been, the appearance of the two children did not suggest worthwhile victims.

'For comfort,' as their mother had said, they both wore soft, old cotton clothes: Laura a green smock which had seen better days but did not look too bad, well washed and ironed, and Edmund an ex-Sunday white sailor suit, disqualified for better wear because the sleeves of the blouse and the legs of the knickers had been let down and the join showed. Both wore what were then known as Zulu hats, plaited of rushes and very wide brimmed, beneath which they must have looked like a couple of walking mushrooms. Most of the things necessary for their stay had been sent on by parcel post, but they still bulged with food packets, presents for the cousins, and coats for themselves in case of rain. Laura had narrowly escaped carrying an umbrella, for, as her mother persuasively said, if there was no rain she could use it as a sunshade; but, at the last minute, she had managed to put this down in a corner and 'forget' it.

They left home at seven o'clock on a lovely August morning. The mounting sun drew moisture in a mist from the stooks of corn in the partly stripped harvest fields. By the roadside all the coarse yellow flowers of later summer were out: goat's beard and lady's finger, tall thickets of ragwort and all the different hawkbits; the sun shone softly through mist; altogether, it was a golden morning.

A new field had been thrown open for gleaning and, for the first mile, they walked with some of their school-fellows and their mothers, all very jolly because word had gone round that young Bob Trevor had been on the horse-rake when the field was cleared and had taken good care to leave plenty of good ears behind for the gleaners. 'If the foreman should come nosing round, he's going to tell him that the ra-ake's got a bit out of order and won't clear the stubble proper. But that corner under the two hedges is for his mother. Nobody else is to leaze there.' One woman after another came up to Laura and asked in a whisper how her mother was keeping and if she found the hot weather trying. Laura had answered a good many such inquiries lately.

But the gleaners soon trooped through a gate and dispersed over the stubble, hurrying to stake out their claims. Then Edmund and Laura passed the school and entered on less familiar ground. They were out on their first independent adventure and their hearts thrilled to the new sense of freedom. Candleford waited so many miles ahead of them and it was nice to know that supper and a bed were assured to them there; but the pleasure they felt in the prospect of their holiday visit was nothing compared to the joy of the journey. On the whole, they would rather not have known where they were bound for. They would have liked to be genuine explorers, like Livingstone in Africa; but, as their destination had been decided for them, their exploring had to be confined to wayside wonders.

They found plenty of these, for it did not take much to delight them. A streak of clear water spouting from a pipe high up in the hedgerow bank was to them what a cataract might have been to more seasoned travellers; and the wagons they met, with names of strange farmers and farms painted across the front, were as exciting as hearing a strange language. A band of long-tailed tits, flitting from bush to bush, a cow or two looking at them over a wall, and the swallows strung out, twittering, along the telegraph wire, made cheerful and satisfying company. But, apart from these, it was not a lonely road, for men were working in the harvest fields on either side and they passed on the road wagons piled high with sheaves and saw other wagons go clattering, empty, back for other loads. Sometimes one of the wagoners would speak to them and Edmund would answer their 'An' where do 'ee s'pose you be off to, young shaver?' with 'We are going over to Candleford'; and they would both smile, as expected, when they were told, 'Keep puttin' one foot in front o' t'other an' you'll be there before dark.'

One exciting moment was when they passed through a village with a shop and went in boldly and bought a bottle of gingerade to wash down their sandwiches. It cost twopence and when they were told they must pay a halfpenny on the bottle they hesitated. But, remembering in time that they each had a whole shilling to spend, more than they had ever had at one time in their lives before, they paid up, like millionaries, and also invested in a stick of pink and white rock each, and, with one end wrapped in paper to keep it from sticking to their fingers, went off down the road sucking.

But eight miles is a long walk for little feet in hot August weather, and the sun scorched their backs and the dust made their eyes smart and their feet ached and their tempers became uncertain. The tension between them reached breaking point when they met a herd of milking cows, ambling peacefully, but filling the narrow road, and Laura ran back and climbed over a gate, leaving Edmund to face them alone. Afterwards, he called her a coward, and she thought she would not speak to him for a long time. But, like most of her attempted sulks, it did not last, for she could not bear to be on bad terms with any one. Not from generosity of heart, for she often did not really forgive a real or imagined injury, but because she so much wanted to be liked that she would sometimes apologize when she knew the fault had not been hers.

Edmund was of a quite different nature. What he said he held to, like a rock. But then he did not say hasty, thoughtless things: what he said he meant and if any one was hurt by it, well, they were hurt. That did not change the truth, as he saw it. When he told Laura she was a coward he had not meant it unkindly; he was simply stating a fact and there was more of sorrow than of anger in his tone. And Laura only minded what he said so much because she was afraid it was true. If he had said she was stupid or greedy, she would only have laughed, because she knew she was neither.

Fortunately, soon after this, they saw what must have looked

like a girls' school out for a walk advancing between the hedgerows to meet them. It was a relief party, consisting of the
cousins and as many of their school friends as they could
muster, with a large tin can of lemonade and some cakes in a
basket. They all flopped down beside a little brook which
crossed the road at that point and the girls fanned themselves
with bunches of willow-herb and took off their shoes to search
for stones, then dipped their toes in the water, and, before long,
the whole party was paddling and splashing, which astonished
Laura, who had always been told it would 'give anybody their
death' to put the feet in cold water.

After that, it did not seem long before Candleford was
reached and the travellers were being welcomed and made
much of. 'They've walked! They've walked the whole way!'
called their aunt to a friend who happened to be passing her
door, and the friend turned and said, 'Regular young travellers,
aren't they?' which made them again feel like the explorers they
admired.

Then there was tea and a bath and bed, thought not to sleep
for a long time, for Laura had a bed in her two middle cousins'
room and they talked a great deal. Talking in bed was a novelty
to her, for it would not have been permitted at home. In her
cousins' home there was more liberty. That night, once or twice
one of their parents called upstairs telling them to be quiet and
let poor little Laura get to sleep; but the talking went on, a little
more quietly, until long after they heard the front door bolt
shot and the window sashes in the lower rooms pushed up.
What do little girls talk about when they are alone together? If
we could remember that, we should understand the younger
generation better than we do. All Laura could remember was
that that particular conversation began with a cousin saying,
'Now, Laura, we want to know all about you,' and that in the
course of it one of them asked her: 'Do you like boys?'

When she said, 'I like Edmund,' they laughed and she was
told: 'I mean boys, not brothers.'

Laura thought at first they meant sweethearts and grew very
hot and shy; but, no, she soon found they just simply meant
boys to play with. She found afterwards that the boys they

knew talked to them freely and let them join in their games, which surprised her, for the boys at home despised girls and were ashamed to be seen talking to one. The hamlet mothers encouraged this feeling. They taught their boys to look down upon girls as inferior beings; while a girl who showed any disposition to make friends of, or play games with, the boys was 'a tomboy' at best, or at worst 'a fast, forward young hussy'. Now she had come to a world where boys and girls mixed freely. Their mothers even gave parties to which both were invited; and the boys were told to give up things to the girls, not the girls to the boys – 'Ladies first, Willie!' How queer it sounded!

Candleford was but a small town and their cousins' home was on the outskirts. To children from a city theirs would have been a country holiday. To Laura it was both town and country and in that lay part of its charm. It was thrilling, after being used to walking miles to buy a reel of cotton or a packet of tea, to be able to dash out without a hat to fetch something from a shop for her aunt, and still more thrilling to spend whole sunny mornings gazing into shop windows with her cousins. There were marvellous things in the Candleford shops, such as the wax lady dressed in the height of fashion, with one of the new bustles, at the leading drapers; and the jeweller's window, sparkling with gold and silver and gems, and the toy shops and the sweet shops and, above all, the fishmonger's where a whole salmon reposed on a bed of green reeds with ice sprinkled over (ice in August! They would never believe it at home), and an aquarium with live goldfish swimming round and round stood near the desk where they took your money.

But it was just as pleasant to take out their tea in the fields (Laura's first experience of picnics), or to explore the thickets on the river banks, or to sit quietly in the boat and read when all the others were busy. Several times their uncle took them out for a row, right up the stream where it grew narrower and narrower and the banks lower and lower until they seemed to be floating on green fields. In one place they had to pass under a bridge so low that the children had to lie down in the boat and their uncle had to bow down his head between his knees until it almost touched the bottom. Laura did not like that bridge, she was always afraid that the boat would stick half-way through and they would never get out again. How lovely it was to glide through the farther arch and see the silvery leaves of the willows against the blue sky and the meadowsweet and willow-herb and forget-me-nots!

Her uncle exchanged 'Good morning's and words about the weather with the men working in the fields on the banks, but he did not often address them by name, for they were not close neighbours as the field workers were at home; and the farmers themselves, in this strange place, were not reigning kings, as they were at home, but mere men who lived by farming, for the farms around Candleford were much smaller.

On one of the first days of their holiday they went harvesting in the field of one of their uncle's customers, their share of the work, after they had dragged a few sheaves to the wagon, being to lie in the shade of the hedge and take care of the beer-cans and dinner baskets of the men, with occasional spells of hide-and-seek round the stooks, or rides for the lucky ones on the top of a piled-up wagon.

They had taken their own lunch, which they ate in the field, but at teatime they were called in by the farmer's wife to such a tea as Laura had never dreamed of. There were fried ham and eggs, cakes and scones and stewed plums and cream, jam and jelly and junket, and the table spread in a room as large as their whole house at home, with three windows with window seats in a row, and a cool, stone-flagged floor and a chimney corner as large as Laura's bedroom. No wonder Mr Partington liked that kitchen so much that his wife, as she told them, could never get him to set foot in the parlour. After he had gone back to the field, Mrs Partington showed them that room with its green carpet patterned with pink roses, its piano and easy chairs, and let them feel the plush of the upholstery to see how soft and deep it was, and admire the picture of the faithful dog keeping watch on its master's grave, and the big photograph album which played a little tune when you pressed it.

Then Nellie had to play something on the piano, for no friendly call was then considered complete without some music. People said Nellie played well, but of this Laura was no judge, although she much admired the nimble way in which her hands darted over the keyboard.

Afterwards they straggled home through the dusk with a corn-crake whirring and cockchafers and moths hitting their faces, and saw the lights of the town coming out, one by one, like golden flowers, as they entered. There was no scolding for being late. There was stewed fruit on the kitchen table and a rice pudding in the oven, of which those who felt hungry partook, and glasses of milk all round. And, even then, they did not have to go to bed, but went out to help water the garden, and their uncle told them to take off their shoes and stockings, then turned the hose upon them. Wet frocks and petticoats and knicker legs resulted; but their aunt only told them to bundle them all up and put them into the cupboard under the attic stairs. Mrs Lovegrove was coming to fetch the washing on Monday. It was a surprising household.

Every few days, when they were out in the town, they would call at Aunt Edith's, at their Aunt Ann's request, 'in case she should be hurt, if neglected'. Uncle James would be about his business; the girls were away on a visit, and even Aunt Edith herself would often be out shopping, or at a sewing party, or gone to the dressmaker's. Then Bertha would take them straight through to her kitchen and give them cups of milk in order to detain them, for although so silent as to be thought simple in the presence of the elders, with the children alone she became talk-ative. What did Molly, or Nellie, think of so-and-so, which had happened in the town? What was Mr Snellgrave up to when he fell down those stone steps? 'Was he a bit tight, think you?' She had heard, though it wouldn't do for Master to know, that he called at the 'Crown' for his glass every night, and him a sides-man and all. Still, it might, as Molly suggested, have been that the steps were slippery after the shower. But you couldn't help thinking! And had they heard that her Ladyship up at Bartons was getting up one of these new fancy bazaars? It was to be held in the picture gallery and anybody could go in who cared to pay sixpence; but she expected they'd have to buy something – crocheted shawls and hand-painted plates and pincushions and hair-tidies – all given by the gentry to sell for the heathens.

'No, not the Candleford heathens. Don't be cheeky, young Nell. The heathen blacks, who all run naked in foreign parts, like they have the collection for in church on missionary Sundays. I expect the Mis'is will go and your mother and some of you. They say there's tea going to be sold at sixpence a cup. Robbery, I call it! but there's them as'd pay as much as a pound only to get their noses inside Bartons, let alone sitting down and drinking tea with the nobs.'

Bertha was not above school gossip, either. She took great interest in children's squabbles, children's tea parties and children's holidays. 'There, did you ever! – I wonder, now, at that!' she would ejaculate on hearing the most commonplace tittle-tattle and remember it and comment on it long after the squabble had been made up and the party forgotten by all but her.

In spite of her spreading figure and greying hair, there was something childlike about Bertha. She was excessively submissive before her employers, but, alone with the children, with whom she apparently felt on a level footing, she was boisterous and slangy. Then she was so pleased with little things and so easily persuaded, that she actually seemed unable to make up her mind on any subject until given a lead. She had an impulsive way, too, of telling something, then begging that it might never be repeated. 'I've been and gone and let that blasted old cat out of the bag again,' she would say, 'but I know I can trust you. You won't tell nobody.'

She let a very big cat out of the bag to Laura a year or two later. Laura had gone to the house alone, found her Aunt Edith out, and was sipping the usual cup of milk in the kitchen and paying for it with small talk, when a very pretty young girl came to the back door with a parcel from Aunt Edith's dressmaker and was introduced to her as 'our young Elsie'. Elsie could not stay to sit down, but she kissed Bertha affectionately and Bertha waved to her from the doorway as she crossed the yard.

'What a pretty girl!' exclaimed Laura. 'She looks like a robin with those rosy cheeks and all that soft brown hair.'

Bertha looked pleased. 'Do you see any likeness?' she asked, drawing up her figure and brushing her hair from her forehead.

Laura could not; but, as it seemed to be expected, she ventured: 'Well, perhaps the colour of her cheeks ...'

'What relation would you take her for?'

'Niece?' suggested Laura.

'Nearer than that. You'll never guess. But I'll tell you if you'll swear finger's wet, finger dry, never to tell a soul.'

Not particularly interested as yet, but to please her, Laura wetted her finger, dried it on her handkerchief, drew her hand across her throat and swore the required oath; but Bertha, her cheeks redder than ever, only sighed and looked foolish. 'I'm making a fool of myself again, I know,' she said at last, 'but I said I'd tell you, and, now you have sworn, I must. Our young Elsie's my own child. I gave birth to her myself. I'm her mother, only she never calls me that. She calls our Mum at home Mother and me Bertha, as if I was her sister. Nobody here knows, only the Mis'is, and I expect the Master and your Aunt Ann, though they've never either of them mentioned it, even with their eyes, and I know I oughtn't to be telling you at your age, but you are such a quiet little thing, and you saying she was pretty and all, I felt I must claim her.'

Then she told the whole story, how she had, as she said, made a fool of herself with a soldier when she was thirty and ought to have known better at that age, and how Elsie had been born in the Workhouse and how Aunt Edith, then about to be married, had helped her to send the baby home to her mother and advanced money from her future wages to get herself clothes, and taken her into her new home as a maid.

Laura felt honoured, but also burdened, by such a confidence; until one day, when they were speaking of Bertha, Molly said, 'Has she told you about Elsie?' Laura must have looked confused, for her cousin smiled and went on, 'I see she has. She's told me and Nellie, too, at different times. Poor old Bertha, she's so proud of "our young Elsie" she must tell somebody or burst.'

Except for these calls and a formal tea-drinking at Aunt Edith's once or twice in every holiday, the children spent their time at Aunt Ann's.

The class to which she and her husband belonged is now

extinct. Had Uncle Tom lived in these days, he would probably
have been manager of a branch of one of the chain stores,
handling machine-made footwear he had not seen until it came
from the factory. Earning a good salary, perhaps, but subject to
several intermediary 'superiors' between himself and the head
of the firm and without personal responsibility for, or pride in,
the goods he handled: a craftsman turned into a salesman. But
his day was still that of the small business man who might work
by his own methods at his own rate for his own hours and,
afterwards, enjoy the fruits of his labour and skill, both in the
way of satisfaction in having turned out good things, and in that
of such comforts for himself and his family as his profits could
afford. What these profits should be, his customers decided; if
he could please them they came again and again and sent others
and that meant success. Except his own conscience as a craftsman, he had nothing but his customers to consider. Twice a
year he went to Northampton to buy leather, choosing his own
and knowing what he chose was good because, owing no merchant a long bill, he was not tied to any and could choose where
he would. It was a simple life and one which many might well
envy in these days of competition and carking care.

His was a half-way house between the gorgeous establishment of their other uncle and their own humble home. There
was nothing pretentious. Far from it, for pretentiousness was
the one unpardonable sin in such homes. But there was solid
comfort and not too close a scrutiny of every shilling spent.
When Aunt Ann wrote out her grocery list, she did not have to
cut out and cut out items, as their mother had to do, and they
never once heard from her the familiar 'No, no. It can't be
done' they were so used to hearing at home.

There were other advantages. Water had not to be drawn up
from a well, but came from a bright brass tap over the kitchen
sink, and the sink was another novelty; at home the slops were
put in a pail which, when full, had to be carried out of doors
and emptied on the garden. And the w.c. – a real w.c. – although not actually indoors, was quite near, in a corner of the
yard, and reached by a covered pathway. Then there was no big
washing-day to fill the house with the steam of suds and leave

behind a mass of wet clothes to be dried indoors in bad weather, for a woman came every Monday morning and carried the week's washing away, and when she brought it back clean at the end of the week she stayed to scrub out the stone-floored kitchen and passage, sluice down the courtyard and clean the windows.

The water was pumped up to a cistern in the roof every morning by the boy who swept out the shop and carried the customers' parcels and, in between, was supposed to be learning the trade, although, as Uncle Tom told him, he would never make a good snob, his backside was too round – meaning that he would never sit still long enough. Benny was a merry, good-natured lad who performed all kinds of antics and made ridiculous jokes, which the children relished greatly. Sometimes, as a great favour, he would let them take a turn with the pump-handle. But he soon seized it again, for he could not stand still a moment. He would jump on the pump-handle and ride it; or stand on his head, or turn somersaults, or swarm up a water-pipe to an outhouse roof and sit, grimacing like a monkey, on the ridge tiles. He never walked, but progressed by hopping and skipping or galloping like a horse, and all this out of sheer light-heartedness.

Poor Benny! he was then fourteen and had all the play of a lifetime to crowd into a very few years. He was an orphan who had been brought up in the Workhouse, where, as he told the children, 'em 'udn't let you speak or laugh or move hardly,' and the recent release of his high spirits seemed to have intoxicated him.

He did not live in the house, but had been put out to board with an elderly couple, and Aunt Ann was so afraid that they would forget he was a growing boy that she seldom saw him without giving him food. A cup of milk and a doorstep of bread and jam rewarded him for the pumping every morning and he never returned from an errand for her but she put an apple or a bun or a slice of something into his hand. No baking was complete without a turnover of the oddments being made for Benny.

All, excepting the poorest, kept house extravagantly in those days of low prices. Food had to be of the best quality and not only sufficient, but 'a-plenty', as they expressed their abundance. 'Do try to eat this last little morsel. You can surely find room for that and it's a pity to waste it,' they would say to each other at table and some one or other would make room for the superfluous plateful; or, if no human accommodation could be found, there were the dogs and cats or a poorer neighbour at hand.

Many of the great eaters grew very stout in later life; but this caused them no uneasiness; they regarded their expanding girth as proper to middle age. Thin people were not admired. However cheerful and energetic they might appear, they were suspected of 'fretting away their fat' and warned that they were fast becoming 'walking miseries'.

Although Laura's Aunt Ann happened to be exceptionally thin and her uncle was no more than comfortable of figure, the usual abundance existed in their home. There were large, local-grown joints of beef or lamb, roasted in front of the fire to preserve the juices; an abundance of milk and butter and eggs, and cakes and pies made at a huge baking once or twice a week. People used to say then, 'I'd think no more of doing it than of cracking an egg,' little dreaming, dear innocents, that eggs one day would be sixpence each. A penny each for eggs round about Christmas was then thought an exorbitant price. For her big sponge cake, a speciality of hers, Aunt Ann would crack half a dozen. The mixture had to be beaten for half an hour and the children were allowed to take turns at her new patent egg-beater with its handle and revolving wheels. Another wonder of her kitchen was the long fish kettle which stood under the dresser. That explained what was meant by 'a pretty kettle of fish'. Laura had always imagined live fish swimming round and round in a tea kettle.

Before they had been at Candleford a week a letter came from their father to say they had a new little sister, and Laura felt so relieved at this news that she wanted to stand on her head, like Benny. Although no hint had been dropped by her elders, she had known what was about to happen. Edmund had known, too, for several times when they had been alone together he had said anxiously, 'I hope our mother's all right.' Now she was all right and they could fully enjoy their holiday.

Ordinary mothers of that day would put themselves to any inconvenience and employ any subterfuge to prevent their children suspecting the advent of a new arrival. The hint of a stork's probable visit or the addition of a clause to a child's prayers asking God to send them a new little brother or sister were devices of a few advanced young parents in more educated circles; but even the most daring of these never thought of telling a child straightforwardly what to expect. Even girls of fifteen were supposed to be deaf and blind at such times and if they accidentally let drop a remark which showed they were aware of the situation they were thought disagreeably 'knowing'. Laura's schoolmistress during Bible reading one day became embarrassed over the Annunciation. She had mentioned the period of nine months; then, with blushing cheeks and downcast eyes, said hastily: 'I think nine months is the time a mother has to pray to God to give her a baby before her prayer is answered.' Nobody smiled or spoke, but hard, cold eyes looked at her from the front row where her elder pupils sat, eyes which said as plainly as words, 'You must think we're a lot of softies.'

After the baby's arrival, if the younger children of the family asked where it had come from, they were told from under a gooseberry bush, or that the midwife had brought it in her basket, or the doctor in his black bag. Laura's mother was more sensible than most parents. When asked the question by her children when very small she replied: 'Wait until you get older. You're too young to understand, and I'm sure I'm not clever enough to tell you.' Which perhaps was better than confusing their young minds with textbook talk about pollen and hazel catkins and bird's eggs, and certainly better than a conversation between a mother and child on the subject which figured in a recent novel. It ran something like this:

'Mother, where did Auntie Ruth get her baby?'

'Uncle Ralph and she made it.'

'Will they make some more?'

'I don't think so. Not for some time at any rate. You see, it is a very messy business and frightfully expensive.'

That would not have passed with a generation which knew its Catechism and could repeat firmly: 'God made me and all the world.'

What impressed Laura most about Candleford, on that first holiday there, was that, every day, there was something new to see or do or find out and new people to see and talk to and new places to visit, and this gave a colour and richness to life to which she was unaccustomed. At home, things went on day after day much in the same manner; the same people, all of whom she knew, did the same things at the same time from week-end to week-end. There you knew that, while you were having your breakfast, you would hear Mrs Massey clattering by on her pattens to the well, and that Mrs Watts would have her washing out first on the line and Mrs Broadway second every Monday morning, and that the fish-hawker would come on Monday and the coalman on Friday and the baker three times a week, and that no one else was likely to come nearer than the turning into the main road.

Of course, there were the changes of the seasons. It was delightful on some sunny morning in February, one of those days which older people called 'weather-breeders', to see the hazel catkins plumping out against the blue sky and to smell the first breath of spring in the air. Delightful, too, when spring was nearer, to search the hedgerows for violets, and to see the cowslips and bluebells again and the may, and the fields turning green, then golden. But all these delights you expected; they could not fail, for had not God Himself said that seedtime and harvest, summer and winter, should endure as long as the world lasted? That was His promise when He painted the first rainbow and set it in the sky as a sign.

But at Candleford these things did not seem so important to Laura as they did at home. You had to be alone to enjoy them properly; while games and fun and pretty clothes and delicious food demanded company. For about a week of her visit Laura wished she had been born at Candleford; that she was Aunt Ann's child and had lots of nice things and was never scolded.

Then, as the week or two for which they had been invited drew
out to nearly a month, she began to long for her home; to
wonder how her garden was looking and what the new baby
was like and if her mother had missed her.

The last day of their holiday was wet and one of the cousins
suggested they should go and play in the attic, so they went up
the bare, steep stairs, Laura and Ann and Amy and the two
little boys, while the two elder girls were having a lesson in
pastry-making. The attic, Laura found, was a storehouse of old,
discarded things, much like the collection Mrs Herring had
stored in the clothes closet at home. But these things did not
belong to a landlady; they were family possessions with which
the children might do as they liked. They spent the morning
dressing up for charades, an amusement Laura had not heard of
before, but now found entrancing. Dressed in apron and shawl,
the point of the latter trailing on the ground behind her, she
gave her best imitation of Queenie, an old neighbour at home
who began most of her speeches with 'Lawks-a-mussy!' Then,
draped in an old lace curtain for veil, with a feather duster for
bouquet, she became a bride. Less realistically, no doubt, for
she had never seen a bride in conventional attire – the girls at
home wore their new Sunday frock to be married – but her
cousins said she did it well and she became very pleased with
herself and full of ideas for illustrating words which she kept to
herself for future use at home, for she felt too much of a novice
to venture suggestions.

All the morning, first one cousin then another had been running down to the kitchen to ask for suggestions for the charades. They always came back munching, or wiping crumbs
from their mouths, and once or twice they brought tit-bits for
the whole party. At last they all disappeared, Edmund included,
and Laura was left alone in her bridal finery, which she took the
opportunity of examining in a tall, cracked mirror which leaned
against one wall. But her own reflection did not hold her more
than a moment, for she saw in the glass a recess she had not
noticed before packed with books. Books on shelves, books in
piles on the floor, and still other books in heaps, higgledy-
piggledy, as though they had been turned out of sacks. Which

they had, no doubt, for she was told afterwards that the collection was the unsaleable remains of a library from one of the large houses in the district. Her uncle, who was known to be a great reader, had been at the sale of furniture and been told that he might have what books were left if he cared to cart them away. A few of the more presentable bindings had already been taken downstairs; but the bulk of the collection still awaited the time when he should not be too busy to look through them.

That attic was very quiet for the next quarter of an hour, for Laura, still in her bridal veil, was down on her knees on the bare boards, as happy and busy as a young foal in a field of green corn.

There were volumes of old sermons which she passed over quickly; a natural history of the world which might have detained her had there not been so many other vistas to explore; histories and grammars and lexicons and 'keepsakes' with coloured pictures of beautiful languishing ladies bending over graves beneath weeping willows, or standing before mirrors dressed for balls, with the caption 'Will he come tonight?' There were old novels, too, and poetry. The difficulty was to know what to look at first.

When they missed her downstairs and came to call her to dinner she was deep in Richardson's *Pamela, or Virtue Rewarded*, and it was afterwards a standing joke against her that she had jumped and looked dazed when Amy hissed into her ear, 'Do you like apple dumplings?'

'Laura's a bookworm, a bookworm a bookworm!' she sang to her sisters with the air of having made an astonishing discovery, and Laura wondered if a bookworm might not be something unpleasant until she added: 'A bookworm, like Father.'

She had brought the first volume of *Pamela* down with them to illustrate Laura's bookworminess and now asked her mother if Laura might not have it to keep. After glancing through it, her mother looked doubtful, for she gathered that it was a love story, though not, perhaps, the full extent of its unsuitability for a reader of such tender age. But Uncle Tom, coming in just then to his dinner and hearing the whole story, said 'Let her keep it. No book's too old for anybody who is able to enjoy it, and none too young, either, for that matter. Let her read what she likes, and when she's tired of reading to herself she can come to my shop and read to me while I work.'

'Poor Laura! You're in for it!' laughed mischievous Nell. 'Once you start reading to Dad, he'll never let you go. You'll have to sit in his smelly old shop and read his dry old books for ever.'

'Now! Now! The less you say about that the better, my girl. Who was it came to read to me and made such a hash of it that I never asked her to come again?'

'Me', and 'Me', and 'Me', cried the girls simultaneously, and their father laughed and said: 'You see, Laura, what a lot of dunces they are. Give them one of their mother's magazines, with fashion pictures and directions for making silk purses out of sows' ears and pretty little tales that end in wedding bells, and they'll lap it ûp like a cat lapping cream; but offer them something to read that needs a bit of biting on and they're soon tired, or too hot, or too cold, or they can't stand the smell of cobbler's wax, or think they hear somebody knocking at the front door and have to go to open it. Molly started reading *The Pilgrim's Progress* to me over a year ago – her own choice, because she liked the pictures – and got the poor fellow as far as the Slough of Despond. Then she had to take an afternoon off to get a new frock fitted. Then there was something else, and something else, and poor Christian is still bogged up in the slough for all she knows or cares. But we won't have *The Pilgrim's Progress* when you read to me, Laura. That is a shade dull for some young people. I've read it a good many times and hope to read it a good many more before I wear my eyesight out getting a living for these ungrateful young besoms. A grand old book, *The Pilgrim's Progress*! But I've something here you'll like better. *Cranford*. Ever heard of it, Laura? No, I thought not. Well, you've got a treat in store.'

They sampled *Cranford* that afternoon, and how Laura loved dear Miss Matty! Her uncle was pleased with her reading, but not too pleased to correct her faults.

Seated on the end of the bench on which he worked, with both arms extended as he drew the waxed thread through the leather, his eyes beaming mildly through his spectacles, he would say: 'Not too fast now, Laura, and not *too* much expression. Don't overdo things. These were genteel old bodies, very prim and proper, who would not have raised their voices much if they'd heard the last trump sounding.' Or, more gently, in a matter-of-fact tone, as if, although it did not matter much how words were pronounced as long as one knew their meaning, it might still be just as well to conform to usage: 'I think that word is pronounced so-and-so, Laura,' and Laura would repeat the syllables after him until she had got it more or less correctly. Having read so much to herself and being a rapid reader, she knew the meanings of hundreds of words which she had never even attempted to pronounce until she came to read aloud to her uncle. Though he must have been sorely tempted to do so, he never once smiled, even at her most grotesque efforts. Years later in conversation he pronounced magician 'magicun' and added, 'as Laura once called one of that kidney', and they both laughed heartily at the not altogether inapt rendering.

XXVI

Uncle Tom's Queer Fish

THE readings were continued the next summer, when Laura again spent her summer holidays with her cousins, and afterwards, when Candleford became for several years her second home. Every afternoon when her cousins could be persuaded to go out or do what they wanted to do without her, she would tap at the door of her uncle's workshop and hear the familiar challenge, 'Who goes there?' and reply, 'Bookworms, Limited,' and, receiving the password, go in and sit by the open window looking out on the garden and river and read while her uncle worked.

Their reading was often interrupted, for customers came and went, or sat down to chat in a special chair with a cushion, 'the customer's chair'. Many sat in that chair who were not there on business, for her uncle had many friends who liked to look in when passing, especially on days when there was something of special interest in the newspaper. 'Just wanted to know what you thought of it,' they would say, and Laura noticed that whatever opinion he had given them was adopted so thoroughly that it was often advanced as their own before they left.

In the evening his workshop became a kind of a club for the young working-men of the neighbourhood, who would sit around on upturned boxes, smoking and talking or playing draughts or dominoes. Uncle Tom said he liked to see their young faces round him, and it kept them out of the 'pub'. Their arrival was the signal for Laura to take up her book and depart; but, when a day caller arrived, she would sit still in her corner, reading, or trying to solve that maddening puzzle of the day, 'Getting the teeth in the nigger's mouth'. The mouth belonged to a face enclosed in a circular glass case and the teeth were small metal balls which were easier to scatter than to get into place. One, two, or three, might with infinite patience be coaxed to rest between the thick lips, but the next gentle jerk, intended to place a fourth, would send them all rolling around beneath the glass again. Laura never got more than three in. But perhaps she did not persevere sufficiently; it was much more interesting to listen.

Uncle Tom had many friends. Some of these, as might have been expected, were fellow tradesmen of the town who looked in upon him to pass the time of day, as they said, or to discuss the news or some business complication. Others were poor people who came to ask his advice on some point, or to ask him to sign a paper, or to bring him something out of their gardens, or merely to rest and talk a few minutes. Few of these ever spoke to Laura, beyond a casual greeting, but she came to know them and could remember their faces and voices when those of others who had been more to her had become dim. But it was those Nellie described as 'Dad's queer fish' that she liked best of all. There was Miss Connie, who wore a thick tweed golf cape and spiked boots, even in August. 'Let Laura take your cape and sit down and cool off a bit,' Uncle Tom would say to her when the sun was raging and there was scarcely a breath of air in the shop, even with both windows wide open. 'No. No, thanks, Tom. Don't touch it, please, Laura. I wear it to keep the heat from the spine. The spine should always be protected.'

Miss Constance kept nineteen cats in the big house where she lived alone, for she could not trust servants; she thought they would always be spying upon her. Sometimes a kitten would thrust its head between the edges of her cape as she talked. 'Now, don't you worry, Miss Constance,' Uncle Tom would be saying. 'You'll get your money all right come quarter day. Some lawyers are rogues, we know, but not Mr Steerforth. And nobody can harm you for keeping your cats, for your house is your own. And don't take any notice of what you heard Mrs Harmer say; though, if you'll excuse me for saying it, Miss Constance, I do think you've got quite enough of them. I wouldn't save any more kittens, if I were you; and, if you can't bear a maid about the place, why not get some decent, respectable woman to come in once or twice a week and clean up a bit? Somebody who likes cats. No. She wouldn't poison them, nor steal your things. Bless you, there are very few thieves about compared to the number of honest people in the world. And don't you worry, Miss Constance, or you'll lose all your pussies. Worry killed the cat, you know,' and at that often-repeated joke Miss Constance would smile and the smile would transform the poor, half-mad recluse she was fast becoming to something resembling the bright, happy girl who had danced all night and ridden to hounds in the days when Uncle Tom had first fitted her for her country shoes.

But even Miss Constance was not quite so strange as the big fat man who wore the dark inverness cloak and soft black felt hat. He was a poet, Laura was told, and that was why he dressed like that and wore his hair so long. He came every market day, having walked from a village called Isledon, six or seven miles away, and, after puffing and blowing and mopping his brow, he would draw out a paper from his breast pocket and say, 'I must read you this, Tom,' and Uncle Tom would say, 'So you've been at it again. Oh, you poets!' To her great disappointment, although she listened intently, Laura could never grasp exactly what his poems were about. There were eagles in most of them, but not the kind of eagles she had read of, which circled over mountains and carried off lambs and babies; these eagles of his were eagles one moment and Pride or Hate the next; and if there were flowers in his poems he had always chosen the ugliest, such as nightshade or rue. But it all sounded very learned and grand, read in his rich, sonorous voice, and she had the comfort of knowing that, if she could not make much sense of it, her uncle could not either, for she heard him say many times: 'You know I'm no judge of poetry. If it were prose now . . . But it's certainly got a fine roll and swell to it. That I do know.'

After the reading, they would settle down to talk about flowers and birds and what was going on in the fields, for the poet loved all these, although he did not write about them. Or sometimes he would talk of his home and children and praise his wife for allowing him to come away into the country alone for a whole summer to write. 'Shows she believes in you as a poet,' Uncle Tom said once, and the poet drew himself up from his chair and said, 'She does and she'll be justified, though perhaps not in my lifetime. Posterity will judge.'

'Fine words! Fine words!' said Uncle Tom after he had gone. 'But I doubt it. I doubt.'

Less odd, and therefore less interesting to Laura, though dearer to her Uncle Tom's heart, was the young doctor with the keen, eager face and grey eyes set deep under heavy dark brows. From what she heard then, she thought, looking back in after years, that he was trying to work up a practice and finding it heavy going. He certainly had a good deal of spare time.

'It's a rotten shame,' he would begin, as he burst into the workshop and turned up the tails of his frock coat to keep them from contact with the customers' chair. 'It's a rotten shame' was the beginning of most of his conversations. It was a rotten shame that cottage roofs should leak, that children living on farms should not know the taste of fresh milk, that wells should be in use of which the water was contaminated, or that families should have to sleep eight in a room.

Uncle Tom was just as sorry about it all as he was; but he was not so angry; though Laura did once hear him say that something they were talking about was damnable. 'You take things too hard,' Laura once heard him say. 'You fret, and it's no good fretting. You can only do what you can, and God knows you're doing your full share. Things'll be better in time. You mark my words, they will. They're better already: you should have seen Spittals' Alley when I was a boy!' And when the young man had taken down his top hat from the shelf which was kept covered with clean paper for its reception, and jammed it down on his head and gone out, still declaring that it was a rotten shame, her uncle said, perhaps to her, perhaps to himself: 'That young fellow-me-lad's going to make a big stir in the world, or else he's going to build up a fat practice, marry and settle down, and I don't know which to wish for him.'

It was the young doctor who named Laura 'the mouse'. 'Hullo, Mouse!' he would say if he happened to notice her. That seldom happened, for he had no eye for plain little girls with books on their knees, unless they were ill or hungry. When one of her pretty cousins burst in at the door, her healthy high spirits stirring the air like a breeze, his face lit up, for she was the type of what he believed all children would be, if they could be properly fed and cared for.

Excepting the doctor, none of those known as Uncle Tom's 'queer fish' seemed to have any work to do or business to attend to, and, excepting Miss Connie, none of them were Candleford people. Some were regular visitors to farmhouses where boarders were taken; others were staying for the fishing at village inns, or had their own homes in one of the surrounding villages. Uncle Tom's chief friend among them, a Mr Mostyn, took a furnished cottage outside the town every summer. How they had first become acquainted, Laura never heard, but by the time of her regular visits to Candleford he was a frequent visitor.

Even in his holiday attire of shabby Norfolk suit and sandals, no one could have mistaken Mr Mostyn for anything but what was then spoken of openly and unashamedly as 'a gentleman'. Unce Tom was a country shoemaker. He had black thumbs, worked in an apron, and carried the odours of leather and wax about with him; but he was the least class-conscious man on earth, and Mr Mostyn appeared equally so, though breeding may have had something to do with that on his side. While Uncle Tom sewed, they would talk by the hour; about books, about historical characters, new discoveries in science or exploration, with many a titbit of local gossip thrown in and many a laugh, especially when Tom told some story in dialect. Or they would sit silent if that suited either of them better than talking. Mr Mostyn would take a book out of his pocket and read; or, in the midst of a conversation, Tom would say, 'Not another word, now, till I've got this seam joined up. I've cut the toecap a bit short, I find.' In fact, they were friends.

But one year, when Laura arrived, she found things had changed between them. Mr Mostyn still called at the workshop once or twice a week and they still talked – talked more than ever before, indeed – but upon a new subject. Mr Mostyn was thinking of changing his creed, 'going over to Rome', Uncle Tom called it, and, surprisingly, for a man who believed in perfect freedom of thought, he did not approve of this step.

It was strange to see how earnest he was about it; for, although he went to church every Sunday, he had never appeared to take any special interest in religion. Mr Mostyn, probably, had hitherto taken less. Laura had often heard him say that he preferred a good long tramp on a Sunday to church-going. Now, something had stirred him; he had been reading Catholic doctrine for months and was on the brink of being received into the Catholic Church.

Uncle Tom must have read, too, at some time, for he appeared to know the authors his friend quoted. 'That's Newman,' he said once. 'Methinks his lordship doth protest too much'; and, at another time, 'He can write like an angel, I grant you, but it's all spellbinding.'

Mr Mostyn gritted his teeth. 'Tom, Tom,' he said, 'your other name is Didymus!'

'Now, look here,' said Tom. 'We've got to get to grips with this. If you want everything thought out for you and to be told what to think and do, give your conscience to some priest to keep; go over to Rome. You couldn't do better. It'll be a rest for you, I don't deny, for you've had your problems, as many and hard as most men; but if, as a reasoning being, you prefer to accept full responsibility for your own soul, you are going the wrong road – you are, indeed!' Then Mr Mostyn said something about peace, and Tom retorted, 'Peace in exchange for liberty!' and Laura heard, or understood, no more.

'Another good man gone over to the old enchantress,' he said, as the door closed behind his friend; and Laura, who was by that time nearly fourteen, asked, 'Do you think it wrong to be a Catholic, Uncle?'

It was some time before he answered. She thought he had forgotten her presence and had been talking to himself. But, after he had polished his spectacles and taken up his work, he answered, 'Wrong? No, not for those born to it or suited to it. I've known some good Catholics in my time; some the religion suited like the glove the hand. It was a good thing for them, but it won't be for him. He's been over a year thinking it out and studying books about it, and if you have to spend a year worrying and arguing yourself into a thing, that thing's against your nature. If he'd been cut out for a Catholic, he'd have just sunk down into it months ago, as easy as falling into a feather bed, and not had to lash and worry himself and read his eyes out. But, for all that, I've been a fool to try to influence him, trying to influence him against being influenced. Never try to influence anybody, Laura. It's a mistake. Other people's lives are their own and they've got to live them, and often when we think they are doing wrong they are doing right – right for them, although it might not be right for us. Come, get that book and see how Lucy Snowe's getting on with her Frenchman, and I'll stick to my last, as every good shoemaker should do, and not go airing my opinions again – until the next time.'

Once a commercial traveller called at the workshop to have a stitch or two put in the shoes he was wearing. He was a stranger to Laura; but not to her uncle, for one of the first questions he asked was, 'How is your wife?'

'Lazier and more contrary than ever,' was the unconventional reply.

Uncle Tom looked grave, but he said nothing. The visitor needed no encouragement, however; he was soon launched on a long story of how he had that very morning taken up his wife's breakfast to her in bed – so many rashers, so many eggs, and toast and marmalade. Breakfast in bed for any one who was not ill was a novel idea to Laura; but her Uncle Tom seemed to look upon it as a slight attention any good husband might pay his wife, for he only said, 'That was very kind of you.'

'And what did I get for my kindness?' almost shouted the husband. 'No thanks, you'll bet! but only black looks and an order to be home on time tonight for once in my life. Home on time! Me, who, as she ought to know by this time, might be held up for hours on end by a customer. Of all the spiteful, contrary cats . . .'

Uncle Tom looked distressed. 'Hush! Hush! my lad,' he interposed. 'Don't say things you'll be sorry for after. How long have you been married? Two years, and no child yet? Well, you wait till you've been married ten before you begin talking like that, and by that time, if you do as you should yourself, it's ten to one you'll not need to. Some women simply can't understand what business is unless they see for themselves. Why not take her out on the round a time or two in that smart little outfit of yours with the high-stepper. The firm's done you well this time, I see, in that respect. A nice bit of horseflesh, if I'm any judge! If you do that, she'll see for herself, and the outing will do her good. It's dull for a young woman, shut up by herself in the house all day, and when, towards night, her man's supper's drying up in the oven through waiting, it gets on her nerves and maybe her welcome's not all a husband might wish, after a trying day and not too many orders in his notebook. And when you get a bit nettled yourself, bite on it, bite on it, my boy; don't go opening your mouth to fill other folks's. They won't think any better of you if you do. Truth of the matter is, most married folks have their little upsets, especially for the first year or two; but they manage to pretend that all is well and that everything in the garden of matrimony looks lovely, and, in ninety-nine cases out of a hundred, before they know where they are, all *is* well, or as well as can be expected in this imperfect world.'

During this long speech the young man had broken in several times with such ejaculations as 'That's all very well' or 'Not

hálf', but he was spared the necessity for any formal comment
upon what was almost a lecture by a sound of scuffling and
'Whoa-a-s!' and 'Come up nows!' in the street, which caused
him to cram on the shoe which Tom had been attending to and
run. But, a few minutes later, very flushed and hot-looking, he
came to the open window and said: 'That mare of mine's got
the spirit of a racehorse. A moment more and she'd been off!
Got an idea I'll bring my wife next week; she could hold the
reins and read her book while I was inside anywhere, and the
outing might do her good. So long, Mr Whitbread. I must go or
she'll kick the cart to bits.'

Laura never knew if the mare kicked the cart to bits; or if the
young couple's own little applecart of happiness was overturned
or steadied; but she can still see the young husband's face
flushed and distorted with indignation beneath the white straw
'boater', moored so modishly to his button-hole by a black
cord, and her Uncle Tom's pale and grizzled and serious, looking up at him through his spectacles as he said: 'Bite on it, my
boy. Bite on it.'

XXVII

Candleford Green

ON one of her visits to Candleford, Laura herself found a
friend, and one whose influence was to shape the whole outward
course of her life.

An old friend of her mother's named Dorcas Lane kept the
Post Office at Candleford Green, and one year, when she heard
that Laura was staying so near her, she asked her and her
cousins to go over to tea. Only Molly would go; the others said
it was too hot for walking, that Miss Lane was faddy and old-
fashioned, and that there was no one to talk to at Candleford
Green and nothing to see. So Laura, Edmund, and Molly
went.

Candleford Green was at that time a separate village. In a
few years it was to become part of Candleford. Already the

rows of villas were stretching out towards it; but as yet the green with its spreading oak with the white-painted seats, its roofed-in well with the chained bucket, its church spire soaring out of trees, and its clusters of old cottages, was untouched by change.

Miss Lane's house was a long, low white one, with the Post Office at one end and a blacksmith's forge at the other. On the turf of the green in front of the door was a circular iron platform with a hole in the middle which was used for putting on tyres to wagon and cart wheels, for she was wheelwright as well as blacksmith and postmistress. She did not work in the forge herself; she dressed in silks of which the colours were brighter than those usually worn then by women of her age and had tiny white hands which she seldom soiled. Hers was the brain of the business.

To go to see Cousin Dorcas, as they had been told to call her, was an exciting event to Laura and Edmund, for they hoped to be shown her famous telegraph machine. There had been some talk about it at home when their parents heard it had been installed, and their mother, who had seen one, described it as a sort of clock face, but with letters instead of figures, 'and when you turn the handle,' she said, 'the hand goes round and you can spell out words on it, and that sends the hand round on the clock face at the other Post Office where it's for, and they just write it down, pop it into an envelope, and send it where it's addressed.'

'And then they know somebody's going to die,' put in Edmund.

'After they've paid three and sixpence,' said their father, rather bitterly, for an agitation was being worked up in the hamlet against having to pay that crushing sum for the delivery of a telegram. 'For Hire of Man and Horse, 3*s*. 6*d*.' was written upon the envelope and that sum had to be found and paid before the man on the horse would part with the telegram. But about that time, the innkeeper, tired of having to lend three and sixpence with little prospect of getting it back, every time the news arrived that some neighbour's father or mother or sister or aunt was 'sinking fast' or had 'passed peacefully away this morning', had, in collaboration with a few neighbours of whom the children's father was one, written a formal and much-thought-out protest to the Postmaster General, which resulted in men coming with long chains to measure the whole length of the road between the hamlet and the Post Office in the market town. The distance was found to be a few feet under, instead of over, the three-miles limit of the free delivery of telegrams. This made quite an interesting little story for Laura to tell Cousin Dorcas. 'And to think of those poor things having paid that sum! As much as a man could earn in a day and a half's hard work,' was her comment, and there was something in the way she said it that made Laura feel that, although, as her cousins said, Miss Lane might be peculiar, it was a nice kind of peculiarity.

Laura liked her looks, too. She was then about fifty, a little, birdlike woman in her kingfisher silk dress, with snapping black eyes, a longish nose, and black hair plaited into a crown on the top of her head.

The famous telegraph instrument stood on a little table under her parlour window. There was a small model office for the transaction of ordinary postal business, but 'the telegraph' was too secret and sacred to be exposed there. When not in use, the dial with its brass studs, one for every letter of the alphabet, was kept under a velvet cover of her own devising, resembling a tea-cosy. She removed this to show the children the instrument and even allowed Laura to spell out her own name on the brass studs – without putting the switch over, of course, or, as she said, Head Office would wonder what they were up to.

Edmund preferred the forge to the telegraph office, and Molly the garden where Zillah, the maid, was picking green-gages bursting with ripeness. Laura liked all these; but, best of all, she liked Cousin Dorcas herself. She said such quick, clever things and seemed to know what one was thinking before a word was spoken. She showed Laura her house, from attic to cellar, and what a house it was! Her parents had lived in it, and her grandparents, and it was her delight to keep all the old family possessions just as she had inherited them. Other people might scrap their solid old furniture and replace it with plush-covered suites and what-nots and painted milking-stools and Japanese fans; but Dorcas had the taste to prefer good old oak and mahogany and brass, and the strength of mind to dare to be thought old-fashioned. So the grandfather's clock in the front kitchen still struck the hours as it had done on the day of the Battle of Waterloo. The huge, heavy oak table at the head of which she carved for the workmen and maid, sitting in higher or lower seats according to degree, was older still. There was a legend that it had been made in the kitchen by the then village carpenter and was too large to remove without taking it to pieces. The bedrooms still had their original four-posters, one of them with blue-and-white check curtains, the yarn of which had been spun by her grandmother on the spinning wheel lately rescued from the attic, repaired and placed with the telegraph instrument in the parlour. On the dresser shelves were pewter plates and dishes, with a few pieces of old willow-pattern 'to liven them up', as she said; and in the chimney corner, where Laura sat looking up into the square of blue sky through the black furry walls, a flint and tinder box, used for striking lights before matches were in common use, stood on one ledge, and on another stood a deep brass vessel with a long point for sticking down into the embers to heat beer. There were brass candle-sticks on the mantelpiece, and, flanking it, a pair of brass warming-pans hung on the wall. These were no longer in use, nor was the sandbox for drying wet ink instead of using blotting-paper, nor the nest of wooden chopping bowls, nor the big brewing copper in the back kitchen, but they were piously preserved in their old places, and, with them, as many of the old customs as could be made to fit in with modern requirements.

The grandfather's clock was kept exactly half an hour fast, as it had always been, and, by its time, the household rose at six, breakfasted at seven and dined at noon; while mails were despatched and telegrams timed by the new Post Office clock, which showed correct Greenwich time, received by wire at ten o'clock every morning.

Miss Lane's mind kept time with both clocks. Although she loved the past and tried to preserve its spirit as well as its relics, in other ways she was in advance of her own day. She read a

good deal, not poetry, or pure literature – she had not the right
kind of mind for that – but she took in *The Times* and kept
herself well-informed of what was going on in the world, especially in the way of invention and scientific discovery. Probably she was the only person on or around the Green who had
heard the name of Darwin. Others of her interests were inter-
national relationships and what is now called big business. She
had shares in railways and the local Canal Company, which was
daring for a woman in her position, and there was an affair
called the Iceland Moss Litter Company for news of which
watch had to be kept when, later, Laura was reading the newspaper aloud to her.

Had she lived later she must have made her mark in the
world, for she had the quick, unerring grasp of a situation, the
imagination to foresee and the force to carry through, which
meant certain success. But there were few openings for women
in those days, especially for those born in small country villages, and she had to be content to rule over her own small
establishment. She had been thought queer and rather improper
when, her father having died and left his business to her, his
only child, instead of selling out and retiring to live in ladylike
leisure at Leamington Spa or Weston-super-Mare, as her friends
had expected, she had simply substituted her own name for his
on the billheads and carried on the business.

'And why not?' she asked. 'I had kept the books and written
the letters for years, and Matthew is an excellent foreman. My
father himself had not put foot inside the shop for ten months
before he died.'

Her neighbours could have given her many reasons why not,
the chief one being that a woman blacksmith had never been
known in those parts before. A draper's or grocer's shop, or
even a public-house, might be inherited and carried on by a
woman; but a blacksmith's was a man's business, and they
thought Miss Lane unwomanly to call herself one. Miss Lane
did not mind being thought unwomanly. She did not mind at all
what her neighbours thought of her, and that alone set her apart
from most women of her day.

She had consented to house the Post Office temporarily in the first place, because it was a convenience badly needed on and around the Green, and no one else could be found willing to undertake the responsibility. But the work soon proved to be a pleasure to her. There was something about the strict working to a time-table, the idea of being a link in a great national organization and having some small measure of public authority which appealed to her businesslike mind. She liked having an inside knowledge of her neighbours' affairs too – there is no denying that – and to have people coming in and out, some of them strangers and interesting. As she ran the office, she had many of the pleasures of a hostess without the bother and expense of entertaining.

She had arranged her Post Office with its shining counter, brass scales, and stamps, postal orders, and multiplicity of official forms neatly pigeonholed, in what had been a broad passage which ran through the house from the front door to the garden. The door which led from this into the front kichen, where meals were taken, marked the boundary between the new world and the old. In after days, when Laura had read a little history, it gave her endless pleasure to notice the sudden transition from one world to the other.

It was still the custom in that trade for unmarried workmen to live-in with the families of their employers; and, at meal-times, when the indoor contingent was already seated, sounds of pumping and sluicing water over hands and faces would come from the paved courtyard outside. Then 'the men', as they were always called, would appear, rolling their leather aprons up around their waists as they tiptoed to their places at table.

The foreman, Matthew, was a bow-legged, weak-eyed little man with sandy whiskers, as unlike as possible the popular picture of a village blacksmith. But he was a trustworthy foreman, a clever smith, and, in farriery, was said to approach genius. The three shoeing-smiths who worked under him were brawny fellows, all young, and all of them bashful indoors; although, by repute, 'regular sparks' when out in the village, dressed in their Sunday suits. Indoors they spoke in a husky whisper; but in the shop, on the days when they were all three working there together, their voices could be heard in the house, above the

roaring of the bellows and the cling-clang of the anvil as they
intoned their remarks and requests to each other, or sang as an
anthem some work-a-day sentence, such as 'Bil-h-l-l, pass me o-
o-over that sm-m-a-ll spanner.' When Matthew was out of the
way, they would stand at the shop door for 'a breather', as they
called it, and exchange pleasantries with passers-by. One had
recently got into trouble with Cousin Dorcas for shouting
'Whoa, Emma!' after a girl; but no one who only saw him at
table would have thought him capable of it.

There, the journeymen's place was definitely below the salt.
At the head of the long, solid oak table sat 'the mistress' with an
immense dish of meat before her, carving knife in hand. Then
came a reserved space, sometimes occupied by visitors, but
more often blank table-cloth; then Matthew's chair, and, after
that, another, smaller blank space, just sufficient to mark the
difference in degree between a foreman and ordinary workmen.
Beyond that, the three young men sat in a row at the end of the
table, facing the mistress. Zillah, the maid, had a little round
table to herself by the wall. Unless important visitors were present, she joined freely in the conversation; but the three young
men seldom opened their mouths excepting to shovel in food.
If, by chance, they had something they thought of sufficient
interest to impart, they always addressed their remarks to Miss
Lane, and prefixed them by 'Ma-am'. 'Ma-am, have you heard
that Squire Bashford's sold his Black Beauty?' or 'Ma-am, I've
heard say that two ricks've bin burnt down at Wheeler's. A
tramp sleeping under set 'em afire, they think.' But, usually, the
only sound at their end of the table was that of the scraping of
plates, or of a grunt of protest if one of them nudged another
too suddenly. They had special cups and saucers, very large and
thick, and they drank their beer out of horns, instead of glasses
or mugs. There were certain small delicacies on the table which
were never offered them and which they took obvious pains not
to appear to notice. When they had finished their always excellent meal, one of them said 'Pardon, Ma-am,' and they all tiptoed out. Then Zillah brought in the tea-tray and Matthew
stayed for a cup before he, too, withdrew. At tea-time they all
had tea to drink, but Miss Lane said this was an innovation of

her own. In her father's time the family had tea alone, it was their one private meal, and the men had what was called 'afternoon bavour', which consisted of bread and cheese and beer, at three o'clock.

As a child, Laura thought the young men were poorly treated and was inclined to pity them; but, afterwards, she found they were under an age-old discipline, supposed, in some mysterious way, to fit them for becoming in their turn master-men. Under this system, such and such an article of food was not suitable for the men; the men must have something substantial – boiled beef and dumplings, or a thick cut off a gammon, or a joint of beef. When they came in to go to bed on a cold night, they could be offered hot spiced beer, but not elderberry wine. They must not be encouraged to talk and you must never discuss family affairs in their presence, or they might become familiar; in short, they must be kept in their place, because they were 'the men'.

Until that time, or a few years earlier in more advanced districts, these distinctions had suited the men as well as they had done the employers. Their huge meals and their beds in a row in the large attic were part of their wages, and as long as it was excellent food and the beds were good feather beds with plenty of blankets, they had all they expected or wished for indoors. More would have embarrassed them. They had their own lives outside.

When a journeyman was about to marry, it was the rule for him to leave and find a shop where the workers lived out. There was no difficulty about this, especially in towns, where the living-out system was extending, and a good workman was always sure of employment. The young men who still lived in did so from choice; they said they got better food than in lodgings, better beds, and had not to walk to their work at six o'clock in the morning.

Miss Lane's own father had come to the Green as a journeyman, wearing a new leather apron and with a basket of tools slung over his shoulder. He had walked from Northampton, not on account of poverty, for his father was a master-man with a good smithy in a village near that town; but because it was the custom at that time that, after apprenticeship, a young smith should travel the country and work in various shops to gain experience. That was why they were called 'journeymen', Miss Lane said, because they journeyed about.

But her own father journeyed no farther, for his first employer had a daughter, Miss Lane's mother. She was an only child and the business was a flourishing one, and, although the new journeyman was the son of another master-smith, her parents had objected to the match.

According to her daughter's story, the first intimation they had of the budding attachment was when her mother found her Katie darning the journeyman's socks. She snatched them out of her hand and threw them into the fire and her father told her he would rather see her in her coffin than married to a mere journeyman. After all they had done for her, she should marry at least a farmer. However, they must have become reconciled to the match, for the young couple married and lived with the parents until the father died and they inherited the house and business. There was a painting of them in their wedding clothes in the parlour; the bridegroom in lavender trousers and white kid gloves (How did he manage to squeeze his smith's horny and ingrained hands into them?), and the dear little bride in lavender silk with a white lace fichu and a white poke bonnet encircled with green leaves.

When she was old enough, little Dorcas had been sent to school as a weekly boarder and the school must have been even more old-fashioned than her home. The girls, she said, addressed each other as Miss So-and-So, even during playtime, and spent some time every day lying flat on the bare board floor of their bedroom to improve their figures. Their punishments were carefully calculated to fit their crimes. The one she remembered best and often laughed about later was for pride or conceit, which was standing in a corner of the schoolroom and repeating 'Keep down, proud stomach', patting the said organ meanwhile. They learned to write a beautifully clear hand, to 'cast up accounts', and to do fine needlework, which was considered a sufficient education for a tradesman's daughter eighty or ninety years ago.

Once, when she was turning out a drawer to show Laura some treasure, she came upon a white silk stocking, which she held up for inspection. 'How do you like my darning?' she asked; but it was not until Laura had drawn the stocking over her own hand to examine it more closely that she saw that the heel and the instep and part of the toe were literally made of darns. The silk of the original fabric had been matched exactly and the work had been exquisitely done in a stitch which resembled knitting.

'It must have taken you ages,' was the natural comment.

'It took me a whole winter. Time thrown away, for I never wore it. My mother turned it out from somewhere and gave it me to darn at such times as the men were indoors. It was not thought proper then to do ordinary sewing before men, except men's shirts, of course; never our own underclothes, or anything of that kind; and as to reading, that would have been thought a waste of time; and one must not sit idle, that would have been setting a bad example; but cutting holes in a stocking foot and darning them up again was considered industrious. Be glad you weren't born in those days.'

Although she could darn so beautifully, she no longer darned her own stockings. She left them to Zillah, whose darns could easily be seen across the room. Probably she felt she had done enough darning for one lifetime.

Belonging to the establishment was a light spring-cart and a bright chestnut mare named Peggy and, three times a week, Matthew and two of the shoeing smiths drove off with strings of horseshoes and boxes of tools to visit the hunting stables. Sometimes the remaining smith was out also and the forge was left, cold and silent and dark, save for the long streamers of daylight which filtered through the cracks in the shutters. Then Laura would steal in through the garden door and inhale the astringent scents of iron and oil and ashes and hoof-parings; and pull the bellows handle and see the dull embers turn red; and lift the big sledge hammer to feel its weight and made the smaller ones tinkle on the anvil. Another lovely sound belonging to the forge was often heard at night when the household was in bed, for then the carrier, returning from market, would fling down on the green in front of the shop the long bars of iron for making horseshoes. *Cling-cling, cling,* it would go, like a peal of bells. Then the carrier would chirrup to his tired horse and the heavy wheels would move on.

All kinds of horses came to the forge to be shod: heavy cart-horses, standing quiet and patient; the baker's and grocer's and butcher's van horses; poor old screws belonging to gipsies or fish-hawkers; and an occasional hunter, either belonging to some visitor to the neighbourhood or one from a local stable which had cast a shoe and could not wait until the regular visit-ing day. There were a few donkeys in the neighbourhood, and they, too, had to be shod; but always by the youngest shoeing smith, for it would have been beneath the dignity of his seniors to become the butt for the wit of the passers-by. 'He-haw! He-haw!' they would shout. 'Somebody tell me now, which is top-most, man or beast, for danged if I can see any difference be-twixt 'em?'

Most of the horses were very patient; but a few would plunge and kick and rear when approached. These Matthew himself shod and, under his skilful handling, they would quiet down immediately. He had only to put his hand on the mane and whisper a few words in the ear. It was probably the hand and voice which soothed them; but it was generally believed that he whispered some charm which had power over them, and he rather encouraged this idea by saying when questioned: 'I only speaks to 'em in their own language.'

The local horses were all known to the men and addressed by them by name. Even the half-yearly bills were made out: 'To So-and-So, Esq. For shoeing Violet, or Poppet, or Whitefoot, or The Grey Lady.' 'All round', or 'fore', or 'hind', as the case might demand. Strings of horseshoes, made in quiet intervals, hung upon the shop walls, apparently ready to put on; but there was usually some little alteration to be made on the anvil while the horse waited. 'No two horses' feet are exactly alike,' Mat-thew told Laura. 'They have their little plagues and peculi-arities, like you and me do.' And the parting words from man to beast were often: 'There, old girl, that's better. You'll be able to run ten miles without stopping with them shoes on your feet.'

Other items which figured in the bills were making hinges for doors, flaps for drains, gates and railings and tools and household requirements. On one occasion a bill was sent out for 'Pair of Park Gates to your own design, £20', and Matthew said it should have been fifty, for he had worked on them for months, staying in the shop hours after the outer door was closed, and rising early to fit in another hour or two before the ordinary work of the day began. But it was a labour of love, and, after they were hung, he had his reward when he, who so seldom went out for pleasure, dressed on a Sunday and took a walk that way in order to admire and enjoy his own handicraft.

So the days went on, and, secure in the knowledge of their own importance in the existing scheme of things, the blacksmiths boasted: 'Come what may, a good smith'll never want for a job, for whatever may come of this new cast-iron muck in other ways, the horses'll always have to be shod, and they can't do that in a foundry!'

Yet, as iron will bend to different uses, so will the workers in iron. Twenty years later the younger of that generation of smiths were painting above their shop doors, 'Motor Repairs a Speciality', and, greatly daring, taking mechanism to pieces which they had no idea how they were going to put together again. They made many mistakes, which passed undetected because the owners had no more knowledge than they had of the inside of 'the dratted thing', and they soon learned by experiment sufficient to enable them to put on a wise air of authority. Then the legend over the door was repainted, 'Motor Expert', and expert many of them became in a surprisingly short time, for they brought the endless patience and ingenuity of the craftsman to the new mechanism, plus his adaptable skill.

XXVIII

Growing Pains

BUT the holidays at Candleford only occupied a small part of
Laura's year. At the end of a month or so a letter would come
saying that school would begin on the following Monday and
she had to return. Excepting the arrival of a new baby or two,
or the settling of a stray swarm of bees on somebody's apple-
tree, nothing ever seemed to have happened in the hamlet while
she had been away. The neighbours would still be discussing the
same topics. The crops were good, or 'but middling', according
to the season. Someone had nearly a half-bushel more corn
from their gleanings than the rest of the hamlet, and that was a
mystery to others, who declared they had worked just as hard
and spent even more hours afield. '*A bit of rick-pulling there,
I'll warrant.*' After a dry summer the water in the wells would
be dangerously low, but it had not given out yet, and, 'Please
God, us shall get a nice drop of rain 'fore long. The time of
year's getting on to when we may look for it.' 'Look for it! He!
He! It'll come whether you looks for it or not. Nice weather for
young ducks and mud up to y'r knees when you goes round to
the well, *you'll* see, before you knows where *you* are.'

She found the hamlet unchanged every year; but, beyond the
houses, everything had altered, for it was still summer when she
went away and when she returned it was autumn. Along the
hedgerows hips and haws and crab-apples were ripe and the
ivory parchment flowers of the traveller's joy had become silver
and silky. The last of the harvest had been carried and already
the pale stubble was greening over. Soon the sheep would be
turned into the fields to graze, then the ploughs would come and
turn the earth brown once more.

At home, the plums on the front wall of the house were ripe
and the warm, fruity smell of boiling jam drew all the wasps in
the neighbourhood. Other jams, jellies, and pickles already
stood on the pantry shelves. Big yellow vegetable marrows

dangled from hooks, and ropes of onions and bunches of drying thyme and sage. The faggot pile was being replenished and the lamp was again lighted soon after tea.

For the first few days after her return the house would seem small and the hamlet bare, and she was inclined to give herself the airs of a returned traveller when telling of the places she had seen and the people she had met on her holiday. But that soon wore off and she slipped back into her own place again. The visits to Candleford were very pleasant and the conveniences of her cousins' home and their way of life had the charm of novelty; but the plain spotlessness of her own home, with few ornaments and no padding to obscure the homely outline, was good, too. She felt she belonged there.

Her freedom of the fields grew less every year, however, for, by the time her last year at school approached, her mother had five children. One little sister shared her bed and another slept in the same room; she had to go to bed very quietly in the dark, not to awaken them. In the day-time, out of school hours, the latest baby, a boy, had to be nursed indoors or taken out for his airing. These things, in themselves, were no hardship, for she adored the baby, and the little sisters, who held on, one on each side of the baby-carriage, were dears, one with brown eyes and a mop of golden curls, and the other a fat, solemn child with brown hair cut in a straight fringe across her forehead. But Laura could no longer read much indoors or roam where she would when out, for the baby-carriage had to be kept more or less to the roads and be pushed back punctually at baby's feeding-time. Her mother's bedtime stories were still a joy, although no longer told to Edmund and her, but to the younger children, for Laura loved to listen and to observe the effect each story had on her little sisters. She was also rather fond of correcting her mother when her memory went astray in telling the old familiar true stories, which did not add to her popularity, of which she had little enough already. She had come to what the hamlet called 'an ok'ard age, neither 'ooman nor child, when they oughter be shut up in a box for a year or two'.

At school about this time she made her first girl friend and wearied her mother by saying, 'Emily Rose does this,' 'Emily

Rose does that,' and 'That is what Emily Rose says,' until she said she was sick of the sound of Emily Rose's name, and could not Laura talk about somebody else for a change.

Emily Rose was the only child of elderly parents who lived on the other side of the parish in a cottage like a picture on a Christmas card. It had the same diamond-paned windows and pointed thatched roof and the same mass of old-fashioned flowers around the doorway. There was even a winding foot-path leading across a meadow to its rustic gate. Laura often wished she lived in such a house, away from interfering neigh-bours, and sometimes almost wished she was an only child like Emily Rose.

Emily Rose was a strong, sturdy little girl with faintly pink cheeks, wide blue eyes and a flaxen pigtail. Some pigtails in the school were as thin as rats' tails and others stuck out at an angle behind the head of the wearer, but Emily Rose's pigtail was thick as a rope and hung heavily to her waist, where it was finished off with a neat ribbon bow and a fluff of little loose curls. She had a way of drawing it up over her shoulder and stroking her cheek with this soft end, which Laura thought very captivating.

Her parents were in somewhat more comfortable circum-stances than the hamlet folk; for not only had they but one child to keep, instead of the usual half-dozen or more, but her father, being a shepherd, had slightly higher wages and her mother took in needlework. So Emily Rose had pretty clothes to set off her flaxen pigtail, a pleasant, comfortable home, and the undivided affection of both parents. But, although she had the self-confidence of one who was seldom thwarted, Emily Rose was not a spoilt child. Nothing could have spoiled one of her calm, well-balanced, straightforward disposition. Hers was one of those natures which are good all through, good-tempered, good-natured, and thorough in all they do; a little obstinate, perhaps, but, as they are usually obstinate with good cause, that also counts as a virtue.

Laura thought Emily Rose's bedroom was worthy of a prin-cess, with its white walls scattered with tiny pink rosebuds, little white bed and frilly white window-curtains tied up with pink bows. There were no babies for her to nurse, and apparently no household tasks were expected of her. She could have read all day and in bed at night, if she had cared to, for her room was well apart from that of her parents. But she did not want to read; her delight was in needlework, at which she excelled, and in wading through brooks and climbing trees. Her way home from school skirted a wood, and she boasted that she had climbed every tree by the pathway at some time or other and this for her own pleasure, without spectators, not because she had been dared to do it.

At home she was petted and made much of. She was asked what she would like to eat, instead of being given whatever was on the table, and if the food she fancied were not forthcoming her mother was quite apologetic. But there were delicious things to eat at Cold Harbour. Once, when Laura called for Emily Rose during school holidays they had sponge fingers and cowslip wine, which Emily Rose poured out herself into real wine-glasses. On another of Laura's visits there was lambs' tail pie. The tails in the pie were those of still living lambs which had been cut off while their owners were still very young, because, Laura was told, if sheep were allowed to have long tails they would, in wet weather, become heavy with wet and mud and injure or irritate them. So the shepherd docked them and took the tails home to be made into a pie or gave bundles of them to friends as a great favour. Laura did not like the idea of eating the tails of live lambs; but it had to be done, for she had been told it was rude to leave anything at all, excepting bones or fruit stones, on one's plate.

At school, that last year, Emily Rose and Laura were known as Class I and had several advantages, although these did not include much education. They were trusted with the *Key* containing the answers to their sums and heard each other's spellings, or anything else that had to be committed to memory. This was partly because the schoolmistress, with all the other classes in the school on hand, had no time at all to devote to them; but also as a mark of her confidence. 'I know I can trust my big girls,' she would say. There were but the two of them and no boys at all in Class I. Most of the children who had been with

Laura in the lower classes had by that time left school for work, or, having failed to pass their examinations, were being kept back in Standard IV to make another attempt at the next examination.

In summer the two 'big girls' were allowed to take out their lessons and do them under the lilac tree in the mistress's garden, and, in winter, they sat cosily by the fire in her cottage living-room, the condition attached to this latter privilege being that they kept up the fire and put on the potatoes to cook for her dinner at the appropriate time. Laura owed these advantages to Emily Rose. She was the show pupil of the school; good at every subject and exceptionally good at needlework. She was so good a needlewoman that she was trusted to make garments for the mistress's own wear, and perhaps that was the chief reason for their being given the freedom of the sitting-room, for Laura remembered her sitting with her feet on a hassock with yards and yards of white nainsook around her, putting thousands of tiny stitches into the nightdress she was feather-stitching, while Laura herself knelt before the fire toasting a kipper for the mistress's tea.

That picture remained with her because it was the day after St Valentine's Day, and Emily Rose was telling her about the valentine she had found awaiting her when she reached home the evening before. She had brought it to show Laura, pressed between cardboard and wrapped in layers of notepaper, all silver lace and silk-embroidered flowers, with the words:

> Roses are red
>   And violets blue,
> Carnations sweet,
>   And so are you,

and when Laura asked if she knew who had sent it, she pretended she had lost her needle and bent down to the floor, looking for it, and, when pressed again, told Laura that her kipper would never be cooked if she pointed it at the window, instead of at the fire.

The lessons set them by their kind but overworked mistress, learning long columns of spelling words, or of the names of towns, or countries, or of kings and queens, or sums to be worked out of which Laura had never grasped the rules, were waste of time as far as she was concerned. The few scraps of knowledge she managed to pick up were gleaned from the school books, in which she read the history and geography portions so many times over that certain paragraphs remained with her, word for word, for life. There were stories of travel, too, and poems, and when these were exhausted there was the mistress's own bookshelf.

The lessons were soon finished; the long lists repeated to each other, parrot fashion; Emily Rose had done Laura's sums for her and Laura had written Emily Rose's essay for her to copy, and the spare hour or two was passed pleasantly enough over *Ministering Children*, or *Queechy*, or *The Wide, Wide World* or Laura would knit while Emily Rose sewed, for she liked knitting, and they would sit there, very cosily, while the fire flared up and the kettle sang on the hob and the school sounds came faint and subdued through the dividing wall.

During their last few months at school they had plenty to talk about, for Emily Rose was in love and Laura was her confidante. It was no childish fancy, she was really deeply in love, and it was one of those rare cases where first love was to lead to marriage and last a lifetime.

Her Norman was the son of their nearest neighbours, who lived about a mile from their cottage. On the evenings when Emily Rose stayed after school for choir practice he would meet her and they would walk through the wood arm in arm, like grown-up lovers. 'But you must only kiss me when we say good night, Norman,' said sensible little Emily Rose, 'because we are too young yet to be properly engaged.' She did not tell Laura what Norman said to that, or whether he always observed her rule about kissing; but when asked what they found to talk about her blue eyes opened wide and she said, 'Just about us,' as though there were no other possible subject.

They had made up their minds to marry when they were old enough and nothing on earth could have shaken that resolve; but, as it turned out, they met with no opposition. When, a year or two later, their respective parents discovered the state of things between them, they were at once asked to each other's houses as accepted lovers, and when Emily Rose went as an apprentice to a dressmaker in a neighbouring village she already wore a little gold ring with clasped hands on her finger and Norman came openly to fetch her home on dark evenings.

The last time Laura saw her she was as little changed as anything human could be after a decade. A little fuller of figure, perhaps, and with her flaxen hair wreathed in coils round her head instead of hanging in a pigtail, but with speedwell eyes as innocently candid and milk-and-rose complexion as fresh as ever. She had two lovely children in a perambulator, 'The very spit and moral of herself,' another stander-by assured her; and, according to the same observer, the kind, steady husband who stood by her side would not have let the wind blow upon her if he could have helped it. She was still the same Emily Rose, kind, straightforward and a little dictatorial; convinced that the world was a very nice place for well-behaved people.

Laura felt old and battered beside her, a sensation she enjoyed, for that was in the 'nineties, when youth loved to pose as world-weary and disillusioned, the sophisticated product of a dying century. Laura's friends away from the hamlet called themselves *fin de siècle* and their elders called them fast, although the fastness went no further than walking, hatless, over Hindhead at night in a gale, bawling Swinburne and Omar Khayyám to each other above the storm.

But the 'nineties were barely beginning when Laura left school and where she would be and what she would be doing when they ended she had no idea. For some months that was her great trouble, that, and the changed conditions at home and a growing sense of inability to fit herself into the scheme of things as she knew it.

Her mother, with five children to keep and care for, was hard-pressed, especially as she still insisted upon living up to her old standard of what she called 'seemliness'. Her idea of good housekeeping was that every corner of the house should be clean, clean sheets should be on the beds, clean clothes on every one of the seven bodies for which she was responsible, a good dinner on the table and a cake in the pantry for tea by noon every Sunday. She would sit up sewing till midnight and rise before daybreak to wash clothes. But she had her reward. She was passionately fond of little children, the younger and more helpless the better, and would talk by the hour in baby language to the infant in the cradle or upon her lap, pouring out love and lavishing endearments upon it. Often when Laura began speaking she would cut her short with a request to go and do something, or take no notice at all of what she said, not from deliberate unkindness, but simply because she had no thought to spare for her older children. At least, so it appeared to Laura.

Her mother told her in after years that she had been anxious about her at that time. She was outgrowing her strength, she thought, and was too quiet and had queer ideas and did not make friends of her own age, which she thought unnatural. Her future and that of Edmund were also causing her anxiety.

Her plans had not changed: Laura was to be a nurse and Edmund a carpenter; but the children themselves had changed. Edmund was the first to protest. He did not want to be a carpenter; he thought it was a very good trade for those who wanted one; but he didn't, he said firmly. 'But it is so respectable and the pay's good. Look at Mr Parker,' she urged, 'with his good business and nice house and even a top hat for funerals.'

But now it seemed that Edmund had no ambition to wear a top hat or to officiate at funerals. He did not want to be a carpenter at all, or a mason. He would not have minded being an engine-driver; but what he really wanted was to travel and see the world. That meant being a soldier, she said, and what was a soldier when his time had expired, regularly ruined for ordinary life, with his roving ideas and, more than likely, a taste for drink. Look at Tom Finch, as yellow as a guinea and eaten up with ague, putting in a day or two here and there on the land and but half alive, for you couldn't call it living, between one pension day and another. Even if he had been well he had no trade in his hands, and what was land work for a young chap, anyhow?

Then Edmund surprised and hurt her more than he had ever done in his life before. 'What's the matter with the land?' he asked. 'Folks have got to have food and somebody's got to grow it. The work's all right, too. It'd rather turn a good straight furrow any day than mess about making shavings in a carpenter's shop. If I can't be a soldier and go to India, I'll stop here and work on the land.' She cried a little at that; but afterwards cheered up and said he was too young to know his own mind. Boys did sometimes have these fancies. He'd come to his senses presently.

Laura's failure troubled her more because she was two years older than Edmund and the time was nearer when she would have to earn her own living. Perhaps she had had doubts about her vocation for some time and that was why she had seemed cold and reserved towards her. The situation came to a head one day when Laura was nursing the baby with a book in her hand and, absent-mindedly, put down the little hand which was trying to clutch her long hair.

'Laura, I'm sorry to say it, but I'm downright disappointed in you,' said her mother solemnly. 'I've been watching you for the last ten minutes with that little innocent on your lap and your head stuck in that nasty old book and not so much as one look at his pretty ways. (Didums, didums neglect him then, the little precious! Anybody who could read a book with you on their lap must have a heart of stone. Come to mum-mums, then. *She'll* not push you pretty pawdy away when you try to play with *her* hair!) No, it won't do, Laura. You'll never make a nurse, sorry as I am to say so. You're fond enough of the baby, I know, but you just haven't got the knack of nursing. A child'd grow up a perfect dummy if it had to depend upon you. You want to talk to them and play with them and keep them amused. There, don't cry. You are as you're made, I suppose. We shall have to think of something else for you to do. Perhaps I could get Cousin Rachel to take you as a apprentice to her dressmaking. But, there, that's no good either, for your sewing's worse than your nursing. We shall have to see what turns up; but there's no denying it's a great disappointment to me, after having had the promise of a start for you and all.'

So there was Laura at thirteen with her life in ruins, not for the last time, but she grieved more over that than her later catastrophes, for she had not then experienced the rebound or learned that no beating is final while life lasts. It was not that she had particularly wanted to be a nurse. She had often wondered if she were suitable for the life. She loved children, but had she the necessary patience? She could keep the older ones amused, she knew; but she was nervous and clumsy with babies. It was the sense of defeat, of having been tried and found wanting, which crushed her.

There was also the question of what she could do for a living. She thought she would like to work on the land, like Edmund. It was long before the day of the land-girl; but a few of the older women in the hamlet worked in the fields. Laura wondered if the farmer would employ her. She was afraid not; and if he had been willing, her parents would not consent to it. But when she said this to Edmund, who had found her crying in the wood-shed, he said, 'Why not?' Then, it appeared, he already had a plan. They would have a little house together and both work on the land; Laura could do the housework, for field-women's hours were shorter than those of the men; or perhaps Laura need not go out to work at all, but just stay at home and keep house as other women did for their husbands. They talked this over every time they were alone together and even chose their cottage and discussed their meals. Treacle tarts were to figure largely on their menu. But when at last they told their mother of their plan she was horrified. 'Don't either of you so much as mention such a silly idea again,' she said sternly, and 'for goodness' sake don't go telling anybody else. You haven't, have you? Then don't, unless you want to be thought mad; for mad it is, and I'm downright ashamed of you for such a low-down idea. You're going to get on in the world, if I have any say in it, and leave working on the land to them as can't do better for themselves. And not a word to your father about this. I haven't told him yet what Edmund said about working on the land, for I know he'd never allow it. And as to you, Laura, you're the eldest and ought to know better than to put such silly ideas into your brother's head.'

So that would not do; even Edmund was convinced of that, though he still said to Laura in private that he would not be apprenticed. 'I want to get about and see things,' he said, 'if it's only things growing.' Evidently the craftsman spirit of his ancestors on one side of the family had passed over his head to come out again in some future generation.

There was scarlet fever at Candleford that year and Laura did not go there for her usual holiday. Johnny came to stay with them instead, and did *not* bring the infection; he had been too carefully guarded. But he made one more in the already over-crowded home; although it must be said that he improved marvellously under her mother's firm rule. It was no longer 'Johnny, would you like this or that?' but 'Now, Johnny, my man, eat up your dinner or you'll be all behind when the next helping's given out.' The fine air and the simple food must have been good for him, for he put on weight and started to shoot up in height. Or perhaps his being there at the time of the turning-point of his health was a lucky accident for which Laura's mother got the credit.

All that winter Laura went on with her brooding. Then spring came and the bluebells were out and the chestnut candles and young bracken fronds were unrolling; but, for the first time since she could remember, she had no joy in such things. She sat one day on the low-hanging bough of a beech and looked at them all. 'Here I am,' she thought, 'and here are all these lovely things and I don't care for them a bit this year. There must be something the matter with me.'

There was. She was growing up, and growing up, as she feared, into a world that had no use for her. She carried this burden of care for months, not always conscious of it; sometimes she would forget, and in the reaction become noisy and boisterous; but it was always there, pressing down upon her, until the neighbours noticed her melancholy expression and said: 'That child looks regular hag-rid.'

This accumulated depression of months slid from her at last in a moment. She had run out into the fields one day in a pet and was standing on a small stone bridge looking down on brown running water flecked with cream-coloured foam. It was a dull November day with grey sky and mist. The little brook was scarcely more than a trench to drain the fields; but overhanging it were thorn bushes with a lacework of leafless twigs; ivy had sent trails down the steep banks to dip in the stream, and from every thorn on the leafless twigs and from every point of the ivy leaves water hung in bright drops, like beads.

A flock of starlings had whirred up from the bushes at her approach and the *clip, clop* of a cart-horse's hoofs could be heard on the nearest road, but these were the only sounds. Of the hamlet, only a few hundred yards away, she could hear no sound, or see as much as a chimney-pot, walled in as she was by the mist.

Laura looked and looked again. The small scene, so commonplace and yet so lovely, delighted her. It was so near the homes of men and yet so far removed from their thoughts. The fresh green moss, the glistening ivy, and the reddish twigs with their sparkling drops seemed to have been made for her alone and the hurrying, foam-flecked water seemed to have some message for her. She felt suddenly uplifted. The things which had troubled her troubled her no more. She did not reason. She had already done plenty of reasoning. Too much, perhaps. She simply stood there and let it all sink in until she felt that her own small affairs did not matter. Whatever happened to her, this, and thousands of other such small, lovely sights would remain and people would come suddenly upon them and look and be glad.

A wave of pure happiness pervaded her being, and, although it soon receded, it carried away with it her burden of care. Her first reaction was to laugh aloud at herself. What a fool she had been to make so much of so little. There must be thousands like her who could see no place for themselves in the world, and here she had been, fretting herself and worrying others as if her case were unique. And, deeper down, beneath the surface of her being, was the feeling, rather than the knowledge, that her life's deepest joys would be found in such scenes as this.

XXIX

Exit Laura

HER mother was stooping to take something out of the oven and as she looked down upon her, Laura noticed for the first time that her looks were changing. The blue eyes were bluer than ever, but the pink and white of her face was weathering. Her figure was hardening, too; slim young grace was turning to thin wiriness; and a few grey threads showed in her hair at the temples. Her mother was growing old, soon she would die, thought Laura with sudden compunction, and then how sorry she would be for giving her so much trouble.

But her mother, still on the right side of forty, did not think of herself as ageing and had no thought of dying for a good many more years to come. As it turned out, barely half of her life was over.

'Gracious, how you are shooting up!' she said cheerfully, as she rose and stretched herself. 'I shall soon have to stand tiptoe to tie your hair-ribbon. Have a potato cake? I found young Biddy had laid an egg this morning, her first and not very big, so I thought I'd make us a cake for tea of those cold potatoes in the pantry. A bit of sugar can always be spared. That's cheap enough.'

Laura ate the cake with great relish, for it was delicious, straight from the oven, and it was also a mark of her mother's favour; the little ones were not allowed to eat between meals.

Her father had put up a swing for the younger children in the wash-house. She could hear one of them now, crying, 'Higher! Higher!' Except for the baby, asleep in the cradle, her mother and she were alone in the room, which, on that dull day, was aglow with firelight. Her mother's pastry board and rolling-pin still stood on a white cloth on one end of the table, and the stew for dinner, mostly composed of vegetables, but very savoury-smelling, simmered upon the hob. She had a sudden impulse to tell her mother how much she loved her; but in the early 'teens such feelings cannot be put into words, and all she could do was to praise the potato cake.

But perhaps her look conveyed something of what she felt, for, that evening, her mother, after speaking of her own father, who had been dead three or four years, added: 'You are the only one I can talk to about him. Your father and he never got on together and the others were too young when he died to remember him. Lots of things happened before they were born that you'll always remember, so I shall always have somebody to talk to about the old times.'

From that day a new relationship was established and grew between them. Her mother was not kinder to Laura than she had been, for she had always been kindness itself, but she took her more into her confidence, and Laura was happy again.

But, as so often happens when two human beings have come to understand each other, they were soon to be parted. In the early spring a letter came from Candleford saying that Dorcas Lane wanted a learner for her Post Office work and thought Laura would do, if her parents were willing. Although she was not one for much gadding about, she said, it was irksome to be always tied to the house during Post Office hours. 'Not that I expect her to stay with me for ever,' she added. 'She'll want to do better for herself later on, and, when that time comes I'll speak to Head Office and we shall see what we shall see.'

So, one morning in May, Polly and the spring-cart drew up at the gate and Laura's little trunk, all new and shiny black with her initials in brass-headed nails, was hoisted into the back seat. and Laura in a new frock – grèy cashmere with a white lace collar and the new leg-of-mutton sleeves – climbed up beside her father, who was taking a day off to drive Polly.

'Good-bye, Laura. Good-bye. Good-bye. Don't forget to write to me.'

'And to me, and address it to my very own self,' cried the little sisters.

'You be a good gal an' do what you're told an' you'll get on like a house afire,' called a kindly neighbour from her doorway.

'Wrap every penny stamp up in a smile,' advised the inn-keeper, closing his double gates after Polly's exit.

As Polly trotted on, Laura turned to look across fields green with spring wheat to the huddle of grey cottages where she knew her mother was thinking about her, and tears came into her eyes.

Her father looked at her in surprise, then said kindly but grudgingly: 'Well, 'tis your home, such as it is, I suppose.'

Yes, with all its limitations, the hamlet was home to her. There she had spent her most impressionable years and, although she was never to live there again for more than a few weeks at a time, she would bear their imprint through life.

XXX

From One Small World to Another

LAURA sat up beside her father on the high front seat of the spring-cart and waved to the neighbours. 'Good-bye, Laura! Good-bye!' they called. 'Mind you be a good gal, now!' and Laura, as she turned to smile and wave back to them, tried not to look too conscious of her new frock and hat and the brand-new trunk (with her initials) roped on to the back seat.

As the cart moved on, more women came to their doors to see what the sound of wheels meant at that time in the morning. It was not the coalman's or the fish-hawker's day, the baker was not due for hours, and the appearance of any other wheeled vehicle than theirs always caused a mild sensation in that secluded hamlet. When they saw Laura and her new trunk, the women remained on their doorsteps to wave their farewells, then, before the cart had turned into the road from the rutted lane, little groups began forming.

Her going seemed to be causing quite a stir in the hamlet. Not because the sight of a young girl going out in the world to earn her own living was an uncommon one there – all the hamlet girls left home for that purpose, some of them at a much earlier age than Laura – but they usually went on foot, carrying bundles, or their fathers pushed their boxes on wheelbarrows to the railway station in the nearest town the night before, while, for Laura's departure, the innkeeper's pony and cart had been hired.

That, of course, was because Candleford Green, although only eight miles distant, was on another line of railway than that which ran through the market town, and to have gone there by train would have meant two changes and a long wait at the Junction; but the spring-cart brought a spice of novelty into her departure which made 'something to talk about', as the saying went there. At the beginning of the eighteen-nineties any new subject for conversation was precious in such places.

Laura was fourteen and a half, and the thick pigtail of hair which had so far hung down her back had that morning been looped up once and tied with a big black ribbon bow on her neck. When they had first known that she was to go to work in the Post Office at Candleford Green her mother had wondered if she ought not to wear her hair done up with hairpins, grown-up fashion, but when she saw a girl behind the Post Office counter at Sherston wearing hers in a loop with a bow she had felt sure that that was the proper way for Laura to do hers. So the ribbon was bought – black, of course, for her mother said the bright-coloured ribbons most country girls wore made them look like horses, all plaited and beribboned for a fair. 'And mind you sponge and press it often,' she had said, 'for it cost good money. And when you come to buy your own clothes, always buy the best you can afford. It pays in the end.' But Laura could not bear to think of her mother just then; the parting was too recent.

So she thought of her new trunk. This contained – as well as her everyday clothes and her personal treasures, including her collection of pressed flowers, a lock of her baby brother's fair hair, and a penny exercise book, presented by her brother Edmund and inscribed by him *Laura's Journal*, in which she had promised to write every night – what her mother had spoken of as 'three of everything', all made of stout white calico and trimmed with crochet edging.

'No child of mine,' her mother had often declared, 'shall go out in the world without a good outfit. I'd rather starve!' and when the time had come to get Laura ready for Candleford Green the calico, bought secretly from time to time in lengths, had been brought out from its hiding-place to be made up and trimmed with the edging she had been making for months. 'I told you it would come in handy for something at some time,'

she had said, but Laura knew by her arch little smile she had
meant it for her all along.

Her father had made and polished the trunk and studded it
with her initials in bright, brass-headed nails, and, deep down in
one corner of it, wrapped in tissue paper, was the new half-
crown he had given her.

The contents of the trunk, the clothes she was wearing, youth
and health, and a meagre education, plus a curious assortment
of scraps of knowledge she had picked up in the course of her
reading, were her only assets. In fitting her out, her parents had
done all they could for her. They had four younger children
now to be provided for. Her future must depend upon herself
and what opportunities might offer. But she had no idea of the
slenderness of her equipment for life and no fears for the distant future which stretched before her, years and years in which
anything might happen. She could not imagine herself married,
or old, and it did not seem possible that she would ever die.

Any qualms she felt were for the immediate future, when she,
who had so far only known her cottage home and the homes of
a few relatives, would be living in some one else's house, where
she would work and be paid for her work and where the work
she was to do had still to be learnt. She was much afraid she
would not know what she ought to do, or where to find things,
or would make mistakes and be thought stupid.

The postmistress of Candleford Green, it was true, was no
stranger, but an old girlhood's friend of her mother. Laura had
been to her house several times and had liked her, and she
thought Miss Lane had liked her. But that only seemed to make
the new relationship more difficult. Should she treat Miss Lane
as an old friend of the family, or strictly as a new employer?
Her mother, when appealed to, had laughed and said: 'God
bless the child! always looking for trouble! What is there to
worry about? Just be your own natural self and Dorcas I'm
sure'll be hers. Though, when it comes to that, perhaps you'd
better not go on Cousin Dorcasing her. That was all right when
you were a visitor, but now it'd better be "Miss Lane".'

As they lurched out of the rutted road which led round the

hamlet, her father urged on the pony. He was not a patient man and there had been too many farewells to suit his taste. 'What a lot!' he muttered. 'You can't so much as hire a horse and cart for a day without creating a nine days' wonder in this place!' But Laura thought it was kind of the neighbours to wish her well. 'Go and get rich and fat,' kind old Mrs Braby had advised; 'and whatever y'do, don't 'ee forget them at home.' Rich she could never be, her starting salary of half a crown a week would leave no margin for saving, and getting fat seemed more improbable still to tall, lanky fourteen – 'like a molern, all legs and wings', as the neighbours had often called her – but she would never forget those at home: that she could promise.

She turned and looked back over green cornfields at the huddle of grey cottages, one of which was her home, and pictured her mother ironing and her little sisters playing round the doorway, and wondered if her favourite brother would miss her when he came home from school and if he would remember to water her garden and give her white rabbit, Florizel, plenty of green leaves, and if he would care to read her new journal when she sent it to him, or would think it silly, as he sometimes did her writing.

But it was May and the warm wind dried her eyes and soothed her sore eyelids, and the roadside banks were covered with the tiny spring flowers she loved, stitchwort and celandine and whole sheets of speedwell, which Laura knew as angel's eyes, and somewhere in the budding green hedgerow a blackbird was singing. Who could be sad on such a day! At one place she saw cowslips in a meadow and asked her father to wait while she gathered a bunch to take as an offering to Miss Lane. Back in her seat, she buried her face in the big fragrant bunch and, ever after, the scent of cowslips reminded her of that morning in May.

When, about midday, they passed through a village, she held the reins while her father went into the inn for a pint of ale for himself and brought out for her a tall tumbler of sweet, fizzing orangeade. She sat in state on her high seat and sipped it gently in the grown-up way she had seen farmers' wives in gigs sipping their drinks before the inn at home, and it pleased her to im-

agine that the elderly clergyman who glanced her way in passing was wondering who that interesting-looking girl in the
spring-cart could be, although she knew very well in sober fact
he was more probably thinking about his next Sunday's
sermon, or trying to decide whether or not he owed a parochial
call at the next house he had to pass. At fourteen it is intolerable
to resign every claim to distinction. Her hair was soft and thick
and brown and she had rather nice brown eyes and the fresh
complexion of country youth, but those were her only assets in the
way of good looks. '*You'll* never be annoyed by people turning
round in the street to have another look at you,' her mother had
often told her, and sometimes, if Laura looked dashed, she
would add: 'But that cuts both ways: if you're no beauty, be
thankful you're not a freak.' So she had nothing to pride herself
upon in that respect, and, being country born and with little
education, she knew herself to be ignorant, and as to goodness,
well, no one but herself knew how far she fell short of that so,
rather than sink into nothingness in her own estimation, she
chose to imagine herself interesting-looking.

Candleford Green was taking its afternoon nap when they
arrived. The large irregular square of turf which gave the village its name was deserted but for one grazing donkey and a
flock of geese which came cackling with outstretched necks
towards the spring-cart to investigate. The children who at
other times played there were in school and their fathers were at
work in the fields, or in workshops, or at their different jobs in
Candleford town. The doors of the row of shops which ran
along one side of the green were open. A man in a white
grocer's apron stood yawning and stretching his arms in one
doorway, an old grey sheepdog slept in the exact middle of the
road, the church clock chimed, then struck three, but those were
the only signs of life, for it was Monday and the women of the
place were too busy with their washing to promenade with their
perambulators in front of the shops as on other afternoons.

On the farther, less-populated side of the green a white
horse stood under a tree outside the smithy waiting its turn to be
shod and, from within, as the spring-cart drew up, the ring of
the anvil and the roar of the bellows could be heard.

Attached to the smithy was a long, low white house which might have been taken for an ordinary cottage of the more substantial kind but for a scarlet-painted letter-box let into the wall beneath a window at one end. Over the window was a painted board which informed the public that the building was CANDLEFORD GREEN POST AND TELEGRAPH OFFICE. At the other end of the building, above the door of the smithy, was another board which read: DORCAS LANE, SHOEING AND GENERAL SMITH.

Except for the sounds of the forge and the white horse dozing beneath the oak tree, that side of the green appeared even more somnolent than the shopping side. Their arrival had not been unobserved, however, for, as the cart drew up, a young smith darted from the forge and, seizing Laura's trunk, bore it away on his shoulder as if it weighed no more than a feather. 'Ma'am! The new miss has come,' they heard him call as he reached the back door of the house, and a moment later, the Post Office door-bell went *ping-ping* and Miss Lane herself stepped out to welcome her new assistant.

Miss Lane was not a tall woman and was slightly built, but an erect carriage, a commanding air, and the rustle as she walked of the rich silks she favoured gave her what was then known as a 'presence'. Bright, dark, almost black eyes were the only noticeable feature in her sallow but not otherwise unpleasing countenance. Ordinarily quietly observant, those eyes could disconcert with a flash of recognition of motives, sparkle with malice, or, more rarely, soften with sympathy. That afternoon, over a deep prune-coloured gown, she wore a small black satin apron embroidered almost to stiffness with jet beads, and, in accordance with fashion, her still luxurious black hair was plaited into a coronet above a curled fringe.

Not quite the Dorcas Lane, Shoeing and General Smith, that might have been expected after reading her signboard. Had she lived a century earlier or half a century later, she would probably have been found at the forge with a sledge-hammer in her hand for she had indomitable energy and a passion for doing and making things. But hers was an age when any work outside the four walls of a home was taboo for any woman who had

any pretensions to refinement, and she had to content herself
with keeping the books and attending to the correspondence of
the old family business she had inherited. She had found one
other outlet for her energy in her post office work, which also
provided her with entertainment in the supervision of her neighbours' affairs and the study and analysis of their motives.

This may sound terrifying as now related, but there was
nothing terrifying about Miss Lane. She kept the secrets with
which she was entrusted in the course of her official duties most
honourably, and if she laughed at some of her customers' foibles
she laughed secretly. 'Clever' was the general village description
of her. 'She's a clever one, that Miss Lane, as sharp as vinegar,
but not bad in her way,' people would afterwards say to Laura.
Only her two or three enemies said that if she had lived at one
time she'd have been burned as a witch.

That afternoon she was in her most gracious mood. 'You've
come just at the right time,' she said, kissing Laura. 'I've had a
most terrible rush, half a dozen in at once for postal orders and
what not, and the telegraph bell ringing like mad all the while.
But it's over now, I think, for the time being, and the afternoon
mail is not due for an hour, so come inside, do, both of you
and we'll have a nice cup of tea before the evening's work
begins.'

Laura experienced a slight shock when she heard of this
recent pressure of business. How, she thought, would she ever
be able to cope with such rushes. But she need not have feared:
the rushes at Candleford Green Post Office existed chiefly in the
imagination of the postmistress, who loved to make her office
appear more busy and important than it was in reality.

Her father could not stay to tea, as he had his Candleford
relations to visit, and Laura watched him drive away with the
sinking feeling of one whose last link with a known world is
vanishing. But, before the day was out, her childhood's life
seemed long ago and far away to her, there was so much to see
and hear and try to grasp in the new one.

As she followed her new employer through the little office
and out to the big front living kitchen, the hands of the grandfather's clock pointed to a quarter to four. It was really only a

quarter past three and the Post Office clock gave that time exactly, but the house clocks were purposely kept half an hour fast and meals and other domestic matters were timed by them. To keep thus ahead of time was an old custom in many country families which was probably instituted to ensure the early rising of man and maid in the days when five or even four o'clock was not thought an unreasonably early hour at which to begin the day's work. The smiths still began work at six and Zillah, the maid, was downstairs before seven, by which time Miss Lane and, later, Laura, was also up and sorting the morning mail.

The kitchen was a large room with a flagstone floor and two windows beneath which stood a long, solid-looking table large enough to accommodate the whole household at mealtimes. The foreman and three young unmarried smiths lived in the house, and each of these had his own place at table. Miss Lane, in a higher chair than the others, known as a carving-chair, sat enthroned at the head of the table, then, on the side facing the windows, came Laura and Matthew, the foreman, with a long space of tablecloth between them supposed to be reserved for visitors. Laura's seeming place of honour had, no doubt, been allotted to her for handiness in passing cups and plates. The young smiths sat three abreast at the bottom end of the table and Zillah, the maid, had a small side-table of her own. All meals excepting tea were taken in this order.

Cooking and washing-up were done in the back kitchen; the front kitchen was the family living- and dining-room. In the fireplace a small sitting-room grate with hobs had replaced the fire on the hearth of a few years before; but the open chimney and chimney-corners had been left, and from one of these a long, high-backed settle ran out into the room. In the space thus enclosed a red-and-black carpet had been laid to accommodate Miss Lane's chair at the head of the table and a few fireside chairs. This little room within a room was known as the hearth-place. Beyond it the stone floor was bare but for a few mats.

Brass candlesticks and a brass pestle and mortar ornamented the high mantelshelf, and there were brass warming-pans on the walls, together with a few coloured prints; one of the first man in this country to carry an umbrella – rain was coming down in sheets and he was followed by a jeering but highly ornamental crowd. A blue-and-white dish of oranges stuck with cloves stood upon the dresser. They were dry and withered at that time of the year, but still contributed their quota to the distinctive flavour of the air.

Everything there was just as Miss Lane had inherited it. Except for a couple of easy chairs by the hearth, she had added nothing. 'What was good enough for my parents and grandparents is good enough for me,' she would say when some of her more fashionable friends tried to persuade her to bring her house up to date. But family loyalty was rather an excuse than a reason for her preference; she kept the old things she had inherited because she enjoyed seeing and owning them.

That afternoon, when Laura arrived, a little round table in the hearthplace had already been laid for tea. And what a meal! There were boiled new-laid eggs and scones and honey and home-made jam and, to crown all, a dish of fresh Banbury cakes. The carrier had a standing order to bring her a dozen of those cakes every market day.

It seemed a pity to Laura that the first time she had been offered two eggs at one meal she could barely eat one and that the Banbury cake, hitherto to her a delicious rarity only seen in her home when purchased by visiting aunts, should flake and crumble almost untasted upon her plate because she felt too excited and anxious to eat. But Miss Lane ate enough for the two of them. Food was her one weakness. She loaded her scone, already spread with fresh farm butter, with black currant jam and topped it with cream while she inquired about the health of Laura's mother and told Laura what her new duties would be. Once or twice during tea the Post Office door-bell tinkled and she wiped her mouth and sailed majestically off to sell stamps, but the hour of her early tea was the quietest hour of the day; after that what she called her 'rush hour' began, and for that Laura was allowed to accompany her.

With what expert speed Miss Lane stamped letters and made up the mail, and with what ceremonious courtesy she answered questions which sounded like conundrums to Laura, was a wonder to hear and see.

The door-bell tinkled all the time as people came in to collect their afternoon mail. There was a delivery of letters in the morning, and the poorer inhabitants of the place only called in the afternoon when they were expecting a letter. 'I s'pose there isn't nothing for me, Miss Lane?' they would say almost apologetically, and would look pleased or disappointed according to her reply. Those of more assured position called regularly and these often would not speak at all, but put their heads inside the door and raise their eyebrows inquiringly. None of them gave their names or addresses, because Miss Lane knew everybody on and around the green and she seldom had to look in the pigeon-holes labelled 'A' to 'Z', because she had sorted the letters and could answer from memory. She often knew from whom the letter was expected and what its contents were likely to be and would console the disappointed callers with: 'Better luck in the morning. There's barely time for an answer as yet.'

Out in the kitchen Zillah and the workmen were at tea. The rattle of their teacups and the subdued hum of their conversation could be heard in the office. This was the only meal of the day at which Miss Lane herself did not preside. Zillah poured out, but she did not occupy her mistress's seat at the head of the table – that was sacred; between each pouring out she retired to her own seat on the settle with her own little table before her. At the other, more formal, meals, the conversation was carried on by Miss Lane and her foreman, with an occasional reference to Zillah when any item of local interest was under discussion, while the young smiths at the foot of the table munched in silence. At tea, with the mistress engaged elsewhere, there was more freedom, and sometimes Zillah's shrill laughter would break through a chorus of guffaws from the younger workmen. In moderation this was tolerated, but one day, when some one rapped loudly upon the table with a teacup and said (Miss Lane said 'shouted'), 'Another pint, please, landlady!' the office door opened and a voice as severe as that of a schoolmistress admonishing her class called for 'Less noise there, please!'

None of them resented being spoken to like children, nor did the young journeymen resent being placed below the salt, nor

Zillah at her separate table. To them these things were all part
of an established order. To that unawakened generation freedom was of less account than good food, and of that in that
household there was an abundance.

Tea was not considered a substantial meal. It was for the
workmen, as Miss Lane counted time, an innovation. She could
remember when bread and cheese and beer were at that hour
taken to the forge for the men to consume standing. 'Afternoon
bavour,' they had called it. Now a well-covered table awaited
them indoors. Each man's plate was stacked with slices of bread
and butter, and what was called 'a relish' was provided. 'What
can we give the men for a relish at tea-time?' was an almost
daily question in that household. Sometimes a blue-and-white
basin of boiled new-laid eggs would be placed on the table.
Three eggs per man was the standard allowance, but two or
three extra were usually cooked 'in case', and at the end of the
meal the basin was always empty. On other afternoons there
would be brawn, known locally as 'collared head', or soused
herrings, or a pork pie, or cold sausages.

As the clock struck five the scraping of iron-tipped boots
would be heard and the men, with leather aprons wound up
around their waists, and their faces, still moist from their visit
to the pump in the yard, looking preternaturally clean against
their work-soiled clothes, would troop into the kitchen. While
they ate they would talk of the horses they had been shoeing.
'That new grey o' Squire's wer' as near as dammit to nippin' my
ear. A groom ought'r stand by and hold th' young devil' or
'Poor old Whitefoot! About time he wer' pensioned off. Went to
sleep an' nearly fell down top of me today, he did. Let's see, how
old is he now, do you reckon?' 'Twenty, if he's a day. Mus'
Elliott's father used to ride him to hounds and he's bin dead
this ten 'ears. But you leave old Whitefoot alone. He'll drag that
station cart for another five 'ears. What's he got to cart? Only
young Jim, and he's a seven-stunner, if that, and maybe a bit of
fish and a parcel or two. No, you take my word for't, old Whitefoot ain't going to die while he can see anybody else alive.' Or
they would talk about the weather or the crops or some new
arrival in the place, extracting the last grain of interest from

every trifling event, while, separated from them by only a
closed door, the new activities of a more sophisticated day were
beginning.

On her first day in the office, Laura stood awkwardly by Miss
Lane, longing to show her willingness to help, but not knowing
how to begin. Once, when there was a brisk demand for penny
stamps and the telegraph bell was ringing, she tried timidly to
sell one, but she was pushed gently aside, and afterwards it was
explained to her that she must not so much as handle a letter or
sell a stamp until she had been through some mysterious in-
itiation ceremony which Miss Lane called being 'sworn in'.
This had to take place before a Justice of the Peace, and it had
been arranged that she should go the next morning to one of the
great houses in the locality for that purpose. And she would
have to go alone, for until she herself had qualified, Miss Lane
could not leave home during office hours, and she feared she
would not know which doorbell to ring or what to say when she
came into the great man's presence. Oh dear! this new life
seemed very complicated.

The dread of this interview haunted her until, at Miss Lane's
suggestion, she went out for a turn in the garden, where, she was
told, she might always go for a breath of fresh air between busy
times in the office. She had been in that garden before, but
never in May, with the apple-blossom out and the wallflowers
filling the air with their fragrance.

Narrow paths between high, built-up banks supporting flower
borders, crowded with jonquils, auriculas, forget-me-nots and
other spring flowers, led from one part of the garden to another.
One winding path led to the earth closet in its bower of nut-
trees half-way down the garden, another to the vegetable
garden and on to the rough grass plot before the beehives. Between each section were thick groves of bushes with ferns and
capers and Solomon's seal, so closed in that the long, rough
grass there was always damp. Wasted ground, a good gardener
might have said, but delightful in its cool, green shadiness.

Nearer the house was a portion given up entirely to flowers,
not growing in beds or borders, but crammed together in an
irregular square, where they bloomed in half-wild profusion.

There were rose bushes there and lavender and rosemary and a bush apple-tree which bore little red and yellow streaked apples in later summer, and Michaelmas daisies and red-hot pokers and old-fashioned pompom dahlias in autumn and peonies and pinks already budding.

An old man in the village came one day a week to till the vegetable garden, but the flower garden was no one's especial business. Miss Lane herself would occasionally pull on a pair of wash-leather gloves and transplant a few seedlings; Matthew would pull up a weed or stake a plant as he passed, and the smiths, once a year, turned out of the shop to dig between the roots and cut down dead canes. Betweenwhiles the flowers grew just as they would in crowded masses, perfect in their imperfection.

Laura, who came from a district often short of water, was amazed to find no less than three wells in the garden. There was the well beneath the pump near the back door which supplied the house with water; a middle well outside the inner smithy door used only for trade purposes, and what was called the 'bottom well' near the beehives. The bottom well was kept padlocked. Moss grew on its lid and nettles around it. At one time it had supplied the house with drinking water, but that was a long time ago.

Every one in any way connected with the place knew the story of the wells. No one had suspected the existence of the one near the house until, one day, while Miss Lane was still a small child, a visitor who had come to tea was on her way to what was still known as 'the little house' half-way down the garden. When she had gone a few yards from the back door a flagstone on the path gave way beneath her feet and she found herself slipping into a chasm. Fortunately, she was a substantially built woman and, by flinging out her arms, she was able to support her upper part above ground while her legs dangled in space. Her screams soon brought assistance and she was hauled to safety, and, the modern treatment of bed and hot-water bottles for shock being as yet undiscovered, Miss Lane's mother did what she could by well lacing the patient's tea with rum, which remedy acted so well that, when passing her cup a third time, she actually giggled and said: 'This tastes a lot better than that old well water'd have done!'

When or why the well had been abandoned and not properly filled in no one ever knew. Miss Lane's grandparents had had no knowledge of it, and they had come to live there early in the century and both they and her parents and herself as a child had walked gaily over it thousands of times, little suspecting the danger that lurked below. However, all ended well. After the well had been thoroughly cleansed and the water tested, it provided an excellent supply close at hand for the house.

When Laura went to bed that night in her new little bedroom with its pink-washed walls, faded chintz curtains, and chest of drawers all for her own use, she was too tired to write more in her new journal than: 'Came to live at Candleford Green today, Monday.' After she was in bed she heard Zillah call the cat, then plod, flat-footed, upstairs. Then the men came up, pad-padding in their stockinged feet, and, last of all, Miss Lane tap-tapping on her high heels.

Laura sat up in bed and drew aside the window curtain. Not a light to be seen, only darkness, thick and moist and charged with the scent of damp grass and cottage garden flowers. All was silent except for the sharp, sudden swish of a breeze in the smithy tree, and so it would be all night unless the hoof-sounds of a galloping horse rang out, followed by the pealing of the doctor's bell. There was no ordinary night traffic on country roads in those days.

XXXI

On Her Majesty's Service

THE interview next morning did not turn out so terrifying as Laura had expected. Sir Timothy smiled very kindly upon her when the footman ushered her into his Justice Room, saying: 'The young person from the Post Office, please, Sir Timothy.'

'What have you been up to? Poaching, rick-burning, or petty larceny?' he asked when the footman had gone. 'If you're as innocent as you look, I shan't give you a long sentence. So come along,' and he drew her by the elbow to the side of his chair. Laura smiled dutifully, for she knew by the twinkle of his keen blue eyes beneath their shaggy white eyebrows that Sir Timothy was joking.

As she leaned forward to take up a pen with which to sign the thick blue official document he was unfolding, she sensed the atmosphere of jollity, good sense, and good nature, together with the smell of tobacco, stables, and country tweeds he carried around like an aura.

'But read it! Read!' he cried in a shocked voice. 'Never put your name to anything before you have read it or you'll be signing your own death warrant one of these days.' And Laura read out, as clearly as her shyness permitted, the Declaration which even the most humble candidate for Her Majesty's Service had in those serious days to sign before a magistrate.

'I do solemnly promise and declare that I will not open or delay or cause or suffer to be opened or delayed any letter or anything sent by the post', it began, and went on to promise secrecy in all things.

When she had read it through, she signed her name. Sir Timothy signed his, then folded the document neatly for her to carry back to Miss Lane, who would send it on to the higher authorities.

Sir Timothy could not have been very busy that morning, for he kept her talking a long time, asking her age and where she came from and how many brothers and sisters she had and what she had learnt at school and if she thought she would like the post office business. 'You've been well brought up,' he said at last, as weightily as if pronouncing sentence in Court. 'And you should do well. Miss Lane is an excellent woman – most efficient, and kind, too, to those of whom she approves, though I should not like to offend her myself. By gad! I should not! I remember one day when she was a girl – but perhaps I had better not tell you that story. Now, I expect you would be glad of some refreshment. Ask Purchase, or Robert, to show you the way to the housekeeper's room. There's sure to be tea or coffee or something going there at this time,' and Laura dropped a little curtsey as she said 'No, thank you, Sir Timothy. No, thank you,' and passed through the door which he courteously held open and down the long resounding stone passage which led to the side door, and was very glad that she saw no one, for when she arrived the footman had teasingly pulled her hair and asked for a kiss.

Out in the park, she turned and looked back at the long, white, battlemented façade of the mansion, with its terraces, fountains and flower-beds, and thought: 'Thank goodness that's over. I don't suppose I shall ever see this place again.' But she erred in her supposition. She was to cross the park, come clanging through the iron swing gate, and pass beneath the tall, rook-noisy elms to the mansion every morning in all weathers for nearly three years.

For the first few days Laura feared she would never learn her new duties. Even in that small country Post Office there was in use what seemed to her a bewildering number and variety of official forms, to all of which Miss Lane who loved to make a mystery of her work referred by number, not name. But soon, in actual practice, 'AB/35', K.21', 'X.Y.13', or what not became 'The blue Savings Bank Form', 'The Postal Order Abstract', 'The Cash Account Sheet' and so on, and Laura found herself flicking them out of their pigeon-holes and carrying them without a moment's hesitation to where Miss Lane sat doing her accounts at the kitchen table.

Then the stamps! The 1d. and ½d. ones she already knew by sight were in 10s. and 5s. sheets which hot, nervous hands were inclined to tear, and those of higher value, neatly hinged in a cardboard-leaved book, ready to be sold for parcels and telegrams, had to be detached just so, working up from the left-hand bottom corner. And the cash drawer, with its three wooden bowls for gold, silver, and copper, and all three bowls at least half full, even the one for sovereigns and half-sovereigns! What a lot of money there must be in the world! Laura would run her fingers through the shining gold coins when the cash was counted at night and placed in the black japanned box ready to be taken upstairs, wrapped in an old woolly shawl as disguise, and stood on the top shelf of Miss Lane's clothes cupboard.

Occasionally there was a banknote in the japanned box, but no Treasury notes, for there were none issued; there was plenty of gold to serve as currency in those days. Gold in plenty flowed through the country in a stream, but a stream to which only the fortunate had access. One poor half-sovereign was doled out on Saturday night to the lowest-paid workers; men who had a trade might get a whole sovereign and a few pieces of silver.

At first, when giving change, Laura boggled and hesitated and counted again, but although she had learned little arithmetic at school she was naturally quick at figures, and that part of her work soon became easy to her. And she liked seeing and speaking and being spoken to by the post office customers, especially the poorer ones, who would tell her about their affairs and sometimes ask her advice. The more important at first would ignore her if Miss Lane was present, or, if she was absent, would ask to see her; but they soon got used to seeing a new face there, and once, when Laura had gone indoors to tea, a gentleman farmer from a neighbouring hamlet actually inquired what had become of 'that charmin' young gal you've got now'. That set the seal of acceptance upon her and, fortunately, it was the only compliment so definitely expressed. Further inquiries of the kind might not have pleased Miss Lane. She liked Laura and was glad to find she was giving satisfaction, but naturally expected to stand first in her customers' regards.

Working hours in such small post offices as that where Laura was employed were then from the arrival of the seven o'clock morning mail till the office was closed at night, with no weekly half-day off and Sunday not entirely free, for there was a Sunday morning delivery of letters and an outward mail to be made up in the evening. Slave's hours, she was told by those employed directly by Government in the larger post offices, where they worked an eight-hour day. And so they would have been had life moved at its present-day pace. At that time life moved in a more leisurely manner; the amount of business transacted in such village post offices was smaller and its nature more simple, there were no complicated forms with instructions for filling in to be dealt out to the public, no Government allowances to be paid, and the only pensions were the quarterly ones to ex-Service men, of whom there would not be more than three or four in such a place. During the day there were long, quiet intervals in which meals could be taken in comparative peace, or reading or knitting were possible, while where two were engaged in the business, as at Candleford Green, there were opportunities of getting out into the fresh air.

Most important of all, there was leisure for human contacts. Instead of rushing in a crowd to post at the last moment, villagers would stroll over the green in the afternoon to post their letters and stay for a chat, often bringing an apple or a pear or a nosegay from their gardens for Laura. There was always at least one pot of cut flowers in the office, pink moss-roses, sweet williams and lad's love in summer, and in autumn the old-fashioned yellow-and-bronze button chrysanthemums which filled cottage gardens at that time.

In time Laura came to know these regular customers well. Some letter or telegram they had received or were sending opened the way to confidences and often, afterwards, she was treated as an old friend and would ask if the daughter in Birmingham had made a good recovery from her confinement, or if the son in Australia was having better luck, or how the wife's asthma was, or if the husband had succeeded in getting the job he was trying for. And they would ask Laura if her people at home were well or compliment her upon a new cotton frock she was wearing, or ask her if she liked such-and-such a flower, because they had some at home they could bring her.

The morning mail arrived from the head office by walking postman at seven o'clock, and it was Laura's first duty of the day to attend to the opening of the mail-bag and the distribution of its contents in what had in times past been one of the numerous out-buildings of the house, wash-house, brew house, or pantry. New-floored and new-ceiled and with sorting-benches placed around, it made a convenient little sorting office, although, with no other means of heating than an oil stove, it was cold there in winter.

Every morning, the postman who had brought the mail remained to sort out his own letters for the village delivery, and the two women letter-carriers who did cross-country deliveries

to outlying houses and farms had their own sorting. The elder
woman, Mrs Gubbins, was an old country-woman who wore
for her round a lilac sunbonnet with apron and shawl. She was a
crabbed old creature who seldom spoke beyond grunting a
'Good morning', except when some local scandal was afoot,
when she could be voluble enough. The other postwoman was
still in her thirties and as pleasant in manner as Mrs Gubbins
was uncouth. Her name was Mrs Macey, and more will be told
about her later.

The morning postman, Thomas Brown, was a stockily built
man with greying hair, who had, as far as was known always led
a quiet, respectable life. Until recently he had taken great
interest in local affairs and had had such good judgement that
he had occasionally been asked to arbitrate in local disputes. A
teetotaller and a non-smoker, his only known vice had been an
addiction to grumbling, especially about the weather, which, he
seemed convinced, was ordered by some one with a special
grudge against postmen.

Then, just before Laura knew him, he had been converted at
a chapel revivalist meeting and the people who had formerly
lain in wait for him on his round to ask his advice about their
worldly affairs – what, for instance, could they ask from the
MFH for those three hens that old fox'd carried off in the
night, or for the cabbage patch the hunt had trampled – now
almost ran in the opposite direction when they saw him coming,
lest he should ask impertinent questions about their souls. 'How
is it with your soul?' he would unblushingly inquire of any
chance-met acquaintance, or, more directly, 'Have you found
salvation?' and, in face of a question like that, what could a man
or woman do but mumble and look silly?

All but Miss Lane, who, suddenly asked in an earnest tone,
'Miss Lane, are you a Christian?' replied haughtily, 'I do not see
that whether I am or not is any business of yours, but, if you
particularly want to know, I am a Christian in the sense that I
live in a Christian country and try to order my life according
to Christian teaching. Dogma I leave to those better qualified
than myself to expound, and I advise you to do the same.'

That last was a shrewd thrust, because he had recently

become a local preacher, but he did not feel it as such, for he only shook his grey head and said mournfully, 'Ah, I see you've not found Christ yet.'

Laura was pleased when she heard that his wife had been converted, for, outside his home, he found little sympathy. His position seemed to her quite clear. He had found, as he thought, a priceless treasure which all mankind might share if they would, and he wanted to make it known to them. The pity was that he himself was so poor an advertisement of the change of heart he wished them to experience. His expression and voice when he spoke of Divine Love failed to light up or to soften, and, although he now declared that he had been the chief of sinners, his outward life had always been so exemplary that there could be no sudden change there to illustrate and enforce his new faith. Moreover, he was still grumbling and censorious.

But at least he had the courage of his convictions. Laura discovered that in him once when one of the higher officials was paying the office a visit of inspection. He was a very great man officially and had arrived, wearing a top-hat and an immaculate morning suit, in the station fly. When the office had been surveyed and a few criticisms made, none of them very severe, because the business was really well run and the delicious tea which followed the survey had softened the edges before they were delivered, he announced that he had to see Postman Brown, then about due with a letter-box collection. Laura, quietly sorting the night mail, could not help hearing what was said at this interview.

'About this new Sunday evening collection, now,' began the surveyor in his high-pitched, public-schoolboyish accent, 'I hear you object to doing it.'

Postman (subdued, but not intimidated): 'Yes, sir, I do object.'

Surveyor: 'On what grounds, may I ask? Your colleagues have agreed, and there is extra pay for it. It is your place, my man, to carry out the duties laid down for you by the Department, and I advise you for your own good to withdraw your objection immediately.'

Postman (firmly): 'I can't, sir.'

Surveyor: 'But why, man, why? What do you usually do on a Sunday evening? Got another job? Because, if so, I warn you that to undertake outside employment of any kind is against the regulations.'

Postman (manfully and with spirit): 'My job on Sunday evenings, sir, is to worship my Creator, who Himself laid down the law, "Keep holy the Sabbath Day", and I can't go against that, sir.'

By that time the man was trembling. He knew that his post and the pension he had so nearly earned hung in the balance. He drew out a big red, white-spotted handkerchief and mopped his forehead. Yet there was still a certain dignity about him far removed from his ordinary demeanour.

The gentleman appeared to less advantage. His easy, urbane, authoritative manner dropped from him, and there was an ugly sneer in the way he pronounced the words: 'Takes a lot out of you, I suppose, this worshipping business! Better attend to the work which provides you with bread and butter. But you can go now. I will report what you have said and you will hear further about it.' Then, to Laura, as Brown went out with a humble 'Good night, sir'; 'A cantankerous man. I know his kind. Out to make trouble. But he will find he will have to fit in the Sunday evening work with his psalm-singing.'

But, although highly placed, it appeared that Mr Cochrane was not all-powerful. Some one at headquarters was more sympathetically disposed to Sabbatarian principles, or perhaps the head postmaster, who was a bit of a psalm-singer himself, interceded for Brown, for, after a few weeks of suspense, he was excused Sunday evening attendance. The other postmen did his collection with pleasure, for it brought them in a little extra pay, and he continued to add to his already high weekly walking mileage by tramping the countryside to preach in little local chapels.

Twice a year the head postmaster from Candleford came to audit the accounts and made a general survey of the office. This was officially supposed to be a surprise visit, with the object of detecting any shortage of cash or neglect of duty, but Mr Rushton and Miss Lane were on such terms that on the morning of the day of his intended visitation the head postmaster would himself come to the telegraph instrument and with his own hands signal to Laura: 'Please tell Miss Lane I shall be paying her a surprise visit this afternoon.'

That saved trouble all round. By the time Mr Rushton's pony-carriage drew up at the post office door, the account books, sheets of stamps, postal orders, licences, and so on, together with the cash, ready-counted in neat piles, would be arranged in readiness on the kitchen table. So the official business did not take long and, that dispatched, the occasion became a social one.

Tea was laid on the round table in the parlour for Mr Rushton's visits, with Miss Lane in her best silk, and a long gold chain twice round her neck and tucked into her waistband, pouring out tea from the best silver teapot, Mr Rushton doing full justice to the country fare (there was once cold duck on the table), and Laura bobbing in and out between her calls to the post office counter. The first time she was trusted to warm the pot and put in the tea from the special caddy for this function, she forgot to put in the tea and nearly dropped on the floor with nervous terror when the other two stared blankly at the crystal stream proceeding from the teapot.

After tea the garden and chickens and pigs had to be surveyed and the pony-cart loaded up with country produce, including a huge, old-fashioned bouquet of flowers for Mrs Rushton.

It was an old-fashioned way of conducting business and Mr Rushton was an old-fashioned postmaster. He was a neat, middle-aged little man, very precise in his speech and manner, and with what many considered an exaggerated sense of his own importance. Pleasant, if somewhat patronizing to well-doers on his staff, but a terror to the careless and slipshod worker. He was under the impression that his own office staff adored him. 'The crew of my little ship', he would say when speaking of those under him, 'the crew of my little ship know who is captain.' It is sad to have to record that the crew in private spoke of their captain as 'Holy Joe'.

That was because in private life Mr Rushton was a pillar of the Methodist Connexion in Candleford town, Sunday School superintendent, occasional preacher, and the ready host of visiting ministers, a great man locally in his Church. Which perhaps accounted for his style of dress. In his black, or very dark grey clothes and round, black soft felt hat, driving his fat grey pony in the lanes, he might himself have been taken for a minister, or even for a clergyman of the Established Church. On his salary of at most two hundred and fifty a year, he was able in those spacious days to keep his own pony carriage, a maid for his wife, and to entertain his friends and educate his children.

He was liked by the Candleford townspeople, but with those in the big country houses he was not a favourite. They thought him a too pedantic stickler for official rules. 'That little jack-in-office', one of the squires called him, and there was a story of a fox-hunting baronet who had terminated an interview in the office marked 'Postmaster' by hurling a stone bottle of ink at the official head. It missed its mark, fortunately, but some of the younger clerks in his office still took a pride in pointing out the faint remaining traces of the splashes on the wallpaper.

At an early stage of their acquaintance, Mr Rushton promised Laura the offer of the next vacancy for a learner in his office. But the vacancy never occurred. His only two women clerks were the daughters of a minister, a friend of his own, and boarded with his family. They were quiet, refined, pleasant young women in the early thirties, of a type to which most women clerks in the post office at that time belonged. The 'young ladies' with the artificial pearls and bad manners belonged to the early years of this century and disappeared before the last war. In Laura's time post office employment was largely the preserve of ministers' and schoolmasters' daughters. It had not become popularized. The pay of a learner in the larger offices was very small, not nearly sufficient to live upon away from home, and the smaller offices, where learners were boarded, demanded a premium. Laura had crept in by a kind of back door and later she was sometimes reminded of that fact. 'Why should I teach you? My parents paid for me to learn' was a spirit not unknown in the service.

For some time Laura hoped one of the Miss Rapleys would marry; but neither of them showed the least disposition to oblige her in that manner, and gradually her hopes of a Candleford vacancy faded. And no other offered which it was possible for her to accept. This is no success story. She remained what was officially known as an assistant throughout her brief official career. But there were compensations, which might not have appealed to everybody, but appealed to her.

The telegraph instrument had been installed in the parlour, where its scientific-looking white dials and brass trimmings looked strikingly modern against Miss Lane's old rosewood and mahogany furniture. It was what was known as the ABC type of instrument, now long superseded even in such small offices by the telephone. But it served very well in its day, being easy to learn and reliable in working. Larger and busier offices had Sounder and Single Needle instruments, worked by the Morse code and read by sound. The ABC was read by sight. A handle, like that of a coffee mill, guided a pointer from letter to letter on a dial which had the alphabet printed around it, clockwise, and this came out and was read on a smaller dial at the other end of the circuit. Surrounding the operating dial were brass studs, or keys, one for each letter, and the operator, turning the handle with one hand, depressed the keys with the finger of the other, and by so doing spelt out the words of a telegram. A smaller dial above, known as the 'receiver', recorded incoming messages.

For a few days Laura, with a book propped open before her to supply the words, practised sending. Round and round went the handle and *blick, blick, blick*, went the keys, slowly and jerkily at first, then more smoothly and quickly. Sometimes a bell attached to the instrument would ring and a real telegram come through, which Miss Lane would take off while Laura tried hard to follow the pointer on the smaller, upper dial. It whirled round so madly that she feared her eyes would never be able to follow it, but, gradually, they became accustomed to note its brief pauses and in about a week she was able to take charge of the simple apparatus.

How to get the telegrams delivered promptly was one of Miss

Lane's problems. A girl named Minnie, who lived in one of the cottages near, could usually be depended upon to do this if she happened to be at home; but although there were only about a dozen incoming telegrams a day on the average, they were apt to come in rushes with long intervals between, and often Minnie had barely had time to get out of hailing distance before another telegram arrived. Then there was running to and fro to find another messenger, or Zillah or the apprentice from the blacksmith's shop would be pressed into the service. Neither of these went willingly, and often they could ill be spared from their work, but it was a strict rule of the establishment that no telegram must be delayed. Another worrying thing about the delivery of telegrams was that even when two came fairly close together they were bound to be for addresses in opposite directions. Many were for farms or for country houses two or even three miles distant, and Minnie trailed many miles about the countryside in a day.

Trailing is the only way to describe her method of progress, for she had an apparently slow, languid walk which was, in fact, deceptive, as she managed to cover long distances and usually be back to time. She was a pretty, doll-faced country girl of fifteen, with wide, rather vacant-looking blue eyes and a great love of finery. She usually appeared at the office in a very clean, if sometimes old, print frock and a flower-wreathed hat. One very hot day in a very hot summer, Miss Lane brought forth from her hoard an old white silk parasol with a deep cream lace frill and presented it to Minnie. Her face as she went off beneath it to deliver her telegram wore an expression Laura never forgot. It was one of utter felicity.

Miss Lane's parlour door opened out into the public portion of the office and it sometimes happened that after attending to the telegraph instrument Laura found herself cut off from the inner side of the counter by what appeared to be a private and confidential conversation between Miss Lane and a customer. Then she would close the door softly and go straight to the bookcase. A few books, such as *Cooking and Household Management*, *The Complete Farrier*, and Dr Johnson's *Dictionary*, were kept on one of the kitchen window-seats, but all the best books were kept behind glass doors above the bureau in the parlour. When one of these was lent to Laura, it had first to be fitted with a brown-paper jacket, for Miss Lane was very particular about her books, most of which had belonged to her father.

The collection was an unusual one to be found in a tradesman's parlour at that time; but her father had been an unusual man, a lover of poetry, especially of Shakespeare, and a student of history and astronomy.

There were *The Works of William Shakespeare* in two large, flat volumes, and Hume's *History of England* in at least a dozen small fat ones, Scott's *Poetical Works* and a number of the Waverley Novels, Cowper's poems and Campbell's and Gray's, Thomson's *Seasons* and many other such books. Any of these, she was told, she might borrow; with one exception. That was Byron's *Don Juan*, a terrible book, she was told, and most unfit for her reading. 'I don't know why I haven't destroyed it long ago,' said Miss Lane. 'Next time there's a bonfire in the garden, I must see about it.'

Laura knew she ought to be, and was, ashamed of herself when, at every opportunity, she stood before the bookcase with goggling eyes and many a guilty glance at the door, devouring another half-canto of *Don Juan*. She slipped the book into her pocket one night and took it to read in bed and narrowly escaped detection when Miss Lane came suddenly into her room to give some instruction about the next morning's mail. She saved herself by tucking the book down into the bed beside her, but the feel of its sharp edges against her side made her so incoherent that Miss Lane glanced round suspiciously. 'No reading in bed, now,' she said. 'You've got no need to wear out your eyesight, and I'm sure I don't fancy being burnt to death in my sleep.' And Laura replied in a small, meek voice, 'No, Miss Lane.'

But she went on reading. She could not help it. How fascinating the book was! She felt she simply had to know what came next, and the blue skies and seas of those foreign shores and the seaside caves and golden sands and the wit of the author and the felicity of his language and the dexterity of his rhymes enchanted her. She was shocked by some of the hero's adventures, but more often thrilled. Laura learned quite a lot by reading *Don Juan*.

When she had finished eating that forbidden fruit, she turned to Shakespeare. Miss Lane said Shakespeare was the greatest poet who ever lived and vowed that when she had time she would re-read every one of the plays herself. But she never did. She had read them all at some time, probably to please her father, and still remembered the stories and a few lines here and there of the poetry. Sometimes, when she was in a good mood, Laura would begin: 'Good morrow, Father,' and she would reply, 'Benedicite. What early tongue so sweet saluteth me?' and go on being the Friar to Laura's Romeo. But much more often, in their off-duty hours, she was deep in *The Origin of Species*, or one of the books on human psychology she had bought at a doctor's sale of furniture. Such books as those and the leading articles in *The Times* were the kind of reading she liked. But, because of her father, she could understand Laura's love of quite other literature.

When Laura had read most of the parlour books, Miss Lane suggested that, as she was fond of reading, she should take out a library ticket at the Mechanics' Institute in Candleford town. Laura took out the ticket and, within a year, she had read and laughed and cried over the works of Charles Dickens, read such of the Waverley Novels as had not before come her way, and made the acquaintance of many other writers hitherto unknown to her. *Barchester Towers* and *Pride and Prejudice* gave her a taste for the work of Trollope and Jane Austen which was to be a precious possession for life.

The caretaker at the Institute acted as librarian during the day. He was a one-legged man named Hussey, and his manner and qualifications bore no resemblance to those of librarians today. He seemed to bear a positive grudge against frequent borrowers. 'Carn't y'make up y're mind?' he would growl at some lingerer at the shelves. 'Te-ak th' first one y'comes to. It won't be no fuller o' lies than t'others,' and, if that admonition failed, he would bring his broom and sweep close around the borrower's feet, not sparing toes or heels. Laura sometimes wondered if his surname was inherited from some virago of a maternal ancestor.

But there was no dearth of books. After she left home, Laura never suffered in that way. Modern writers who speak of the booklessness of the poor at that time must mean books as possessions; there were always book to borrow.

XXXII

The Green

IN Laura's time Candleford Green was still a village, and, in spite of its nearness to a small country town which was afterwards to annex it, the life lived there was still village life. And this, she soon discovered, was as distinct from that of a hamlet, such as that in which she had been bred, as the life of a country town was from that of a city.

In the hamlet there lived only one class of people; all did similar work, all were poor and all equal. The population of Candleford Green was more varied. It had a clergyman of its own and doctor and independent gentlewomen who lived in superior cottages with stabling attached, and artisans and labourers who lived in smaller and poorer ones, though none so small and poor as those of the hamlet. Then there were shopkeepers and the schoolmaster and a master builder and the villa people who lived on the new building estate outside the village, most of whom worked in Candleford town, a couple of miles away. The village was a little world in itself; the hamlet was but a segment.

In the large country houses around lived squires and baronets and lords who employed armies of indoor servants, gardeners, and estate workers. The village was their village, too: they attended its church, patronized its shops, and had influence upon its affairs. Their ladies might be seen, in mellow tweeds and squashed hats, going in and out of the shops in the morning, or bringing flowers with which to decorate the church for some festival, or popping into the village school to see that all was going on there as they thought it should be. In the afternoon, the same ladies in silks and satins and huge feather boas would pass through the village in their carriages, smiling and bowing to all they met, for it was part of their duty, as they conceived it, to know every inhabitant. Some of the older village women still curtsied in acknowledgement, but that pretty, old-fashioned if somewhat servile custom was declining, and with the younger, or more enlightened, or slightly higher socially, smiles and a jerk of the head by way of a bow had become the usual response.

Every member of the community knew his or her place and few wished to change it. The poor, of course, wished for higher wages, the shopkeepers for larger shops and quicker turnovers and the rich may have wished for higher rank and more extensive estates, but few wished to overstep the boundaries of class. Those at the top had no reason to wish for change and by others the social order was so generally accepted that there was no sense of injustice.

If the squire and his lady were charitable to the poor, affable to the tradesmen, and generous when writing out a cheque for some local improvement, they were supposed to have justified the existence of their class. If the shopkeeper gave good value and weight and reasonable credit in hard times, and the skilled workman had served his apprenticeship and turned out good work, no one grudged them their profits or higher wages. As to the labouring class, that was the most conservative of all. 'I know my place and I keep it,' some man or woman would say with a touch of pride in the voice, and if one of the younger and more spirited among them had ambition, those of their own family would often be the first to ridicule and discourage them.

The edifice of society as it then stood, apparently sound but already undermined, had served its purpose in the past. It could not survive in a changing world where machines were already doing what had been men's work and what had formerly been the luxuries of the few were becoming necessities of the many; but in its old age it had some pleasant aspects and not everything about it was despicable.

Along one side of the large oblong stretch of greensward

which gave the village its name ran the road into Candleford
town, a pleasant two miles, with its raised footpath and shady
avenue of beech trees. Facing the road and the green on that
side, shops and houses and garden walls were strung closely
enough together to form a one-sided street. This was known as
'the best side of the green' and many who lived there complained of the Post Office having been established on the opposite, quieter side 'so out of the way and ill-convenient'. The
Post Office side of the green was known as 'the dull side', but
Miss Lane did not find it dull, for, from the vantage point of her
windows, she had a good view of the more populous road and
of all that was going on there.

The quieter road had only the Post Office and the smithy and
one tall old red-brick Georgian farmhouse where, judging by its
size and appearance, people of importance must once have
lived, but where then only an old cowman and his wife occupied one corner. The windows of their rooms had white lace
curtains and pot plants; the other windows stared blankly in
long rows out on the green. Rumour said that on certain nights
of the year ghostly lights might be seen passing from window to
window of the upper storey, for the house was supposed to be
haunted, as all unoccupied or partly occupied large houses were
supposed to be at that date. But old Cowman Jollife and his
wife laughed at these stories and declared that they were too
cosy in their own rooms on winter nights to go looking for
ghosts in the attics. 'Us knows when we be well off,' John would
say, 'wi' three good rooms rent-free, an' milk an' taties found;
we ain't such fools as to go ferritin' round for that which might
fritten us away!'

Between these few buildings on the quiet side were rickyard
and orchard and garden walls with lilacs, laburnums, and fruit
trees overhanging. This greenery with the golden or dun thatch
of the pointed-topped ricks and the sights and sounds of the
farmyard and smithy gave this side of the green a countrified
air which some of the more go-ahead spirits of the place resented. They said the land occupied by the gardens and orchards ought to be developed. There was room there for a new
Baptist chapel and a row of good shops, and these would bring

more trade to the place and encourage people to build more houses. But, for a few more years, the dull side of the green was to remain as it was. The farmyard sounds of cock-crow and milking-time and the *tang, tang* of the forge were to blend with the strains of gramophone music and the hooting of motor horns before the farmhouse was demolished and its stock driven farther afield and the smithy gave place to an up-to-date motor garage with petrol pumps and advertisement hoardings.

Except for the church and vicarage, which stood back among trees at one end of the green with only the church tower show-ing, and roomy old inn which had known coaching days and now, after a long eclipse, was beginning to call itself an hotel, at the other, these two roads were almost all there was of the village. There were labourers' cottages out in the fields and a group of these called 'Hungry End' stood just outside the village at the farther end, and there was the new building estate on the Candleford road, but neither of these was included in the view from the Post Office.

Between the two roads lay the green with its daisies and dan-delions and grazing donkey and playing children and old men sunning themselves on the two backless benches: or, in rainy weather, deserted but for a few straggling figures crossing from various angles with umbrellas and letters to post in their hands.

The road past the shops was the favourite promenade and meeting place, but on a few occasions the green itself became the focus of attention, and the greatest of these was when, on the morning of the first Saturday in January, the Hunt met there in front of the roomy old inn. Then riders in scarlet would rein in their mounts to reach down for a stirrup-cup, and their ladies, in tight-fitting habits with long, flowing skirts, would turn on their side-saddles to wave their hunting-crops to their friends, or gather in groups to gossip while their mounts backed and fidgeted, and the waving white sterns of the pack moved hither and thither in massed formation at the word of command of the Huntsman, there known as the whipper-in. If one of the hounds strayed a yard, he would call it by name: 'Hi, Minnie!' or Spot, or Cowslip, or Trumpeter, and the animal would look lovingly into his face as it turned in meek obedience, which always seemed wonderful to Laura, in view of the fact that within a few hours the same animal might be helping to tear a living fellow creature limb from limb.

But few there thought of the fox, beyond hoping that the first covert would be successfully drawn and that the day's sport would be good.

The whole neighbourhood turned out to see the Meet. Both roadways were lined with little low basketwork pony-carriages with elderly ladies in furs, governess-cars with nurses and children, farm carts with forks stuck upright in loads of manure, and butcher's and grocer's carts and baker's white-tilted vans, and donkey-barrows in which red-faced, hoarse-shouting hawkers stood up for a better view. Matthew used to say that it was a funny thing that everybody's errand led them in that direction on Meet Morning.

On the green itself school-teachers, curates, men in breeches and gaiters with ash sticks, men in ragged coats and mufflers, smartly dressed girls from Candleford town, and local women in white aprons with babies in their arms pressed forward to see all there was to be seen, while older children rushed hither and thither shouting, 'Tally-ho! Tally-ho!' and only missed by a miracle being hit by the horses' hoofs.

Every year, as soon as the Meet had assembled, Matthew would hang up his leather apron, slip into his second-best coat, and say that he must just pop across the green for a moment; Squire, or Sir Austin, or Muster Ramsbottom of Pilvery had asked him to run his hand over his mare's fetlock. But the smiths were to get on with their work, none of their 'gaping an' gazing', they had seen 'osses before and them that rode on 'em though to judge by some of their doings you'd think they didn't know the near from the off side.

As soon as he had disappeared, the smiths left anvil and tools and forge and fire to take care of themselves and hurried out to a little hillock a few yards from the smithy door, where they stood close-packed with their fringed leather aprons flapping about their legs.

No one was likely to have business at the Post Office counter that morning, but the telegraph instrument had to be attended to, and, although that was furnished with a warning bell which could be heard all over the house, both Miss Lane and Laura found it necessary to be in constant attendance.

From the window near the instrument the green, with its restive horses and swaying crowds, its splashes of scarlet coats and its white splash of hounds, could be viewed in comfort. Miss Lane could recognize at sight almost every one there and give little character sketches of many for Laura's benefit. That gentleman there on the tall grey was 'out-running the constable'; he had got through a fortune of so much in so many years and was now in 'queer street'. The very horse he sat upon did not belong to him; he had got it to try out, as he happened to know; Tom Byles, the vet, had told her only yesterday. And that lady there with the floating veil was a perfect madam; just look at all those men around her, did you ever, now! And that pretty quiet little thing was a cousin of Sir Timothy's, and that fine, handsome young fellow was only a farmer.

'Poor young things!' she said one day when a man and a girl rider had, ostensibly to soothe the restlessness of their mounts, detached themselves from the main body of the Hunt and were riding at a walking pace backwards and forwards before the Post Office windows. 'Poor young things, trying to get in a word together. Think they are alone, no doubt, and them with the eyes of all the field upon them. Ah, I thought so! Here comes her mother. It'll never do, my poor dears, it'll never do, with him a younger son without a penny to bless himself, as the saying goes.'

But Laura, as yet, had less sympathy with lovers. Her eyes were fixed on a girl of about her own age in a scarlet coat and a small black velvet jockey cap, whose pony was giving her trouble. A groom came up quickly and took its reins. Laura thought she would like to be dressed like that girl and to ride to hounds across fields and over streams on that mild January morning. In imagination she saw herself flying across a brook, *her* hair streaming and *her* gloved hands holding the reins in such a masterly fashion that other riders near called out 'Well done!' as she had heard riders near her home call out when witnessing a feat of horsemanship.

When the Hunt moved off to draw the appointed cover, men and women and boys and girls would follow on foot as long as their breath lasted. Two or three working men of the tougher kind would follow the Hunt all day, pushing through thorn hedges and leaping or wading brooks, ostensibly on the chance of earning a sixpence or two for opening gates for the timid or pointing out directions to the lagging horsemen; but, actually, for the fun of the sport, which they thought well worth the loss of a day's pay and a good dressing down by the Mis'is when they got home torn and tired and hungry at night.

In summer what grass there was on the green was cut with the scythe by the man who owned the donkey which grazed there. It is doubtful if he had any legal right to the grass, but even if not, his gain in donkey fodder was well repaid to the community by the newly cut hay scent which seemed to hang about the village all the summer. One of Laura's most lasting impressions of Candleford Green was that of leaning out of her bedroom window one soft, dark summer night when the air was full of new-made hay and elderflower scents. It could not have been late in the evening, for a few dim lights still showed on the opposite side of the green and some boy or youth, on his way home, was whistling 'Annie Laurie'. Laura felt she could hang there for ever, drinking in the soft, scented night air.

One other scene she remembered at the time of year when it is still summer, but the evenings are closing in. Then youths were on the green flying kites on which they had contrived to fix lighted candle-ends. The little lights floated and flickered like fireflies against the dusk of the sky and the darker tree-tops. It was a pretty sight, although, perhaps, the sport was a dangerous one, for one of the kites caught fire and came down as tinder. At that, some men, drinking their pints outside the inn door for coolness, rushed forward and put a stop to it. Madness, they called it, stark staring madness, and asked the youths if they wanted to set the whole place on fire. But how innocent and peaceful compared with our present menace from the air!

Those who did not care for the dull side of the green would
point with pride to the march of progress on the opposite side.
To the fine new plate-glass window at the grocer's; the plaster-
of-paris model of a three-tiered wedding cake which had recently appeared among the buns and scones at the baker's next
door; and the fishmonger's where, to tell the truth, after the
morning orders for the big houses had gone out, the principal
exhibits were boxes of bloaters. But how many villages had a
fishmonger at all? And the corner shop, known as the 'Stores',
where the latest (Candleford Green) fashions might be studied.
Only the butcher lagged behind. His shop stood back in a
garden, and the lambs and hares and legs of mutton behind its
one small window were framed in roses and honeysuckle.

Interspersing the shops were houses; one, a long, low brown
one where Doctor Henderson lived. His red lamp, when lighted
at night, made a cheerful splash of colour. Less appreciated by
those who lived near was the disturbing peal of his night bell
followed by some anxious voice bawling up to him through the
speaking-tube. Some of his night calls came from outlying
hamlets and farms, six, eight, or even ten miles distant, and
those from the poor had to be brought on foot, for bicycles
were still rare and the telephone was, as yet, unknown there.

The doctor, dragged from his warm bed at midnight, had
often to saddle or harness his own horse before he could start
on his long ride or drive, for even if he kept a man to drive him
around in the day time, that man might not be available for
night work. And yet, swear as he might, and often did, on the
journey, damning horse, messenger, roads, and weather, the
doctor brought cheer and skill and kindness to his patient's
bedside.

'She'll be all right now our doctor's come,' the women downstairs would say, 'and he's that cheerful he's making her laugh
between her pains. "That's my fifth cup of tea," he says. "If I
have any more" – but I'd better not say what he said'd happen –
only it made Maggie laugh and she can't be so bad if she's
laughing.' And that was said of a man who, after a hard day's
work, had been dragged from his bed to spend the night in a
tiny, fireless bedroom overseeing a difficult delivery.

Laura's mother used to say, 'All doctors are heroes', and she spoke feelingly, for the night before Laura was born the doctor came from the nearest town through one of the worst snow-storms in then living memory. He had to leave his horse and gig at a farmhouse on the main road and walk the last mile, for the by-road to the hamlet was blocked to wheeled traffic by drifts. No wonder he said when Laura at last put in an appearance: 'There you are! Here is the person who has caused all this bother. Let us hope she will prove worth it!' Which saying was kept as a rod in pickle to be repeated to Laura when she mis-behaved during her childhood.

From her Post Office window in summer, Laura could see the grey church tower with its flagstaff and the twisted red-brick chimneys of the Vicarage rising out of massed greenery. In winter, when the trees were bare, there were glimpses of the outer tracery of the east window of the church and the mellow brick front of the Vicarage with rooks tumbling and cawing above the high elm-tops where they nested in early spring.

At the time when Laura arrived at Candleford Green a clergyman of the old type held the cure of souls of its inhabi-tants. He was an elderly man with what was then known as a fine presence, being tall and large rather than stout, with rosy cheeks, a lion-like mane of white hair, and an air of conscious authority. His wife was a dumpy little roly-poly of a woman who wore old, comfortable clothes about the village because, as she was once heard to say, 'Everybody here knows who I am, so why bother about dress?' For church and for afternoon calls upon her equals, she dressed in the silks and satins and ostrich feathers befitting her rank as the granddaughter of an earl and the wife of a vicar with large private means. She was said by the villagers to be 'a bit managing', but, on the whole, she was popular with them. When visiting the cottagers or making pur-chases at the shops, she loved to hear and discuss the latest tit-bit of gossip, which she was not above repeating – some said with additions.

The church services were long, old-fashioned and dull, but all was done decently and in order, and the music and singing were exceptionally good for a village church at that date. Mr Coulsdon preached to his poorer parishioners contentment with their divinely appointed lot in life and submission to the established order of earthly things. To the rich, the responsibilities of their position and their obligations in the way of charity. Being rich and highly placed in the little community and genuinely loving a country life, he himself naturally saw nothing wrong in the social order, and, being of a generous nature, the duty of helping the poor and afflicted was also a pleasure to him.

In cold, hard winters soup was made twice a week in the vicarage washing-copper, and the cans of all comers were filled without question. It was soup that even the very poor – connoisseurs from long and varied experience of charity soups – could find no fault with – rich and thick with pearl barley and lean beef gobbets and golden carrot rings and fat little dumplings – so solidly good that it was said that a spoon would stand in it upright. For the sick there were custard puddings, home-made jellies and half-bottles of port, and it was an unwritten law in the parish that, by sending a plate to the vicarage at precisely 1.30 on any Sunday, a convalescent could claim a dinner from the vicarage joint. There were blankets at Christmas, unbleached calico chemises for girls on first going out in service, flannel petticoats for old women, and flannel-lined waistcoats for old men.

So it had been for a quarter of a century, and Mr and Mrs Coulsdon and their fat coachman, Thomas, and Hannah, the parlourmaid who doctored the villagers' lesser ailments with herb tea and ointments, and Gantry, the cook, and the spotted Dalmatian dog which ran behind Mrs Coulsdon's carriage, and the heavy carved mahogany furniture and rich damask hangings of the vicarage seemed to the villagers almost as firmly established and enduring as the church tower.

Then, one summer afternoon, Mrs Coulsdon, dressed in her best, drove off in her carriage to attend a large and fashionable bazaar and sale of work got up by the country notabilities, and, in addition to her many purchases, brought back with her the germ which killed her within a week. Her husband caught the infection and followed her a few days later and they were buried in one grave, to which their coffins were followed by the

entire population of the parish, and sincerely mourned, for that
one day at least, even by those who had scarcely given them a
thought before. The *Candleford News* had a three-column account of the funeral, headed: 'The Candleford Green Tragedy,
Funeral of Beloved Vicar and His Wife', and the grave and the
surrounding sward, covered with wreaths and crosses and pathetic little bunches of cottage-garden flowers, was photographed and copies were sold at fourpence each and framed
and hung upon cottage walls.

Then the parishioners began to wonder what the new Vicar
would be like. 'We shall be lucky if we get another as good as
Mr Coulsdon,' they said. 'He was a gentleman as was a gentleman, and she was a lady. Never interfered with anybody's
business, he didn't, and was good to the poor'; and 'Dealt with
the local shops and paid on the nail,' added the shopkeepers.

Months later, after every room in the vicarage had been overhauled by workmen and the greater part of the garden and
paddock had been torn up to get at the drains, which were
naturally suspect, the new Vicar arrived, but he and his family
belonged so much to the new order of things that they must be
given a later place in this record.

It sometimes seems to us that some impression of those now
dead must be left upon their familiar earthly surroundings. We
saw them, on such a day, in such a spot, in such an attitude,
smiling – or not smiling – and the impression of the scene is so
deeply engraved upon our own hearts that we feel they must
have left some more enduring trace, though invisible to mortal
eyes. Or perhaps it would be better to say at present invisible,
for the discovery of sound waves has opened up endless possibilities.

If any such impressions of good old Mr Coulsdon remain,
one may be of him as Laura once saw him, brought to a halt on
one of his daily progresses round the green. He stood, well-fed
and well-groomed, in a world that seemed made for him,
gravely shaking his head at a distant view of the gambols of the
village idiot, as if asking himself the frequent question of lesser
mortals, 'Why? Why?'

For Candleford Green had its village idiot in the form of a

young man who had been born a deaf mute. At birth he was
probably not mentally deficient, but he had been born too early
to profit by the marvellous modern system of training such
unfortunates, and had, as a child, been allowed to run wild
while other children were in school, and the isolation and the
absence of all means of communicating with his fellows had
told upon him.

At the time when Laura knew him, he was a full-grown man,
powerfully built, with a small golden beard his mother kept
clipped and, in his quieter moments, an innocent rather than a
vacant expression. His mother, who was a widow, took in washing, and he would fetch and carry her clothes-baskets, draw
water from the well, and turn the handle of the mangle. At
home the two of them used a rough language of signs which his
mother had invented, but with the outside world he had no
means of communication and, for that reason, coupled with
that of his occasional fits of temper, although he was strong and
probably capable of learning to do any simple manual work, no
one would give him employment. He was known as Luney
Joe.

Joe spent his spare time, which was the greater part of each
day, lounging about the green, watching the men at work at the
forge or in the carpenter's shop. Sometimes, after watching
quietly for some time, he would burst into loud, inarticulate
cries which were taken for laughter, then turn and run quickly
out into the country, where he had many lairs in the woods and
hedgerows. Then the men would laugh and say: 'Old Luney
Joe's like the monkeys. They could talk if they'd a mind to, but
they think if they did we'd set 'em to work.'

If he got in the way of the workmen, they would take him by
the shoulders and run him outside, and it was chiefly his wild
gestures, contortions of feature, and loud inarticulate cries at
such times which had earned him his name.

'Luney Joe! Luney Joe!' the children would call out after
him, secure in the knowledge that, whatever they said, he could
not hear them. But, although he was deaf and dumb, Joe was
not blind, and, once or twice, when he had happened to look
round and see them following and mocking him, he had threat-

ened them by shaking the ash stick he carried. The story of this lost nothing in the telling, and people were soon saying that Joe was getting dangerous and ought to be put away. But his mother fought stoutly for his liberty, and the doctor supported her. Joseph was sane enough, he said; his seeming strangeness came from his affliction. Those against him would do well to see that their own children were better behaved.

What went on in Joe's mind nobody knew, though his mother, who loved him, may have had some idea. Laura many times saw him standing to gaze on the green with knitted brows, as though puzzling as to why other young men should be batting and bowling there and himself left out. Once some men unloading logs to add to Miss Lane's winter store allowed Joe to hand down from the cart some of the heaviest, and, for a time, his face wore an expression of perfect happiness. After a while, unfortunately, his spirits soared and he began flinging the logs down wildly and, as a result, hit one of the men on the shoulder, and was turned away roughly. At that, he fell into one of his passions and, afterwards, people said that Luney Joe was madder than ever.

But he could be very gentle. Once Laura met him in a lonely spot between trees and she felt afraid, for the path was narrow and she was alone. But she felt ashamed of her cowardice afterwards, for, as she passed him, so closely that their elbows touched, the big fellow, gentle as a lamb, put out his hand and stroked some flowers she was carrying. With nods and smiles, Laura passed on, rather hurriedly, it must be confessed, but wishing more than ever she could do something to help him.

Some years after Laura had left the district she was told that, after his mother's death, Luney Joe had been sent to the County Asylum. Poor Joe! the world which went very well for some people in those days was a harsh one for the poor and afflicted. For the old and poor, too. That was long before the day of the Old Age Pension, and for many who had worked hard all their lives and had preserved their self-respect, so far, the only refuge in old age was the Workhouse. There old couples were separated, the men going to the men's side and the women to that of the women, and the effect of this separation on some faithful

old hearts can be imagined. With the help of a few shillings a
week, parish relief, and the still fewer shillings their children –
mostly poor like themselves – could spare, some old couples
contrived to keep their own roof over their heads. Laura knew
several such couples well. The old man, bent nearly double
upon his stick, but clean and tidy, would appear at the Post
Office periodically to cash some postal order for a tiny amount
sent by a daughter in service or a married son. 'Thank God
we've got good children,' he would say, with pride as well as
gratitude in his tone, and Laura would answer: 'Yes, isn't Katie'
– or Jimmy – 'splendid!'

In those days, if any one in a village was ill, it was the custom
for neighbours to send them little dainties. Even Laura's
mother, out of her poverty, would send a little of anything she
thought a sick neighbour might fancy. Miss Lane, who had ten
times the resources of Laura's mother, did things in style. In
cases of sickness, as soon as she heard the patient had 'turned
the corner', she would kill or buy and have cooked a fowl in
order to send a dinner, and Laura, being the quickest walker,
was deputed to carry the covered plate across the green. It was
an act of kindness which blessed giver and receiver alike, for the
best cut from the breast of the bird was always reserved for
Miss Lane's own dinner. But perhaps that was not a bad plan;
anticipation of the enjoyment of her own tit-bit may have acted
as a stimulus to her good intention, and the invalids got the
next-best cuts and broth was made from the bones for them
later.

Zillah could be trusted to cook the chicken, but, once, when
one of Miss Lane's own friends fell ill, she herself brought out
from somewhere a cooking apron of fine white linen and, with
her own hands, made him a wine jelly. The history of that jelly
was far removed from that of those we now buy in bottles from
the grocer. To begin upon, calf's feet were procured and simmered for the better part of a day to extract the nourishment.

Then the contents of the stewpan were strained and the stock
had another long boiling in order to render it down to the desired strength and quantity. Then more straining and sweet-
ening and lacing with port, sufficient to colour it a deep ruby,

and clearing with eggshells, and straining and straining. Then it was poured into a flannel jellybag, the shape of a fool's cap, which had to hang from a hook in the larder ceiling all night to let its contents ooze through into the vessel placed beneath, without squeezing, and when, at last, all the complicated processes were completed, it was poured into a small mould and allowed yet one more night in which to set. No gelatine was used.

What Miss Lane called 'a taster' was reserved for herself in a teacup, and of this she gave Laura and Zillah a teaspoonful each that they might also taste. To Laura's untutored palate, it tasted no better than the red jujube sweets of which she was fond, but Zillah, out of her greater experience, declared that a jelly so strong and delicious would 'a'most raise the dead'.

Few would care to take that trouble for the sake of a few spoonfuls of jelly in these days. Laura's aunts delighted in such cookery and her mother would have enjoyed doing it had her means permitted, but already it was thought a waste of time in many households. On the face of it, it does seem absurd to spend the inside of a week making a small jelly, and women were soon to have other uses for their time and energy, but those who did such cookery in those days looked upon it as an art, and no time or trouble was thought wasted if the result were perfection. We may call the Victorian woman ignorant, weak, clinging and vapourish – she is not here to answer such charges – but at least we must admit that she knew how to cook.

Another cooking process Laura was never to see elsewhere and which perhaps may have been peculiar to smithy families was known as 'salamandering'. For this thin slices of bacon or ham were spread out on a large plate and taken to the smithy, where the plate was placed on the anvil. The smith then heated red-hot one end of a large, flat iron utensil known as the 'salamander' and held it above the plate until the rashes were crisp and curled. Shelled boiled, or poached, eggs were eaten with this dish.

Bath nights at Candleford Green were conducted on the old country system. There was near the back door an old out-building formerly used as a brew-house. Miss Lane could remember when all the beer for the house and the smiths was brewed there. In Laura's time it came from the brewery in nine-gallon casks. The custom of home brewing was fading out in farmers' and tradesmen's households; it saved trouble and expense to buy the beer from the brewery in barrels; but a few belonging to the older generation still brewed at home for themselves and their workmen. At the Candleford Green Post Office Laura issued about half a dozen four-shilling home-brewing licences a year. One woman there kept an off-licence and brewed her own beer. There was a large old yew tree at the bottom of her garden, and her customers sat beneath its spreading branches on the green, just outside her garden wall, and consumed their drinks 'off the premises' in compliance with the law. But, as she brewed for sale, hers must have been a more expensive licence, probably issued by the magistrates.

Miss Lane's brew-house had become a bath-house. It was not used by Miss Lane or by Zillah. Miss Lane took what she called her 'canary dip' in a large, shallow, saucer-shaped bath in her bedroom in a few inches of warm rain water well laced with *eau de cologne*. In winter she had a bedroom fire on her weekly bath night, and in all seasons the bath was protected by a screen – not, as might be supposed, to preserve Victorian modesty, but to keep off draughts. On the farm churning days a quart of butter-milk was delivered for Miss Lane's toilet. That was for her face and hands. When, where, and how Zillah bathed was a mystery. When baths in general were mentioned, she said she hoped she knew how to keep herself clean without boiling herself like a pig's cheek. As she always appeared very fresh and clean, Laura supposed she must have bathed by the old cottage method of washing all over in a basin. The smiths, on account of the grubby, black nature of their work, needed baths frequently, and for them, in the first place, the brew-house had been turned into a bathroom. Wednesdays and Saturdays were their bath nights. Laura's was Friday.

In one corner of the bath-house stood the old brewing copper, now connected by a length of hose-pipe, passing through the window, with the pump in the yard for filling purposes. A tap a few feet above floor level served to draw off the water when hot. On the brick floor stood the deep, man-length zinc bath used by the smiths, and standing up-ended in a corner when not in use was the hip bath for Laura and for any visitor to the house who preferred, as they said, 'a good hot soak to sitting in a saucer'. There was a square of matting rolled up, ready to be put down by the bather, and a curtain at the window and another over the door to keep out prying eyes and cold air.

To Laura the brew-house baths seemed luxurious. She had been used to bathing at home in the wash-house in water heated over the fire in a cauldron, but there every drop of water had to be fetched from a well and, fuel being equally precious, the share of hot water for each person was small. 'A good scrub all over and a rinse and make way for the next' were her mother's instructions. At Candleford Green there was unlimited hot water – boiling water which filled the small building with steam, for the fire beneath it had been lighted by the smithy apprentice before he left work, and by eight o'clock the water in the copper was bubbling. With curtains drawn over window and door and red embers glowing beneath the copper, Laura would sit, with her knees drawn up, in hot water up to her neck and luxuriate.

She was often to think of those baths in later years when she stepped into or out of the few inches of tepid water in her clean but cold modern bathroom or looked at the geyser, ticking the pennies away, and wondered if it would be too extravagant to let it run longer. But perhaps the unlimited hot water did less to make the brew-house baths memorable than the youth, health, and freedom from care of the bather.

The community was largely self-supporting. Every household grew its own vegetables, produced its new-laid eggs and cured its own bacon. Jams and jellies, wines and pickles, were made at home as a matter of course. Most gardens had a row of bee-hives. In the houses of the well-to-do there was an abundance of such foods, and even the poor enjoyed a rough plenty. The problem facing the lower-paid workers was not so much how to provide food for themselves and their families as how to obtain the hundred and one other things, such as clothing, boots, fuel, bedding and crockery ware, which had to be paid for in cash.

Those with an income of ten or twelve shillings a week often had to go short of such things, although the management and ingenuity of some of the women was amazing. Every morsel of old rag they could save or beg was made into rugs for the stone floors, or cut into fragments to make flocks to stuff bedding. Sheets were turned outside into middle and, after they had again become worn, patched and patched again until it was difficult to decide which part of a sheet was the original fabric. 'Keep the flag flying!' they would call to each other when they had their Monday morning washing flapping on the line, and the seeing eye and the feeling heart, had the possessor of these been present, would have read more than was meant into the saying. They kept the flag flying nobly, but the cost to themselves was great.

XXXIII

Penny Reading

IN those days, when young or progressive inhabitants of Candleford Green complained of the dullness of village life, the more staid would say, 'It may be dull in some villages; but not here. Why, there's always something going on!' which the dissatisfied could not deny, for, although there was none of the amusement they desired, amusements of a kind were plentiful.

No films, of course, for twenty years had yet to pass before Candleford town had its Happidrome, and no dancing for the ordinary villager except dancing on the green at holiday times in summer. But there were in winter the Church Social, with light refreshments and indoor games, and monthly Penny Readings, and a yearly concert in the schoolroom. Between these highlights of the social year, there were sewing parties which met at each of the members' houses in turn, when one of the members read aloud while the others sewed garments for the heathen or for the poor in cities, and tea was provided by the hostess of the occasion. The work parties were for the better-to-do. The cottagers had their Mothers' Meetings, which were very similar, except that there the members sewed for themselves and their families materials provided at under cost price by the ladies of the Committee, and there was no tea.

The reading aloud must have made slow progress, judging by the amount of talking done at both types of sewing party. The repetition of every spicy item of village gossip was prefaced by: 'Mrs So-and-So was saying at the working party – ' Or: 'I heard somebody say at the Mothers' Meeting – ' The fact was that both were clearing-houses for gossip, but that did not make them less enjoyable.

In summer there were 'the outings'. That of the Mothers' Meeting, after weeks of discussion of more or less desirable seaside resorts, always decided for London and the Zoo. The Choir Outing left in the small hours of the morning for Bournemouth or Weston-super-Mare; and the Children's School Treat Outing went, waving flags and singing, in a horse wagonette to the vicarage paddock in a neighbouring village, where tea and buns were partaken of at a long trestle table under some trees. After tea they ran races and played games, and returned home, tired and grubby, but still noisy, to find even a larger crowd than had seen them off waiting on the green to welcome them and join in their 'Hip-hip-hooray!'

The Penny Reading was a form of entertainment already out of date in most places; but at Candleford Green it was still going strong in the 'nineties. For it the schoolroom was lent, free of charge, 'By kind permission of the Managers', as stated upon the handbills, and the pennies taken at the door paid for heating and light. It was a popular as well as an inexpensive entertainment. Everybody went; whole families together, and all agreed that the excitement of going out after dark, carrying lanterns, and sitting in a warm room with rows and rows of other people, was well worth the sum of one penny, apart from the entertainment provided.

The star turn was given by an old gentleman from a neighbouring village, who, in his youth, had heard Dickens read his own works in public and aimed at reproducing in his own rendering the expression and mannerisms of the master.

Old Mr Greenwood put a tremendous amount of nervous energy into his reading. His features expressed as much as his voice, and his free hand was never still, and if the falsetto of his female characters sometimes rose to a screech, his facetious young men were almost too slyly humorous, and some of his listeners felt embarrassed when the deep, low voice he kept for pathetic passages broke and he had to pause to wipe away real tears, his rendering still had an authentic ring which to Dickens lovers was, as the villagers said about other items, 'well worth listening to'.

The bulk of his audience did not criticize; it enjoyed. The comic passages, featuring Pickwick, Dick Swiveller, or Sairy Gamp, were punctuated with bursts of laughter. Oliver Twist asking for more and the deathbed of Little Nell drew tears from the women and throat-clearings from the men. The reader was so regularly encored that he had been obliged to cut down his items on the programme to two; which, in effect, was four, and, when he had finished his last reading and, with his hand on his heart, had bowed himself from the platform, people would sigh and say to each other: 'Whatever comes next'll sound dull after that!'

They showed so much interest that one would naturally have expected them to get Dickens's books, of which there were several in the Parish Library, to read for themselves. But, with a very few exceptions, they did not, for, although they liked to listen, they were not readers. They were waiting, a public ready-made, for the wireless and the cinema.

Another penny reader whose items Laura enjoyed was a Mrs Cox, who lived in the Dower House on one of the neighbouring estates and was said to be an American by birth. She was middle-aged, dressed unconventionally in loose, collarless frocks, usually green, and had short iron-grey hair which hung loose in curls, like a modern bob. She always read from *Uncle Remus*, and her rendering of Brer Rabbit and Brer Fox and the tar-baby may have owed something to some old black mammy of her childhood. The rich huskiness of her tone, her plantation dialect, and her flashing smile when delivering some side-thrust of wit were charming.

For the rest, some of the readings were well chosen, some ill chosen. A few poems were interspersed between the prose passages, but these seldom rose higher than 'Excelsior', or 'The Village Blacksmith', or 'The Wreck of the Hesperus'. Once Laura had the honour of choosing two passages for the father of one of her friends, who had been invited to read and could not, as he said, think of anything likely, not if his life depended upon it. She chose the scene from *The Heart of Midlothian* in which Jeanie Deans is granted an audience by Queen Caroline and the chapter about the Battle of Waterloo from *Vanity Fair* which ends: 'Darkness came down on the field and city; and Amelia was praying for George, who was lying on his face, dead, with a bullet through his heart.' The man who read them said he thought they went down very well with the audience, but Laura did not notice any marked interest.

For the homely Penny Reading, second-best wear was considered sufficient; that being the last outfit before the newest, which, sponged and pressed and smartened up by the addition of a new ribbon bow and lace collar, had to serve another term for better wear before being taken into everyday use. At the annual concert the audience appeared in churchgoing Sunday best. The young ladies contributing to the programme wore white or pale-coloured frocks with a modest 'v' neck and elbow sleeves, and the village girls who appeared on the platform their last summer's frock with a flower in their hair, or an ivy wreath, or a bright ribbon bow. For the Church Social, summer frocks were worn by the girls – last year's in most cases, but, in a few, next year's made in advance and worn with the collar tucked in to give it an evening-dress appearance. The older women wore black silk if they had it; if not, the stiffest and richest fabric they possessed or could afford to buy for the occasion.

The fashion in dress was by that time more simple than it had been. The bustle had long passed away, and with it had gone panniers, waterfall backs, and other drapings on skirts. The new plain skirt was long and full and slightly stiffened at the hem to

make it stand out well round the ankles, and, with it went a
blouse or bodice, as the upper part of a frock was still called,
with balloon sleeves and a full, loose front, often of a con-
trasting colour. Small waists were still fashionable, but the standard of smallness had changed. Women no longer aimed at an
eighteen- or twenty-inch span, but were satisfied with one of
twenty-two, -three, or -four inches, and that had to be attained
by moderate compression; the old savage tight-lacing was a
thing of the past.

In hairdressing, the Royal, or Alexandra, fringe was the rage.
For this the hair was cut above the forehead and curled, or,
rather, frizzed to reach back almost to the crown. Considering
that this style of hairdressing was introduced by the then Princess of Wales whose beauty and goodness and taste as a leader
of fashion was unchallenged, it is strange that it should have
been condemned by many as 'fast'. As in the case of bobbing
during the last war, men and older women objected extravagantly to the fringe; but they had to get used to it, for, like the
bob, it was a becoming fashion and it had come to stay. Fringes
were worn all through the 'nineties.

Laura, dressing for the Church Social in the cream nun's
veiling frock in which she had been confirmed and in which her
cousins Molly and Nellie had been confirmed before her, wondered if she might venture to cut and curl a few locks on her
own forehead. If Miss Lane or her mother noticed them and
objected, she could say they were little loose ends she had curled
up to make them tidier, or, if they passed unnoticed, she could
cut and curl more, and so get a fringe by instalments. The stem
of a new clay pipe borrowed from Matthew's bedroom served
her as a substitute for curling-tongs when heated in the flame of
her candle, and she pushed her hat low down on her brow
before going downstairs. There were comments and some criticism afterwards. Her brother told her she looked like a young
prize bull, and her mother said, 'It suits you, of course, but
you're too young to go thinking of fashions.' But, by degrees,
she got her fringe, and a troublesome job it was to keep it in
curl in wet weather.

The Church Social was strictly a villagers' affair. No one

came from the great houses and the clergyman only looked in once during the evening. The presence of the curate and Sunday-School teachers guaranteed propriety. When the mothers had assisted with clearing away the tea and the long trestle tables had been removed, they seated themselves around the walls to watch the games. After 'Postman's Knock' and 'Musical Chairs' and 'Here we go round the Mulberry Bush', a large ring was formed for 'Dropping the Handkerchief' and the fun of the evening began. '*I wrote a letter to my love and on the way I dropped it. One of you has picked it up and put it in your pocket,*' chanted the odd man or girl out as they circled the ring, handkerchief in hand, until they came to the back of the person they wished to choose and placed the handkerchief on his or her shoulder. The chase which followed took so long, round and round the ring and always eventually out of one of the several doors, that two separate handkerchiefs kept two couples going in the Church Social version of the game. There was supposed to be no kissing, as it was a Church function, but when the pursuer caught the pursued somewhere beyond the door with a smudged roller towel upon it, who could say what happened. Perhaps the youth sketched a stage kiss. Perhaps not.

As the evening went on, the women and girls and young men and boys in the ring whirled hand in hand, faster and faster, the girls' blue and pink and green skirts standing out like bells and the young men's faces getting redder, until some one called out, 'Time for "Auld Lang Syne"!' and hands were crossed and the old song was sung and people went home, in families or couples, according to age. Dancing would have been better perhaps, but 'Dropping the Handkerchief' served much the same purpose in that unsophisticated day.

From such festivities some of the older girls were seen home by young men. The engaged, of course, were already provided with an escort, and for that office to certain unattached pretty and popular girls there was keen rivalry. The young and not in any way outstanding girls, such as Laura, had to find their way home through the darkness alone, or join up with some family or group of friends which happened to be going their way.

One year and one year only at the Church Social, after the singing of 'Auld Lang Syne', a young man approached Laura and said, bowing gravely as was the custom, 'May I have the pleasure of seeing you home?' This caused quite a sensation among those immediately surrounding the pair, for the young man was the reporter for the local newspaper and so looked upon as an outsider at such gatherings. His predecessor had sat about with a bored air between his dashes out to the 'Golden Lion', and once, when invited to join hands in the final singing, had refused and stood aloof in a corner scribbling in his note-book. But he was a middle-aged man and inclined to give himself airs. This new reporter, who had appeared for the first time at Candleford Green that evening, was only a year or two older than Laura, and he had joined in the games and laughed and shouted as loudly as anybody. He had nice blue eyes and an infectious laugh, and, of course, the note-book in which he scribbled shorthand notes was also attractive to Laura. So, when he asked her if he might see her home, she was delighted to murmur the conventional 'That would be very kind of you'.

As they circled the green in the mild, damp air of the winter night, he told Laura about himself. He had only left school a few months before and was being given a month's trial by the Editor of the *Candleford News*. The month of trial was almost over and he would be leaving Candleford in a day or two, not because he had proved unsatisfactory – at least he hoped not – but because a much better opening had now been found for him by his parents on a newspaper in his home town, far up in the midlands. 'After that, Fleet Street, I suppose?' suggested Laura, and they both laughed at that as an excellent joke and agreed that they both felt they must have met before at some-time, somewhere. Then they had to discuss the party they had come from and to laugh at some of the oddities there. Which was wrong of Laura, who had been carefully trained never to make fun of the absent. The only excuse that can be found for her is that it was the first time she met any one from the outside world near her own age and upon anything like equal terms, and that may have gone to her head a little.

They laughed and chattered until they came to the Post Office door; then stood talking in hushed voices until their feet grew cold and her companion suggested that they should take another turn round the green to restore their circulation. They took several turns, for they began talking about books and forgot how late it was growing, and they might, indeed, have continued walking and talking all night had not a light appeared at the Post Office door, when Laura, after a hasty 'Good night', hurried there to find Miss Lane looking out for her.

Laura never saw Godfrey Parrish again, but for some years they wrote to each other. His were amusing letters, written on the best editorial notepaper, thick and good, with a black embossed heading. As his letters often ran to seven or eight pages, his editor must sometimes have marvelled at the rapidity with which his private stock of notepaper became depleted. In return, Laura told him of any amusing little incident which occurred and what books she was reading, until, at last, the correspondence languished, then ceased, in the usual manner of such pen-friendships.

Beyond having a friend or relative to stay with her occasionally, Miss Lane did little entertaining. She said she saw as much of her neighbours as she desired at the Post Office counter. But once a year she gave what she called her 'hay-home supper', and that to those of her household was a great occasion.

She had two small paddocks beyond her garden in one or other of which Peggy, the old chestnut mare, took her ease when her services were not required to draw the smiths with their tools in the spring-cart to the hunting stables. Every spring one of the paddocks was shut up for hay. Its yield was one small haystack, a quantity quite out of proportion to the bustle and excitement of the hay-home supper, but the making of hay for the pony's winter fodder and the supper for all those who had worked for her in any capacity during the year was part of the traditional business and domestic economy handed down to Miss Lane by her parents and grandparents. Excepting Laura, the younger smiths, and Miss Lane herself, who was ageless, all at the hay-home supper were elderly or old. There were grey and white heads all around the table and the custom itself was

so hoary that that must have been one of its last mani-
festations.

For the haymaking a queer old couple named Beer were engaged, not for the day, week, or season, but permanently. On
some fine summer morning, without previous notice, Beer
would come with his scythe to the back door and say: 'Tell
Mis'is that grass be in fine fettle now an' th' weather don't look
too unkind like; and with her permission I be now about to
begin on't.' When he had the grass lying in swathes, his wife
appeared, and together they raked and turned and tossed and
tedded, refreshed at short intervals by jugs of beer or tea provided by Miss Lane and carried to them by Zillah.

Beer was a typical old countryman, ruddy and wizened, with
very bright eyes; shrivelled and thin of figure and sagging at the
knees, but still sprightly. His wife was also ruddy of face, but
her figure was as round as a barrel. Instead of the usual sun
bonnet, she wore for the haymaking a white muslin frilled cap
tied under the chin, and over it a broad-brimmed black straw
hat, which made her look like an old-fashioned Welsh-woman.
She was a merry old soul with a fat, chuckling laugh, and when
she laughed her face wrinkled up until her eyes disappeared. She
was much in request as a midwife.

When the hay was dried and in cocks, Beer came to the door
again: 'Ma'am, ma'am!' he would call. 'We be ready.' That was
the signal for the smiths to turn out and build the hayrick, with
Peggy herself and her spring-cart to do the carrying. All that
day there was much running to and fro and shouting and mer-
riment. Indoors, the kitchen table was laid with pies and tarts
and custards and, in the place of honour at the head of the
table, the dish of the evening, a stuffed collar chine of bacon.
When the company assembled, large, foaming jugs of beer
would be drawn for the men and for those of the women who
preferred it. A jug of home-made lemonade with a sprig of
borage floating at the top circulated at the upper end of the
table.

For the stuffed chine the largest dish in the house had to be
used. It was a great round joint, being the whole neck of a pig,
cut and cured specially for the hay-home supper. It was lavishly

stuffed with sage and onions and was altogether very rich and highly flavoured. It would not have suited modern digestions, but most of those present at the hay-home supper ate of it largely and enjoyed it. Old Mr Beer, in the little speech he made after supper, never forgot to mention the chine. 'I've been a-meakin' hay in them fields f'r this forty-six 'ears,' he would say, 'in your time, ma'am, an' y'r feather's an' y'r gran'fer's before yer, an' th' stuffed chines I've a-eaten at the suppers've always bin of the best; but of all the chines I've tasted in this kitchen that of which I sees the remains before me – if remains they can be called, f'r you wants to put on y'r spectacles to see 'em – wer' the finest an' fattest an' teastiest of any.'

After Miss Lane had replied to the speech of thanks, home-made wine was brought out, tobacco and snuff handed round, and songs were sung. It was a point of strict etiquette that every guest should contribute something to the programme, irrespective of musical ability. The songs were sung without musical accompaniment and many of them without a recognizable tune, but what they may have lacked in harmony was more than made up for in length.

Every year when Laura was present Mr Beer obliged with his famous half-song, half-recitation, relating the adventures of an Oxfordshire man on a trip to London. It began:

Last Michaelmas I remember well, when harvest wer' all over,
Our chaps had stacked up all the be-ans and re-aked up all th' clover,

which lull in the year's work gave one Sam the daring idea of taking a trip to Town:

For Sal went there a year ago, along wi' Squire Brown,
Housemaid or summat, doan't know what,
To live in Lunnon town,
An' they behaved right well to Sal an' give her cloathes an' that,
An' Sal 'aved nation well to them and got quite tall and fat.

So Sam thought, if 'Measter' approved, he would pay his sister a visit. 'If "Measter" refused permission', Sam said in quite a modern spirit:

Old Grograin then must give I work, a rum old fellow he!
He grumbles when he sets us on, but, dang it! what care we.

But he had still his mother to deal with. She 'cried aloud to break
her heart at parting thus with me'; but cheered up and began to
look into ways and means:

Well, since you 'ull so headstrong be, some rigging we must get,
I'll wash 'ee out another shirt, an' sprig 'ee up a bit,

and gave as her parting advice:

Now, Sam, 'ave well where you be gwain,
Whatever others does to you, be sure don't turn again.

To which Sam replied:

Yes, very purty, fancy that now, blow me jacket tight!
If they begins their rigs wi' me, I'll purty soon show fight,

and cut himself a good stout ash stick before setting out in his
'holland smock, as good as new' on foot to 'Lunnon town'.

To her children's disgust in after years, Laura's memory left
him, newly arrived, on London Bridge, asking passers-by if they
knew 'our Sal, or mayhap Squire Brown', but there were
stanzas and stanzas after that – that one song, in fact, accounted
for a good part of the evening. But no one then present found it
too long, for the younger smiths had slipped, one by one, out of
the door, and those left, excepting Laura and Miss Lane, were
old and loved the old, slow, country manner of rejoicing.

They sat around the table. Mrs Beer with her arms folded on
her comfortable stomach and one ear always open to catch
what she called 'a bidding', for 'My dear, 'tis a mortal truth that
babbies like to come arter dark. For why? So's nobody should
see their blessed little spirits come winging'; Beer himself beaming on all and inclined to hiccups towards the end of the evening; the old washerwoman's worn fingers fingering her muslin
cap, only worn on special occasions; Zillah, important and
fussy, acting the part of a second hostess; and Matthew, with his
old blue eyes shining with gratification at the laughter which
greeted his jokes. Miss Lane, very upright at the head of the

table in her claret-coloured silk, looked like a visitant from another sphere, well weighted down to earth, though, by her gold chains and watch and brooches and locket; and Laura, in pink print, ran in and out with plates and glasses, because it was Zillah's evening off. That was the hay-home supper, a survival, though perhaps not more ancient than a couple of hundred years or so – a mere babe of a survival compared to the Village Feast.

The maypole had long been chopped up for firewood, the morris dance was fading out as one after another the old players died, and Plough Monday had become an ordinary working day; but at Candleford Green the Feast was still a general holiday, as it must have been from the day upon which the church was dedicated, far back in the centuries.

Some kind of feast may have been held on the green before that time, some pagan rite, for even in the respectable latter part of the nineteenth century there was more of a pagan than a Christian spirit abroad at the Feast celebrations.

It was essentially a people's holiday. The clergy and the local gentle-people had no hand in it. They avoided the green on that day. Even the youngest of country house-parties had not yet discovered the delights of hurdy-gurdy music and naphtha flares, of shouting oneself hoarse in swingboats and waving paper streamers while riding mechanical ostriches. With one exception to be mentioned hereafter, only a few of the under-servants from the great houses appeared on the green on Feast Monday.

For those who liked feasts there were booths and stalls and coconut shies and shooting-galleries and swingboats and a merry-go-round and a brass band for dancing. All the fun of the fair, in fact. From early morning people poured in from the neighbouring villages and from Candleford town.

Candleford Green people were proud of this display. It showed how the place had come on, they said, for the largest and most brilliantly painted and lit merry-go-round in the county to find it worth while to attend their Feast. Old men could remember when there had been only one booth with a two-headed calf or a fat lady, and a few poor stalls selling

ginger bread or the pottery images still to be seen in some of
their cottages, representing a couple in bed in nightcaps, and the
bedroom utensil showing beneath the bed-valance.

In those early days there had been no merry-go-round, but
for the children, they said, there was Old Hickman's whirligig,
apparently the parent of the modern merry-go-round. It was
made entirely of wood, with an outside circle of plain wooden
seats which revolved by means of a hand-turned device in the
centre. It was a one-man show. When Old Hickman grew tired,
a boy bystander was invited to take his place at the handle,
the promised reward being a ride for every twenty minutes'
labour. While the old men were still boys, this primitive
merry-go-round collapsed and they made a rhyme about it,
which ran:

> Old Jim Hickman's whirligig broke down,
> Broke and let the wenches down.
> If that'd been made of ash or oak,
> I'll be blowed if that'd have broke.

Old Hickman's whirligig had broken down and gone to the
bonfire fifty years before, and only Laura cared to hear about
it. That, she was told, was because she was 'one of the quiet,
old-fashioned sort'. But 'still waters run deep', they would
remind her, and there were plenty of sweethearts to go round
and suit all.

There were plenty of sweethearts on the green on Feast
Monday, pairs and pairs and pairs of them, the girls in their best
summer frocks, with flowers or feathers in their hats, and the
young men in their Sunday suits, with pink or blue ties. With
arms round each other's waists, they strolled from one sight to
the next, eating sweets or sections of coconut; or took turns on
the merry-go-round or in the swingboats. All day the roundabout organ ground out its repertoire of popular tunes, in competition with the brass band playing a different tune at the other
end of the green. Swingboats appeared and disappeared over the
canvas roofs of the booths, and the occupants, now head
upwards, now feet upwards, shrieked with excitement and
cheered each other on to go higher and still higher, while, below,

on the trampled turf, people of all ages threaded the narrow passages between the shows, laughing and shouting and eating – always eating.

'What crowds!' people cried. 'It's the best Feast we've ever had. If the green could only always look like this! And I do dearly love a bit of good music.'

The noise was deafening. The few quiet people who stayed indoors put cotton-wool in their ears. One year when a poor woman was dying on Feast Monday in a cottage near the green her friends went out and begged that the band would stop playing for an hour. The band, of course, could not stop playing but the bandsmen offered to muffle the drumsticks, and, for the rest of the afternoon the drum's *dum, dum, dum* sounded a *memento mori* amidst the rejoicings. Very few noticed it, the other noises were too many and too loud, and by teatime its resonance was restored, for the woman had died.

Every year, among the cottagers and show folk and maid-servants and farm-hands at the Feast, there was one aristocratic figure. It was that of a young man, the eldest son of a peer, who for years frequented all the feasts and fairs and club-walkings of the countryside. Laura knew him well by sight, for his an- cestral mansion was not far from her own home. From her window at Candleford Green Post Office she once saw him, leaning languidly against the pay-box of a coconut shy, sur- rounded by a bevy of girls who were having 'tries' at the coco- nuts at his expense. His dress was that of a country gentleman of his time, tweed Norfolk suit and deerstalker cap, and that, and his air of ironic detachment, set him apart from the crowd and helped out his Childe Harold pose.

All day he was surrounded by village girls, waiting to be treated to the different shows, and from these he would select one favourite with whom to dance the evening through. His group was a centre of interest. 'Have 'ee seen Lord So-and-So?' people would ask, just as they might have asked, 'Have 'ee seen the fat lady?' or 'the peep-show?' and they openly pointed him out to each other as one of the sights of the Feast.

The heroine of a modern novel would have seized such an opportunity to go out into the throng and learn a little at first-hand about life; but this is a true story, and Laura was not of the stuff of which heroines are made. A born looker-on, she preferred to watch from her window, excepting one year when her brother Edmund came and took her out and knocked off so many coconuts from the 'shy' that its proprietor refused his penny for another go, saying in aggrieved tones: 'I know your sort. You bin practising.'

Early in the evening the merry-go-round packed up and departed. It had only stopped there to put in a day on its way to a larger and more remunerative fair in the locality. After its organ had gone, the strains of the band music could be heard and the number of dancers increased. Shop girls and their swains arrived from Candleford town, farm workers from outlying villages came, arm in arm with their girls; men- and maid-servants from the great houses stole out for an hour, and an occasional passer-by, attracted by the sounds of revelry, came forward and found a partner.

Stalls and booths were taken down and their owners departed; tired family parties trailed home through the dust and unattached men retired to the public-houses, but for many there the fun was only beginning. The music went on and the pale summer frocks of the girl dancers glimmered on in the twilight.

XXXIV

Neighbours

IN the early 'nineties the change which had for some time been going on in the outer world had reached Candleford Green. A few old-fashioned country homes, such as that of Miss Lane, might still be seen there, especially among those of the farming class, and long-established family businesses still existed, side by side with those newly established or brought up to date; but, as the older householders died and the proprietors of the old-fashioned businesses died or retired, the old gave place to the new.

Tastes and ideas were changing. Quality was less in demand than it had been. The old solid, hand-made productions, into which good materials and many hours of patient skilled craftsmanship had been put, were comparatively costly. The new machine-made goods cost less and had the further attraction of a meretricious smartness. Also they were fashionable, and most people preferred them on that account.

'Time, like an ever-rolling stream, bears all its sons away,' and its daughters, too, and the tastes and ideas of each generation, together with its ideals and conventions, go rolling downstream with it like so much debris. But, because the generations overlap, the change is gradual. In the country at the time now recorded, the day of the old skilled master-craftsman, though waning, was not over.

Across the green, almost opposite to the post office, stood a substantial cottage, end to end with a carpenters' shop. In most weathers the big double door of the workshop stood open and white-aproned workmen with their feet ankle-deep in shavings could be seen sawing and planing and shaping at the benches, with, behind them, a window framing a glimpse of a garden with old-fashioned flowers and a grape-vine draping a grey wall.

There lived and worked the three Williams, father, son, and grandson. With the help of a couple of journeymen, they not only did all the carpentry and joinery of the district at a time when no doors or mantelpieces or window-frames came ready made from abroad, but they also made and mended furniture for the use of the living and made coffins for the dead. There was no rival shop. The elder William was the carpenter of the village, just as Miss Lane was the postmistress and Mr Coulsdon the vicar.

Although less popular than the smithy as a gathering place, the carpenters' shop had also its habitués: older and graver men, as a rule, especially choirmen, for the eldest William played the organ in church and the middle William was choirmaster. Old Mr Stokes not only played the organ, but he had built it with his own hands, and these services to the Church and to music had given him a unique local standing. But he was almost as much valued for his great experience and his known wisdom. To him the villagers went in trouble or difficulty, and he was never known to fail them. He had been Miss Lane's father's close and intimate friend and was then her own.

At the time Laura knew him he was nearly eighty and much troubled by asthma, but he still worked at his trade occasionally, with his long, lean form swathed in a white apron and his full white beard buttoned into his waistcoat; and, on summer evenings, when the rolling peal of the organ came from the open door of the church, passers-by would say: 'That's old Mr Stokes playing, I'll lay! And he's playing his own music, too, I shouldn't wonder.' Sometimes he *was* playing his own music, for he would improvise for hours, but he loved more to play for his own pleasure the music of the masters.

The second William was unlike his father in appearance, being short and thick of figure while his father was as straight and almost as thin as a lath. His face resembled that of Dante Gabriel Rossetti so closely that Laura, on seeing the portrait of that poet-painter in later years, exclaimed, 'Mr William!' For, of course, he was called 'Mr William'. His father was always spoken of respectfully as 'Mr Stokes', and his nephew as 'Young Willie.'

Like his father, Mr William was both musician and craftsman of the old school, and it was naturally expected that as a matter of course these gifts would descend to the third William. It had been a proud day for old Mr Stokes when young Willie's indentures were signed, for he thought he saw in them an assured future for the old family business. When he was at rest, and his son, there would still be a William Stokes, Carpenter and Joiner, of Candleford Green, and, after that, perhaps, still another William to follow.

But Willie himself was not so sure. He had been legally apprenticed to his grandfather's business, as was the custom in family establishments in those days, rather because it was the line laid down for him than because he desired to become a carpenter. His work in the shop was to him but work, not a fine art or a religion, and for the music so sacred to his elders he had but a moderate taste.

He was a tall, slim boy of sixteen, with beautiful hazel eyes and a fair – too fair – pink-and-white complexion. Had his mother or his grandmother been alive, his alternating fits of lassitude and devil-may-care high spirits would have been recognized as a sign that he was outgrowing his strength and that his health needed care. But the only woman in his grandfather's house was a middle-aged cousin of the middle William, who acted as housekeeper: a hard, gaunt, sour-looking woman whose thoughts and energies were centred upon keeping the house spotless. When the front door of their house was opened upon the small bare hall, with its grandfather's clock and oilcloth floor-covering patterned with lilies, an intruding nose was met by the clean, cold smell of soap and furniture polish. Everything in that house which could be scrubbed was scrubbed to a snowy whiteness; not a chair or a rug or a picture-frame was ever a hairbreadth out of place; horsehair chair and sofa coverings were polished to a cold slipperiness, table-tops might have served as mirrors, and an air of comfortless order pervaded the whole place. It was indeed a model house in the matter of cleanliness, but as a home for a delicate, warm-hearted orphan boy it fell short.

The kitchen was the only inhabited room. There the three generations of Williams took their meals, and there they carefully removed their shoes before retiring to the bedrooms which were sleeping-places only. To come home with wet clothes on a rainy day was accounted a crime. The drying of them 'messed up the place', so Willie, who was the only one of the three to be out in such weather, would change surreptitiously and leave his clothes to dry as they might, or not dry. His frequent colds left him with a cough that lingered every year into the spring. 'A churchyard cough,' the older villagers said, and shook their heads knowingly. But his grandfather did not appear to notice this. Although he loved him tenderly, he had too many other interests to be able to keep a close watch over his grandson's physical well-being. He left that to the cousin, who was absorbed in her housework and already felt it a hardship to have what she called 'a great hulking hobble-de-hoy' in the house to mess up her floors and rugs and made enough cooking and washing up for a regiment.

Willie did not care for the music his grandfather and uncle loved. He preferred the banjo and such popular songs as 'Oh, dem Golden Slippers' and 'Two Lovely Black Eyes' to organ fugues – except in church, where he sometimes sang the anthem, looking like an angel in his white surplice.

Yet, in other ways, he had a great love of and craving for beauty. 'I do like deep, rich colours – violet and crimson and the blue of these delphiniums – don't you?' he said to Laura in Miss Lane's garden one day. Laura loved those colours, too. She was almost ashamed to answer the questions in the Confession Books of her more fashionable friends: *Favourite colours?* Purple and crimson. *Favourite flowers?* The red rose. *Favourite poet?* Shakespeare. The answers made her appear so unoriginal. She almost envied previous writers in the books their preferences when she read: *Favourite flower?* Petunia, orchid, or sweet-pea; but she had not as yet the social wit to say, 'Favourite flower? After the rose, of course?' or to pay mere lip service to Shakespeare, so she was obliged to appear obvious.

Willie was fond of reading, too and did not object to poetry. Somehow he had got possession of an old shattered copy of an anthology called *A Thousand and One Gems* and when he came to tea with Miss Lane, who had known his mother and had a special affection for him, he would bring this book, and after office hours Laura and he would sit among the nut-trees at the bottom of the garden and take turns at reading aloud from it.

Those were the days for Laura when almost everything in literature was new to her and every fresh discovery was like one of Keats's own *Magic casements opening on the foam.* Between the shabby old covers of that one book were the 'Ode to a Nightingale', Shelley's 'Skylark', Wordsworth's 'Ode to Duty', and other gems which could move to a heart-shaking rapture. Willie took their readings more calmly. He liked where Laura loved. But he did honestly like, and that meant much to Laura, for none of those she had previously known in her short life, except her brother Edmund, cared twopence for poetry.

But one incident she shared with Willie remained more vivid

in her memory than the poetry readings or the scrapes he got into with other boys, such as being let down into a well by the chain to rescue a duck which had spent a day and a night, quacking loudly, as it searched in vain for a shore to that deep, narrow pool into which it had tumbled, or the time when the hayrick was on fire and, against the advice of older men, he climbed to the top to beat the burning thatch with a rake.

She had gone one day to his home with a message from Miss Lane to the housekeeper and, finding no one at home in the house, had crossed the yard to a shed where Willie was working. He was sorting out planks and, intending to tease and perhaps to shock her, he showed her a pile at the farther end of the shed in the semi-darkness. 'Just look at these,' he said. 'Here! Come right in and put your hand on them. Know what they're for? Well, I'll tell you. They're all and every one of them sides for coffins. I wonder who this one's for, and this and this. This nice little narrow one may be for you; it looks about the right size. And this one at the bottom' – touching it with his toes – 'may be for that very chap we can hear kicking up such a row with his whistling outside. They're all booked for somebody, mostly somebody we know, but there aren't any names written on them.'

Laura pretended to laugh and called him a horrid boy, but the bright day seemed to her suddenly to become dark and cold, and, afterwards, whenever she passed that shed she shivered and thought of the pile of coffin boards waiting in the half-darkness until they should be needed to make coffins for people now going happily about the green on their business and passing the shed without a shudder. The elm or the oak which had yet to make her coffin must then have been growing green, somewhere or other, and Willie had no coffin tree growing for him, for his was a soldier's grave out on the veld in South Africa.

He, the youngest, was the first of the three Williams to go. Soon after, the middle William died suddenly while working at his bench, and his father followed him next winter. Then the carpenters' shop was demolished to make way for a builder's showroom with baths and tiled fireplaces and w.c. pans in the window, and only the organ in church and pieces of good woodwork in houses remained to remind those who had known them of the three Williams.

Squeezed back to leave space for a small front garden, between the Stores and the carpenters' shop, was a tall, narrow cottage with three sash windows, one above the other, which almost filled the front wall. In the lowest window stood a few bottles of bullseyes and other boiled sweets, and above them hung a card which said: *Dressmaking and Plain Sewing.* This was the home of one of the two postwomen who, every morning, carried the letters to outlying houses off the regular postman's beat.

Unlike her colleague, who was old, grumpy and snuffy, Mrs Macey was no ordinary countrywoman. She spoke well and had delicate, refined, if somewhat worn, features, with nice grey eyes and a figure of the kind of which country people said: 'So-and-So'd manage to look well-dressed if she went round wrapped in a dishcloth.' And Mrs Macey did manage to look well-dressed, although her clothes were usually shabby and sometimes peculiar. For most of the year on her round she wore a long grey cloth coat of the kind then known as an 'ulster', and, for headgear, a man's black bowler hat draped with a black lace veil with short ends hanging at the back. This hat, Miss Lane said, was a survival of a fashion of ten years before. Laura had never seen another like it, but worn as Mrs Macey wore it, over a head of softly waving dark hair drawn down into a little tight knob on the neck, it was decidedly becoming. Instead of plodding or sauntering country fashion, Mrs Macey walked firmly and quickly, as if with a destination in view.

Excepting Miss Lane, who was more of a patron than a friend, Mrs Macey had no friends in the village. She had been born and had lived as a child on a farm near Candleford Green where her father was then bailiff; but before she had grown up her family had gone away and all that was known locally of fifteen years of her life was that she had married and lived in London. Then, four or five years before Laura knew her, she had returned to the village with her only child, at that time a boy of seven, and taken the cottage next to the Stores and put the card in the window. When the opportunity offered, Miss

Lane obtained for her the letter-carrier's post and, with the four shillings a week pay for that, a weekly postal order for the same amount from some mysterious organization (the Freemasons, it was whispered, but that was a mere guess) and the money earned by her sewing, she was able in those days and in that locality to live and bring up her boy in some degree of comfort.

She was not a widow, but she never mentioned her husband unless questioned, when she would say something about 'travelling abroad with his gentleman', leaving her hearer to conclude that he was a valet or something of that kind. Some people said she had no husband and never had had one, she had only invented one as a blind to account for her child, but Miss Lane nipped such suspicions in the bud by saying authoritatively that she had good reasons which she was not at liberty to reveal for saying that Mrs Macey had a husband still living.

Laura liked Mrs Macey and often crossed the green to her house in the evening to buy a screw of sweets or to try on a garment which was being made or turned or lengthened for her. It was as cosy a little place as can be imagined. The ground floor of the house had formerly been one largish room with a stone floor, but, by erecting a screen to enclose the window and fireplace and cut off the draughty outer portion, where water vessels and cooking utensils were kept, Mrs Macey had contrived a tiny inner living-room. In this she had a table for meals, a sofa and easy chair, and her sewing-machine. There were rugs on the floor and pictures on the walls and plenty of cushions about. These were all of good quality – relics, no doubt, of the much larger home she had had during her married life.

There Laura would sit by the fire and play ludo with Tommy, with Snowball, the white cat, on her knee, while Mrs Macey, on the other side of the hearth, stitched away at her sewing. She did not talk much, but she would sometimes look up and her eyes would smile a welcome. She seldom smiled with her lips and scarcely ever laughed and, because of this, some villagers called her 'sour-looking'. 'A sour-looking creature,' they said, but any one with more penetration would have known that she was not sour, but sad. 'Ah! you're young!' she once said when Laura had been talking a lot, 'You've got all your life before you!' as though her own life was over, although she was not much over thirty.

Her Tommy was a quiet, thoughtful little lad with the man-of-the-house air of responsibility sometimes worn by fatherless only sons. He liked to wind up the clock, let out the cat, and lock the house door at night. Once when he had brought home a blouse which Mrs Macey had been making out of an old muslin frock for Laura and with it the bill, for some now incredibly small amount – a shilling at the most, probably ninepence – Laura, by way of a mild joke, handed him her pencil and said, 'Perhaps you'll give me a receipt for the money?' 'With pleasure,' he said in his best grown-up manner. 'But it's really not necessary. We shan't charge you for it again.' Laura smiled at that 'we', denoting a partnership in which the junior partner was so very immature, then felt sad as she thought of the two of them, entrenched in that narrow home against the world with some mysterious background which could be felt but not fathomed.

Whatever the nature of the mystery surrounding the father, the boy knew nothing about it, for twice in Laura's presence he asked his mother, 'When will our Daddy come home?' and his mother, after a long pause, replied: 'Oh, not for a long time yet. He's travelling abroad, you know, and his gentleman's not ready to come home.' The first time she added, 'I expect they're shooting tigers', and the next, 'It's a long way to Spain.'

Once Tommy, in all innocence, brought out and showed Laura his father's photograph. It was that of a handsome, flashy-looking man posing before the rustic-work background of a photographer's studio. A top-hat and gloves were carefully arranged on a little table beside him. Not a working man, evidently, and yet he did not look quite like a gentleman, thought Laura, but it was no business of hers, and when she saw Mrs Macey's pained look as she took away the photograph she was glad that she had barely glanced at it.

At one end of the green, balancing the doctor's house at the other end, stood what was known there as a quality house, which meant one larger than a cottage, but smaller than a mansion. There were several such houses in the neighbourhood of Candleford Green, mostly occupied by ladies, elderly maiden or widowed, but here there lived only one gentleman. It was a white house with a green-painted balcony, green outside shutters, and a beautifully kept lawn with clipped yew trees. It was a quiet house, for Mr Repington was a very old gentleman and there were no young people to run in and out or to go to parties or hunting. His maidservants were elderly and uncommunicative, and his own man, Mr Grimshaw, was as white-headed as his master and as unapproachable.

Sometimes, on summer afternoons, a carriage with champing horses, glittering harness, and cockaded coachman and footman would stand at the gate, while, from within, through the open windows, came the sounds of tinkling teacups and ladies' voices, gossiping pleasantly, and every year, at strawberry time, Mr Repington gave one garden party to which the local gentlepeople came on foot because his stabling accommodation and that of the inn was strained to the utmost by the equipages of guests from farther afield. That was all he did in the way of entertaining. He had long given up dining out or dining others, on account of his age.

Every morning, at precisely eleven o'clock, Mr Repington would emerge from his front door, held ceremoniously open for him by Grimshaw, visit the Post Office and the carpenters' shop, stand for a few minutes to talk to the Vicar or any one else of his own class whom he happened to meet, pat a few children on the head and give a knob of sugar to the donkey. Then, having made the circuit of the green, he would disappear through his own doorway and be seen no more until the next morning.

His dress was a model of style. The pale grey suits he favoured in summer always looked fresh from the tailor's hand, and his spats and grey suède gloves were immaculate. He carried a gold-headed cane and wore a flower in his button-hole, usually a white carnation or a rosebud. Once when he met Laura out in the village he swept off his panama hat in a bow so low that she felt like a princess. But his manners were always courtly. It was not at all surprising to be told that he had formerly held some position at the Court of Queen Victoria. Which perhaps he had, perhaps not, for nothing was really known about him, excepting that he was apparently rich and obviously aged. Laura and Miss Lane knew and the postman may have noticed that he had many letters with crests and coronets on the flap of the envelope, and Laura knew that he had once sent a telegram signed with his Christian name to a very great personage indeed. But, his servants being what they were, such things were not matter for village gossip.

Like all those of good birth Laura met when in business, his voice was quiet and natural, and he was pleasant in his manner towards her. One morning he found her alone in the office, and perhaps intending to cheer what he may have thought her loneliness, he asked: 'Do you like ciphers?' Laura was not at all sure what kind of a cipher he meant – it could not be the figure nought, surely – but she said, 'Yes, I think so,' and he wrote with a tiny gold pencil on a leaf torn from his pocket-book:

> U O A O, but I O thee.
> I give thee A O, but O O me,

which, seeing her puzzled look, he interpreted:

> 'You sigh for a cipher, but I sigh for thee
> I give thee a cipher, but O sigh for me.'

And, on another occasion, he handed her the riddle:

> The beginning of Eternity,
>   The end of Time and Space,
> The beginning of every end
>   And the end of every place,

to which she soon discovered that the answer was the letter 'E'.

Laura wondered in riper years how many times and in how many different environments he had written those very puzzles to amuse other girls, unlike her in everything but age.

There were a number of small cottages around the green, most of them more picturesque than that occupied by Mrs Macey. Of these Laura knew every one of the occupants, at least well enough to be on speaking terms, through seeing them at the post office. She did not know them as intimately as she had known similar families in her native hamlet, where she had been one of them and had had a lifelong experience of their circumstances. At Candleford Green she was more in the position of an outside observer aided by the light of her previous experiences. They appeared to have a similar home life to that of the Lark Rise people, and to possess much the same virtues, weaknesses, and limitations. They spoke with the same country accent and used many of the old homely expressions. Their vocabulary may have been larger, for they had adopted most of the new catchwords of their day, but, as Laura thought afterwards, they used it with less vigour. One new old saying, however, Laura heard for the first time at Candleford Green. It was used on an occasion when a woman, newly widowed, had tried to throw herself into her husband's grave at his funeral. Then some one who had witnessed the scene said dryly in Laura's hearing: 'Ah, you wait. The bellowing cow's always the first to forget its calf.'

The Candleford Green workers lived in better cottages and many of them were better paid than the Lark Rise people. They were not all of them farm labourers; there were skilled craftsmen amongst them, and some were employed to drive vans by the tradesmen there and in Candleford town. But wages for all kinds of work were low and life for most of them must have been a struggle.

The length of raised sidewalk before the temptingly dressed windows of the Stores was the favourite afternoon promenade of the women, with or without perambulators. There *The Rage* or *The Latest*, so ticketed, might be seen free of charge, and the purchase of a reel of cotton or a paper of pins gave the right of entry to a further display of fashions. On Sundays the two Misses Pratt displayed the cream of their stock upon their own persons in church. They were tall, thin young women with frizzy Alexandra fringes of straw-coloured hair, high cheek-bones and anaemic complexions which they touched up with rouge.

At the font they had been given the pretty, old-fashioned names of Prudence and Ruth, but for business purposes, as they explained, they had exchanged them for the more high-sounding and up-to-date ones of Pearl and Ruby. The new names passed into currency sooner than might have been expected, for few of their customers cared to offend them. They might have retaliated by passing off on the offender an unbecoming hat or by skimping the sleeves of a new Sunday gown. So, to their faces, they were 'Miss Pearl' and 'Miss Ruby', while, behind their backs, as often as not, it would be 'That Ruby Pratt, as she calls herself', or 'Pearl as ought to be Prudence'.

Miss Ruby ran the dressmaking department and Miss Pearl reigned in the millinery showroom. Both were accepted authorities upon what was being worn and the correct manner of wearing it. If any one in the village was planning a new summer outfit and was not sure of the style, she would say, 'I must ask the Miss Pratts,' and although some of the resulting creations might have astonished leaders of fashion elsewhere, they were accepted by their customers as models. In Laura's time the Pratts' customers included the whole feminine population of the village, excepting those rich enough to buy elsewhere and those too poor to buy at all at first-hand.

They were good enough girls, enterprising, hard-working, and clever, and if Laura thought them conceited, that may have been because she had been told that Miss Pearl had said to a customer in the showroom that she wondered that Miss Lane had not been able to find some one more genteel than that little country girl to assist her in her office.

At the time of her marriage, it was said, their mother had been looked upon as an heiress, having not only inherited the Stores, then a plain draper's shop with rolls of calico and red flannel in the window, but also cottages and grazing land, bringing in rent, so it may be supposed she felt justified in marrying where her fancy led her. It led her to marriage with a smart young commercial traveller whose round had brought him to the shop periodically, and together they had introduced modern improvements.

When the new plate-glass windows had been put in, the dressmaking and millinery departments established, and the shop re-

named 'The Stores', the husband's efforts had ended, and for the
rest of his life he had felt himself entitled to spend most of his
waking hours in the bar parlour of the 'Golden Lion' laying
down the law to other commercial gentlemen who had not done
so well for themselves. 'There goes that old Pratt again, shaking
like a leaf and as thin as a hurdle,' Miss Lane would say when
taking her morning survey of the green from her window, and
Laura, glancing up from her work, would see the thin figure in
loud tweeds and white bowler hat making for the door of the
inn and know, without looking at the clock, that it was exactly
eleven. Some time during the day he would go home for a meal,
then return to his own special seat in the bar parlour, where he
would remain until closing time.

At home his wife grew old and shrivelled and complaining,
while the girls grew up and shouldered the business, just in time
to stop its decline. At the time Laura knew them their 'Ma', as
her daughters called her, had become an invalid on whom they
lavished the tenderest care, obtaining far-fetched dainties to
tempt her appetite, filling her room with flowers, and staging
there a private show of their latest novelties before they were
displayed to the public. 'No. Not that one, please, Mrs Perkins,'
Miss Pearl said to a customer in Laura's hearing one day. 'I'm
ever so sorry, but it's the new fashion, only just come in, and
Ma's not seen it yet. I'd take it upstairs now to show her, but she
takes her little siesta at this hour. Well, if you really don't *mind*
stepping round again in the morning . . .'

If, through absent-mindedness or a lost sense of direction, Pa
wandered in his hat and coat into the showroom, he was gently
but firmly led out by a seemingly playful daughter. 'Dear
Papa!' Miss Pearl would exclaim. 'He does take such an
interest. But come along, darling. Come with your own little
Pearlie. Mind the step, now! Gently does it. What you want is a
nice strong cup of tea.'

No wonder the Pratt girls looked, as some people said, as if
they had the weight of the world on their shoulders. They must
in reality have carried a biggish burden of trouble, and if they
tried to hide it with a show of high spirits and simpering smiles,
plus a little harmless pretension, that should have been put

down to their credit. Human nature being what it is, their shifts and pretences only served to provoke a little mild amusement. But, by the time Laura went to live at Candleford Green the Pratts' was an old story, until, one summer morning, a first-class sensation was provided for the villagers by the news that Mr Pratt had disappeared.

He had left the inn at the usual time, closing time, but had never reached home. His daughters had sat up for him, gone after midnight to the 'Golden Lion' to inquire, and then headed the search in the lanes in the early dawn, but there was still no trace, and the police were about, asking questions of early workmen. Would they circulate his photograph? Would there be a reward? And, above all, what had become of the man? 'Thin as he was, he couldn't have fallen down a crack, like!'

The search went on for days. Stationmasters were questioned, woods were searched foot by foot, wells and ponds were dragged, but no trace could be found of Mr Pratt, dead or alive.

Ruby and Pearl, their first grief abating, took counsel with friends as to whether or not to wear mourning. But, no, they decided. Poor Pa might yet return, and they compromised by appearing in church in lavender frocks with touches of mauve, half, or perhaps quarter, mourning. As time went on, the back door, which, so far, had been left on the latch at night in case of the return of the prodigal father, was again locked, and perhaps, when alone with Ma, they admitted with a sigh that all might be for the best.

But they had not heard the last of poor Pa. One morning, nearly a year later, when Miss Ruby had got up very early and, the maid still being in bed, had herself gone to the wood-shed for sticks to boil a kettle to make tea, she found her father peacefully sleeping on a bed of brushwood. Where he had been all those months he could not or would not say. He thought, or pretended to think, that there had been no interval of time, that he had come home as usual from the 'Golden Lion' the night before he was found and, finding the door locked and not liking to disturb the household, had retired to the woodshed. The one and only clue to the mystery, and that did not solve it, was that in the early dawn of the day before that of his reappearance a cyclist on the Oxford road, a few miles out of that city, had passed on the road a tall, thin elderly man in a deerstalker cap walking with his head bent and sobbing.

Where he had been and how he had managed to live while he was away was never found out. He resumed his visits to the 'Golden Lion' and his daughters shouldered their burden again. By them the episode was always afterwards referred to as 'Poor Pa's loss of memory'.

The grocer's business next door to the Pratts was also a thriving and long-established one. From a business point of view, 'Tarman's' had one advantage over the Stores, for while the draper's depended chiefly on the middle state of village society, the poor not being able to afford to buy their models and the gentry despising them, the grocer catered for all. At that time the more important village people, such as the doctor and clergyman, bought their provisions at the village shops as a matter of principle. They would have thought it mean to go further afield for the sake of saving a few shillings, and even the rich who spent only part of the year at their country houses or their hunting boxes believed it to be their duty to give the local tradesmen a turn. If there happened to be more businesses than one of a kind in a village, orders were placed with each alternately. Even Miss Lane had two bakers, one calling one week and the other the next, but in her case it may have been more a matter of business than of principle, as both bakers had horses to be shod.

This custom of local dealing benefited all the inhabitants. The shopkeeper was able to keep more varieties of goods in stock and often of a better quality then he would otherwise have done, his cheerful, well-lighted shop brightened the village street, and he himself made enough money in the way of profit to enable him to live in substantial comfort. A grocer had to be a grocer then, for his goods did not come to him in packets, ready to be handed over the counter, but had to be selected and blended and weighed out by himself, and for quality he was directly responsible to his customers. The butcher, too, received no stiff, shrouded carcasses by rail, but had to be able to recognize the points in the living animal at the local market sufficiently quickly and well to be able to guarantee the succulent joints and the old-fashioned chops and steaks would melt in the mouth. Even his scrag ends of mutton and sixpen'orth of pieces of beef which he sold to the poor were tasty and rich with juices which the refrigerator seems to have destroyed in present-day meat. However, we cannot have it all ways, and most villagers would agree that the attractions of films and wireless and dances and buses to town, plus more money in the pocket, outweigh the few poor creature comforts of their grandparents.

Above the grocer's shop, in their large, comfortable rooms, lived the grocer, his wife, and their growing-up family. This family was not liked by all; some said they had ideas above their station in life, chiefly because the children were sent to boarding-school; but practically every one dealt at their shop, for not only was it the only grocery establishment of any size in the place, but the goods sold there could be relied upon.

Mr Tarman was a burly giant in a very white apron. When he leaned forward and rested his hands on the counter to speak to a customer, the solid mahogany seemed to bend beneath the strain. His wife was what was called there 'a little pennicking bit of a woman', small and fair and, by that time, a little worn, though still priding herself upon her complexion, which she touched with nothing but warm rain water. In spite of the fine lines round her mouth and eyes, which the rain water had not been able to prevent, the effect justified her faith in its efficiency, for her cheeks were as fresh and delicately tinted as those of a child. She was a generous, open-handed creature who gave liberally to every good cause. The poor had cause to bless her, for their credit there in bad times was unlimited, and many families had a standing debt on her books that both debtor and creditor knew could never be paid. Many a cooked ham-bone with good picking still left on it and many a hock-end of bacon were slipped by her into the shopping baskets of poor mothers of families, and the clothes of her children when new were viewed by appraising eyes by those who hoped to inherit them when outgrown.

By neighbours of her own class she was said to be extravagant, and perhaps she was. Laura ate strawberries and cream for the first time at her table, and her own clothes and those of her girls were certainly not bought at the Miss Pratts'.

The baker and his wife were chiefly remarkable for their regularity in adding a new unit to their family every eighteen months. They already had eight children and the entire energies of the mother and any margin the father might have left after earning their living were devoted to nursing the younger and keeping in order the elder members of their brood. But theirs was a cheerful, happy-go-lucky household. The only dig ill-natured neighbours could get in at Mrs Brett was the old one then often heard by young mothers: 'Ah! You wait! They makes your arms ache now, but they'll make your heart ache when they get older.'

The parents were too old and too otherwise engaged and the children were too young to be friends for Laura, and she never heard what became of them; but it would not be surprising to learn that those healthy, intelligent, if somewhat unmanageable Brett children all turned out well.

There were a few other, lesser shops around the green, including the one which was really a cottage where an old dame sold penny plates of cooked prunes and rice to the village boys in the evening. She also made what was known as sticky toffee, so soft it could be pulled out in lengths, like elastic. She took snuff so freely that no one over twelve years of age would eat this.

But we must return to the Post Office, where Laura in the course of her duties was to come to know almost every one.

XXXV

At the Post Office

SOMETIMES Sir Timothy would come in, breathing heavily and mopping his brow if the weather were warm. 'Ha! ha!' he would say. 'Here is our future Postmistress-General. What is the charge for a telegram of thirty-three words to Timbuctu?

Ah! I thought so. You don't know without looking it up in a
book, so I'll send it to Oxford instead and hope you'll be better
informed next time I ask you. There! Can you read my handwriting? I'm dashed if I can always read it myself. Well, well.
Your eyes are young. Let's hope they'll never be dimmed with
crying, eh, Miss Lane? And I see you are looking as young and
handsome as ever yourself. Do you remember that afternoon I
caught you picking cowslips in Godstone Spinney? Trespassing,
you were, trespassing; and I very properly fined you on the spot,
although not as yet a J.P. – not by many a year. I let you off
lightly that time, though you made such a fuss about a
mere –'

'Oh, Sir Timothy, how you do rake up things! And I wasn't
trespassing, as you very well knew; it was a footpath your
father ought never to have closed.'

'But the game birds, woman, the game birds – ' And, if no
one else happened to come in, they would talk on of their
youth.

For Lady Adelaide, Sir Timothy's wife, the footman usually
did business while she sat in her carriage outside, but occasionally she herself would come rustling in, bringing with her a
whiff of perfume, and sink languidly down in the chair provided
for customers on their side of the counter. She was a graceful
woman, and it was a delight to watch her movements. Laura,
who sat behind her in church, admired the way she knelt for the
prayers, not plumping down squarely with one boot-sole on
each side of a substantial posterior, as most other women of her
age did, but slanting gracefully forward with the sole of one
dainty shoe in advance of the other. She was tall and thin and,
Laura thought, aristocratic-looking.

For some time she took no more notice of Laura than one
would now of an automatic stamp-delivering machine. Then,
one day, she did her the honour of personally inviting her to
join the Primrose League, of which she was a Dame and the
chief local patroness. A huge fête, in which branches from the
surrounding villages joined, was held in Sir Timothy's park every
midsummer, and there were day excursions and winter-evening
entertainments for the benefit of Primrose League members. It

was no wonder the pretty little enamelled primrose badge, worn as a brooch or lapel ornament, was so much in evidence at church on Sundays.

But Laura hesitated and grew red as a peony. In view of her Ladyship's graciousness, it seemed churlish to refuse to join; but what would her father, a declared Liberal in politics and an opponent of all that the Primrose League stood for, say if she went over to the enemy?

And she herself did not really wish to become a member; she never did wish to do what everybody else was doing, which showed she had a contrary nature, she had often been told, but it was really because her thoughts and tastes ran upon different lines than those of the majority.

The lady looked her in the face, her expression showing more interest than formerly. Perhaps she noticed her embarrassment, and Laura, who admired her sincerely and wanted to be liked by her, was about to cave in when 'Dare to be a Daniel!' said an inward voice. It was a catchword of the moment derived from the Salvation Army hymn, 'Dare to be a Daniel. Dare to stand alone', and was more often used as a laughing excuse for refusing a glass of beer in company or adopting a new style of hairdressing than seriously as a support to conscience; but it served.

'But we are Liberals at home,' said Laura apologetically, and, at that, the lady smiled and said kindly: 'Well, in that case, you had better ask your parents' permission before joining,' and that was the end of the matter as far as she was concerned. But it was a landmark in Laura's mental development. Afterwards she laughed at herself for daring to be a Daniel on so small a matter. The mighty Primrose League, with its overwhelming membership, was certainly not in need of another small member. Her Ladyship, she realized, had asked her to join out of kindness, in order that she might qualify for a ticket for the approaching celebrations, and had probably already forgotten the episode. It was better to say clearly and simply just what one meant, whoever one was talking to, and always to remember that what one said was probably of no importance whatever to one's listener.

That was the only decided stand Laura ever took in party politics. For the rest of her life she was too ready to admire the good and to detest what she thought the bad points in all parties to be able to adhere to any. She loved the Liberals, and afterwards the Socialists, for their efforts to improve the lot of the poor. Stories and poems of hers appeared before the 1914 War in the *Daily Citizen*, and, after the war, her poems were among the earliest to appear in the *Daily Herald* under Mr Gerald Gould's literary editorship; but, as we know on good authority, 'every boy and every girl that's born into this world alive, Is either a little Liberal, Or else a little Conserva*tive*', and, in spite of her early training, the inborn cast of her mind, with its love of the past and of the English countryside, often drew her in the opposite direction.

A frequent caller at the Post Office was an old Army pensioner named Benjamin Trollope, commonly called 'Old Ben'. He was a tall, upright old fellow, very neat and well-brushed in appearance, with a brown wrinkled face and the clear, straight gaze often seen in ex-Service men. He kept house with an old companion-in-arms in a small thatched cottage outside the village, and their bachelor establishment might have served as a model of order and cleanliness. In their garden the very flowers looked well-drilled, geraniums and fuchsias stood in single file from the gate to the doorway, every plant staked and in exact alignment.

Ben's friend and stable-companion, Tom Ashley, was of a more retiring disposition than Ben. He was one of those old men who seemed to have shrunken in stature and, by the time Laura knew them, he had become little and bent and wizened. He stayed mostly indoors and made their beds and curry and cobbled their garments, only coming once a quarter to the Post Office for his Army pension, when, no matter what time of year or what kind of weather, he complained of feeling cold. Ben did the gardening, shopping, and other outdoor jobs, being, as it were, the man of the house while Tom acted as housewife.

Ben told Laura that they had decided to rent that particular cottage because it had jessamine over the porch. The scent of it reminded them of India. India! That name was the key to Ben's

heart. He had seen long service there and the glamour of the
East had taken hold of his imagination. He talked well, and his
talk gave Laura a vivid impression of hot, dry plains, steaming
jungles, heathen temples, and city bazaars crowded with the
colourful life of the land he had loved and could never forget.
But there was something more which he felt, but could not
express, sights and scents and sounds of which he could only
say: 'It seems to get hold of you like, somehow.'

Once, when he was telling her of a journey he had once made
to the hills with a surveying party in some humble capacity, he
said: 'I wish you could have seen the flowers. Never saw anything like it, never in my life! Great sheets of scarlet as close-
packed as they grasses on the green, and primulas and lilies and
things such as you only see here in a hothouse, and, rising right
out of 'em, great mountains all covered with snow. Ah! 'twas a
sight – a sight! My mate says to me this mornin' when we found
it was rainin' and his ague shakin' him again, "Oh Ben," he says,
"I do wish we were back in India with a bit of hot sun"; and I
said to him, " 'Taint no good wishin', Tom. We've had our day
and that day's over. We shan't see India no more." '

It was strange, thought Laura, that other pensioners she knew
who had served in India had left that land with no regrets and
very few memories. If asked about their adventures, they would
say: 'The places have got funny names and its very hot out
there. In the Bay of Biscay on the way out every man jack of us
was seasick.' Most of them were short-service men, and they
had returned cheerfully to the plough-tail. They appeared to be
happier than Ben, but Laura liked him best.

One day a man known as 'Long Bob', a lock-keeper on the
canal, came in with a small package which he wished to send by
registered post. It was roughly done up in soiled brown paper,
and the string, although much knotted, was minus the wax seals
required by the regulations. When Laura offered him the loan
of the office sealing-wax, he asked her to seal and make tidy the
package for him, saying that his fingers were all thumbs and he
hadn't got no 'ooman now to do such fiddling little jobs for him.
'But maybe,' he added, 'before you start on it, you'd like to
have a look at that within.'

He then opened the package and brought forth and shook out a panel of coloured embroidery. It was a needlework picture of Adam and Eve, standing one on each side of the Tree of Kr. ledge with a grove of flowering and fruiting trees behind them and a lamb, a rabbit, and other small creatures in the foreground. It was exquisitely executed and the colours, though faded in places, were beautifully blended. The hair of Adam and Eve was embroidered with real human hair and the fur of the furry animals of some woolly substance. That it was very old even the inexperienced Laura could sense at the first glance, more by something strange and antique-looking about the nude human figures and the shape of the trees than by any visible sign of wear or decay in the fabric. 'It's very old, isn't it?' she asked, expecting Long Bob to say it had belonged to his grandmother.

'Very old and ancient indeed,' he replied, 'and I'm told there's some clever men in London who'll like to see that pictur'. All done by hand, they say, oh, long agone, before old Queen Bess's day.' Then, seeing Laura all eyes and ears, he told her how it had come into his possession.

About a year before, it appeared, he had found the panel on the towing-path of the canal, carelessly screwed up in a sheet of newspaper. Inspired rather by strict principles of honesty than by any idea that the panel was valuable, he had taken it to the Police Station at Candleford, where the sergeant in charge had asked him to leave it while inquiries were made. It had then, apparently, been examined by experts, for the next thing Long Bob heard from the police was that the panel was old and valuable and that inquiries as to its ownership were in progress. It was thought that it must have been part of the proceeds of some burglary. But there had been no burglary in that part of the county for several years, and the police could get no information of any more distant one where such an article was missing. The owner was never found, and, at the end of the time appointed by law, the panel was handed back to the finder, together with the address of a London sale-room to which he was advised to send it. A few weeks later he received the, to him, large sum of five pounds which its sale had realized.

That was the recent history of the needlework panel. What of its past? How had it come to lie, wrapped in a fairly recent newspaper, on the canal tow-path that foggy November morning?

Nobody ever knew. Miss Lane and Laura thought that by some means it had come into the possession of a cottage family, which, though ignorant of its value, had treasured it as a curiosity. Then, perhaps, it may have been sent by a child as a present to some relative, or as part of an inheritance from some old grandmother who had recently died. The loss by a child of 'that old sampler of Granny's' would be but a matter of cuffing and scolding; poor people would not dream of making what they called a 'hue and cry' about such a loss, or of going to the police. But this was mere supposition; the ownership of the panel and how it came to be found in such an unlikely place remained a mystery.

The office was closed to the public at eight, but, every year, for several Saturday evenings in later summer, Laura was in attendance until 9.30. Then, as she sat behind closed doors reading or knitting, she would hear a scuffle of feet outside and open the door to one, two, or more wild-looking men with touzled hair and beards, sun-scorched faces, and queerly cut clothes with coloured shirts which always seemed to be sticking out of their trousers somewhere. These were the Irish farm workers who came over to England to help with the harvest. They were keen workers, employed on piecework, who could not afford to lose one of the daylight hours. By the time they had finished work all the post offices were closed, postal orders could not be procured on Sunday, and they had to send part of their wages to their wives and families in Ireland, so, to help them solve their difficulty, Miss Lane had for some years sold them postal orders, secretly, after official hours. Now she authorized Laura to sell them.

Laura had been used to seeing the Irish harvesters from a child. Then some of the neighbours at home had tried to frighten her when naughty by saying, 'I'll give you to them old Irishers; see if I don't, then!' and although not alarmed at the threat beyond infancy – for who could be afraid of men who did no one any harm, beyond irritating them by talking too much and working harder and by so doing earning more money than they did? – they had remained to her strangers and foreigners who came to her neighbourhood for a season, as the swallows came, then disappeared across the sea to a country called 'Ireland' where people wanted Home Rule and said 'Begorra' and made things called 'bulls' and lived exclusively upon potatoes.

Now she knew the Irish harvesters by name – Mr McCarthy, Tim Doolan, Big James and Little James and Kevin and Patrick, and all the other harvesters working in the district. More and more came from farther afield as the knowledge spread that at Candleford Green there lived a sympathetic postmistress who would let a man have his postal order for home after his week's work was done. By the time Laura left the village, the favour had had to be extended to Sunday morning, and Miss Lane was trying to harden her heart and invent some reason for withdrawing the privilege which had become a serious addition to her work.

At the time now recorded there were perhaps a dozen of these Saturday-evening clients. None of the older men among them could write, and when Laura first knew them these would bring their letters to their wives in Ireland already written by one of their younger workmates. But soon she had these illiterates coming stealthily alone. 'Would ye be an angel, Missie darlint, an' write just a few little words for me on this sheet of paper I've brought?' they would whisper, and Laura would write to their dictation such letters as the following:

'*My Dear Wife*, – Thanks be to God, our Blessed Lady and the saints, this leaves me in the best of health, with work in plenty and money coming in to give us all a better winter than last year, please God.'

Then, after inquiries about the health of 'herself' and the children, the old father and mother, Uncle Doolan, Cousin Bridget, and each neighbour by name, the real reason for getting the letter written surreptitiously would emerge. The wife would be told to 'pay off at the shop', or to ask such and such a price for something they had to sell, or not to forget to 'lay by a bit in the stocking'; but she was not to deny herself anything she fancied; she should live like a queen if the sender of the letter had his way, and he remained her loving husband.

Laura noticed that when these letters were dictated there were none of the long pauses usual when she was writing a letter for one of her own old countrymen, as she sometimes did. Words came freely to the Irishman, and there were rich, warm phrases in his letters that sounded like poetry. What Englishman of his class would think of wishing his wife could live like a queen? 'Take care of yourself' would be the fondest expression she would find in his letters. The Irishman, too, had better manners than the Englishman. He took off his hat when he came in at the door, said 'please', or, rather, 'plaze', more frequently, and was almost effusive in his thanks for some small service. The younger men were inclined to pay compliments, but they did so in such charming words that no one could have felt offended.

Many gipsies frequented the neighbourhood, where there were certain roadside dells which they used as camping-grounds. These, for weeks together, would be silent and deserted, with only circles of black ash to show where fires had been and scraps of coloured rag fluttering from bushes. Then one day, towards evening, tents would be raised and fires lighted, horses would be hobbled and turned out to graze, and men with lurchers at their heels would explore the field hedgerows (not after rabbits. Oh, no! Only to cut a nice ash stick with which to make their old pony go), while the women and children around the cooking pots in the dell shouted and squabbled and called out to the men in a different language from that they used for business purposes at cottage doors.

'There's them ole gipos back again,' the villagers would say when they saw blue smoke drifting over the treetops. 'Time they was routed out o' them places, the ole stinkin' lot of 'em. If a poor man so much as looks at a rabbit he soon finds hisself in quod, but their pot's never empty. Says they eat hedgehogs! Hedgehogs! He! He! Hedgehogs wi' soft prickles!'

Laura liked the gipsies, though she did sometimes wish they

would not push with their baskets into the office, three or four at a time. If a village woman happened to be there before them she would sidle out of the door holding her nose, and their atmosphere was, indeed, overpowering, though charged as much with the odours of wood-smoke and wet earth as with that of actual uncleanliness.

There was no delivery of letters at their tents or caravans. For those they had to call at the Post Office. 'Any letters for Maria Lee?' or for Mrs Eli Stanley, or for Christina Boswell, they would say, and, if there were none, and there very often were not, they would say: 'Are you quite sure now, dearie? Do just look again. I've left my youngest in Oxford Infirmary,' or 'My daughter's expecting an increase,' or 'My boy's walking up from Winchester to join us, and he ought to be here by now.'

All this seemed surprisingly human to Laura, who had hitherto looked upon gipsies as outcasts, robbers of henroosts, stealers of children, and wheedlers of pennies from pockets even poorer than their own. Now she met them on a business footing, and they never begged from her and very seldom tried to sell her a comb or a length of lace from their baskets, but one day an old woman for whom she had written a letter offered to tell her fortune. She was perhaps the most striking-looking person Laura ever saw in her life: tall for a gipsy, with flashing black eyes and black hair without a fleck of grey in it, although her cheeks were deeply wrinkled and leathery. Some one had given her a man's brightly coloured paisley-patterned dressing-gown, which she wore as an outdoor garment with a soft billy-cock hat. Her name was Cinderella Doe and her letters came so addressed without a prefix.

The fortune was pleasing. Whoever heard of one that was not? There was no fair man or dark man or enemy to beware of in it, and though she promised Laura love, it was not love of the usual kind. 'You're going to be loved,' she said; 'loved by people you've never seen and never will see.' A graceful way of thanking one for writing a letter.

Friends and acquaintances who came to the Post Office used often to say to Laura: 'How dull it must be for you here.' But although she sometimes agreed mildly for the sake of not ap-

pearing peculiar, Laura did not find life at the Post Office at all
dull. She was so young and new to life that small things which
older people might not have noticed surprised and pleased her.
All day interesting people were coming in – interesting to her, at
least – and if there were intervals between these callers, there
was always something waiting to be done. Sometimes, in a few
spare moments, Miss Lane would come in and find her reading
a book from the parlour or the Mechanics' Institute. Although
she had not actually forbidden reading for pleasure on duty, she
did not altogether approve of it, for she thought it looked un-
businesslike. So she would say, rather acidly: 'Are you sure you
can learn nothing more from the Rule Book?' and Laura would
once more take down from its shelf the large, cream,
cardboard-bound tome she had already studied until she knew
many of the rules word for word. From even that dry-as-dust
reading she extracted some pleasure. On one page, for instance,
set in a paragraph composed of stiff, official phrases, was the
word 'mignonette'. It referred only to the colour of a form, or
something of that kind, but to Laura it seemed like a pressed
flower, still faintly scented.

And, although such callers as the gipsies and the Irish harvesters appealed to her imagination because they were out of
the ordinary, she was even more interested in the ordinary
country people, because she knew them better and knew more
of their stories. She knew the girl in love with her sister's husband, whose hands trembled while she tore open her letters
from him; and the old mother who had not heard for three
years from her son in Australia, but still came every day to the
Post Office, hoping; and the rough working man who, when
told for the first time, ten years after marriage, that his wife had
an illegitimate daughter of sixteen and that that daughter was
stricken with tuberculosis, said: 'You go and fetch her home at
once and look after her. Your child's my child and your home's
her home'; and she knew families which put more money in the
Savings Bank every week than they received in wages, and other
families which were being dunned for the payment of bills, and
what shop in London supplied Mrs Fashionable with clothes,
and who posted the box containing a dead mouse to Mrs

Meddlesome. But those were stories she would never be at liberty to tell in full, because of the Declaration she had signed before Sir Timothy.

And she had her own personal experiences: her moments of ecstasy in the contemplation of beauty; her periods of religious doubt and hours of religious faith; her bitter disillusionments on finding some people were not what she had thought them, and her stings of conscience over her own shortcomings. She grieved often for the sorrows of others and sometimes for her own. A sudden chance glimpse of animal corruption caused her to dwell for weeks on the fate of the human body. She fell into hero-worship of an elderly nobleman and thought it was love. If he noticed her at all, he must have thought her most attentive and obliging over his post-office business. She never saw him outside the office. She learned to ride a bicycle, took an interest in dress, formed her own taste in reading, and wrote a good deal of bad verse which she called 'poetry'.

But the reactions to life of a sensitive, imaginative adolescent have been so many times described in print that it is not proposed to give yet one more description in this book. Laura's mental and spiritual development can only be interesting in that it shows that those of a similar type develop in much the same way, however different the environment.

A number of customers rode up to the Post Office door on horseback. A mounting-block by the doorstep, with an iron hook in the wall above to secure the reins, had been provided for these. But the hook was seldom used out of school hours, for, if boys were playing on the green, half a dozen of them would rush forward, calling: 'Hold your 'oss, sir?' 'Let me, sir.' 'Let me!' and, unless the horse was of the temper called 'froxy', one of the tallest and stoutest of the boys would be chosen and afterwards rewarded with a penny for his pains. This arrangement entailed frequent dashes to the door by the customer to see what 'that young devil' was 'up to', and a worrying haste with the business within, but no horseman thought of refusing the job to a boy who asked for it, because it was the custom. The boys claimed the job and the reward of one penny as their right.

The gentlemen farmers to whom most of the horses belonged had fresh, ruddy faces and breezy manners and wore smartly cut riding breeches and coats. Some of them were hunting men with lady wives, and children away at boarding schools. Their farmhouses were comfortably furnished and their tables well covered with the best of food and drink, for everybody seemed in those days to do well on the land, except the farm labourer. Occasionally the rider would be a stud groom from one of the hunting stables. Then, after doing what little business he had, he would ask for Miss Lane, pass through to the kitchen, from which the chinking sound of glasses would soon proceed. Bottles of brandy and whisky were kept for these in a cupboard called 'the stud-grooms' cupboard'. No one in the house ever touched these drinks, but they had to be provided in the way of business. It was the custom.

The sound of a bicycle being propped against the wall outside was less frequent than that of a horse's hoofs; but there were already a few cyclists, and the number of these increased rapidly when the new low safety bicycle superseded the old penny-farthing type. Then, sometimes, on a Saturday afternoon, the call of a bugle would be heard, followed by the scuffling of dismounting feet, and a stream of laughing, jostling young men would press into the tiny office to send facetious telegrams. These members of the earliest cycling clubs had a great sense of their own importance, and dressed up to their part in a uniform composed of a tight navy knicker-bocker suit with red or yellow braided coat and a small navy pill-box cap embroidered with their club badge. The leader carried a bugle suspended on a coloured cord from his shoulder. Cycling was considered such a dangerous pastime that they telegraphed home news of their safe arrival at the farthest point in their journey. Or perhaps they sent the telegrams to prove how far they really had travelled, for a cyclist's word as to his day's mileage then ranked with an angler's account of his catch.

'Did run in two hours, forty and a half minutes. Only ran down two fowls, a pig, and a carter', is a fair sample of their communications. The bag was mere brag; the senders had probably hurt no living creature; some of them may even have dismounted by the roadside to allow a horsed carriage to pass, but every one of them liked to pose as 'a regular devil of a fellow'.

They were townsmen out for a lark, and, after partaking of refreshment at the hotel, they would play leap-frog or kick an old tin about the green. They had a lingo of their own. Quite common things, according to them, were 'scrumptious', or 'awfully good', or 'awfully rotten', or just 'bally awful'. Cigarettes they called 'fags'; their bicycles their 'mounts', or 'my machine' or 'my trusty steed'; the Candleford Green people they alluded to as 'the natives'. Laura was addressed by them as 'fair damsel', and their favourite ejaculation was 'What ho!' or 'What ho, she bumps!'

But they were not to retain their position as bold pioneer adventurers long. Soon, every man, youth and boy whose families were above the poverty line was riding a bicycle. For some obscure reason, the male sex tried hard to keep the privilege of bicycle riding to themselves. If a man saw or heard of a woman riding he was horrified. 'Unwomanly. Most unwomanly! God knows what the world's coming to,' he would say; but, excepting the fat and elderly and the sour and envious, the women suspended judgement. They saw possibilities which they were soon to seize. The wife of a doctor in Candleford town was the first woman cyclist in that district. 'I should like to tear her off that thing and smack her pretty little backside,' said one old man, grinding his teeth with fury. One of more gentle character sighed and said: ' 'T'ood break my heart if I saw my wife on one of they,' which those acquainted with the figure of his middle-aged wife thought reasonable.

Their protestations were unavailing; one woman after another appeared riding a glittering new bicycle. In long skirts, it is true, but with most of their petticoats left in the bedroom behind them. Even those women who as yet did not cycle gained something in freedom of movement, for the two or three bulky petticoats formerly worn were replaced by neat serge knickers – heavy and cumbersome knickers, compared with those of today, with many buttons and stiff buttonholes and cambric linings to be sewn in on Saturday nights, but a great improvement on the petticoats.

And oh! the joy of the new means of progression. To cleave the air as though on wings, defying time and space by putting what had been a day's journey on foot behind one in a couple of hours! Of passing garrulous acquaintances who had formerly held one in one-sided conversation by the roadside for an hour, with a light *ting, ting* of the bell and a casual wave of recognition.

At first only comparatively well-to-do women rode bicycles; but soon almost everyone under forty was awheel, for those who could not afford to buy a bicycle could hire one for sixpence an hour. The men's shocked criticism petered out before the *fait accompli*, and they contented themselves with such mild thrusts as:

Mother's out upon her bike, enjoying of the fun,
Sister and her beau have gone to take a little run.
The housemaid and the cook are both a-riding on their wheels;
And Daddy's in the kitchen a-cooking of the meals.

And very good for Daddy it was. He had had all the fun hitherto; now it was his wife's and daughter's turn. The knell of the selfish, much-waited-upon, old-fashioned father of the family was sounded by the bicycle bell.

XXXVI

'Such is Life!'

CANDLEFORD was a pleasant and peaceful place, but it was no second Garden of Eden. Every now and again, often after months of placidity, something would occur to disturb the even current of village life.

Sometimes these events were sad ones: a man was gored by a bull, or broke his neck by falling from a loaded wagon in the harvest field, or a mother died, leaving a brood of young children, or a little boy playing by the river fell in and was drowned. Such tragedies brought out all that was best in village life. Neighbours would flock to comfort the mourners, to take the motherless children into their own care until permanent homes could be found for them, or to offer to lend or give anything they possessed which they thought might be of use to the afflicted.

But there were other happenings, less tragic, but even more disturbing. A hitherto quiet and inoffensive man got drunk and staggered across the green shouting obscenities, an affiliation case brought unsavoury details to light, a sweetheart of ten years' standing was deserted for a younger and fresher girl, a child or an animal was ill-treated, or the usually mild and comparatively harmless village gossip suddenly became venomous. Such things made the young and inexperienced feel that life was not as it had appeared; that there were hitherto unsuspected dark depths beneath the sunny surface.

Older and more experienced people saw things more in proportion, for they had lived long enough to learn that human nature is a curious mixture of good and evil – the good, fortunately, predominating. 'Such is life!' Miss Lane would sigh when something of the kind came to her ears, and once she continued in the same breath, but more briskly, 'Have another jam tart, Laura?'

Laura was shocked, for she then thought tart and tears should be separated by at least a decent interval. She had yet to learn that though sorrow and loss and the pain of disillusionment must come to all, if not at one time then at another, and those around the sufferer will share his or her sorrow to some extent, life must still go on in the ordinary way for those not directly implicated.

At Candleford Green there was no serious crime. Murder and incest and robbery with violence were to its inhabitants just things read about in the Sunday newspapers – things to horrify and to be discussed and to form theories on, but far removed from reality. The few local court cases were calculated rather to cause a little welcome excitement than to shock or grieve.

Two men were charged with poaching, and as this had taken place on Sir Timothy's estate he retired from the Bench while the case was tried. But not, it was said, before he had asked his fellow magistrates to deal lightly with the offenders. 'For,' he was supposed to have added, 'who's going to stump up to keep their families while they are in gaol if I don't.' Sentence was passed with due regard to Sir Timothy's pocket. That case caused but a mild interest and no dissension. A poacher, it was agreed, knew the risks he was running, and if he thought the game was worth the candle, well, let him take the consequences.

Then there was the case of the man who had systematically stolen pigwash from a neighbour. The neighbour, who kept several pigs on an allotment some distance from his dwelling, had bought and collected the pigwash from an institution in Candleford town. The thief had risen early and fed his own pig from his neighbour's pig-tubs every morning for weeks before the leakage was discovered, a watch set, and he was caught, dipper in hand. 'A dirty, mean trick!' the villagers said. A fortnight in gaol was too short a sentence.

But over the case of Sam and Susan, neighbours quarrelled and friends were divided. They were a young married couple with three small children and had, as far as was known, always lived peaceably together until one evening when a dispute arose between them, in the course of which Sammy, who was a great, strapping fellow, fell upon his frail-looking little wife and gave her a bad beating. When this was known, as it was almost immediately, for such bruises and such a black eye as Susan's cannot long be hidden, there was a general outcry. Not that a wife's black eye was an entirely unknown spectacle in the village, though it was a rare one, most of the village couples being able to settle their disputes, if any, in private, but on account of the relative sizes of the couple. Sammy was so very big and tall and strong and Susie so slight and childish-looking, that every one who heard of or saw the black eye called out at once. 'The great big bully, him!' So far opinion was unanimous.

But Susie did not take her whacking in the ordinary way. Other wives who had in the past appeared with an eye blackened had always accounted for it by saying that they had been chopping firewood and a stick had flown up and hit them. It was a formula, as well understood and recognized as their more worldly sisters' 'Not at home', and good manners demanded that it should be accepted at its face value. But Susan gave no explanation at all of her state. She went in and out of her cottage in her usual brisk and determined way about her daily affairs and asked neither sympathy nor advice of her neighbours. Indeed, several days had passed before it became known that, with her black eye and her bruises still fresh, she had gone to the Police Station at Candleford town and had taken out a summons for Sammy.

Then, indeed, the village had something to talk about, and talk it did. Some people professed to be horrified that a great, strapping young fellow like Sam should have been such a brute as to lay hands on his nice little wife, good mother and model housewife as she was, and far and away too good for him. They thought she did quite right to go to the police. It showed her spirit, that it did! Others said Susan was a shrew; as all those thin, fair-haired, vinegarish little women were bound to be, and nobody knew what that poor fellow, her husband, may have had to put up with. It was nag, nag, nag, they'd be bound, every moment he was at home, and the house kept that beastly clean he had to take off his coal-heaving clothes in the shed and wash himself before he was allowed to sit down to his supper. Two parties sprang quickly into being. To one Sam was a brute and Susan a heroine, and if the other did not actually hold up Sam as a hero, they maintained that he was an ill-used young man and that Susan was a hussy. It was a case of one quarrel breeding many.

But Susan had another surprise in store for them. In due course, Sam came up before the Court and was sentenced to one month's imprisonment for wife-beating. Susan came home from the Court and, still without saying a word as to her intention to any one, packed her three small children into the perambulator, locked up the house, and marched off to Candleford Workhouse, as it appeared she had then the right to do, having no official means of support while her husband was in prison. She could quite well have stayed at home, for the tradesmen would have given her credit and the neighbours would have helped, or she could have gone to her parents' home in a neighbouring village, but she chose her own course. The step lost her many of her warmest supporters, who had been looking forward to standing by her with sympathy and material aid, and caused the opposition to condemn her more fiercely. She said afterwards she did it to shame Sam, and in this no doubt she succeeded, for it must have added to his humiliation to know that his wife and children were chargeable to the parish. But the period spent in the poorhouse must have been punishment to herself as well. It was common knowledge that life in such establishments was not a bed of roses for a respectable young woman.

However, it all ended happily. A sight Laura could never forget was that of the reunited family returning to their home after Sam's sentence had expired. They passed the Post Office, talking amiably together, Sam pushing the perambulator and Susan carrying a string bag containing the few little luxuries they had purchased on their way for their second house-warming. Each of the children clutched a toy, that of the little toddling boy being a tin trumpet which he tootled to let people know they were coming. Afterwards Sammy became a model husband, almost excessively gentle and considerate, and Susan, while still keeping the reins in her own hands, took care not to pull too hard on them for Sammy's comfort.

A family dispute about some land at one time caused great excitement. An old man of the village had many years before inherited from his parents a cottage and a couple of small fields which he had so far enjoyed without question. Then a niece of his, the daughter of a younger brother long dead, put in a claim for part of the land, which she said, ought rightfully to have gone to her father. It was an unsound claim, for the house and land had been left by will to the eldest son, who had always lived at home and assisted his parents in working their small holding. Eliza's father had been left a small sum of money and some furniture. Apparently she had the notion that while money and furniture could be left by will according to the testator's fancy, land had always to be divided between the sons of a family. Even had it been a just claim, it should, after that lapse of time, have been settled in Court, but Eliza, who was a positive, domineering kind of person, decided to take possession by force.

She was living in another village at the time, and the first intimation her uncle had of her intention was when one morning a party of workmen arrived and proceeded to break down the hedge of one of the fields. They had orders, they said, to prepare the site for a new cottage which Mrs Kibble, the owner of the land, was about to have built. Old James Ashley was a peace-loving man, a staunch Methodist, and much respected in the village, but at such an affront, understandably, his anger flared up and the workmen were quickly sent about their more lawful business. But that was only the beginning of a quarrel which lasted two years and provided much entertainment for those not affected.

About once a week the niece appeared, a tall, rather handsome woman, who wore long, dangling gold earrings and often a red shawl. She always refused to step indoors and talk it over reasonably, as her uncle suggested, but planted herself on the plot she called hers and shouted. She might well have relied on her own voice and human curiosity for an audience, but to make sure of one she had provided herself with an old-fashioned dinner-bell which served both to announce her arrival and to drown any rejoinders made by her opponent. He, poor old man, stood no chance at all in the contest. It was contrary both to his own nature and his religious beliefs to take part in a brawl. He would often go in and shut the door and draw down the blind, hoping, no doubt, that his niece would soon tire of shouting abuse if he appeared to take no notice. If something she said was more than he could bear in silence, he would open the door, poke out his head, and, keeping a firm hold on his temper, make some protestation, but, as whatever he said at such times was drowned by a clanging of the bell, it had little effect on village opinion, and certainly none on his niece's behaviour.

His title to his modest estate was so clear that it was surprising how many of the villagers sided with Eliza. They said it was a shame that before his father's body was cold, old Jim should have seized all the land, when it stood to reason it ought to have been divided. These admired Eliza for her spirit and hoped she would insist upon getting her rights, perhaps also hoping subconsciously that she would continue to provide them with entertainment. More thoughtful and better-informed people maintained that the right was on old Jim's side. 'Right's right, and wrong's no man's right,' they quoted sententiously. In the meantime wrong, plus a dinner-bell, appeared to have the best of it.

But old Jim, though an unworldly man, had no intention of parting with any of his property. When he found that lawyers' letters had no effect upon niece Eliza, he did at last take the case to Court, where it was quickly settled in his favour, and Eliza of the bobbing earrings disappeared from the Candleford Green scene. After that, for a time, life in the village seemed strangely silent.

But such disturbances of the peace were well spaced out and few – too few for the tastes of some people. The one constable stationed at Candleford Green had plenty of leisure in which to keep his garden up to the standard which ensured him his customary double-first at the annual Flower Show for the best all-round collection of vegetables and the best-kept cottage garden. After the bicycle came into general use, he occasionally hauled up before the Bench some unfortunate who had exceeded the speed limit, or had been found riding lampless after lighting-up time; but, still, for three hundred days of the year his official duties consisted of walking stiffly in uniform round the green at certains hours by day and taking gentle walks by night to meet his colleague on point duty.

Though not without a sense of the dignity due to his official position, he was a kindly and good-tempered man; yet nobody seemed to like him, and he and his wife led a somewhat isolated life, in the village but not entirely of the village. Law-abiding as most country people were in those days, and few as were those who had any personal reason for fearing the police, the village constable was still regarded by many as a potential enemy, set to spy upon them by the authorities. In Laura's childhood, she knew a woman who declared that she 'went all fainty, like' at the sight of a policeman's uniform, just as some other sensitive people are supposed to do when they smell a rose, or if a cat enters the room. And small boys had a catch which at that time they shouted from behind hedges at a respectful distance after a policeman had passed them:

> There goes the bobby with his black shiny hat
>> And his belly full of fat
>> And a pancake tied to his nose,

a relic, it is to be supposed, from the days before policemen wore helmets.

Of those other offences which do not come within the scope of the law and yet may destroy the peace of a village, Candleford Green had its share. In those days, when countrywomen read little and the cinema had yet to be invented, the thrills which human nature appears to demand had to be extracted from real life. This demand was abundantly met by the gossips. Candleford Green had several of these talented women who could take some trifling event and so expand, distort, and embroider it that by the time a story had made the round of the village, gathering a little in the way of circumstantial detail here and there, and came at last to the ears of the persons concerned, it would bear so little resemblance to the facts of the case that it was indignantly repudiated.

And, indeed, it was annoying to a proud housewife to be told that people were saying that on a certain day last month she had been compelled to raise money by selling her one easy chair, or that a hire-purchase firm had taken it away in default, when what had really happened was that the easy chair had been carried away to be reupholstered, and, far from being penniless, its possessor had the money saved up and actually in her pocket at that moment to pay for the renovation. And it was still more annoying for a young man to have his sweetheart's recent coldness accounted for by the story going the rounds that he had been seen going into the house of a fascinating young widow. Which he had, not as a victim to her fascination, but to investigate the cause of a smoking chimney which his employer, who was also her landlord, had asked him to see to.

Such stories did no great harm. Those concerned who happened to possess a sense of humour would laugh at them as a pack of lies invented by a few gossiping old women who would have been better employed mending the holes in their stockings. Others would go from house to house trying to track down the originator of the gossip. They never succeeded, though most of those they interviewed were in some measure guilty; but the pursuit served to take off the edge of their indignation.

But every few years at Candleford Green, and no doubt in other such villages, stories no more true to fact were circulated which did definite harm. One such was that a young girl, at home for a time from her place in service, was pregnant. There was no truth whatever in the story. She was anaemic and run down and her kindly employers had sent her home for a few weeks' rest and country air, but soon, not only her supposed condition, but also the name of her seducer, was common talk. She was a modest, sensitive girl and in her then weak condition suffered greatly.

Another outlet for the few who had venomous minds was the sending of so-called comic valentines addressed in disguised handwriting. The custom of sending daintily printed and lace-bedecked valentines by friends and lovers had by that time died out. Laura was born too late ever to receive a genuine valentine. But what were known as comic valentines were still popular in country districts. These were crude coloured prints on flimsy paper representing hideous forms and faces intended to be more or less applicable to the recipient. A valentine could be obtained suitable to be sent to one of any trade, calling, or tendency, with words, always insulting and often obscene, calculated to wound, and these, usually unstamped, passed through the village post offices in surprising numbers every St Valentine's Eve.

Laura once took one out of the posting-box addressed to herself, with the picture of a hideous female handing out penny stamps and some printed doggerel which began:

> You think yourself so la-di-da
> And get yourself up so grand

and went on to advise her always to wear a thick veil when she went out, or her face would frighten the cows. Underneath the verse was scrawled in pencil: 'Wat you reely wants is a mask.' She thrust it into the fire and told nobody, but for some time all pleasure in her own appearance was spoiled and the knowledge that she had an enemy rankled.

But scandalous gossip and the sending of anonymous valentines was but the work of a few of the evil-minded people such as may always be found in any place. The majority of Candleford Green dwellers were kind, as majorities always are. Education had already done something for village life. The old dark superstitions had gone. Poor, ugly, old lone-living women were no longer suspected of witchcraft, although there was one man still living in the village who firmly believed that he had known a witch in his childhood and that she had caused by her magic all manner of misfortunes. Under the influence of her evil eye children had pined and died, horses had gone lame, cows had slipped their calves, and fires had broken out in rickyards.

A disease known locally as the 'scab' had at that time ravaged the sheepfolds and ruined farmers, and, as old Nanny had been known to collect the scraps of wool torn from the sheeps' backs by the bushes, probably to warm her poor old body in some way, the villagers had held her responsible. They said she burned the wool by night, they had smelt it sizzling when passing her cottage; and, as the wool shrivelled, the sheep upon whose backs it had grown developed the scab. Women who offended old Nanny speedily lost their looks, and sometimes their husbands' affections, or their crockery fell from the shelves and got broken. In fact, as one of his hearers once said, old Nanny seemed to have played the very devil with the place. But that was all long before Laura's time, before her father or mother were born. In the eighteen-nineties in that part of the country ordinary people either disbelieved altogether in witchcraft, or thought it one of the old unhappy things of the past, like the gibbet and transportation.

A few innocent charms and superstitious practices were all that remained of magic. Warts were still charmed away by binding a large black slug upon the wart for a night and a day. Then the sufferer would go by night to the nearest crossroads and, by flinging the slug over the left shoulder, hope to get rid of the wart. Fried mice were still given to children as a specific for bed-wetting. The children were told the mouse was meat and ate it without protest, but with what result is unknown. No one would at a table spoon salt on to another person's plate, for 'help you to salt, help you to sorrow'. After Michaelmas blackberries were unfit for food because on Michaelmas Day the devil dragged his tail over them. If a girl began to whistle a tune, those near her would clap their hands over her mouth, for 'A whistling maid and a crowing hen is no good either to gods nor men'. On the other hand, as far as Laura ever heard, one might walk under a ladder with impunity, for the absence of which inhibition she had cause to be thankful in after years, when the risk of a spat-tering of paint on one's clothing was a trifle compared to that of stepping off the curb and being run over by the traffic.

The funerals of the country poor were at that time a deeply moving sight. At Laura's home the farmer lent one of his farm wagons, freshly painted in bright reds and blues and yellows, or newly scrubbed, to carry the coffin. Clean straw was spread on the bed of the wagon to prevent jolting, and the tired labourer rode to his last rest as he had during his lifetime so many times ridden home from the harvest field. At Candleford Green, the coffin was carried on a wheeled hand-bier propelled by friends. Both were what was called 'walking funerals', the mourners following the coffin on foot. Sometimes there would be but three or four mourners, perhaps a widow supported by her half-grown children. In other instances the procession was quite a long one, especially if the dead had been aged, when sons and daughters and grandchildren, down to the youngest who could toddle, would follow the coffin, the women in decent if shabby and unfashionable mourning, often borrowed in parts from neighbours, and the men with black crape bands round their hats and sleeves. The village carpenter, who had made the coffin, acted as undertaker, and the cost of the funeral, but £3 or £4, was covered by life insurance. Flowers were often placed inside the coffin, but there were seldom wreaths; the fashion for those came later.

The extravagant expenditure on funerals by those who could least afford it was never a feature of country life. A meal to follow the funeral was certainly provided, and the food then consumed was the best the bereaved could obtain. Those funeral meals of the poor have been much misunderstood and misrepresented. By the country poor and probably by the majority of the poor in towns they were not provided in any spirit of ostentation, but because it was an urgent necessity that a meal should be partaken of by the mourners as soon as possible after a funeral. Very little food would be eaten in a tiny cottage while the dead remained there; evidences of human mortality would be too near and too pervasive. Married children and other relatives coming from a distance might have eaten nothing since breakfast. So a ham, or part of a ham, was provided, not in order to be able to boast, 'We buried 'im with 'am', but because it was a ready-prepared dish which was both easily obtained and appetizing.

Those funeral meals have appeared to some more pathetic than amusing. The return of the mourners after the final parting and their immediate outbursts of pent-up grief. Then, as they grew calmer, the gentle persuasion of those less afflicted that the widow or widower or the bereaved parents, for the sake of the living still left to them, should take some nourishment. Then their gradual revival as they ate and drank. Tears would still be wiped away furtively, but a few sad smiles would break through, until, at the table, a sober cheerfulness would prevail. They had, as they told themselves and the others told them, to go on living, and what greater restoratives have we poor mortals than a good meal taken in the company of loving friends? It is possible that the sherry and biscuits provided in more prosperous households after the funerals of that day were sometimes partaken of by sincere and simple-minded people as a much-needed restorative, and not always in order to provide an opportunity for some Victorian father to utter pompous platitudes while he warmed his hinder-parts before the fire.

Ghost stories and stories of haunted houses were still repeated. A few of the more simple people may have believed they were literally true. Others enjoyed them for the sake of the

thrill, as we now enjoy reading mystery stories. The more educated scoffed at them as old women's tales. It was an age of
materialism, and those in any measure in touch with current
ideas believed in nothing they could not feel, or see, or smell.

Laura's mother was the only person she knew at that time
who had an open mind on the subject of the supernatural, and
she leaned rather to the side of unbelief. She told her children
that she had in her time been told many ghost stories, some of
which had almost convinced her that there *was* something outside the range of ordinary earthly life, but, she would say, there
was always some little loophole for doubt. Still, nobody on
earth knew everything; ghosts might have appeared and might
appear again, though, she thought, it was doubtful if any happy
spirit would wish to leave the glories of Heaven to wander on
the earth on dark, cold, winter nights, and as to those who had
gone to the bad place, they would not be given the opportunity.

She was never convinced, one way or the other. Yet she was
the one person Laura ever came into close touch with and for
whose absolute integrity she could vouch who had had an experience which could only be explained by taking into consideration the possibility of the supernatural. It concerned not
the dead, but the dying. Laura had a family of cousins on her
mother's side, one of whom had married and lived at that time
in a neighbouring village, near her old home. Another sister,
also married, lived in yet another village, the two, with Laura's
home hamlet, arranged like the three points of a triangle.

One of the sisters, Lily, was at the time very ill, and, for a
week or more, the other sister, Patience, had been going daily
by a direct route which did not pass Laura's home to help with
the nursing, returning at night to her own home duties. But on
the morning in question, when about to set out, she had the
sudden idea of passing by Laura's home in order to collect the
rent of a cottage they owned in the hamlet. The tenant was a
reliable one, and it had been decided the night before that the
rent-collection could wait. But money is always needed at such
times and she probably wished to take some little extra luxury
or comfort to her sister. No one knew that she was thus going

out of her way and she met no one on the quiet country road between the two places.

She collected the rent, then, having to pass her aunt's cottage, looked in at the door upon her. She found her busy with her weekly ironing and alone in the house except for the small baby in the cradle, her husband being at work and her elder children at school for the day. In reply to her aunt's anxious inquiry, Patience said sadly: 'Very, very, ill. It is only a matter of days now, I'm afraid. She may even go today.'

'Then,' said her aunt, 'I'll come with you,' and, after she had bundled away her ironing and put her infant in the perambulator, they hurried off together without seeing or speaking ing to anybody. Their way lay for the greater part through fields and across a wild heath, and they still saw no one who knew them or could possibly guess their errand.

In the meantime, as they journeyed, in the village of their destination the nurse was washing and making comfortable the invalid. They were alone in the house, together in the one room. Poor Lily was a little peevish, for she was in a weak state – as it proved, actually dying – and objected to being disturbed by the nurse's ministrations.

'Come, come! You must let me make you look nice. Your sister will be here directly,' said the nurse cheerfully.

'I know,' said Lily. 'I can see her. Aunt Emma is with her. They're just coming over Hardwick Heath and they're picking some blackberries.'

'Oh, no, my dear,' said the nurse. 'You mustn't expect your aunt so early in the day as this. She doesn't even know you're so ill, and she's got her young baby to see to. And they wouldn't be picking blackberries. They'd be hurrying on to see you.'

Shortly afterwards they arrived. And blackberries had been picked, for the aunt, not having had time to take flowers from her own garden, had gathered a little bouquet of harebells and other heath flowers, which she had backed with early-turned yellow and crimson bramble leaves and a few sprays loaded with fruit.

XXXVII

'Ta-ra-ra-boom-de-ay!'

AFTER she had become accustomed to her new surroundings at Candleford Green, Laura was happier, or at least gayer, than she had been since early childhood. Because of her age, or the overflowing abundance of Miss Lane's table, or because something in the air or the life suited her, her thin figure filled out, a brighter colour appeared in her cheeks, and such an inrush of energy and high spirits took hold of her that she would dance, rather than walk, about the house and garden, and felt she could never tire.

This may have been partly due to her release from home cares. At home she had been a little mother to her younger brothers and sisters and the sharer in many of her mother's perplexities. Now she was the youngest in a houseful of adults, the elder of whom treated her as a child. Miss Lane was, at times, even indulgent to her, calling her 'my chick' and making her presents of small, pretty things, which she knew would please her. The old servant, Zillah, tolerated her when she found that she had now some one at hand willing to run upstairs 'to save her poor feet', or to whisk the washing off the line and bring it indoors when it started to rain, or to creep into the low henhouse to collect the eggs for her. She would still sometimes refer to Laura as 'that lafeting little thing' and tell her to wait until the black ox trod on her toes, and, once, in a very bad-tempered moment, she foretold that 'Our missis'll rue the day when she brought that hoity-toity little piece to live along with her', but that was only because Laura had accidentally left footprints on her newly scoured flagstones. Often she was quite pleasant, and on the whole their relations may be described as a state of armed neutrality.

There was no neutrality about Matthew. As he said, if he liked anybody, he *liked* them; if not, they had better keep out of his way. His liking for Laura took the form of kindly teasing. He quizzed her about her clothes and accused her of altering the shape of her best hat once a fortnight. She had re-trimmed it once and he, happening to come into the kitchen while she was doing it, had asked what she thought she was up to. When she said she was trying to make the crown a little lower, he had offerered to take the hat out to the forge and lower the crown with his sledge-hammer on the anvil, and that episode furnished him with a standing joke which he repeated every time Laura appeared in anything new. That is a sample of Matthew's jokes. He had scores of similar ones which he was constantly repeating with the intention of amusing her.

Matthew was a small, bent, elderly man with weak blue eyes and sandy whiskers. No one looking at him would have guessed at his importance in the eyes of the local farmers and land-owners. He was a farrier as well as a smith, and such a farrier, it was said, as few neighbourhoods could boast of. Horses, indeed, appeared to be more to him than human beings: he understood and could cure so many of their ailments that the veterinary surgeon had seldom to be sent for by the Candleford Green horse-owners.

A cupboard, known as 'Matthew's cupboard', high up on the kitchen wall, held the drugs he used. When he unlocked it, bottles of all shapes and sizes could be seen; big embrocation bottles, stoppered glass jars containing powder or crystals, and several blue poison bottles, one of which must have held at least a pint and was labelled 'Laudanum'. He would hold this last bottle up to the light, shake it gently, and say: 'A wineglass of this wouldn't do some folks I know much harm. Their head-aches and whimseys 'udn't trouble them no more, nor other folks neither.'

That was another of Matthew's jokes. He had no enemies, and, as far as was known, no intimate friends among his own kind. His affections were reserved for animals, especially for those he had cured of some sickness or injury. If a cow had a difficult calving, or a pig went off its food, or an infirm old dog had to be put away, Matthew was sent for. He had a tame thrush which he had found in the fields with a broken wing and brought home to treat. He had succeeded to some extent in mending its wing, but it could still only flutter, not fly, so he bought a round wicker cage for it which he kept hung on the wall outside the back door. He released it every day during his dinner-hour, when it would follow him round the garden, *hoppity-hop*.

The younger smiths, who called Laura 'Missy', had little to say to her in public, but when they met her alone in the garden they would offer to reach her a pear or a greengage, or show her some new flower which had come out, or ask her if she had seen old Tibby's new kittens in the woodshed, blushing the while in a way which delighted Laura, who loved to come soundlessly upon them in her new rubber-soled shoes.

Those new lightweight shoes in which Laura hopped and skipped when she should have walked were the thin black rubber ones with dingy-looking, greyish-black uppers, now known as 'gym shoes'. They were known then by the ugly name of 'plimsolls' and had for some time been popular for informal seaside wear by otherwise well-dressed women and children. Now they had been introduced into country districts as a novelty for summer wear, and men and women and girls and boys were all sporting their 'softs'. They were soon found unsuitable for wear in wet weather and on rough country roads, and newer and smarter styles in buck-skin or canvas superseded them for tennis and croquet, but for a summer or two they were 'all the rage', and the young, hitherto accustomed to stiff, heavy leather shoes, luxuriated in them.

Miss Lane still kept to the old middle-class country custom of one huge washing of linen every six weeks. In her girlhood it would have been thought poor looking to have had a weekly or fortnightly washday. The better off a family was, the more changes of linen its members were supposed to possess, and the less frequent the washday. That was one reason why our grandmothers counted their articles of underwear by the dozen. And the underwear then in fashion was not of the kind to be washed out in a basin. It had to be boiled and blued and required much ironing. There may have already been laundries, though Laura never heard of one in that district. A few women in cottages took in washing, but most of it was done at home.

For the big wash at Miss Lane's, a professional washer-woman came for two days, arriving at six o'clock on the Monday morning in a clean apron and sun-bonnet, with a second apron of sacking and a pair of pattens in a large open basket upon her arm. Charwomen, too, carried these baskets, 'in case', as they said – meaning in the hope that something or other would be given them to put into them. They were seldom disappointed.

All day on the two washdays, steam and the smell of soapsuds came in great puffs from the window and door of the small, detached building known as the 'washhouse', and the back yard was flooded with waste water flowing down the gutter to the open drain, while the old washerwoman clattered about in her pattens, or stood at her wooden washtub, scouring and rinsing and wringing and blueing, and Zillah, as red as a turkeycock and in a fiendish temper, oversaw and helped with the work in hand. Indoors, Laura washed up and got the meals. If Miss Lane wanted anything cooked, she had to cook it herself, but cold food was the rule. A ham or half a ham had usually been boiled a few days before.

Soon, sheets and pillow-cases and towels were billowing in the wind on a line the whole length of the garden, while Miss Lane's more intimate personal wear dried modestly on a line by the henhouse, 'out of the men's sight'. All went well if the weather happened to be fine. If not, very much the reverse. The old country saying which referred to a disagreeable-looking man or woman: 'He' – or she – 'looks about as pleasant as a wet washday' would have lost its full flavour of irony if used in these days.

On the evening of the second washday, the washerwoman departed with three shillings, wages for the two days, in her pocket, and in her basket whatever she had been able to collect. The rest of the week was spent by the family in folding, sprinkling, mangling, ironing and airing the clothes. The only pleasant thing about the whole orgy of cleanliness was to see the piles of snowy linen, ironed and aired and mended, with lavender bags in the folds, placed on the shelves of the linen closet and to know that six whole weeks would pass before the next upheaval.

Laura's modest stock of three of everything was, of course, inadequate for such a period; so, before she had come there, it had been arranged that her washing should be sent home to her mother every week. The clothes Laura sent home one week were returned by her mother the next, so Laura received a parcel from home every Saturday. It had had a cross-country journey in two different carriers' carts, but it still seemed to smell of home.

It was her treat of the week to open it. She would bundle the clean clothes, beautifully ironed and folded as they were, higgledy-piggledy upon her bed and seize the little box or package she always found within containing a few little cakes her mother had baked for her, or a cooked home-made sausage or two, or a tiny pot of jam or jelly, or flowers from the home garden. There was always something.

But before she put the flowers in water or tasted a crumb of the food, she would read her mother's letter. Written in the delicate, pointed Italianate handwriting her mother had been taught when a child by an old lady of ninety, the letter would usually begin, 'Dear Laura'. Only on special occasions would her mother write, 'My own dear,' for she was not demonstrative. After the beginning would come the formula: 'I hope this will find you still well and happy, as it leaves us all at home. I hope you will like the few little things I enclose. I know you have got plenty and better where you are, but you may like to taste the home food', or 'smell the home flowers'.

Then followed the home news and news of the neighbours, all told in simple, homely language, but with the tang of wit and occasional spice of malice which made her conversation so racy. She always wrote four or five pages and often ended her letters with 'My pen has run away with me again', but there never was a word too much for Laura. She kept her mother's letters to her for years and afterwards wished she had kept them longer. They deserved a wider public than one young daughter.

At that time Laura had, as it were, one foot in each of two

worlds. Behind her lay her country childhood and country traditions, many of which were still current at Candleford Green.
Miss Lane's and several similar establishments also still
flourished there; but new ideas and new ways were seeping in
from the outer world which was still unknown at Lark Rise, and
with these Laura was becoming acquainted through friends she
was making of her own age.

Some of these she came to know through talking to them
over their post-office business; others through her relatives in
Candleford town, or because they belonged to families approved of by Miss Lane. They had most of them been brought
up in different circumstances from those of her own childhood
and they spoke of 'poor people' and 'cottage people' in a way
which grated on Laura; but they were lively and amusing and,
on the whole, she enjoyed their company.

When she met one of these girls in the street, she would sometimes be invited to 'Come into the wigwam and have a palaver',
and they would go up carpeted stairs into the crowded, upholstered drawing-room over the shop and exchange
confidences. Or the friend would play her latest 'piece' upon the
piano for Laura and Laura would sit and listen, or not listen,
but just sit and take mental notes.

There was a piano in every drawing-room and there were
palms in pots and saddle-bags suites of furniture and hand-
painted milking-stools and fire-screens, and cushions and antimacassars in the latest art shades; but, beyond bound volumes of
the *Quiver* and the *Sunday at Home* and a few stray copies of
popular novels, mostly of a semi-religious character, there were
no books to be seen. The one father who was a reader remained
faithful to those works of Charles Dickens which his parents
had taken in monthly parts. Most of the fathers of such families
found sufficient reading in their *Daily Telegraph*, and the
mothers, on Sunday afternoons, dozed over *Queechy* or *The
Wide Wide World*. The more daring and up to date among the
daughters, who liked a thrill in their reading, devoured the
novels of Ouida in secret, hiding the book beneath the mat-
tresses of their beds between whiles. For their public reading
they had the *Girls' Own Paper*.

And that was in the 'nineties, afterwards to be named – by a presumably more innocent generation – the 'Naughty Nineties'. The clever, witty, but, oh! so outràgeous! books of the new writers of the day were, no doubt, read in some of the large country houses around, and they may even have found their way into rectories; but no whisper of the stir they were making in the outer world of ideas had penetrated to the ordinary country home. A little later, the trial of Oscar Wilde brought some measure of awareness, for was it not said that he was 'one of these new poets'? and it just showed what a rotten lot they were. Thank God, the speaker had always disliked poetry.

The tragedy of Oscar Wilde did nothing to lessen their natural distrust of intellect, but it did enlighten the younger generation in a less desirable manner. There were vices, then, in the world one had not hitherto heard of – vices which, even now, were only hinted at darkly, never described. Fathers for weeks kept the newspapers locked up with their account books. Mothers, when appealed to for information, shùddered and said in horrified accents: 'Never let me hear that name pass your lips again.'

Miss Lane, when asked outright what all this fuss was about, said: 'All I know is that it's some law about two men living together, but you don't want to bother your head about things like that!' 'But what about Old Ben and Tom Ashley?' Laura persisted, and was told that those two innocent old comrades had already had their windows broken with stones after dark. People thought, after that, they would leave the village, but they did not. Whoever heard of old soldiers running away? All that happened was that Tom, who had formerly spent most of his time indoors, went out more, and that Ben's walk made him look more than ever as if he had a ram-rod down his back. It was those who had thrown the stones who slunk round corners when they saw Ben or Tom coming.

But although, until that time, not only out of the main stream of ideas but unaware of its existence, before the decade was ended the Candleford Greenites had a Yellow Book of their own in the form of the all-conquering weekly periodical called *Answers*. Already its green counterpart, *Tit-Bits*, was taken by

almost every family, and the snippets of information culled
from its pages were taken very seriously indeed. Apparently it
gave deep satisfaction to the majority of the younger people to
know how many years of an average life were spent in bed and
how many months of his life a man spent shaving and a woman
doing her hair. 'If all the sausages eaten at breakfast in this
country on one Sunday morning were stretched out singly, end
to end, how many miles do you suppose they would reach?' one
neighbour, newly primed, would ask another. Or, in lighter
mood, 'What did the cyclist say to the farmer whose cockerel he
had run over?' and, only too often, the answer came pat, for the
neighbour had just read *his* copy of *Tit-Bits*. The title of *Tit-
Bits* furnished a catchword which could always be used with
effect when an unfamiliar taste was discovered or an unfamiliar
opinion expressed. Then 'Don't try to be funny. We've read
about you in *Tit-Bits*!' said scathingly was, in the slang of the
day, 'absolutely the last word'.

The girls Laura saw most of at that time were tradesmen's
daughters, living at home, employed only in keeping their
fathers' business books or in helping their mothers with the
lighter housework. These were known as the 'home birds';
others belonging to the same families were away from home,
earning their own living as shop assistants in one of the big
London stores, or as school-teachers or nursery governesses.
One was in training as a nursing probationer in a London hospital and another was book-keeper and receptionist at a
boarding-house. Tradesmen's daughters no longer went into
domestic service, unless one, after an apprenticeship to dressmaking and a second apprenticeship to hair dressing, became a
lady's maid. Nor did they associate much with the domestic
staffs in the big houses, and this not because of snobbishness, but
because their lives and interests ran along different lines. The
village social system in which the first footman is paired off with
the grocer's daughter and the second footman with the post-
office girl as a matter of etiquette belongs to the world of
fiction.

The home birds were not all of them content with light
household duties and, for pleasure, the choir practices and tea-

drinkings and village concerts their mothers in their time had found sufficient amusement. A few of the boldest among them were already beginning to talk about their right to live their own lives as they wished. According to them, their parents' old-fashioned ideas were their main obstacle. 'Pa's so old-fashioned. You'd think he had been born in the year dot,' these would say. 'And Mama's not much better. She'd like us to talk prunes and prisms and be indoors by ten o'clock and never so much as look at a fellow before he had shown her a certificate of good character.' Far from feeling under any obligation to those who had brought them up and, as Laura in her inexperience thought, been so generous to them, they seemed to think their parents existed chiefly to give them whatever they happened to wish for most at the moment – one of the new safety bicycles, or a sealskin coat, or an outing to London. The parents, on their side, preached circumspect behaviour, obedience, and gratitude as a daughter's first duties, and many clashes ensued.

'I didn't ask to be born, did I?' one girl reported herself as saying to her father, and his retort, 'No; and if you had you wouldn't have been if I had known as much about you as I do now,' was repeated by her as an instance of the ignorance and brutality with which she had to contend.

'Straining at the leash, I am. Straining at the leash,' said Alma dramatically when telling the story to Laura, and Laura, looking round the pretty bedroom and at the new summer outfit, complete with white kid gloves and a parasol, laid out on the bed for her admiring inspection, thought that, at least, the leash was a handsome one. But she did not say so, for even she, brought up in a harder school, could understand that it must be annoying to be treated as a child at twenty, and to be forbidden to do this or do that because it was 'not the thing', and have to depend for every little thing on a parent's generosity.

But the rebellious daughter was the exception. Most of the girls Laura knew were contented with their lot. They enjoyed helping in the house and making Mama bring it up to date and giving tea-parties and playing the piano. Some of these were of the type then called 'sunbeams in the home': good, affectionate, home-loving girls, obviously created for marriage, and most of them did marry and, there can be no doubt, made excellent wives for their own male counterparts.

Laura cannot be said to have been really popular with any of them. Her Candleford town connections vouched for her to some extent, but her own personal antecedents were too humble and her dress and accomplishments fell too short of their own standards for her to rank entirely as one of themselves. Perhaps she was most valued by them as the possessor of a ready ear for confidences and for what they called 'repartee' – a light, bantering form of conversation then much in fashion. But Laura enjoyed their company, and it was good for her. She no longer looked, as the neighbours at home had sometimes said, as if she had all the weight of the world on her shoulders.

Those were the days of Miss Lotty Collins's all-conquering dance and song, 'Ta-ra-ra-boom-de-ay!' and the words and tune swept the countryside like an epidemic. The air that summer was alive with its strains. Ploughmen bawled it at the plough-tail, harvesters sang it in the harvest field, workmen in villages painted the outside of houses to its measure, errand boys whistled it and schoolchildren yelled it. Even housewives caught the infection and would attempt a tired little imitation of the high kick as they turned from the clothes-lines in their gardens singing 'Ta-ra-ra-boom-de-ay'.

Early in the morning, while dew still roughened the turf of the green, Laura's friend at the grocer's, dusting the drawing-room, at sight of the keys of the open piano, would drop her duster, sink down on the music stool, and from the open window the familiar strain would be wafted:

> Such a nice young girl, you see,
> Just out in Society.
> Everything I ought to be.
> Ta-ra-ra-boom-de-ay!
> A blushing bud of innocence,
> Pa declares a great expense.
> The old maids say I have no sense,
> But the boys agree I'm just immense,
> Ta-ra-ra-boom-de-ay! Ta-ra-ra-boom-de-ay!

Then the madness would seize her and she would pirouette about the room and come down with such weight from the high kick that her father, honest tradesman, would call urgently to her from the foot of the stairs to remember the drawing-room was immediately over the shop and customers might come in any moment. But, even he, having worked off his annoyance, would go back to his books or his scales humming between his teeth the prevailing tune.

During the day, when the master's back was turned and the shop for the moment was clear of customers, the young men behind the counter would gather up their white aprons in their hands and kick and dance a parody. Ta-ra-ra-boom-de-ay! Ta-ra-ra-boom-de-ay! Were there such things as death and want and grief and misery in that world? If so, youth possessed a charm to banish them from its thoughts in 'Ta-ra-ra-boom-de-ay'.

It would seem that the silly, light-hearted words of the song fitted the tune to perfection; but they were often 'improved' upon. One version, sung by lounging youths beneath the chestnut tree on the green, perhaps nearer the end of the long run of the song, went:

> Lotty Collins has no drawers.
> Will you kindly lend her yours?
> She is going far away
> To sing Ta-ra-ra-boom-de-ay!

But that was sung with the intention of annoying any girl who might happen to be passing. And she would be annoyed. Shocked, too, to hear such an intimate undergarment mentioned in public, and little think that the garment, under that name at least, would pass with the song.

Laura enjoyed life at Candleford Green. In summer the sun seemed to shine perpetually and the winter flew past before she had done half the things she had saved for the long evenings. She was young and she had gay new friends and nicer clothes than she had ever had before and was growing up and could kick as high as anybody to the tune of 'Ta-ra-ra-boom-de-ay!'

But something within her remained unsatisfied. She had her hours of freedom. Every other Sunday, if Miss Lane could spare her, which was not always, she would dress with care and walk into Candleford town for tea with her relatives. She was welcomed warmly, and the hours she spent with her favourite uncle and aunt were pleasant hours, even though her cousins of her own age were away. She enjoyed the Candleford Green village entertainments and the laughing, high-spirited company of her village friends, and Miss Lane's garden was lovely and green and secluded and she spent many happy hours there. But none of these pleasures seemed entirely to satisfy her. She missed – missed badly and even pined for – her old freedom of the fields.

Candleford Green was but a small village and there were fields and meadows and woods all around it. As soon as Laura crossed the doorstep, she could see some of these. But mere seeing from a distance did not satisfy her; she longed to go alone far into the fields and hear the birds singing, the brooks tinkling, and the wind rustling through the corn, as she had when a child. To smell things and touch things, warm earth and flowers and grasses, and to stand and gaze where no one could see her, drinking it all in.

She never spoke of this longing to any one. She accused herself of discontent and told herself, 'You can't have everything,' but the craving remained until, unexpectedly, it was gratified in fullest measure and in a way which seemed to her to be wholly delightful, though, on this latter point, very few of those she knew were inclined to agree.

XXXVIII

Letter-Carrier

ONE cold winter morning, when snow was on the ground and the ponds were iced over, Laura, in mittens and a scarf, was sorting the early morning mail and wishing that Zillah would hurry with the cup of tea she usually brought her at that time.

The hanging oil lamp above her head had scarcely had time to thaw the atmosphere, and the one uniformed postman at a side bench, sorting his letters for delivery, stopped to thump his chest with his arms and exclaim that he'd be jiggered, but it was a fact that on such mornings as this there was bound to be a letter for every house, even for those which did not have one once in a blue moon. 'Does it on purpose, I s'pose,' he grumbled.

The two women letter-carriers, who had more reason than he to complain, for his round was mostly by road and theirs were cross-country, worked quietly at their bench. The elder, Mrs Gubbins, had got herself up to face the weather by tying a red knitted shawl over her head and wearing the bottoms of a man's corduroy trouser-legs as gaiters. Mrs Macey had brought out an old, moth-eaten fur tippet which smelt strongly of camphor. As the daylight increased, the window became a steely grey square with wads of snow at the corners of the panes. From beyond it came the crunching sound of cart-wheels on frozen snow. Laura turned back her mittens and rubbed her chilblains.

Then, suddenly, the everyday dullness of work before breakfast was pierced by a low cry of distress from the younger postwoman. She had an open letter in her hand and evidently it contained bad news, but all she would say in answer to sympathetic inquiries was: 'I must go. I must go at once. Now, immediately.' Go at once? Go where? And why? How could she go anywhere but on her round? Or leave her letters half-sorted? were the shocked questions the eyes of the other three asked each other. When Laura suggested calling Miss Lane, Mrs Macey exclaimed: 'No, don't call her here, please. I must see her alone and in private. And I shan't be able to take out the letters this morning. Oh, dear! Oh, dear! What's to be done?'

Miss Lane was downstairs and alone in the kitchen, with her feet on the fender, sipping a cup of tea. Laura had expected she would be annoyed at being disturbed before her official hours, but she did not even seem to be surprised, and in a few moments had Mrs Macey in a chair by the fire and was holding a cup of hot tea to her lips. 'Come. Drink this,' she said. 'Then tell me about it.' Then to Laura, who had already reached the door on her way back to her sorting, 'Tell Zillah not to begin cooking breakfast until I tell her to,' and, as an after-thought: 'Say she is to go upstairs and begin getting my room ready for turning out,' a message which, when delivered, annoyed Zillah exceedingly, for she knew and she knew Laura would guess that the upstairs work was ordered to prevent listening at key-holes.

The sorting was finished, the postman had gone reluctantly out, five minutes late, and old Mrs Gubbins was pretending to hunt for a lost piece of string in order to delay her own exit when Miss Lane came in and carefully shut the door after her. 'What? Not out yet, Mrs Gubbins?' she asked coldly, and Mrs Gubbins responded to the hint, banging the door behind her as the only possible expression of her frustrated curiosity.

'Here's a pretty kettle of fish! We're in a bit of a fix, Laura. Mrs Macey won't be able to do her round this morning. She's got to go off by train at once to see her husband, who's danger-ously ill. She's gone home now to get Tommy up and get ready. She's taking him with her.'

'But I thought her husband was abroad,' said the puzzled Laura.

'So he may have been at one time, but he isn't now. He's down in Devonshire, and it'll take her all day to get there, and a cold, miserable journey it'll be for the poor soul. But I'll tell you more about that later. The thing now is what we are going to do about the letters and Sir Timothy's private postbag. Zillah shan't go. I wouldn't demean myself to ask her, after the dis-graceful way she's been banging about upstairs, not to mention her bad feet and her rheumatism. And Minnie's got a bad cold. She couldn't take out the telegrams yesterday, as you know, and nobody can be spared from the forge with this frost, and horses pouring in to be rough-shod; and every moment it's getting later, and you know what old Farmer Stebbing is: if his letters are ten minutes late, he writes off to the Postmaster-General, though, to be sure, he might make some small allowance this morning for snow and late mails. What a fool I must have been to take on this office. It's nothing but worry, worry, worry – '

'And I suppose I couldn't be spared to go?' asked Laura

tentatively. Miss Lane was inclined to reconsider things if she appeared too eager. But now, to her great delight, that lady said, quite gratefully, 'Oh, *would* you? And you don't think your mother would mind? Well, that's a weight off my mind! But you're not going without some breakfast inside you, time or no time, or for all the farmers and squires in creation.' Then, opening the door: 'Zillah! Zillah! Laura's breakfast at once! And bring plenty. She's going out on an errand for me. Bacon and two eggs, and make haste, please.' And Laura ate her breakfast and dressed herself in her warmest clothes, with the addition of a sealskin cap and tippet Miss Lane insisted upon lending her, and hurried out into the snowy world, a hind let loose, if ever there was one.

As soon as she had left the village behind, she ran, kicking up the snow and sliding along the puddles, and managed to reach Farmer Stebbing's house only a little later than the time appointed for the delivery of his letters in the ordinary way by the post-office authorities. Then across the park to Sir Timothy's mansion and on to his head gardener's house and the home farm and half a dozen cottages, and her letters were disposed of.

Laura never forgot that morning's walk. Fifty years later she could recall it in detail. Snow had fallen a few days earlier, then had frozen, and on the hard crust yet more snow had fallen and lay like soft, feathery down, fleecing the surface of the level open spaces of the park and softening the outlines of hillocks and fences. Against it the dark branches and twigs of the trees stood out, lacelike. The sky was low and grey and soft-looking as a feather-bed.

Her delivery finished, and a little tired from her breathless run, she stopped where her path wound through a thicket to eat the crust and apple she had brought in her pocket. It was an unfrequented way and the only human footprints to be seen were her own, but she was not alone in that solitude. Everywhere, on the track and beneath the trees, the snow was patterned with tiny claw-marks, and gradually she became aware of the subdued, uneasy fluttering and chirping noises of birds sheltering in the undergrowth. Poor birds! With the earth frozen and the ponds iced over, it was indeed the winter of their discontent, but all she could do for them was to scatter a few crumbs on the snow. The rabbits were better off: they had their deep, warm burrows; and the pheasants knew where to go for the corn the gamekeeper spread for them in such weather. She could hear the *honk* of a pheasant somewhere away in the woods and the cawing of rooks passing overhead and Sir Timothy's stable clock chiming eleven. Time for her to be going!

In spite of a late start and a leisurely return, Laura managed to reach the office only a few minutes later than the official time fixed for that journey, which pleased Miss Lane, as it saved her the trouble of making a report, and that, perhaps, made her more communicative than usual, for, at the first opportunity, she told Laura what she knew of Mrs Macey's story.

Her husband, Laura now learned, was not a valet, although he might at one time have been one; nor was he travelling with his gentleman. He was by profession a bookmaker, which interested Laura greatly, as she at first concluded that he was in some way engaged in the production of literature. But Miss Lane, who knew more of the world, made haste to explain that his kind of bookmaker had something to do with betting on race-horses. In the course of his bookmaking, she said, he had been involved in a public-house quarrel which had led to blows, and from blows to kicks, and a man had been killed. The crime had been brought home to him and he had been given a long sentence for manslaughter. Now he was in prison on Dartmoor, nearing the end of his sentence. A long, long way for that poor soul to go in that wintry weather; but the prison authorities had written to say he was dangerously ill with pneumonia and the prison doctor thought it advisable that his wife should be sent for.

Miss Lane had known all the time where he was, though not what crime had caused him to be there, and she had not breathed a word to a living soul, she assured Laura, and would not be doing so now had not Mrs Macey said, as she went out of the door: 'Perhaps Laura will go over and feed Snowball. I'll pay for his milk when I get back. And tell her whatever you think fit about where we are going. She's a sensible little soul and won't tell anybody if you ask her not to.'

Poor Mrs Macey! No wonder she had been distressed. The strain of the journey in such weather and the ordeal at the end of it were not the whole of her trouble. As far as Tommy knew, his father was a gentleman's servant travelling abroad with his employer. Now, at some point on their journey, she would have to tell him the truth and to prepare him for whatever might follow.

Furthermore, her husband's sentence would expire in a year and, if his conduct had been good, he would be released sooner – unless – unless – well, unless he died now through this illness, which Miss Lane thought would be the best thing that could happen for all parties. Still, a husband was a husband, and often the worst husbands were most mourned for. She would not pretend to say whether his wife would be relieved or sorry if the Lord saw fit to take him. All she could say was that she had never seen a poor creature more upset by bad news, and her heart ached at the thought of her, setting off on such a journey, to the end of the earth, as one might say, and snow on the ground, and a prison hospital and all manner of humiliations at the end of it. However, dinner was ready, and Zillah had made a delicious damson jam roly-poly with a good suety crust. Laura must feel hungry after her cold walk, and she felt a bit peckish herself. 'So come along; and not a word of what you've been told to anybody. If any one asks you, it's her mother who's ill, and she's gone to London to nurse her.'

A week later, Mrs Macey returned, sad and subdued, but not in mourning, as Miss Lane had half-expected. She had spent a night in London and left Tommy with her friends there, for she had only come back to settle up her small affairs and to pack her furniture. Her husband was recovering and would shortly be released, and she had decided to make a home for him, for a husband is a husband, as Miss Lane had so sagely remarked, and although Mrs Macey obviously dreaded the future, she felt she must face it. But she could not let her husband come to Candleford Green to make a nine days' wonder. She would find a couple of rooms near her friends in London, and the Prisoners' Aid people would find him a job, or if not, she could earn their keep with her needle. She was sorry to leave her nice little cottage – she had had a few years' peace there – but, as Laura would find, you can't always do what you like or be where you would wish in this world.

So she went with her boxes and bundles and with Snowball mewing in a basket. Someone else came to live in her cottage and very soon she was forgotten, as Laura, in her turn, would be forgotten, and as all the other insignificant people would be who had sojourned for a time at Candleford Green.

But her going had its effect upon Laura's life, for, after a good deal of discussion among her elders and hopes and fears on Laura's part, it was arranged that she should undertake what was still known as 'Mrs Macey's delivery'. Miss Lane was quite willing to spare her for two and a half hours each morning. She had suggested the plan, pointing out that it would not only give her more fresh air and exercise, but also put another four shillings a week in her pocket.

It was really most generous of Miss Lane; and four shillings a week was considered quite a substantial addition to larger incomes than Laura's in those days; yet Laura, sent home for a week-end to obtain her parents' consent to the arrangement found them less pleased with the plan than she had expected. Except in letters from Laura, neither of them had heard of postwomen before, and the idea of letters being delivered by any one but a man in uniform struck them as odd. Her father thought she would demean herself and get coarse and tomboyish trapesing about the country with a letterbag strapped over her shoulder. Her mother's objection was that people would think it funny. However, as it was Miss Lane's suggestion and Laura herself was bent on the plan, they gave, at last, a grudging consent, her father stipulating that she should keep strictly to her official timetable and favour nobody, and her mother that she should never forget to change her shoes in wet weather.

An order for a pair of stout waterproof shoes at her father's expense was forthwith sent off to her shoemaker Uncle Tom, and it may be recorded here as a testimonial to the old hand-made product that that one pair of shoes outlasted the whole of Laura's time as a postwoman. They might have been worn several years longer had not her taste in shoes changed. They were still well worth the gipsy's fervent 'God bless you, my lady' when exchanged for a basket of plaited twigs filled with moss and ferns.

Laura had been away from the hamlet less than seven months, and nothing appeared to have changed there. The men still worked in the fields all day and worked on their allotments or talked politics at the village inn in the evening. The women still went to the well on pattens and gossiped over garden hedges in their spare moments, and to them the affairs of the hamlet still loomed larger than anything going on in the outside world. They were just as they had been from the day of her birth, yet to her they seemed rougher and cruder than formerly. When they chaffed her about the way she had grown, saying it was plain to see there was plenty to eat and drink at Candleford Green, or commented on her new clothes, or asked her if she had found a sweetheart yet, she answered them so shortly that one good old soul was offended and told her it was no good trying to make strange with one who had changed her napkins as a baby. After that well-merited reproof, Laura tried to be more sociable with the neighbours, but she was young and foolish, and for several years she held herself aloof from all but a few loved old friends when visiting her home. It took time and sorrow and experience of the world to teach her the true worth of the old homely virtues.

But home was still home; nothing had changed there. Her brother had come part of the way to meet her and her two little sisters were waiting on the road nearer home. As they neared the house, with their arms about her, she saw her father, ostensibly examining a branch of a damson tree the last snowstorm had broken, but with an eye on the road. He kissed her with more feeling than he usually displayed. 'Why, Laura!' he exclaimed. 'It's fine to see you!' Then, hastily skirting the sentimentality he detested: 'Quite the prodigal daughter. Well, we haven't exactly killed the fatted calf, for we hadn't one handy, but your mother has killed her very best fowl and it's about done to a turn by this time.'

It was delightful to sit in the familiar room with all the old, familiar things around her, with a fire 'half-way up the chimney', as her mother said, and she usually so frugal. Delightful to have a long secret chat with her brother in the woodshed, to be embraced and made much of by her little sisters and to ride her baby brother on her back round the garden with the wind blowing through their hair.

When her mother called her at five o'clock on the Monday morning to get up and prepare for her long walk back and she tiptoed downstairs and saw the lamplit room and savoured the bacon and potatoes frying for her breakfast, the new interests which had come into her life seemed of small account compared with the permanence of this life at home, to which she felt she belonged. Her father had already gone on his way to work. The children upstairs still slept. For the first time during her visit, she was really alone with her mother.

While Laura ate they conversed in whispers. How glad she was, her mother said, to know she was happy, and how pleased to see her well grown. 'You won't be a little bit of a thing like me. Nobody will ever call *you* a pocket Venus,' which certainly no one was ever likely to do, and that not for reasons of size alone. Then there was news of the hamlet doings, some of it very amusing when told by the speaker, some of it a little saddening, and, at last, they came to Laura's own affairs. First of all, her mother wanted to know why Laura had not been home before. 'Every few weeks,' she reminded her had been the agreement, and she had been away seven months. Miss Lane had kept saying, 'You must wait until we hear of some one going that way to give you a lift,' but to this explanation Laura's mother retorted: 'But what was the matter with walking? You could walk here one day and back the next easily enough, as you are doing now'; to which Laura agreed. She had longed to walk home many a time and had several times suggested that she should, but had never been firm and strong enough to insist in face of Miss Lane's objections.

'You must stick up for your rights, my dear,' said her mother that morning. 'And don't forget what I've always told you; don't try to be clever, or go speaking ill of anybody just to show off your own wit. I know how it is with these clever people, like

Dorcas Lane. They think they can see through everybody, and so they can to some degree, but they see so far through people that they sometimes see more than there is there and miss the things that are. And, of course, it was very kind of her to give you that nice fur and fur cap. They'll keep you warm this cold weather. But you don't want to go on accepting a lot of things like that from somebody who, after all, is no relation. You have got your own wages now and can buy what you want, or, if not, we'll buy it for you and if you want any advice as to what to buy or where to buy it, you've got your two aunts in Candleford town.'

Laura blushed again at that, for, although she was supposed to go to see the Candleford relatives on alternate Sundays, she had not been there for weeks. Something had always turned up to prevent her going. Snow or rain, or one of Miss Lane's bad headaches, when she could do no other than offer to get off the Sunday evening mail, though it was not her turn to do so. 'I don't like keeping you from your friends,' Miss Lane would say, 'but I really must lie down for an hour.' Or: 'Really, you can't want to go out in this weather. When you've got off the mail, we'll have a good fire in the parlour and make ourselves cosy and read. Or we might have down that box from upstairs I told you about, and I'll show you the letters my father had from that gentleman about Shakespeare. After all, Sunday's the only day of the week we have to ourselves, with Zillah and the men away.' And, if Laura still looked a little regretful, she would add: 'I believe you think more of your Uncle Tom than you do of me.' Laura did. She thought more of that particular uncle in one way than she did of any one else she knew, for no one else, she felt sure, could equal him in wisdom, wit, and sound, homely common sense. But she was fond of Miss Lane, too, and did not wish to displease her, so she stayed.

She did not attempt to describe to her mother a position she had scarcely begun to realize; but her looks and manner must have betrayed something of it, for her mother repeated: 'You must stand up for your rights, child. Nobody will think any the better of you for making a doormat of yourself. But you'll be all right. You've got a head well screwed on to your shoulders,

and a conscience to tell you right from wrong, I should hope';
and they talked of other things until it was time for Laura to
go.

Her mother put on her thick cape and walked to the turn of
the hamlet road with her. It was a raw, grey winter morning,
with stars paling in a veil of cottage chimney smoke. Men,
about to start on their way to work, stood lighting pipes at
garden gates, or shuffled past Laura and her mother with a gruff
'G'marnin!' Although not frosty, the air was cold and the two
snuggled closely together, Laura's arm in her mother's, under
the cape. She had grown so much that she had to lean down to
her mother, and they laughed at that and recalled the time when
she, a tiny mite, had said: 'Some day, when I'm grown up, I'll
be the mother and you'll be my little girl.' At the turn of the
road they halted and, after a close embrace, her mother said
good-bye in the old country words: 'Good-bye. God bless
you!'

Then, almost immediately, as it seemed to Laura when looking back, it was spring. The countryside around Candleford
Green was richer and more varied than that near her home.
Instead of flat, arable fields, there were low, green hills, and
valleys and many trees and little winding streams. Her path as
postwoman led over much pasture land and she often returned
with her shoes powdered yellow with buttercup pollen. The
copses were full of bluebells and there were kingcups and
forget-me-nots by the margins of the brooks and cowslips and
pale purple milkmaids in the water-meadows. Laura seldom
returned from her round without more flowers in her hand than
she knew what to do with. Her bedroom looked and smelled
like a garden, and she stood as many pots and vases about the
kitchen as Zillah would permit.

The official time allowance for the journey was so generous
that she found that, by walking quickly on her outward way,
she could deliver her letters and still have an hour to spare for
sauntering and exploring before she need hurry back home. The
scheme had evidently been drawn up for older and more sedate
travellers than Laura.

Soon she came to know every tree, flower-patch and fern-clump beside her path, as well as the gardens, houses, and faces of the people on her round. There was the head gardener's cottage, semi-Gothic and substantial against the glittering range of glasshouses, and his witty, talkative Welsh wife, kindly, but difficult to escape from; and the dairymaid at the farmhouse who had orders to give her a mug of milk every morning and see that she drank it, because the farmer's wife thought she was growing beyond her strength; and the row of half a dozen cottages, all exactly alike in outward appearance and inside accommodation, but differing in their degree of comfort and cleanliness. Laura wondered then, as she was often to do in her after-life, why, with houses exactly alike and incomes the same to a penny, one woman will have a cosy, tasteful little home and another something not much better than a slum dwelling.

The women at the cottages, clean and not so clean alike, were always pleasant to Laura, especially when she brought them the letters they were always longing for, but seldom received. On many mornings she did not have to go to the cottages, for there was not a letter for any one there, and this left her with still more time to loiter by the pond, reaching out over the water for brandyballs, as the small yellow water-lily was called there, or to brood with her hand over bird's eggs in a nest, or to blow dandelion clocks in the sun. Her uniform in summer was a clean print frock and a shady straw hat, which she would sometimes trim with a wreath of living wild flowers. In wet weather she wore her stout new shoes and a dark purplish waterproof cloak, presented to her by one of her Candleford aunts. She carried a postman's pouch over her shoulder and, for the first part of her outward journey, Sir Timothy's locked leather private postbag.

The only drawbacks to perfect happiness on her part were footmen and cows. The cows would crowd round the stiles she had to get over and be deaf to all her mild shooings. She had been used to cows all her life and had no fear of them in the open, but the idea of descending from the stile into that sea of heads and horns was alarming. She knew they were gentle creatures and would never attack her; but, accidentally, perhaps – . Their horns were so very sharp and long. Then, one morning, a cowman saw her hesitating and bade her, 'Coom on.' If she approached and climbed over the stile quickly, he said the cows would disperse. 'They dunno what you want to be up to. Let 'em see that you've got business on the other side of that stile and that you be in a hurry and they'll make way for 'ee. They be knowin' old craturs, cows.' It was as he had said: when she came to and crossed the stile in a businesslike way, they moved politely aside for her to pass, and they soon became so used to seeing her there that they dispersed at her approach.

The footmen were far less mannerly. At the hour at which she reached the great house every morning, their duties, or their pleasure, lay in the back premises, near the door at which Sir Timothy's postbag had to be delivered. At the sound of the doorbell, two or three of them would rush out, snatch the leather postbag from Laura's hand and toss it from one to the other − sometimes kick it. They hated that postbag because their own private letters were locked therein, and if Sir Timothy was out on the estate or engaged in his Justice Room, they had to wait until he was ready, or chose, to unlock it. They accused him of examining the handwriting and postmarks of their correspondence and of asking inquisitive questions about it. Which he may at some time have done, for, in Laura's time, they had betting tips and bookmakers' circulars addressed to the Post Office to be called for.

It was this matter of the postbag which had caused their animosity towards Laura. When she had first appeared as postwoman they had asked − or, rather, told − her to bring up to the house with the bag their letters addressed to the Post Office. Miss Lane, who was a stickler for strict observance of the official rules, would not permit her to do this. If a letter was addressed to the Post Office to be called for, she said, called for it must be, and although Laura, who thought it unfair that their letters should be inspected, like those of small boys at school, had softened Miss Lane's message to them when delivering it, they were annoyed and under a show of boisterous horseplay visited their annoyance upon Laura.

They would creep silently up behind her and clap her heavily upon the shoulders, or knock her hat over her eyes, or ruffle her hair with their hands, or try to kiss her. The maids, several of whom were often present, as the housekeeper and the butler were at that time taking their morning coffee in the house-keeper's room, would only laugh at her discomfiture, or join in the sport, putting pebbles down her neck, or flicking her face with their dusting-brushes.

'You look as if you'd been drawn through a quickset hedge backward,' remarked the head gardener's wife one day when Laura was more than usually dishevelled; but, when told what had happened, she only laughed and said: 'Well, you're only young once. You must get all the fun you can. You give them as good as they give you and they'll soon learn to respect you.' She dared not tell Miss Lane, for she knew that lady would com-plain to Sir Timothy and there would be what she thought of as 'a fuss'. She preferred to endure the teasing, which, after all, occupied but a few minutes during an outing in which there were rich compensations.

Excepting the men working in the fields, she seldom saw any one between the houses on her round. Now and then she would meet the estate carpenter with his bag of tools, going to mend a fence or a gate, and occasionally she saw Sir Timothy himself, spud in hand, taking what he called 'a toddle round the estate', and he would greet her in his jovial way as 'our little Post-mistress-General' and tell her to go to Geering, the head gar-dener, and ask him to show her through the glasshouses and give her some flowers. Which was kind of him, but unnecessary, as Mr Geering had, on his own responsibility, conducted her several times through the long, warm, damp, scented hothouses, picking a flower here and there to add to her bouquet. *My* glasshouses, the gardener called them; *our* glasshouses, said his wife when speaking of them; to the actual owner they were merely *the* glasshouses. So much for the privilege of owner-ship!

Once she saw Sir Timothy in a more serious mood. That was after a night of high wind had brought down two magnificent elm trees on the edge of the ha-ha, and he called to her to come and look at the damage. It was a sad sight. The trees were lying with their roots upended and their trunks slanting across the ditch to the ruin of broken branches and smashed twigs on the lower level. Sir Timothy appeared to be as much distressed as if they had been the only trees he possessed. There were tears in his eyes as he kept repeating: 'Wouldn't have lost them for worlds! Known them all my life. Opened my eyes upon them, in fact, for I was born in that room there. See the window? It's this damned sunk fence is to blame. No root room on one side. Wouldn't have lost them for worlds!' And she left him lamenting.

Although so few people were seen there at the early hour of Laura's passing, the park was open to all. Couples went there for walks on summer Sundays, and the poorer villagers were permitted to pick up the dead fallen wood for their fires; but the copses and other enclosures were barred, especially in the spring, when the game birds were nesting. There were notice boards in such places to say trespassers would be prosecuted and, although Laura considered herself to some extent a privileged person, she climbed into them stealthily and kept a lookout for the gamekeeper. But he was an old man, getting beyond his work, people said; his cottage stood in a clearing in a wood on the other side of the estate, and she never once sighted him.

She went in and out of the copses, gathering bluebells or wild cherry blossom, or hunting for birds' nests, and never saw anyone, until one May morning of her second year on the round. She had gone into one of the copses where a few lilies-of-the-valley grew wild, found half a dozen or so, and was just climbing down the high bank which surrounded the copse when she came face to face with a stranger. He was a young man in rough country tweeds and carried a gun over his shoulder. She thought for a moment that he might be one of Sir Timothy's nephews, or some other visitor at the great house, though, of course, she should have remembered that no guest of Sir Timothy's would have carried a gun at that season. But, when he pointed to a notice board which said *Trespassers will be prosecuted* and asked, rather roughly, what the devil she thought she was doing there, she knew he must be a gamekeeper, and he turned out to be a new underkeeper engaged to do most of the actual work of the old man, who was failing in health, but refused to retire.

He was a tall, well-built young man, apparently in the middle twenties, with a small fair moustache and very pale blue eyes which, against his dark tanned complexion, looked paler. His features might have been called handsome but for their set rigidity. These softened slightly when Laura held out her half-dozen lilies-of-the-valley as an excuse for her trespass. He was sure she had meant to do no harm, he said, but the pheasants were still sitting and he could not have them disturbed. There had been too much of this trespassing lately – Laura wondered by whom – too much laxity, too much laxity, he repeated, as if he had just thought of the word and was pleased with it, but it had got to stop. Then, still walking close on her heels on the narrow path, as if to keep her in custody, he asked her if she would tell him the way to Foxhill Copse, as it was his first morning on the estate and he had not grasped the lie of the land yet. When she pointed it out and he saw that her own path led past, he unbent sufficiently to suggest that they should walk on together.

By the time they reached the copse he had become quite human. His name, he told her, was Philip White. His father was head gamekeeper on an estate near Oxford and he had so far worked under him, but had now come to Candleford Park on the understanding that when poor old Chitty died or retired he would take his place as head gamekeeper. Without actually saying so, he managed to convey the impression that by consenting to serve under Chitty for a time he was doing, not only Sir Timothy, but the whole neighbourhood a favour. His father's estate (he spoke of it as his father's in the way the Geerings spoke of 'our glasshouses') was larger and better preserved than this, and belonged to a very great nobleman with an historic title. He did not claim the title as a family possession, but it was evident that he felt its reflected glory.

Laura glanced up at him. No. He was perfectly serious. There was no smile on his face, not even a twinkle in his pale eyes; the only expression there was one of a faint interest in herself. Before they parted she had been shown a photograph of his sister, who worked in a draper's showroom in Oxford. It was that of a smiling girl in evening dress for some dance, with her fair hair dressed in curls high on her head. Laura was much impressed. 'All in our family are good-looking,' he said as he slipped the photograph back into his breast pocket. She had also been given a description of his parents' model cottage on the famous estate and been told of the owner's great shoots, to which dukes and lords and millionaires appeared to flock, and would probably have heard much more had not her conscience pricked her into saying: 'I really must go now, or I shall have to run all the way.' She had not told him anything about herself, nor had he asked any questions beyond inquiring where she lived and how often she passed that way. Happening to look back as she climbed over the stile, she saw him still standing where she had left him. He raised his hand in a wooden salute, and that, she thought, was the last she would see of him.

But she had not seen the last of Philip White. After that he always seemed to appear at some point on her walk. At first he would spring out of some copse with his gun and seem to be surprised to see her; but soon he would stroll openly along the path to meet her, then turn and walk by her side through the park until just before they came in sight of the great house windows. Beyond telling Miss Lane as an item of news on the first morning that a new under-keeper had come and that he had asked her the way to Fox'lls, Laura mentioned these meetings to no one, and as they met on the loneliest part of her round no one she knew ever saw them together. But for weeks they met almost daily and talked, or rather Philip talked and she listened. Sometimes he would take the hand which swung by her side and hold it in his as they walked on together. It was pleasant at sixteen to be the object of so much attention on the part of a grown man and from one who was spoken of respectfully by the villagers as Keeper White, while to her in secret he was Philip. 'Call me Philip,' he had said at their second meeting. 'I wouldn't allow any one else here to call me it, but I'd like it from you,' and she called him by that name occasionally. Never 'Phil'; it would not have suited him. He called her 'Laura', and once or twice when they passed through the kissing gate, he gave her a shy, cold, wooden kind of kiss over the bars.

She supposed they were sweethearts and sometimes looked

into the future and saw herself feeding the pheasant chicks hatched out under hens in the little coops under the green clearing where old Chitty's cottage stood. She felt she could be happy for life in that pretty cottage on the green, surrounded by waving tree-tops. On one of her walks last spring she had seen the margins of the green and the earth under the trees starred with white wild anemones, swaying in the wind, and it had looked to her then a perfect paradise. But then came the dampening thought that Philip would be there, too, at least some of the time, and she was not sure that she liked Philip well enough to be able to endure his perpetual company.

He was so self-satisfied, so sure that he and everything and everybody belonging to him were perfect, and he had no interests whatever outside his own affairs. If she tried to talk about other people or of flowers she had found, or some book she was reading, it was never long before he brought the conversation back to himself again. 'That's like *me*,' he would say, or, 'What *I* think about it is – ' or, '*I* couldn't stand that sort of thing,' and she, who loved to listen to most people and found nearly everybody else interesting, wanted to run straight away across the park and fields and leave him talking to himself.

But she was constitutionally incapable of that. And if she tried to offend and quarrel with him, she could not. She knew that from some of the stories against himself he repeated, without the least idea that they were against himself. If she told him openly that she thought they ought not to walk together, as it was against official rules, she would still have to meet and pass him frequently, for it was one of his duties to patrol every part of the estate. There really seemed to be nothing she could do about it, except to bound on a few yards in front as they approached the kissing gate.

Then, when she least expected it, the whole affair came to a head and was over. It was just upon closing time one evening, and she had taken some forms to Miss Lane, who was already seated at the kitchen table about to begin on her accounts, when the office doorbell tinkled and she hurried back to find Philip there. That, to begin with, was a surprise to her, for he had never been in the office before – an embarrassment, too, for she knew that Miss Lane, sitting quietly at the kitchen table with the door wide open, would hear every word that was said. But there he was, looking full of importance, and all she could do to cope with the situation was to say 'Good evening' in what she hoped was a businesslike voice. She almost prayed that he would say, 'Three penny stamps' or something of that kind and go. He might squeeze her hand, if he liked; she did not care if he kissed her, if only he kissed her quietly and Miss Lane did not hear. But she was not to be let off so easily.

Without any formal greeting, he pulled a letter out of his pocket and said: 'Can you get off for a few days at the end of this week? Well, as a matter of fact, you must. I've got this letter from our Cath' – his sister – 'and she says our Mum says I'm to bring you. Saturday to Monday, she says, or longer if we can manage it, but, of course, I can't. Nobody can afford to leave my job for long together – too many bad characters about. Still, I think I have earned a day or two and Sir Timothy's quite agreeable, so you'd better arrange about it now and I'll wait.'

Laura looked at the open door; she could positively feel Miss Lane listening. 'I'm s-s-sorry – ' she began feebly, but the idea of any one trying to refuse an invitation from his family was unthinkable to Philip. 'Go and ask,' he commanded; then, more gently, but still too, too audibly: 'Go and ask. You've got the right. Everybody takes their girl for their people to see; and you are my girl, aren't you, Laura?'

The papers on the kitchen table rustled, then again dead silence, but Laura was no longer thinking of the danger of being overheard so much as wondering what she should say.

'You are my girl, aren't you, Laura?' asked Philip once more, and for the first time since she had known him, Laura detected a faint note of uneasiness in his voice. She herself was trembling with consternation, but when she said, 'You've never asked me,' her voice sounded flippant, perhaps coquettish, for Philip took one of her trembling hands and smiled down upon her as he said magnanimously: 'Well, I thought you understood. But don't be frightened. You will be my girl. Won't you, Laura?' That was inadequate enough as a declaration of love, but

Laura's answer was even more inadequate: 'No – no thank you, Philip,' she said, and the most unromantic love scene on record was over, for, without another word, he turned, went out of the door and out of her life. She never saw him again to speak to. On one occasion, months afterwards, she had a momentary view of his distant figure, gun on shoulder, stalking across one of the open spaces of the park, but, if he ever came her way again, he must have chosen a time of day when she was not likely to be there.

But Miss Lane was still with her and had to be dealt with. Laura expected at least a severe scolding. A letter might even be written to her mother. But when Laura returned to the kitchen Miss Lane, who was carefully ruling a line in red ink, did not even look up. 'Who was that?' she asked in a casual tone when she had finished, and Laura, trying to sound casual too, replied: 'Sir Timothy's new gamekeeper.' No more was said at that moment, but, as she folded her accounts and slipped them into the large brown paper envelope with the printed address, 'Accountant-General, G.P.O., London', Miss Lane eyed Laura closely and said: 'You seem to know that young man very well,' 'Yes,' admitted Laura. 'I've met him on the round sometimes.' And Miss Lane said, 'Umph! So I gathered.'

So there were no reproaches. On the contrary, Miss Lane appeared in a better temper than usual for the rest of the evening. As they were lighting their candles to go up to bed, she said thoughtfully: 'I don't see why you should ever leave here. You and I get on very well together, and perhaps, after my time, you might take my place in the office.'

In after years Laura sometimes looked rather wistfully back on that evening when an apparent choice was offered her between two widely differing paths in life. It would have been pleasant to have lived all her days in comparative ease and security among the people she knew and understood. To have watched the seasons open and fade in the scenes she loved and belonged to by birth. But have we any of us a free choice of our path in life, or are we driven on by destiny or by the demon within us into a path already marked out? Who can tell?

Choice or no choice, Laura's sojourn at Candleford Green

was to be but of a few years' duration. And, if the choice had
been hers and she had remained there, her life might not have
been as happy and peaceful as she afterwards imagined it would
have been. Her mother's judgement was usually sound, and she
had often told her: 'You're not cut out for a pleasant, easy life.
You think too much!' Sometimes adding tolerantly: 'But we are
as we are made, I suppose.'

XXXIX

Change in the Village

THE gradual change which was turning the formerly quiet and
secluded village of Candleford Green into the suburb of a small
country town was accentuated by the death of Mr Coulsdon
and the arrival of the new vicar. Mr Delafield was a young man
in the early thirties, somewhat inclined to premature bulkiness,
whose large, pink, clean-shaven face had a babyish look, which
his fair hair, worn rather long and inclined to curl, did nothing
to dispel. Dignity did not enter into his composition. He would
run out to post a letter or to buy a cucumber for lunch in his
shirt-sleeves, and, even when fully dressed, the only evidence of
his sacred calling was his collar. Well-worn flannels and a Norfolk jacket were his usual everyday wear. Very dark grey, of
course; any lighter shade would have been too revolutionary, as
would anything more daring in the way of headgear than the
black-and-white speckled straw boater he wore in summer in
place of the round, black, soft felt hat of the other local
clergy.

He looked like a very big boy, and an untidy boy. Miss Lane
once said that she longed to take a needle and thread and set
forward the top button of his trousers, so that he could button
in the bulge at his waist. He probably thought Miss Lane's
appearance as unsatisfactory as she did his, for he had come
there with a townsman's ideas of the country, according to
which a village postmistress should have worn a white apron
and spoken the dialect. But he had come to his country living

determined to be friendly with all his parishioners, and although Laura felt sure he did not like that sardonic little glint of amusement in her eyes when he tried to talk improvingly to her, he was always pleasantly breezy in his manner, and she, in time, came to admit that he had a boyish charm.

The verdict of others varied. The old order had changed and, in changing, had gone somewhat ahead of the times in the depth of the country. Some complained that his 'Hail fellow, well met!' attitude to everybody annoyed them. All men were brothers in church, of course, but outside they thought a clergyman ought to 'hold on to his dignity'. 'Look at poor old Mr Coulsdon! He was a gentleman, if ever there was one!' Others liked Mr Delafield because he was 'not proud and stuck up', like some parsons they could name. By the majority, judgement was suspended. 'You've got to summer and winter a man before you can pretend to know him' was an old country maxim much quoted at that time. On one point all churchgoers agreed; the new Vicar was a good preacher. He had a surprisingly deep, rich voice for one of his boyish appearance, and he used this to advantage in the pulpit.

Pride was certainly not one of Mr Delafield's failings. He had a charming way of relieving any old woman he met of any burden she was carrying. Once Laura saw him crossing the green with a faggot of sticks on his shoulder, and, on another occasion, he helped to carry home a clothes-basket of washing.

On leaving the Post Office, he would vault over the railings of the green to bowl for small boys playing cricket with an old tin for wicket. But that was in his early days; before he had been there long, Candleford Green cricket was put upon a proper footing, with an eleven of young men and practice nights for boys. On Saturday afternoons in summer he himself played with the eleven, and soon other local teams were challenged and the white flannels of such players as possessed them enlivened the pleasant, summery scene on the greensward.

Before long he had got together a club for boys which met in the schoolroom on winter evenings. The noise the boys made,

said those who lived near, made life pretty well unbearable; but
the boys' parents were pleased to have them kept out of mischief, and those who lived near their former winter evening
haunts were not sorry. Then a timely Confirmation ceremony
brought together the nucleus of a Girls' Guild which had its
headquarters in the now disused servants' hall at the vicarage.
Mrs Delafield was Lady President of this, but as she had two
children and kept but one young maid in a house where there
had formerly been four, she had little time for the supervision
of the weekly meetings, and help had to be obtained from the
ladies of the congregation. The Pratts, *Miss* Ruby and *Miss*
Pearl, as the Vicar and his wife were careful to insist upon when
naming them to the girls, saw and seized here their opportunity,
and soon what they did not know about the vicarage household
could easily, as people said, have been written on a threepenny
bit.

The Delafields were poor. Soon after their arrival they gave
out that, as the living was but a poor one and they had no
private means, the charities of the former Vicar would have to
be discontinued. 'I know myself what it is to be poor,' the Vicar
would say frankly when sympathizing with one of the cottagers,
and, although his hearer might smile incredulously as she mentally compared his idea of poverty with her own, his frankness
would please her.

After a time, the tradesmen hinted that the new vicarage
family was long-winded in paying its bills. 'But,' they would
add, 'so far they've always paid up in the end, and they don't go
running to another shop with their bit of ready money as soon
as they owe you a few pounds, and they aren't extravagant,'
which, from a shopkeeper's point of view, was not altogether a
bad character to give a customer.

The Delafields had a succession of untrained young maids, of
whom they expected trained service, and, in consequence, they
were as often without a maid as with one. And they fared little
better with the women brought in 'to oblige'. One excellent
charwoman in her own line of washing and scrubbing was so
taken aback on her first appearance at the vicarage by having a

written list of the dishes she was expected to cook for dinner thrust into her hand that she seized her coarse apron and basket and bolted.

But what struck the Miss Pratts more than the scrappy meals and undusted rooms at the vicarage was what they called Mrs Delafield's 'singularity'. Her style of dress was what Miss Ruby called 'arty'. She wore long, loose frocks, usually terracotta or sage green, which trailed on the floor behind her and had low necks which exposed the throat when other women were whaleboned up to the ears.

For church on Sundays the Delafield children wore white kid slippers and openwork socks, but at all other times they ran about barefoot, which shocked the villagers and could not have been very comfortable for themselves, although they appeared to enjoy scrabbling with their toes in the dust or taking impressions of their own footprints in mud. Their ordinary everyday dress was a short brown holland smock, elaborately embroidered, which for comfort and beauty would have compared favourably with the more formal attire of other children of their class had it not invariably been grubby.

'Those awful children!' some people called them, but to others their intelligence and good looks made up for their lack of manners. And, 'Thank heaven,' somebody said, 'we ain't expected to "Miss" them!' It was something of a privilege to be able to say 'Elaine' or 'Olivia' when speaking to or of them, at a time when other quality children were 'Master' or 'Miss' in their cradles. The village had taken its lead in this matter from the Vicar, who always spoke to them of his children by their plain Christian names. Other parents added the prefix, often emphasizing it. One child Laura knew who, being the youngest of her family, retained the name and status of baby while a toddler, was spoken of by her parents to the servants and estate workers as 'Miss Baby'.

The change at the vicarage did as much as anything to hasten the decline of the old servile attitude of the poorer villagers. With all his failings, or what they considered failings, Mr Delafield did at least meet them on a purely human footing and speak to them as one man to another, not as one bending down from a pedestal. The country gentlemen around still loomed larger than life-size upon their horizon, but the Vicar lived amongst them, they saw him and spoke to him daily, and his example and influence were greater. Some still sighed for the fleshpots and blankets of the old régime, others regretted its passing from love of the stately old order, but a far larger number rejoiced, if insensibly, in the new democratic atmosphere of parochial life. The parish was soon to be proud of its Vicar.

From the first Mr Delafield's sermons had been praised by his congregation. 'Keeps you awake, he do', said some who had formerly been in the habit of nodding in sermon time. Their duty towards their neighbour and the importance of honesty and truthfulness had been topics too familiar to keep their eyes open, but when a sermon began: 'The other day I heard a man in this parish say – ' or 'You may have read in your newspapers last week – ' they sat up and listened.

Quite often the thing heard or read was amusing, and, although, of course, there could be no laughter in church, a slight stir of smiling appreciation would lighten the atmosphere and prepare the congregation to settle down happily to listen to the lesson or moral to be drawn. It was never a severe one. Hell was never mentioned, nor, for the matter of that, heaven, and earth was depicted as not as bad a place, after all, if people bore one another's burdens and pulled together. If, sometimes, the deep, melodious voice in the pulpit preached repentance, it was not so much repentance of the sins common in country villages as those of the world in general. No one present could ever feel hurt or offended by anything he said in his sermons. Indeed, a member of his congregation was heard to say in the churchyard one Sunday morning: 'A sermon like that makes you feel two inches taller.'

Those comfortable words, that eloquent voice, and the telling pauses when, leaning far over the edge of his pulpit, he searched the faces and seemed to look into the very hearts of his congregation, soon won for him the reputation of being the best preacher in the neighbourhood – some said in the county. People from surrounding parishes and even from Candleford

town itself were soon coming to hear him preach. On summer
Sunday evenings the church was often so well filled that late-
comers had to stand in the aisle. Even Miss Lane, who was not a
frequent churchgoer, attended a service. Back at home her only
comment was: 'All very pleasant! But pass me my Darwin,
please. Like the birds, I need a little grit in my food.' But the
lack of enthusiasm shown by one crusty old woman was but as
a grain of sand on the seashore compared to the rising tide of
the new Vicar's popularity as a preacher, which reached its
high-water mark on Harvest Thanksgiving Sunday, when the
Candleford News sent a reporter to take down the Vicar's
sermon verbatim. Copies of the issue containing the sermon
were bought in great numbers to be posted to sons and daughters in London, in the North of England, or out in the Colonies.
'Just to show them,' their parents said, 'that Candleford Green's
no longer the poor little stick-in-the-mud spot they may be
thinking.'

As Mr Delafield's popularity as a preacher increased and
brought renown to the village, his small unconventionalities
were accepted as the little, amusing, lovable peculiarities of
genius. His wife had no longer difficulties with her maids and
charwomen, for an elderly farmer's daughter proposed herself
and was accepted as mother's help. By the time Laura left
Candleford Green, the ladies of the congregation were almost
fighting over decorating the church and the turns they had
agreed to take at relieving Mrs Delafield of the family mending.
So many pairs of carpet slippers were worked for Mr Delafield
that only a centipede could have worn out all of them, and
Elaine and Olivia were so frequently asked out to tea, and so
feasted when there, that, had they not been sent away to a
boarding school, their digestions would have been ruined. By
his poorer parishioners, though not perhaps as respected as Mr
Coulsdon had been, the new Vicar was more beloved, because
more human.

Mr Delafield's cure of souls at Candleford Green was but
brief. A year or two after Laura had left there she was told in a
letter that he had accepted a London living and was to hold a
special service in his new church for the Candleford Green

Mothers' Meeting on its annual outing. But he left his mark on the village, not only by the spiritual comfort he had been able to bring to many, but also by breaking down prejudices.

Then, about that time, came a rise in wages. Agricultural workers were given fifteen instead of ten or twelve shillings a week, and skilled craftsmen were paid an agreed rate per hour, instead of the former weekly wage irrespective of the time put in, and although at the same time prices were rising, they had not as yet risen in proportion. The Boer War, when it came, sent prices soaring, but that was still several years in the future.

Meanwhile, Queen Victoria had her Diamond Jubilee and 'Peace and Plenty' was the country's watchword. Rural councils were established and some of the progressive Candleford Green villagers were able to voice their improvement schemes and to get a few of them carried out. There were rumours of scholarships for village schoolchildren; the County Council sent a cookery expert to lecture in the schoolroom; and there were evening classes, no longer called 'night school', for the older boys. Housing was still left to private enterprise, but the demand for more modern homes did not go unregarded.

When one of the Candleford Green villagers had a stroke of good luck in the way of a better job or higher wages, his wife's reaction to the good news would usually be to exclaim: 'Now we can go to live in one of the villas!' Sometimes her ambition was realized and they exchanged their old, inconvenient, though thick-walled and warm old cottage with its large, fertile garden for one of a row of small houses on the newly opened building estate on the Candleford Road.

The new house might prove to be damp and draughty, for the walls were thin and the woodwork ill-fitted, and the garden at the back of the house, formerly part of a damp, tussocky meadow, left in the rough by the builder, would certainly turn out what her husband would call 'a heartache'; but, as compensation, she would enjoy the distinction conferred by owning a smart front door with a brass knocker, a bay window in the parlour, and water laid on to the kitchen sink. Plus the *éclat* of living in one of the villas.

Although the speculative builder had left the making of the

back garden to his tenant, he had finished the small plot in front
by laying a few feet of turf round a small centre flower bed.
Ornate iron railings enclosed this small space and a red-and-
blue-tiled path led up to the front door. Outside, at the edge of
the sidewalk, young trees had been planted, of which some had
already died and others were pining, but, lining the favourite
and most built-up road, a sufficient number survived to give
colour to its name of Chestnut Avenue.

In Laura's time, a few of the villas were occupied by ambitious Candleford Green families which had migrated; more
had been taken by clerks and shopmen from Candleford town
who fancied a country life or wished to reduce their rent. Six
shillings a week for a five-roomed villa was certainly not excessive, but no doubt it repaid the builder-owner well enough for his
outlay. Laura's uncle, who was also a builder in Candleford,
declared that the villas were run up of old oddments of second-
hand stuff, without proper foundations, and that the first high
wind would blow half of them down; but his pessimism may
have been due to professional rivalry, though, to do him justice,
it must be said that he spoke the truth when he frowned and
shook his head and declared: 'Never touch a cheap job. Not my
line.'

Chestnut Avenue stood, apparently firmly, as long as Laura
lived near and may quite probably be standing now, let at treble
the rent to trebly paid wage-earners, with the chestnut trees
fully grown and candled with blossoms and a wireless mast in
every back garden. As they were built, almost before the paint
was dry the villas were occupied and the new tenants tied back
their lace curtains with blue or pink ribbon and painted on the
gate the name of their choice: 'Chatsworth' or 'Naples' or
'Sunnyside' or 'Herne Bay'.

Laura, although conscious of disloyalty to 'the trade', per-
sonified for her by her father and uncle, still thought the
Chestnut Avenue houses stylish. She had just enough taste, or
sense of humour, to think some of the names chosen for them
by the occupiers were unsuitable – 'Balmoral' was the latest
addition – but she saw nothing amiss with the wide-ribbon pale
blue or pink curtain ties, though she herself would have pre-

ferred green or yellow. Except for the ex-villagers whom she already knew, the villas were occupied by a class of people which was new to her, the lower fringe of the lower middle class, of which she was to see a great deal later.

Her first introduction to this, to her, new way of life she owed to a Mrs Green of 'The Shack', the wife of a clerk in the Candleford Post Office. She had come to know the husband in the way of business, he had introduced her to his wife, and an invitation to tea had followed.

The Greens' villa was only distinguishable from the others by its name and by the maidenhair fern which stood in place of the usual aspidistra on a little table exactly in the centre of the small space between the draped curtains at the parlour window. Mrs Green said aspidistras were common, and Laura soon discovered that she had a great dislike of common things and especially of common people. The people who lived next door, she told Laura, were 'awfully common'. The man was a jobbing gardener, 'a clodhopper' she called him, and his wife wore his cloth cap when she hung out her washing. They were toasting herrings, morning, noon, and night, and the smell was 'most offensive'. She thought the landlord ought to be more particular in choosing his tenants. Laura, who was used to the ways of those she called 'clodhoppers' and their wives, and herself enjoyed a good bloater toasted on the coals for supper, heard this with wonder. Of course men who worked on the land were common, there were so many of them, but then there were a good many men in every other trade or calling, so why complain of the number? When it gradually dawned upon her that Mrs Green used the word 'common' in a social sense, she was rather afraid that she would be thought common, too; but she need not have feared, for that lady did not think of her at all, excepting as the possessor of eyes and ears.

Mrs Green was a small, fair woman, still under thirty, who would have been pretty had not her face habitually worn a worried expression which sharpened her features and was already destroying her bloom. Her refinement, or perhaps her means, did not run to visits to a dentist and, to hide decaying teeth, she cultivated a thin, close-lipped little smile. But her hair was still very pretty and beautifully cared for, and she had pretty hands which she rubbed with cold cream after washing the tea things.

Her husband was also small and fair, but his manners were more simple and his expression was opener and franker than that of his wife. When he laughed, he laughed loudly, and then his wife would look at him reproachfully and say in a pained voice, '*Al*bert!' He had not had the same training in the art of keeping up appearances as his wife, for while she, as she said, had come down in the world, having been born into what she vaguely termed 'a refined family', he had begun to earn his living as a telegraph messenger and worked his way up to his present position, which, though still modest, was in those days something of an achievement. Left to himself, he would have been a pleasant, homely kind of fellow who would have enjoyed working in his garden and afterwards sitting down in his shirt-sleeves to a bloater or tinned salmon for tea. But he had married a genteel wife and she had educated him as far as possible up to her own standard.

They were both touchingly proud of their home, and Laura on her first visit had to be shown every nook and corner of it, including the inside of the cupboards. It was furnished in accord with its architectural style. The parlour, which they called the 'drawing-room', had a complete suite of furniture upholstered in green tapestry, and there was a green carpet, but not quite the right shade of green, on the floor. Photographs in ornate frames stood on little tables and a set of framed pictures on the walls illustrated the courtship of an insipid looking couple – 'Lovers' Meeting', 'The Letter', 'Lovers' Quarrel', and 'Wedded'. There was not a book or a flower in the room and not so much as a cushion awry to show that it was lived in. As a matter of fact, it was not. It was more a museum or a temple or a furniture showroom than a living-room. They sat in state in the bay window on Sunday evenings and watched their neighbours pass by, but took their meals and spent the rest of their time in the kitchen, which was a much pleasanter room.

In the bedroom above the parlour there was one of the new duchess dressing-tables and a wardrobe with a long looking-glass door. These pieces of furniture Mrs Green pointed out as 'the latest', a description she also applied to many other treasured objects which she seemed to regard as models of fashion and elegance. Knowing only the cottage simplicity of her own home and the substantial but old-fashioned comfort of Miss Lane's and her Candleford relatives' houses, Laura had to accept her word for this. The people whom she had hitherto known just put what they had or could get into their homes, old things and new things, side by side with each other, with, perhaps, a few yards of new chintz or a new coat of paint to smarten things up occasionally. So, naturally, they did not make a show of their houses, beyond sometimes pointing out some special treasure which had 'belonged to my old granny' or been in our family for years and years'.

There were no such out-of-date objects in the Greens' home; everything there had been bought by themselves when setting up house or later, and the date of purchase and even the price were subjects for conversation. Seven pounds for the drawing-room suite and ten pounds for that in the bedroom! Laura was amazed; but then, she reflected, the Greens were comfortably off; Mr Green's weekly salary must be at least two pounds.

Everything was beautifully kept, furniture and floors were highly polished, windows gleamed, curtains and counterpanes were immaculate, and the little kitchen at the back of the house was a model of neatness. Laura found out afterwards that Mrs Green worked herself nearly to death. With only one child and a house only a little larger than theirs, she worked twice the number of hours and spent ten times the energy of the cottage women. They, standing at their doors with their arms folded, enjoying a gossip with a neighbour, would often complain that a woman's work was never done; but the Mrs Greens were working away while they gossiped and, afterwards, when they were indoors having 'a set down with a cup o' tay', the Mrs Greens, wearing gloves, were polishing the silver. For, of course, forks and spoons and any other metal objects possessed by a Green housewife were known collectively as 'the silver', even if there was not one single hallmark to be seen upon any of them.

At the tea-table it was the turn of the Greens' only child to be chief exhibit. Doreen was seven and, according to her parents, there never had been and never again would be such an intelligent child. 'So cute. You should hear some of her sayings,' and specimens were repeated forthwith, the little girl meanwhile munching her cake with a self-conscious expression. She was a pretty, well-mannered child, well dressed and well cared for, and not so much spoiled as might have been expected. Her parents adored her, and it came as a shock to Laura to hear one of them say and the other repeat that they did not intend to have any more children. Not *intend* to have more! What say would they have in the matter? If married people had one child, they almost always had more – a good many more in most cases. Laura had sometimes heard the mother of a seventh or eighth say that she hoped it would be the last, 'Please God', but she had never before heard one say definitely that it would be. Miss Lane, when told of this incident, said she didn't think much of the Greens for talking like that before a girl of Laura's age; but, as a matter of fact, people nowadays had learned how to limit their families, and a good thing, too, she thought. 'But you don't want to trouble your head about anything to do with marriage,' she concluded, 'and if you take my advice you won't ever do so. Leave marriage to those who are suited for it.' But Laura thought she would like some children, a girl and two boys, perhaps, and to have a house of her own with lots of books in it and no suites of furniture at all, but all sorts of odd, interesting things, such as Miss Lane had.

Her acquaintance with the Greens brought Laura for the first time in contact with the kind of people among whom much of her life was to be spent. It was a class newly emerging in this country, on the borderline between the working and middle classes. Its main type had many good points. Those belonging to it were industrious, frugal and home-loving. Their houses were well kept, their incomes well managed, and their ambitions on their children's behalf knew no bounds. No sacrifice on the part of the parents was too great if, by it, they could give a better start in life than their own to their offspring. The average number of children in a family was two, but there were many only children and nearly as many childless homes; a family of three was unusual.

The men's suits were kept well brushed, sponged and pressed by their wives, and the women had the knack of dressing well on little. Many of them were able to make, alter, and bring up to date their own clothes. They were good cooks and managers; their homes, though often tasteless, were substantially furnished and beautifully kept; and, although when alone they might take their meals in the kitchen, they had elaborate afternoon tea-cloths and fashionable knick-knacks for the table for festive occasions.

Those were the lines along which they were developing. Spiritually, they had lost ground, rather than gained it. Their working-class forefathers had had religious or political ideals; their talk had not lost the raciness of the soil and was seasoned with native wit which, if sometimes crude, was authentic. Few of this section of their sons and daughters were churchgoers, or gave much thought to religious matters. When the subject of religion was mentioned, they professed to subscribe to its dogmas and to be shocked at the questioning of the most out-worn of these; but, in reality, their creed was that of keeping up appearances. The reading they did was mass reading. Before they would open a book, they had to be told it was one that everybody was reading. The works of Marie Corelli and Nat Gould were immensely popular with them. They had not sufficient sense of humour to originate it, but borrowed it from music-hall turns and comic papers, and the voice in which such gems were repeated was flat and toneless compared to the old country speech.

But those who had left village life and all it stood for behind them were few compared to the number of those who stayed at home and waited for change to come to them. Change came slowly, if surely, and right into the early years of this century many of the old village ways of living remained and those who cherished the old customs were much as country people had been for generations. A little better educated, a little more democratic, a little more prosperous than their parents had been, but still the same unpretentious, warm-hearted people, with just enough malice to give point to their wit and a growing sense of injustice which was making them begin to inquire when their turn would come to enjoy a fair share of the fruits of the earth they tilled.

They, too, or, rather, their children and grandchildren, were to come in time to the parting of the ways when the choice would have to be made between either merging themselves in the mass standardization of a new civilization or adapting the best of the new to their own needs while still retaining those qualities and customs which have given country life its distinctive character. That choice may not even now have been determined.

But only a few of the wisest foresaw that the need for such a choice would arise when, for Laura, what appeared to be an opportunity offered and, driven on by well-meant advice from without and from within by the restless longing of youth to see and experience the whole of life, she disappeared from the country scene. To return often, but never as herself part of it, for she could only be that in her native county, where she had sprung from the soil.

On the last morning of her postwoman's round, when she came to the path between trees where she had seen the birds' footprints on the snow, she turned and looked back upon the familiar landmarks. It was a morning of ground mist, yellow sunshine, and high rifts of blue, white-cloud-dappled sky. The leaves were still thick on the trees, but dew-spangled gossamer threads hung on the bushes and the shrill little cries of unrest of the swallows skimming the green open spaces of the park told of autumn and change.

There was the stable tower with its clock-face and, near it, though unseen, was the courtyard where she had been annoyed – foolishly annoyed, she thought now – by the horseplay of the footmen. The chief offenders had gone long before and with those who had taken their places she knew quite well how to deal, even if they had been offensive, which they were not, for she was nearly three years older. There, where the path wound past the two copses, she had met Philip White – he, too, had left the estate – and away to the left were the meadows where the cows had obstructed her path. Farther on, quite out of sight, was the Post Office where, doubtless, Miss Lane was at that moment dispensing stamps with the air of a high priestess, still a little offended by what she considered Laura's desertion, but not too much so to have promised her as a parting gift one of her own watches and chains. And around the Post Office and green was the village where she had had good times and times not so good and had come to know every one of its inhabitants and to count most of them as her friends.

Nearer at hand were the trees and bushes and wild-flower patches beside the path she had trodden daily. The pond where the yellow brandyball waterlilies grew, the little birch thicket where the long-tailed tits had congregated, the boathouse where she had sheltered from the thunderstorm and seen the rain plash like leaden bullets into the leaden water, and the hillock beyond from which she had seen the perfect rainbow. She was never to see any of these again, but she was to carry a mental picture of them, to be recalled at will, through the changing scenes of a lifetime.

As she went on her way, gossamer threads, spun from bush to bush, barricaded her pathway, and as she broke through one after another of these fairy barricades she thought, 'They're trying to bind and keep me.' But the threads which were to bind her to her native county were more enduring than gossamer. They were spun of love and kinship and cherished memories.

PENGUIN MODERN CLASSICS

TARRY FLYNN
PATRICK KAVANAGH

'A work of art' *Irish Times*

A man's mother can be a terrible burden sometimes. For Tarry Flynn – poet, farmer and lover-from-afar of beautiful young virgins – the responsibility of family, farm, poetic inspiration and his own unyielding lust is a heavy one. The only solution is to rise above it all – or escape over the nearest horizon.

Like *The Green Fool*, his autobiography, Patrick Kavanagh's *Tarry Flynn* is an idyllic and beautifully evocative account of life as it was lived in Ireland in the 1930s.

PENGUIN MODERN CLASSICS

THE OUTCRY
HENRY JAMES

'A highly topical comedy' Toby Litt

The Outcry, a witty satire on money, art and the media, was Henry James's last completed novel.

Inspired by a real-life contemporary scandal, this tantalizingly little-known work centres on the outcry caused when a brash American comes to England intent on buying up her finest art treasures. Mr Breckenridge Bender's hobby is pursuing expensive works of art – and Lord Theign has the '*ideally* expensive' painting that he is looking for. Theign needs the money to pay off his wayward daughter's gambling debts, but his friends and relations are violently opposed to the sale and plot to save the picture. Old money and values clash with the new, and the ensuing battle causes a public sensation.

Edited with an Introduction by Toby Litt

PENGUIN MODERN CLASSICS

THE FORSYTE SAGA VOLUME TWO

THE WHITE MONKEY/ THE SILVER SPOON/ SWAN SONG

JOHN GALSWORTHY

'The *Forsyte Saga* was such a cracking good story … compulsive, as well as very modern and outrageous' *Sunday Times*

In this second part of John Galsworthy's splendid trilogy of love, power, money and family feuding, a new generation has arrived to divide the Forsyte clan with society scandals and conflicting passions. Set in the years following the First World War, the story moves to Soames Forsyte's daughter Fleur. She is now married to Michael Mont, but when her old love Jon returns after seven years, desire is rekindled and loyalties begin to divide. Still insulated from reality by their wealth and class, the Forsytes try to resist but cannot ignore the threat of change and 'the stealthy march of passion'.

PENGUIN MODERN CLASSICS

THE FORSYTE SAGA VOLUME ONE

THE MAN OF PROPERTY/ IN CHANCERY/ TO LET

JOHN GALSWORTHY

'An immortal achievement … The Forsytes are intimately human … it is, at all levels, readability itself' *Financial Times*

John Galsworthy's magnificent, well-loved *Forsyte Saga* traces the changing fortunes of the wealthy Forsyte dynasty through fifty years of material triumph and emotional disaster. This first volume begins as the nineteenth century is drawing to a close, and the upper middle classes, with their property and propriety, are becoming a dying section of society. The Forsytes are blind to this fact, clinging to their conventions and their 'brilliant respectability'. As dignified Soames Forsyte struggles to uphold the old moral code in the face of the social revolution resulting from the Great War, his wife Irene's extraordinary beauty causes even more disruption. The bitter feud between them will come to split the Forsyte family for two generations.

PENGUIN MODERN CLASSICS

THE RECTOR'S DAUGHTER
F. M. MAYOR

'A tender masterpiece of love and sacrifice that rings true even in our uninhibited times' Elizabeth Buchan, *The Times*

Mary was plain, shy, middle-aged and reliable. Her life centred on her father, the aged and difficult Canon Jocelyn, and on the quiet duties of a rector's daughter deep in the country. She never dreamed that her lonely life was to be shaken to the core by an unlooked-for love affair. The devastatingly honest and deeply moving portrayal of Mary's longing 'to love and be loved' makes her a touching and genuinely memorable heroine. Since its first publication in 1924 this, Mayor's only major work, has come to be appreciated as one of the great works of British women's fiction.

'A masterpiece ... it is about love; filial love and married love and extreme sexual passion, and about the anguish, despair and intermittent bliss of every hopeless relationship between man and woman' Susan Hill, *Daily Telegraph*

With an Introduction by Susan Hill

PENGUIN MODERN CLASSICS

THE GO-BETWEEN
L. P. HARTLEY

'Magical and disturbing' *Independent*

When one long, hot summer, young Leo is staying with a school-friend at Brandham Hall, he begins to act as a messenger between Ted, the farmer, and Marian, the beautiful young woman up at the hall. He becomes drawn deeper and deeper into their dangerous game of deceit and desire, until his role brings him to a shocking and premature revelation. The haunting story of a young boy's awakening into the secrets of the adult world, *The Go-Between* is also an unforgettable evocation of the boundaries of Edwardian society.

'On a first reading, it is a beautifully wrought description of a small boy's loss of innocence long ago. But, visited a second time, the knowledge of approaching, unavoidable tragedy makes it far more poignant and painful' *Express*

Edited with an Introduction and Notes by Douglas Brooks-Davies

Contemporary ... Provocative ... Outrageous ...
Prophetic ... Groundbreaking ... Funny ... Disturbing ...
Different ... Moving ... Revolutionary ... Inspiring ...
Subversive ... Life-changing ...

What makes a modern classic?

At Penguin Classics our mission has always been to make the best
books ever written available to everyone. And that also means
constantly redefining and refreshing exactly what makes a 'classic'.
That's where Modern Classics come in. Since 1961 they have been an
organic, ever-growing and ever-evolving list of books from the last
hundred (or so) years that we believe will continue to be read over and
over again.

They could be books that have inspired political dissent, such as
Animal Farm. Some, like *Lolita* or *A Clockwork Orange*, may have
caused shock and outrage. Many have led to great films, from *In Cold
Blood* to *One Flew Over the Cuckoo's Nest*. They have broken down
barriers – whether social, sexual, or, in the case of *Ulysses*, the
boundaries of language itself. And they might – like *Goldfinger* or
Scoop – just be pure classic escapism. Whatever the reason, Penguin
Modern Classics continue to inspire, entertain and enlighten millions
of readers everywhere.

'No publisher has had more influence on reading habits than Penguin'
Independent

'Penguins provided a crash course in world literature'
Guardian

The best books ever written

PENGUIN 🐧 CLASSICS

SINCE 1946

Find out more at www.penguinclassics.com